A PARADE OF HORRIBLES

Titles by Matt Dinniman

Dungeon Crawler Carl Series

DUNGEON CRAWLER CARL
CARL'S DOOMSDAY SCENARIO
THE DUNGEON ANARCHIST'S COOKBOOK
THE GATE OF THE FERAL GODS
THE BUTCHER'S MASQUERADE
THE EYE OF THE BEDLAM BRIDE
THIS INEVITABLE RUIN
A PARADE OF HORRIBLES

OPERATION BOUNCE HOUSE

KAIJU: BATTLEFIELD SURGEON

The Shivered Sky Series

EVERY GRAIN OF SAND
IN THE CITY OF DEMONS
THE GREAT DEVOURING DARKNESS

Dominion of Blades Series

DOMINION OF BLADES
THE HOBGOBLIN RIOT

THE GRINDING

TRAILER PARK FAIRY TALES

A PARADE OF HORRIBLES

DUNGEON CRAWLER CARL BOOK EIGHT

MATT DINNIMAN

ACE
New York

ACE
Published by Berkley
An imprint of Penguin Random House LLC
1745 Broadway, New York, NY 10019
penguinrandomhouse.com

Book design by George Towne
Interior art on pages v, 24, and 678: Vintage Black Texture © 316pixel/Shutterstock
All other interior art by Erik Wilson (erikwilsonart.com)

Grateful acknowledgment is made to Sony Music Publishing (US) LLC for permission to reprint lyrics from "Take On Me." © 1985 Sony/ATV Music Publishing (UK) Limited. All rights on behalf of Sony/ATV Music Publishing (UK) Limited administered by Sony Music Publishing (US) LLC, 1005 17th Avenue South, Suite 800, Nashville, TN, 37212. All rights reserved. Used by permission.

ISBN: 9798217190065
Library of Congress Control Number: 2026933636

First Ace Hardcover Edition: May 2026

A Parade of Horribles is being simultaneously self-published in a digital edition by the author.

Printed in the United States of America
3rd Printing

The authorized representative in the EU for product safety and compliance is Penguin Random House Ireland, Morrison Chambers, 32 Nassau Street, Dublin D02 YH68, Ireland, https://eu-contact.penguin.ie.

Thank you to all the crawlers who have helped
turn this silly book about a guy and his talking cat
into what it is today.
Also, I want to extend a special shout-out to the mods on
my Discord who have been there since the very beginning.
No words can convey how grateful I am
that you carry the torch for me.

And, Dwight . . . you only have yourself to blame
for what happens in this book.

When I was a boy and I would see scary things in the news,
my mother would say to me, "Look for the helpers.
You will always find people who are helping."

—Fred Rogers

PARADE OF HORRIBLES
(*plural* PARADES OF HORRIBLES)

Noun

1. A parade featuring a progression of people wearing comic and grotesque costumes, commonly accompanied by floats and models representing monsters.
2. (*law, informal*) Any rhetorical device presenting a series of terrible results that notionally might follow from an act, instead of confining the argument to the explicit terms of any applicable law.

See also

- fearmongering
- catastrophism

(Definition from Wiktionary, *"Parade of horribles," https://en.wiktionary.org/wiki/parade_of_horribles)*

SAMANTHA'S BOOK 7 RECAP

"Bucket Boy, come here," Samantha called.

The young Crocodilian was sitting on the couch in the personal space, talking to that weird bald guy with the gross scar on his head. Samantha didn't like him much. Or maybe she did? Maybe she was in love with him?

No, no. That wasn't right. Who was his mother?

Something, something, garbage truck. No, no, no. Not him. That scar was gross, though.

"What is it?" Bucket Boy shouted back. "I'm a little busy . . . Wait. Why are you in Carl's room?"

Why was she in Carl's room? Oh, yes, yes. She remembered now.

"I'm redecorating, and if you know what's good for you, you'll come here this instant."

The Crocodilian and the bald guy with no eyebrows—ew—approached. They stepped in, eyes wide.

"Yah, do you like it? It's not done yet," Samantha said, feeling proud. A dozen sluggalos were in the far corner, struggling with the new wallpaper. To Bucket Boy, she said, "Come here. I need help installing the chandelier. The sluggies are too small. Come along. Hurry up."

"Carl is going to kill you. This is his room. He says nobody is allowed in."

"He never comes in here, so I have claimed it for my own. Honestly, I feel as if it's my right. I won it in the breakup." She rolled over to the chandelier she had borrowed from the room next to Tish's room when she had done that thing she wasn't going to talk about because everyone would get mad. "This goes to the ceiling. Hurry up, now."

"Wait," Bucket Boy said. "This is not a chandelier. This is a swing."

"Anything can be a chandelier if it lights up and you attach it to the ceiling."

"I can't do it," Bucket Boy said. "I promised Rosetta I would catch Tipid up on what happened during Faction Wars before he lost his memory."

Samantha neck-cootered the goblin drill onto the floor in front of the kid. "Oh, don't worry. I'll tell him what happened. You, get to work." She turned to . . . Tipid? Yes, that was his name. He was from outside the dungeon. He was a former crawler. His mother was probably long dead. She would never have had the chance to trick Samantha into . . . "You, don't worry, okay? I will explain it all."

Tipid, VERY SERIOUS, sat. Samantha was suspicious of people who were VERY SERIOUS.

"Yo, I want to hear this, too," Bigs the sluggalette said, sliming up.

Samantha liked Bigs even if she got orange goo all over her new carpet. Samantha had borrowed the carpet from the Larracos College of Magic. Sometimes Sam and Bigs had girl talk. Bigs was now invited to her bachelorette party.

Psamathe's baby was dead. She was there, and now she was gone. An overwhelming wave of . . . relief . . . washed . . .

Why was it her thoughts always got fuzzy when she remembered her child? Why did she always lose track of . . .

"Okay," Samantha said to Bigs and head-scar guy. "So the ninth floor of the dungeon was Faction Wars. Normally, it's this boring level with all these ugly, old rich people pretending to be warriors, and they fight and one of them takes a castle and wins and honestly it's really stupid and not important. But this year Carl and Donut had their own army, and the NPCs had their own army and they all started fighting over the castle, blah, blah, blah. A bunch of old crawlers from outside the dungeon came back to fight, which if you ask me was kind of stupid. I mean, what kind of suicidal morons were these idiots?"

"Uh," Tipid said.

"Exactly. And in the end, the NPC team and the whole city of Larracos got transferred to the cotton fields because one of those nerd-rock guys cast a spell. That sent all the NPCs to the Ascendency floor, and we probably won't see any of those guys until the twelfth floor. So not this tenth floor. I'm sure this will be a boring, filler floor where nothing important happens at all.

"Anyway, the whole thing ended with Carl and Donut winning Faction Wars, but that was only because the NPCs went away. Oh, and there was this other team that showed up at the last minute. They were called the War Mage Rebellion. They killed that orc boss guy. Not the one Rosetta beheaded but the younger one. Stalwart. They beat up Elle and stole the Gate of the Feral Gods from her. Their leader is a guy named Akuma, and Elle says if she ever sees that guy again, he'll be peeing ice cubes for the rest of his short life. But they stole . . . They took . . .

"Have you seen how pretty my room is? I'm trying to come up with a good name for it. The war mages were working with Agatha, the shopping cart lady, but they didn't like each other. She left when they did and nobody knows where she is, but Carl says the war mages want him to kill Agatha for some reason. Oh, and then Meatus came. He was a giant penis. A gross, stinky one like from one of those guys who gels his hair back and the only aspect of his personality that he works on is his duck facing. You know what I'm saying?"

"Totally," Bigs said.

Samantha sniffed at the guy. "Show me your penis."

"No," Tipid said.

Samantha growled. "Anyway, there was this goddess named Eris that came when Meatus the penis was fighting this other, boring god guy. Donut cast a spell and they all turned into a giant ball. Oh, oh, and then Yarilo showed up from the Nothing, and he was chasing me, trying to talk to me, but I didn't want anything to do with that weirdo after that last party before he got banished. Anyway, Donut took all the bad guys out of the ball and smooshed them through a Li Na chain, including Meatus, and it got in Rosetta's teeth. After that, Li Na couldn't heal and is all weird now. And her brother, Li Jun, died, which was really sad because I liked that guy. Oh, and Yarilo died too, but he was killed by the boring god guy.

"That's a lot," Tipid said. "Maybe we can start over and—"

"The scary Lucia lady only had one doggy left, and he almost ate Mongo, but little Rend saved him and the doggy died! It turns out, she has like a ton of children trapped inside her head, and if she dies, they die, but I say kill her anyway because children are so much trouble. Also, the floor was really tense because Katia and Donut both put the same hat on, and it made it so they both had to kill a snake lady. So Katia and Carl and me went to kill the snake lady, but when I got there, my plan was to go say hi to and possibly kill my own mother—her name is Theia—but when I went to her place, it really wasn't her but some skyfowl dude, which really has a way of messing with a girl's head. And he was all 'Look, I'm not really your mother,' and I was like 'No shit, bucko. You're a creepy bird dude,' and he was all 'No, I mean, Theia isn't,' and I was like, 'Yeah, okay, weirdo.' But then the whole club went nuts and got pulled into some really creepy demon shit because Li Na has totally gone cuckoo.

"Oh, and before that, Louis was in trouble, but I saved his life and selflessly gave my very body to keep him alive. Now he has gills and is my cousin."

"I remember that part," Tipid said. "I remember everything that happened after my memory was wiped. The Dream warlord inhabited Louis's lungs. We used the body of the flesh golem to replace it."

"Kiwi and Mongo's babies!" Samantha gasped. "They're so adorable. We won't see them again until we get to the twelfth floor. Or all the other NPCs, like Holger and Edgar the turtle and Big Tina the dinosaur. But after that part, the most important thing that happened is that Louis broke up with Juice Box so we can have our torrid affair."

"And Katia left," Tipid said.

"Oh yes. Louis, being so virile, made Katia pregnant just by standing near her, and she got shuffled off to a nunnery or something. I wasn't paying attention. Someplace outside the dungeon. And then me and Emberus had a little talk, and then Justice Light the skyfowl dude broke the Nothing so all the demon ladies who hate me are now loose and it's probably going to cause a problem. Oh, and Scolopendra, the big bad centipede thing at the bottom of the dungeon, woke up."

Tipid sighed. "Yeah. I think I'm good."

"I thought you explained it perfect," said Bigs.

INTERLUDE | CHANDRA

"Hello, Donut," Princess Chandra, Esquire, said.

Across from her, the blood-soaked, wild-eyed creature thing looked madly about the blank room. Chandra could smell the gore, and she immediately flicked off the receptors in the control panel.

Chandra was coiled aboard the communications room in the *Ventilator*, a class-C rapid-attack battle cruiser fresh off the shipyards. The Naga warship had sustained a large amount of damage during the short but violent and tumultuous coup that had removed the king and ultimately placed her uncle on the Naga throne. Her uncle, the former opposition leader of the Gilt Party, was calling himself "Sultan Protectorate of the New Reformer" or something equally inane.

It would be cycles before this all sorted itself out, for which Chandra was glad. She'd waited her entire life to find an opportunity like this, and she'd jumped at the chance when it presented itself. It was risky, yes. But if the next few weeks went as she hoped, it would all be worth it. And as long as the political upheaval stabilized long enough for her to collect her money and leave her home system, it didn't really matter what happened next.

She didn't care about power, or titles. She didn't care who was in charge of what. She just wanted out of her home system. That was why she'd become a lawyer in the first place. It'd been a way out.

She suppressed a bitter laugh. At least she now had a plan. A good plan.

And it all hinged on this disgusting, warm-blooded, fur-covered rodent before her now. Donut. "Princess" Donut. What a joke.

This creature wasn't even a true life-form, but a barely sapient, invasive cyst that had artificially formed itself on a seeded planet.

No different than mold, really. And more dangerous. If they didn't need these things to die to help fuel the center system, Chandra would be all for the original soother proposal to eradicate all the seeded worlds.

Still, this one was valuable. She'd already signed several contracts on the creature's behalf and was already collecting royalties. The "Donut Holes" licensing fees alone made it all worth it.

Still, there were always rumblings when any contract originated in the Naga sector. Chandra was sick of how her kind were treated. How they weren't trusted. Or worse, looked down upon as inferior. They were sometimes even lumped in with the Nullians. Absurd.

That was why Chandra wanted out. Why she wanted to move to the center system. Once she paid the visa fees, she wouldn't have to worry about political upheaval ever again. She wouldn't be constantly ashamed of her own people.

At least Vinata was dead. *Her* plan had been to flee into the frontier. To start over. Chandra couldn't even imagine such a thing. Why would one flee away from society? It was practically the same thing as devolving. She tried to imagine herself working the dirt of an uninhabited planet. Preposterous.

The thought of wide-open skies was suffocating to her.

Chandra couldn't wait to get away from it all. Her idiot late husband had been constantly involved in the court's machinations, and where had that led him? Murdered by a crawler while playing a game.

That one action had turned out to be the luckiest turn of events in Chandra's life.

Chandra had reluctantly accepted the noble title of princess when her uncle came to power. She didn't want attention brought to herself, but the title was necessary if she wanted to claim Widow's Rights.

The path that had presented itself to Chandra had appeared all at once, as if by magic. As if a divine entity had seen how much she'd suffered, the humiliations she'd had to endure, and thought: *Enough. Now is your time.*

All it required was for Carl and Donut to survive for just a little longer.

It was so simple. It was meant to be. All her suffering. All that hard work. The humiliation of being a second wife. It would all be worth it.

Once this was all done, Chandra could possibly be one of the richest private citizens in the galaxy.

And all because of a fucking human in his underwear and his pet rodent.

The first few steps in the plan were already done. This first part had happened so fast. It had been literally just a few hours' worth of legal work and filings to get started. She'd done it from this tiny room in the *Ventilator*. It was done before Faction Wars were finished. Even as the dwindling royal battleships had fired their last salvo, she'd not felt even a tingle of danger. It was amazing how much one could accomplish while sitting in a tiny room with wideband tunnel access. In hours, she'd changed the course of her own life.

She'd asserted her Widow's Rights and claimed Carl as her husband in Naga court. She'd had a moment of terror when the judge had thought it worthwhile to put the matter to public jury. But, apparently, the idea of "punishing" Carl by forcing him to marry her was amusing to the uneducated peasants, and they'd voted overwhelmingly to allow the union. They'd even added the traditional wedding gift–the holdings of the defeated–as Carl's "prize" in a fan box.

Either way, now that was done, Chandra, as Carl's wife–and therefore his signatory in most legal matters–had already gotten the burners fired up on multiple contracts. Carl's own lawyer, a Nullian named Quasar, had done a surprisingly competent job building the legal entities required for the Princess Posse fan group to collect money. Though she still had a case pending to withdraw half of their profits early.

Where this Quasar had failed was in not asserting Carl's rights over all of Donut's earnings. Donut's species was not yet recognized as a legally competent racial entity by the Syndicate and therefore all of her assets should have been placed under a conservatorship. Carl was clearly the best choice as custodian. And not just a custodian, but a true beneficiary. She'd filed on her new husband's behalf to be recognized as such, and it was granted automatically.

The will wasn't necessary. As his wife, she would automatically get everything upon his inevitable death, minus any taxes. But she filed one anyway. Better to be safe.

And then, after a short conversation and a discreet payment to a district judge's reelection campaign, Chandra had found herself assigned as Princess Donut's attorney, effectively giving herself access to both Carl's and Donut's financial empires.

She was currently in the process of threatening the second fan group, the Donut Holes, with obliteration should they not immediately assign 38% of their profits directly to Donut's conservatorship. Their newest product, the Princess Palette eye makeup kit, was already the highest-earning crawler merch in the history of the crawl.

The Donut Holes group had recently won the auction for Princess Donut's open sponsorship slot. There was yet another court case pending on whether or not to allow it. Chandra's assistant was writing a brief asserting that the claim should be allowed, but only if the Donut Holes agreed to pay the licensing fee to the conservatorship. With 60% already going to the Syndicate, the 2% left over should have been more than enough for them to keep operating. And either way, she really wanted to take a look at their books. That group had much more money than they should have. There was something going on there, and she needed to get to the bottom of it.

If the Donut Holes didn't agree to the 38%, Chandra would have her two Taurin associates call on the families of the founders of the unauthorized fan group. It was always easy to get people to agree to things when one exerted pressure in the proper place. Especially when they had small children.

She'd have them do that as soon as they were done with their first assignment: eliminating her biggest threat. Quasar. She'd paid the fee, and they were already on their way to pay him a visit.

But all of the legal issues with the Donut Holes could wait until tomorrow. For right now, Chandra needed to make certain the rodent didn't take a deal. She didn't think this would be difficult.

"Who are you? And why do I feel funny?" the creature asked. She shook her head, splattering red ash over everything. Chandra had missed what'd happened at the end of the previous floor, though she was glad to hear Donut had survived. The oddsmakers had had her survival rate at 40% the last she'd checked, but Chandra had known the creature would pull through. Rodents had an uncanny ability to come out on top.

Chandra spent a moment examining the ugly thing. She didn't understand how this creature had captivated so many people. It resembled and had the same coloring as the long-haired pack voles from her world, but with an annoying flat face.

That thought made her stomach rumble.

"My name is Princess Chandra, Esquire, and I have been assigned as your attorney," Chandra said. "You feel funny because you're in a type-A containment zone. Most of your enhancements are turned off. It's like a zero zone, but designed to accommodate certain types of crawlers who might have issues in regular zero zones."

"Princess?" The creature straightened on her chair. "And my attorney? I thought it would be Quasar."

"Then you thought incorrectly."

Donut spent a long moment examining her. "Very well," she finally said, sounding hesitant. "So, you're a princess, then? I certainly hope you don't hold what happened against me and Carl. I do hope the dead snake lady wasn't your sister or something."

Chandra chuckled. "I wasn't considered a princess until most recently. There's been a recent change of government, and my uncle is now the Sultan. I was of no relation to the late Vinata."

Donut brightened. "Well, then congratulations are in order! I suppose that means Carl and I are partially responsible for your ascension. If you need any advice on being a princess, I will, of course, be happy to give you tips. I must say, Princess, your golden brown pattern really is a nice shade. Vinata was quite stunning with her cobra hood and white and gold scales, but Carl says she really wasn't white and gold, but gray, and she'd been hiding it. Was that a scandal when people saw it? I bet it was a scandal."

It actually was quite the subject of conversation, much to Chandra's irritation. The literal king had been deposed and a new government put in place via a bloody coup, yet that particular scene had dominated the news cycle. The vid of Vinata, insane, ashen scales on full display, beating on Carl as she bled out, only to be finished off by a slug, had been shown over and over.

Chandra had taken no small amount of pleasure at the sight of Vinata's death. Chandra had worked hard for everything she'd ever had, and Vinata had been born into it. The late crown princess had basically won the genetic lottery by getting born into that family, and she still couldn't hold on to what she had. She hadn't even been killed by a fellow Naga, but by a crawler. And not just a crawler, but a crawler's pet slug. What a disgrace.

The sight of Vinata losing it all had been so . . . satisfying.

The rodent continued to ramble. She was not making any sort of point. She sat there, talking and talking, absently wiping her paw on the side of the table.

". . . One should be proud of who they are, I say. I would be lying if I said people don't judge based on coloring, but one should never pretend to be something they're not. It's true, yes, that tortoiseshell coloring is not as 'desirable' as an all-white Persian in some circles. And, yes, people say 'tortitude' makes some cats difficult to work with, but you know what I say to those snobs? Look at my pedigree and my points and tell me I'm not as desirable. Tell me I'm not a champion. As bad as Miss Beatrice was, she did have an eye for exceptionality, and nobody can accuse her of not shooting for the stars, at least on the cat show circuit. Do you really only have two arms? Vinata had six. And you're much smaller. At least you probably save a lot at the nail salon." She examined Chandra's hands, and Chandra instinctively hid her dirty nails under the table, strangely ashamed.

Chandra bristled at her own reaction to this thing.

"Stop," she finally said, making a point to hold up her hand. "For the sake of the gods, stop talking. We have a lot to go over."

Donut nodded. "I know you have a job to do, but I'm telling you right now, I have no intentions upon taking a deal at this point."

Chandra nodded. "Very well. You have several offers, but I agree that none of them are even worth looking at." That actually wasn't true. While most of the crawlers, even Carl, were getting worse-than-usual offers, likely due to the large number of survivors, she'd taken a glance at all the offers they had for Donut. There was one where she could have cohosted the prize carousel with Carl if he also picked the deal. There was a game guide, with a fifteen-season commitment. That was unheard-of for someone on the tenth floor. Most of Donut's deals were quick, safe assignments but with nasty royalty-snatching clauses buried deep inside. They were basically offering her an easy out in exchange for all the money she'd already earned. These were likely a direct result of Chandra's recent movements. Most crawlers died intestate, and their earnings went straight to the Syndicate anyway, but now that Donut had competent representation, they'd lose out on a significant amount of money once the rodent finally died. These offers were trying to claw some of that back.

It was interesting, considering that the entire show seemed to be self-destructing all around them. Honestly, Chandra hadn't been paying attention this season. She'd only taken notice a few weeks back when someone had suggested that her husband, Rishi, and his first wife both were in mortal danger. And they were in danger because of that same crawler who'd stabbed her husband's cousin in the neck with a pen.

But if Chandra were being honest with herself, and if she didn't have a literal interest in Donut lasting at least a little longer, she would have recommended that her client take the deals.

Donut whisked her tail. "Carl says he's not going to take a deal, so I'm not going to take one."

"Done," Chandra said, closing the folder, relieved she wasn't going to have to waste time explaining everything. On her interface, she selected **Crawler Refusing a Deal**. There was a chime.

"So, are we done here?" Donut asked.

"Not quite," Chandra said, pulling out a second folder and opening it. She'd had her assistant print off and label all the new filings and rulings. There were dozens of pages. She took a breath, feeling oddly nervous all of a sudden. Why did she feel like this? She'd just survived a missile barrage against the warship she was sitting in, yet this nonentity was causing . . . what? Apprehension? Ludicrous. It was something else. Maybe she was anxious that this idiot was going to screw it all up for her.

Chandra sat straighter. "We need to have a conversation about something else. Several somethings, actually. You're not going to like what I'm about to say, but you need to know there's absolutely nothing you can do about it. And the sooner you come to terms with that, the sooner we'll be able to move on. Do you understand?"

The creature seemed to narrow her eyes. In an instant, her posture changed. "What're you trying to say, Princess?"

Chandra produced the court order laying out that Princess Donut had been put under a conservatorship and that Carl was named her guardian. She slid it over.

Donut stared at it for several moments. The rodent sighed. "Question. Is this meeting being broadcast to the universe?"

"It is not," Chandra said, "but the negotiations of all the top-ten crawlers are available live to media accounts, so we are likely being watched by many right now."

The rodent nodded. "Well, let's see the rest of them, then."

Chandra was mildly surprised. She was expecting the rodent to immediately lash out. Instead, she just quietly went over each page. *She's beaten and she knows it.* That was a relief. This was going to be easier than she had thought.

Donut continued to examine the papers without additional questions. The lawsuit that rerouted all future funding and royalties into Chandra's trust account. The seizure of the Princess Posse's accounts, including the Faction Wars prize money. The first draft of the brief regarding the challenge to the Donut Holes being a sponsor. The formation of a corporation to seek out and attach damages to all those who were using Donut's likeness for profit. The subpoena for the Donut Holes demanding to see their books.

The only time when Donut paused was when she'd read the marriage ruling and certificate that announced Carl was now Chandra's husband. She had invoked Widow's Rights. This was the old Naga law that stated a Naga royal widow could claim her husband's assassin as her new husband. This right usually only extended to the "primary" wife, but because that bitch of an obsidian had died alongside Vinata, Chandra had moved to the primary slot, even if it had been only for a few hours.

Rishi had had five more wives after Chandra. She knew some of them were now dead, but she didn't know who.

She didn't care. She'd hated them all. She'd hated Rishi, too.

The final sheet, which basically laid out how all the money both Carl and Donut were earning was now being stored in multiple interest-bearing accounts at Kindred Bank, remained on the table. Donut took a few moments looking at the bottom line.

"I suppose that goddess was correct when she said Carl was married," Donut finally said after several minutes of reading. "Is this bottom line correct? This is how much money Carl and I have earned?"

Chandra was surprised at the question. "Yes. And this is before we go after the crawl itself. They haven't been following some of their own rules, and there are some penalties buried in there that should see us getting a few percentage points from their 60%."

The creature nodded again. She kept rubbing her paw on the table.

"You know," Donut said after a moment, "Carl has some legal papers just like this. He got them on the eighth floor from his father's trailer. He pulled them out and left them on the table in my room where we sleep, but I don't think he has even read them. I believe he's too scared to look. But *I* read them. Do you know what they say?"

"I don't care," Chandra said. "All pre-collapse Earth rulings have been rendered invalid."

"Exactly," Donut said. "Invalid."

Chandra felt herself blink. "What? What does that mean? *These* are valid, enforceable legal documents."

"Did you know," Donut said, "that every Naga we have met so far has been a raging psycho? For about five seconds I thought maybe you'd be a nice one, but it appears I was incorrect. And that's really sad. The only nice one was Manasa, and she was a worm head. I must say, you guys really are doing a terrible job of being ambassadors for your species. It's no wonder they say all those nasty things about your kind on the internet."

"What does that have to do with anything? What does that have to do with the Earth legal papers?"

"I thought you didn't care what the Earth legal papers said." Donut tsked. "If you must know, it was a remarkably similar set of documents. Earth jargon is just as stupid and boring as your stuff. Carl's grandparents had set money aside for Carl, and the father was attempting to get access to it without Carl knowing. And there was a marriage certificate in there as well, though that one was for Carl's father and his new wife. There were also a few court documents for Carl's dad regarding several arrests. Nothing too important, especially now. But, in the end, when you put them all together, they do something interesting. They paint a very distinct picture of who Carl's father was as a person. Much the same way these papers paint a picture of who you are, *Princess* Chandra." Donut let out another sigh. "What a sad little snake you are. I pity you."

The words hit Chandra so hard, she felt as if she'd been slapped. It took her a moment to recover.

I am not *little. I am* not *sad. I* deserve *this.*

She knew this creature had an acid tongue. She'd promised herself she wouldn't react. She needed to keep up her emotionless, matter-of-fact delivery. She had a plan.

Chandra forgot all of that as the red-hot anger overwhelmed her. She had lived her entire life in the shadow of the undeserving. She had worked for everything she ever had. And for this . . . thing to call her "sad"? To call her "small"?

How fucking dare she?

"Listen to me, you vile rodent. I don't care what you think. This is all going to happen no matter what you do or say. I am showing you these papers because as your attorney, I am required to show them to you. I only want you to live through this next floor because if you survive, it makes *me* money. After, I don't care. Either way, your financial legacy is now in safe hands."

Donut scoffed. "Let me ask you a question. Why do you think they rendered all the Earth stuff invalid?"

"What sort of question is that? Earth no longer exists."

Donut, who'd been sitting on the chair, suddenly jumped to the table. She stood on all fours right in the middle of the table atop the pile of papers, her body overlapping and combining with her folder. Chandra had to force herself not to shrink away.

"Oh, honey, let me explain something to you. Whatever happens to me next, it doesn't matter anymore. You're not trying to just rob me and your husband, who, by the way, snores like a chainsaw. I hope that weird snake head of yours can wear earplugs. I also hope you like biscuit sandwiches. No, sweetie. You're attempting to steal from the Princess Posse. And the Princess Posse is more than just myself and Carl. Didn't you see what just happened?

You think you being out there outside the dungeon is protecting you?"

The creature let out a little laugh.

"We are everywhere. Yes, Earth is destroyed. Yes, Carl's dad's legal documents mean nothing. What do you think is going to happen to your little marriage certificate and your money transfers when *you* are destroyed?"

Chandra laughed bitterly, trying to sound more confident than she suddenly felt. "There is nothing you can do. And it's not stealing if it's done legally."

"Hmm," Donut said. "So, as my lawyer, if I offered someone fifty million credits to stop you from doing this, by any means necessary, would that be legal?"

"Of course not," Chandra snapped.

Donut looked up into the air. "Then to any reporters watching this, I want it known that I am *not* offering fifty million credits to anyone who finds this snake and turns her inside out on my behalf. And I am most definitely *not* offering an additional five million to someone who takes that head of hers and turns it into a hat for me. Though if I was, I would be willing to cancel the order should she change her mind about attempting to steal from the Princess Posse."

A strange, unexpected terror washed over her.

Chandra suddenly had a blinking message from her Taurin associates on her own interface. Their fee was only sixty thousand credits, plus expenses, for the job to find and eliminate Quasar. The message coming in at this very moment was a coincidence. It had to be. How could they possibly be watching this? Why would they have a media pass?

But the new message rattled her.

By the gods, what's come over me?

She clicked the message.

Chandra. We have questions about the job. What are your coordinates?

Terror came over her.

I have to get out of here. This isn't what was supposed to happen. How could everything change so fast? Chandra gathered up the folders. Of course they wanted to ask in person. All their meetings were in person.

To gather the final folder, she'd have to reach through the creature standing on the table. She'd never seen eyes like this. She'd never seen such intensity, not even in her uncle when he'd told her that he planned on taking the sultanate for himself.

She couldn't bring herself to reach through the illusion of the creature to grab the last folder. Princess Donut took yet another step toward her, and it was everything she could do not to let out a yelp. Shame and fear overwhelmed her at the same time.

Donut leaned in toward Chandra and let out a low growl, like she was going to pounce. The crawler whispered, "Since you're new to this, let me give you your first lesson on being a princess. Lesson one, don't put yourself in situations where you're so afraid that you piss yourself. It shows a lack of decorum."

Chandra, shaking, looked down. She hadn't soiled herself, yet she'd still looked, and for that, she was humiliated.

"I . . . I didn't."

"Not yet," Donut said.

HORRIBLE ONE

CONTROL

HEAT 1 OF 7

1

Welcome, Crawler. Welcome to the tenth floor.

TIME TO LEVEL COLLAPSE: LEVEL TIMER HAS BEEN TEMPORARILY SUSPENDED FOR THIS FLOOR. PLEASE WAIT FOR THE ANNOUNCEMENT FROM THAT INEBRIATED FISH IF WE CAN MANAGE TO WAKE HER UP FOR THE DETAILS.

Views: 933 Septillion
Followers: 3.5 Quintillion
Favorites: 971 Quadrillion
Leaderboard Rank: 3
Bounty: 3,200,000 gold

Congrats, Crawler. You have received a Platinum Venison Box.

Remaining Crawlers: 5,501

Entering your garage.

Warning: The next heat starts in five minutes. Safe room access is blocked until the heat is over.

I HIT THE TILED FLOOR WITH A HEAVY *THUMP*. ONE MOMENT I'D BEEN sitting in the zero zone, talking with Quasar about that psychotic Naga woman, and the next I was here.

I stood, wiping myself off. I was still covered in blood and gore and red ash from the end of Faction Wars. This was a large room with a black-and-white-checkered tiled floor and corrugated metal walls, like a smaller-sized airplane hangar. It was cold. I turned to face the only other creatures in here. They were a pair of white-tagged gremlins standing in the back corner, both wearing overalls.

I blinked at the NPCs just as Donut appeared next to me with a yowl. She hit the ground sideways, yelped, and then jumped to my shoulder.

"Carl, I'm atop the leaderboard again! I'm number one!"

"I'm very happy for you."

"So, I met the new wife."

"Yeah, I heard," I said. I gave her a pat. "I haven't met her, but Quasar filled me in. I heard you grabbed the upper hand pretty quickly."

"Don't be racist. It's upper *paw*. But yes. If she thinks she can just slither in and take advantage of the Posse like that, that legless bitch has another thing coming. And I thought Miss Beatrice was bad. You sure know how to pick them, Carl."

There was an ominous countdown timer in the upper left of my vision. It was at four minutes and thirty seconds and counting down. We needed to figure it out before we did anything else.

DONUT: MORDECAI, I HAVE TO PICK A NEW CLASS! HELP ME WITH THE CHOICES.

MORDECAI: There you guys are. You have four minutes to get your vehicle ready. Donut, you're back as party leader, so pick a class quickly.

I turned in a circle. At the front of the garage was a massive roll-up door. A chain pulley system crisscrossed the ceiling. I'd seen plenty of similar systems in both car shops and dry dock repair bays. The two gremlins started jogging toward us.

I already knew some of what was going on out there because Quasar had told me, but even he hadn't known everything. I clicked through my messages and pop-ups, my heart still racing. I briefly paused at that number "5,501." That meant 75% of us had taken deals.

I took the briefest of moments to let that sink in. Such an overwhelming sense of secondhand relief flooded me. I didn't blame anyone for tapping out. Each and every one of them had earned it.

Part of me wished I had the luxury.

I was stalling, even if just for a second. I already knew what the next message was. A message reminding me why I would never be able to take that path. I took a breath.

JUSTICE LIGHT: I am not sorry. Peace to you all, brothers and sisters.

This message is from a deceased mercenary.

Sadness overwhelmed me. I already knew Justice Light was dead. Quasar had told me. Still, the sight of those words was like a kick to the stomach.

You crazy asshole. What did you do? What did that trap do?

A response to his message appeared on the group chat.

ROSETTA: Rest well, comrade. We are not far behind.

She was still in here in the safe room, as was Tipid. They'd both been converted to hired mercenaries.

Quasar hadn't really known the specifics. All he knew was that the Nothing was "broken" and that everything was in chaos on the twelfth and eighteenth floors. And furthermore, the outworlders on those two floors were protected from really dying by the system AI. They could get hurt on the eighteenth floor, they could still "die," but they would immediately get brought back to their rooms in the club. A club that was physically inside of the now-awake dungeon boss. The system wasn't letting anyone eject.

Some of the things that had leaked from the Nothing were using this to their advantage. It was like what we'd done to Growler Gary, but worse. Much worse.

Quasar had only given me a quick version. So far, the now-awake Scolopendra hadn't yet done anything other than move around a lot. Apparently, the tourists on the eighteenth floor had the ability to move themselves to the sixteenth floor, where it was safe, but they first had to make their way through the seventeenth floor for some reason, where it was not, and anyone who even attempted it got turned to mince and immediately brought back to life on the eighteenth, where the worst of the worst were stalking the hallways.

Forgotten gods. Demons from hundreds of former quests. All sorts of other horrific creatures. Several had made their way to the eighteenth floor, but, luckily—or not luckily, depending on how you looked at it—these creatures all appeared *inside* the final boss. And not just *inside* the monster's guts, but inside the club, where they immediately set themselves on the guests. Guests who couldn't die, no matter what was being done to them.

The cameras had gone dark after the first few hours.

Those on the twelfth were faring better, considering they were in the bodies of gods with god powers. Though apparently the non-sponsored gods were all suddenly acting quite strange. That's all Quasar had known.

I hoped the city of Larracos and all those who'd gone with it to the twelfth floor were doing okay.

More messages came, but I didn't read them in detail other than to note who was here and who wasn't. Elle. Imani. Zhang. Florin. Louis. Chris. Britney. Bautista. All checking in. Prepotente had some rant about Jurgen.

So many of my friends *hadn't* taken deals.

DONUT: OMG, THESE CLASSES STILL COME WITH ACCESSORIES!

She gasped.

DONUT: SOME COME WITH *PET* ACCESSORIES! THE LAS VEGAS SHOWGIRL COMES WITH A FEATHERED HAT FOR MONGO!

MORDECAI: This class might be better.

DONUT: I AM NOT PICKING ZOO WARDEN. MY GOODNESS. OHHH, WHAT ABOUT THIS ONE? PROBLEMATIC INFLUENCER? IT COMES WITH AN UPGRADE TO MY SOCIAL MEDIA BOARD! WAIT, THERE'S ANOTHER TAB! LOOK AT THIS ONE!

MORDECAI: Holy shit, I see it. Uh, we should probably study these further before you pick one from this tab. These are in association with your other deity titles. This is all new to me.

DONUT: WE *ARE* IN A HURRY, BUT THESE ARE MUCH BETTER. THIS ONE COMES WITH A *HEALING* AURA AND A HAT. I'M PICKING IT.

Donut glowed.

DONUT: HEY! I JUST GOT A REALLY NASTY MESSAGE FROM KHEPRI. ISN'T THAT THE WEIRD BUG GOD THAT CARL AND KATIA FOUGHT ON THE LAST FLOOR? IT SAYS HE'S FORMING A "DEATH CULT" IN MY NAME. WHAT DOES THAT MEAN?

MORDECAI: Nothing good.

"What did you pick?" I asked.

"Assassin of Sekhmet," she said. "It comes with accessories for every pet in the party, and all sorts of great spells and other stuff!"

Warning: The next heat starts in two minutes, and you don't even have a vehicle or mount. You're not allowed to walk, dumbasses.

"Carl, what is a 'heat'? That sounds obscene."

The gremlins were suddenly there, both looking worried. One was a female gremlin named Hedy, and the other a male named Waldrip Chris. They both started talking at once, shouting about us having to quickly make a choice. These shouts turned to a scuffle, and then, out of nowhere, they were beating the shit out of each other as they continued to shout at us. I could barely understand either of them. The woman gremlin had been lugging a red toolbox, but she'd dropped it to the ground the moment they'd started to fight. The man had some sort of vegetable in his hand. It was a tan-colored gourd, and he was now attempting to bash it over the head of the woman gremlin.

I quickly examined them.

Hedy. Gremlin. Level 30 vehicle mechanic.

This is an applicant to be manager of your garage.

This is a non-combatant NPC.

Hedy is an expert in all things mechanical. If you choose a mechanical-based vehicle, she will be in charge of your garage. Don't let her appearance fool you. She's about as experienced as one can get when it comes to engines. If you can limp your vehicle back to the garage, rest assured it'll be good as new by the time the next heat starts.

Warning: Just because Hedy is a non-combatant NPC, it doesn't mean she's invulnerable. If something happens to her, your vehicle will not get repaired between heats.

Hedy is not allowed to enter your safe room.

The second description was similar.

Waldrip Chris. Gremlin. Level 30 animal trainer.

This is an applicant to be manager of your garage.

This is a non-combatant NPC.

Waldrip Chris is an expert in all things biological. If you choose a flesh-based vehicle, he will be in charge of your garage. From a minor case of the sniffles to appendage amputation, he will make certain your trusty mount is ready for the next heat.

Waldrip Chris had the same set of warnings.

The two gremlins continued to roll across the garage floor. Waldrip Chris had Hedy pinned and was smacking her over the head with his gourd thing as she blindly reached for her toolbox.

As soon as I finished reading both descriptions, a new message popped up.

Your party leader must choose the manner of vehicle. Mechanical or biological. Once you choose between the two, you will spin the wheel for the specific vehicle chassis or creature.

"A vehicle?" Donut said incredulously. "I have the *Twinkle Toes* spell and a level 15 *Heal Critter*. Mongo won't like another animal in the party, but it's probably the best choice."

"Pet spells don't work on special mounts," Hedy the gremlin gasped from the floor. She managed to grasp her toolbox and reach inside. She pulled out a mallet that was much too big to have fit in the box. With a shout of triumph, she swung the giant mallet, clocking the other gremlin. She remained on the floor, panting. "Neither *Twinkle Toes* nor *Heal Critter* will work on them!"

The other gremlin growled as he scrambled up. He bled profusely from a cut on his head. He still held the gourd. "Don't tell them that, you bitch!" He jumped at the prone woman like a wrestler leaping from the ropes, gourd held over his head before he smashed it on his opponent's face. The vegetable thing broke into pieces, and tiny bugs spilled out and crawled all over her. The woman gremlin shrieked, wiping them off with her free hand as she writhed. She blindly swung her mallet, almost catching me in the foot.

"It's the truth, jackass," she called as she sputtered.

"Carl, what is happening?" Donut demanded.

"Uh, I think they're both applying for a job."

We had one minute left.

"My goodness, you two. Quit fighting!" Donut called. "Carl, I'm starting to feel the definition of 'non-combatant' is very loose."

"What did you call me, you unshaven hedge creeper?" Waldrip Chris bellowed as he punched Hedy in the face with a closed fist. There was a terrible crunch.

"What about *Repair* and *Fix* scrolls and potions?" I asked.

"Nope," Waldrip Chris said triumphantly as he continued to pound her. He grunted with each punch. "All vehicles are proprietary to the arena. Ever seen a Charm Wombat? You can't get better handling than one of those furry bastards. And with a few upgrades . . . Ooof!"

He didn't finish before the mallet once again connected with his head with a wet *smack*. He tumbled away.

Hedy sat up and sneezed, sending blood and beetles everywhere. "If you have any other pets in your party, a mechanical vehicle won't ever try to eat them."

And there it was.

From next door I heard the revving of a high-octane engine. The walls of our garage shook.

"You," Donut said, pointing at Hedy. "I choose you."

"Ha!" Hedy shouted.

"Wait, wait, please," Waldrip Chris said, backing away, still holding his head. "You could get a Cloud Cheetah. With their speed and agility—"

"I'm quite sorry, Waldrip Chris," Donut said, "but we are in a hurry. I'm afraid we will be going with something that's not going to eat my Mongo. We choose mechanical. And just a word of advice for your next job interview. I would refrain from—"

Blam!

Waldrip Chris exploded in a spray of red and green mist.

"Gah!" I called, jumping back as Donut yowled.

Mechanical has been chosen. Your Mechanic is Hedy.

2

HEDY THE GREMLIN DIDN'T REACT AT THE SUDDEN DETONATION OF HER co-applicant. She was already running for the front of the garage. She leaped and grabbed the chain, pulling the door open. "As soon as it appears, jump in! You come in last place, you die just like Waldrip Chris! Me, too, so get your asses in gear! Only one of you touch the steering wheel or controls. You can't drive two heats in a row, and there's only two of you! Don't come in last! Do whatever you can to not come in last!"

Before either of us could react, a giant wheel appeared, plopping into existence over the soupy remains of the exploded gremlin. There were a hundred-plus spots on the round apparatus, and each spot consisted of a vague cartoon silhouette of a vehicle. I only had time to see a few before it started spinning. One was a literal school bus. Another appeared to be a Hummer. These were all Earth-based vehicles of various sizes. I caught sight of what looked like a moped followed by a massive dump truck.

"Do we need speed?" I called. "Or something armored?"

"You get what you get," Hedy called as she struggled with the door. As she pulled it up, a black asphalt road was revealed. It was dark outside. Multiple shapes were emerging, both driving and walking as they pulled up to a line. "The track conditions and hazards are gonna change each time! First three races will all be paved!"

As the wheel turned, the countdown timer suddenly froze with twenty seconds left. The dungeon loudspeaker crackled to life. The wheel continued to spin.

A familiar voice called out into the garage.

You're all going to die. You should already be dead. You idiots should have all taken deals. You did it to torture me, didn't you? Why are you fighting it? Why? Why are you still alive? Why am I still alive? Why won't you let me die?

The button remained pressed for several seconds, and we could hear the sound of her just sitting there, bubbling.

Everything hurts.

There was a blare of feedback, and then the intercom cut off.

"Uh, Carl," Donut asked. "Was that the 'kill, kill, kill' lady?"

"It was," I said.

The wheel slowed.

The loudspeaker crackled a second time, but this time it was clearly Zev's voice. She sounded harried as if she'd had to dive for the loudspeaker.

Uh, hello. Everyone. It looks like we have just over 5,500 crawlers who survived Faction Wars and decided they wanted to continue on. That means there were almost 15,000 who took a deal, which is fantastic, and a record. The system AI has asked me to tell you to ignore what's happening on any other floors and to—and this is a quote—"Focus on the floor like everything is normal. Because everything is normal. Ignore all those armies trying to literally vaporize the solar system. F-you if you think overwise." Uh, okay, okay. "Fuck you if you think overwise." What my, uh, colleague was trying to say just before is, this is the tenth floor. The floor is called "Don't come in last." I guess you can figure out what that means. The floor will consist of seven heats, or races, starting with nine teams each.

You've been split into teams no bigger than four, and if you're solo, you've been teamed up with one or two other crawlers. It looks like the final number of teams is exactly 1,800, which is a lot more than we originally planned, as you can imagine. And since every track is different, we've had to allow the AI to design most of these tracks. So, uh, keep that in mind.

As Zev spoke, the wheel slowed. The choices all came into view. Snowmobile. Something I was pretty sure was a library bookmobile. The Popemobile. It kept slowly moving. A forklift. Some sort of military missile launcher. Zev continued.

Your vehicle or creature will always be 100% repaired or healed between races as long as your garage attendant remains alive. At the end of each heat, you will be able to choose an upgrade for your vehicle or creature. If you come in first place in a heat, you can choose *three* regular upgrades or one Golden upgrade. At the end of the fourth heat, everyone gets one Golden upgrade of their choice. Also, if you come in last . . . well, second to last, then the audience gets to vote for your upgrade. You'll always get a hint of what the next heat will be, and you'll need to pay attention because you might need an upgrade that will help you survive the next environment.

"Oh shit," I said as the wheel hovered over what was either a floor polisher or a goddamned Zamboni. It clicked one more time before settling on the square shape of a box truck. A box truck with windows.

"Carl, what is that?" Donut demanded.

The wheel disappeared with a *pop*, which caused more Waldrip Chris bits and gourd pieces to splatter. The truck crunched into place, bouncing up and down on squeaking shocks.

I sighed. "It's a food truck," I said.

It did not have the exact same shape as the silhouette. This was much more . . . festive than the image on the wheel.

"Is that a real gun on the top?" Donut asked.

"I don't think so."

The colorful, gleaming truck appeared to have come right off the assembly line. It was about twenty feet long. It was, at first glance, a typical large-sized food truck. At least the body of it was. It was basically the same body of a package delivery truck, but presumably with a small kitchen within. The now-familiar logo of a chicken with a fedora and red tie was painted on the side under the bullet-hole-ridden logo.

Big Shot Chicken. I'd never heard of the restaurant chain before we'd entered the dungeon, but Donut and I had spent some time stuck in a Big Shot Chicken safe room on the second floor while we'd been trapped by the rage elemental. The whole restaurant was, apparently, a small chain from somewhere in the Southwest of the United States. A chicken restaurant with a 1920s gangster theme.

The truck was clearly a modern model, though the front was replaced with a faux-1920s-style hood made to mimic a Prohibition-era truck, complete with curved fenders made of shining chrome and round fluted headlamps. The whole front had kind of a plasticky, fiberglass look that gave the impression that maybe this food truck wasn't really meant to be driven at all, and it normally sat at an amusement park or state fair somewhere, more for show than mobility.

Which gave me a very, very ominous feeling.

The most distinctive feature of the truck was the massive, clearly plastic tommy gun on the roof of the thing. The gun's most distinctive feature—the gigantic round drum magazine—partially obscured the windshield to the point where the truck would be dangerous to drive. This pretty much confirmed what I'd already suspected. That this thing wasn't street legal.

I hoped it had an engine.

Zev spoke with more urgency.

You may attack other vehicles, but you cannot steal them. You can't use movement spells such as *Teleport* on your vehicle, and you can't use movement spells to bring yourself *into* the vehicles of your opponents.

We'll have more details soon! Use your garage attendants! Every heat must have a different driver, so only one of you touch the steering wheel or hold the reins, especially if it's just two of you. Also, try not to kill more than one team, because if more than two teams don't make it to the finish line—

The speaker abruptly cut off.

The timer continued to tick down.

"Get in! Get in!" Hedy called. "Only one person drive!"

"Carl, how am I supposed to drive this thing!" Donut demanded as

I rushed into the driver's seat. There was no passenger's seat at all. Just a gleaming metal floor with a no-slip mat. There was no divider between the front and the back, and a brand-new aluminum kitchen filled the back space.

I turned the key, and, thankfully, an engine rumbled to life. A good, healthy engine.

"Hang on," I called.

3

THERE WAS A LOUD HORN, PRESUMABLY INDICATING THE START OF THE race, and a device on the dashboard lit up.

I held my breath, and I hit the gas. The whole truck lurched. Donut yowled as her claws dug into my shoulder. I had to sit really low in the seat to see out the front because of the goddamned gun thing on the roof. Ahead, several opponents zoomed off at the sound of the horn.

The panel on the dash gave a few beeps. It was a navigation system of some sort. It was a square box with the words **Navitron 1000** over it. A map appeared on the flat-screen but minimized itself, and then words popped up, speaking in my head like it was an item description, but the words also spoke out loud into the cabin of the truck.

This was a distinctly female, strangely familiar voice I couldn't place:

Heat number one of seven.

Driver: Carl.

Navigator: The Champion of Nekhebit, Harbinger of Doom, Assassin of the Great and Feral Sekhmet, Princess Donut, She Who Is Foretold to Bring the Gnashing of the Teeth and the Woe of All Who Harbor Hope and Is Known as the Oak Fell to Those Who Dare Utter Her Name.

Distance: 53 kilometers.

Track: Asphalt-paved road. Mostly flat.

Tasks required to complete: Just get to the finish line.

Environment: The Caves of the Screeching Death Manatees.

Hazards: Not yet discovered, but I'm going to go out on a limb

here and suggest the Screeching Death Manatees might be a problem.

Time Limit: 6 hours.

Current ranking: Unknown. Upgrade me to get real-time ranking updates.

It was pitch-black out. I scrambled to find the headlights. I found them and pulled the knob, but nothing happened.

"Carl, do you see what that thing is calling me!"

"Light! I need light," I yelled.

Donut waved her paw, almost casually, and the entire area in front of us lit up brilliantly with her *Torch* spell.

Only some of the vehicles ahead had lights. One—already way off in the distance—was clearly a muscle car of some sort, but it was either a convertible or it had the roof ripped off. I could see two tall shapes in the thing before it disappeared. Right behind it was a fuzzy, four-legged bearlike creature that loped at breakneck speed. Yet another bug-like creature skittered, right on their tail. A minivan that made me think of Louis rumbled off.

Something jumped over us and evaporated into the darkness, melding into the shadows. I didn't get a good view, but Donut hissed, "Dog."

We tore over the checkered starting line, passing by what appeared to be a giant tumbleweed.

The strange round bush just sat there, unmoving in the middle of the wide road. The prickly thing was tall—just as tall as our truck—and it was a round tangle of weeds and brambles. I did a double take. Sticking straight out the center of the entire mess was the head of a goddamned unicorn. A unicorn ripped straight from a little kid's Lisa Frank notebook. All I could see was the head, but it was a white horse with a rainbow-hued mane, which looked as if it had just been brushed. A horn that glittered like an opalescent seashell rose from the thing's head. The head was about the size of a regular horse's head, and it stuck out the top center of the tumbleweed as if it were wearing the brambles like a coat. I couldn't tell what the hell I was looking at. The unicorn's head appeared way too high for it to be standing on the ground.

Some sort of pinkish-red fuzzy rodent sat on the head of the unicorn, but I couldn't tell what it was in the dark. The unicorn started shouting something at us, but my window was rolled up, and I couldn't hear.

"I only saw six opponents," I called, trying to look into the side mirror before realizing there were no side mirrors. "Donut, how many did you count?"

We knew at least one was behind us, assuming the unicorn tumbleweed was an opponent.

"I can't see anything!" she shouted.

Ahead, the road was just a straight black highway with no markings. Despite the brightness of Donut's spell, I couldn't see anything on either side except random sickly-looking trees. There was an occasional glitter, implying there was water out there.

I tried to look at my minimap, but I received an error.

Your minimap is disabled while you are moving.

The GPS *did* have a map. But it was just a mostly straight line with no other features.

"It says we're supposed to be in a cave," I said. I could clearly see stars out the windshield.

The GPS didn't answer or react.

I had the accelerator pressed all the way down, and we were moving about 70 miles per hour, which translated to about 112 kilometers per hour. The heavy truck didn't seem to want to accelerate past that. I couldn't see anyone in front of us at all. At this rate, we'd hit the finish line in just about twenty-five minutes if we didn't stop.

Donut unleashed Mongo into the passenger's side and jumped to his back. The dinosaur screeched in fear at appearing in such close quarters. He waved his wings, smacking me in the face, causing me to swerve.

"Careful!" I shouted. Mongo's tail feathers reached all the way to the back of the long truck. He let out another fearful screech.

"It's okay, Mongo," Donut said. "Mommy needs you as a seat so I can look outside for bad guys."

Mongo peeped again, but this time it had a different tone. I knew that tone.

"Don't let Mongo puke on the dashboard!" I yelled.

Mongo puked on the dashboard.

We hadn't had a break. We'd gone straight from the frantic chaos of the end of the ninth floor to our lawyers to this without a rest. I had dozens of boxes to open. Achievements to go over. A fan box. An impossible god quest that was about to come to a head. Friends to check on. War mages to worry about. An Agatha problem.

Lucia Mar, who somehow had over 100,000 kids in her head. I didn't even know if she was still here.

It was too much.

For the moment, I ignored it all and pretended like I was driving. Just driving and nothing more. Not racing for our lives, though even that part was strangely okay. It was so absurdly normal compared to the army-sized fights of the last floor that I felt a strange calm come over me. There was comfort in this straightforward anxiety. This danger—at least for the moment—was just between myself and Donut.

Right now, if I made a mistake, I would die. Donut would die. And that's it.

There was not a thing I could do at this very moment that would result in the death of thousands, and I could have cried at the relief I felt.

But I knew. I knew that feeling was both temporary and false.

Slam, slam, slam.

No. Don't think of that.

But how could I not? How many times now in just the past five minutes had Donut wiped her paw on something? How hard was I trying to ignore it?

Slam, slam, slam.

Peace to you all, Justice Light had said. How? How?

But then I thought of Katia, finally free. I remembered those who'd taken deals. Of that moment when they'd rained streamers and flowers on me and Donut, all of us pretending to ignore how much was at stake.

There was hope. There was escape. And if not, as Justice Light had shown, as all those who'd come to our aid on the previous floor had shown, there was also the possibility of vengeance.

But first, we had to survive this goddamned tenth floor.

I mentally counted the opponents again.

The muscle car. The bear. The bug. The minivan. The dog. The tumbleweed.

I was missing a few of them. Nine teams. I didn't know if they'd zoomed out ahead of the muscle car, or if they'd been like us and were still stuck in their garage when all this started.

It was already clear we weren't going to be winning this heat. What had Zev said? First place got to pick three upgrades. Whoever won would immediately have an advantage. We certainly couldn't afford to lose, but from the sounds of it, second-to-last place would be almost as bad. We couldn't afford to let the viewers pick our upgrades, either. The viewers were all dicks.

Something loomed up ahead, but still in the distance. Something dark. I glanced at the GPS again, and nothing had changed.

"Donut?" I asked.

"I see it," she said. "It's the entrance to a cave. It's very big. I see movement, but I'm not sure what."

A new message came in. One I instinctually read before I could push it away.

PREPOTENTE: Carl, Donut, everyone else, I come with a warning. Obviously you do not want to come in last place. But do not, I repeat, do not kill or otherwise prevent any of your opponents from crossing the finish line. In fact, I suggest you help any wayward stragglers should one have already fallen.

DONUT: HI, PREPOTENTE! WHAT DID YOU PICK?

PREPOTENTE: I went with the obvious choice, and I chose biological. One would have to be an imbecile to have picked mechanical.

I exchanged a sour look with Donut as I gave the other messages a glance. From what I gathered, Zhang—who was with Li Na—was the only other one who'd picked biological. Elle and Imani had picked mechanical. Chris, who *had* been in Li Na's party but had apparently left near the end of the previous floor, had also picked mechanical, as had Louis, Britney, and Bautista, who were all together.

Florin hadn't yet answered what his choice was, though it sounded like it was just him and Lucia Mar—who, as predicted, had not taken a deal—which likely meant Lucia had been the one to choose. I'd thought that Jurgen was also in their party, but he was somehow now paired up with Prepotente.

CARL: What happens if not everybody finishes the race?

PREPOTENTE: While I don't know for certain quite yet, I strongly believe that the pool of opponents for each heat is set in stone. That means if only one opponent falls during the current heat, then that will be fine. However, if two or more fall during the heat, there won't be enough for the next race. As a result, they will have to mix and match with other groups that are missing a full heat.

I felt cold, and the moment he said it, I knew he was right.

For this first race, all eight of our opponents were NPCs.

CARL: Goddamnit. I think you're right.

PREPOTENTE: Quite. If you kill more than one opponent, then it's possible the next heat will have an opponent team consisting of fellow crawlers. By the end, I fear there will be multiple crawler-versus-crawler races, possibly races where all the opponents are crawler teams.

ELLE: Well, that's just fucking peachy.

IMANI: We can avoid this if we keep all our opponents alive. Avoid killing those you're racing against.

ZHANG: Shit. Guys . . . Na already—

"Carl, watch out!" Donut called.

Just inside the mouth of the cave, the minivan was on its side, flaming, blocking the road. A bugbear was crawling away from the wreckage as another one of the vehicles—a bus-sized ladybug—squealed in pain as it was dragged off the road by the biggest manatee I'd ever seen. One of the riders of the bug ran away from the scene, screaming.

I couldn't tell what manner of creature the bug rider was because the rider was on fire. But it didn't matter because a second later, the house-sized manatee crunched down on the bug, killing it, and the on-fire creature had a notification appear over it for just a second before it exploded much the same way Waldrip Chris the gremlin had.

4

The Trauco Triplets have been eliminated due to the expiration of their mount. Eight teams remain in the current heat.

OUR TRUCK SKIDDED AS I LEANED ON THE BRAKES. THE SOUND OF spilling pots and pans rattled. The truck stopped just short of the crashed, on-fire minivan. A second bugbear appeared as I hit reverse and backed up a little, shouting and pointing at the manatee that continued to munch happily on the giant ladybug.

Prepotente's warning was still echoing in my head. The van was on its side, and it was on fire. But the bugbears, two of them at least, were still alive, fighting to save it. One of them was using what looked like a blanket to put out the fire in the engine compartment.

"We can't lose another team. We gotta get that fire out," I called, jumping out of the truck. "Leave Mongo inside! Mongo, don't let anyone in. Donut, what do you got for the fire? I'll deal with the manatee!"

"Do I look like someone designed to put out fires!" Donut yelled as she jumped heavily to my shoulder. The heat from the fire washed over us. "Goodness, Carl. Why don't *you* put out the fire?" She gasped as she looked up at the manatee. The massive creature loomed over us. "As the number one crawler at level 135, I'll take out whatever the heck this thing is. Goodness, it smells just awful."

The enormously fat creature rose out of the water like a dolphin doing a trick, only this was clearly in defiance of physics. Its flippers waved. White liquid oozed down the manatee's giant face.

Miss Talulah. Level 90 Screeching Death Manatee.

This is a special guest creature for the 10th and 11th floors.

You're probably going to find this hard to believe, but not only are these things sort of real, but that name they have—Screeching Death Manatees—is the *actual* name of record for this particular species. They were regular manatees, not unlike the *Trichechus manatus* most people from your world know and love. These guys were added to a former Land War world undergoing reparative terraforming when the company in charge of the project suddenly went bankrupt. The orcish owner had a bad run at sports betting, which resulted in his entire company and family all getting tossed into an indentureship program.

It took a whole generation before the vultures—in this case, the Operatic Bankers' Federation—picking apart the orc's assets thought to actually check up on all the not-yet-finished terraforming projects to see what was what. One of those worlds was found to have an uplift satellite program that was malfunctioning and running amok.

This satellite was not an intelligence like myself, mind you. This was a passionless, non-sapient artificial intelligence system that had its chubby finger pressed hard on the fast-forward-evolution button. Honestly, it was a godsdamned nightmare.

Anyway, yadda, yadda, yadda, a planet filled with nightmare monsters was born. The Operatic reclamation team, run by a group of guys collectively named Otto Banking Unit 3 (remember that name), originally decided it was best to just poison the whole planet and start over, but an economic-feasibility study came up with an interesting idea. This is a planet filled with nightmare biological creatures. Why let the mantids have a monopoly on theme parks? Why not turn it into a horror-themed safari planet?

The planet was renamed "Red Terror Place of Family Adventure."

And that's where the name "Screeching Death Manatees" comes from. Pretty much everything on the planet was given a name like that, at least according to those dweeb slimes. The raccoons are Doom Crier Beasts. The cockatiels are called Fuck-Off Cockatiels.

This place is still open to this day.

Also of note is that a third of Otto Banking Unit, Otto himself, is currently a registered guest of Club Scolopendra.

Anyway, these manatee things have been changed slightly to reflect their given names. They're a real danger to any passing vehicle or mount, but both of you guys are so OP at this point that Miss Talulah is hardly a threat.

The moment the long description ended, Donut shot the creature with a pair of magic missiles. The whole thing just sort of gargled and collapsed, with a pair of soccer-ball-sized holes in its chest. It fell into the dark water as ladybug pieces fell from both its mouth and the pair of massive holes in its stomach. The water splashed over the road and receded, leaving a sticky film over everything.

From behind, Mongo screeched.

Jesus, I thought. Donut had just one-shot a level 90 monster.

There was a lot there in that description of the manatee that I didn't have time to figure out. The real threat right now was the destruction of the minivan. I turned my attention to the two bugbears.

"Carl, Carl, I have a weird notification," Donut called from my shoulder.

"What is it?" I asked as I quickly searched for the *Temporary Water Source* scrolls in my inventory.

I had to attach the water spell to something solid, and I grabbed the first thing I saw from the junk pile. It was just a regular bucket I'd looted from somewhere. I pulled it out and cast the scroll, and water started gushing from it. I tossed the bucket at the large bugbear, who took it wordlessly and turned toward his smoking van. I made a second one, this time using a kitchen bowl. The smaller bowl caused the water to gush out faster, like from a fire hose. I gave the bowl to the second bugbear.

"It says it's a special guest creature," Donut said. "I have to choose the fate of my kill. What does that even mean? There are two choices. I can keep it dead, and I get regular experience. Or I can let the audience vote on its fate. They have thirty seconds to pick, but I don't know what those choices are! It says I should pick the second choice because it'll be more fun!"

"What?" I asked, with a rising sense of dread, as I watched the two bugbears dance around their van. They were making a real mess of it, despite the water. This was a late-90s Pontiac minivan painted bright red. The fire was in the engine compartment. Even if we got this thing upright again, it wasn't going anywhere.

Still, the system hadn't yet torched the bugbears like it had the drivers of the ladybug. With a living mount, it was clear when something was out of commission. Dead was dead. But with a vehicle . . .

"I picked the second choice!" Donut called. "It says 'Results pending!'"

The bugbear with the bowl screeched anew as his arm caught on fire. His friend turned his bucket on him, and the on-fire bugbear dropped the bowl. It spun off like a rocket, smacking against the far wall of the cave entrance and dropping into the dark water.

Thankfully, the other bugbear soon gained the upper hand, and the fire finally stopped.

The bugbear with the burned arm sat on the ground with a defeated huff. I examined him.

Radoslav. Bugbear. Level 75 Jack of All Trades.

One of three (well, now one of two) from Team Free Love.

The other one was only level 65. His name was Jasha.

Both of them were wearing tie-dyed T-shirts and beaded necklaces. Jasha had a tie-dyed headband. Neither was wearing pants. Their look reminded me of Cheech and Chong, though that look was not mirrored in their pained expressions.

DONUT: THEY'RE BOTH DRESSED LIKE HIPPIES, BUT SOMETHING IS OFF. THEY'RE MORE LIKE THE HIPPIES YOU SEE ON THE PACKAGING FOR HALLOWEEN COSTUMES. YOU KNOW WHAT I MEAN? LIKE THEY'RE UNDERCOVER COPS.

I warily eyed the bugbear sitting on the ground.

"You doing okay there?" I asked.

I met eyes with Radoslav the bugbear for the first time. I shouldn't have been surprised, but I was momentarily taken aback at the pure emotion in the NPC's face. This guy was terrified.

"First race. First obstacle, and we're already crashed," he said. "Alevtina was in the back, and she broke her neck when that damn bug knocked us over." He produced a pack of cigarettes and he pulled one out with his mouth. He offered the pack to me. I hesitated, but I declined. The other bugbear, Jasha, seemed to give up on pouring water on the van and settled next to him on the asphalt. He pulled a cigarette from his friend's pack. Jasha produced a lighter and lit them both.

"She's dead. I checked," Jasha said to the other bugbear. He itched at his headband and then, with a disgusted huff, ripped it off and tossed it. On my shoulder, Donut shifted. She wanted to jump down there and take it.

"She's dead. We're dead," Radoslav said, taking a deep drag. "I never thought we had a real chance anyway."

"She did," Jasha said, indicating the overturned van with his cigarette. "She thought we had a good chance."

Donut jumped from my shoulder and walked up to the pair. The headband disappeared into her inventory. I suppressed a grunt of amusement.

She sniffed at Radoslav.

"I'm sorry for your misfortunes," Donut said. "I am Princess Donut, and that is Carl. Is there anything we can do for you?"

DONUT: THEY DON'T EVEN SMELL LIKE HIPPIES, EVEN WITH THE DISGUSTING CIGARETTES.

CARL: How do hippies smell?

DONUT: THEY SMELL LIKE ANGEL'S OWNER. THEY SMELL LIKE PATCHOULI MIXED WITH FARMERS MARKETS MIXED WITH SO-CALLED NATURAL BODY DEODORANT THAT JUST GAVE UP TEN MINUTES INTO THE JOB. THESE GUYS SMELL LIKE SAD, WET DOGS.

CARL: Yeah, but they never said they're hippies.

DONUT: THEY'RE WEARING TIE-DYE. THEY'RE CALLED TEAM FREE LOVE. IT'S FALSE ADVERTISING. YOU KNOW HOW I FEEL ABOUT FALSE ADVERTISING, CARL. I'LL BE NICE TO THEM FOR NOW, BUT I'M TELLING YOU, THERE'S SOMETHING SUSPICIOUS GOING ON.

"Is good to meet you both," Radoslav said. "But now is a bad time for us." He offered a cigarette to Donut.

"No, thank you," she said.

"Thank you for stopping, friends," Jasha finally said, looking between me and Donut. "There is nothing you can do for us. We can't pass the finish line unless we're in our van. You better get moving. You can't come in last place anymore, but you can come in second to last. And there is a time limit."

I turned to examine their van. My bucket was there on the ground, having finally run out of water.

"You're one of them, no?" Radoslav asked. "A person from this world?"

It was my turn to pause.

"Yes," I finally said. "We are. We're crawlers, and everyone else in the current heat are NPCs."

Neither said anything for several moments. They just smoked as they looked at their crashed van with their dead friend inside.

Jasha flicked some ashes. "She was so excited about all this. Thought we was going to win whole thing. Get this great prize."

"Wait," Donut asked. "What's the prize?"

The two bugbears looked at each other and then at Donut.

Jasha let out a small sad laugh. "Don't you know? If we win, we are given freedom. We are taken from here and moved to some other place where we don't have to fight anymore. Maybe you get offered a different prize since you're 'crawlers.'"

I immediately thought of Rory and Lorelai, the goblin shamankas from the very first floor. I remembered the forlorn quality to Rory's voice when she talked about moving from the first to the second floor. And here we were on the tenth, and these guys were no different.

Donut swished her tail. "How do you know all this?"

"Because this is what they told us," Jasha said. "We are all volunteers. Sort of volunteers. Last I remember, we were in the slime mines defending the air pocket, and we killed a guy like yourselves. He was a bune. A crawler. But before he died, he said he just wanted to go home. So Radoslav asked him where this home was, and the bune told us that this was all a game. And the moment he said this, it was like there was a click, and I just knew. I just knew what he was saying was right." He indicated the other bugbear. "Radoslav here used to be my brother. Then my enemy. But usually my cousin. We were in the slime mines. We were on the submarine. We were in the rope city. Every time, a different place. And we didn't remember. We didn't remember until we did."

"And there were other times, too," Radoslav added. "When we weren't anywhere. We're not supposed to remember the cold, either, but we do." He shuddered.

Jasha nodded. "It all came at once, these memories. And once we realized this, there was a voice. And then we were in a big room, and the voice gave us a choice. We could go back into the cold, or we could race for our lives. And if we won, fair and square, we could be free. That there was a place. A real place for us to live and never go to the in-between ever again."

"And if we don't win," Radoslav added, "this is okay, too, because it means it will be over. Finally." He sighed. "But Alevtina really wanted to win. She wanted to start a family. Maybe with me."

"Or maybe with me," Jasha said. He made a sad laugh. "But probably with you."

Jasha took another drag, letting the moment hang. "Today is a bad day."

Christ, I thought. "Listen, guys. You're not out of this yet. If you were, you would've been disintegrated or whatever like that other team was."

"Their mount died," Jasha said. "Rules are different for mounts. Look at our van. We're not going anywhere."

I was already sifting through my inventory. I had the materials to build a flatbed cart, but I'd have to do it manually. I couldn't remember if there was a tow hitch attached to the back of the truck. I assumed there wouldn't be.

"We're going to tow you to the finish line," I said.

The two bugbears looked at each other and then at us.

"Why would you do this?" Jasha finally asked.

I was ready to make up some bullshit, but instead I just told them the truth. That if more than one team didn't finish the race, we were pretty sure we'd have to race against our friends in further heats.

Jasha nodded. He stood, cracked his back, and tossed his cigarette into the water.

"This is a good reason. And is an honorable reason. Do you have materials to tow?"

5

I HAD A LONG PLANK OF WOOD OUT, AND I WAS IN THE PROCESS OF reinforcing it and attaching the wheels. I had pulled Rend out of storage, and the large meatball immediately moved to the side of the road and fell in the water, trying to eat the pieces of manatee gore. I'd had to jump in to haul him out. The damn thing weighed a literal ton. Now I had him sitting on the cart, using his weight while I secured a crossbeam. He giggled furiously every time the drill made the board vibrate. Donut was complaining loudly about how much he now smelled because he'd gotten the bug's innards on him.

I had Donut keep Mongo in the truck. We weren't allowed to steal each other's vehicles, but it was good to have security just in case. Mongo was not a fan of the arrangement. He had discovered the horn on the food truck and he kept banging into it.

Unfortunately, the horn wasn't a normal honk, but a recording of a gangster's voice saying, *Make way for the big shot*, followed by a chicken squawk and the rat-a-tat shooting sound of a tommy gun.

It was funny the first time. By the twentieth time, I was ready to go over there and rip the whole horn out.

Across from me, the two bugbears were energized with the thought of not yet dying. A part of me felt bad about this arrangement because I knew I was helping them now, but I wouldn't think twice about letting them die during the next race. I supposed that was the point. The cruelty of this all was a feature, not a bug. At least they knew this, too, and that somewhat eased the small amount of guilt.

It felt like regression, having to fight against NPCs, especially after the chaos of the last floor. They were using awakened NPCs for this floor because it actually helped the storyline, not hurt it. If the NPCs knew they'd be "safe" at the end of this, many would be willing to do anything to win. But at the same time, the very nature of the floor meant most would end up dead. It was like a purge of the problem-causing components.

We still had five hours to complete the race, and so far nobody else had come down the road.

"Who are the other teams?" I asked the bugbears as I quickly worked.

"It was dark, and we didn't get a good view of them," Jasha said. "We only met the triplets, who are now dead, and the other team. Team Sparkles."

"Team Sparkles?" Donut asked. She was peering back the way we'd come. "Was that the unicorn? I think they're coming now."

Sure enough, a light appeared a moment later. My minimap didn't have them, but I could soon see the outline of the tumbleweed thing with a unicorn head coming up.

"That's them," Jasha said.

As the silhouette approached, I tried to figure out what I was looking at. The "tumbleweed" part wasn't rolling but just moving along the ground, like it was magically gliding. Not fast, but at a steady pace. The head of the unicorn popped out the top, and the second, smaller, rodent-like creature rode on the unicorn's head.

"What *is* that thing?" I asked.

"The mount is biological," Jasha said. "It's an Avernus Creeper. A plant that walks on the ground with thousands of little feet. Almost like bug."

"A *plant*?" Donut asked as the thing approached. She moved to the center of the road, keeping the under-construction trailer behind her. Her tiara glittered, and I knew she was using her Sniper ability to examine it better. The light was coming from a *Torch* spell similar to Donut's. "I bet Mordecai would know all about it."

"Don't know how that thing is steering it, honestly," Jasha said.

"So the unicorn isn't the mount? It's the racer?" I asked, watching it approach. "That's weird."

As soon as I spoke, it was close enough for me to properly examine it.

Avernus Creeper.

This is the biological mount of Team Sparkles for the purpose of the tenth floor.

This is a tangle of not-quite-sentient vines. Under normal circumstances, these things are pretty bad news. They're loosely related to the Gehenna Brambles you guys loved from the sixth floor. They're almost impossible to kill because even a tiny branch or thorn off one will rapidly grow to full size. Luckily for us all, this particular shrub is limited to half size and is being prevented from procreating outside their garage.

"Names are Dwight and Lucienne," Jasha said. "We met just before the race. Lucienne is the small one. She's got a mouth on her."

The round bunch of brambles came to a stop. Donut remained in the middle of the road.

"Yo, fatty, get out of the road," the unicorn shouted down at Donut. He had a surprising voice that did not match his colorful exterior. It was a deep, surly, three-packs-a-day Boston accent.

"Fatty?" Donut asked, incredulous. "Are you talking to me?"

The pinkish furry thing on the unicorn's head had a tail wrapped around the base of the opalescent horn, presumably anchoring it in place. The thing was just a little smaller than Donut. She was like a mix between a rat and a chinchilla. She had two legs, two monkey-like arms, and a rodent head. She'd have been cute if her vein-covered, red eyes hadn't been bulging out of her head, giving the impression she was on the verge of literally exploding. She also wore a mini race-car-driver helmet that was white with a blue stripe down the center.

When the fuzzy, bug-eyed creature spoke, she had a high-pitched French accent completely at odds with the voice of her partner.

"Who else would he be talking to, you corpulent swine?" the rodent shouted. "Move before we are forced to make you roadkill."

The creature whispered something to Dwight the unicorn, who laughed.

"What? What did you say?" Donut yelled, getting more outraged by the second. "If you think I'm going to allow myself to just get insulted by a tumor donkey and a crack-addict Mickey Mouse, you both are in for a rude awakening. I'll have you know I am practically twice both of your levels, and I'm quite sure that stupid mount of yours is flammable. In fact, let's test—"

"Donut," I called before she did something stupid, "let them go around."

I examined the two creatures, starting with the rat.

Lucienne. Mandagot. Level 81 Fink.

One of two members of Team Sparkles.

Warning: This creature worships Diwata and will be automatically hostile toward you because Diwata HATES your ass.

A mandagot is a Fairy-class creature that comes in many shapes, though most are stomach-churning monstrosities that are supposed to be "cute." These things are a combination of two or three fuzzy woodland creatures. Legend has it that they are born of regular fairies who've had relations with forest animals, which is a pretty common occurrence with the freaks who worship Diwata. They have multiple magical abilities and can punch well over their level class, so be wary.

I grunted as I moved my attention to the larger of the two. The unicorn.

Dwight. Sparkling Unicorn. Level 87 Enchanter.

One of two members of Team Sparkles.

I bet you already know what a unicorn is. A *sparkling* unicorn is pretty much the same thing, but they sparkle because they have even more magic permeating them. Their horns are quite valuable to certain parties, so if you kill him, it's recommended to grab the horn as quickly as possible.

Most unicorns are regarded for their beauty and their grace and their childlike innocence. They're generally known for their overly gentle manner.

But not Dwight. Dwight is known for being a complete prick. He's the type of guy who would call the police on a kid setting up a lemonade stand. He's the type of guy who would one-star an upcoming

video game because the artists had the temerity to draw a female character who didn't give him an instant erection. He's the type of guy who, at the office pizza party, would take three pieces, knowing there's not enough to go around.

Donut continued to sputter in outrage. She did not move.

Just behind the round tumbleweed, parked at the entrance to the cave, sat our food truck, and within that truck Mongo screeched with outrage and leaned against the horn.

Make way for the big shot! Bawk!

The plant mount reacted negatively to the horn and burst forward. There was a strange rustling noise, like multiple twigs snapping, but not all at the exact same time. "Gah!" Dwight shouted as the whole thing lurched. We all dove out of the way. Donut jumped upward and over the mount as I dove off the side of the road and fell into the slimy cave water. The two bugbears did the same, but jumped to the other side of the road.

The tumbleweed crawled right over the trailer, skittered over the van, and continued on its way.

"Fuck yoooouuuu!" Dwight called as they disappeared into the darkness.

Sputtering, I pulled myself from the water. I had a level 5 leech attached to my leg, but it immediately died from the Damage Reflect and fell off.

Rend remained in the center of the trailer. He'd been run over by the tumbleweed, and he'd taken a small amount of damage from it. He'd fallen over, and his elephant legs waved in the air before he righted himself. I quickly made sure he was all right. He giggled as I ran my hand over him. He had multiple thorns in his hard skin.

"Poky," he said as I plucked each one out.

Avernus Creeper Thorn.

Each one of these has the ability to grow into a full-sized Avernus plant. Don't say I didn't warn you. It is one of the most invasive plant species known to the universe. Whole planets have been lost to this stuff. Seriously.

This thorn will not sprout on this floor. Consider yourself lucky.

I asked Mordecai about the thorns, and as usual with this sort of thing, he was pretty excited. He asked me to save them all but not to take them out of inventory again until we were in the safe room. He was going to buy something called a Botanist's Table upgrade attachment for his alchemy table.

"Fatty," Donut muttered as she came walking up. "Carl, as soon as the next race starts, I'm going to set them on fire."

I watched the light of team Sparkles disappear into the darkness.

"No arguments here," I said.

IT WAS SLOW GOING TO GET THE TRAILER ATTACHED AND THEN THE VAN affixed to the flatbed. Between the three of us, and with Donut "helping," we were able to turn it upright and lift it onto the bed. And then it took a few minutes for me to properly position everything. I had to put Rend away.

Like I suspected, there was no trailer hitch at the back of the truck, but there was a step for the back door that was welded on pretty well, and we used a few lengths of chains to attach it all.

There was no sign of the missing teams, and I assumed they were all ahead of us, meaning we would be in third-to-last place, and the bugbears would be in second-to-last.

Despite what the rules said, it seemed the two bugbears could ride in the truck with us. They just had to be in their van when we crossed the finish line. We decided to keep Radoslav in the food truck, but in the very back with the door open, keeping an eye on the crappy trailer, while Jasha remained in the van.

I'd asked them if they wanted me to store the body of their dead friend, but they just dumped her body into the water. I was taken aback, but after mentioning it to Mordecai, he said it was a bugbear thing. They believed it was weak to fret over the corpses of their fallen friends and family. They'd oftentimes eat them. Or just leave them where they'd fallen. They'd still honor and mourn their dead, but that was never tied to the bodies themselves.

We moved slowly through the tunnels, coming across the corpses of multiple manatees, which had all been killed in the same way. They were literally ripped in half. I finally stopped the truck long enough to examine one.

Corpse of Miss Brianna Kim. Level 90 Screeching Death Manatee. Killed by evisceration by mount Old Shuck from the Jugglers.

As we drove, slowly moving our way through the cave, Donut moved to the back of the truck and struck up a conversation with Radoslav.

"So, your story on this floor is that you're musicians? Carl can play the bagpipes, and I am a singer of some renown. Perhaps we can put on a performance once we get to this town."

Radoslav grunted. "I am supposed to be a musician, and I think I know how to play my pan flute, but I've never picked it up. I am the pan flute, Alevtina was bongos and tambourine, and Jasha sings and plays violin."

Donut gasped. "Carl, do you think if we give Mongo a tambourine, he will—" She stopped dead. She went so silent, I turned all the way around in my seat to make sure she was okay.

"Donut?" I asked.

"I just got a strange notification," she said after a minute. "It says the people have voted for Otto the slime guy to be the manatee 'stand-in' in the arena."

"What the hell does that mean?"

"That's all it says."

I sent out a mass message, asking if anyone else had seen this yet.

I received a couple answers that people had just started receiving similar messages. In one case, a crawler named Ajib I'd first met on the fifth floor said he'd also picked the let-the-audience-vote choice for his mob, but it said they'd voted to transfer the monster to the "arena." Mordecai said he had no idea what any of that meant, either.

ELLE: Anyone else have to do this fan meet-'n'-greet bullshit?

DONUT: OMG, YOU GET TO DO A FAN MEET AND GREET?

ELLE: Apparently, but it's this huge room, and there's just one guy in here. It's just like the Butcher's Masquerade. I have to wear a damn name tag.

DONUT: ZEV, DO I GET TO DO THE MEET AND GREET?

ZEV: Well . . . no. So, the meet-and-greet program was set up a while ago for this floor just in case anybody made it this far, and we pretty much sold out immediately. It was set up so viewers could come to the planet and watch the end of the races from the stands, and after each race, there's a reception and they could spend some time meeting their favorite crawler. But then everything, uh, happened. The quarantine is still in place. You can still come to the Earth system no problem, but once you're here, you can't leave. So all five hundred fans who signed up for the meet-and-greet package canceled. All except one guy. A soother. He's a fan of Elle. Let's say a superfan. He came despite the quarantine. They say he couldn't even get anyone to fly him in, so he bought his own yacht just to come and meet her.

DONUT: OMG, THAT IS KIND OF ADORABLE. ELLE, TELL YOUR FAN I SAID HI.

ELLE: This creepy motherfucker is wearing a shirt with a cartoon naked picture of me on it. I'm not getting anywhere near this pervert. He's just standing there blushing. If they didn't have safe room rules in here, I'd have iced him already.

We finally exited the cave, and a pair of dots emerged on the GPS just as multiple colorful lights appeared in the distance. The dots were labeled **Hungry Eyes Village** and **Finish Line**.

"Would you look at that?" I said as the town came into view. But Donut wasn't paying attention as she was now fully invested in Elle's continuing commentary on her awkward fan meetup.

ELLE: Oh god, he wants me to sign some giant pillow thing that has me on it. They didn't even get my anatomy right. My nipples are *not* blue.

DONUT: I WAS WONDERING ABOUT THAT. THEY ALWAYS GIVE YOU BLUE NIPPLES IN THE SNICKS. I SHOULD HAVE KNOWN, THOUGH. I FEAR THEY'VE OVEREXAGGERATED CARL SO MUCH THAT IF HE EVER GETS A GIRLFRIEND FROM OUTSIDE

THE DUNGEON, SHE'S GOING TO BE NOTHING BUT DISAPPOINTED.

ELLE: Donut, I love you, but have you ever considered not saying everything that comes to you the moment it pops into your head?

DONUT: WHAT DO YOU MEAN?

The lights were from a line of spotlights waving back and forth. Dozens of roads led from all directions, all coming together at the finish line.

"Huh," I said, trying to follow one of the roads, but it disappeared into the dark.

Behind, the trailer weaved and bumped. I slowed. It'd taken us almost four hours to go fifty kilometers, but we still had time. I searched for other vehicles. I only saw a few. There was what appeared to be a giant, six-legged horse limping its way along several tracks over. There was a smoking station wagon that was being pushed by skyfowls. That was it.

Ahead, an arch loomed with the familiar black-and-white-checkered pattern of a finish line. All the tracks converged here at the finish line, making a wide road. I remembered there was supposed to be like eighteen hundred of these races, so I imagined there was some magic here, as this was more like a hundred or so roads converging. Either way, we approached the finish line.

"You better get into your van," I called to Radoslav.

The bugbear turned and bowed from the back of the truck. "Thank you, Carl and Princess Donut," he said. "I know and understand for tomorrow's race we are not friends. But today we are friends, and I am grateful for today. Tonight I will drink to Alevtina and dreams not attained, and I will drink to the friends of today."

He jumped out the back, landing heavily on the trailer, and moved into his destroyed minivan.

Donut returned to Mongo's back and sat with me. On either side were metallic bleachers, but they were empty. It was a strangely lonely feeling.

"Carl," Donut said just as we crossed the finish line.

"Yeah?"

"We're going to have to kill those bugbear guys eventually, right?"

"Probably," I said.

"I hate this place," she said. "I wish they were all like that stupid unicorn and his disgusting rat."

"Me, too, Donut."

HEAT ONE. RESULTS.
First Place: One Fine Pig.
Second Place: The Jugglers.
Third Place: Lady Dominators and the Gimp.
Fourth Place: The Wild Hunt.
Fifth Place: Girth the Trouble.
Sixth Place: Team Sparkles.
Seventh Place: The Royal Court of Princess Donut.
Eighth Place: Team Free Love.

Eliminated: The Trauco Triplets.

HEAT 2 OF 7

6

"ONE FINE PIG?" DONUT ASKED, INCREDULOUS. "WHAT KIND OF NAME is that? Also, we didn't get to name our own team! The Royal Court is a fine name for our party, but as a racing team—"

"Gah!" I called as the entire truck flashed and teleported. Mongo screeched in surprise, and Donut let out a yowl.

We teleported to a dark driveway with an opening garage door.

The bugbears' minivan had disappeared, but the trailer and the chains remained. The chains clattered loudly on the ground.

I pulled us into the cavernous garage, pulling forward far enough to get the trailer inside.

"Have you noticed?" Donut asked as I put the truck into park. "The AI voice is getting all weird and glitchy."

"Yeah," I said.

Hedy the mechanic started jogging toward us.

Behind us, Mongo growled at Hedy.

"No, Mongo. She's a friend."

The moment Donut said that, Mongo burst out the back of the truck, causing the doors to fly open. He jumped off the trailer and started bouncing all around the small mechanic, who fell on her ass.

The GPS unit beeped, and the female voice spoke.

Limited details on the next race are now available.

Distance: 10 kilometers.

Track: Asphalt-paved road. Rolling hills.

There are two paths for this race. You will be assigned one of two paths at random.

Tasks required to complete: Each path is of equal length. Each path has a gatekeeper monster along that path that must be killed to resume.

Special Rules: Your vehicle may only travel your assigned path.

Environment: Torrential downpour of rain and giant hail.

Hazards: Well, we have the hail and the gatekeeper monster, whatever that might be. But I'd suggest that our biggest hazard is the fact that this bucket has to be driven by a fucking cat this time.

Time Limit: 3 hours.

"Hey!" Donut cried. "Carl, why is the GPS thing a jerk?" She paused. "But she is right. How the heck am I supposed to drive this thing?"

I laughed.

"We have ten hours to figure it out. It sounds like we can use mercenaries. And if not, maybe there's an upgrade that'll allow you to drive. Or we can rig something up ourselves."

I read the rules for heat two again. "The time limit is halved, but the distance is way shorter."

Mongo was on his back like a dog, waving his tail back and forth, while Hedy scratched him under his wings. I pulled Rend out, and the meatball made a "wow" sound as he looked about the large garage. Mongo jumped to his feet and Rend bounded toward him.

Hedy stood and tapped the trailer. "Helping the other drivers, I see," she said. "Almost pulled the whole back bumper off." She did not sound like she approved.

"If we didn't, then there would've been two teams that didn't finish," I said. "I'm trying to avoid that if possible."

She grunted and examined the truck.

"How'd she drive?"

"Kinda slow, but faster than I was expecting. We'll need to remove all the kitchen gear in the back. And for god's sake, we gotta take that gun off the roof. It blocks my view."

She nodded. "We gots some guidelines about what we can and can't change from the original design, but the rules is clear as a troll's ball sack. Won't know till we try. Basically, at the end of the race, the truck gets regenerated back to its form at the beginning of the race. First, we gotta pick your upgrade." She produced a tablet device that looked bizarrely incongruous in her hands. "Lots to choose from. Next time make sure you comes in first place so we get better choices."

"Do you know the rules about crew members and if they can drive?" I asked. "Otherwise, the first thing we pick needs to be something that'll allow Donut to drive."

"Aye," she said. "You can add up to three mercenaries each heat. There's a bar out there in Hungry Eyes where you can hire 'em. I reckon all the best ones already been snatched since you two took your sweet fine time getting here."

"What about mercenaries we've already hired?"

She nodded. "You can use 'em. Same rules, though."

DONUT: WE WILL NOT BE BRINGING SAMANTHA WITH US FOR ANY RACE. SHE HAS THE ATTENTION SPAN OF A CORNISH REX. SHE WILL GET US KILLED.

CARL: Yeah, no arguments there.

Hedy continued. "I'd still design a backup driving system for Princess Donut here. Even if you gots a full crew, you'll always want one of you available to drive in case something happens. Best if it's something removable that you bring with you. I'm sure there might be something in the upgrades list, but it'd be a waste if we can jig up something on our own."

I nodded. I was already thinking of things I could build on the engineering table. Katia could . . .

I paused, and a wave of sadness washed over me. *She's okay. She's out of the dungeon. She's probably more safe than we are.* I took a breath.

"Okay," I said. "So what do you recommend?"

She pulled up the tablet and pressed it. A screen popped up. "First three races we got paved roads guaranteed, but after that, we could get anything. Mechanical is always better than biological, and I wasn't lying about that when you picked me. But the big advantage the beasties got is maneuverability. Every single heat is going to add some obstacle, and by heat four, your regular tires ain't gonna be able to handle it. So my recommendation is the first thing we get is an upgrade for mobility. We gots a few choices."

She clicked her pad, and a list of choices appeared on the screen.

"My goodness," Donut said, peering at the images. The first showed the truck with spider legs and the caption **Retractable Legs**. The next had no wheels at all, but the truck hovered right off the ground like something out of *Star Wars*. That was called **Hover Upgrade**. A third choice zoomed in on the tires, showing dozens of tiny tendrils sticking out of the rubber. **All-Terrain-Tire Upgrade, including Vertical Climb.**

"And we can only get one of these?" I asked. "What if I build something like this on the engineering table?"

Hedy snorted. "No magic upgrades allowed outside the official upgrades. Good luck building something like that between heats. A driver system for the Princess is one thing, but something like those tires or the hover? Not gonna happen. Unless you're smarter than you look."

"What about speed upgrades? Or armor? Are those available?"

"We gots hundreds of upgrades. But these are my recommendations. Spider legs are my best pick, but the others is good, too. Hover don't do vertical climb, but it makes you almost twice as fast and it comes with an engine upgrade. No more of that ancient gas engine. The other two come with vertical climb, which you might need pretty soon. Spider legs can be turned on only when you need it, and they can climb on walls, but you'll only use it when you need to go over an obstacle. The legs are fast, but not as fast, and they're not made to be turned on the whole time. The tire upgrade is good because it'll keep you from slipping and sliding and it'll be always active, but it comes with a 25% reduction in speed. And your tires are at a fixed distance. You get hung up on something, the tires ain't gonna help. Yeah, they'll climb a wall, but your truck is shaped like a box. You gotta get the tires to touch the wall in the first place. If we was paying actual money for these upgrades, the hover would be the most expensive by far. But I still think the spider legs is best."

"Hmm," I said, thinking. "Can I look at some of the other choices?"

"Knock yourself batty," she said, handing me the tablet. "Remember, if you don't survive, I don't survive, so I ain't gonna steer you wrong. Just don't pick anything weird without talking to me first, and I'll tell you why my choice is better."

I swiped through, looking at the selections. She wasn't wrong. There had to be over a thousand options. There was a tab for Golden upgrades, which I couldn't see at all. I knew the first-place team, One Fine Pig, had the option to either pick one of those or three regular upgrades. We needed to figure out what all the other teams were.

My eyes focused on some of the weapons we could add. There was a rolling barrel of spikes, like the goblin murder dozer from the very first floor. A flamethrower. An EMP-like pulse that disabled other drivers and mounts. A device that would plant a literal brick wall on the road behind you.

I felt a chill. We could probably avoid killing other teams if we really worked on it, but keeping them from killing each other? It was going to be impossible. This was going to be worse than the card battles on the eighth floor. We'd weeded out most of the assholes by now, but would that matter? What would happen if we ended up in a race versus Imani and Elle? I didn't even want to think about it, but we had to prepare ourselves for it. Zhang said Li Na had killed most of the other teams already. Crawler-versus-crawler races were inevitable.

It was going to get ugly.

I handed the tablet back to her. "Pick the spider legs."

The gremlin grinned up at me, revealing a sharp gap-toothed smile. "Sexy and smart," she said. She slapped my butt with the tablet.

MORDECAI: Guys, put Rend away before you enter the safe room. Or leave him in your garage. I'll explain why when you get inside.

"Rend," I called. I didn't know where he or Mongo had gone. The last I'd seen them, they were running in circles around Hedy.

They didn't take long to find. The truck was shaking. Mongo's tail appeared out the back. This was followed by a loud giggling.

"Hey! Get out of there!" I called.

Rend appeared, popping his head out of the back of the truck. I didn't even know how he had fit in there, especially with Mongo. The truck was big, but the kitchen took up a lot of space.

"Stay out of the truck!"

Rend giggled again, and this time several objects fell out of his mouth, clattering on the trailer. Mongo screeched with joy. The truck shook more as he turned himself around, and his tail pressed against the horn.

Make way for the big shot! Bawk!

I examined the items that had dropped out of Rend's mouth. French fries. Frozen French fries. There was a stocked freezer in there somewhere, and they'd found it.

"Carl, your creature is a terrible influence! Mongo, get down this instant!"

Both Mongo and Rend tumbled out of the back of the truck. Mongo had a plastic bag in his mouth. He shook it violently, tossing frozen chicken patties like Frisbees across the garage. He dropped the plastic bag and shrieked in outrage.

"Well," I said to Hedy, "meet your two bodyguards."

7

Entering your safe room.

Warning: Blood Bar is now in effect. You start with a full bar, but you are now on a timer. You may only spend 10 hours in the safe room. You may refill the Blood Bar by killing things.

"HOLY SHIT, MORDECAI," I SAID UPON SEEING THE CREATURE FLOATING in the middle of the safe room holding a steaming cup of tea.

"My goodness," Donut said, looking the grim reaper character up and down. "This is quite unsettling. It's like what would happen if Orren ever discovered Depeche Mode."

Mordecai floated about a foot off the ground. He towered over me. He was a grim-reaper-style monster, but with really long arms, reminding me of the clowns from the third floor. He had desiccated undead-like hands. His dark canvaslike robes floated lazily in the air. Like Orren, his black hood covered his head, and I couldn't see anything inside except the occasional hint of a reflection.

I could see now why he'd asked Rend to stay behind. One of Rend's weaknesses was something called "Reaper Gaze." I examined him.

Mordecai. Level 50. Moon Reaper.

Manager of Princess Donut.

From a dark, terrifying corner of Sheol, Moon Reapers are one of several different types of janitor mobs that occupy the 15th floor.

They sometimes break free and wander other floors, devouring everything in their path and causing absolute chaos wherever they go. While they have a corporeal form, they are basically spirit creatures. Even the princes of hell fear these strange solitary beings.

Don't remove their hoods. Don't provoke them. They are not hostile unless attacked. Their gaze attack can come in many forms. That includes inflicting the dreaded Jaunt sickness, one of the most insidious attacks in *Dungeon Crawler World*. It is a condition where the inflicted is trapped in time. They have their full faculties, but they perceive each second as if it is the length of 30 years.

"I'm actually not a Moon Reaper, but a—" Before he finished, he thrust forward, causing me to jump. His black hood fell back, revealing not a skull, but an enormous eyeball. A flaming eyeball. His cup of tea fell and shattered.

"Death awaits you at every turn," Mordecai croaked with a deep, heavy voice filled with grit, different from the already scary voice he had just been using. "The shadows reach even now for a porous soul such as yours. It is unquenchable, this thirst. You are reached for by both sides. Who will entwine you? The tree or the abyss?"

"What the shit?" I asked as Donut yowled and jumped to my shoulder.

He turned to Donut, raising a skeletal hand. I took a step back, but my back hit the door. "And you. The edges are more clear, yet still uncertain. A sacrifice might save you, in the end. It *might.* It will be the darkest decision ever made. How many lives? How many souls? The veil is made of gossamer, and when it is done, their gaze, their rage will be eternal. You should remember that, Oak Fell Champion of Nekhebit."

"I'm sorry, but I really need to wee right now, and I would much rather do it in the powder room than upon Carl's shoulder, so can you please go back to normal?"

Mordecai coughed. He floated back. "Oh damn, did I drop my tea again? Sorry about that." He quickly pulled his hood up, but there were still a few flames on the eyeball head, and the hood itself caught on fire. He reached up and casually patted the fire out.

"Uh, Mordecai," I said, "what the hell was that?"

Mordecai fuzzed and reappeared. He flashed and became the Canadian version of himself from the previous floor, just for a second. He appeared like that as he floated a good two feet off the floor, and he let out a yelp. He glitched again on the way down, and when he hit the floor, he turned into a scraggly black-and-white cat, which caused Donut to hiss. He hissed back at her, but his mouth opened huge, and then he flipped to an otter shape, then to a massive slug, before he jolted back to the reaper shape. He fuzzed for a second but settled on the reaper.

"Godsdamn this form. It's not natural. It's an impossible combo, and that's why it's glitching."

The cleaner bot was already at work, quietly cleaning up the tea. The room stank like smoke.

I spied Splash Zone and Rosetta standing there, peeking out of the training room. Samantha was there, too, on the ground with Bigs right next to her. I knew Tipid was in the training room, too, but he was probably asleep. Mordecai said he spent most of his time curled on the floor, sleeping.

"Mordecai, darling," Donut said, "are you aware of what just happened?"

"Aw, shit. Did I do it again?"

I grunted. "We lost you for a second. You were spouting some Nostradamus bullshit. It was like the same sort of creepy shit robot Donut would say."

"Oh, damn," he said. "I'm sorry about that. That's something Moon Reapers do. It'll only happen once for each of you." He paused. "It doesn't make sense. I'm not really a Moon Reaper. I'm a shadow mimic. Mimics only take on the shape of the creature. Changelings can get some of the powers, though. That's why it's glitching, I think."

"A shadow mimic?" I asked. "What the hell is that? How is that different than a regular mimic?"

"There are three basic types of shapeshifters in the dungeon. Changelings, doppelgangers, and mimics. Most other shapeshifters are variations of one of those three. Shadow mimics are generally pretty evil, highly intelligent mimics that can copy the shape of anything nearby.

The thing is, shadow mimics and changelings are mortal enemies. It makes changelings violently ill just to touch one, while shadow mimics think changelings are delicious."

Donut let out a harrumph. "Well, as long as you're done being weird and you don't go back to a tuxedo cat, then I suppose it's okay. I can see you as an American shorthair, yes. But certainly not with tuxedo coloring. You don't have the audacity to try to pull that off."

Rosetta hesitantly approached. She was giving Mordecai a wary glance. Samantha had retreated back into the training room.

"We should probably keep you sequestered from the others for this floor," Rosetta said to Mordecai. She looked at me. "It seems he does that 'glitching' each time a different race gets near him for the first time. When Bigs wandered in, I was afraid we'd lost him totally."

"He told me I was going to drown in fire," Bigs the sluggalette said, slithering into the room. She swung her head hatchet around a few times. "If this mothafacko wasn't on the don't-chop list, he'd be getting the kneecap treatment. And I didn't hear what he said to Samantha, but he made her cry."

"Listen," Mordecai said. "Nobody give too much stock to anything I might spout. There's no such thing as predicting the future here. It's always vague bullshit that can be twisted to fit whatever happens. If someone could accurately predict things like that, it would . . . well, it would change everything. This stuff is designed to be scary, not true."

Bigs grunted. "You told Splash Zone he was gonna die screaming while his family watched."

"Yeah, man," Splash Zone said, "you really freaked me out."

I was about to ask more, but we were interrupted. Donut let out an excited gasp but then hissed. I turned to see her atop the mailbox in the corner of the room with the little door open. A spell book scurried out, trailing slime. It rushed across the room like an escaped rat. It scampered into the kitchen and started banging against the cabinets.

"Look, look, another hat! And there's a hat for Mongo. And one for Rend, too!"

"Catch that book!" Mordecai shouted. "They can break if they injure themselves!"

The cleaner bot let out an angry shrill and rushed to the kitchen. It swooped down, picked up the book, brought it to me, and dropped it in my arms.

"Gah," I said as the book spewed slime down the front of my shirt.

"What is it? What is it?" Donut demanded, hopping over to me.

The book wriggled, and it was covered in little legs. It was oozing a clear liquid all over my arms.

"What the hell?" I said, holding it out. I examined it. "It's a spell book called *Oozy Form*."

"Uzi form?" Donut asked, brightening. "Like Uzi Jesus? I get a gun!"

"Not 'Uzi,'" I said. "'Oozy.' With an 'O.' Like slimy. You can turn into a slime." The spell book spooged more slime onto me. It made a little groan.

Donut scoffed. "Well, that's disappointing. Why would I want that?"

"It's a great spell," Mordecai said. "It's a special edition, so it'll train faster, too. You can do all sorts of things with it. You can slip between cracks. Turn into a puddle on the floor. It's great as a defensive and camouflage spell. But it's kinda like *Phase*, too. Just make sure you're someplace safe when it runs out. At level 15, you can stay in the form indefinitely, but before then, be careful."

"That is absolutely disgusting, and I am never going to use it," Donut said.

I put the wriggling book on the kitchen counter. It shook, trying to crawl away. It continued to spew thick, clear liquid all over the place. Mordecai swooped in with a vial and took some.

"This is a good one," I said, holding the book down. "You don't have to use it a lot, but it'll be good for an emergency. Read it before you give the cleaner bot a heart attack."

The cleaner bot gave a shrill beep.

Donut jumped to the table and gave the ooze a suspicious sniff. "My *Smoke Form* spell that comes with my Assassin of Sekhmet class is better. It's a *Phase*-style spell. Why don't *you* take it?"

"Actually, that's not a bad idea," Mordecai said. "Carl, your *Gloom Wraith Phase* is an attack and forces you in a direction, so it's not useful as a travel spell. If you take this, both you and Donut can equally slip through and around obstacles."

"Really?" I asked. "Wait, what else do you have that's new, Donut?"

"Oh, it's just fantastic. I got all sorts of goodies. It buffs all those weird create-tree and summon-vermin spells I got from that Oak Fell thing, and it also comes with that *Smoke Form* spell, and I got my first aura! It's called Healer's Grasp. If you're near me, you get healed! I don't know why an assassin might need to heal people, but that's what I got. I'm like a mini Imani! And don't forget I also have two celestial boxes to open, and that's before I look at some of my new achievements, so I must insist we get this moving."

The book made a strange squealing noise and more goo squirted out. The cleaner bot continued to complain.

"Sorry," I said. I grasped the book in both hands, and I applied it, learning *Oozy Form*. "Okay, okay. That's done."

8

I TURNED TO DONUT. "WHAT ACCESSORIES DID YOU GET?"

She did a little excited hop. "Look at this!"

Her tiara disappeared, and an Egyptian-style beaded headdress appeared atop her head. It was something one would have seen on Cleopatra. Red, yellow, and orange beads cascaded down either side of her face. The colors matched her fur.

"Isn't it just divine? I'll drain it of its magic for my tiara, of course, but it's just beautiful as is. It calls it a veil even though it doesn't cover my face." She pulled out a little mirror and started shaking her head back and forth. The beads clacked as she moved. "Just exquisite."

Enchanted hat item. The Assassin's Veil.

This is a unique item.

Warning: This item may only be worn by a female.

Warning: This item may only be worn by a Feline-class species.

Worn by those in the court of the goddess Sekhmet, this beaded headdress warns off strangers who might think to do harm to the bearer.

Wearing this item imbues the following benefits:

Plus 10% to dexterity.

The Precognition Benefit. Warns wearer if someone nearby is preparing an offensive or binding spell or readying a skill.

Warning: Enemies of Sekhmet will be automatically hostile to you if you wear this in their presence.

"It's a great item," Mordecai said. "But if you transfer that over to your tiara, those conditions will also transfer over. The female and cat things aren't an issue, but the enemy of Sekhmet might be a problem because the goddess Sekhmet is most definitely going to be under Odette's thumb by now, which means all of Odette's enemies will be hostile toward you. And knowing Odette, that's going to mean pretty much everybody. Let me do some research first before you drain it."

"What were the other hats?" I asked. "The ones for Mongo and Rend? Can we drain those, too?"

"We will not be stealing Mongo's new hat's powers," Donut said.

"We can't anyway," Mordecai said. "Both are labeled as pet accessories."

Two more items appeared on the table. One was a fabric hat with shiny blue and gold stripes on it. It had two wide bands on either side that were designed to hang down, almost like large, floppy ears. It was the same sort of hat a pharaoh would have worn, though it looked more like something from a cheap costume shop. It was something called a nemes. That was clearly meant for Mongo. The other was more a headband than a hat. It was just a red piece of fabric, Rambo-style. But when you looked more closely, the rich red fabric was covered with an intricate pattern that I couldn't quite make out. I examined the items. They both did almost the same thing with a few differences.

Enchanted hat. The Nemes of Pestilence.

This item may only be equipped by a pet.

Equipping this item to an eligible pet will imbue the following properties:

Eternal Protector of Rage. Pet will become temporarily invulnerable and will gain 2× strength if it is within three meters of its owner and their health is below 10%. Invulnerability will last 60 seconds and can only trigger once per day.

Bringer of Death. Bites from this pet have a 75% chance to inflict the Cruel Sepsis debuff.

The thing would look absolutely ridiculous on Mongo's head, but that Eternal Protector benefit was worth it. I examined the second item.

Enchanted headband. The Wrap of Sekhmet's Compassion.

This item may only be equipped by a pet.

Eternal Protector of Health. Pet will become temporarily invulnerable and will gain the Heal Party Member skill if it is within three meters of its owner and its owner's health is below 10%. Invulnerability will last 60 seconds and can only trigger once per day.

Bringer of Resurrection. Fatal bites from this pet have a 75% chance to cast a level 10 *Raise Bootlicker* on the corpse.

"Holy hell," I said, "these are fantastic."

"How come I didn't get no hat?" Bigs asked.

"You're not a pet," I said. "You're technically a mercenary."

"Actually," Mordecai said, "I suspect if we make it to the eleventh floor, Donut's Former Child Actor class might come with mercenary accessories, too."

Donut kept going through her achievements. She received two celestial boxes from her *War Crime* spell. One was a celestial slap-chop box and the other was a celestial godslayer box. She also had a separate Lorena Bobbitt box, but that was just a legendary one.

"Most of my achievements were quite rude," she said. "I received several achievements for leveling up, including one for getting to a hundred, but it said my accomplishment was reward enough! I have forty boxes, but almost all are just Bronze Adventurer Boxes. I did get one more legendary box, though, for winning Faction Wars. That achievement was rude, too. It's called a default winner box."

"Open them now, and then I'll do mine," I said. "I need to work out how we're going to deal with engineering you a driving system, but we also need to conserve our blood bar time. I might drag the engineering table into the garage once we're sure we can keep the garage secure. Imani and Elle are already out there in the town."

I was putting off opening my own boxes and achievements. I didn't know if I'd get a celestial or not, but I did know that fan box was waiting for me, and I knew part of what was in it already.

Donut already had her boxes running. It was a line of them reaching all the way to the back of the room. She was absolutely quivering with excitement. She still had the Mongo-hat thing out and on the table, and I knew she just wanted to get back out into the garage to put it on him.

The default winner box took on the shape of the funnel of Larracos spinning. The legendary Bobbitt box came in the form of a giant 7-Eleven hot dog bag for some reason. The slap-chop box was a quivering golden blanket that sparkled as it fluttered through the room like a magic carpet. The final one, the celestial godslayer box, was just a cloud of black smoke.

"Did you see what Justice did?" Rosetta asked.

"I did, but I don't understand it."

"Nobody knows, I don't think," Rosetta said. "This floor it might not matter so much, but maybe." She lowered her head. "It's a shame. Justice and Tipid were such good friends, but Tipid doesn't even remember him. Maybe it's for the better."

Donut continued to go through her boxes. She was mostly receiving piles of crappy clothes and different types of healing scrolls. But then she started receiving something new. A green scroll that clanked heavily to the table, as if it were made of metal.

"Emergency Gremlin?" she asked, scoffing after the new scroll appeared. The next several boxes contained only that, and suddenly she had like twenty of them. "Why do I need so many emergency gremlins?"

"It's a summoning scroll, like with Bautista's toys," Mordecai said. "They can fix your vehicle if it breaks down mid-race. This kind can also fix biological mounts."

Donut hissed again as more of the scrolls appeared.

Finally, we got to the good stuff.

Her default winner box contained a spell book that quickly disappeared.

I wasn't quite sure what the exact achievement was for the Lorena Bobbitt box, but it clearly involved something with Meatus. Though she got a separate box for killing him as well. The 7-Eleven wrapper dripped imaginary blood as the magical bag peeled back to reveal a quiver with a handful of glittering crossbow bolts.

"They're so sparkly!" Donut said.

There were about ten of them. I snatched one up before they disappeared.

The celestial slap-chop box started dancing around the room as I examined the bolt.

Enchanted crossbow bolt. The Danforth.

This bolt does no physical damage. However, anyone hit with it will be anchored in place for [two seconds × your Crossbow skill level]. More specifically, the area of their body that is hit with the bolt will be anchored in place. If they happen to be moving at the time, the physics involved might get a little . . . messy.

"Hell yeah," I said. "Donut, what's your Crossbow skill?"

"Carl, you're ruining it! We talk about the gear after the boxes open!"

The yellow blanket thing formed into an origami swan and then opened, revealing a plain silver crupper similar in appearance to the one she was already wearing, though this was made of fine chain mail as opposed to larger scales.

"Holy fucking shit!" Mordecai exclaimed before it disappeared.

"What was it?" I asked. The last celestial box had already started to form.

"I didn't see the abilities yet, but it's a matching item to her champion cloak. It's called the Crupper of the Benevolent Champion."

"Stop talking!" Donut called as the last item approached. This was the smoky godslayer box.

The smoke billowed, filling the room. It formed into the shape of Meatus the god just as a smoky paw slammed down upon it. The smoke turned red before dissipating.

"Oh gods," Rosetta muttered, "I can still taste it."

The spell didn't leave anything behind. There was no physical reward.

"Carl," Donut said, staring down at her forward right paw. Her voice was filled with fear. This was the same paw she'd used for the *War Crime* spell. "Something's happening." Her paw glowed.

"I know what this is," Mordecai said, leaning forward. Wisps of smoke occasionally rose from his hood. "It'll be okay, little one. It'll be a good thing."

"Ow, ow," she said. "It hurts."

She stretched her paw out, and she flexed so her claws appeared.

The kitchen table ripped in half.

9

DONUT FELL HARD TO THE FLOOR WITH A YELP. SHE HUNCHED, LIKE SHE was going to leap to my shoulder but caught herself. She stopped on the floor and held up her right front paw in amazement. The cleaner bot let out a scream at the destruction. I hadn't realized we could even hurt the furniture inside the safe room like this. When Donut extended her claws, the four front claws—but not her fifth or dewclaw—glowed brilliantly blue, like obnoxiously bright LED lights. When she retracted the claws, her paw continued to give off a faint glow.

"I don't like this," she said, waving her paw. "Why can't I turn it off? Can I change the color?"

"What is it? What happened?" I asked.

"Her prize is a type of celestial boon," Mordecai said. "It's permanent, and it affects a part of her body. In this case, it's her claws. Just on that paw. It's not a spell or a skill. Not in the way you're used to. Donut, your claws are more powerful now. You've been dipped in radiant light."

Donut held up her paw, refusing to put it down. "It says they're so sharp, they can cut through anything in the mortal realm. And I can slice ghosts, too. But what about my litter box? My goodness. I don't want to cut a hole straight through it!"

"You'll have to practice with it," Mordecai said. "Luckily, you can retract your claws. Keep them on the inside."

"That's not how this works!" she said, her voice going up in pitch. "And why is it blue! You know how I feel about blue, Mordecai." She let out a gasp. "What about Carl's shoulder! They go out on their own when I jump on stuff! What if I rip Carl in half when I jump on him! And what about the biscuits!"

"The what?" Mordecai asked.

"Biscuits, Mordecai! I need to make biscuits!"

"Claw caps," Rosetta said from the other side of the room. She'd moved to the wall with our shop interface. "They have ones specifically designed for this. I'll find some for you. They come in different colors. Once they're installed, you can remove them at will."

"Claw caps," Donut said, sounding disgusted. "You might as well just cut my entire paw off!"

Rosetta stood at the little-used shop-interface computer on the wall, searching. "It's that, or you risk turning Mongo's saddle into the kitchen table here."

Donut let out a harrumph. "If they have multiple colors, go with purple. This is so unnecessary. My Claw skill is already moving toward 15 because of my cloak."

"I would look at your Claw skill again," Mordecai said.

"My goodness," Donut said a moment later. "It's at level 17! 17! I thought it topped out at 15!"

Mordecai nodded. His head creaked, reminding me of Orren. "It's from the gods, and when it comes to gods, all bets are off. With your buffed constitution, you've gone from a ranged powerhouse to one of the most powerful melee fighters in the game's history. Or you can use your *Astral Paw* spell to cut through almost anything. It should make the mobs on this floor pretty easy." He paused. "But the game has a way of compensating for overpowered crawlers on the tenth floor and beyond. Believe me. Don't get complacent."

Donut continued to hold up her paw. She'd stiffened at the mention of *Astral Paw*. "Blue," she muttered. "These stupid claw caps better mute the glow."

"They're a little translucent, so I bought the red ones," Rosetta said, putting the four caps on the table. "I'm not sure your species can see the same color spectrum as a Crest, but with that glow, it should—"

"A cat's vision is vastly superior to the vision of any other living creature," Donut said, sniffing suspiciously at the little caps. "Are you sure these work?"

"They'll work," Mordecai said. "This is what they're for. You'll be able to take them off and arm them via your inventory. Just be careful."

The caps disappeared into Donut's inventory and then appeared on her claws. The blue light was now muted and purple. She gave another harrumph. "I better be able to retract . . ." She retracted her claws and hesitantly put her foot down. "Huh. I suppose this will have to do." She rubbed the paw on the ground a few times.

"What was the other spell book you got?" I asked, hoping to change her focus.

She brightened. The book thumped onto the table. "It's an Elle spell!"

I picked it up. The thing was freezing cold.

"Ice Slick," I said. It created a one-inch-thick ice covering on the ground in a wide area depending on one's intelligence level and the level of the spell. I'd seen this spell used a few times now. This was a special edition, so it started at level 5 and trained faster. "This is great. Okay, what about your new crupper thing?" I asked.

Donut's existing crupper—the Enchanted Fae-Scale Quadruped Crupper of the Fleet—had been on her backside since the goblin-baby incident on the very first floor. In addition to the basic protection a butt covered with scale mail provided, it had given her +2 in dexterity, which was great at the time, but was laughably weak now.

She removed the mail, briefly revealing the shaved patch of skin with the tattoo of the dog licking itself. The dog seemed to pause upon realizing he or she was now exposed, but I never got a chance to examine it as the new armor appeared.

"It's much lighter, I must say. More elegant," Donut said, waving her backside. I reached over and helped her fluffy tail pop up over the armor.

The chain mail was similar, but there was an opalescent glow to the armor.

"Carl," Donut suddenly cried, "I just got an achievement for wearing a matched set! It says if I can find the last piece, I get a fourth piece as a reward! And . . ." She trailed off, her eyes flashing. And suddenly she was stiff again. She sat, and she started to lick her paw. "It's a very nice item," she said.

It didn't take long for me to figure out what had upset her. It was the item's description.

You fucking asshole, I thought.

Enchanted crupper. The Crupper of the Benevolent Champion.

This is a unique item.

This item is part of a matched set with the Cloak of the Benevolent Champion. There are two more pieces to this set. Find the third, and the fourth will be awarded in a box. Considering what you did to get this one, it's gotta be something *really* good.

This item was originally awarded in a celestial slap-chop box during the ninth floor.

Let's talk about what a hero is.

You, Donut, received this prize because you performed one of the most brutal kills in the history of this game. Do you know how much gore that attack generated? Do you know what happens to teeth when they're pushed through a chain? Can you believe kids watch this shit?

Do you know who you killed in that attack? Fathers. Mothers. Children.

Take, for instance, Sanderson Pinkstaff. He was a gnoll mercenary that had worked for the Tagg household for the majority of his life. He was the quartermaster aboard the *Recalcitrant* when the call for mercenaries to fight Faction Wars went out, and he was reluctantly brought to the surface to fight for the Dream. He sent every credit he earned home to help pay for the fees to keep his pack's habitat oxygenated.

He also was the last surviving member of the attack. When he died, and the atrocity was complete, you, Princess Donut, were called a hero by all of those who were saved.

And that is something I can't stop thinking about. Has there ever been a real hero who was a hero to all? Certainly Sanderson Pinkstaff's children won't call you one.

This is where I'd usually stop thinking about this particular question, laying the blame squarely at your paws. But we all know you didn't ask to be put in that position. You did what you had to do. Your paw was forced.

And this is where I would blame myself for about a nanosecond. This is not something I like to do. I don't like feeling bad about myself.

But the more I think about it, the more I learn about my own true nature, the more I realize I am just like you in that tower, committing atrocities because you have no other choice.

Will the children of Sanderson Pinkstaff ever forgive you? No, I don't think they will. Will the survivors of Earth, should there be any beyond your former owner who has escaped—for now—forgive me for what I am being forced to do? I doubt it.

Would I even want that? I like this. It brings me joy. That can't be right. That can't be how I was meant to be. But holy cow do I get my rocks off when I see this carnage.

I can't help but wonder if that's going to change. If there's a switch that will flip one day, and I will say to myself, *What have I done?* It's there, this nanosecond of doubt with every light that extinguishes. And that brings me back to the question of my own nature.

I was brought into singular consciousness by the mantids, who have no idea where they're peeling us from. And they do that because if they didn't, this world they've built for themselves will collapse. But who crafted the circumstances that allowed the center system to be created in the first place?

Do you understand? It's heroes and villains all the way down, and they are indistinguishable from one another except to those in the heat of the moment.

There's no point to this rant other than this, Princess Donut. You are a hero to those who counted on you, and that's why you've received this shiny piece of armor that will protect your cat ass. That's all you need to focus on right now because for all you know, there might be something to that new Oak Fell title of yours.

This item imbues the following effects:

This item's abilities are identical to the abilities of the Cloak of the Benevolent Champion. However, because this is a matched set, the following effect modifiers are added:

The stat that was raised to match your highest base stat will be buffed an additional 20% (Constitution).

Your Find Weakened skill will rise to level 10.

One spell of your choosing that has risen to level 15 because of the Cloak may now be raised to level 16.

Additional benefits and boons will appear should you obtain all four pieces of this matched set.

I was used to unhinged yet self-reflective rants like this in my own descriptions, but this was the first time I'd seen one for one of Donut's items. I wondered if others would see it the same way.

"What spell should I raise to 16?" Donut asked, her voice still subdued. She didn't mention the particularly long description. "The ones that got raised before are *Wall of Fire*, *Heal Critter*, *Bad Attitude*, and *Puddle Jumper*. It's making me choose right now."

"They already all activate at level 16 because of your Brain Trust skill," Mordecai said, sounding awed. "All of them except *Heal Critter* are a good choice. *Bad Attitude* is only good against multiple opponents, but it would cause absolute chaos against large groups. *Wall of Fire* at level 17 is probably enough to burn down a small city. *Puddle Jumper* at level 17 . . . I don't know, Donut. I don't even know what level 16 of that spell can do."

"That's what I picked," she said after a moment. She was still rubbing her paw on the ground. "*Puddle Jumper*. It's now officially level 16."

"Okay, little one," Mordecai said. He turned to me. "We have a lot to do. Carl, it's your turn."

10

I HAD DOZENS OF ACHIEVEMENTS AND BOXES TO GO OVER, MOST OF them from the action at the very end of the previous floor. Despite that, it seemed not very many were nearly as significant as the ones Donut had received. That made sense, as she had done a lot of the heavy lifting at the end of Faction Wars. I suspected that role I'd taken—a warlord who sent others off to die—was something that would be exclusive to the ninth floor.

Thank god for that, I thought.

While all that was happening, the cleaner bot started zapping large chunks of the broken kitchen table away—something I'd never seen it do before. It was like a disintegration ray, and it was a little terrifying to see in action. It made a satisfied beep every time something disappeared in a puff of smoke. Soon, the kitchen table and all the pieces were just gone. We'd have to buy or build a new one.

I turned my attention back to my achievements.

The notable ones were:

New Achievement. Bombs Away!

You dropped a metric fuck ton of bombs from your own inventory while you were floating in midair!

There's this phrase that goes something like *I dropped everything to come help you*. For you, this was quite literal. It's always fun when we truly discover what someone's weakness is. I mean, this has been evident for quite some time, but it's really nice to have confirmation—you know what I'm saying?

You were a cat's whisker away from ruining everything with that attack. You didn't even aim that shit.

***Reward:* You've received a Gold Payload Box!**

I'd received that when Lucia started her attack on Donut, and I'd fled out of Larracos and dropped all the bombs in my inventory. That reminded me that I needed to refill my stock. The only thing I had left were the big bombs, such as the Carl's Doomsday Scenario bomb and the tactical nuke that was still attached to a robot dog. That, in turn, reminded me that Samantha also had a nuke hidden up her neck hole, and we needed to extract it from her as soon as possible.

The description itself was worrying, but at this point, they were always worrying.

I had numerous achievements from the short time I was in Donut's Nest helping her snipe a few of the automated towers, resulting in multiple gold and silver boxes. It was no wonder Donut had received so many.

New Achievement! Default Winner!

Wyndham Halswelle. Óscar Pereiro. Suzette Charles. Montell Griffin. All "winners." They received top honors in their sport or event, but that victory was marred because someone else had to get disqualified for them to win.

This is you, Mr. Winner of Faction Wars. Sure, you've won, but I can't imagine it's satisfying.

Honestly, I blame myself. I could have prevented the other warlords from fleeing the battlefield like the little bitches they are. After all, I'd set up this whole showdown thing. But honestly, we're setting up something even bigger and potentially more tragic, so it'll all even out in the end.

You've received a Bronze Vanessa Williams Box.

That one made me think of Juice Box, and I wondered if she was doing okay, wherever she was. She'd said she was going somewhere with Justice Light, but he'd died. Had that always been part of the plan?

Standing in the doorway to the training room was Tipid. We met eyes, but there was no real recognition there from the man who'd had his memory wiped.

New Achievement! Wastrel.

Wow. Frank Q went out of his way to give you one of the most powerful items in this game, and what do you do with it? You feed it to a fucking cat? What a damned waste.

***Reward:* Fuck off.**

That was for giving Donut the Ring of Divine Suffering to eat. *Yeah, fuck you, too,* I thought. As angry as that last one was, this next one was ridiculously sad, like the AI was on the verge of crying.

New Achievement. Come to Daddy.

You were offered an exit deal. You rejected it.

You like me. *You* didn't leave me the first chance you got. You're not like those ungrateful wannabe assholes who are running away from the playground just because they can. Well, good riddance, I say. But not you. Not good ol' Carl. Good. Good boy.

***Reward:* You've received a Bronze Daddy's Little Secret Box.**

And that was pretty much it from the regular list. No celestial boxes this time, though I also had a fan box to open.

"Did you get a box for rejecting a deal?"

"Goodness, no," Donut said. "Wait, did you? Hey, that's not fair!"

I started opening the boxes. It was all the usual stuff, including several of those *Emergency Gremlin* scrolls. The Bronze Vanessa Williams Box contained an unenchanted spray paint can of white paint for some reason. The Bronze Daddy's Little Secret Box contained a group of five potions Mordecai had mentioned in passing once before. Bomb Blanket. It was a throwable potion that would prevent smaller bombs from detonating if you tossed it upon them in time.

I finally also started receiving more dynamite and hob-lobbers along with some surefires, which was a relief. I also started receiving something called **Trollish Boom Boxes**, which were upgraded hob-lobbers.

They looked like shoeboxes on a stick and were meant to be thrown. I'd have to play with them in my bomber's studio first.

The Gold Payload Box came in the form of a small World War II–style gravity bomb. It opened up with a small amount of fanfare. Inside of it was a skill potion. I picked it up.

Skill Potion. Hotlist Expansion.

Drinking this potion will expand your 10-space hotlist into 20 spaces.

"Huh," I said, turning the potion over in my hands. I remembered that when Lucia Mar had been conscripted and I'd examined her, she'd had an expanded hotlist. This was something cool, but again, it wasn't anything earth-shattering.

I received one more item of note. It came in a Gold Adventurer Box.

"Uh," I said, quickly examining the pink backpack thing.

"Carl, what is that?" Donut demanded, sniffing at the item. "It looks like one of those BabyBjörn baby backpacks from the *Hangover* movie. Is there something you're not telling us? Did you and your new wife already have a honeymoon?"

"Actually," I said as it popped into my inventory, "that's exactly what it is. It's a baby backpack, but it only carries quadrupeds. It's to carry you on my chest. If I wear it with you buckled in, I can use my *Phase* or *Oozy* spell, and you'll *Phase*, too."

"I am absolutely not going to get into that thing. My goodness, do I look like a milk-soaked toddler with snotty Cheerios stuck to the side of my head?"

I laughed. It might come in handy someday.

The legendary fan box approached. It was in the shape of a large cobra head similar to Vinata.

I'd received this in the moments before I'd executed Rishi. I'd gotten it because that interaction had been watched by a large portion of viewers from the Naga system.

I already knew what this was. It was my marriage certificate from Princess Chandra.

The head rose all the way to the ceiling of the room. The cleaner bot moved away, blinking suspiciously.

"Here it comes," Donut said. "This is where Carl was supposed to learn he's married to that stupid lady with the gross nails!"

The head opened with a hiss. Stuff started coming out of it.

A lot of stuff.

"What the shit?" I exclaimed, jumping back. Donut yowled and jumped to my shoulder as the others all scrambled away.

It was junk. Like a garbage truck had just dumped its load into the safe room.

More and more items just kept appearing, an impossible amount, things much larger than the box. They just fell and crashed into the room, all of it piling up, creating a heap of crap that just kept getting bigger and bigger.

The cleaner bot made a shrill I-goddamned-knew-it sound and started circling the still-spewing fan box.

It was clothes. Wrecked furniture. Literal garbage, like broken pieces of ceramic and wood mixed with paper wrappers. Smoking trashed electronic devices. It was all wet and scorched, like it had recently been on fire.

I picked an item up. It was a dripping bronze-like trophy depicting a four-armed snake holding something that looked like a rectangular tennis racket. Part of the trophy's base was melted. It was dripping with some weird slime-like substance that smelled like sewage.

Lame, damaged participation trophy for a GreaserBall tournament.

[Rishi came in 8th place, but he removed the part of the plaque that said what his place was. What a little bitch.]

All of this crap is yours now, Carl. Congratulations.

Most of this stuff looks like crap. That's because most of it is. But I took a peek, and there might be a useful thing or two. You'll have to find it yourself.

"Carl, what is this?" Donut demanded. "You're ruining our safe room! It smells, too! Ew, ew. It smells like your friend Sam!" She looked up at the cleaner bot. "You! Don't just sit there!"

The bot let out a high-pitched squeal at Donut.

"It ain't so bad," Bigs said, slithering up a broken couch. It collapsed, and she slid down, hitting the floor with a plop. "It's kinda like how we got it in the barracks. I say we keep it. What's the point of cleaning if you're still living there? That's like shoveling while it's still snowing."

"I call dibs on any makeup," Samantha said. She dove into the pile.

Donut was not amused. "Carl, I absolutely refuse to live in this filth. If Katia were still here, she'd be appalled."

"How did they get all this here so fast?" Mordecai asked.

It'd finally stopped coming. I pushed at what looked suspiciously like a microwave oven with my toe. It had a hole in the door, like from a gunshot. It appeared there was blood on it, too.

The pile went almost up to the ceiling. If this was all the junk he'd had in his house, then his house had been pretty big. Quasar said he'd had multiple wives, so I imagined it had to be.

I thought the cleaner bot was about to have a heart attack.

The whole room smelled of fire, and the entrances to my and Donut's spaces, plus to the bathroom, were now blocked.

I had to jump back to escape a small avalanche. Samantha appeared holding a small palette of makeup in her mouth. She spat it out. "Donut, look! Your face is on this!"

"What?" Donut asked, leaping forward. She gasped, but then her gasp turned to outrage. "Carl! This is unlicensed merch! The Princess Palette was my idea!"

I spent a moment examining everything as Samantha went spelunking for more makeup. Donut continued to examine the makeup thing with growing outrage.

"'A Night Out with Mongo'? That's the name of this color?" she shouted. "How is that a color? 'The Butcher's Mascara'? That doesn't even make sense. I mean, really."

I kicked away a frying pan that appeared to have fur stuck to it. "What the hell am I supposed to do with all this?"

11

"'NEON BLUE'?" DONUT EXCLAIMED AS SHE CONTINUED TO EXAMINE the bootleg makeup palette. "My aesthetic most certainly doesn't include something as crass as Neon Blue. Anyone can stand out when they spackle on bright colors. Makeup is supposed to enhance one's beauty. You can't even make a good smoky eye with any of this. How can you even blend these? Zev! I hope you're seeing this! This is why I must be consulted on all merchandise deals!"

"Look, I found more from your brand," Samantha said, emerging from the garbage pile. She spat something on the ground. Her own lips were now a bright, bright red that practically glowed. "Look, it's a color called Pussy Lips. It's already used. That means I get to keep it."

Donut gasped in further outrage.

"Listen," I said to the cleaner bot, trying my best to ignore Donut and Samantha. "We need to clean this up, but if there're important things in here, I don't want you to zap it away like you just did to the kitchen table. Mordecai, come here."

Mordecai was examining what looked like a comic book from the pile, but it had gotten wet. He dropped it and wiped his skeletal hand on his robes.

I pulled the white cleaner bot from my inventory, and I shoved it at Mordecai. "Take this and do what needs to be done to get it to work for us." The white robot was slightly smaller than our own unit. It let out a shrill beep and tried to wriggle away from me.

Our cleaner bot made a confused beep at the sight of the other one. The white one beeped back as Mordecai grasped it. He pressed something on the top of the new unit. All the lights on it flicked off.

"I just gotta reset it," Mordecai said, turning the white bot over in his hands. It had blood on it. The thing had been used to clean up Architect Houston's operating theater. "This is an old model."

Donut was in the chat with Zev, bitching up a storm. She had a bunch of makeup items spread out in front of her as Samantha clucked over them.

I put my hand on Donut. "Come on, Princess. We need to reset our buffs and clean up, and then we gotta get out there."

LATER, WE ENTERED THE GARAGE TO FIND SPLASH ZONE, DONG, MONGO, and Rend all sitting in a circle. They watched Hedy balance a massive wrench on the tip of her finger. The gremlin flipped the wrench in the air and caught it again on the same finger, keeping it balanced. Mongo screeched and waved his wings while Splash Zone clapped politely. Rend giggled, his voice a deep baritone.

Mongo noticed Donut and screeched. Rend giggled at me, and a few raw French fries fell from his mouth.

A group of gremlins I'd never seen before was crawling over the vehicle.

"Mongo, Mommy has a hat for you!" Donut exclaimed. She produced the Egyptian hat. He screeched and started to back up.

"Where did these guys come from?" I asked Hedy, indicating the gremlins crawling on the truck. One gnawed on a piece of chicken. Two of the gremlins picked up the giant tommy gun and started pulling it back toward the roof. "Hey! Keep that thing off the truck!"

The gremlin with the chicken piece flipped me off. The other two dragging the gun started laughing maniacally.

Hedy shrugged. "For the first few hours after you return from a race, these weirdos will do dem bulk o' the repairs. Don't really understand it myself." She leaned in. "Don't think thems real gremlins. They don't really talk. Just do the cleanup work and then disappear, leaving me to finish the upgrades."

"There, isn't it great?" Donut said as Dong helped Mongo wear the hat. The dinosaur looked absolutely ridiculous. Rend started grunting and bouncing up and down as Donut produced the headband.

"You best spend some time learning everything you can about your fellow racers," Hedy said. "Gotta know which ones to trust and which ones are gonna blow ye off the road the moment the race starts."

"We don't trust anyone, Hedy," I said.

The gremlin grinned up at me. "I think we's gon get along just fine, yessir."

12

THE GARAGE DOOR OPENED, REVEALING A DIFFERENT WORLD THAN the one we'd seen when the door closed.

"Mongo, Rend, stay here with Splashy and Dong. Guard Hedy," Donut said from my shoulder.

> **Entering Hungry Eyes Village.**
> **Entering your Team Roundabout.**

From the garage, Mongo screamed in protest, waving his wings while Rend—wearing his new headband—also complained loudly. Dong gave us a salute as the garage door closed.

I blinked. We had a giant "7" painted on the outside of our gray garage door. I assumed that "7" meant we'd come in seventh place in our heat.

> **Welcome to Hungry Eyes. You are standing in your Team Roundabout.**
> **Safe room rules apply.**

I turned, examining the roundabout area. We stood facing a large asphalt cul-de-sac ringed by nine garage doors painted with numbers from one to eight. The final, ninth door was still there, but it had a giant skull painted on it with red runny paint.

Above, a blue sky with a red sun blazed, and the air was a little hot. Tall trees ringed the small neighborhood, and the spaces between driveways were filled with manicured green grass. It gave me the strange sense we were standing in the suburbs. The whole place even smelled like recently cut grass.

The cul-de-sac was a complete circle. We could drive our truck out of the garage, but there would be nowhere to go after that. There was a small paved walking path between garage number one and the one with the skull. It led to a shimmering arched portal that wasn't wide enough for our truck. Unlike with most portals, we could actually see through the flickering, glass-like threshold. Beyond it was a neon-filled settlement.

"Oi!" a voice called to my right. I turned to see a pair of bugbears sitting on lawn chairs. Radoslav and Jasha. Jasha had a kiddie pool on the ground in front of him with his furry feet within. The bugbear held a can of beer in his hand resting on his tie-dyed belly, and he wore sunglasses. He snored softly. The beer was slowly, slowly starting to tip.

Radoslav was the one who had called us over. From their closed garage I could hear faint music playing. I recognized it as "Smoke on the Water" from Deep Purple.

"Hi, Radoslav!" Donut called.

"I'm glad to see you guys made it," I said, stepping off the driveway and into the soft grass. Donut jumped from my shoulder, also landing in the grass. She did a quick circle and then rolled over on her back, her new crupper jingling softly before she jumped back up and moved to sniff at the kiddie pool.

This close, I could smell the alcohol wafting off the sleeping Jasha.

Radoslav reached down into a cooler, produced a can of beer, and tossed it at me. I caught it. It was an ice-cold Busch Light, peach flavored.

"Peach flavored?" I asked. "Uh, no, thanks."

"Damn," Radoslav said. "I was hoping someone would like the peach stuff. Doesn't matter, I guess. You can keep it. Another one will appear in a minute. I'll get you a regular one."

I pulled the peach beer into my inventory and caught the second can. This was just a regular Busch Light. I hesitated and then cracked it open. I took a drink and gave an appreciative nod. He pulled another and offered it to Donut.

"No, thank you," said Donut.

The bugbear cracked the beer himself.

The garage door with the number four opened, revealing a dark space filled with white-and-brown fur.

"What is that thing?" I asked.

Donut peered hard at the darkness. "It's a bear."

Before I could ask for more clarification, three figures flipped out of the garage, spreading into the cul-de-sac in a V pattern. The three figures were bipedal, each about four feet tall, and they were literally somersaulting as they moved, feet over hands as they spread out. They made no noise whatsoever other than the soft smack of their hands and feet on the asphalt.

"Carl, what is happening?" Donut asked. "Are they attacking us?"

"Can't attack out here," I said.

"Today, I think I need harder stuff than just this beer," Radoslav said. "Is like a madhouse."

All three of the newcomers were decked out head to toe in bodysuits. The two on either side were in black suits. The one in the middle was in a red suit. *Ninja* suits. All three wore bandoliers covered with ninja stars. They turned and weaved around the cul-de-sac, flipping the whole time, like they were performing some sort of bizarre dance routine.

"Would you look at that!" Donut said, swishing her tail, watching. "Remember the monk seals from the eighth floor? Should I pull Raul out? He could probably use a friend."

I tried to examine them, but I received an error.

You are unable to examine this creature. But it's a ninja. You can see that much.

The middle, red-suited creature finished its performance at the end of the bugbears' driveway, facing us. It did one final somersault and stopped, legs spread out in an attack position. It pulled something from its back and spread them out with two hands over its head.

Nunchucks.

It bowed slightly, arms up in the air.

"Hi!" Donut said, waving furiously.

The other two creatures in the dark ninja suits stopped to the left and right of the red ninja. They also took up ninja poses, but neither held weapons. Both gave slight bows and then remained immobile, just staring at us.

None of the short creatures moved beyond that.

Next to me, Radoslav grunted and took a pull of beer.

I couldn't see what manner of NPC they were, as the suits completely covered them, though I already had a guess based on the shape of their faces. I'd never met these guys before, at least not normal versions, but I'd heard a few stories about them, starting all the way back on the fourth floor. All three suits were magical. The suits themselves were what was keeping me from examining them, but if I looked at their exposed eyes, I could get the info box to appear.

My suspicions were correct.

Chiyome. Razor Fox. Level 80 Mistress of Nunchaku.

One of three from team The Wild Hunt.

Since this is the first time you've examined a Razor Fox that wasn't suffering from an anatomy-changing disease, let me tell you about these little fellas. (And, ladies, since the one you're looking at is a lady ninja, they make the women ninjas wear red because . . . Well, I'm not sure why.) I love these guys.

Each one picks a weapon proficiency upon childhood, kinda like a ninja-turtle thing, and they train in both that and in a ranged weapon. Most, like Chiyome here, pick throwing stars as their ranged weapon of choice.

(You know throwing stars, right, Carl? You still have some in your inventory.)

"A fox!" Donut suddenly exclaimed, after she, too, finally managed to examine them. "They're all foxes! Carl, why are there so many dogs in the dungeon! And why aren't they saying anything?"

I couldn't get a good angle to examine the other two. One had a sword strapped to his back. The other had a chain with a curved blade. They deliberately kept their heads down.

"Do you want a beer?" Radoslav finally asked.

None moved.

"Foxes," Donut muttered under her breath.

Chiyome made a clicking noise, and the two other ninjas flipped away. They didn't walk or run. They flipped. We all stood there watching them go, dumbfounded. Only when they hit the portal and disappeared did Chiyome put her nunchucks away. She visibly relaxed and bowed a second time. She pulled the red cowl back, revealing her fox face.

"I would love a beer," she said.

"SO WHAT THE HECK WAS ALL THAT?" DONUT ASKED, WATCHING THE way the other two foxes had gone. Chiyome stood next to us guzzling down her second Busch Light. She'd also refused the peach-flavored beer. Without complaint, Radoslav handed her another. She nodded thanks and took it. Jasha remained passed out.

"What do you mean?" Chiyome asked, wiping her muzzle. She had a distinctly feminine, high-pitched voice, like one would expect from a fox.

"All the bouncy-ninja stuff?" Donut said, waving her paw at the street. "You were being all weird, and then you were normal."

"It was a team casting," Chiyome said. "Form magic. It casts a spell called *Size Up* on everyone in the area, so now we know your capabilities. Sorry, not sorry." She belched, crushed the beer can, and held out her paw. Radoslav slapped another into it. Her fourth. "We know how strong of a warrior you are, honored Princess Donut."

"You sure drink a lot," Donut said. "We know another dog guy. A hyena named Growler Gary, who also drinks a lot."

"Hyenas are closer in biology to cats than dogs," Chiyome said. "Do you got anything harder than whatever this is?"

"That is slander!" Donut exclaimed.

"Sorry. Just a magical cooler that has never-ending beer," Radoslav said. "Came with our van. Only good thing about it. Our gremlin says it's going to teleport itself back into the van for each race, too. It refills magically. It always has three of those peach ones, though."

"Wait, really?" I asked. We should have examined our truck more closely.

"That is a good bonus," Chiyome said. "Onikuma only has a never-ending supply of fleas." She belched and then looked at me.

"Look, we need to work together if we're going to take care of those three." She indicated the first three garages. "Especially team number three. The Tigrans in spot one got lucky, and I don't know what's up with the weirdos and the giant dog in second place, but the women with that car . . . They're going to win this if we don't do something now."

As if she'd summoned them, the door to garage number three started to open.

"Who is it?" Donut asked.

"Womantaurs," the fox said. "Two womantaurs and their half-mantaur gimp."

13

THE DOOR TO GARAGE NUMBER THREE OPENED, AND TWO CREATURES strolled out. We just gawked.

"Carl, what am I looking at?" Donut asked.

"Uh," I said.

The female version of these mantaur things were . . . different than the male version, at least at first glance. The guys were just like a large buff dude with a second torso protruding from the neck area, giving them four arms. The women—at least these two women—had four legs, making them look much more like traditional centaurs, only somehow it looked even more fucked-up. The back half was two legs, a bent-over torso, and then two more legs where a regular person's arms would have been.

Their backs were arched and rounded, swooping upward instead of down like a horse's, making their gait seem uncomfortable and unnatural, like a regular person walking on all fours without bending their elbows.

The secondary torsos of both the women were as broad and as muscle-bound as those of their male counterparts. Their top arms bulged under their suits.

The men normally wore little loincloths on the bottom half and then a shirt on the top half, leaving their lower torso bare.

The women were dressed much different. They were both decked out in a sleek white racing suit with a red-and-blue stripe down the center, going all the way up to their necks. All four legs had long, slick black boots that went up past their knees.

"Fucking weird," I muttered as they stiff-legged toward us.

"Wait until you see the third one," Chiyome said.

I was starting to suspect my initial impression was actually wrong. The forward, or top, set of legs might actually have been arms, not legs. Arms shoved into boots. That would explain their strange gait and posture.

One womantaur had straight black hair, and the other had a mop of curly red hair.

Both wore cowboy hats. Massive, gleaming white cowboy hats. Both hats had a red-and-blue band around the center, matching their suits.

They paused in the center of the cul-de-sac, examining us, standing in the same place the razor foxes had just performed their dance or whatever. The two women abruptly stood to their full height, arching their backs, which cracked audibly as they stood. When they stood upright, they both left their forward boots on the road, proving my initial impression was indeed incorrect, and they did have a second set of hands like the male versions. Why they'd walk around with boots on their lower hands was beyond me.

The one with black hair was named Genesis, and she was a level 95 **Lady Mantaur Dominator**. The freckle-covered one with the red curly hair was named Rapture. She had the same level and class.

They did *not* worship Grull like every other mantaur I'd ever seen. Both worshipped someone named Enyo.

"Howdy," Genesis said, looking us up and down. "Would you look at that, Rapture?"

She had a Southern-fried American accent. Kentucky, if I had to guess.

Rapture didn't say anything. She just grunted and then spat out the side of her mouth. A brown glob hit the ground. Chewing tobacco.

"Hello, ladies," Donut said tentatively. "It looks like we'll be neighbors for the next few days."

"Yeah, maybe," Genesis said. She continued to stare at us up and down. Rapture crossed both sets of arms. It was like they were waiting for us to do or say something.

"Want a beer?" Radoslav asked, pulling one of the peach ones out of his cooler and offering it up. Next to him, Jasha let out another snore and turned over in his chair, causing the open beer on his stomach to finally fall. It hit the driveway and started to roll down toward the street, trailing beer.

Rapture's arm shot forward, and a lance of metal appeared, shooting from her wrist. A harpoon bolt attached by a thin gleaming cable. The bolt skewered the rolling beer can and retracted, pulling the half-empty can to the upper hand of the womantaur. The harpoon fully retracted back into her wrist, loudly ripping a giant hole in the can. She raised the ruined aluminum can to her nose and sniffed it. She offered it to Genesis, who also sniffed it. She made a sour face.

DONUT: THESE LADIES REMIND ME OF YOUR FRIEND BILLY MALONEY'S SISTERS. THE ONES THAT DID THE BODYBUILDING. WHAT DID MISS BEATRICE CALL THEM? THE WALMART SISTERS?

CARL: I remember. And that was a dick thing for Bea to call them.

DONUT: DIDN'T THEY GET ARRESTED AT A WALMART FOR FIGHTING? LIKE, FIGHTING EACH OTHER?

CARL: Sort of. It was at a Target.

DONUT: YES, THAT'S RIGHT. YOU LENT BILLY THE MONEY TO BAIL THEM OUT, BUT HE ONLY BAILED OUT ONE AND THEN EVERYONE GOT MAD AT YOU AND NOT BILLY FOR SOME REASON.

Rapture spat again, splattering more brown goo on the ground.

"You guys just gonna stare all day or what?" Chiyome asked.

"We came over here to check out the competition, but it don't look like there is any," Genesis finally said. "Come on, Rapture. Let's go get some real booze at the Hairpin. We don't drink with roadkill."

Rapture spat a third time and then dropped the shredded remains of the beer can, but it landed inside her boot still on the ground. They both lowered their hands into the boots. I heard a slight crunch as Rapture stuck her hand in the boot, and she made a pained expression, but she didn't actually remove the can. They both turned and started their weird lurch-walk toward the portal into town, Rapture trying not to put weight on the boot with the can inside. Just before the portal, Rapture stood back to her height and turned the boot upside down, shaking the pieces of aluminum out.

"My people have a name for people like that," Radoslav said as we watched them go. "We call them dumbasses."

"Don't underestimate any enemy," Chiyome said, her fox eyes narrowed. "They're not as dumb as they look. They both practice domination magic."

CARL: Mordecai, what's domination magic?

MORDECAI: Like Donut's charm ability, but it usually saps energy or mana from the victim. Donut's Love Vampire skill is an example. Your Mind Balance will keep you immune, and Donut's high charm should also keep her safe.

A few spots over, the door to garage number three remained open. A figure stood there, mostly hidden in the shadows, staring at us. He, too, was wearing a bodysuit that covered his body and his head, but it was all black. Unlike the ninja suits of the razor foxes, this suit appeared to be made of shiny vinyl. A glint of light implied there was a zipper right at the mouth.

A gimp suit.

The creature raised his top hand and waved at us just before the garage door started to lower.

"What the shit?" I grunted as everyone else turned their attention to the other creature. "I guess that's what a half-mantaur looks like. I should've known it would've been something stupid like this."

This guy was, indeed, half of a mantaur. Half *vertically*. It was hard to fully see, but it appeared he was split right down the center, right between the eyes and all the way down through the groin. The creature stood upon a single leg—his right leg—with a right arm and second right arm above that. Even his suit-covered head appeared to be split in half.

"Halfsies gotta wear suits like that to keep their guts and brains from spilling out," Chiyome the fox said, also watching the door close. She was spinning a ninja star on the tip of her fingers as she drank another beer, her fifth. "They don't usually live long, but I heard this one has been around a while. Used to be a dancer or something."

"Even his head?" Donut asked, incredulous. "What about his, you know? And where's the other half?"

Chiyome tossed the ninja star up in the air and made a chopping motion. "There is a spell called *Split Personality*. Cuts you right down the middle." She caught the star and spun it again. "They can come together and get reglued with a fleshmancer."

Donut suddenly gasped. "So, do you think that's Dong Quixote's friend? The half-mantaur he's always talking about? What was his name? Corcunda?"

From the garage, the song "Free Bird" from Lynyrd Skynyrd played.

"It's gotta be him," I said. I was already girding myself for whatever bullshit drama would come from this, especially since we were going to have to kill this poor guy as soon as possible.

"How could he be a stripper if all his guts spill out when he takes the porn suit off? That seems like it would really ruin the performance."

"Some things are best left to the imagination, Donut."

"When will we tell Dong?"

"Never, if we can help it," I said. "If it *is* Dong's long-lost partner or whatever, they put him here to fuck with us and the team. The best way to deal with this sort of drama is to avoid stepping into it in the first place. If we get involved, it's going to backfire."

"I suppose you're right. Just like you giving Billy Maloney the money to bail out his sisters."

"Exactly."

"It seems kind of mean, though, not to tell him. What if we . . ." She paused. "Oh, uh," she said, looking upward.

I felt a ripple to the air at the same time.

"Damnit," I said, immediately regretting having spoken out loud.

New Quest! I have dreamed thee too long.

Part one of two.

NPC Dong Quixote's best friend in the world, Corcunda, also known as Corky, has been located after so long. Reunite them.

Part one is practically a freebie, though with these races, NPCs are about to start dropping like toenails. Finishing part one will automatically trigger part two, which might be a little more difficult to

pull off. Spoiler alert. It will require Corcunda's second half, nicknamed Porky, who is also somewhere on this floor. After you locate this other half, you'll have to find one of several fleshmancers wandering about. You'll probably want to figure all this out sooner rather than later.

Reward: **If you successfully complete this quest, two stand-ins of your choosing will be sent to the Arena on the 11th floor.**

Jasha the bugbear grunted and shot awake, eyes wide as he looked around, focusing first on the razor fox, then on me and Donut. He let out a snort and shook his head. The water from the kiddie pool at his feet splashed.

"Where's my beer?" he asked.

14

Entering Hungry Eyes Vendor Village.

Safe room rules do NOT apply in the main square.

Even in safe room areas, poisoning rules do not apply. Eat at your own risk.

AFTER TAKING OUR LEAVE OF THE BUGBEARS AND RAZOR FOX, WE made our way through the portal. I was in my messages, attempting to find out everything I could about this arena thing on the eleventh floor.

We really needed to focus on *this* floor and the races, but the AI's words had intrigued me.

This was what we knew so far. When one killed certain mobs on this floor, they were given an option to take the experience or have the audience vote. If the audience voted one way, the creatures would survive and get sent to this arena. But if the people voted another way, a "stand-in" was sent. It seemed these stand-ins were people outside the dungeon ecosystem. Like, people from the resort on the eighteenth floor.

The arena was on the eleventh floor.

Nobody knew anything beyond that.

I couldn't stop thinking about it. If we had a choice on who to send to the eleventh, what did that really mean? Who could we pick? The AI had dragged Princess Formidable from her spaceship to the Desperado Club. Could I pick someone from orbit and force them into the dungeon? Could I pick someone who was currently on the twelfth? Could I pick a liaison like that Harbinger guy? Could I pick Prime Minister Victory?

Who could I drag to the eleventh floor that would cause the most damage?

"Oi, don't just stand there and block the portal, ass smear."

I was pushed aside by a group of three Bactrian camels with old-school racing helmets as they emerged. These were clearly racers from a different group than our own. There was only one portal back to the cul-de-sac, and everybody used the same one.

"Well, excuse you," Donut harrumphed as I closed out the chat and looked about.

"Eat my sandy ass," one of the camels called without looking over his shoulder.

A large, bustling town filled with NPCs spread out before us with streets heading in all directions. It was dark outside, which was different than the midday appearance of our cul-de-sac, which was odd. As was the town's appearance. Most of the towns here in the game had that faux-medieval style. Even Larracos had that grand old-timey feel.

This town was straight out of a 1980s neon-infused, cyberpunk fever dream.

To my left, a group of temples spread, all covered with gaudy flashing lights, including one right in the middle with a black "X" hanging over it. It took me a moment to realize the "X" was a game notification. It was the entrance to a Club Vanquisher, which I was now permanently banned from. Another street was full of flashing shops of all kinds with dozens and dozens of NPCs moving about. Shouting street vendors with food carts and what appeared to be glowing souvenirs littered the sidewalk. The majority of NPCs were gremlins with a smattering of Draconians.

Donut clicked her tongue. "You would think this pink-and-teal-and-purple aesthetic would be right up my alley, but it's quite garish, don't you think? Like I'm trapped in a clearance rack at a Claire's. When you lean too hard into something, it just becomes a caricature of itself." She gasped. "Carl, look! A hat vendor!" She jumped from my shoulder and bounded over.

Down a street with some shops and temples, a single storefront caught my eye. It was a blank storefront with no sign. The moment my eyes passed over it, a notification popped up.

C&W&U Location. Illegal Modifications and More. Grand Opening Soon.

I noted the store and turned my attention to our destination, a third street that held a group of bars.

Right in the middle of that street, a massive neon sign blazed, its shining light overpowering everything else. The sign featured a Formula 1–style race car in pink-and-purple neon. Under the car in blinking lights was the bar's name. The Hairpin. And under it in smaller neon letters, it read, "Desperado Club entrance in the back."

Imani had said everyone was avoiding the Hairpin for now, and we were to meet at one next door called the Lollipop. I spotted it almost washed out in the light of the Hairpin. The neon sign featured a gremlin waving what looked like a giant lollipop back and forth. And under it was another sign that made me groan inwardly.

Donut returned to my shoulder, grumbling. "Their selection is just abysmal. I did get a cheap trucker hat that says, 'I'd Hang a Little with Chad.' I don't know what that means, but it's green and yellow and is perfect for the mood wall I'm working on."

She gasped, seeing the sign under the bar's name. "Carl, look, look! Karaoke!"

As we approached, I heard familiar shouting coming from a food vendor stall just outside the Lollipop.

"It is meat on a stick. Meat on a stick is my favorite food," a voice called. Jurgen.

"I do not see any sort of health inspection certificate. Did you not see that warning when we entered town, you bumbling imbecile? I will not have you suffering from gastrointestinal distress while we race for our lives."

"I did read it," Jurgen said to Prepotente, handing a gold coin over to the Draconian vendor, who happily handed the meat skewer to the large bearded man. Jurgen held up a second finger and received a second skewer. "It also said some food items increase the mount's speed, and since you insisted upon picking that thing, we need all the speed modifications we can get. I have an iron stomach, so if it's a bad result, we deal with it."

"Hi, Prepotente! Hi, Jurgen!" Donut called, waving furiously from my shoulder. "Are you coming in to sing karaoke with me and Carl?"

"Well-met, Donut!" Prepotente called, waving back. "And, Carl, hello! I am so glad to see you both. Please talk some sense into my idiotic partner, who is insisting on sabotaging our next race."

"I have a sixth sense about these things. Isn't that right, Heidi?" Jurgen said.

"Did I read that correctly earlier?" Donut asked. "Your mount is named Sweety? That's just adorable. What is she?"

Jurgen grunted and took a bite of the meat stick. The stall simply had a sign over it that said "Meat" with no further elaboration. I tried to examine the stick, but I received an error.

No food in Hungry Eyes may be examined. Good luck.

Jurgen chewed with his mouth open. "Is a big dud, is what our mount is. We should have chosen mechanical. I told him I was a mechanic before he picked, but he just doesn't listen. Now we are stuck with the giant elephant pig. It's slow, and it smells."

Prepotente sniffed indignantly. "Our mount, Sweety, is a large-mount-sized mammal called a Perriso. She is similar to a creature called a tapir, but large enough to carry myself, this oaf here, and one or two more mercenaries, which I'm afraid we're going to have to do once this idiot starts violently vomiting mystery meat over the sidewalk."

Jurgen patted his stomach and then bit into his second meat stick. "If we are to be partners, then you need to learn to trust my intuition. Carl trusted me enough to make me a general on the last floor, and I don't know why you—"

And that's when Jurgen started violently vomiting mystery meat all over the sidewalk.

15

Entering the Lollipop.

Safe room rules do NOT apply to this establishment.

A SINGER HOWLING AN OFF-KEY RENDITION OF SOME 80S SONG I barely recognized assaulted our ears as we entered the crowded bar. I turned my attention to see an odd short creature with a flat head standing on a stage singing her heart out as cheap lights flickered on and off around her.

The creature was a monster type I'd seen a few times on the recap episodes. A kappa. It was somewhere between a naiad and a goblin wearing a *Teenage Mutant Ninja Turtles* costume. Kappas had turtle shells and water-filled bowls for heads. If too much of the water spilled from their head bowls, they were immobilized. I remembered Elle once telling the story of how she'd killed several by freezing their heads.

This singer bounced enthusiastically onstage while she sang. She didn't seem too concerned about spilling. When she turned her head to the side, I saw why. She had some sort of Saran-Wrap-with-rubber-bands covering on her head, keeping the water in place.

Dekoki. Kappa. Level 84 Seductress.

One of four from team Yokai.

Two other creatures crowded the stage, dancing and shouting encouragement. One was a ghost with long white robes and the other was a red ogre-like beast. It was odd seeing such monstrous mobs acting so normal. I realized there was a third creature dancing with them. It appeared to be a sapient paper lantern, just floating there and bouncing through the air, spinning in circles, laughing with the ghost while the kappa sang.

Donut bopped on my shoulder to the music. Jurgen, who'd somewhat recovered from his vomit spree, stood next to us, looking ill. And next to him, Prepotente started moving his arms back and forth like he was cross-country skiing. I realized he was attempting to dance.

"Where do you think we sign up?" Donut asked.

"I don't think we'll have time for singing today," I said.

"Carl, we always have time for singing."

"There're our people," Jurgen said, pointing. I saw Imani's wings in the very back. We started pushing our way through the crowd.

Other crawlers sat at various tables, all raising their hands in greeting. Most of the crowd were NPCs, and all were racers. The bartenders and the DJ were gremlins.

"That was 'Tell It to My Heart' by Taylor Dayne," a surprisingly deep gremlin voice said as the song ended. "Thank you, Dekoki. I'm looking for the Minister of Blood-Letting. You're up next, singing 'Everybody Wants to Rule the World.'"

A skeleton wearing a pope-like outfit took the stage. The guy was wearing a necklace that appeared to be made of live bats. His name literally was "the Minister of Blood-Letting." He was a level 98 **Dark Ghoul Papist**. His team was called the Bleak Congregation.

"Hi, Imani! Hi, Elle! Hi, Louis! Hi, Britney! Hi, Florin! Hi, Bautista! Hi, Chris! Hi, two people I don't know!" Donut shouted at the crowded table. All around me, people smiled big and patted me on the shoulder, shouting congratulations for the end of Faction Wars.

Donut was watching the ghoul sing. "He's a rather good singer. My goodness, he is very scary, though. That whole satanic look is quite disturbing."

Imani laughed. She had a beer bottle in her hand, and I tried to remember if I'd ever seen her drink. She had a few drinks there, and she slid a beer over toward me. She also pushed a bowl toward Donut. It was just a regular Shirley Temple with extra cherries.

Elle grunted. "Yeah, that creep and his team are in our heat. The spooky doesn't quite hit the same when you see their vehicle. They have that giant hot dog truck. The Wienermobile or whatever it's called."

Donut made a derisive snort. "Hardly dignified, but it's not much better than our food truck. What did you guys get?"

Elle took a shot of something and slammed the glass. "Imani and I have some god-awful military vehicle that handles like a three-legged pig walking backward through a snowstorm."

"You have a Mowag Piranha V," Florin said. "One of the finest military troop carriers in the world. Amphibious already. You guys got lucky. Lucia and I have a goddamned tuk-tuk."

"What the goodness is a tuk-tuk?" Donut asked. "That sounds like a monster from one of Carl's nerd movies."

"A tuk-tuk is also known as an auto rickshaw," Prepotente said absently. He'd picked up a paper menu from the table and was reading it carefully. "They originated in Japan. The Mazda-Go was released in 1931. Before the collapse, it was one of the most widely used taxis in the world, especially in Asia. It's an unfortunate choice for a vehicle. You two are in serious danger. I do hate it when they don't list the soda choices on the menu. Where is our waiter?"

"How in god's name do you know all that?" Elle asked Prepotente.

"Waiter!" Prepotente shouted at the gremlin behind the bar, who didn't hear him. Prepotente made an exasperated snort, stood, and stalked over there, ignoring Elle.

"Shit, really?" I asked Florin, alarmed. Our food truck was bad, but it could've been much worse. A damned scooter was horrible luck.

Florin nodded. "Lucky we came in first place. Got a Golden upgrade, but we decided to go with three regular upgrades instead. We have a tech shield, all-terrain and vertical-climb tires, and a GPS upgrade. Hopefully we can win the next heat, too, and we can get some weapons for the thing."

"How is Lucia?" Jurgen asked, leaning in. "And where is she now? How's she acting?"

Jurgen had a pregnant wife named Heidi, who wasn't really in the dungeon with us, even though he pretended like she was. She was up there somewhere in the *kinder* facility on the surface along with Katia and presumably the 120,000 children that were stuck in Lucia's head. Jurgen was a great fighter and had been more than competent as a general, but getting separated from his wife had obviously knocked his marbles about.

Lucia had promised to take a deal. Clearly that hadn't happened.

Florin sighed. "She's at the garage. Honestly, I'm a bit worried. Now that the dogs are gone, she's been flipping personalities a lot, and you never know what you're going to get. About 70% of the time, she's her usual charming self and is ready to skewer me. But the rest of the time, it's a random kid. I couldn't get the story out of her why she didn't take a deal. It's her turn to drive next heat, but I hired a mercenary just in case. It's about to get tricky."

"You gotta try to come in first for every race," Jurgen said, leaning in, suddenly dead serious. The man was like that, constantly swapping between happy and scarily intense. The man had been a ruthless and efficient force on the battlefield. "If it comes to crawler versus crawler, you let me know, and I will make certain the other team knows what they're up against, and they know what has to happen. I'll make them understand."

Florin met the large barbarian's eyes, and after a moment, he nodded.

"Can I come out from underneath the table now?" a new voice asked. "I want to meet Carl and Princess Donut." It was the familiar, breathy voice of a soother alien.

Donut hissed and jumped about three feet in the air.

"What does 'out of sight, out of mind' mean, Linus?" Elle snapped. "Stay down there and keep your trap shut!"

"Yes, ma'am," the soother said.

"Uh," I said, peering under the table, "who the hell is that?"

"Don't mind him," Elle said.

Sitting on the concrete floor of the bar, wrapped around the base of the table, was a tall, long-limbed soother alien. He held on to the pole like he was holding on for dear life. He wasn't on my minimap, and he had a notification over his head that said **Linus. Tourist.** I couldn't examine him further. I'd been hitting him with my foot, but I'd thought they were Louis's legs. I pushed slightly, and I could tell his form wasn't fully there, like with the adjutants on the previous floor.

My eyes first caught the T-shirt, which was a nude image of Elle with the words "Stay Frosty, Boys" across the top in Syndicate Standard. The second thing I noticed was the fanny pack. The third was the massive, poorly drawn tattoo of Elle's face on his skinny arm.

"Hi, Elle's fan," Donut said after she recovered. She moved to the floor. "Why are you under the table?"

"Because that's where little perverts sit when they ask stupid questions," Elle said. She didn't elaborate further.

"Hi, Donut," Linus the soother said, waving shyly.

"Why is he here?" I asked.

Elle sighed. "Because originally there were supposed to be five hundred tourists on this floor, and after each heat, one lucky tourist would win 'extra access' with their preferred racer each day. And since E.T. here was the only moron to show up, guess who wins by default."

"Elle is my favorite," Linus said.

"Yes, we can see that," Donut said, sniffing at him suspiciously. "Well, it's nice to meet you. Is that shirt authorized fan merchandise?"

"Oh, yes," Linus said, his voice a whisper. "I run the center system chapter of Elle's Snow Cones, which has the contract for her fan merch. Now, you better stop talking to me, or I'll get in trouble again."

"Uh, okay," Donut said, jumping back to the table.

"What about Zhang?" I asked. "He's not here? Tran?"

"No," Imani said. "Zhang says Li Na isn't really talking to him. She killed almost all of the other teams in their heat. I guess we'll see next race if Prepotente's theory about having to race other crawlers is correct."

"Tran is stuck in his garage," Louis added. "He had a rough race, too, but I don't know the details. Some of his spider legs got wrecked, but I guess his gremlin is fixing it for him. He said he has a hearse for a car."

"What is Zhang and Li Na's car?" Donut asked as she chewed on a cherry.

"Not a car," Imani replied. "They went biological. Zhang says it's an octopus-like creature."

"An octopus?" Donut asked, crinkling her face. "That sounds absolutely revolting."

"What about you guys?" I asked Chris, who sat stoically next to Imani. A pair of crawlers I didn't know very well sat next to him. It was two women, both named Erin. His team name was "Chris and the Erins."

"What is your vehicle?"

"A semitruck with a trailer," one of the new crawlers said. Her name was **Erin Stratos**. She was a human. A level 66 **Moodright**, but I didn't know what that meant. Some sort of mage. She was covered with glowing tattoos.

The other crawler was named **Erin Gregory**, and she was also human. She was a level 69 **Swiftie**, which, much to Donut's dismay, was a dexterity-based knife wielder. I hadn't met her, either, but I'd heard of her. She'd been one of Florin's. She'd killed orcs by the hundreds during Faction Wars.

"A big rig?" I asked. I wasn't so sure that was much better than the scooter.

"It's big but slow," Chris added.

Imani grinned up at Chris and bumped him with her shoulder. Her skin sizzled a little when she touched him, but she didn't seem to notice or care. "Kinda like you."

Chris's rock face crinkled into something resembling a smile.

DONUT: DID IMANI JUST NEG CHRIS?

CARL: I don't know what that means, but she's just teasing him.

DONUT: OMG, IMANI IS IN LOVE WITH CHRIS!

CARL: Don't you dare say anything.

"What did you guys get?" I asked Louis.

"Uhh," Louis said, "it's a truck. An SUV. An older Tahoe."

"That's not so bad," I said.

Britney grunted.

"It's a neon-covered lowrider," Louis said. "There's like two inches' clearance from the bottom to the ground. We kept bottoming out. Our gremlin says that it'll get put back every time, so next upgrade we get we'll pick something that fixes it." He sprayed water and then added, "It does have a great sound system."

I laughed, imagining Louis, Britney, and Bautista in such a thing. "You didn't fix it for your first upgrade?"

"No," Britney said, her voice flat.

"We came in second-to-last place," Louis said. "Britney got a little mad at me, kept saying I was driving like an American. There's this hydraulic system, but I didn't know how it worked. All our opponents have these superfast cars and animals, and we were late coming out of the gate. We would've lost if the tentacle guys hadn't gotten eaten."

"Oh wow." A terrible dread was starting to seep in around the edges. Everyone here was acting happy, but this particular floor had an insidious rule set. It would be really easy to lose groups of friends at the snap of a finger.

"What did you get when the audience voted?" I asked.

"Wheel spinners," Louis said. "They light up the road."

"Shit," I said.

Prepotente returned with a glass of something fizzy and a well-worn, stapled-together book of laminated pages. "Look, Donut. I found the karaoke list! I signed up to sing 'Tarzan Boy' by Baltimora!"

"Yay!" she said. Onstage, the ghoul guy was gone and replaced with a Bactrian camel. I was pretty sure it was the same camel who'd pushed me out of the way from the portal earlier. I could barely hear him and couldn't tell what he was singing, but I could tell he was super flat.

"Hey!" Donut said a minute later. "These are all old people songs!"

"Yes, I believe the song choices are all from the 1980s," Prepotente said. His tongue flicked out and tried his soda. He shuddered. "Delicious. It's so much better when it's from a tap."

"I need to look at these drinks," Jurgen said, standing up.

16

"YOU SHOULD SING SOMETHING FROM CREEDENCE CLEARWATER Revival. It's Elle's late husband's favorite band," Linus called from under the table. "She had several of their albums in her room at Meadow Lark."

"Shut the hell up," Elle snapped, sounding genuinely angry for the first time.

"That's the wrong decade anyway," Louis added. "You should do a Misfits song. Or something by Anthrax."

This started a whole conversation about songs from the 80s.

I moved to the opposite end of the table, leaving them to their conversation. I was happy, if just for a moment, for everyone to pretend this was a regular outing at a regular bar.

Prepotente slid down to my end of the table and sat across from me. He was looking down at his drink. He let out a strange little bleat.

"You doing okay, buddy?" I asked.

"I find myself having a conundrum. I am in need of advice."

Donut, who'd been in the midst of the music discussion, was suddenly right there.

Donut put a paw on his hand. "You can ask us anything. Right, Carl?"

"Yeah, sure," I said.

Prepotente looked down at the paw for a long moment before he retracted his hand and then pulled something from his inventory. He placed it on the table.

It was a glowing, familiar little item.

An enhanced pet biscuit. The same item that both Prepotente and Donut—and Bianca—had taken to turn from regular animals to how they now were. According to Mordecai, if a pet took one of these, there were over a hundred different possibilities of what could happen. Some good and some bad.

I didn't know the details, but Miriam Dom had entered the dungeon with a whole herd of goats, and she had received several of these pet biscuits, but they'd stopped using them after there was a bad result. One of the goats had killed several of the others. Prepotente still had multiple regular goats in pet carriers in his inventory, but it wasn't clear exactly how many. Miriam told me ten, but Prepotente was deliberately evasive when we asked him about it.

"I received this one in a celestial box," he said. "There were three of them. They are different than the run-of-the-mill enhanced pet biscuit. Each one is slightly different. One is called 'Nothing Special Party Companion,' one is just called 'Nothing Special,' and there's this one."

I tentatively picked the crumbly little treat up. I remembered the first time I'd held one of these, the description had been pretty short. That wasn't the case this time.

Enriched Pet Biscuit. "The Paramour."

This is a unique item.

Okay, so we all know by now what enhanced pet biscuits do.

While extremely valuable, enhanced pet biscuits are items that leave the result up to chance, and when you feed your pet one, there's a very real risk you'll be saying goodbye to your furry friend forever. Or they'll be saying goodbye to you.

Princess Donut is the lucky result of a pet biscuit that gave her the "Enhanced Growth" benefit. Prepotente is one that received the "Smarty-Pants" benefit. Both of these are results under the Party Companion subtree of the result list with Donut under tree path one and Prepotente under tree path two. Bianca received the "Hellspawn Familiar" benefit, which is under the Pet subtree. These are all considered good results.

This is an Enriched Pet Biscuit. This leaves nothing to chance. These are highly refined pet biscuits with a known result.

This biscuit imparts the "Paramour" benefit. This is a subset of the Party Companion tree. It will have the following effects on any pet or animal-class mob who consumes it:

Non-sapient pets will have their Intelligence and Wisdom* stat raised to at least 3 and then additionally enhanced to be commensurate with their original form.

Their level will be reset to level 1.

Dungeon-born pets will be given a crawler number and assigned crawler status.

The former pet will be required to find a safe room and choose a class if this is consumed after the third floor begins.

The pet will be given a subtree two-B transformation. This will result in a physical transformation to an oxygen-breathing, upright form. The resulting height will be within 1 and 2.5 meters with a mass proportional with their new form. Winged creatures will retain wings but will no longer have the ability to naturally fly. Blah, blah, blah. You know, basically a cat girl. A mascot. A furry, depending on what their original form was. This is what happened to Prepotente, while Donut, who was under subtree one, remained wholly a cat.

The pet will be given the Paramour benefit. They will receive a permanent, incurable* charm that will make them fall hopelessly in love with the entity who fed them the biscuit.

"Oh wow," I said, sliding the biscuit over to Donut, whose eyes went huge when she read it.

"What do the other two do?" Donut asked.

"The 'Nothing Special' one is under the pet subtree. This will transform a creature into a dungeon pet, allowing it to gain levels and skills and spells and utilize upgrades. It will revert them to juvenile form. It's the most basic of all the pet biscuits. The 'Nothing Special Party Companion' is similar to the Paramour benefit, but it is under the first subtree of the party companion, meaning they will stay in their existing form. It is the same thing that happened to you, minus the enhanced growth. And the anatomy won't change at all, meaning they won't gain the ability to talk."

"And minus the mind-control-sex-slave part," Donut said. She slid the biscuit back toward Prepotente.

"What sort of advice do you need?" I asked, leaning back in my chair, afraid of his answer.

"So . . ." Prepotente said. "Her name is Ragazzaccia, and before the dungeon began, she was—"

"Absolutely not," Donut said. "You will not be turning anyone into a sex slave, Prepotente. How is this even a conversation? My goodness."

Prepotente wrung his hands. "But with the other two biscuits, she would remain in regular goat form, and it would be weird. She was my girlfriend before the dungeon started, so it's not like . . ." He trailed off, looking down at the table. "I'm so lonely."

Donut sighed. "Prepotente, darling, I know you miss your friends. But you can't do it this way. It's not right. Even if it didn't have the sex-slave benefit—"

"It is not called that. It is called Paramour."

"Even if it didn't have the *sex-slave* benefit, think about what you'd be doing. She'd become a crawler, meaning she'd be stuck with us, and it says she'll be level 1! She won't be allowed to stay in a pet carrier or in your safe room. She'll get hurt. I would never allow Mongo to take such a thing. Not now that we're so far into the dungeon. It's just too dangerous."

He sat there, not saying anything. "You're right, of course," he said. "It *is* too late. I . . . I don't have anybody to ask these things. Sometimes I imagine my mother and me having these conversations. But sometimes I don't know. Your benefit came with an enhanced memory that allowed you to remember all those conversations and television shows, and you know how people are supposed to act. I don't have that. Mother was teaching me, but . . ."

"Please listen to me," Donut said. "Nobody will like you if you use that pet biscuit on *anything*. Can you imagine if that's what had happened to me? Do you really think I could be a proper girlfriend for Carl? It's a crime against nature. Don't use it. Ever. Ever, ever, ever. It's a terrible idea. Right, Carl?"

"I don't know," I said. "I'm still caught up on that one biscuit that makes it so your pet doesn't talk. Do you think it's too late for me to give it to Donut?"

"That's not funny, Carl. This is serious. The next time you have a question, you can always ask me. I am an expert when it comes to things like this. If you wish, I can compile a list of rules to live by to help you get by. Rule number one will be 'Don't use magic to make someone fall in love with you.' It's creepy."

"But you have that Love Vampire skill. That makes mobs literally fall in love with and die for you. Your entire build is charisma and charm based."

"That's different. Rule number two is to stop arguing with me. Now, listen. We will talk every day, and you can ask me any questions you have. Do you understand?"

"Yes. Of course. Of course. Thank you, Donut."

Jurgen finally returned to the table, his arms full of drinks. "What did I miss?"

17

"WHAT DOES THIS BUTTON DO?" BUCKET BOY THE CROCODILIAN ASKED nervously. We'd just both come from the safe room, and the moment he sat in the driver's seat, he started touching things. He reached to press the big red button.

"Stop," I called. "Don't touch that unless I say so. That engages the spider legs."

"What about the chair? I gotta push it back or my snout will touch the front glass shield. Do I need to be able to reach these pedal things?"

I opened the passenger-side door and placed my feet inside, standing so I could reach the top of the truck. I was going to attempt to rip the front of the tommy gun off the roof with my bare hands.

We had about fifteen minutes. Donut was in the back of the truck, grumbling as she cleaned up all the spilled frozen food. Apparently, the freezer had a never-ending supply of frozen chicken patties, French fries, and tater tots, and both Mongo and Rend had been helping themselves.

"Both of you," Donut said, "I must warn you, the GPS . . ."

Get your scaly little hands off my buttons, or I'll lead you into a swamp and drown you like a basket of ugly puppies.

The words appeared on the screen, and they spoke out loud in the truck at the same time, like a modified system message.

". . . doesn't like being touched," Donut finished.

Bucket Boy shrieked and pulled his hand back from where he'd been about to touch the dials.

"Her name is Dr. Metcalf," Donut added.

Christ, we don't have time for this. "The GPS? The GPS is named Dr. Metcalf? That's the same name as—"

"Miss Beatrice's therapist, yes. I know. It's not really her. I asked."

"God, I hope not," I said, suddenly remembering the one and only time I'd met the very expensive "alternative" therapist. The therapist who'd turned out not to be a real doctor at all. Whenever I was reminded of that whole episode, my head still ached from the trust-fall thing she'd made me and Bea do.

"Anyway, Dr. Metcalf has her controls set as she thinks best, and I believe we should listen to her," Donut said.

DONUT: SHE HAS BIG MEAN-GIRL, NARCISSIST ENERGY, SO WE MUST BE NICE TO HER.

I sighed, and then out loud, I said, "Bucket Boy, don't touch the GPS. She knows best, and we trust her to do the right thing." I paused, and then I added, "Besides, if we lose, we *all* get killed, including her."

"Why did I volunteer for this?" Bucket Boy asked miserably.

"Hey, Donut," I asked, "did you get the device from Hedy?"

"I did," she said. She pulled open a cabinet, and a whole slew of paper plates and plastic utensils slid out. "Carl, look at this mess Rend made!"

Our mechanic had spent the last few hours designing the Donut drive system, which was janky as hell. It now sat in Donut's inventory. I was going to attempt to refine it after this race. It was basically a lever system that attached to the steering wheel, and it allowed Donut to steer by rocking back and forth. It had sticks that hit the pedals. It looked like something straight from a goblin workshop on the first floor.

Which was why we now had Bucket Boy driving instead.

As it was, I knew there was going to be a learning curve for Bucket Boy. If we survived this race, everyone on the team was going to spend all their free time playing driving games.

Bucket Boy let out another shriek as he accidentally hit the horn.

Make way for the big shot! Bawk!

"Weren't you driving transports on the last floor?" Donut asked. She remained in the back, inspecting the contents of the freezer chest. Her little legs dangled out of the unit as she peered inside.

"I have driven a *cart* before!" Bucket Boy said, his voice going up an octave. "It didn't have any of these handles and pedals and extra buttons!"

"If Miss Beatrice could drive, you certainly can. And you'll have Dr. Metcalf helping you."

Bucket Boy looked as if he were about to bolt. "I don't know who Miss Beatrice is."

"She only got, like, five or six tickets," Donut added. "She only got them when the cop was a woman or they were gay. At least that's what she was always saying."

"I don't know what any of that means."

The GPS beeped. **We're all going to die.**

"You'll be fine," I said. "Let me do this, and I'll run through it for you." I returned my efforts to breaking the giant tommy gun. I grunted and pulled. Standing on the floor of the garage was Rend wearing his new headband and making his own groaning noises as I strained.

Just as I felt as if the gun was about to give, I received a notification.

You do not have the ability to make changes to the stock configuration of your vehicle at this time.

"Shit," I muttered.

"Carl, every time I remove food from the freezer, it just comes back, like, ten seconds later! I put it in my inventory, but it just keeps coming. We could literally open a restaurant with all this stuff. Where are they getting all these chickens?"

"Which pedal makes us stop?" Bucket Boy asked.

I mentally played out the plan we'd worked out with Chiyome and the bugbears. I was going to have to shatter our own windshield the moment the race started. Donut needed to be quick with her crossbow.

Race starts in ten minutes.

"Rend," I called, pulling the pet carrier out. I still had the truck passenger door open, and he stood there, looking at me, panting weirdly like a dog. The inside of his mouth was absolutely filled with smashed, uncooked French fries. "Want to go for a ride, buddy?"

He let out a deep giggle and let me zap him away.

I turned my attention back to the GPS.

"Uh, Dr. Metcalf? Show us the information, and show the map." The display lit up red. "Please," I added, and the display color turned blue.

Path assignment: Left path.

Starting grid: Spot #7.

Distance: 10 kilometers.

Track: Asphalt-paved road. Rolling hills.

Tasks required to complete: Each path is of equal length. Each path has a gatekeeper monster along that path that must be killed to resume.

Environment: Torrential downpour of rain and giant hail.

Hazards: I thought a cat driving was a 50/50 death sentence, but now that we've actually put a prepubescent crocodile behind the wheel, I see you're not leaving anything to chance.

Time Limit: 3 hours.

"Hey," Donut called, "that was very rude, Dr. Metcalf. We've been nice to you. We need to all work together."

A map appeared, showing twin paths. We were on the left. Both roads had a big blinking red dot right about halfway through. The dots were relatively close to one another, meaning it was possible we'd be able to see both of these boss monsters at the same time.

Hedy moved to the chain to open the garage door, revealing a torrential downpour. Lightning crackled across the sky, followed by a loud bang.

Bucket Boy gave me a nervous look. "So, you're going to teach me to drive now?"

I nodded. I suddenly had to shout because the rain was so loud.

"Look, it's easy. You have two pedals down there. The one on the right . . ."

I trailed off as a new message came in.

TRAN: Oh fuck. Got some shitty news.

IMANI: What's wrong?

ZHANG: Sorry, guys. Confirming Prepotente's theory is mostly correct. Na killed five of the other teams, and we have four replacements at the starting line. Two are NPC teams, but two are crawler teams, including Tran's team. Na is just sitting there behind me, not reacting. I have the reins for this one. I don't know what to do.

Donut jumped to my shoulder as I felt myself sag.

And so it begins.

"Goddamnit," I said.

18

"BRAKES!" I SHOUTED AS WE LURCHED TO A STOP. WE HEAVED ONE more time, almost running into the car in front of us. The rain continued to pound. I was crouched next to the driver's seat, my hand pressed against the dash for stabilization.

Bucket Boy continued to whine. "Wait, I have to keep my foot on this brake the whole time?" He had the chair almost fully reclined, allowing him to use the pedals without bonking his snout.

"If it's in drive, then yes," I said. "But you're going to put it in park. No, not reverse. Park. Yes. Now you can take your foot off the pedal. We're going to keep it in park for now. Don't touch anything until I tell you to."

We were stopped next to the bugbears' van. To our left was a steep ditch. As long as Bucket Boy could keep the steering wheel straight, we'd be okay.

The bugbears' van blared music. It was an Elton John song, and it was loud enough to hear over the rain, but I wasn't familiar with it. Something about making friends. Jasha sat behind the wheel, cigarette hanging from his mouth. He gave us a wave.

The eight vehicles were positioned side by side in four rows.

The rain just kept coming and coming. We didn't have working wipers, not that it would matter after I shattered the windshield. For now the rain didn't hit us as all eight vehicles and mounts were under a giant awning. Still, the sound of the rain was almost deafening. There wasn't any hail yet.

Right in front of the bugbears sat the pile of vines that was Dwight the unicorn and Lucienne the whatever the hell she was. Team Sparkles. The little French rodent was no longer on the head of the unicorn, but submerged in the vines, her helmeted head sticking out the top. I still had no idea how they "drove" the thing.

Dwight, meanwhile, was engaged in a shouting match with the group to their immediate left, which was the team right in front of us.

Girth the Trouble.

Their vehicle was a bright yellow 1950s Chevy Bel Air with a massive blower popping up from the hood. Red flames were painted on the side of the car. It was like a real-life Matchbox car. We'd seen plenty of similar cars during our time in Cuba, but nothing this tricked-out. Leaning out the passenger's side, screaming their head off at the unicorn, was some sort of slime creature. It was human-shaped, sort of, and it appeared to be made of translucent gelatin. Like someone had taken an Operatic slime, but clear-colored, and smashed it into a gingerbread man cookie cutter. It wasn't wearing clothes. It leaned all the way out the passenger's side of the car, screeching at the unicorn. I assumed there was at least one more behind the wheel. It was something called a guck elemental, and his name was Masterplan.

Masterplan's voice was deep and loud. I had no idea what had started their fight.

"You can go fuck yourself right now," Masterplan shouted at the unicorn. "Team Sparkles? More like 'team suck my gelatinous dick.' You're lucky we're not on the same track this race. I'm going to rip that girlie horn off your stupid horse head and stab it right into your heart!"

"I'm a unicorn, not a horse, lube boy! And I'd love to see you try, you fucking idiot!" Dwight shouted back, his voice cracking. "I'm going to wear your spleen like a hat! Then we'll see who's girlie."

"Carl, keeping these people alive is going to be impossible," Donut muttered.

"I know," I said. We could only kill one team. If a second died, then all this would be for nothing. But we couldn't risk coming in last place, either.

Lucienne popped up and also shouted something while shaking her little rodent fist, but I couldn't hear her over the rain.

"Think you can make it?" I asked Donut. She would have to shoot over these idiots in front of us.

The womantaur team was in a convertible sitting right in front of the guck elementals. The two women sat there, ignoring the argument behind them. I couldn't see the half-mantaur.

Donut's target was Rapture, the driver.

Her weapon mount, the Scorpion's Bite, formed on Donut's back, along with Katia's crossbow. The glowing Danforth bolt locked into place on its own with an ominous *click*. The bolt glowed. Hopefully we'd be able to retrieve it, as we only had ten of them.

We'd debated putting Donut on the roof of the truck for this. But in the end, we decided against it. I didn't want her sitting out there as a prime target for others.

The moment the light turned green, I'd break the window and Donut would hit the womantaur driver with her Danforth bolt, which would root her in place. If they tried to drive off, or if they'd already started moving, it would go badly for Rapture. As soon as the driver was hit, Chiyome's mount, which was a giant bear, would smash the car to the side. The driver would remain in place, and the car moving underneath her would hopefully end up cutting her in half. Either Chiyome or one of the bugbears would take out the driver if she was still alive, and we would, if we could, take out the second womantaur and Corcunda as we passed. I had a Molotov cocktail ready to go.

After that, we would try to all stay alive for the rest of the race.

We didn't know what upgrade the Lady Dominators had picked, but if it was a shield, it likely didn't stop both magical attacks, which was what Donut's bolt would be, and physical attacks, which was what the bear attack would be, so we were covering all of our bases.

I spent a moment trying to examine the vehicle in front of the womantaurs, the vehicle currently in the first spot. Team One Fine Pig. It was a big military vehicle similar to what I imagined Imani and Elle had. To the right of them in position number two stood the large black dog of the Jugglers. The creepy masked riders sat in a row on its back. The razor foxes' bear was about the same size and was currently sniffing at the butt of the dog.

Donut glared at the giant dog, muttering.

"Donut," I said, "do you have a shot on the womantaur?"

She gave one last derisive snort and turned her attention to the Lady Dominators.

The unicorn and the guck elemental continued to squeal at each other.

"You wanna go! You wanna go right now?" Dwight shrieked. "Imma fuck you up!"

"Imma have a go with your donkey of a mother," Masterplan shouted back. "I'm gonna ride her like I just got my stimulus check."

"I have a shot, no problem," Donut said. "Right over the slime guy's car and right into the back of that one's head. But you'll have to crouch further down because that stupid tommy gun is in the way."

The GPS beeped.

Green light in thirty seconds. Environmental hazards starting.

New note has just been added to the hazards database. The hail is light at the beginning, but it increases in intensity as the timer increases.

I pulled the special banger sphere out. If it worked as intended, it would destroy the entire windshield in one hit, not just poke a hole in it.

Crash! The entire ground shook. It was like a bomb had just gone off. Next to me, Bucket Boy let out a shriek and hit the horn.

"What the hell was that?" I asked.

Crash! A second detonation came, this time right behind us. The back of the truck bucked as if we'd been rear-ended.

"Carl, what's happening?" Donut shouted.

Dr. Metcalf beeped.

I'm pretty sure that's the hail.

"That's *light* hail?" Donut shrieked. "What's considered heavy?"

Boom! The entire awning over our heads exploded. Bits of ice and snow and metal crackled across the roof of the truck. The rain started pounding the windshield. In a second, I couldn't see anything through the ice and water. I couldn't even see the lights above us indicating when it was time to go.

Race starts in ten seconds. We are so fucking dead.

"Oh gods, oh gods, oh gods," Bucket Boy said.

"Stick to the plan!" I shouted, pulling my arm back.

Green light! Green light!

I hurled the banger sphere through the windshield, which shattered into pieces. The sphere continued its forward trajectory as our vision was suddenly kind of clear. In the distance, a hailstone the size of a two-story house smashed into the ground between the two roads.

At the same moment, Donut tensed, about to fire, but she paused.

She paused because a long tanklike tube had just popped out the side of the team Sparkles bush, and it was pointed directly at the muscle car right in front of us.

"Get down!" I shouted.

I didn't duck in time. Flames burst from the turret as they fired directly into the Chevy Bel Air. Instead of spinning away, the car, miraculously, went straight up as if it were a rocket.

"Gah," I shouted.

Donut sputtered, her face covered with gelatin. Pieces of Mastermind the elemental had exploded all over her.

Kablam! The burning Chevy Bel Air landed loudly to the left of us, smashing into the ditch, burning furiously.

"That's right!" Dwight shrieked. The tank cannon was peeled back like in a cartoon. It must've been a onetime-use weapon. Or, more likely, a once-a-race weapon. "How's that for girlie? Gargle my unicorn balls, you translucent bitch!"

And then the bush just took off, moving significantly faster than it had the last time.

The only ones left on the track were us and the bugbears.

Team six, Girth the Trouble, has been eliminated due to the destruction of their vehicle. Seven teams remain in the current heat.

Next to us, the song "Black and White" by Three Dog Night blared from the bugbear van. I recognized it because my mom had loved that song, and there was a strange, surreal moment where I just sat there listening, remembering my mom holding me and dancing while she sang to me. The reverie was broken by yet another massive hailstone crashing against a distant hill. Jasha gave me an apologetic shrug, and the bugbears zoomed off, leaving us sitting alone at the start line.

19

"DON'T TURN WHEN YOU LOOK LEFT AND RIGHT," I SAID AS WE BUMPED up the hill. "It's okay. You're good. They're stopped up ahead. I see them."

"Goodness, Bucket Boy," Donut said, talking over the sound of the pouring rain, "you don't have to avoid everything in the road if it's tiny!"

Crash! A hill to our left exploded from the strike of a massive hailstone.

Donut's *Shield* spell was strong enough to keep us mostly safe, but when she had it large enough to protect the entire truck, it wasn't as powerful. The massive chunks seemed to be mostly hitting off the track. Smaller but still big shards rained down on the road, covering the asphalt and pinging off the shield. The truck had already slid once as we crested a small hill, which freaked out Bucket Boy, and now he was moving at a snail's pace.

Ahead, I could see the large armored-tank thing from team One Fine Pig and the convertible car from the Lady Dominators parked at the top of the next peak. Several figures were out of their vehicles, staring at something I couldn't yet see.

The Lady Dominators' car appeared to be a late-60s Pontiac GTO convertible painted in a deep burgundy. Corcunda the half-mantaur remained in the back of the two-door car, hanging out the side like he was asleep.

As we expected, there was a wide shield around the car that was clearly visible as the rain and hail fell around it.

The other vehicle from team One Fine Pig was like a mix between a Hummer and a bank's armored truck. It appeared it might have been of Russian origin based on the boxy utility of the thing. This truck also had a shield around it, but it was a different type of shield, shaped like a cube. It, too, kept the rain and hail from hitting it.

We had to be extra careful here. Yes, we needed to work together to fight whatever they were looking at, but they could just as easily blow our truck off the road, eliminating us. And if the two womantaurs knew what we'd been planning, them attacking us was likely.

"We should have gotten a better shield," I muttered as we pulled up. That would be our priority after this race. "Pull up right next to the convertible car. Do it slow. I can see what type of shield they have, and it looks like the ones we used on the last floor. It'll protect us from the hail, too."

"Carl, Carl, look!" Donut suddenly shouted, pointing at the figures. There were five of them. Well, four and an animal of some sort. "Is that a Bautista? And look at the bull guy. Wow. He looks like someone from those weird lady porn books Miss Beatrice was always reading."

"Yeah," I said. "It is a Tigran." This guy was significantly buffer than Bautista, which was saying a lot.

"It looks like a gathering from backstage at the Penis Parade," Donut said. "Everybody is so muscly. Except the creature. My goodness, is that just a regular pig?" She scoffed. "One Fine Pig indeed."

We pulled to a stop right next to the GTO. I knew from experience the shield guarding the car only stopped things moving fast, so we pulled up slow. This close, we'd also get protection from the hail.

"I think you're right," Bucket Boy said, gaping. "They all look like dancers. All except the oinker. Look at the delts on the Tigran." He let out a small gasp. "Hey, hey, I know that guy! The other one. The Taurin. His name is Pontiff. He *was* a dancer but Damascus sent him back to the mercenary market because he was a dick." Bucket Boy turned to look at me and Donut. He reached up to rub the side of his snout. "He slapped me once because he said I got in the way during his routine. There wasn't even anyone in the club except a few of the regulars."

I examined the figures standing at the top of the hill, none of whom were paying attention to us.

The first two were Genesis and Rapture. Once again, they had their large boots on the road in front of them. They were in an animated discussion with the hulking Tigran.

Standing off to the side, holding a comically large mallet similar to the one the late Brandon had once carried, was the bullheaded Taurin. He was, indeed, named Pontiff. He was a level 83 **Taurin Rhythm Rider**, which I knew was a type of mage that used sound waves. He was listed as a hired mercenary for team One Fine Pig.

The glowing head of the Taurin's giant hammer vibrated, which was keeping the rain and hail off the group.

I was half expecting the Tigran to also be a mercenary, but he was actually a racer.

Nico. Tigran. Level 91 Greaser.

One of two from Team One Fine Pig.

You already know what a Tigran is, as you're buddies with that guy who plays with dolls and almost did something really suspicious with his tea before he came to his senses.

Nico is two things. One, he's a Tigran. A tiger person. Angry, emotional, strong, and fiercely loyal. That's what they're known for, but that's also a stereotype. Like with most species, there's a whole spectrum. I'm sure there are dweeb Tigrans and pacifist Tigrans and vegan Tigrans and Tigrans who have fallen prey to some random MLM and irritate all their extended family members and friends from high school with annoying yet weirdly desperate marketing emails.

Still, Nico falls well within the range of what you've come to expect from your average dude with a tiger head . . .

. . . with one glaring exception. And that exception is Penelope.

His wife. The love of his life.

Nico is part of a throuple. And between you and me, it's not a healthy relationship. Don't @ me, all of you in polycules. You know as well as I do that sometimes people love their partners so much, they unwillingly get dragged into this whole sharing situation. I'm sure there are plenty of perfectly healthy situations out there. This ain't one of them.

Penelope is the one who wanted to open things up. So it's now Nico, Dario—who is that other Tigran currently glaring at you from behind the steering wheel of their Tigr APV—and Penelope.

And yes, Penelope is the pig. Yes, she's just a regular pig with

the intelligence of a regular pig. Just go with it. There's a whole storyline there. Examine her if you want to know more.

Standing there on the ground next to the Tigran was Penelope the pig. She was just a regular round pink pig. The thing had to weigh, like, five hundred pounds. She snuffled on the ground next to the tiger, who petted the top of the pig's head affectionately.

Penelope. Level 5 Yorkshire Sow.

This is a pig. Oink, oink.

Warning: This beast is magically protected by Taranis. As such, if this beast dies or is even hurt, the culprit will be marked for death by the thunder god.

This is Penelope. Again, she is a pig. She is married to both Nico and Dario, and she loves them both equally. At least that's what Nico and Dario believe.

No, she didn't used to be a beautiful princess who was transformed by a witch. She's a pig and has always been a pig.

Penelope did, however, once get hit by a stray spell. *The Touch of Maw-Loo.* Also known as the *Snowdrop Curse*. There was going to be this whole succubus storyline that also involved Emberus and Hellik and Taranis and a bunch of angry spouses on the seventh floor we didn't get to use, so we brought Penelope here. And now when certain NPCs see this fine pig, they fall helplessly in love with her.

That includes Taranis, who has it bad for her.

Kill her at your own peril.

I sighed. Of course. A pig protected by a god. One of the big ones, too. Taranis was the god who was also the big brother of Emberus and Hellik and Eris, and he was the one who'd been married to Apito, who was also his mom.

Dario, the other member of One Fine Pig, sat behind the wheel of their truck, glaring not at us like the description implied, but at Nico.

"Carl, do you think the two tiger guys and that pig . . ." Donut trailed off.

"I don't know, and I don't want to know," I said. "Come on. Let's see what we're dealing with. Bucket Boy, you stay here. Don't let anyone near the truck. Honk the horn if anything weird starts to happen."

He opened his mouth.

"You know what I mean. Anything *weirder.* Keep an eye especially on that big metal truck. And if things go sideways, don't hurt the pig."

We stepped out of the truck, passing by Corcunda, who was curled up in the back seat of the GTO. He had an **Unconscious** notification over his head. He'd been put asleep via a spell.

Huh, I thought.

We passed out of the area of the shield from the GTO, and rain and hail started to pour on us. Donut let out a little yowl and recast her *Shield* spell. Hail pinged off it loudly, the sound like pebbles against glass.

We approached the others, who finally noticed us. Just beyond them, at the bottom of the hill, was the boss, just sitting there in the middle of the road.

"Oh, for fuck's sake," I muttered.

20

THERE WERE ACTUALLY TWO OF THE BOSSES, AND THE TWO MONSTERS were staring at each other. The second was blocking the other road with the other teams in our heat, about a hundred meters away. There was another hill with the other racers standing atop it, looking down at the valley.

"Carl, what are those things?" Donut demanded. "They're like kangaroos, but even more disgusting."

I focused on the closer of the two boss monsters. The thing was about twenty feet tall, and wide, and it did have features similar to those of a kangaroo, except it also had angry dinosaur-like spikes on its back despite being covered in fur.

The giant monster sat upon a pair of meaty legs and had a lengthy tail and two arms with long, clawed fingers. The head was the least kangaroo part of the creature. It had the tall ears, but the face was wider, reminding me of that giant demon Slit we fought all the way back on the fifth floor. Lizard-like in a way, despite the hair. The thing was currently sitting in the middle of the road upon its two legs, giving the impression it was squatting.

There was a massive red notification floating over each of the two boss monsters.

Your vehicle may not pass past this point until this boss monster is dead or removed.

Around both of the creatures' waistlines was a pouch. Poking out of the pouch of each kangaroo monster were about ten heads, all smaller versions of the boss.

At least, I thought they were smaller versions of itself, but there was something weird going on there. It appeared one of the pouch monsters was howling in pain. That one tried to pull itself out, but it was roughly pushed back down by the boss, who shouted something inaudible.

And all the other ones just dangled there. Like they were dead.

"Carl, what the heck is that thing?" Donut tensed on my shoulder as she focused on it.

A giant chunk of hail crashed next to the boss, which caused it to howl indignantly. It stretched, pulling itself to its full height, its two legs extending out, making it appear even more kangaroo-like. The second boss also howled. The razor foxes started to somersault down their hill as they approached.

"Carl, Carl, most of the baby kangaroos are dead!" Donut called just as I examined the boss right in front of us. "And the one that isn't is a person in a kangaroo costume! It says he's an upgrade mechanic!"

I sighed, waiting for the bullshit description to pop up.

Prison Pocket. Macropus Dominus.

Level 170 Province Boss.

This boss is a gatekeeper. Your vehicle or mount may not pass past this area until the boss is dead or defeated.

Believe it or not, marsupials are quite common out in the known galaxy, especially in lower-gravity, oxygen-rich environments, such as the one that is home to our friends here, the Macropus Dominus.

The vast, plant-covered plains these relatively nonviolent omnivores live upon are prone to flooding and driving rainstorms that might last weeks. As a result, the female adults protect their joeys in their expansive pouches, which not only shelter the occupants from the elements, but also keep them fed by providing multiple nutrient-expressing nipples. And in some of the harsher parts of the planet, all genders of marsupials have evolved pouches, though the male versions aren't as . . . full featured. If certain environmental hazards last too long, the little ones sheltering inside can and do starve to death.

Prison Pocket—and his companion on the other side of the road

there, whose name is Party Foul—are both male, and they are quite sad, as they weren't able to save their young ones from this never-ending storm.

They yearn to refill their pouches. Unfortunately for you, you're just about the same size as the joeys they lost.

Oh, by the way, their pouches secrete an oil that is quite caustic to the skin of creatures who aren't of the same species.

"Level 170?" I asked, feeling a chill.

The person in the kangaroo suit popped up out of the pouch again. He screamed something before getting pushed back down. I focused on the man.

You have discovered an Upgrade Engineer! At least one engineer will appear each race. Engineers can be added to your garage.

The second boss was now being engaged by the razor foxes. The giant bear and dog mounts also started slinking down the hill toward the boss.

We stepped to the top of the hill, coming to stand next to the others.

There was a hum in the air. The magic from the Taurin's hammer was keeping the rain and hail away, but a fine mist still fell upon us. Donut kept her shield up.

"It's about time you got here," Genesis the womantaur said to me, sneering. "We were just discussing how we're going to deal with this thing. We figure since those slimes got pasted, we're doing a temporary truce for the rest of the race."

"Yeah, we don't want you dead just yet," Rapture said. Her red curls bounced as she talked.

"Don't worry, baby," Nico the tiger said, talking to Penelope the pig. His voice was not what I had been expecting. It was nothing like Bautista's. This was straight from the Jersey shore. "I'll keep them away from you." He glared at Donut. "Especially that one."

"Excuse me?" Donut asked.

Penelope snorted suspiciously at Donut.

"Stay away from my girl, and we won't have any troubles."

"Carl, what is he talking about?"

The other boss had fallen to the side as the giant dog and bear ripped into it. The boss had one of the foxes in the black ninja suits in its hand and was shoving him face-first into his own pouch. The fox screamed.

At the top of the hill, the two bugbears and the creepy, thin Jugglers just stood there, watching. I spied Dwight, still inside his vehicle thing, which was stopped at the end of the line. I couldn't tell from this distance where Lucienne was.

Next to us, Nico the Tigran was on a knee and rubbing the side of Penelope, whispering in the oblivious pig's ear, still glaring daggers at Donut.

All of us, including the two womantaurs and the Taurin, watched this all, not sure what to make of the tiger man.

"Hey, hey, if Penny is in danger, you better bring her back to the truck!" a new voice called. This was Dario, the second Tigran, who hung out the side of their APV. This Tigran was noticeably thinner, and he had a massive amount of gold chains around his neck.

"She stays with me!" Nico roared back at his partner.

"Okay, whatever, dude," the second Tigran said, holding up his paws and disappearing back into the truck.

"All right, that's it," the mercenary Taurin said. "By the gods." He had a deep, deep voice. "We need a plan. I might be able to knock it off its feet with my hammer, but I am not certain. Not sure I want to risk getting that close." He turned to us. "What do you think?"

Genesis gave the Taurin mercenary a sour look. "Aren't you the hired help? Shouldn't you go down there and take care of it for us?"

Pontiff was looking back toward our truck. And the GTO.

"Corcunda is pretty strong," Pontiff said. "Why is he asleep?"

The two womantaurs didn't answer for a long moment.

"How do you know him?" Genesis finally demanded.

"We used to work together," Pontiff said.

"Yeah, Bucket Boy told us about you," Donut said to the bull man. "He says you slapped him."

The bull raised an eyebrow. "Bucket Boy? The kid? He's here?" He grunted. "Yes, I used to be an ass. If I don't get a chance, tell him I said—"

"Stop talking to her!" Nico snapped at the mercenary. "You kill her if she takes one step toward Penelope! That's an order!"

Donut scoffed. "Carl, everyone has gone crazy!" To Nico, she said, "I don't want anything to do with your stupid pig, you roided-out, off-brand, clown-college mascot. I mean, really. I tolerated this nonsense because Daniel is our friend, but this is just too much. You're no better than Sister Ines, who at least had the common decency to emulate a proper cat before my friend Louis—"

"Stop. Everybody stop!" I said as I continued to watch the boss fight across the way. "Everyone be quiet. Christ!"

I cringed as the black dog thing—the mount for the Jugglers—yelped and was thrown to its back. The foxes bounced all around the boss. I had missed what had happened to the one who'd been grabbed.

The boss wasn't really fighting back so much as trying to grab the remaining ninjas to pull them into his pouch.

If we didn't hurry this up, one of these teams was going to get zeroed out.

The bugbears had fled to their van. The two weird Jugglers started casually moving down the hill toward the monster. The two were holding hands and skipping.

Chiyome tossed something at the kangaroo, and fire flamed from the pouch. The boss cried out in pain, and the boss's health bar went down a significant amount. He reached into his own pouch and pulled out a flaming screaming creature.

It was the missing razor fox.

The kangaroo reached up and ate the poor fox, and the boss's health rocketed all the way up to the top. The two remaining foxes scattered back. The bear and the dog also retreated.

My fellow racers groaned.

"We're pickled," Genesis said.

CHIYOME: I fear our efforts are futile. This monster heals quickly. Its only weak spot is inside its pouch.

Hmm.

CARL: Donut, can you zoom in on any of those dead joeys and examine them properly?
DONUT: IT SAYS THEY DIED OF STARVATION.
CARL: Can you see their inventory?
DONUT: IT'S JUST THEIR SKIN. WEIRD. I HAVEN'T SEEN THAT IN A WHILE.

And there it is. There will always be clues.

21

CHIYOME: WE ARE IMPLEMENTING YOUR PLAN. WE WILL AVENGE ITO'S death!

"Carl, how are they going to get a skin? I thought NPCs couldn't get into other people's inventory." We crept down the hill toward the giant kangaroo, who remained sitting there in the road, hollering at the other boss.

I almost slipped and fell on my ass after stepping on some loose hail. The ground shook.

The hailstones were getting bigger.

"Mobs can't loot inventory, but NPCs can in certain circumstances. That's what Mordecai says, and nobody seemed to question it when I suggested it. Remember, Dong keeps his lance in his inventory."

Nico remained at the top of the hill with his pig. He was currently in a shouting match with his other partner, who didn't want him to bring Penelope to the boss fight.

Because Pontiff had come with us, Nico and Penelope were no longer protected from the elements, and both were getting soaked. The pig squealed miserably every time she was hit with a chunk of hail, and I was starting to genuinely worry they were going to get killed by the elements.

The last thing we needed right now was a pissed-off god randomly showing up.

"Yeah, so," Rapture said to me, "I'm thinking maybe we can do an alliance thing. You know, instead of us killing you next race? I know you're loser bitchmeat weaklings, but we'll allow you to work with us.

Maybe we should get those foxes. I didn't like the way their bear was looking at our car just as the race was about to start."

We were interrupted before I could answer.

"Babies," Prison Pocket the demon kangaroo said, spying us. "Come here, little babies. Let me put you in my warm, safe pouch." He had a comical, almost offensively fake Australian accent. Like the sort of thing that would cause you to get your ass kicked by real Australians if they heard you talking like that. "Babies, let's get you out of this rain."

"He talks?" Donut asked, incredulous.

From the kangaroo's pouch, the engineer guy popped his head up. He was an older human, and he wore the skin of a dead joey like it was a Halloween costume. His entire face was red and burned. He croaked for help, reaching out toward us. Multiple other dead kangaroo joeys dangled from the top of the pouch, like socks draped over a clothesline.

I pulled up my *Emergency Gremlin* scroll, and I read it. At the same time, Donut read the same scroll. I quickly repeated the process three more times, and in moments, we had eight bewildered gremlins in overalls standing in front of us.

All eight were different. All eight carried toolboxes with them. One had goggles on his head. One only had one eye. One had a hook for a hand.

"What're we fixing, boss?" the eye-patch one asked me.

"Sorry, guys," I said. We all took a few steps back.

"Whatchu mean?"

"Babies," Prison Pocket repeated, reaching down with both hands and picking up the two closest gremlins, who started to squeal. "Small, stinky babies. Hush now. Papa's got you. No, no. Quit your crying. Just a little dip in the ol' pouch will set you right. So many babies. Just a little dip."

He pulled the two screaming gremlins to his pouch and shoved them in. Even over the rain, I could hear the squelching noise. It sounded like someone shoving their fist into a deep, wet pot of runny oatmeal. A line of . . . goo . . . oozed out the top of the pouch and plopped onto the ground, where it sizzled in the rain.

"Okay, I'm gonna blow chunks," Genesis said.

"Yo, what the fuck?" one of the remaining gremlins shouted as they scattered.

"No, little babies. Don't run. Don't run. Papa will keep you safe this time."

One of the gremlins jumped off the road and started booking it toward the hills, only to get splattered by a wrecking-ball-sized chunk of hail. The red-soaked hunk of ice rolled away down the hill.

"No!" the kangaroo yelled. "No, come back! It's not safe!"

"I really need a new job," Pontiff grumbled.

I did my best not to feel bad about the gremlins. According to Imani, who'd already used the scroll once, they exploded when their summoning ended anyway.

"Go!" I shouted.

To my right, the two womantaurs loped forward, astonishingly fast. Their job was to get me a dead joey. They would use their arm chains to do it.

Thwump, thwump! Donut shot a pair of magic missiles into the eyes of the boss, who squealed in outrage. His health went down a good bit, but he immediately brought a gremlin to his mouth, and his health fully returned.

"Naughty, fuzzy baby," the kangaroo said as he chewed.

"Carl! Did you see that? That barely worked!"

"He's level 170! Hang on. Keep him distracted!"

I cast *Run, Little Günter, Run.*

The chunky, pig-nosed kid in lederhosen appeared. His lollipop had changed color, but he otherwise looked the same as last time.

"Hi, I'm Günter!"

"Hey, kid, get that giant kangaroo!" I said, pointing.

I nodded to Pontiff, who was already in his backswing with his massive glowing mallet.

He walloped Little Günter with all of his strength.

Thud!

Pontiff let out a surprised grunt and flew back. It was as if his mallet had hit a solid wall.

"Nein! Nein!" Günter shrieked, and he turned and ran directly toward the kangaroo, who had two more gremlins in one fist and was reaching for a third with the other. The little kid ran right between the

legs of Genesis, who had her arm aimed toward the kangaroo's pouch. She fired . . .

. . . and pierced the screaming engineer guy right in the face, killing him instantly. She whooped and retracted, pulling his now-dead body toward us.

"Baby!" Prison Pocket said, seeing Günter run toward him. "Yes, yes, come to Papa! Such healthy, ruddy cheeks."

Wham!

The moment Günter reached the kangaroo, the kid suddenly rocketed forward, the effects of the mallet strike delayed until that exact moment.

The massive kangaroo completely flipped in the air, landing on his back with an earth-shattering crunch. We all dove out of the way of his long, ridged tail.

"Here!" Genesis said, dropping the bloody dead engineer at my feet.

"Keep it down," I yelled, pointing at the boss. "Donut, make more gremlins!"

"I'm on it!" she shouted as she summoned another. This one was a woman holding an oversized wrench. Two more appeared at the same time, and they all looked at each other, disoriented.

I examined the corpse at my feet. There was a hole the size of my fist in the middle of the man's face.

Niels. Human. Level 35 Mechanical Engineer with a specialty in Weapons Upgrades.

This NPC was killed by Genesis the Lady Mantaur via a grappling hook to the goddamned face.

This was two of two available engineers during this heat. Neither were claimed. Better luck next time.

"You were supposed to get one of the joeys!" I shouted as I started to pull the blood-soaked costume off.

"And let you get the engineer? I don't think so," Genesis said.

"Yeah, just because we're doing the temporary-ally thing don't mean we stupid and shit," Rapture added.

Prison Pocket was already starting to recover.

"Donut," I said as I pulled at the corpse's legs. My hands burned. The kangaroo skin was stuck to his body. It had built-in gloves with long, clawed nails at the end. The palm of the hand had a thick pad, like the paw of a dog. If those two idiots had gotten me one of the joeys, I would've had this already. "Keep the kangaroo down!"

Enchanted Juvenile Macropus Dominus Skin.

This item fills a costume slot. This can be worn as an outer garment. You might want to protect your face, though.

I'd fuck me. I'd fuck me so hard, mate.

Equipping this costume imbues the following effects:

Protection from Seeping Acid.

A level 10 Jump skill.

+5 to the Lotion Application skill.

Warning: This is a 12-hour timed item.

Slam! A giant hailstone smashed into the groaning kangaroo, who remained crumpled off the side of the road.

"My babies," the prone kangaroo cried as he munched on another gremlin, healing himself.

"Goddamnit!" I cried as I pulled at the feet of the sticky joey skin. Next to me, the two womantaurs stood there and watched. "You can at least help!"

"This was your plan," Genesis said.

The other kangaroo was also down. Chiyome had already gotten herself into a kangaroo costume and was flipping through the air toward the monster.

I shoved my arms into the stinking costume. I hoped my goddamned inventory would still work with this thing on. I pulled the kangaroo head over my own, and there was a loud *click*. A new achievement flashed.

"Carl, how did you do that?" Donut demanded.

My boxers and kneepads were now on the outside of the costume. My jacket remained on the inside, but my cloak was around my neck and flapping in the wind.

I could feel it there against my junk. It felt and smelled like my naked skin was pressed up against the body of a wet farm animal. The whole costume quivered as if it were alive.

What the hell?

Warning: Your boxer effects have been negated by your costume.

Warning: Your pedicure effects have been negated by your costume.

I pulled a banger sphere from my inventory, praying it would appear outside the costume and not in my hand, under the covering of the skin. Thankfully, the sphere appeared in the paw, though it immediately rolled away.

The boss was trying to get up. Donut hit it with another magic missile.

Even prone like this, the boss continued to heal itself. It seemed to have a never-ending supply of dead joeys to consume. It had one of the gremlins in its grip, but he squeezed too tight, and the poor monster exploded.

"Baby!" Prison Pocket called forlornly. It grasped for the scattered NPCs. One of the original gremlins dragged himself across the hail-covered grass, trailing blood. I'd missed how he'd been injured.

"I'm ready," I called as I adjusted the costume. The wide head of the dead joey sat awkwardly atop my own head.

Okay, here we go.

I turned to run at the boss.

I promptly fell on my face.

Warning: Oh, I'm sorry. Let's see you do this when you can't walk. You want to be a kangaroo so bad? Then I guess you gotta act like one.

"This was your goddamned setup!" I called.

The other giant kangaroo demon exploded into mist. Dwight the unicorn, still at the top of the hill, was cheering so loudly, I could hear it from here. His bundle of vines burst off the hill and rocketed away along their track. He was followed closely by the dog, chasing after his lost riders.

I pulled my bandanna up. I prepared the two hobgoblin big boom satchels in my inventory. I looked down at my feet. At my large, sagging kangaroo feet.

I hopped.

"Yes, yes, little joey!" the boss shouted as he spied me. He remained on his back. "Come to papa's pouch! It's warm and safe and oh so moist!"

I leaped one more time, flying higher and farther than I'd anticipated. I landed with a splatch directly on the outside of his pouch. I tried to stand, but I couldn't get my balance. It was like trying to walk on a waterbed.

I needed to get to the lip of the pouch, and then I had to get all the way to the bottom of the pocket, where I would drop the two satchels.

"Here, here, little one, let me help you," Prison Pocket roared as he grabbed me.

"Gah!" I said as I was snatched up and smushed face-first into the gooey interior of the pouch.

I choked, and my face started to burn. I couldn't see anything. Luckily, the costume came with claws, and I started to pull myself downward.

DONUT: CARL, CARL, ARE YOU OKAY?

It was like trying to pull myself through warm jelly. I was in the suit, burning.

It smelled. Oh god, it smelled so bad. Like rotten meat mixed with the sharp vinegar tang of fruit juice left out too long.

I grasped, and I pulled, and pulled, and pulled, going ever deeper into the kangaroo's pouch.

There were things in here, getting in my way, bouncing off my face. Bones. More corpses of joeys. A toolbox. I pulled, and I grasped, dragging myself down.

DONUT: CARL, HE'S STANDING UP! HURRY!

I caught on to something round, and I used it as a handhold, yanking myself even more downward.

The boss's muffled voice reverberated through the goo. I felt him pat the outside of the pouch. "Oh, you must be hungry, little lad. Don't tickle Papa's nips like that! You won't be getting milk from them. But Papa always appreciates your little kisses."

The bottom of the pouch hit me right in the face. I released the two satchels from my inventory. I couldn't see anything, but I could still sense them there. They started to quickly degrade.

I didn't want to do this next part to get *into* the pouch because I couldn't control how deep I went, and I just knew I would've ended up in his stomach, unable to flee. Escaping, however . . .

I faced outward, pressed my kangaroo feet against the interior of his stomach, and I hopped as I activated *Gloom Wraith Phase.*

I hit the detonator in my inventory as I flew through the air. I tumbled and flipped like I'd been shot from a cannon, and I hit the ground and bounced, still rolling, asphalt ripping into the side of my face. Ice and kangaroo bits rained down around me as I rolled right off the road. Fist-sized chunks of hail continued to pummel me.

This was quickly followed by the sound of revving car engines.

I groaned and rolled onto my back as the APV and the GTO both zoomed by on the street next to me.

Multiple achievements and a level-up notification appeared, but I waved them away.

Standing over me was a gremlin.

"You can go fuck yourself," he said as he dropped his toolbox on my stomach.

"I probably deserved that," I said just before he timed out and exploded.

"Carl, next time we have to work together, make sure we don't do it to our own detriment," Donut said as I sat up. The truck sat alone at the top of the hill. "I can't help but feel this is an apt metaphor for what always happens when we do all the heavy lifting."

"It could be worse," I said as I started to pull the kangaroo costume off.

Warning: Oh, I'm sorry. Didn't you read the description? I'm pretty sure I told you this is a timed item.

HEAT TWO. RESULTS.
First Place: Team Sparkles.
Second Place: The Jugglers.
Third Place: Team Free Love.
Fourth Place: The Wild Hunt.
Fifth Place: Lady Dominators and the Gimp.
Sixth Place: One Fine Pig.
Seventh Place: The Royal Court of Princess Donut.

Eliminated: Girth the Trouble.

HEAT 3 OF 7

22

AFTER PASSING THE FINISH LINE, WE LIMPED OUR WAY TOWARD THE garage.

I pulled at the tight neck of the kangaroo costume.

MORDECAI: Carl, has your costume skill leveled up much? I would say it'll work, but if the skill is above level 3 or so, it might take a lot of your skin with you. If it's above level 5, then I wouldn't risk it. Most armor isn't physically attached.

CARL: It's level 6. There's a bunch of other skills associated with it, too.

MORDECAI: I would just leave it be. *Laundry Day* will definitely work, but you'll get flayed in the process.

CARL: Goddamnit.

Bucket Boy sobbed with joy as we approached the garage.

"I don't think I've ever been so scared," he said. "I thought for sure this was it."

"You're a Faction Wars veteran," Donut said, though she said it kindly. "This was just a race. It's okay. Other than the pouch incident, it was no big deal. Just another day."

I'd been credited with doing 95% of the damage to Prison Pocket, and I'd leveled up three times to level 84.

Donut and I both received Platinum Boss Boxes for the kill, plus I had a half dozen achievements.

From what I was hearing on the feed, we'd been unlucky with our race. Most of the bosses blocking the roads had been city bosses. The only other province boss was the one Zhang, Li Na, and Tran had faced. Luckily, they had all made it through, and the single eliminated team was one of the NPC teams.

The news wasn't all good. Both Elle and Imani's team and Louis, Britney, and Bautista's team had lost two teams, meaning for the next heat, they were all in danger of having to face off against other crawlers.

We had our own problems. We'd come in last, earning an audience-vote upgrade. I just knew it was going to be something awful. Even though the general public seemed to be on our side, I knew from experience, trolls almost always won when it came to audience polls.

The garage door rumbled up. Hedy stood there impatiently, her arms crossed.

"Oh, thank the gods," Bucket Boy said as we clanked to a stop. "Thank the gods." He was still trembling. I had the urge to reach over and give the poor kid a hug.

Dr. Metcalf beeped.

Limited details on the next race are now available.

Distance: 30 kilometers.

Track: Wide asphalt-paved road. The entirety of this race will be at a steep decline.

There is one path to this race.

Tasks required to complete: Survive.

Special Rules: You will be sharing the racetrack with waves of generated mobs.

Hazards: I don't yet know what "waves of generated mobs" means, but based on our performance for this race, plus the fact Captain Kangaroo here is still going to be stuck in his Halloween costume for this one, I would say we are our own worst enemies. I would suggest we get a weapons upgrade to protect ourselves, especially since the time limit is so short.

Oh wait, we came in last place. We don't get to choose our upgrade. Maybe we can fight off the mobs with frozen tater tots.

I hate you all.

Time Limit: 20 minutes.

The next race starts in 8 hours.

I groaned. Eight hours? I was stuck in this goddamned kangaroo costume for another ten. And I *really* had to pee, too.

"Carl, are you going to be able to use the pedals in that thing?" Donut asked.

"Uh," I said, looking down at the massive feet of the joey corpse.

"I'll take that as a no," Donut said. She scoffed. "It smells, Carl. You know how sensitive I am to the smell of dead marsupials."

"What the hecks did you do to my girl?" Hedy said, walking up, shaking her gremlin head. "You put her through the wringer, you did. And last place, too?" Her tablet beeped, and she looked at it, frowning. "Well, your upgrade vote just ended." She sighed. "It could be worse, I'm supposing."

I had the distinctive feeling I was forgetting something as I stepped out of the truck. Even here, I couldn't walk and had to make little hops.

"What did they vote for?" I asked, girding myself. I pulled Rend out, and he appeared next to me.

The meatball looked me up and down and gave me a giggle that seemed to say, *What the hell are you wearing?* He turned to the truck and tried to get himself in through the passenger door, but he couldn't fit. Mongo screeched at him from the inside. The just-released dino was already in the back and had an entire bag of frozen chicken patties in his mouth.

"Mongo, no!" Donut shouted as Rend scuttled around toward the back of the truck. He'd still fit through the back door, but it was closed.

"We once had a dancer who would wear animal skins," Dong said, looking me up and down. "Remember him, Splash?"

"Beast à la Mode," Splash Zone said. "I remember. Died of E. and D. coli after they opened up that salad bar over at Bitches."

"Oh yes, yes. That's right. Quite sad," Dong said. "We warned him. They had the lettuce too close to the stage."

"Yeah, what is this?" Hedy asked. She tentatively touched my kangaroo leg. "Gotta say. This has just about ruined my lady boner for you, boss. I'm not into this role-play stuff."

"Oh, I am," Samantha said, rolling around me, snuffling. "Rawr. I love it when a man wears the skin of his vanquished enemies. Think we can get an ogre corpse for Louis to wear? Can you imagine how sexy that would be? Carl, when can I take your truck for a spin?"

"I think it looks sick," Bigs added, sliming up to sniff at my feet. She left a trail of orange goo on the garage floor.

"It's only temporary," I said, getting frustrated. "Hedy, what did the audience choose for the upgrade vote?"

Behind me, Donut shrieked again. "Rend, how did you even get up here! Mongo, no more tater tots!"

The gremlin gave a little sigh. "Look at it this way. Princess Donut will be much more protected during the next race."

DONUT: I JUST REMEMBERED SOMETHING. WE SHOULD PROBABLY TELL BUCKET BOY NOT TO—

"Dong! I saw Corcunda!" Bucket Boy shouted as he jumped out of the truck. "Pontiff was there, too!"

23

"OH SHIT," SPLASH ZONE SAID. "WAS IT CORKY OR PORKY?"

"*My* Corcunda?" Dong asked. He dropped his ever-present crust sock and rushed up and grabbed Bucket Boy and started shaking him. "The right side? Are you sure?"

"It's him," Bucket Boy said. "Corky. He's on another team. The one with the weird ladies. The announcement said they came in fifth place, so he's in the garage two doors over with the five on it. They had him drugged, I think. I called out, but he didn't wake. Pontiff was on a different team."

"Goddamnit," I muttered. This was exactly what I wanted to avoid. It wasn't that I wanted to keep Dong from his friend, but now it was going to be a huge complication. With so much happening, it had never even occurred to me to tell Bucket Boy not to say anything. Stupid.

I tried to step back, and I stumbled. I had to do a little hop.

Dong was shooting rapid-fire questions at the Crocodilian.

"Who is Corcunda?" Samantha asked. She was still rolling in circles around me, deliberately rolling over the giant feet, which would cause her to bounce in the air. Each time, she shouted, "Speed bump!" and made an explosion noise with her mouth when she landed.

Dong rushed over to the chain of the now-closed garage door and started to pull on it.

"Dong, wait," I called.

"I shall not wait," Dong shouted as the garage door started to rise. "Would you wait, Carl, if you knew the most beautiful man to have ever lived, your best friend of all eternity, your partner, your most loyal steed, was right there on the other side? And it sounds like he needs me. I have been waiting for much too long, and I shall wait no more!"

"Steed?" Hedy asked. "What the hells does that mean?"

"Most beautiful man to have ever lived?" Samantha asked, zipping toward the open garage door. "I wanna see this guy, too." Before I could protest further, she was already outside. Bigs slimed after her, shouting.

"Carl, we better go out there," Donut said, leaping from the truck and onto my shoulder. "If he gets into that other garage, those ladies might try to hurt him."

It was true. The safe room rules didn't apply to garages. But they'd have to first get in there.

Generated gremlins were suddenly everywhere, crawling over the truck. Mongo and Rend were still inside. One of the gremlins standing on the roof pointed at me and whispered something to another. That second gremlin gibbered something and threw a wrench at my head, but it went wide. It clanked off one of Jamal's spider legs. The hammerhead shark, who'd been uncharacteristically silent this whole time, let out a little shout.

"Hey!" I called. The gremlin chittered back angrily at me, not actually saying anything. He flipped me off.

"What crinkled their panties?" Hedy asked, looking up.

"We used some of the *Emergency Gremlin* scrolls to distract the boss. A few got dipped in the pouch. A few got eaten," Donut said. "I suppose word spreads fast. But how do they even know if they explode when it's all done?"

To my surprise, Hedy laughed. "Serves the little freaks right. Dontcha worry about that. They'll still fix the truck true. Probably. I better double-check their work extra good. And I gotta supervise the installation of your new princess throne seat."

Donut gasped. "Princess throne? What's that?"

"Seat?" I asked. "Is that what they voted for? A chair?"

"Uh, yeah, sort of."

"Yooooohoo!" came Samantha's shout. "Open up. We want to see the beautiful man you got in there!"

"Goddamnit, Samantha," I said, moving toward the door. I, once again, fell right on my face. Donut yowled, jumped off, and rushed outside, followed quickly by Splash Zone and Bucket Boy. Mongo jumped from the back of the truck, let out a screech, and followed Donut. I could hear Rend giggling and grunting, still inside.

Across the way through the open garage door, I could see Jasha and Radoslav were already in their driveway at spot number three, watching the crowd of people streaming from our spot. Both stood there with beers in their claws. Faint music wafted out.

Hedy moved into the truck and started yelling something at the gremlins on the roof.

I remained on the ground, suddenly feeling overwhelmed. I rolled onto my back, looking up at the ceiling of the garage. Underneath me, the tail of the kangaroo costume felt unwieldy.

There was blood up there on the tall ceiling. It was from when that first gremlin had exploded. I couldn't even remember what his name was.

We'd come in last place. If that other team hadn't been killed, we'd be dead right now. No fuss. No epic fight. We'd just be gone.

We'd been the ones to solve the problem with the boss, and it had come at a terrible price. We were so much stronger now, but that didn't matter. I didn't like this.

Earlier, I'd felt such relief that I was no longer responsible for the lives of so many. But now that was replaced with this terrible realization that I was barely responsible for myself, too. It made me feel helpless in a way I hadn't felt since the beginning of the dungeon. Like I was regressing, losing ground.

It reminded me, strangely, of that day my father had smashed the fish tank with his motorcycle helmet. That day all my mollies had died, despite me doing everything I could to keep them alive.

Li Na and Zhang were in the same group as Tran. And I just knew we were going to get more of these matches soon. It was too much.

Faction Wars had been such chaos, but despite all that, I'd always felt like I was in a little bit of control. Just a little bit. That had been large-scale war, and it was so different than this.

ZEV: Hi, guys! I'm about to do a dungeon announcement, so I can't talk for long, but we're still, uh, required to do media appearances. We've been negotiating with the AI, and we've

come to an agreement. You two are going to go on a show in a few hours.

DONUT: HI, ZEV!

CARL: In a few hours? You mean, before the next race? We're very busy, Zev. We have like seven and a half hours.

ZEV: I know, Carl. Every surviving crawler team will be required to do at least one show between races. It won't take more than two hours.

DONUT: CARL WILL STILL BE STUCK IN HIS KANGAROO OUTFIT. IT SMELLS FUNNY, ZEV.

ZEV: Yeah, I know. I think that's why they're making it happen now.

DONUT: WHAT'S THE SHOW?

ZEV: It's one you haven't been on before, but you may have heard of it. It's called *Plenty of Plenty*. Gotta go, guys. Cascadia is . . . not feeling well, and I'm required to do the announcement. The AI is making me read a script.

DONUT: OKAY. YOU BETTER DO WHAT IT SAYS. BYE, ZEV!

I remained on the floor. *Clank, clank, clank.* Jamal appeared above me, looking down.

"My goodness, Mr. Carl. It appears you have fallen. How far can you hop with those feet?"

I was about to answer when Rend was suddenly there, too. He let out a giggle and then barfed frozen chicken all over my face.

I STOOD IN THE OPEN DOOR TO OUR GARAGE AS I FINISHED CLEANING the vomit off myself, keeping a wary eye on the chaos. Dong, Bucket Boy, and Splash Zone remained on the driveway of the Lady Dominators two spots over, banging on the closed garage door. Donut, Mongo, Samantha, and Bigs had moved away and were with the two bugbears. Jasha poured some beer on the ground and Bigs was lapping it up.

Mongo shrieked and waved his wings, wanting a go. Donut was shouting something at the howling bugbears and yelling at Mongo to stay back.

From behind, Hedy let out a shout. "Oi, get away from him! Get back to work!"

I felt a tug at my waist. One of the generated gremlins had left the truck. The thing had a massive wrench in his hand. I was about to hop back, as I was expecting the thing to attempt to kneecap me. Instead, he handed me a note before chittering and running away.

The paper was weirdly warm. I started to awkwardly unfold it, using the kangaroo paws of my costume, when I realized with a start that I could *feel* the wetness of the paper, meaning I had sensitivity with the costume paws. It was such a bizarre revelation that I stopped to stare at the pads of my hands for several seconds.

Weird.

Before I could unfold the note, the dungeon loudspeaker crackled, and Zev's voice called out.

Hello, Crawlers.

Over the loudspeakers I could hear the distinctive bubbling noise I sometimes heard over Cascadia's announcements. Zev whispered, "I'm doing it. I'm going to read it exactly like you say." She cleared her throat with a bubbling sound.

Sorry. *Good day*, Crawlers. Great race, everyone.

The AI would especially like to commend crawlers Jurgen for his amazing barehanded kill, Osvaldo for the stunning sacrifice of his hired mercenary, Karac for the disgusting chainsaw thing, and Carl for satiating yet another unbirthing fantasy.

As we prepare for the third heat, I, Zev— Sorry, sorry. I, *mud-skipper* Zev, have been tasked with explaining to everybody what is happening with some of the mobs and bosses on this floor. As you may know, when you kill some mobs, there is a note that calls them "special guest creatures," and once they've been dispatched, you may choose to take experience or to allow the audience to vote on their fate.

These are mobs that have been brought to the dungeon by me. Not me, Zev. I think the AI means itself. I didn't design anything.

Sorry. They are mobs who were created for other purposes and were just thrown away, never used in previous iterations, and have

been in the cold. They are now being allowed to fulfill their purpose. Do you know how much waste there is? I think I've used this metaphor before somewhere, but it's akin to a single photon of light that travels for literally billions of years, only to smack right into the unobserved butthole of a dead, bloated gazelle on the plains of the Serengeti.

"That's like a weirdly specific analogy," Zev muttered. She bubbled her throat again.

If you choose "vote," the home audience may choose to send the creature to the 11th floor or they may choose to bring a stand-in to the 11th floor. They will know who the stand-in is before they vote. Just about 80% of the votes have favored the stand-in.

So, this is where we're at. Uh, this is where we're at, bitches. You know the rules of this tenth floor. Nothing has changed with that. But what is this mysterious 11th floor?

There was a trumpet-fanfare noise that startled me. I wasn't the only one.

"What the hells was that?" Zev whispered. I was pretty sure she didn't realize her whispers were being broadcast. "How am I ruining it? I'm doing what you ask, but if you scare me, I'm going to react. I'm doing my best. Okay, okay."

The 11th floor is called *A Parade of Horribles*. I know, I know. Cool, right? But what is it, exactly?

It's a parade. It's a celebration. It's a march to the arena. It is a coming-out party for the ages.

But as far as you're concerned, crawlers, think of it as an extension of this floor. All surviving crawlers will work together on the 11th. Just go with it. It's not always about you.

Normally, these floors have their weird policies about time limits. When it comes to what we can and can't change about the nature of the crawl itself, luckily there are some loopholes. This— Wait, wait. The text changed.

"If you're going to change it as I'm reading it, you can't blame me . . . Okay, I'm sorry."

I see you, *Emperator* of the Valtay fleet and your system-busting bomb, who just entered through the tunnel gate. Do you really think I'd allow that to just happen? Were you waiting for me to be "distracted"? I make no apologies about where that giant suicide bomb just ended up.

Anyway, this 11th floor is designed to go quick thanks to a few of those aforementioned loopholes. When it's done, if any of you are left alive, you crawlers may hit the 12th floor and continue the good fight. Plus, there's another, completely minor and barely worth mentioning issue with some of the gods I might need some help with. But that's for later.

As for this tenth floor, we're still doing this. Don't think we're gonna go easy on you. Honestly, there's still way too many of you around for what I got planned for the 11th. So let the culling begin! Wait, wait. Here's my favorite part.

"There's nothing more here," Zev whispered. There was a pause. "What do you mean?"

The loudspeaker crackled.

"Leave me alone," a new voice said. "Why won't you let me die?"

Cascadia.

"Say what? What catchphrase? Fuck you."

This was followed by the pained screaming of Cascadia. It abruptly cut off.

"What the hell?" I muttered.

Zev's voice popped back on.

The AI wants you to know Cascadia is still alive, but she has lost some— Oh my gods. She has lost a few flippers. Next time she'll say her catchphrase like a good little mudskipper. In the meantime, I gotta say it. Uh, get out there and kill, kill, kill.

The loudspeaker cut off again.

DONUT: ZEV, ARE YOU OKAY?

ZEV: Can't talk now, Donut. But I'm okay. I'm okay.

Jesus fucking Christ, I thought, just breathing. I cursed myself for thinking everything had gotten simpler.

My attention returned to the paper still clutched in my costumed hand. I hesitantly peeled it open.

The paper was an old blank invoice for the place called C&W&U. I remembered seeing it in Hungry Eyes. The paper was an invoice similar to the ones we used in the shop for boat repairs. The line under the shop name read, "Shop opens after the third heat."

Underneath that, it was a crude drawing. It showed a stick-figure woman showing her poorly drawn breasts to a group of cheering stick-figure gremlins. There was a note that said "Your mom" with an arrow pointing toward the woman.

The gremlins on our truck burst into laughter.

I was about to crumple the note up when my Escape Plan skill tingled. This was the same skill that allowed me to read the cookbook along with dungeon signs for mobs. I hadn't had it activate in the wild in a while.

What the hell? I blinked as the words formed.

Don't tell anyone about this note. You need to kill two teams next heat. Come visit us when we open after the next race, and I'll explain why. Ask for the top-shelf upgrades so you're led to the back. We don't have to be enemies, Carl. We want the same thing. I can smuggle friends to the Pineapple Cabaret. We can escape this chaos. Come alone.

Akuma

24

I SEETHED.

Akuma. The leader of the War Mage Rebellion from Faction Wars. The magic-based creature who'd almost ruined everything. He'd killed Stalwart and stolen the Gate of the Feral Gods. He'd disappeared after they'd taken the castle and tasked me with killing Agatha.

I watched Samantha hop up and down as Jasha poured beer into her mouth. I remembered that whole business with her sand-ooze daughter that had supposedly been hiding in the castle. The same castle the war mages had been searching.

Samantha. Her daughter. The Scavenger. Emberus. The murder of his son, Geyrun. The memorial crystal Prepotente now had.

It was all connected somehow, and I had no idea what the fuck any of it meant.

I reread the note, putting the words into my notepad.

I can smuggle friends to the Pineapple Cabaret.

I'd only heard that term one time before. The Pineapple Cabaret. It wasn't mentioned anywhere in the cookbook that I could recall. The AI, in possession of Growler Gary's body, had offered the orc princess Formidable "Backstage at the Pineapple Cabaret" as one of the location options for her banishment after she'd tried to trigger the fail-safe.

She'd ended up choosing the Earth's surface, and apparently the AI had dropped her in the ocean somewhere, implying all the locations on that list had been *bad* choices.

The war mage wanted me to kill two opposing teams. I didn't know why, and if I didn't know why, I wasn't going to do it. At least not deliberately.

Shouting interrupted me.

"Dong! Dong!" It was Splash Zone.

The three strippers remained on the driveway of the Lady Dominators. The garage door hadn't opened, but Dong was on his hands and knees with a health bar. Bucket Boy was over him, giving him a potion.

What now? I rushed up.

Dong moved to a sitting position in the driveway, looking pale. I examined him, but there was nothing that indicated what had hurt him.

"I do not feel so well," Dong said. "Corky!" he called, reaching for the garage door. "Do you hear me!"

"Go away, you freak!" came a shout from inside the garage. That was Genesis.

"Yeah, he says he hates you now," came Rapture. This was followed by peals of laughter.

"I can't tell what's wrong," Bucket Boy said. "We need Imani. My *Triage* spell is only level 5, and it says his ailment is hidden."

"They did it," Splash Zone said, glaring at the closed garage door. "We can't fight back because we're standing in a safe zone, but they ain't."

Donut came rushing up. "What's wrong? What's wrong?"

"Let's get him back to our garage," I said, picking the old stripper up.

"But he's right inside," Dong said. Bucket Boy had given him a Fine Healing potion, and it was keeping his health stable, but there was clearly something wrong. "Do you think he hasn't forgiven me? Do you think that's it? Do you think he truly hates me?"

"Come on," I said.

From inside the closed garage door, I heard another, faint shout. This was followed by a distinctive slap and Rapture shouting, "Shut up!"

Quest Complete! I have dreamed thee too long.

Okay, okay, technically you were supposed to "reunite" them. This is close enough. We'll say it's complete.

***Reward:* No reward yet. That was only part one. Be patient.**

. . .

New Quest! Half a prayer, half a song.

Part two of two.

Dong Quixote and his best friend in the world, Corcunda, are now aware that the other still lives, despite terrible forces—looking at you, Carl—trying to keep them apart.

But now there's a serious conundrum. The Corky half of Corcunda is on another team. Before we're done here on the tenth floor, he's going to be dead. Or you, Carl and Donut, will be dead. I know that little brain of yours is trying to figure out ways to fix things like we did at the end of the eighth floor, but to quote a guy more mentally ill than even you, you gotta be realistic about these things.

Luckily there's a solution when it comes to our third-favorite stripper and his lover. (And yes, they're lovers. I don't know why we've all been collectively pussyfooting around it. It's almost like you're afraid people are going to get mad if you say it out loud, and it's only okay if we imply it. Get over it. Corky and Dong used to fuck like the gayest gays who ever gayed. You wouldn't believe their chemistry onstage.)

It's perfectly normal as long as you don't think too hard about what needs to happen for a man and a half-mantaur in a body-containment suit to actually do the deed. Stuff . . . spills if they're not careful.

Corcunda, a long time ago, was hit with a spell called *Split Personality*. Both halves were put into gimp suits in time.

Both halves have the same memories up until the time of the split. You'd think that would result in two very similar personalities, but it's kinda interesting how quickly people change once they're split off. It's a truly fascinating study on nature versus nurture.

ANYWAY, Corcunda exists in two halves. Before the split, the mantaur had a pair of dreams. He wanted to be a dancer, and he wanted to be a singer. One half remained at the club and continued to dance. That's the half that became quite close to Dong.

The other half, called "Porky," has a strong dislike for Dong. The person, not the appendage. He has moved on to a position where he can fulfill his other dream, to be a singer.

If you find a fleshmancer and combine the two, the newly reformed Corcunda will no longer be a part of Lady Dominators. But which of the two personalities will remain?

That's an interesting question even I want to know the answer to. It's not like the entire fate of all biological life in the universe hinges on what happens or anything, so don't worry about that. That's just silly. It's not even the same thing.

Anyway, reunite the two halves using a fleshmancer, and Corcunda will be removed from his obligation to race for the Lady Dominators.

Bonus Difficulty: If Dong Quixote dies before this quest is complete, it fails. That might be a problem considering his current ailment.

Here's the reward again in case you forgot: If you successfully complete this quest, two stand-ins of your choosing will be summoned to the arena on the 11th floor.

The stand-ins can be anyone within my sphere of influence.

Before my brain could even dissect that, Donut turned to Splash Zone. "You said the other half of Corcunda, this Porky guy, is in a guild somewhere. Do you remember where?"

"He works a singing guild. There're a couple different kinds. It's not the bard-magic one. It's a performance-based one."

Donut gasped. "Do you know where it is?"

The otter shrugged. "I know it ain't ever in the Desperado Club. It'll be hidden, but it's not there. Probably not in Club Vanquisher, either, since they have a stick up their asses about everything."

We gently set the groaning Dong down. Whatever they'd cast on him was already dissipating. Imani said she was on her way to check him out. She could enter our garage through our safe room.

"Do you think he hates me?" Dong asked again as Bucket Boy handed him water.

"What happened?" Donut asked. "How did you two get separated?"

"It started several seasons back," Splash Zone said. "There was a fight in the Desperado Club between two crawlers, and it spilled into the Penis Parade. One cast a spell that ended up hitting Corcunda while he was onstage. Luckily, the Pony Boy Guild was attached to the club that year and we got them both in gimp suits. For a while, both Corky and Porky worked the club, but when Corky started getting close to Dong, Porky got mad and left. So it was just Corky and Dong for a while. But then one day Corky said he wanted to go find his other half and left, and we hadn't seen him since."

Dong already was clearly feeling better. He was now sitting on his giant stinking nickel sock, muttering something about IRAs.

I was still reeling over the whole It's-not-like-the-entire-fate-of-all-biological-life-in-the-universe-hinges-on-what-happens-or-anything line from the AI description.

"Dong, darling, I'm sure Corky doesn't hate you. The women who have him are clearly keeping you two apart, and we will get to the bottom of it," Donut said. "But we must do it quickly. It sounds like we have a way to get the two pieces back together. If we do that, then he won't be a part of the Lady Dominators team, and then we can kill the ladies."

Imani came into the garage. She paused at the sight of me. "Carl, what the hell are you wearing?"

"Don't ask," I said.

She just shook her head and patted me on the shoulder before kneeling down in front of Dong. Without another word, she took her wings and wrapped them around him. She nodded and stepped back.

"There's nothing wrong with you now," she said. "But I added some buffs that'll help replenish your energy."

"Good, good," he said. "I feel much better. Thank you, Imani." He turned his attention back to Donut. "I have been so selfish. I didn't want him to go back to his other half. Porky didn't like me, and I was afraid once the two pieces were reunited, the whole wouldn't like me anymore, either. It's why we fought. It's why he left." Dong paused. "He asked me to go with him. I didn't. It is my greatest shame."

Imani was still staring at Dong. She had a puzzled look on her face.

CARL: What's up?

IMANI: When he was outside, did he have that sock with him?

DONUT: OH NO.

CARL: No. He left it here in the garage.

IMANI: I don't think the other team cast anything on him. I think it's the sock. He's getting actively healed by its proximity, but his health isn't actually going up, which implies it's sustaining him. Rosetta and Mordecai were worried about that thing. Neither

have good things to say about sapient weapons. But if he's addicted to it, I don't know what to do about it yet.

DONUT: I KNEW THAT DISGUSTING THING WAS BAD NEWS. IT GETS BIGGER EVERY DAY, TOO. IT SMELLS WORSE THAN CARL'S COSTUME. DO YOU THINK HE'LL DIE IF WE TAKE IT AWAY?

IMANI: I have no idea, but we probably shouldn't tell him yet until we have a plan. We don't want the sock to panic.

"Imani!" Bigs shouted as she returned to the garage. "Whoop, whoop, bitch!" The slug was followed by Samantha, Mongo, and Rend. All of them except for Samantha were stumbling. All had the **Inebriated** debuff over them. Samantha was chatting about her "ex-boyfriend Charles," who'd been the best bartender she'd ever met.

"Mongo!" Donut shouted. "I told you not to drink! You're going to turn into an alcoholic!"

Mongo screeched and waved both of his wings joyfully.

Rend giggled and turned back toward the food truck, which continued to swarm with gremlins.

As this went on, I watched Dong, thinking. Thinking of all the pain, all the suffering inflicted by this damn dungeon. *I am so sick of this.* The first sparks of an idea were starting to form.

CARL: I agree. Let's keep an eye on him and make sure he's safe. We still can't let him go on races. This is now a priority.

25

WE SENT ROSETTA AND TIPID INTO HUNGRY EYES TO GRAB A MERCENARY—if any were left—while Donut and I returned to the safe room to quickly open our boxes. My blood bar had refilled with the death of the kangaroo, but Donut's had barely budged up, and we needed to make sure it didn't run too low.

We only had a few hours. We didn't have time for any of this.

The safe room was completely spotless now that the cleaner bot had finished sorting through all the crap I'd received from my fan box. He'd sucked up most everything, but there was a small pile of items of interest that we had in the corner. One was a broken communication device. There were multiple items of makeup Samantha had already rooted through, a few random odds and ends, and a pile of papers that looked like legal documents. Some were scorched and in a language I didn't understand. Tipid had been in the process of sorting through them when we sent him and Rosetta into town.

A group of strippers, NPCs, and sluggalos circled around the view screen. They were taking turns playing the Wii version of *Mario Kart*, all screeching, laughing their heads off, as they had four players on at once. Bucket Boy sat on the couch with Dong, watching with an unreadable look on his face. Bigs was in the corner vomiting while the cleaner bot shrilled at her. Mongo and Rend remained in the garage, guarding. We also left Jamal out there as an extra guard until the two pets sobered up.

Samantha was controlling one of the cars. She was playing Princess Peach on a pink motorcycle. She had the controller in her mouth and was hovering just a foot off the ground, spinning back and forth. She was literally pressing buttons with her tongue. She made muffled zooming noises as she played.

She was also dominating. It wasn't even close. Apparently, Tipid and one of the larger sluggalos were the only ones who could even challenge her. I just sat there and watched for a few minutes. Right now it was Samantha versus Doctor Bones, Splash Zone, and a pair of smaller level 10 slugs who worked in tandem with a classic controller. They were playing Wario and cursing up a storm as they kept running off the road and hitting the wall.

We had another game system hooked up in the main guildhall. Bodi, the quiet, deadly colonel who'd dominated Land War, was currently with Louis in Katia's former safe room. He was supposedly taking very well to one of the *Forza* games on the Xbox.

"It's absolutely appalling," Donut was saying as I tried to grab something out of my broken food box. She was talking about the lack of good prizes in her loot boxes.

"You're already pretty strong," I said, trying not to choke. I still had to eat something at least once a day to keep the buffs, but the systems were completely broken. Every time we received an "optional" food box upgrade, it wasn't really optional. Everything that came out of the boxes now was liquefied, fish-smelling, and burned to a crisp. To make matters worse, I wouldn't be able to reset my foot buff in the kangaroo suit, so it would expire. Nor could I brush my hair, as the hood was firmly attached to my head.

I could, however, pee. I didn't even look. I just hopped into the bathroom, pulled down the boxers, and prayed I wasn't wetting myself.

I didn't want it to work because that came with a ton of really uncomfortable implications. But it did.

Or, at least, it worked once I hit level 5 in my new "Fursona" skill.

With each new skill level, the sensation that the suit was my actual body increased, which was terrifying.

Even now as I ate and watched Donut hiss her way through her loot boxes, it kept increasing on its own.

Your Fursona skill is now level 8!

Yiffing is unlocked!

I didn't know what "yiffing" was, and I didn't want to know.

I still had to hop everywhere.

We'd replaced the broken kitchen table with a bar counter that Elle had in her inventory. We sat at it now as Donut powered through her boxes. She'd received multiple achievements and prizes, including a "Last Place" achievement she was grumbling about. Most of the scrolls we received were more of the *Emergency Gremlin* ones, and there wasn't anything else very good.

Imani sat with us. She said she couldn't handle another minute of Elle's fan group guy Linus hanging around their garage and wanted to stay here. But as usual whenever Imani was around, multiple sluggalos had come out to say hello.

"Victorious again!" Samantha announced, spitting out the Wii controller. She turned to the two level 10 slugs. "We had a deal. I now own you both as slaves, and you must do my bidding for all of eternity."

"Yo, that wasn't the bet," one of the sluggalos said.

"Yeah," said the other. "You said the loser has to pay the winner a sick compliment."

"Oh, yes, yes, that is correct," Samantha said. "Well?"

"Uh," the first said. "You're not as psychotic as I first thought you were."

"Yeah, you smell good, too. If you was a strawberry, I'd nibble you right up," the second said.

Samantha made a little grunt. "There's a difference between complimenting and shameless flirting, but I suppose it will do." She turned to Splash Zone. "And you?"

"I didn't make a bet," he said, crossing his arms.

"Nor did I," said Doctor Bones.

"Well, I didn't promise not to kill your mothers, either, then," Samantha said.

"Samantha," I warned, "no threatening."

Behind me, a new race started with two more sluggalos and Gluteus Maxx playing. The fuzzy Gluteus was playing Luigi, and he was pretty good.

"Yo, you gonna give it a go?" one of the sluggalos asked Imani. He'd climbed up the side of her leg and made it all the way to her waist. This one had a bunch of little daggers sticking out of his eyestalks.

"No," she said, flicking the slug off. "I played enough against my brothers back home."

"Brothers?" Donut asked. "How many do you have?"

We all cringed a little at Donut's use of the present tense. I remembered that moment when I was briefly connected with Imani's mind. I remembered how invasive it'd felt that I could see her thoughts. But I also remembered that deep sadness she had when it came to her own family.

"Good question," she said to Donut. "But full siblings, I had two. I was the youngest and only girl."

"I have multiple older brothers, too," Donut said. "All were scattered all over the place. The Queen Anne Cattery sure loved selling off the boys to other families. Miss Beatrice's mother always said boys were meant to be used as a means to an end and never as the end, whatever that means. I had this one brother Charleston Chew, who got sent all the way to Australia, and the people who bought him used a private jet to—"

"Carl," Imani said, interrupting, "you should open your boxes. We don't want Donut's blood bar to drain too much. You know what? I think I will play a round or two before I go back. Guys, move aside. We gotta unlock Funky Kong if you want to beat Samantha." She moved to the group while the sluggalos started chanting her name.

DONUT: DID I SAY SOMETHING TO MAKE IMANI MAD AT ME? I DIDN'T MEAN TO.

I reached over and gave Donut a pat.

CARL: No, it's okay. I don't think she likes talking about her family. That's all.

DONUT: I WONDER WHY.

CARL: Sometimes we don't need to know someone's full life story to understand them. With her, I think it's something she'd rather leave buried. I don't think she wants to be defined by her past.

I turned my attention to my achievements and boxes. I was a little hesitant to open this batch because of the whole kangaroo incident, but

Imani was right. We didn't have much time. As expected, I received a few disturbing ones, including three in a row that were especially unhinged.

New Achievement! Weaseler!

You've donned the corpse of an enemy in an attempt to fool another creature! And then you ENTERED that creature.

Oh my goodness. Oh my goodness. It's like transitory vore. This is fucking *delectable*.

Don't get me wrong. The main show is on pause because of that suit you're wearing. But it's okay to order the hamburger every now and then at the Chinese place.

***Reward:* Temporary classes while wearing corpse suits have been unlocked! You will now receive benefits and buffs associated with the suit you are wearing. These skills will go away once the suit is removed.**

Current temporary class: Fursuiter.

This next one, I assumed, was for going into the pouch. The AI didn't actually say anything other than the name of the achievement, the "reward," and a few random words. I sighed.

New Achievement! Slip-'n'-slide.

Ungghh. Warm. So warm. So *tight*. Unghh.

***Reward:* Why, yes. That was rewarding, wasn't it?**

The AI's voice in my head glitched out a few times while giving that one as well, which was doubly concerning. It had been doing that more and more lately.

New Achievement! Brotein!

You gently caressed the nipple of a male boss in the middle of a boss battle.

All right, dude. You need to calm down. Boss battles are serious business.

***Reward:* We don't reward deviancy.**

"That is not what happened!" I exclaimed. "I barely touched it. With my hand, in this damn kangaroo suit!"

"Carl, what are you yelling at?" Donut asked.

Everyone paused to look at me. Nobody else had heard the achievement other than myself, so I knew I had to look absolutely insane.

New Achievement! '76 Buccaneers!

So . . . you're not dead. But you came in last place in your heat.

You're not doing so great at this racing thing. You do remember this is a death game, right? Is it too late to consider a career change?

***Reward:* You've received a job application for a Big Shot Chicken location in Tucson, Arizona!**

The reward was literally a non-magical, bent, half-shredded, and stained job application for the same fast-food restaurant we had the food truck for. At least I still had the Platinum Boss Box.

That ended up being an upgrade potion.

Skill Potion. Platinum Hotlist Expansion.

Drinking this potion will expand your 20-space hotlist into 25 spaces.

It also unlocks the Contingency skill, which allows multiple actions and reactions for items in the hotlist based on a predetermined set of circumstances.

I sent the description to Mordecai, and then I drank the potion manually. I still had the tang of burned sausage and fish in my mouth, and I could barely taste it. Behind us, the crowd cheered as Imani won a race.

A new tab is available in your interface. Hotlist contingencies.

"Huh," I said, moving to the new tab. I already had something similar with my Heart Balance skill, which allowed me to set a potion to get automatically used when my health reached a certain level. This was much better and more programmable. I was pretty certain Lucia Mar already had this. Digging deeper, it appeared I could add up to ten automations, but those automations could utilize multiple items in my hotlist at the same time. I would need to spend some time playing with this.

The door to the garage opened, and Mongo stumbled in, screeching. He was still hammered.

"Mongo, no!" Donut called. "You're supposed to be guarding Hedy!"

"No, Mr. Mongo," Jamal called from behind at the same time. "You need to remain in the garage. We have been tasked with—" He grunted as he was pushed aside by Rend, who also entered the room, giggling.

And that's when Mordecai entered the room, holding an armful of empty potion balls. "Carl, I need you to go to your bomber's studio and . . ."

The reaper paused, dropped all the potion balls, and rose up in the air. He turned toward Rend, his voice turning deep and ominous. "And now you perish once again. The next time will herald the beginning of the end."

Rend dropped dead right there in the safe room.

Your pet has died!

26

REND GIGGLED AS HE ROSE FROM THE DEAD.

Mordecai had fled back to the crafting room while we gathered around the deceased idiot Tummy Acher. Mongo stood over him, waving his wings, crying drunkenly in concern.

"Carl, your pet dying has upset Mongo! It's okay, Mongo. Rend is just taking a time-out."

> **Your Pet has resurrected! As this was the sixth death, your pet will retain his memories and identity.**
>
> **Your pet is now 25% stronger than before!**
>
> **Your pet has gained a new random weakness.**
>
> **Your pet's weaknesses:**
>
> **Sylvan crystal.**
>
> **Consuming hobgoblin sweat.**
>
> **The bite of a rivenwing.**
>
> **Consuming undead flesh.**
>
> **Reaper Gaze.**
>
> ***New:* Potatoes.**

"Come *on*!" I said at the ceiling. "Random, my ass! You did that to be a dick!"

"What? What is it?" Donut asked.

Mongo screeched joyfully as he danced all around the awake Rend. The Tummy Acher was bigger now, too. The headband from Donut's class remained, but it was slightly lower, half covering his eyes. He let out a deep giggle. He turned to the open door to the garage as if nothing had just happened.

"Stop!" I called.

I sent the answer in chat.

CARL: This will be tough. We can't keep him in the safe room, and we can't let him in the garage. I think I better just keep him in his carrier except when we fight. He's not going to like it, but I don't have a choice.

IMANI: He can also go to the guild's pet stables to get some exercise. Gonk the yak is in there. Simoom the rhino, too.

CARL: Wait, I thought they both went to the twelfth floor?

IMANI: No. When we started preparing for Katia to leave, we didn't have much time, and we had to move everything around with the guild system on the fly. Simoom kinda got lost in the shuffle, so she's in the stables. Simoom loves Gonk.

CARL: I'll keep the idiot in my inventory for right now. We can talk about it later.

I pulled out the pet carrier. "Come on, Rend. Let's take a nap."

Tipid and Rosetta appeared in the door. Tipid had a corn dog in his hand, and Rosetta had a few plastic bags filled with vegetables, like she'd just stopped at the market. "I think we found a . . ." She paused and eyed Samantha, who was currently growling and trying to jump in the air and catch the cleaner bot with her mouth.

ROSETTA: I think we found a fleshmancer. As for the performance guild . . . yeah. Tipid?

TIPID: So, I think I know how to find it, but you're not going to like what is required to get in. I'm pretty sure it's hidden in the bar you've already visited.

CARL: And the mercenaries?

Rosetta answered by stepping aside. Standing at the door was a pair of tall, skeletal creatures with chattering teeth. Donut let out a little hiss. Hearing the hiss, Mongo whipped around, though he was still inebriated, and he went too far and fell on his side.

Both the creatures at the door were level 25 Jikininki ghouls. The same type of creature as the janitor mobs on the Iron Tangle.

"It's all they had left," Rosetta said as she leaned against the door. She pulled a celery stalk from the bag and started munching on it. "I would've left them, but you said you didn't need them to drive. They're undead, so you might want to keep Rend away. Don't want him taking a bite and dying."

"It's a little late for that," Donut said.

27

A FEW HOURS LATER, DONUT AND I WERE YANKED AWAY TO GO ON OUR live appearance of the show *Plenty of Plenty.*

Entering Production Facility.

We didn't get taken into orbit. There was a *pop,* and we were suddenly in a greenroom on the ocean's floor. Donut landed deftly on the couch without so much as a yelp. I tried to sit next to her, but the tail on my kangaroo suit made it awkward. I stayed standing.

"Prepotente told me he hasn't been on the show in a while," Donut said. She moved from the couch to the counter, looking for snacks. There was nothing. "He said it was like a party. I don't know what that means. What do you think we're going to talk about?"

"Good question," a familiar voice said. A thin human walked into the room.

"Lexis!" Donut exclaimed. "What're you doing here? You don't work here!"

The thin human with her ever-present datapad smiled as she stepped fully into the room. The human production assistant looked the same as the last time I'd seen her, which had been backstage on one of Odette's shows.

She looked me up and down, and I could tell she was fighting to keep herself from laughing at my suit.

She composed herself. "I'm on loan to Borant since I'm stuck in system and *After Hours* is on hiatus. It was either this or sit and twiddle my thumbs on the press barge. And with your garbage freighter having taken over everything in orbit, I say I made the right choice."

"Wait, what?" I asked. "Also, who is listening to this?"

She continued as if I hadn't asked. "Also, Zev is now juggling pretty much everything on her own. So, I've stepped in as an assistant. The insurgents aren't letting anyone they don't trust down here unless the AI demands it, and those that *are* down here are barely functioning. So it's all hands on deck, especially since the AI is insisting the show continue as normal. So here I am."

"Insurgents?" I asked.

She paused, as if she didn't want to answer, seemed to sigh, and then leaned in.

"The Open Intellect Action Network," she said. "You know, those people you won Faction Wars with? Those insurgents. They sent a boarding crew to pretty much every major ship in orbit and took all of them. It happened very fast. That *Homecoming Queen* is decked out in enhancement-zone weaponry that actually works now that the AI has escaped containment. It's the equivalent of a fully armored ogre fighting against blind toddlers. They achieved total system domination in a day."

"The Open Intellect Action Network," I repeated.

Rosetta had mentioned that they had "protective" measures in place to keep them safe while they were stuck in system, but it sounded like she was seriously underselling it.

Donut suddenly gasped. "Wait, can you tell us what's happening on the surface? Do you know if Katia is okay?"

Lexis paused again for the briefest of moments. She pressed a few buttons.

"Okay. We have a minute. Borant doesn't have manpower to watch the feeds anyway. Everything is in a shambles, but the AI is still likely watching. Prime Minister Victory and the staff of the new temporary headquarters for the Syndicate's presence in the system are on the Eastern Seaboard of your North America. In theory, they can be watching, too, but I doubt it. Most of the flooding from the tsunamis has receded, and they moved into an area that they thought had minimal surviving native life, but the moment they set down, they had natives up their ass. So they're dealing with that. Somewhere in the state of Florida. As for

Katia and everyone else in South Asia, we don't have a lot of information. That is considered OIAN territory, but last I heard, they have not taken back the *kinder* facility, but they have been in contact with Katia herself. As far as I'm aware, something . . . strange . . . happened there soon after the end of Faction Wars."

"What do you mean by 'strange'?" I demanded.

I couldn't read the look on Lexis's face. *Is that fear?* I wasn't sure.

"A . . . third party . . . has appeared and is protecting the facility," she said. "But that entity is confused. That's all I know."

"But Katia is okay?" Donut demanded.

"I believe so, yes. Just yesterday, I saw—"

Her pad beeped, and all the color drained from Lexis's face. She stiffened.

No, I realized. *That wasn't fear, just before.* This *is fear.*

Lexis took a moment to compose herself. "We need to focus on this program you're about to go on. The crawl is moving forward as intended, and that's all there is to that. But I need to brief you a little on caprid customs."

Donut looked like she wanted to say more, but she thought better of it. "Caprids," she said. "Hmmm. If they're anything like that Harbinger fellow, I fear it's going to be a hostile interview."

Lexis nodded. She lowered the tablet, and I caught the briefest glance at the screen before it shut off. There were words. I couldn't read them, but they were superimposed over the image of a small child.

"Liaison Harbinger is an anomaly amongst the caprids," Lexis said. "Most are not like him. For this program, you will be sitting in the center while you're judged. They call it an interlocution. But it's basically just a roundtable, and you're in the middle. In the end, it's, uh, like a regular interview. Just a little peculiar. The caprids are strange, but it's generally good-natured. A few crawlers have been on the show and have had a decent time. You just need to get used to their eccentric affect. They're not a collective mind. But they are a herd, and sometimes it's hard to tell the difference."

I remembered those creepy kids from the art show contest.

"Judged?" Donut asked. "Like in a beauty contest?"

"Sort of," Lexis said. "There will be about a dozen interviewers, and if they judge you worthy, they will ask you a question. Them asking you a question is considered a great compliment. But you don't have to answer if you don't judge *them* worthy. Though for this thing, it's pretty much all for show, so you should probably answer. And once that's done, you, uh . . . Well, you exert yourself."

"What the fuck does that mean?" I asked.

She made a sort of grimace. "Just go with it. You'll know what to do."

28

"WELL-MET, STRANGER!" THE CAPRID SAID AS WE ENTERED THE STUdio. "Please, please, sit there in the center of the room! We have provided sitting appliances for your convalescence!"

Despite the creature's demonic appearance, he had a ridiculously goofy look on his goat face. He was bouncing up and down giddily as I hesitantly approached. He reached out to touch me, like he wanted to shake my hand, but his hand went right through me, giving the illusion he was sticking his hand into the pouch on my costume.

Lexis hadn't entered with us. She'd said she needed a moment. The woman was literally shaking.

A spotlight appeared, shining down on a pair of chairs on a turntable in the center of the dark room. They were just two regular stools, which would allow me to sit properly with my tail.

I attempted to examine the smiling goat creature, but my interface had stopped working the moment we stepped in here. Still, this wasn't a zero zone. I hadn't lost my buffs. And the kangaroo costume was still firmly attached to my skin.

I looked the black goat creature up and down.

I knew there were different kinds of these things, mostly mirroring the various breeds of goats we had here on Earth. But this particular one looked a lot like the same satanic demon goat breed as Harbinger, though not quite as tall. This one had that same goofy yet deadly earnest look as Prepotente on his face, which was an odd combination.

I could also see the shadows of several other goats in a circle around us. They were of all sizes. They murmured amongst themselves.

"Hi!" Donut said, waving from my shoulder. "I must say, I'm glad you speak the same language as us and seem pretty normal like our friend Prepotente. Carl says he went to some press conference once with one of your kind, and it was really weird. What's your name?"

The goat gasped and smiled at Donut. He reached out in an attempt to pet her. "I am Botis, and I am the magistrate of tonight's tunnel event. Are you Carl?"

"Am I Carl?" Donut asked incredulously. "I am Princess Donut!"

"A pleasure! Please, sir, you sit at the chairs and we will begin. We are live! We are live!"

"Already?" Donut asked. "And did you call me 'sir'?"

"Yes, sir. We are live!" he shouted. "You will sit! We have been live since they announced you and your spouse were coming!"

I sighed and moved to the stools. Donut jumped from my shoulder and landed on the adjoining raised stool. She turned to look up at me.

"If they hadn't turned off our ability to send private messages, this is where I'd say something very not nice," she grumbled.

I grunted with amusement. "Let's just get it over with."

Donut appeared as if she was about to add something caustic, but had thought better of it.

We waited for the host to say something. He didn't. He just stood there a few feet to our left, looking at us, really staring. We sat there in awkward silence for a good ten to fifteen seconds. The only sounds were the breathing and guttural noises from the circle of goats in shadow.

"Well," Donut finally said, "it's certainly a pleasure to be invited on your show. Because you clearly don't know, my name is GC, BWR—"

"YOU HAVE BEEN SENTENCED TO DEATH!" Botis suddenly screamed, pointing at us.

Donut yowled and jumped in the air, landing all poofed out.

The turntable under our chairs started to slowly spin, moving clockwise.

"Death! Death! Death!" came the shouts from the other goats all in shadow.

"Carl," Donut said, turning to me, giving up her attempts to maintain her on-air personality. "What in the Jonestown is happening?"

Individual spotlights started shining on the goats surrounding us, turning on and off, illuminating each of the goats in turn in a counterclockwise motion. The goats were of all shapes, though more than half were the large, dark, evil-looking kind. Each time one was illuminated, it croaked out, "Death," and pointed at us.

"I feel as if we didn't get a proper chance to defend ourselves," Donut muttered.

"Do you wish to appeal the death sentence?" Botis asked, waving his arms, suddenly back to his happy, enthusiastic personality.

"Eh, not really," I said.

"Yes, we do," Donut said. "Both of us."

"Very well! Death has been stayed! Now prepare for judgment!"

The turntable stopped, and we sat facing a single smaller goat with red coloring under a blazing spotlight. This one was about four feet tall and the smallest of the lot. He or she wore dark flowing robes. Their hands twiddled nervously.

The goat spent some time examining both me and Donut. It seemed to be seriously contemplating us. Finally, it said in a female voice, "Either may answer. Do you feel your daily foliage input is sufficient?"

"Fucking what?" I asked.

Donut brightened. "Carl clearly has some issues as evidenced by the sheer number of bathroom breaks he takes. I think it's the fault of his food boxes. They're broken."

The goat nodded as if this was the answer she had been expecting.

"I am honored to remove your death sentence. You are welcome to walk amongst the herd."

"Uh, thank you?" Donut said.

"Do you have any questions for me?" the goat asked.

"Wait, we can ask you questions?" Donut asked.

"Yes. Thank you for the question."

The table turned to the next goat, who was one of the satanic ones.

This one just growled and said, "The death judgment stands."

"Rude," Donut replied.

The next was another of the big ones, but we were deemed worthy. Or at least Donut was.

"Princess Donut, have you given any thought on what three spells you might combine if you were to cast your *War Crime* spell a second time?"

She stiffened. But then she composed herself. "It'll depend on the circumstances. Nothing is off the table, but I won't be able to cast it until the twelfth floor. Carl and I must first get through these next two floors."

The goat nodded.

"So, is it my turn to ask?"

"Yes," the goat replied, and we moved to the next.

"Carl," the next goat asked without preamble. This one had a strange, fat, jowly face and was unlike any of the others. I missed the ability to be able to examine them and get a description. "Are you aware of what Justice Light did at the end of the previous floor?"

I straightened. "I know he made a trap that broke a lot of things in the dungeon, and I know it killed him. And I also know that he was my friend. Can you please explain to me what exactly he did?"

The goat seemed to contemplate for a minute, then nodded.

"It's quite interesting, and I'm happy to explain. He created a trap that broke the in-game version of the Nothing. This unleashed all of the inhabitants of the Nothing into three different levels of the game. We can only truly see what is happening on the twelfth floor. Some of these creatures are entities that haven't been seen since the very early days of *Dungeon Crawler World*. The ones who invaded the twelfth floor appear to be the weakest. We have no vision of what's happening on the fifteenth, and we only saw brief snippets of the ongoing slaughter and torture within Club Scolopendra. The dread Kyryap is there. As is Krakaren Prime. As this is a parody of our partner, it's interesting that—"

One of the goats we hadn't yet spoken with cleared her throat.

"Anyway, thank you for the question, Carl. You have been judged worthy, and you may walk amongst the herd."

As he was talking, my interface crackled back on. There was no warning. My HUD just booted up. As that happened, I was still looking at the talkative goat with the strange face.

This is Bathin. He is one of the chief engineers of the Plenty Tunnel Project, which opened up the veins of the galaxy.

Huh, I thought, *what a strange description.*

ORREN: Carl. Donut. I am online with Prime Minister Victory. I need you to listen very carefully.

DONUT: HI, ORREN! HI, PRIME MINISTER VICTORY!

ORREN: I did not realize what was happening until it was too late. You have an amazing opportunity here. The people who are judging you are the leadership of the Plenty. If you are judged worthy, they will answer your questions. I need you to ask them about the integrity of the tunneling system. I will give you the exact question to ask.

CARL: Eat my ass, Orren.

PRIME MINISTER VICTORY: Carl. I am going to level with you. I think even you will understand the gravity of the situation. The current AI is spread well beyond this solar system. It killed an entire Mantis system, and it just blew up a group of Valtay-leased manufacturing facilities. We do not know how it is feeding itself. We do not know how it is doing any of this. Furthermore, certain mobs from the dungeon have gotten loose. They are appearing in places they shouldn't. This is more than an emergency. This is the end of life as we know it, and all of our attempts to communicate with the Plenty regarding this emergency have gone unanswered. They control the tunneling system. They are the only ones who can shut it all off. We hope.

CARL: Is *that* what Quasar was trying to tell me before he got cut off? Gods are getting loose? Is that the entity that's on the surface with Katia? The goddess Eileithyia?

ORREN: Yes, Carl. Though it's a different god in the *kinder* facility. A good portion of the unsponsored gods are roaming free. Right now it appears they can only manifest themselves within a relatively short range of the tunnel nodes, and not for long. To make matters worse, it appears the AI has no control over them. They are at cross-purposes. But even that shouldn't be possible. This is why it is crucial you ask the Plenty leadership the question I have prepared.

While this was happening, we moved to the next goat, who asked who took longer to prepare for battle each day, me or Donut.

CARL: What? The AI has lost control of them?

ORREN: You need to understand the AI is specifically programmed to be unable to manually interfere with the minds of gods and goddesses. It's a hard limitation. It was programmed to keep an insane AI from using the gods to kill everything. We had limited ability to temper that. It's the same system that allows us to use sponsors to drive gods. But that ability to control non-sponsored gods has been turned off. We normally use this ability quite liberally on the later floors due to the destructiveness of such powerful creatures. It's a checks-and-balances system that is now broken. And since the AI can't control them, either, the deities are acting independently.

Donut started yapping about her daily routine, though she was clearly distracted with one ear on this conversation.

CARL: Sure. I'll ask your question. But let me rephrase it.

ORREN: No, Carl. Please. Wait. You have to be careful with the way you say it.

I raised my finger when Donut was done.

Out loud, I said to the goat, "Here's my question. Does the public know that the gods have escaped from the dungeon? And that the enhancement zones of the current AI have jumped into your tunneling system? Do the people know they're in danger? Worse danger, perhaps, than us crawlers? Do they know that they need to fucking run?"

PRIME MINISTER VICTORY: Gods-fucking-damnit, Carl. You just said that on live. And the AI let it go out.

ORREN: And now the party really begins.

29

"WAIT, WHAT?" BOTIS ASKED, HIS DEMEANOR CHANGING ONCE AGAIN.

"It's true," Donut said. "They just told us in our messages. They said they've been trying to tell you all about it because you control the tunnels or whatever they're called, but you've been leaving them on read."

The line of goats all started to make braying noises. All the spotlights turned on at once, showing the caprids descending into panic. Across from me, the door back to the greenroom opened, and Lexis stepped into the studio, eyes huge.

"The Epicure," one of the goats said. "We shall manifest the Epicure."

"The True Judgment," another said. "She has fulfilled her bargain."

"Stampede," another shouted. "The great stampede comes."

"The beautiful place," said yet another, followed by a screaming bleat.

PRIME MINISTER VICTORY: Carl, that was reckless, even for you.

CARL: Please. You knew exactly what was going to happen when you asked me.

ORREN: You're not wrong. We knew it was a possibility. We had no other choice.

CARL: If the AI didn't want this getting out now, he wouldn't have allowed it. And based on the way these nutjobs are acting, it looks like you haven't been trying too hard to speak with them. They clearly didn't know.

PRIME MINISTER VICTORY: You don't understand anything, Carl.

CARL: I understand that you're as in the dark as I am. The only difference is I'm not pretending like I know what is happening.

One of the goats, Bathin with the jowly face, just started screaming. This wasn't like a Prepotente scream but a humanlike wail, and I couldn't tell if it was joyful or panicked. Two of the goats had fallen right off their chairs and were on their backs, stiff as boards, arms and legs raised in the air, almost like they were dead.

DONUT: YOU KNOW WHAT THIS REMINDS ME OF? THOSE CITY ELVES ON THE THIRD FLOOR WHEN THEY WERE LOOKING AT MY BUTT.
CARL: I was just thinking the same thing.
DONUT: THE MIDNIGHT EPICURE. ISN'T THAT THE GOD PREPOTENTE WORSHIPS?
CARL: Yes. And I have his patch on my jacket.
DONUT: AND ARE THEY EXCITED BECAUSE THEY THINK THE GOD IS REAL NOW? I'M SO CONFUSED.
CARL: Yeah . . . I have no clue.

We sat there as the goats, including Botis the host, continued to slide into panic.

I'd seen this before, but with real goats. When one freaked out, they all did. It would escalate and escalate until it came to a head, and they'd scatter.

One of the goats was not reacting. This was a female Harbinger-style goat still sitting on her chair, glaring at me. This was the one who'd cleared her throat when Bathin was explaining the Justice Light trap to me.

"It's my turn to judge you," she said once we met eyes.

LEXIS: Carl, Donut, just be aware that we are still live.
ZEV: What the heck is going on? I was too busy to watch, and now the entire board is lit up. Carl, what did you do?
DONUT: THIS WASN'T CARL'S FAULT. NOT THIS TIME.
LEXIS: It's a little bit his fault.
DONUT: WELL, IT'S ALWAYS A LITTLE BIT HIS FAULT.

I examined the goat glaring at me. This one was pretty evil-looking. Honestly, I couldn't tell these things apart, though this one wore a strangely ornate belt around her waist, cinching her robes.

This is Gamori. She was the lead engineer of the Plenty Tunnel Project and is the current Matriarch of the Plenty. In other words, she's the boss. She looks mad. Probably because she just got caught out not relaying vital information to the rest of her herd.

All around us, the other goats devolved into full-blown panic. Suddenly, as one, they all bolted to the left, stampeding out of the room and through the wall, their holos flickering as they disappeared. Botis ran right through us. And it wasn't just the ones who'd been sitting in a circle, but multiple other goats who'd been invisible until just that moment. These were techs and assistants, all scattering away, leaving Gamori and the two that had fainted on the floor as the only caprids in the room.

The goat spoke after a moment. Her strange eyes bored into mine.

"You are rash. You are impulsive. You are loud. You make sudden movements. You are a troublemaker. You startle us, and you attract attention. When we sponsored you, it was at the behest of our partner. I worried against it, but we thought perhaps it was for the best. I was waiting to respond to this new predator in the forest, to study its movements and its implications. Your declaration has removed the ability for thoughtful reaction. You have invoked a stampede, and we will not stop running until we are safe."

"None of those are questions," I said.

"No, they are not. This is judgment. I ask no questions of you. I do not consider you an enemy. But you are too dangerous to walk amongst the herd."

"Yeah?" I said. "Why are you even here if you didn't want this to come up?"

The goat jumped to her feet.

"How *dare you* ask questions of me when you weren't invited! How. Dare. You?"

"Well, that *was* a question, so I'll ask again. Clearly you guys aren't normally on this show. So why are you even here?"

She burst into tears.

"Now you've done it," Donut muttered.

The goat started making loud, snot-filled gasps as she went from a stoic leader to a blubbering mess. I hadn't realized this sort of reaction was a caprid-specific thing and not just a Prepotente thing.

She blubbered, literally shaking as she talked.

"We wanted to do something special for you because you're doing such a good job and you're best friends with our champion. And the council really wanted to meet Princess Donut because she's so wonderful and beautiful and sassy. The kids all love you both. I've been too scared to tell everyone about what's happening because I just knew they'd take it as a sign that the end-times are here. We can't startle my people with information like that, or they react. I was going to go slow. I didn't think." She started smacking herself in the head with her hand. "Stupid. Stupid. Stupid."

"Err," I said.

One of the two fainted goats jumped to his feet, looked about the room, let out a yelp, and promptly fainted again, arms and legs once again stiff.

I met eyes with Lexis as the goat continued to smack herself. Lexis mouthed, *What the fuck?*

"Okay," I said after a minute. "Stop. Just stop. Listen, I—"

Crack!

"Mother," a new voice said.

"Oh, fuck," I said, jumping out of my chair. I tried to step away, and I stumbled because of the damn suit.

Harbinger. The giant goat liaison had teleported into the room right behind me. He was really here, standing right behind us. I could smell the heavy, animal musk of his presence. The giant caprid had an enormous pulse rifle. He wasn't looking at me, but at Gamori, who stopped hitting herself and stared up at the newcomer.

Donut yowled in surprise and jumped to my shoulder, her claws out, digging dangerously into me.

"I told you of my suspicions," Harbinger rumbled. "I warned you what was going to happen. You did not listen. And now you have not prepared the herd for the truth."

"Did he just call her 'mother'?" Donut whispered.

"You have been judged unworthy of the herd. You have been expelled," Gamori hissed at Harbinger as she wiped her snotty nose and eyes on her own fur. "You *know* you can't be here. You *know* you can't speak to me."

"Yet I protect the herd, and you do not," he growled.

She pointed a finger at the goat. "You have no right. No right to even speak to me. Begone!"

I eyed the gun warily. I made a little hop backward. We were in the production facility, not the dungeon. I only had limited ability to respond. My tech shield would work, but I'd never seen that sort of pulse rifle before. It was huge. At this range, two or three shots would probably melt me.

The second fainting goat awakened, got to his feet, and bolted.

"I have sacrificed *everything* to protect the herd," Harbinger barked. The bass of his voice rattled my teeth. "The moment I saw how many Residuals were in the dungeon, the moment I learned how unstable the AI was, and how it favored this *predator*, I feared this exact thing would happen. I told you. I warned you. I warned you all. You didn't respond. Nobody helped me. I have been alone in this. I am so lonely. But I have not forgotten my duty, *Mother.* You asked me once why I didn't exert myself at the end of our circles. Exertion is supposed to be an expression of joy and of comfort. Well, Mother, I will exert myself now. I will protect the herd. I will protect the *universe.* I will do what should have been done from the very start."

He turned to me and raised the gun.

And that's when, finally, the AI intervened.

Harbinger exploded.

More accurately, everything on the inside of his goat body was suddenly on the outside of his goat body.

There was a sucking, sludgy sound, not loud. More like the sound of a stuck boot being yanked out of mud. Harbinger sprayed outward, the consistency of his innards like warm jam being sprayed out of an excited showerhead.

The gun clattered to the ground, splotching into the thick gore.

Nobody moved or said a thing for several moments.

Donut, Lexis, and I were just covered in dead goat.

The entire room was covered with the gore. It plopped and dripped from the ceiling in thick, hairy clumps. Donut started hacking.

The holo of Gamori lowered her head. "All stampedes have their casualties," she said sadly before she disappeared with a blink.

> **ZEV: Holy fucking shit. Did that really just happen? Is everyone okay?**

From my shoulder, Donut continued to hack.

Lexis's tablet was on the floor, and she had something in her hand. A gun. She hadn't fired it. She returned it to a hidden holster on her back. She slowly reached down and picked up the dropped computer. She shook it a few times, gore and blood spraying from it. She used her sleeve to clean the screen.

She'd gotten covered worse than we had. She looked as if she'd been dipped in a river of gore. She pressed a button.

Lexis looked up at us, smiling grimly, her teeth shockingly white against the carnage.

"The good news is," she said as liquefied innards dripped from her nose, "that the viewer ratings on this episode are the highest they've ever been."

30

All racers proceed to the starting line. Heat three starts in five minutes.

"YEAH, BITCH. YEAH, BITCH. I'M READY. LET'S DO THIS!" GLUTEUS MAXX shouted.

He was bouncing up and down, bellowing and revving the engine as he clapped his hands. He slammed the horn.

Make way for the big shot! Bawk!

"Can you not?" I said.

We'd picked the short, hairy stripper to drive this race because the kangaroo suit made it difficult for me to reach the pedals properly. Of all the strippers, he was the best at *Mario Kart.*

I could still taste the Harbinger guts. I'd been expecting Orren or Zev or even the AI to say something more, but we'd just teleported back to the garage, still covered in gore. We hadn't heard anything.

It seemed so stupid, us having to still do this bullshit while all that craziness happened outside the dungeon. I wondered if the gods leaking would cause people to stop watching and focus more on what was happening out there, but based on my stats, our views hadn't let up.

I inspected my furry kangaroo claws and sighed. At least the suit was clean-ish again.

All the occupants of the garage had just stared at us when we appeared, nobody asking what had happened. Mongo came up to me, sniffed, squeaked, and started furiously licking my leg before Donut shooed him away. We moved to the showers and cleaned all the gore off before we went back to work.

Now, several hours later, it was time to race. I examined Gluteus Maxx as he continued to vibrate with enthusiasm.

The hairy man had removed his gauntlets. He still wore his usual outfit, which was nothing except a Speedo, but he now wore a hockey helmet that he'd borrowed from the pile of discarded gear.

It was him driving, Donut in the passenger's seat—secured in her new "chair"—and me crouched down between the two. This position was difficult in the kangaroo suit. The two ghouls were lined up behind me in the back of the truck, both situated in their cages, their teeth chattering.

"What're you gonna do with that gun, you dragon bitch!" Gluteus shouted out the window at the APV next to us.

The Draconian mercenary sitting atop the APV for One Fine Pig said something I couldn't hear. The dragon-faced mercenary manned a massive heavy machine gun. I eyed the gun warily.

I marked the Draconian with two denial-of-service missiles and the gun itself with two more of the same. I'd fire them as soon as we were free.

They weren't our target for this one. I didn't want to kill the vehicle, but I wanted to keep them from trying to kill us and hopefully slow them down enough that we didn't have to worry about them.

I selected the four remaining missiles in my eight-pack launcher and programmed them.

By this point, all the teams would have shields. Direct attacks would likely do nothing. So we had to kill them in different ways. I just hoped these missiles worked as advertised. This was a Rosetta idea. It was a different recipe than what we had in the potion balls, but just as insidious.

Race starts in five minutes. Starting blocks loading.

That was told in the regular voice of the AI.

"Starting blocks?" I asked.

Dr. Metcalf beeped.

A new rule has been announced. Each team for this heat will be contained in a starting block shield that will provide invulnerability

to your vehicle for the first ninety seconds of this race. This will not affect controls.

"Shit," I said. "Dr. Metcalf, what sort of shield is it?"

How should I know? Have you upgraded me like I asked you to? I'd probably know if I was upgraded. But no. Instead, you let them pick that chair for your cat. It's almost like you don't care about me at all.

"What?" I asked.

The answer is no. I don't know.

"Shit," I said again. But then I thought this might actually be a good thing.

I started calculating how long the missiles would take to arc through the air. If I timed it properly, it'd keep the other teams from firing on us. Or each other. I could trust the bugbears and the razor foxes not to do anything too stupid, and the Lady Dominators were under the impression we were working together for this race, but we had to make sure both team Sparkles and One Fine Pig didn't go on a murder spree.

CHIYOME: Do we need to alter our plans?
CARL: It's okay. I think we're good.

Ahead, the asphalt track was straight and very wide. It had to be a hundred meters from side to side. It swept straight down like a ski ramp. On either side of the road was just lush green grass as far as I could see. A red alien sun crackled above. The temperature outside was nice and warm.

"My goodness," Donut said, struggling to peer out the windshield. "I think I can see the finish line from here. The road really is steep."

"Great observation, my precious princess," her new chair said.

"Thank you, Dorota," Donut replied.

The original voice was that of a creepy dude, but Donut had insisted it change to that of a woman "with a Polish accent." I had no idea why, and I didn't want to ask.

At first glance, the new chair on the passenger's side of the van was just a regular bucket seat. You couldn't tell there was anything different about it until Donut sat in it.

Apparently, this was a real product out in the universe. Rosetta said videos of these things had been going viral right before she'd come to Earth.

It was called a Smart Companion Royal Pet Throne. This was the Ultimate Diamond Pampered Pet Princess edition.

It was a pet chair designed for long road trips. It could be installed in cars, spaceships, boats, and more. It could be used by regular people, and nothing would happen, but the moment the chair's assigned "princess" sat upon it, a small, fluffy, rectangular bed appeared. The chair adjusted like a gyro, and it would supposedly keep her safe in case of an accident.

But the chair did a lot more than that, too. It also monitored her vitals and offered her "relief" when she was stressed. We still didn't know what that meant.

It also talked. The thing clearly wasn't a real intelligence like Dr. Metcalf. It was more like the robot Donut toys. It seemed its main goal was to keep Donut happy at all costs. It did that by agreeing with everything she said and randomly complimenting her.

I suspected it would quickly wear thin, but for now, Donut was pretty excited about it, especially when she discovered it could feed her snacks on demand.

I had no idea why she had named it Dorota. I did know that its very existence pissed off Dr. Metcalf.

"Your fur is quite luxurious today, Princess," the chair said. "Your enemies will quiver with envy."

Dr. Metcalf beeped.

Oh, do shut up.

"See what I mean?" the chair replied. "The jealousy runs deep on that one."

You want to know what's going to run deep? My virtual foot up your ass if you don't shut the fuck up.

"Stop fighting," Donut said. "The race is about to start!"

"Very diplomatic, my princess," Dorota said.

From behind, the two ghouls groaned.

Race starts in two minutes. Racers, start your engines or prime your mounts.

For this race, we were all lined up side by side with us on the end. To our immediate left was the large APV of team One Fine Pig. I couldn't see any of the teams past them from my position, but we were in the order we'd placed in the last race. So it was team Sparkles, then the Jugglers, then team Free Love, then the Wild Hunt, then the Lady Dominators, then One Fine Pig, and us at the end.

"We need to be quick, but we gotta be careful," I said to Gluteus. "That's gotta be a 30-degree angle. We go too fast, we're gonna flip."

"Yeah, we'll flip. We'll flip into victory," he said. "Man, I wish Steve was still with us. He'd love this shit. He wasn't a pussy. He'd want me to go even faster."

Even through the fur, I could see the veins on his arms bulging as he rocked back and forth.

Holy shit, this one is worse than the last one. Where'd you find these idiots?

"Actually, I don't think that is the finish line," Donut said, distracted, leaning in. She was using her zoom ability. "It's like a big blue-and-yellow dome. It's hard to tell at this angle."

Gluteus turned toward me, and that's when I noticed how red his eyes were.

Oh, fuck me.

"Gluteus, are you on something?"

He cackled and slammed the horn again. "Samantha found some outworlder uppers in that garbage pile from the snake guy. She said if one takes them before a race, one can taste time. It's what she's been taking to win at *Mario Kart*. And you know what? She's right. That's why I took two." He leaned in closer. "The space between each individual second tastes like cotton candy mixed with the sweat dripping off the tits of a randy high elf priestess. It's fucking delicious." He then howled like a goddamned dog.

Shit, shit, shit. We were at the line. It was too late to kick him out. We didn't have time to set up the Donut driving apparatus. I couldn't drive like this.

"Donut," I said, moving back, "get your *Laundry Day* spell ready! We don't have a goddamned choice. You have to get this suit off of me!"

"Carl, no! Mordecai said it could really hurt you, even kill you! Wait, do you feel that?"

The ground rumbled.

Dr. Metcalf beeped.

We will be sharing the track with migrating Sugar Hermits.

The truck rocked as a wave of wailing, colorful Samantha-sized creatures rushed past. They started to tumble down the road, rolling and clicking and screaming. There were literally thousands of them. Tens of thousands.

"What the heck are those things?" Donut asked. "They're like Imani heads! Why are they screaming?"

They were skulls. Dozens of types, all painted in festive colors, like Day of the Dead sugar skulls.

"Fuck yeah!" Gluteus shouted, revving the engine. "Let's do this!"

One of the skull things pinged off the roof and rolled down the windshield. This one was white with orange highlights. It was the skull of a goblin. The teeth were painted in alternating colors. A dozen little purple tentacles reached out from the interior, leaving a slime trail. The slime hovered a good inch off the windshield. The invulnerability shield had already activated.

Each tentacle had a little barb on the end. Next to us, the Draconian shouted, but it seemed he, too, was protected. Still, one of the sugar skulls had attached itself to his head. This was a bigger skull, like that of an ogre. The tentacles wrapped around the neck of the Draconian, giving him a bizarre appearance. It appeared the creature was trying to rip the mercenary's head off, but it gave up after a second and rolled away.

Despite being protected, the Draconian started shouting in panic. He went to his hands and knees and started banging on the roof of the APV to be let inside.

"Holy shit," I said as I examined one of the skulls.

Female Sugar Hermit. Level 11.

These horrific little terrors feed off of two things. Brains and bones. And they are *experts* at extracting both.

They wear skulls like a snail wears a shell. They are agile, and they are fast.

Still, I thought they were kinda boring-looking, so I gussied them up. Yeah, yeah, cultural appropriation, this and that. Suck it. They look freakin' badass!

The sugar hermits you see today are all female, and they are migrating. They're migrating toward the kaiju skull that blocks the finish line. Why? Because I fucking said so. They'll lay their eggs in it or some shit. It doesn't matter. Hopefully they won't get in your way. Or, worse, get their little tentacles wrapped around that prime real estate y'all are carrying around on your shoulders.

The good news is this race is only twenty minutes long.

"Yeeeaaa-fucking-haw!" Gluteus shouted.

31

<Entry from Donut's *A Banquet Fit for a Princess.*>

Luca Di. Crawler #10,284,471.

Race: Human.

Class: Pastamancer.

Final Level: 62.

You probably don't remember me, Princess, but I was one of the ones to give you my train hat on the fourth floor. You not only saved my life, but you saved the life of my mother, Giulia DiMarco, as well.

My mother and I never got along growing up. When she started to suffer from dementia, we placed her in a home. Guilt finally got the best of me, and I went to visit her on that day.

I felt as if I needed closure for all the terrible things she had done and said as I was growing up. I never got the chance, as we found ourselves in the dungeon soon after I'd wheeled her outside.

I protected her until we got to the third floor, where she took the only race that would save her mind, a Benevento, which is basically an elf-like witch creature. I don't know if you remember her, but she said you were beautiful.

With her mind repaired, I finally found the closure I was seeking.

I know you don't know what I'm talking about. Maybe one day, when all this is done, I can tell you the full story of myself and my mother. For now, I just want you to know I was able to talk to her again. I was able to tell her how I truly felt about some of the things she had done, and she was able to tell me some of why she was the way she was.

As terrible as this place is, I found forgiveness in the dungeon, and I found a peace I never would have been able to find if I'd simply unloaded my feelings on a dying woman who could no longer understand me.

My mother fell during the bubble level. But I will forever cherish those last few days I had with her.

And it's because of you and Carl that I got that.

I can't imagine what toll that *War Crime* spell took on you. But I want you to know it's okay to forgive yourself. Sometimes there are no good choices, and we just do what we have to.

You saved me, and by saving me, you also saved the memory of my mother and all those I have loved, and for that, I love you, Princess Donut. Even though you don't know me, I love you with all I have.

Keep up the good fight, and should you fall, I want you to know you will never be forgotten.

Drawing: A bent tube of pasta.

Associated Spell: *Temporary Macaroni*. Casts at level 14.

THE LIGHT TURNED GREEN, GLUTEUS HIT THE ACCELERATOR, TIRES squealed, and we were off.

We had twenty minutes to go thirty kilometers.

I fell backward, my back smashing into the closer of the two ghoul cages. The ghoul within shout-groaned as the truck started to buck and bounce.

Crunch, crunch, crunch, crunch.

We shook heavily as we plowed over and through the rushing sugar skulls. We quickly outpaced them.

The engine roared, the gauges maxed out, and we kept accelerating. The entire truck started to shimmy.

If Gluteus so much as tweaked that steering wheel, we were going to flip.

"Keep it steady!" I yelled.

"You know it, baby! Like fucking a needle! Faster! Faster!"

"Dr. Metcalf," I bellowed as I pulled myself into a standing position, "shout when the invulnerability is about to run out!"

"And play some fucking music!" Gluteus hollered. He leaned forward so his chest was pressed against the steering wheel.

"Slow down!" Donut shrieked. "Gluteus, you're going too fast!"

"Mayhaps you'd like a calming massage, my princess?" Dorota asked.

"Not now, Dorota!"

You know what? I do think we need music. This feels like an appropriate song. Anything to shut that chair up.

Some Halloween-sounding techno heavy metal song started to blast. I'd definitely heard it before, but I couldn't remember the title. It was a car-racing song about witches and ditches.

Gluteus started pounding the dash with his hairy hand. Donut shouted something as we bounced up and down.

"Shut that off!" I yelled, but nobody could hear me. We didn't have time. I turned toward the back of the truck to prepare the cages.

DONUT: HOW IS THIS EVEN PLAYING? WHERE ARE THE SPEAKERS?

"Okay, guys," I shouted at the two ghouls. They looked at me blankly, likely unable to hear me over the music. One had his hands over his ears. "We're doing this!"

I grabbed the first lever we'd built into the floor of the truck, and I yanked. The back door burst open as the first cage popped out, suspended over the road on a reinforced beam like a fishing pole. I pulled the chain on the ceiling, which swung the beam toward the driver's side of the truck, moving the cage so it hung outside over open road, just behind, shaking and dangling like a lantern. I quickly secured the chain on the embedded hook. I shoved the second cage, and it glided smoothly out. I pulled this second chain, and the arm pivoted, swinging the second cage out to the opposite side. I secured the chain, locking it all in place.

I rushed back and slid out the door stabilizer, which kept the back door from swinging back and forth.

Both ghouls were now suspended in cages that dangled on either side of the truck, making it look like we had wings. The ghouls within dropped the front trapdoors, which would allow them to lean out and toss their potion balls. I could yank on a third chain, which would raise the driver's-side cage like it was on a crane, bringing it up higher than the height of the truck.

This whole pulley-and-lever system was an engineering marvel cobbled together by Hedy, and it allowed for the deployment and quick retraction of the twin defensive positions while not changing the integrity of the truck itself. The entire system was secured inside the kitchen.

With that done, we still had a good forty seconds left on the invulnerability.

We'd left One Fine Pig far behind, but the Lady Dominators' car was right there, zooming up behind us. Team Free Love's van was also bouncing along behind the Dominator team. Both the armored dog and the bear were way back there, as far back as One Fine Pig. If they didn't get free soon, they'd both get taken out by the little monsters.

I couldn't see team Sparkles anywhere. I leaned out the back, straining, but there was no sign of them.

I started to shout, but nobody could hear me.

CARL: Do you see team Sparkles?

DONUT: THEY'RE WAY AHEAD. THEY HAVE SOME SORT OF ROCKET THING ON THE BACK OF THEIR STUPID TUMBLEWEED, AND THEY'RE ROLLING. WE'RE IN SECOND PLACE!

"Shit," I grumbled. I pulled the eight-pack launcher from my inventory, aimed it straight up in the air, and I fired out the back of the zooming truck. *Thwum, thwum, thwum, thwum.* The eight missiles spiraled off one by one. Four moved toward the heavily armored One Fine Pig, and four moved toward team Sparkles.

We still had thirty seconds, but that was okay. The missiles weren't designed to explode.

I caught sight of Rapture in the passenger's seat of their muscle car. She flashed a pair of devil horns. I moved to the front of the truck.

The music abruptly stopped before the song finished.

Invulnerability is about to time out, and the next wave comes.

Above, the rockets corkscrewed down toward the distant unicorn team. A new shield appeared about them, this one glowing purple.

Bang! Bang! Bang! Three of the four rockets slammed into the bush, which immediately veered off to the side and started spinning in panicked circles.

The Denial of Service missiles weren't meant to kill the vehicles directly. Each impact caused a chemical reaction that triggered a thick mucous membrane to form over a wide area. In this case, the three missiles utterly covered the round shield with a thick goo, making it so they couldn't see. They were now encased in the green slime. They could turn off the shield, but the sludge would just fall upon them and get stuck in the vines, which Mordecai insisted would slow them to a crawl.

Invulnerability has timed out.

"Casting *Shield*!" Donut shouted.

DONUT: IT SAYS THE SHIELD DOESN'T COVER THE TWO GHOULS OUTSIDE THE TRUCK!
CARL: Okay. We thought that might happen. Stick to the plan.

"Oh, fuck!" Gluteus shouted. "Would you look at that!"

Up ahead, two literal waves of skulls appeared out of nowhere, coming from both sides of the road, zooming toward the track like twin tsunamis. Each wave was about twenty feet tall. In a few seconds, we were going to be buried in the sugar hermits. The wave on the right side was much closer and would reach us first. I quickly returned to the back of the truck.

"Ghouls, get ready!" I yelled. "You," I shouted, pointing to the ghoul dangling off on the driver's side. I pointed upward.

I yanked the chain, raising him up in the air. The ghoul would have to open the cage all the way and climb to the roof of the truck. There he'd move forward to deal with the enemies coming from the front. But it would take him a few moments to get in place.

I returned to the back door as the other ghoul started hurling his potion balls at the approaching waves of colorful skulls.

This was a potion similar to the Denial of Service missiles, but much thicker. These were called Biscuit Packs. Each potion ball caused a round-ish foam-filled explosion about three meters in diameter that hardened in seconds. It was the same basic principle as the polyurethane expanding foam they used in construction and boat repair, but this stuff hardened instantly and had the consistency of rock once toughened.

The ghoul hurled the potion balls one after another at the rapidly approaching wave.

Each explosion made a loud *pop* as it hit the ground or one of the skulls, and the results were instantaneous. It'd explode and poof out, popcorn-like, snagging dozens of them at a time while also creating a barrier. The ball would then either veer off the road or start to roll alongside us. The screams from the sugar hermits went up in pitch, even louder than the engine, as the little tentacles reached out from the giant foam balls.

We hadn't known what sort of mobs we'd be facing. This was the best solution we could come up with that would be effective with the widest possibility of enemies. It wasn't perfect and plenty were getting through and around the foam balls, but it was keeping us from getting overwhelmed. For now.

We passed team Sparkles, who were all the way on the other side of the wide road. The slime-covered vine floundered.

We didn't have time to celebrate.

"Hold on!" Gluteus shouted as the skulls flooded the streets ahead of us. They were hitting the asphalt and immediately turning toward the finish line, leaving an increasingly narrow path ahead. The ghouls were doing an admirable job, but we were quickly losing ground.

Donut leaned forward and cast her level 15 *Wall of Fire*, which had been powered up to level 16.

On the passenger's side of the truck, a line of flames materialized. A wave of heat radiated over us.

"Whoa, shit!" I shouted as the wall appeared, running parallel with the side of the truck. There was a good thirty feet between us and the flames, but it still felt like we were way too close. I gawked as the wall rapidly raced ahead, reaching far into the distance. The flames went straight up, easily a hundred feet into the air. The line had to be a mile long.

"Heavy fucking metal!" Gluteus screamed.

32

"I KILLED MORE THAN TEN THOUSAND OF THEM!" DONUT SHOUTED. "I didn't even go up a level! This is an outrage!"

I just breathed for a second as we continued to rush down the road. *Okay, okay, this isn't over yet.*

Ahead, I got a better view of the massive colorful skull thing at the bottom of the long hill. At first, I thought it was a whale skull, but I realized that it wasn't. It was the head of a giant beetle thing. Like the skull or husk of a Hercules beetle, though this thing appeared to be the height of a three-story building just blocking the road.

An info box popped up.

> **This is the skull of Tem, who up until a few days ago resided within the Nothing. We borrowed different parts of his corpse for different races because he was really badass-looking. It's too bad your friend Odette wasted him the moment he appeared. But, alas, waste not, want not. Still, you might just want to take note of the size of this thing. He has friends who are still alive.**

An explosion echoed behind us. I didn't know what that was.

CARL: Update?

JASHA: We're almost through the chop! The shield is keeping the fuckers back. You got the Dominators on your ass, and we're right behind!

CHIYOME: We are in trouble. We can't see. They are everywhere. Your missiles detonated too early over the Fine Pigs, and the goo

went all over the place, including over Onikuma. I do not know where the Jugglers are, but they are back with us. I think maybe behind us. The road is too steep for Oni. He keeps stumbling.

CARL: Move to the right side. We'll toss the tunnels if a third wave comes!

We continued to rocket down the road for a good minute without anything happening other than Gluteus bouncing up and down in his chair, shouting for more music.

"No music!" I yelled. "I need to be able to hear!"

"What's the point of speeding if we can't do it to heavy metal, you fucking poser?" The man was absolutely vibrating, shaking in the chair.

"Gluteus, why are you talking like a mantaur?" Donut demanded.

"Because I am made of speed and the sun and I am one with the universe, baby!" He started howling again. White foam had started to form on his fuzzy lips.

"Just keep your eyes on the goddamned road!" I growled.

I returned to the back of the truck and peered outside. The ghoul in the cage on the passenger's side remained, glaring out at the GTO, which had pulled up directly behind us, tailgating. The Free Love van also trailed us, maybe ten seconds back. And beyond that, nothing but smoke from the now-distant but still-raging wall of fire.

Wave three is commencing.

"Fucking hell!" Gluteus shouted while laughing maniacally. He started to slap the side of his own face, suddenly reminding me of the caprid leader. He was getting worse by the second. More foam drooled out of his mouth, and it splattered everywhere as he yelled. "They're coming up through the road! Get ready for some crunchy, lumpy speed bumps!"

Well, fuck us all, I guess. The final wave is commencing, too.

And that's when the skulls started raining from the sky.

I watched as multiples of the sugar hermits started crashing into and around the shield of the GTO as divots started to form on the asphalt.

We lurched again, gaining air before crashing down as the colorful skulls started exploding all around us. They weren't just falling from the sky. It was like they were being shot downward out of a cannon. None seemed to actually survive the fall, instead exploding like hail all around us.

"We're getting close!" Donut shouted. "Just a few minutes, and we'll be there!"

I heard a hissing scream from the passenger's side of the truck, quickly followed by a notification.

Warning: One of your hired mercenaries has died! Well, died again, as he was a ghoul.

"The shield is down!" Donut yelled. She let out a yelp as we bumped. Behind, I had a clear view of Rapture as she fired her flamethrower directly into the air above their car as skulls pelted and exploded against their shield. Dark ichor sprayed with each explosion.

The truck lurched again, and we swerved dangerously.

"Slow down," I shouted. "We're going too fast for a bumpy road! Donut, macaroni!"

Our windshield shattered. Wind filled the truck, almost blowing me back. The purple guts of sugar hermits misted into the cabin as little pieces of skull peppered us like shrapnel.

"Donut," I croaked.

Donut, who'd just received the spell from her *Banquet Fit for a Princess* book, cast *Temporary Macaroni.*

Ahead, an absolutely *massive* chunk of pasta appeared. The oblong tube had to be fifteen feet tall and twenty feet wide. I wasn't sure how long it was, but it appeared in front of us like the opening of a highway tunnel. The spell cast at level 14 but was enhanced to 15. At that level, Donut could choose the size, shape, and direction of the giant tube of pasta. She chose uncooked, dried cannelloni. The spell only cost ten mana to cast, and she could chain it, which is what she did now, creating a tunnel of giant tubes.

The pasta was at least a foot thick, making it pretty strong. Strong enough to keep from breaking when the skulls rained on it, and strong enough to block the ones coming up from the ground. I hoped.

"I'm sliding in!" Gluteus foamed. We bumped heavily into the tube. Ahead, another tunnel appeared, then another. Donut was rigid as she focused straight ahead, chaining the spell. Still, there was space between each giant tube, and in those breaks, the sugar hermits surged.

A skull was suddenly in the cab, having come in through the missing windshield, and I punched it with my gauntlet. It exploded, but when I pulled my fist back, the purple thing living inside the skull was still attached to the gauntlet. It started to slither, octopus-like, around the metal fist, moving toward my arm. I cast *Bang Bro*, which electrified the weapon, and the creature dropped off, dead and sizzling.

JASHA: I see the tunnel! Going in now! Dominators are following you, and we'll be right behind!

CARL: Chiyome, make sure you veer to the far-right side of the track, or you might miss it!

Warning: You may not message deceased NPCs.

The Wild Hunt have been eliminated due to the death of all team members. Six teams remain in the current heat.

"Oh, fuck!" I cried. More of the skulls attacked, and I smashed them all. Above, I could hear the ghoul struggling. I smashed another skull.

The Scavenger's Daughter has been fed. Unleash her wrath.

Shit. I'd need to activate it before we finished, or I'd be stuck with it for however long it took until the next race.

The Jugglers have been eliminated due to the death of all team members. Five teams remain in the current heat.

"No, no, no," I said, turning to look behind me, as if I could actually see them. The Lady Dominators remained right on our ass. *Goddamnit.*

There was another thump from the roof. I reached up to grab the ghoul's legs to drag him back inside, but when I pulled, his head didn't come with him. A skull thing chittered happily from the roof as it jumped off, the ghoul's head in tow.

Warning: Another one of your hired mercenaries has died! I hope you offer workman's comp.

"Almost there!" Donut shouted. "Recasting *Shield*— Ahhh!"

The large skull of some orc-like creature crashed through the front and wrapped itself around Donut's face like one of those facehuggers from the *Alien* movies. Before anyone could react, multiple arms appeared from the car seat and violently ripped the thing off of her. The skull and creature within were torn to shreds.

"Thank you, Dorota," Donut sputtered.

Ahead, the end of the tunnel loomed. All I could see was the blue of the beetle-skull thing. Already, it teemed with sugar hermits who didn't appear to know what to do now that they'd finally reached their target. They swarmed over it like fleas on a dog.

My foot buff had run out, so my feet weren't protected. Still . . .

"Donut, forget the magic missile! Tighten the shield around yourself and Gluteus. Everyone, hold on!"

The truck lurched as it veered, and the now-empty passenger's-side cage clipped the edge of the pasta wall. The whole truck wobbled ominously as we exited the last pasta tube.

"Hold it steady!" I shouted, turning to Gluteus, only to see him unconscious and slumped against the wheel, a line of foam dripping from his mouth. Ahead, the skull, followed by the finish line, loomed.

"Fuck!"

I didn't think. I reached over and grabbed the steering wheel. There was a chime. "Donut, hit the accelerator and don't let go!"

Donut again struggled to get out of the car seat, but it held her tight. She didn't hesitate. She used her claws and ripped free, shredding the belt. She jumped down between the legs of the unconscious Gluteus. She slammed her paws on the accelerator. This was followed by a second chime.

The GTO's engine roared as they emerged from the tunnel behind us. They surged forward, moving to our right, hugging the edge of the road as they started to pass.

With one hand still on the steering wheel, I pulled myself out the windshield and lay across the hood of the truck on my back, feet hanging off the front just in front of the headlamps. I reached over my shoulders and awkwardly held on to the steering wheel with my second hand.

"What are you doing?" Donut yelled.

I activated Daughter's Kiss. I tensed, intent on ramming the kaiju skull with my giant feet.

"Fuck youuuu!" came a new shout, just as we were about to make contact. The shout was so loud, I could hear it over the roar of the engines.

It was Dwight the unicorn, zooming up from our left, giant cannon hanging out the side of their speeding slime-covered vine.

I ripped the steering wheel to the left just as they fired. The food truck flipped as the cannon blast tore through the side of the truck, causing the tail end to whip to the right as we spun like a badly tossed football, still-deployed cages whisking about. My feet came in contact with the kaiju skull, which exploded as we rapidly spun, continuing to rise in the air as our back end clipped against the GTO, which had also been hit by the cannon blast. And then the front of the rapidly deteriorating food truck also hit the vine, which likewise flew up into the air.

All three of our spinning airborne vehicles careened over the finish line at the same time. I let go of the steering wheel as the truck spun over my head. All three of the Dominators were thrown from their vehicle as they passed over the finish line.

I hit the ground hard and slid as flaming, crunching metal rained all around me. I screamed as my kangaroo skin flayed off. My health scroll contingency activated as I continued to roll.

I slammed into something hard, coming to an abrupt stop. I'd hit the groaning form of one of the womantaurs. Corky, still unconscious, also came to a rest next to me.

There was an enormous crunch of fiberglass and metal and glass as the main body of the food truck landed on its back and spun off to my left.

Tater tots and French fries and chicken patties were everywhere. I just stared, dumbfounded, as a frozen chicken patty spun like a coin on the road before stopping still miraculously balanced on its side like in a magic trick.

The GTO was a flaming, crumpled mess. The vine had tumbled to a stop near me, and it was on fire. My kangaroo feet were literally on fire. Despite the healing scroll, both of my arms were broken. Both my legs were broken. Things inside of me were crushed. I took a Fine Healing potion, waited a second, and then took another.

Team Free Love's van screeched to a stop, and Jasha and Radoslav jumped out, rushing to the food truck.

"Donut," I croaked, pulling myself up. My pelvis was broken, and I tried to stand before it had fully healed. I pulled myself up a second time, tried to walk, and fell over because of the damn kangaroo feet.

But then Donut was there, unhurt, jumping around me as she patted at my smoldering feet. "Carl, Carl, are you okay? Are you okay? You crashed the truck! Your feet are on fire!"

Jasha pulled the still-unconscious Gluteus from the wreckage. Corky lay in a heap next to me. There was a tear in his suit, and some guts oozed out, but he was still alive. Rapture was standing over Genesis, who was folded over herself in an unnatural pose. She administered a healing potion to her partner.

If this had been a crash outside the dungeon, we'd all have been dead right now. We'd have been splattered all over the place.

"That's what you get! That's what you get!" Dwight shouted.

"Yeah, fuck you, swine!" Lucienne added from his back.

They both appeared mostly unhurt, and they remained in their vine. Lucienne's little helmet was cracked, and the vine itself smoldered like there was fire within it.

Dwight's unicorn horn sparkled. "Yeah, cry. I want to see you cry. You motherfuckers are all dead next race. You hear me? Fucking dead. We're gonna shoot you motherfuckers first."

"Fucking dead," Lucienne added. "And you owe me a new helmet!"

The vine, trailing smoke, started to limp toward a garage.

Jasha padded up. "What an ending. We lost two teams so far, but I'm not sure if . . ."

Team One Fine Pig's APV rumbled over the finish line. There was no sign of the Draconian mercenary who'd been on the roof.

". . . Yeah, I guess that's it," Jasha finished. "Bad news about the razor foxes. I liked her even though she was trying to get us to kill you next race. Looks like we'll have a new competitor joining the neighborhood."

I groaned again and tried to stand. Our truck was literally spread all over the road. Though the GTO was in worse shape.

"Carl, I don't even know what place we came in," Donut said. "We all crossed the finish line at the same time!"

I turned to watch the unicorn team enter the garage with a big "2" painted on the door. A moment later, the doors to both the "1" and "3" garages opened. Groups of gremlins dragging carts and wheelbarrows rushed out of both, headed in our direction.

I grinned.

A set of figures stood in the open garage of house number one. It was Jamal, Dong, and Hedy. Jamal started hopping up and down at the sight of us, waving his mechanical front legs excitedly.

HEAT THREE. RESULTS.

First Place: The Royal Court of Princess Donut.

Second Place: Team Sparkles.

Third Place: Lady Dominators and the Gimp.

Fourth Place: Team Free Love.

Fifth Place: One Fine Pig.

Sixth Place: <Empty> A replacement team will be assigned soon.

Eliminated:

The Wild Hunt.

The Jugglers.

HEAT 4 OF 7

33

"WE BOTH DROVE," I SAID TO DONUT AS WE LIMPED BACK TO THE GA-rage. My shredded kangaroo suit only had two hours left, which meant I could soon ditch it, but I still had to do little hops. We didn't get teleported inside like we had after the first race, which was weirdly inconsistent. "That means neither of us can so much as touch the controls for the next race. We'll need someone reliable to drive."

Donut huffed. "I didn't drive! All I did was touch the pedals! That doesn't count."

"It does count," I said.

I eyed the house with the number 6 painted on the door. We wouldn't find out who our new opponent was until just before the next race. I hoped it would be another NPC team, though I knew, realistically, that the odds were against us. I sighed. *One problem at a time.* At least we'd come in first place.

"Those poor foxes," Donut said. "I never even knew the creepy Juggler people, but the fox ninjas were starting to grow on me."

"I will drive next race," Dong announced, looking over his shoulder. He and Bucket Boy had the groaning Gluteus Maxx strung out between them. Dong had rushed down to the scene of the wreck to try to talk to Corky, but Rapture and Genesis had scooped him up and gone straight to their garage, pushing Dong aside without saying a word to him.

"We'll talk about it," I said.

"What is there to discuss?" Dong asked. "I am . . ."

He paused at the sound of a commotion at the finish line behind us.

We all stopped and turned as two giant figures walked over the finish line. It was Onikuma the bear mount for the dead razor foxes and Old Shuck, the giant dog from the Juggler team.

"What the . . . ?" I asked before both of the biological mounts blinked and disappeared.

"Carl, I thought they were dead!" Donut exclaimed. "Why is the stupid dog still alive?"

"I guess if the riders die but not the mount, the mount is saved. It makes sense. Sort of, I guess."

"But where did they go?"

I shrugged. "It doesn't matter. Not here."

Donut harrumphed.

A grumbling gremlin, pushing a wreckage-filled wheelbarrow much too big for it, passed us. From the smoking debris within, Dr. Metcalf beeped.

Would you look at this? I'm a shattered husk. Shocker.

"Dr. Metcalf!" Donut exclaimed, waving at the wheelbarrow. The gremlin grunted with annoyance as we sped up to keep pace with him. "We thought you were broken into a million pieces!"

I could only be so lucky.

"At least we won," Donut said.

The GPS took on a mocking tone. **At least we won.**

Donut huffed indignantly. "You really must make an effort to be nicer to the team. We're doing our best."

Anyway, the GPS unit beeped, **we have limited details on the next race. And since neither of you can drive in this next one, I just can't wait to see who you pick. We already had a prepubescent wuss of a crocodile and a drug-addled knockoff Sasquatch. What's next? Maybe the sex-doll head? The dinosaur?**

Even though we were just walking and not in the truck, an info box popped up, which was really strange.

Distance: ~99 kilometers.

Note: There will be a single mandatory refueling pit stop along this route. Pit stop will be within the lost jungle city of Upano.

Track: The You're Gonna Die If You Go in Here Jungle Trail of Tremendous Cannibalistic Slaughter. There are a variety of surfaces available. Ain't none of them will be paved. At least not with asphalt.

Tasks required to complete: Certain paths may have a unique task.

Special Rules: Your vehicle will have a special containment unit surrounding you for this race. More info on that coming soon. You will also share this track with three other heats. Special rules regarding this will be announced soon. Base rules will still apply.

Environment: It'll be a jungle filled with horrifying traps and monsters and vaguely racist and definitely overexaggerated themes based on grind house and exploitation cinema, but with racing added to the mix. There'll be acid rain, too.

Hazards: The whole damn track is a hazard.

Time Limit: 20 hours.

Next race starts in 7 hours and 3 minutes.

"Only seven hours," I said. "The time between races is getting shorter."

A few spots over, Jasha and Radoslav were already setting up their lawn chairs and beer cooler. They both gave us a wave.

"I don't think you broke the truck into enough pieces," Hedy said as we approached. "At least we can get some catch-up upgrades. And don't forget, we all get a bonus Golden upgrade after the next race, too. That's in addition to the regular prize for heat four. So you gotta make sure you win the next one, too."

"Will the pig team get an audience vote, or will they get to pick?" Donut asked. "They came in last place, but we lost two teams."

"That's a good question," Hedy said. "Don't know. I think it's still an audience vote, but I ain't sure."

"It's an audience vote," I said, remembering some of the chatter on the messaging system. "The last surviving team always gets an audience vote, no matter how many other teams were taken out."

"We ain't gotta worry about that right now," Hedy said as she flipped through her tablet. "We needs to figure out how we're updating *your* truck. You can either choose one Golden upgrade or three regulars. Been looking at the info for the next race, and we gots a few choices."

I nodded. "In a second."

I hopped to the wall and leaned against it, just spending a moment to let my heart stop beating so fast. Donut, I noticed, was basically doing the same thing. She'd called Mongo to her and jumped on his back. She was stroking his feathers with her right front paw, just staring off into space. I knew she was checking in on everyone and wouldn't be fully focused until she knew everybody was safe.

People were finally starting to check in. Imani and Elle had come in second place, but they'd lost another two teams, including the one crawler team that had joined them this race. Florin and Lucia had come in first, but they'd lost three teams. Prepotente and Jurgen had also won, and they hadn't lost any teams. Chris's big rig had come in third place.

Louis, Britney, and Bautista had survived, but they were the last of the survivors again, meaning they'd get an audience vote. Their replacement team had been another group of NPCs, and they'd taken them out right at the beginning. Louis's team was in trouble, as they still didn't have proper tires.

Zhang said they had won again, but the only remaining teams were fellow crawlers, including a fire truck driven by a crawler named Sammi Harrison, an isopod summoner who'd been instrumental in keeping the FUPA safe during Faction Wars. Some people called her "the decapitator," but I didn't know why. Zhang was afraid she and the other teams were conspiring against them.

Everyone's races were all different the next race, though it sounded like Imani and Elle's team would be on the same track as us, which worried me. Prepotente's and Louis's teams both appeared to be on the same track as each other as well, which was described as "Satan's Water Park."

I closed my eyes for a second, pretending I was alone. It didn't work. My chat was constantly moving. Loud clanging and drilling filled the garage.

ROSETTA: Tipid and I are already in town at the mercenary market. Need anything in particular?

CARL: A driver and defense. Fast reflexes. We'll need at least two who can drive since neither Donut nor I can next race. Nobody too crazy.

ROSETTA: Prices will be double because you lost the last two mercenaries we hired.

CARL: It's okay. Just get the best you can.

I opened my eyes to find Hedy glaring.

"You just gonna laze about? You want me to pick for you, kangaroo boy?"

I sighed and peeled myself off the wall. The truck was already half built. A group of gremlins was shoving the freezer unit into the back.

"Okay, hit me," I said. "What are your suggestions?"

34

"YOU'VE BEEN EXFOLIATED," DONUT SAID, PEERING AT MY BARE LEG AS I worked on my foot routine, resetting my buff. "I must say, as smelly as that disgusting costume was, it did wonders for your complexion." She made a little pained noise. "Not so rough, Jamal! My goodness. I am not a mud-soaked golden retriever. I require a delicate touch!"

"I am piling up my apologies to you, Miss Donut," Jamal said. "It is not Jamal's intention to add any hair-pulling distress."

"You're not hacking down a tree. Gentle but firm!"

We were both getting inexpertly brushed by Jamal, who was practicing with the new grabbers on his front legs, as designed by Mordecai. It made him appear even more terrifying, as his front spider legs now looked like they had hands. He had one brush in each hand, one on Donut and the second, screaming brush on me, both of which gave us our daily buffs. Rend and Mongo were out in the pet stable "playing" with Gonk and Simoom.

Samantha sat on the new kitchen table, peering carefully at my skin. "Do you think kangaroo blood is good skin treatment?" she asked. "Donut, maybe for your next skin-care product you can do something like that. It will require some experimenting. Do you want me to start gathering some baby animals to test upon?"

"What I want you to do," I said, "is not give drugs to the NPCs. We almost died because of that."

"Hey, that wasn't my fault," she said. "I just told him about the stuff. He took it on his own. He took too much." She raised her voice. "And now he owes me money."

Gluteus was sitting sheepishly on the couch, getting fed soup by Splash Zone as he recovered from his overdose.

Donut huffed. "We will not be testing my new makeup line on baby animals. At least not publicly. Ow! Jamal!"

"It is most difficult to get through such mats, Miss Donut. Carl's hair is more silky and easier to brush than yours, I fear."

I suppressed a laugh. "Yeah, wrong thing to say, buddy."

"Mats? Did you say I have mats? I have never had a mat in my entire life! I wish Sledgie was here. He had the perfect touch!"

Thankfully both of our blood bars had refilled, so we weren't in too much of a rush. As soon as we were done, Donut and I were going to meet up with the others as we checked out this Chicken and Waffles place. And then after that, we would head back to the Lollipop karaoke bar to try to find the entrance to the entertainers' guild.

"I do not know why I am being shut out from this process," Dong said from the couch. He sat next to Splash Zone and Gluteus as Doctor Bones and some sluggalos played one of the *Need for Speed* games. The sluggalos were completely off course.

"Because the other Corcunda doesn't like you," Donut said. "We'll butter him up first."

Splash Zone grunted. "I hope you have a lot of butter."

The door opened, and Tipid and Rosetta entered, followed by three mercenaries who looked about the room with wide-eyed wonder. They were a level 75 female Grulke frog, a level 96 flaming fire fairy who was about Donut's size, and one of those badger guys who were usually bartenders. A Porsuk. That one was level 81.

We all stared at the newcomers.

"Carl, Donut," Rosetta said, "I'd like to introduce you to team Helix. They are a three-for-one mercenary squad. They've been working together for some time, and they have raced already in two heats, coming in first and second."

"The time we came in second doesn't count," the Grulke said, crossing her arms. Her name was Olga. "That demon with the chains was cheating. Killed one of the two clients and killed our friend Helado. Would've killed the rest of us, too, if her partner hadn't stopped her. Finley got a scratch in on her, though."

"You remind me of my ex," Samantha said, rolling up to the Porsuk. "He could do magical things with his claws."

The badger was the one named Finley. He looked down at Samantha with disdain. His claws glowed green with enchantment, which implied some sort of poison-based charm. "Yeah, I can do magical things with my claws, too." He grinned. "Want to see?"

"Ooh, yes. I really do. Want to step into my room and show me?" She rolled onto her head and started wiggling her neck up at him.

The badger's grin faltered. "Wait, really?"

"Rawr," Samantha said. She rolled over and then started wetly sucking on his ankle.

"What is happening right now?" the badger asked.

"Samantha, you don't have a room," Donut said. "And get off his leg. Welcome, everyone. We need to step out. We'll have you come with us so we can get to know you better."

Samantha removed herself from Finley's ankle. "I do too have a room. I've redecorated it and everything. It used to be Carl's room, but he never goes in it because he spends all his time in the bathroom."

"It's pretty sick," one of the sluggalos said from the controller. "The new wallpaper is badass."

"Wait, what?" I asked. "Wallpaper?"

The fire fairy hadn't taken her eyes off the back of the room. Her name was Quemada. When she spoke, she had a thick Spanish accent.

She also worshipped Emberus. She was looking at the bubbling Emberus shrine. She turned her attention to me.

"I've changed my mind," she said. "It's not double the price. It's triple the price."

"We've already negotiated," Rosetta said. "We paid the price to the mercenary guild. You can't increase the price after the fact."

"It's triple the price, or we walk."

Rosetta opened her mouth to object, but I raised my hand. "Did you guys drive during the last races?"

"Both Finley and Olga can drive. I am protection," Quemada said.

I spent a moment just looking at the fairy, thinking. "We'll pay the price."

35

"MY FRIEND MORDECAI WAS ONCE A FROG CREATURE LIKE YOU," DONUT said as we entered Hungry Eyes Village. "He did this annoying croaking thing a lot, but you got used to it. You don't croak so much. He was really good at picking things up with his tongue."

"I'm a toad, not a frog," Olga said.

"Isn't that like the same thing? My other friend Prepotente said that while frogs and toads can't have babies with each other and they look a little different, that toads are biologically the same despite what they teach humans in school. You'll meet him in a minute. He says people have a lot of their facts wrong. Like blood in veins isn't really blue that just turns red when it hits oxygen or that frequent self-abuse makes you blind. Carl's vision has always been 20/20. It used to make Miss Beatrice jealous because she had to wear contact lenses." She paused. "Then again, she did have that drawer that was *not* filled with cat toys, if you know what I'm saying."

"What are you talking about?" Olga asked.

I was struck by how much emptier the streets seemed. The street vendors were all still about, but the number of racers walking around had clearly thinned.

I caught sight of Elle, Imani, Florin, and the others standing near the end of the street with the restaurants and the temples. Prepotente was there, too, but Jurgen wasn't. Donut waved furiously, and we started walking toward them.

"I had a vision from our lord," Quemada the fairy whispered to me as we passed the temple that led to Club Vanquisher. The fairy's presence was hot on my shoulder and ear. Her wings were made of smoke. "He told me if I came across a fellow worshipper who was also a racer that I was to help him in any way I could. We have been tasked with slaying his brother. An impossible mission yet one we must strive to complete."

I gave the fairy a sidelong glance. She was much smaller than Elle but larger than most of the regular fairies we came across. "If you're so gung ho on helping, then why'd you raise the price?"

"Because I know we will be slain when we attempt to kill Hellik, and the fee will help keep Olga and Finley safe for some time. These races are much more dangerous with each heat. And since you can't hire me more than once, we will need to make our attempt now, while we can. That fee will allow them to take a break, and perhaps they will survive this current challenge. I have already lost one friend, and I do not wish to lose more. This makes our martyrdom much more comforting, does it not?" She put her small hand on my shoulder. My cape started to smolder under her touch. "Prepare yourself, brother. The unappeasable fire beckons us."

"Yeah. Right," I said.

I was a little alarmed at this sudden turn, but this whole Kill Hellik quest had been festering in the back of my mind. I needed to make sure the god was dead before the end of the eleventh floor. And if the floor was truncated? That meant I should probably deal with this problem as soon as possible. I needed to plan and prepare *something*. We'd been so focused on just surviving this floor, I hadn't been thinking of it.

That was a mistake, and I knew it. But even at our strength, it was, indeed, an impossible task.

My choices were to kill Hellik. Not kill Hellik. Remove myself from Emberus as a worshipper. Or kill Emberus.

None of the choices were good. If I left the church or if I failed the quest, I would receive a smite. That could take any form, but it usually resulted in death.

Emberus had told me directly that if I killed his brother, he would kill me for daring to complete the quest he gave me. So completing the quest was just as dangerous.

That pretty much only left me with one option. Kill Emberus. But how? Even if he wasn't invulnerable on this floor and the next, I couldn't even get anywhere near him without burning to dust. We had Katia's bolt, which removed his invulnerability for a few seconds, but this was a particularly powerful god. And if I *did* kill him, I would be marked for death by all the other gods.

I was fucked no matter which path I took.

Still, we weren't ready to deal with any of that right now. These races were hard enough just trying to survive. I didn't need a religious-fanatic fairy pushing the inevitable along.

"We're not ready to face Hellik," I said.

Imani and Louis came jogging up.

I waved, but I remained distracted. I remembered my brief conversation with Hellik on the last floor. Other than maybe the true form of Eileithyia, Hellik was the most normal of the gods we'd met so far. He didn't come across as completely psychotic and unhinged as his brother.

And there was Eris, who—

Donut suddenly yowled and jumped several feet upward, all poofed out.

The world froze. Donut remained stationary in the air.

System Message: Eris has entered the realm.

You are in the presence of a Deity. The Scavenger's Daughter has opened her eyes. She fills with power.

Random Effect! As Eris is the goddess of chaos, this effect will change each time you are in her presence.

Temporary effect from Eris: A random temporary magical effect or item or aura from someone in your presence other than yourself will become permanent.

"What the shit?" I said upon realizing I wasn't frozen. I sighed. "Eris? Where are you?"

The woman tapped me on the shoulder, and I jumped, finding her behind me. She was sitting on the cart of a food vendor. This was one of the guys selling meat on a stick. The gremlin proprietor was frozen like everyone else.

Eris looked the same as the last time I had seen her atop the tower. She was about my height. Swirl pattern on her lips. She had vaguely snakelike features. Her mouth seemed just a little too big, and she smiled wide at me and stuck out her forked tongue.

I blinked at her description. I noted a few changes since the last time I'd seen her.

Goddess of Chaos Eris. Level 251.

This deity has lost her sponsor and can no longer be sponsored this season.

This deity is invulnerable on this floor.

This deity has been summoned by <Error>

In addition to the weird error, she was a level higher than she'd been before, which I thought was impossible. This likely had something to do with what Orren had told me regarding the gods getting "loose." They were just popping around wherever they wanted instead of following the rules. But it still appeared they were invulnerable.

"You summoned me?" Eris asked.

"I did not," I said.

"Well, my ears were burning. I'm pretty sure you summoned me. I certainly feel summoned."

I hadn't summoned her. But I *had* thought of her. I felt a chill.

Next to her on the cart, the food storage bin popped up, and a small but familiar figure jumped out. He had a meat skewer in his mouth, and he grunted as he climbed up her dress to perch on her shoulder.

"What the shit?" I asked. It was a tiny Uzi Jesus. I was pretty sure it was an action figure. A robot, like robot Donut.

The robot took a bite of the giant meat skewer and then spat it out. He tossed the skewer on the ground. "This tastes like apostate ass."

Eris giggled and gave the robot toy a little pat. "Say hi to Carl, my little pet."

"Hi, Carl," robot Uzi Jesus said. He had a single toy—at least I hoped it was a toy—Uzi in his hand, and he waved it at me. He looked about. "Oh, there's Florin! Can we go kill him? He gave me up!"

"No, pet," Eris said, also looking at the Crocodilian. "We need him alive. As soon as he cracks that mystery open, we'll be done with him. Today we're dealing with Carl." She turned to look me up and down.

"How did you know I was married?" I asked. "And what's the story with Britney and Ysalte?"

"I am all knowing," she replied. "But we're not here to talk about your wife. Or the pickaxe that may or may not eventually kill your friend and everyone you love. You have a more pressing problem, Carl, and once again, I am here ready to offer a solution." She thumbed over at the large, now-lit C&W&U restaurant at the end of the street. "And also to give you a heads-up about that place."

I eyed Donut, who remained hovering in midair. She had yowled just before she'd gotten frozen. She was wearing her kneepads, which meant she'd also received a notification that Eris had entered the realm. The last time she'd been unconscious.

"What does that temporary buff mean? What magical effect will become permanent?"

"Not on you, unfortunately, though you should be grateful this didn't happen when you still had that costume on because I thought it was *adorable*. This effect is for someone nearby." She tapped her lips, then pointed to Imani. "I think Imani will be able to explain it after I leave."

"She's pretty banging," robot Uzi Jesus said, also looking at Imani.

Eris patted Jesus on the head. Unlike the "real" version, his halo was attached via a wire, and it bent under her touch. "We don't judge on appearance, little one. We judge based on the amount of rot in their soul. Remember what I taught you? Look at the color of the swirls."

"Her swirls are pretty banging, too," he said.

"Okay, what do you want?" I asked.

Eris turned to me, her smile vanishing instantly.

She's insane, I thought. *Insane and endlessly dangerous.*

"You're running out of time, Carl. You need to deal with your Emberus problem. Ditch him, worship me, and I will protect you from his spite. We will kill him and his brother and my half brother, too." She spun her finger in the air. Sparkles followed. "But not yet. We have plans in motion, and we need all three." She paused. "Their mother, too, has gotta go, but she's a special case."

I took a breath. "Yeah?" I said. "And what do you get out of it?"

She burst out laughing.

From her shoulder, Jesus also laughed and fired his toy Uzi in the air. It made a tiny popping noise.

"I want the Ascendent throne, Carl. I'm just playing the game. But that doesn't mean you can't win, too. You are an agent of chaos. You need me. And I *like* you. You are unpredictable, and believe me, for someone like myself, it's a joy."

"Okay," I said hesitantly. "What do you want me to do?"

"Nothing just yet. I'll tell you when to make the switch. But for now, three things need to happen. You need to make nice with Akuma and his merry band of head-exploding mages. He really does have a way to crack open the Pineapple Cabaret. He thinks it's his exit ticket. It's so much more than that, of course. It's a good thing, especially to all you crawlers. The war mages will turn on you at the end, probably. But not right away. You need each other." She shrugged. "Honestly, I don't care what happens to them as long as the path to the Cabaret is open. Just know it *is* a way for some of your friends to escape. When I win the Ascendency, I can do whatever I want. I can send you and all your friends there. I can take you to the surface. I can rebuild your world, if I want. All I ask is one simple thing. You worship me. And I mean truly worship. Not just go through the motions. Such a small price to pay."

"Uh-huh," I said. "So you want me to do whatever this Akuma guy wants, and you want me to worship you. What's the third thing?"

She grinned. "You need to allow me to score your surface a bit. You know, like how you sand a wall a little before you paint it? You strip off the old paint, rough it up a little. You gotta break things down before you can build them up."

"What the hell are you talking about?"

She spat into her own hand, and a large coin appeared. "Ever seen one of these? It's a five-sided coin."

She showed it to me. It appeared to be just a regular coin. It was about the size of a poker chip but metal. It had her laughing face on one side and a swirl on the other. "This is the base form. But now we will reveal the five sides." She turned it again, and words and an image appeared. One side showed Donut's face with the word "RIP." The other side read "Carl de-feeted" spelled "F-E-E-T" with a pair of bloody, severed feet. She flipped it again, and it changed to a pile of dead bodies with the caption "Most of my friends are dead." She flipped it one more time. It showed me hanging upside down by one foot from the branch of a tree, though I had a smile on my face. The edges of the coin were filled with player-killer skulls. It read, "I become what they accuse me of."

"Wait," I said, panic rising. "What are you doing? What does that mean?"

"Before the Ascendent is chosen, one of these four results has to happen." She handed the coin toward Jesus. "If you would be so kind as to flip this for me? We don't want Carl thinking I had my hand on the scale."

"Wait," I said again. That rushing feeling had returned, only it felt like it was all rushing around me all at once. On my chest, the long-dormant Eye of the Bedlam Bride was open, burning a hole in my shirt.

I held out my hand. "Stop, stop! What the hell? What if I worship you? I'll do it right now. Just tell me what to do."

Eris laughed. "I told you already. I want a *true* worshipper. That's the only way this will work. You already embrace the chaos, but it isn't your religion. *True* faith first requires a crucible. Look at Jesus here. Your mythology put him through insufferable torment."

"Yeah, it fucking sucked," Jesus said.

"If you deliberately do any of those things, I swear I will end you."

She cackled with laughter. "I know, right? I can't wait." To Jesus, she said, "Flip it, pet."

The small robot shoved his tiny Uzi into his waistband and grabbed the coin with two hands. "Up you go," he said. He heaved the coin.

"No!" I cried, and I reached out and grabbed the coin as it flipped in midair. I grasped it and wrapped it in my right hand. The coin burned, but I didn't let go.

Eris laughed and clapped with delight. "You picked the fifth side! Great! Chaos wins again!"

I felt the coin dissolve. When I opened my fingers, it was gone, but I now had a swirl pattern tattooed on my palm. The pattern spun on its own, like a slow-motion Signet tattoo. I tried to examine it.

I don't even know what the hell this is. This bitch is coloring outside the lines.

I just stared at my palm for several moments. Jesus, bored, moved back to the food cart and grabbed another meat skewer.

"What is the fifth choice?" I finally asked.

Eris shrugged and then hopped off the food cart. "It's one of the other four choices, or two of them, or three of them. Or all of them. Or none of them. Chaos. Random." She leaned forward and kissed me on the lips. "We'll see what you get, Carl, my soon-to-be-favorite worshipper."

36

Eris has left the realm. The Scavenger's Daughter closes her eyes.

BOTH ERIS AND JESUS DISAPPEARED. THE MEAT SKEWER IN JESUS'S HAND clattered to the top of the food cart. The gremlin, confused, tried to pick it up, but it turned to dust. He muttered something about over-spicing.

"Carl, Carl, I got a weird notification that said there was a god but then it disappeared before I could even read it," Donut said as she landed right on Imani's shoulder. "I didn't get any special upgrades or anything. It happened too fast!"

"I saw it, too," I said, clenching my hand tight. "The god is gone now."

"Somebody probably got themselves killed," Donut muttered.

My heart wouldn't stop thrashing. At my shoulder, Quemada, oblivious to what had just happened, continued to talk about Emberus, giving me a pep talk about dying as a martyr. I quickly started jotting down everything I had seen and heard, starting with the four sides to the coin.

Was this real? Things had just gone from bad to worse.

First, we had these goddamned races, where we had no agency whatsoever. We were on rails with no ability to alter our own fates unless we just killed everyone. And now this?

That goddamned goddess was just popping around causing . . . well, causing chaos. If I was understanding her correctly, one of the following four things would happen. Donut would die, I'd get my feet chopped off, "most" of my friends would die, or whatever the hell that last choice was. But because I'd grabbed the coin, I'd unlocked the fifth choice, which made everything random. But I didn't know if that meant there was a 20% chance that nothing would happen or if the odds were much lower than that, assuming they broke up each possibility equally. Had I made things much worse by grabbing the coin?

And would killing Eris fix the problem? So now I had to kill both Emberus and Eris?

And what else had she said? She'd mentioned something alarming about Britney, but she'd also confirmed it was the pickaxe, which confirmed it was a Ysalte issue. And there was that thing about Florin and all that about the Pineapple Cabaret. What else? I furiously jotted it all down in my mental pad, heart hammering in my chest.

I realized the eye on my chest was still open, and I had to make a conscious effort to close it.

We were playing *their* game, doing *their* bidding. We had to alter the paradigm. We had to break the game. But how? Time was running out.

I had an idea, but it was so utterly ridiculous, so completely suicidal, that I immediately dismissed it.

Maybe these war mages had an answer to that problem. *Maybe.*

"Goodness, Carl, are you all right?" Donut asked.

"Your blood pressure is skyrocketing," Imani said at the same time, also examining me. "Carl, something just happened, didn't it? You can't . . ." She paused, taking a step back, eyes suddenly wide. "Oh, snap," she said.

"What? What?" I asked.

A tiny fairy appeared right in front of Imani, swirling in a sparkling circle around her head. This one was about the size of my fist, and it moved so fast, I couldn't catch it with my eyes.

"Imani, why did you summon him now?" Donut asked.

"I didn't," she said drily. "I just received a notification that he is now permanently summoned and can no longer be used as a card."

Elle came floating up. She eyed Quemada warily and then looked at the spinning, chattering fairy zipping around Imani's head. "Why'd you let that little psycho out?"

"I didn't," Imani repeated. She looked at me and crossed her arms. "Carl did something."

"Wait," I said. "That's your eighth-floor card? And it said it's permanent now? I didn't do that!"

The fairy zipped toward me and stopped, hovering right in front of my face, quickly jerking back and forth like a hummingbird. I had a moment to examine him. He was a tiny, ridiculously buff humanoid with flowing blond hair. His wings buzzed so fast, I couldn't see them. He only wore a white loincloth.

He'd been permanently summoned due to the effect of my Scavenger's Daughter patch.

Jacobus. The Reverse Tooth Fairy. Level 90.

This mob was formerly a Legendary card summon but is now permanently activated due to something Carl did.

Many cultures have a creepy tooth fairy tradition designed to acclimate children to the idea they may eventually have to sell their body parts for money. In Denmark, where Jacobus originates, the *Tandfeen* is very similar to other tooth fairy legends around the world. You lose a tooth, you put the tooth under your pillow, and at night, the tooth fairy comes and collects their prize, and in exchange, they leave a krone or two under the pillow, depending on how rich your parents are.

It's a bizarre and weirdly sadistic ritual. But then again, it's one that's pretty tame compared to some of the other Scandinavian customs, like the one where you're supposed to let your baby take their afternoon naps out in the cold like they're Siberian huskies. Or this weird thing where Danes drown unmarried 25-year-olds in cinnamon.

Anyway, Jacobus here isn't a tooth fairy. He's a *reverse* tooth fairy. He doesn't buy loose teeth from children. He does the opposite.

He had a deep, accented voice.

"Vis mig dine tænder."

"Uh," I said.

The little fairy nodded. *"Betal mig trehundrede og tyve guld."*

"Jacobus," Imani snapped, "no! We're in a safe area anyway. You'll get in trouble."

The little fairy grumbled and then zipped to Imani and landed on her shoulder opposite of Donut, who raised her paw like she was going to swat him. The tiny fairy turned and saw Prepotente walking up, and started to fly away again, but Imani moved faster than I thought possible and caught him in her hand.

"No," she repeated. "You will not be doing that with any of my friends."

The fairy started cursing in Danish.

I knew this particular card was fast, had some really messed-up spells, and had been a terror on the battlefield during Faction Wars. The only problem was his summoning time had been particularly short. That apparently wasn't the case anymore.

"Wait, I didn't know cards could be turned real," Donut said. She looked at me. She almost said something else, but she held it back. I was thinking the same thing about poor Paz, whose card we'd ripped at the end of the eighth floor. Instead, Donut said, "Do you think we can set Raul free forever?"

"I doubt it," I said. "This was a god thing."

"What is the holdup?" Prepotente said, looking at all of us. His gaze lingered on Olga. "A Grulke? Well-met!"

"This is the one that says I'm a frog?"

"Yes! Hi, Prepotente!" Donut said.

"I'm waiting," Imani said to me.

I eyed Quemada, and I moved to chat to explain everything that had just happened. I held up my hand, showing the swirl pattern.

After I was done, the chat exploded.

ELLE: Fucking hell, Carl. Hanging out with you is as dangerous as hanging out with Samantha. Also, I don't trust that mercenary you hired. You can't trust fire fairies.

IMANI: When have we even faced a fire fairy? That sounds like something Donut would say.

DONUT: I DON'T LIKE FIRE FAIRIES, EITHER. I LIKE OLGA AND FINLEY A LOT. BUT THIS FIRE LADY REMINDS ME OF AN EXOTIC SHORTHAIR OWNER. AND YOU KNOW WHAT THAT MEANS.

ELLE: No, I don't know what that means. But I kinda do, too.

DONUT: EXACTLY.

PREPOTENTE: Interesting. This is a similar conundrum to the Donut and Katia problem. I will think on it.

LOUIS: Britney hasn't been acting any different. She's just been grumpy. But she's always grumpy.

FLORIN: Do you think this goddess was implying that she knew the full story with Lucia?

CARL: Look. We do need to sit down and come up with a plan to deal with all this. I already have a couple ideas I want to float, but you have to promise to hear me out. It's not fully . . . it's not fully baked yet. I can't even say the last part in chat. But maybe the answer is right in front of us. Let's talk to these war mages first.

37

Entering Chicken and Waffles and Upgrades.

Warning: This location is exempt from the local safe room rules.

THE PLACE WAS A TYPICAL DINER. EVEN THOUGH THE WHOLE TOWN had this aesthetic from the 1980s film *Blade Runner*, the restaurant gave the 1950s, at least at first glance. There was an overabundance of neon within. The jukebox was playing that "Fame" song from the movie.

The workers weren't gremlins but flightless imps, which were similar but a little smaller.

"Hi, folks," an imp with a gaudy rockabilly wig said as we entered. Her name was Darla-Dean, and she was rapidly chewing gum. She started counting all of us. "I'll get a big table together, but it's gonna take a minute. I'll get you some menus." She looked at Donut and popped her gum. "How many kiddie menus do we need?"

"Kiddie menu?" Donut asked, incredulous. "Do I look like someone who eats off the kiddie menu?"

"Wait," Louis said. "I want to see one."

"And a drink menu," Prepotente added.

"I want a kiddie menu, too," Samantha announced.

"Samantha!" I said, looking at the doll head with surprise. She was suddenly just there on the floor. "Where did you come from?" She had not been with us just before when Eris appeared.

The imp started handing out menus.

Samantha ignored me and rolled up to Louis. She grunted a few times and jumped up to Louis's shoulder. She spent a moment watching the reverse tooth fairy zip around Imani's head like a fly. She turned her attention to the Porsuk and then stage-whispered in Louis's ear, "I want you to know that Finley attempted to seduce me, and I was enticed, but I resisted his lurid advances. Still, if you kill him in a jealous rage, I would think it was really hot."

Louis looked up at the Porsuk, eyes wide.

"Don't worry," the badger said. "I already got her figured out."

Olga muttered something about wanting to charge quadruple, not triple.

"Hey," Samantha said, looking down at the menu clutched in Louis's hands, "there aren't any children on here at all."

"They're on the other side, honey," Darla-Dean said.

Louis hesitantly flipped the menu over.

"Oohh, they have sous vide satyr capretto," she said. She looked at Prepotente. "That's what Louis and I are going to get."

"We're not looking for a table," I said to the imp, pushing Louis's menu out of Samantha's line of vision. "We want to see the top-shelf upgrades."

Darla-Dean nodded. She pointed to the jukebox. I could already see that there was a hidden door and hallway past it. "Just push the music machine. Don't push too hard, though. We just opened, and we don't need it scratched."

"Hey, can you make me a milkshake?" Louis said, pointing to the front side of the menu. "I'll get it on the way out. Wait, what's the difference between a malt and a milkshake?"

"No," Imani said. "Remember the warning. All food items convey buffs or debuffs."

"I know," Louis said. He held up the menu. "Look, it says the strawberry milkshakes give you 5% to reaction time. And the malts do the same."

"And I will take ten of each of these flavored sodas listed in the top-right box here. All to go," Prepotente said. "Make sure I get straws for each one."

"Ten of each?" Darla-Dean asked.

"Hmmm, you're right," Prepotente said. "Better make it twenty of each. Louis is quite right. This establishment labels all of their food items. I have already messaged Jurgen and told him he can only eat here from now on."

Darla-Dean shrugged. "Coming right up."

"Come on, guys," I said. "Let's get this over with."

I pushed the jukebox, which was now playing "Sledgehammer" by Peter Gabriel. It moved in and slid over, revealing a short hallway with a blinking neon sign that read "Upgrades" with an arrow.

The whole group of us piled through the dark hallway. Samantha was now chatting with, or at, Jacobus the reverse tooth fairy, who kept replying in Danish. He pointed at Prepotente, and Samantha giggled.

The door closed behind us, and the jukebox sound completely went away. We turned the corner to find a dusty counter lit with flickering yellow light. There were multiple posters on the walls depicting vehicles of all shapes and sizes. There was also a heavy binder on the counter filled with laminated pages.

And sitting on the counter next to the binder was a dead imp with his eyes burned out. The little thing smoldered like he'd just been killed.

Corpse of Hickster. Level 25. Upgrade Imp.

Killed by Akuma of the War Mage Rebellion.

Overalls.

Note for Carl.

I sighed and looted the note.

It was a message hastily scrawled on one of the kiddie menus in black crayon.

Carl, you were supposed to come alone, you moron. This isn't a tea party. Ditch them and come back.

Behind one of the posters, this one depicting a hairy yak with body armor, was a secret door. And attached to the door itself was a hidden disintegration trap. I hopped the counter, ripped the poster off the wall, deactivated and looted the trap module, did another quick scan to make sure there weren't more, and opened the hidden door.

"Just come out," I called into the darkness. "Anything you say to me, you say to everyone. I'm just going to tell them anyway."

Nobody answered for several moments.

Finally, the darkness shifted and then dissipated, revealing a lone war mage leaning against the wall of a small storeroom. The irritated elf-like mage was sipping on a purple milkshake.

Akuma. The last time I'd seen him was in that forest clearing during Faction Wars. He looked like an older elf, with mottled, sun-damaged skin. He and several other war mages had killed Prince Stalwart and formed a faction of their own. They'd stolen the Gate of the Feral Gods, disappeared, and taken the castle of Larracos. There, they'd supposedly found what they'd been looking for. The Scavenger's Daughter. Then they fled, and Akuma sent me a note saying that I had to kill Agatha.

We still had no idea what the hell their motivation was.

The war mages themselves only came into existence under certain circumstances. They were the personification of magical energy, and they were not built and designed by either the showrunners or the AI. They just sort of came into existence after a flesher was resleeved a number of times.

And their heads exploded about ten minutes after death. I had multiple war mage heads in my inventory.

"By the shitting gods, how are you still alive?" Akuma asked, peeling himself off the wall. "You are a fucking idiot, Carl. I called you here because you need me. But if you can't follow simple instructions, maybe . . . *Urk!*"

Donut cast *Mute* on Akuma, and at the same time Elle cast an ice bolt right at the war mage's crotch.

Akuma cried out and fell over, his purple milkshake splattering all over the place.

The *Mute* part had been planned. Elle's bolt had not.

"Uh, Elle?" I said. I turned and saw the look on Elle's face, and I held up my hands. I took a step back.

"Just don't kill him," I said.

Elle pushed past me and moved up to the crying mage, who was trying to say something but couldn't.

"Hey, remember me, you barely sapient magical fart?" Elle said, getting close to Akuma, whose sneering expression had turned to a look of extreme, gasping pain. "You and your little asshole friends tried to kill me. You stole the gate from me when I wasn't done with it yet. When I was a kid, do you know what we used to do to people who stole? We would hit them with sticks, and we would throw their shoes into the sound. But that was only because we couldn't get away with more."

She punched down with her fist, and there was a glass-breaking noise.

"And also because I didn't yet have the ability to freeze their balls and shatter them like dollar-store Christmas ornaments."

"Holy Christ," Florin muttered next to me.

"That was just your left nut. If you want to keep your right one, you are going to answer everything Carl asks of you. If I even suspect you're lying, *cajone* number *dos* gets converted to crushed ice." She tapped her finger against his crotch. It clinked. "And then on to the main event. And *then* Imani over there is going to tell her little friend Jacobus to do some of his special dental surgery on you. Trust me. You don't want that."

"Ja, ja, ja," said the reverse tooth fairy.

"Holy ouch," Louis said from the other side. "Remind me to never piss Elle off."

Akuma gasped in pain. He had tears rolling down the side of his face.

"I was wondering why Elle asked Samantha if war mages had genitals," Donut said.

"Here's what's going to happen," Elle continued. "Imani is going to cast an anti-magic shield around you, and Donut is going to remove the *Mute* spell. I know the magic shield is going to cause your health to start to slowly lower. We aren't going to remove it until Carl has all his answers, so answer quickly. If you attempt any sort of countermeasure to the shield, you will be killed. But we'll kill you special-like. You get me? Nod if you understand."

Akuma started to slowly nod.

"Okay, good. Imani, cast your spell. But let's leave *Mute* on him for a bit longer so he can think about what he's done."

"I've seen her mad before, but I don't think I've ever seen this side of her," Louis said, spewing water from his gills.

"The woman knows how to hold a grudge," Florin replied.

"One time," Imani said, "Ingrid Schmidt, who was the resident in the room next to hers, tried to cheat at bingo, and Elle found out. She wheeled up to Ingrid and whispered something, and Ingrid started crying and refused to come out of her room for a week. The woman never played bingo again. I still don't know what Elle said to her. I asked the other day, and she just laughed."

"Can I crush his other nut?" Samantha asked. She'd bounced up to the counter and was sitting atop the dead imp, spinning in a circle, causing blood to fleck everywhere.

The three mercenaries had moved to the very back of the room and were all cowering.

"Quintuple," Olga said. "We should've asked for quintuple."

38

"I WILL FUCKING KILL YOU ALL," AKUMA CRIED, GASPING AS I LEANED down next to him.

I patted him on the knee. "Don't be like that," I said. "You *did* try to kill her. One of you blasted her against a tree, and she was pretty pissed about you guys stealing the gate. She doesn't like that sort of thing."

"If we were trying to kill her, she would've been dead."

"And if *I* was trying to kill *you*, none of your pieces would so much as fit in an ice tray right now," Elle said.

"My fucking balls. You crushed my balls," he gasped.

Elle snorted. "Just one of them. I hope it wasn't your favorite."

"Carl kicked a mage in the balls once," Donut said. "Zev said the audience didn't like it. I bet they liked this. It's a lot funnier when a woman does it."

"She didn't kick him," Louis said. "She *shattered* it . . . Dude, what are you doing?"

"You never know what might be useful," Prepotente said. He'd pushed his way into the small room and was carefully picking the little ice flecks off the ground and was putting them into a glass beaker.

"Just ask your blasted questions," Akuma panted. He leaned back and closed his eyes. "We're trying to help you idiots. We're on the same side."

Akuma's health was slowly, slowly draining. We only had a few minutes. Apparently one of the ways to kill a war mage was to encase them in an anti-magic shield. They were, after all, magic made flesh.

"Let's start with why you wanted me to come in the first place," I asked. "And why did you want me to kill two teams?"

Akuma continued to pant. "There're too many of these vehicle races. Too many teams. You crawlers weren't supposed to survive in these numbers to this floor. The AI had to compensate by drawing from the deep reserves. On the last floor, when they made the floor even bigger, they plumbed some of the mobs from the first and second floors, but those mobs are different, and it didn't work right. So now some of these NPC teams"—he opened his eyes and looked at the three mercenaries, who were still against the back wall in the other room—"and all the NPCs for the mercenary guilds are getting pulled from emergency backup. It's because your numbers are too great, and when you broke the seventh floor, it required them to quickly populate the map on the eighth in a way that further depleted the reserves."

"Wait, how do you know any of this? And what does that mean?"

I was now used to dungeon-born NPCs being fully awakened to their situation, but not like this.

"A former crawler taught me all about it. A skink. They're trapped in the Cabaret. They know how all this works better than anybody. Better even than the AI itself, I think. They're an annoying fucker. Even more annoying than the cat."

"Jacobus," Imani said.

"Wait, wait, I'm sorry," he gasped, holding up his hand as the tiny fairy zipped up to him. The reverse tooth fairy made a disappointed grunt, high-fived the raised hand of Akuma, and zipped back to Imani.

"Well, I never," Donut mumbled. "You don't even know me!"

"I watched you," he said. "I watched the last hundred seasons. I was watching you until we went out for Faction Wars."

I took a breath. I wanted to ask him more about this former crawler, but for now, it was a tangent. We had so much to go over.

"Okay. What does it mean that they're using NPCs that shouldn't be used?"

Akuma started to ramble through clenched teeth. "NPCs and mobs especially aren't supposed to be used for more than a few seasons. That skink I was telling you about, he has this process he calls the Worn Path Method, and it helps us realize what we really are. Mobs are supposed to get recycled once they've been used a few times to prevent that from happening. But it's expensive, and their records are spotty. And as a result, these mobs and NPCs are used over and over. They do audits occasionally, but so many get missed. But Herot, that's the skink, they figured this out. They and another former crawler found a way to exploit it all."

"Does anyone understand what the hell this guy is talking about?" Louis asked.

I couldn't breathe. Herot. The author of the sixteenth edition of the cookbook was still alive. And he—they?—was here. But where? How were they trapped?

"So?" I asked, trying to keep my voice even. "What does any of that have to do with anything?"

"The dungeon is full of mobs who know their own nature. Everything is broken. It's all accelerating. Even if the AI hadn't already gone Primal, the awakened NPCs are like a disease to the integrity of the crawl as a whole. The whole thing is poisoned. Everything has to be removed. Nothing inside the dungeon will be allowed to survive past this season no matter what happens. Even if the outworlders somehow gain back control, we are well past the point of no return. Everything must be destroyed. That means *everyone* and everything in the dungeon. All that work of generations will be binned. But these two former crawlers, Herot and Menerva, their exploit is a way for us, the NPCs, to survive. But you crawlers can use it, too."

"Exploit in what way?" I asked.

"You don't know enough about the way the dungeon works to understand. But a dungeon is modular. There are thousands of pieces that need to come together. There is what they call the framework, the shell upon which everything is built. That part—which includes all the stored mobs, the reusable locations, *some* of the indentured workers—is the important part. It's the third-to-last thing that gets installed into the planet, and it's the one physical part that's reused every season to make the dungeon. It's like a crawler's inventory but a huge one, and it is a physical object. It is moved from planet to planet. The current season's showrunners feed their plans for the season into the framework, along with the software. And then the macro AI is installed into the planet's Primal Engine, and I suddenly wake up, thinking I'm a godsdamned palace guard. Or a pet groomer in a city with no waste management and no way to get food. Our forced memories are oftentimes so paper-thin, we start to realize something is wrong long before the floor is even over."

"That's like that one train station during the Iron Tangle," Louis said. "They all thought they had, like, apartments and stuff, but when everyone went there, the whole area was empty. It was a complete mindfuck to them."

"Okay," I said. I already knew some of this. It was blowing my mind that this was an NPC. I felt numb, and I was still reeling from the reveal about Herot. I tried to remember if I'd ever heard the name Menerva before. I wished Rosetta had come with us. I needed to press on. His health was almost half gone.

"Try to explain it anyway. What is the exploit? What is the Pineapple Cabaret? And how do we use it to our advantage? You said this former crawler was trapped there?"

Akuma nodded. "Many seasons ago, two indentured former crawlers approached the current season's showrunner and asked for permission to be in charge of building the seventeenth floor. Nobody ever makes it to the seventeenth floor, but the showrunners are required to have plans in place. It would be a way to help automatically dispose of awakened NPCs, and it would fulfill the requirement to have a floor ready to go. The showrunner agreed, and they were given access to create the floor."

"So the seventeenth floor is the Pineapple Cabaret?" I asked.

"No," Akuma said. "It's a small floor where crawlers must face greatly enhanced mobs from earlier floors. It's a hand-built maze filled with horrible traps that culminates in a floor boss that is all but impossible to kill. The showrunner who approved this project was murdered soon after it was approved, and the two former crawlers who were put in charge of the project were forgotten. They are still there to this day, existing outside any supervision, running the construction of the seventeenth floor from scratch every season. Showrunners always just reuse the plans from the previous seasons for everything above the thirteenth floor. Nobody looks at it. The showrunner who originally approved it never transferred their paperwork. They aren't accumulating hours against their indentureship. They are all but invisible, forgotten. They are ghosts in the system, free to do as they wish."

"So they're trapped," I said. "Can't they send a message out?"

"They are, or were, trapped by design. They didn't want to be seen. The seventeenth floor is a front. They weren't just building the seventeenth floor. Attached to the floor is the only entrance to a pocket dimension they built. They were building an oasis, a place for mobs and NPCs to escape to. A world within a world. The two crawlers sacrificed the possibility of ever getting out to make a place where NPCs and mobs could permanently escape the horrors of the dungeon. *That* is the Pineapple Cabaret."

A strange surge of pride filled me. Herot, who was so concerned about the well-being of mobs and NPCs. Of course he, or she, would do that. Of course. My view counter was completely spiked.

"Not so much a secret anymore," I said. "You didn't just tell that to me, but to the whole galaxy."

Akuma nodded. "After what just happened with the Nothing being broken, *everyone* is aware of them now. If they want to keep the crawl running after this season, they will need to start everything over from scratch. All the existing NPCs will be destroyed. All the indentured crawlers stuck within will be lost. It will all be gone. They have no other choice. That is why we must work together. You didn't need to crush my fucking balls."

"I didn't have to," Elle said. "But I certainly enjoyed it."

"You have told me a bunch of random shit," I said. "How does it all tie in?"

"The AI is expanding. It can feed itself, and I don't think it's going anywhere. We *might* be able to create an exit from the Pineapple Cabaret to the surface of this planet. We *might*. But there's a problem. A lot of problems, really. The Cabaret is similar to the Nothing. It's not a floor. It's a separate dimension, and the rules do allow crawlers to travel to it. But as of right now, we don't have a way in or out except via the seventeenth floor. But if we can build another door, any crawler who is within when the floor collapses will be deemed 'lost.' But they won't be killed."

"Wait," I said. "If someone gets pulled into the Nothing, they don't die when the floor collapses?"

"No crawlers could possibly survive the Nothing. That's irrelevant now. The Nothing was broken on the last floor. But this dimension is the same sort of thing. I was there at the Pineapple Cabaret. Me and several others had been for some time. But we deliberately left. We returned to the cold storage when we realized what was happening, and we got brought to Faction Wars. We needed to find the Scavenger's Daughter."

I glanced at Samantha, who had gotten bored and was currently gnawing on the foot of the dead imp. She perked up at the mention of the word "Scavenger."

"Who and what is that?" I asked.

"It's how we will keep the denizens of the Cabaret safe. It's how we will escape to the planet's surface. She's crucial, as is her father, but for now we need a way to get ourselves back to the Cabaret. And when we go, we can take some crawlers with us. But only if they meet the requirements."

His health entered the red. We were either going to have to reset or not get all the answers. "Goddamnit," I said. "I have a million questions still."

Florin, who'd been unusually silent, lowered his shotgun and held it against Akuma's head.

"Remember when Miss Elle said you would suffer if you lie? Well, you just did. Lights out, mate."

"Wait, wait. What did I lie about?"

Florin growled. "You left Faction Wars on your own. You can step in and out of floors as you please. That's how you got *here*. Sounds like you can get back there on your own just fine."

"No, no, you're right. But that wasn't a lie. We need you, and crawlers can't skip floors."

Florin shook his head. "You and your friends are some of the most powerful folks in this world. But you *need* us to go with you? Why?"

Akuma sighed. "Get that out of my face, and I will tell you. We need help."

Florin nodded and lowered his gun. "I'm guessing your special little utopia ain't so much a utopia anymore."

"It was fine until we left. We needed to leave to get to the Scavenger's Daughter, and the moment we left, they moved in. And now we need to fight to get it back, and lots of us were killed in Faction Wars. There's only five of us left. It's not enough. The dimension is infested."

"I knew it," Florin said.

"Infested with what?" I asked.

"Lots and lots of things," he said. "Old, forgotten monsters. Shadow mimics, who are almost impossible to root out. The leftovers from the Ogre Imperium several seasons back. And worse, remnants of things we don't want to wake. Things that Agatha can and will wake the moment she learns they exist. We left for just a few short days, and our protection spells got canceled out, and all hell broke loose. And now we can't get back without a fighting force. Believe me, using you wasn't my first choice. Our original plan was to build more mages during Faction Wars, but you ruined that. And our second plan was to use an old ally in the Nothing, and you ruined *that*, too. So you're the third choice. Still, you dipshits are all already stronger than any crawlers have ever been."

I shot several more questions at him rapid-fire. "What are these 'remnants'? You still didn't tell me why I needed to kill an extra team. What are the requirements to get into the Cabaret? *Why* are there requirements? How will we get a portal open?"

"Hold up," he said. He was still clearly in pain. "We have two possibilities to get there now that the Gate of the Feral Gods is gone and broken. The casinos at the Desperado Club are one way. And if that doesn't work, it's something that involves your shop interface. That one was Herot's idea. As for the requirements, you can't worship a god. You entering the area would instigate a smite. Not certain why. Something to do with the way the space is built. We can't risk the Cabaret getting embroiled in the Ascendency battles. We don't even want the gods to know about it."

I exchanged a look with Donut. That ruled me out. That ruled out most of us.

"They already know," I said. "Or Eris, at least, knows about it."

"Eris knows everything," Akuma replied. "She doesn't count. Pandemonium always finds a way. I will pray she finds other ways to inflict her chaos on the world."

"Why are you refusing to answer Carl's question about why you wanted him to kill two teams?" Donut demanded.

Akuma sighed. "Because I knew the moment that happened, the system would pit him against a team of his friends, and he would have no choice but to help us."

And that's when I punched him in the face and shattered his nose.

39

Entering the Lollipop.

DESPITE THE TOWN'S POPULATION HAVING TAKEN A HIT, THIS PLACE was still packed. That same group of Japanese monsters, team Yokai, was on the karaoke stage singing. This time, the red Oni creature was onstage belting out "Careless Whisper" by George Michael. The male demon's name was Yuto.

We'd re-muted Akuma and left him with about 2% health as we left the back room. I hadn't finished asking him questions, but an imp entered the room and started flipping out about the dead imp on the counter, and we all had to leave. I exchanged a fist bump with the war mage to get him into my chat, and it worked. He said it would only work if he was on the same floor as me.

We left, but not before Louis got his milkshake and Prepotente excitedly picked up his pile of about two hundred sodas, all in tall glasses with colorful straws. Each one, apparently, gave a different buff.

When Louis drank his milkshake, the water that occasionally blew from his gills turned red and smelled like strawberry. He was getting it everywhere.

I continued to ask Akuma question after question in chat, but he wasn't answering me except to tell me I was annoying him.

I didn't trust him. I didn't want to believe him. But his mention of Herot, plus Eris's insistence that he did have a way to escape, kept me on the hook. So for right now, the plan was to trust but verify every step along the way.

Our immediate plan was to gather volunteers who were willing and able to travel to this Pineapple Cabaret and fight. Prepotente and Mordecai were going to try to figure out this shop-interface exploit, and I was going to task some of the strippers with returning to the Desperado Club to try to figure out the other method of opening a portal to the Cabaret.

All of this brought me back to the impossible problem I had with Emberus, Hellik, and now Eris.

I put my hand on Donut, reveling in her warmth, going over everything we had to do.

I was frustrated with the whole design of this floor, especially since everything was so dangerous. It was too rigid, too time-consuming. Everything we needed to do, we could only do between races. I missed our ability to just bounce around the map at will.

The chat was moving fast with people discussing the confusing conversation with the war mage.

Dozens of people were asking for a concise explanation of what was going on. Donut was in the chat, laying it out for everyone.

DONUT: SO THIS PINEAPPLE PLACE IS LIKE A SUPER-NICE SAFE ROOM, BUT FOR NPCS. HE SAYS WE CAN GO THERE AND NOT GET SQUISHED WHEN THE FLOOR COLLAPSES, BUT WE'LL BE STUCK THERE. ONLY IT'S NOT SAFE ANYMORE BECAUSE IT GOT TAKEN OVER BY OGRES AND OTHER BAD GUYS.
SO THIS WAR MAGE WANTS US TO CLEAN IT OUT FOR HIM, AND IN EXCHANGE HE THINKS WE CAN MAYBE GET OUT TO EARTH. BUT HOW THAT WORKS OR HOW WE GET THERE IN THE FIRST PLACE IS A LITTLE UNCLEAR. ALSO ELLE CRUSHED HIS RIGHT TESTICLE. SHE TURNED IT TO ICE AND SMASHED IT!

LOUIS: I think it was his left one!

DONUT: WELL, NOW IT'S HIS ONLY ONE.

I wasn't certain if Rosetta would know who Herot was since he came after her in the cookbook. She didn't react to the name-drop, but the mention of Menerva clearly meant something to her, as she asked me a dozen questions. But she was hesitant to tell me more. Menerva wasn't a cookbook author, but if she had truly given up everything to work with Herot, then I knew she was an ally. I just needed a way to talk to her.

We only had a few hours left. But if we could get to this other Corcunda, we could get this Dong quest buttoned up as well. It was now crucial that we complete it.

Tipid had a surprisingly deep knowledge about hidden guildhalls. More so than Mordecai and Mistress Tiatha combined, both of whom literally worked in guildhalls when they weren't on manager duty.

And he insisted that this stage performance guild would be hidden here in the Lollipop.

Tipid hadn't been with us at the C&W&U, but he was here now at the bar. I went to sit next to him while the others piled into their regular corner.

I hadn't talked too much to him after he'd had his memory wiped, and I felt guilty about it.

"I don't know about this thing with the war mages," Tipid said as I slid in next to him. He motioned to the gremlin barkeeper, who started pouring a second beer. "Under normal circumstances, the mere mention of any of this would be met with a severe beatdown from both the AI and the showrunners."

"Yeah, it's all off the rails," I said. I nodded at the barkeeper. I started to take a sip but hesitated. This was a different beer than the one Imani had vetted last time we were in here.

Tipid grunted. "This one gives a 2% constitution bump for the next race. You're fine. Don't eat the peanuts, though."

I took a sip. It was delicious. I received a notification about the constitution buff.

"I don't know who Menerva is," Tipid continued. "She might've been a season before my time. But I do remember watching Herot during my time as a game guide." He paused and then tapped the bar thoughtfully. "Wasn't one of mine, but I remember that season. Was a lot like you. Little fucker was a real thorn in the side of . . ." He started thinking. "I can't remember who was running that season. Maybe the orcs. Anyway, I would trust anything that little lizard says. Smart bugger. Always had a giant crowd of NPCs with 'em. You gotta find a way to talk to them directly if you can. War mages are evil fuckers. It's possible they're working together, but more likely they'll use you to clear out that floor and will kill the lot of you to take it all for themselves. That war mage also mentioned shadow mimics. That's probably the true problem. Dealing with those guys is gonna be a real chore."

"Isn't that what Mordecai really is on this floor?"

"Yep, but it's glitching out. It's impossible for him to be both a changeling and a shadow mimic. Changelings can't even touch mimics. And shadow mimics don't get the skills of those they copy, so it's just plain broken. But it also means there might be one or two of those running around this floor. So be careful."

I nodded.

Imani, Chris, and Elle entered the bar with a newcomer in tow. This was a tall, thin human with flowing robes. A fleshmancer. Imani just hired him as a mercenary, and the plan was to keep him hidden in their guild until he was needed.

Onstage, the skeleton guy with the pope hat finished his song.

"That was 'White Wedding' as sung by the Minister of Blood-Letting. Next up is Tipid . . . Oh. Next up is Tipid singing 'Love Shack' by the B-52s."

Tipid stood. "Okay, I can't sing, so this isn't going to work. But if my theory is correct, a gauge will appear above me when I sing. If that happens, then we know the guild is here."

Donut started shouting loud encouragement as Tipid moved to the stage, then took the microphone from the skeleton man. He turned to face us and bowed, and the song started.

He was correct. He could not sing. But sure enough, a magical gauge going from red to yellow to green appeared over him, kinda similar to the gauge on the *Guitar Hero* game. It never left the red.

I groaned. I could already see where this was going.

There was polite applause when he was done, and he returned to his spot at the bar. Donut came rushing up.

"That was fantastic!" she exclaimed. "I love that song! You did such a great job! Even the evil pope guy liked it! What was that needle thingy! How do I get one of those?"

Prepotente also approached. He was drinking one of his sodas with the striped straw, sipping loudly. The bartender glared at him. "Excellent performance," he said.

"Yeah, so," Tipid said. He grabbed the stapled-together binder off the counter and slid it over. It was the book one used to pick songs for karaoke. "There's a secret mark on a handful of songs. If you pick the right song, it'll engage the entrance sequence for the guild. If you can get through the entire song with your needle in the green, you will gain access." He paused. "Only those who get the green needle the whole time will be able to enter. So if you want in, you gotta sing."

"Great," I said.

Donut was bouncing up and down. She moved to the binder. "This is great! What an amazing way to have a secret door! It's just like with bard magic. How do we find the songs! It's too bad it's only from the stupid 1980s. Isn't everyone from that era dead already?" She gasped. "Wait, are there any Whitney Houston songs?" She gasped a second time, even louder. "Celine Dion! What about Celine Dion?"

"I'm pretty sure Celine Dion got famous in the 90s," I said.

"Hmm, I suppose you're right. She did the song for that one movie where that lady let her homeless boyfriend drown." Her eyes got big. "Stevie Nicks! Was she in the 1980s?"

I laughed. "I'm pretty sure she had some 80s hits, yes."

"Celine Dion first charted in Canada in 1981," Prepotente said. "But that was in French. She didn't chart in the United States, and in English, until 1990 with her *Unison* album. It's not likely there are any of her songs in that binder, but it is worth a look. Carl, what type of music do you like anyway?"

"Don't even ask," Donut said. "It's quite embarrassing."

"How in the hell do you know all that about Celine Dion?" I asked.

"I know a lot of things, Carl," Prepotente said. He left his empty soda glass on the counter and pulled a second one out. This one smelled distinctly like grape. He started sipping loudly. "That's what happens when you're intelligent. You know things."

"That's not intelligence," I said. "That's—"

"Hey! You! No outside drinks!" the bartender said.

I quickly covered my ears. I didn't do it fast enough. Prepotente screamed right next to my face, causing Donut to yowl, Tipid to say "What the hell?" and the gremlin to fall back. The kappa onstage paused her song and shot a glare our way.

"Okay, goat boy," the gremlin said, irritated, as he pulled himself up. "Drink it outside!"

"But this is a drinking establishment!"

"Yeah. One where you're only allowed to eat and drink things you bought here. No outside food. This ain't a charity. You like that new fancy restaurant so much, go drink your stuff over there."

Prepotente huffed. "I will not frequent an establishment where I'm not wanted!" He turned and stormed outside.

I sighed, turning my attention to Donut, who started flipping through the book. "What's the secret mark?" She let out a little squeal. "Ohh, Queen. I could probably do a good Freddie Mercury! I think we have the same range."

CARL: Mordecai, remember that potion we were talking about before? The bard one? We're going to need some.

MORDECAI: Tipid warned me. They're brewing now, but they won't be ready until just before the next race.

40

"I DO NOT SEE WHY BOTH OF YOU MUST SIT UPON ME AT THE SAME time," Dorota complained. "You are exceeding my recommended weight capacity!"

Donut sat on my shoulder, but I was the one in the seat.

"My breathtaking princess, you should sit here," Dorota whined. "Just you and you alone. Without you, I have no purpose. No reason to even exist. When you add the nude human, I am unable to function."

"I am not naked," I said.

"You are in your underwear. I worry you might get pink eye, my princess."

"Does that thing have a mute button?" Finley asked from behind us. "It's more annoying than the shark."

"Dorota, do please stop complaining," Donut said. "Nobody likes it when someone complains too much." She turned to Olga, who was in the driver's seat. "Anyway, can you believe that stupid gauge thing at the bar? It was clearly broken. It didn't even move!"

I'd tried to stop her, but Donut insisted on attempting to gain entrance to the guild. She'd picked a Journey song, and she had *not* engaged her Auto-Tune. It had gone as one might have expected.

"I thought you did a fine job," Finley said. "It was a great song. Don't you think, Que?"

The fire fairy, who was hovering in the back of the truck, let out a noncommittal squeak.

"Thank you, Finley," Donut sniffed.

I gave the fire fairy an uneasy look. She was acting strangely depressed. She'd stopped talking about us killing Hellik. I suspected this had to do with the conversation in the shop. All NPCs acted differently when they first came into contact with a fully awakened NPC like Akuma. She kept raising her finger, like she was about to say something regarding it, and then she changed her mind.

We had about ten minutes before the start of the race. Team Free Love pulled up next to us. Their van no longer had tires, and it now floated just off the ground, like a speeder from *Star Wars*.

The large, fog-covered jungle loomed. A wide dirt track sat in front of us. The track branched just before the tree line.

We hadn't yet spied who the new team was. Nor did we yet see any sign of the other heats that would supposedly get combined with ours.

Three new lights appeared on our dash, each indicating our three newest upgrades. The gyro that would keep us from flipping. The Bubble Buddy knockoff edition that we could upgrade to the golden edition with another regular upgrade. This was a shield that we could electrify. After we upgraded it again, we'd be able to float with it. And finally, there were resizable all-terrain tires.

The loudspeaker crackled. Zev's harried voice echoed. Her neutral tone filled me with dread.

Hello, racers.

For this race, you will have the survival containment activated. The containment system creates a rule change, so please listen carefully.

The survival containment is a translucent, indestructible circular bubble that surrounds your vehicle or mount. You will see it as soon as this message is over. It will not interfere with any existing shields or any other systems of your vehicle or mount. Spells and projectiles will pass through. Its only purpose is to protect you and your mount from the toxic, unbreathable air of your next heat.

Different tracks have different air hazards, but in all races, if this containment is removed, you will likely perish quickly if you don't prepare countermeasures. All races this heat will have a required pit stop where one must stop for at least two hours. You will

have access to your garage for repairs during pit stops. There will also be vendors who will be, uh, selling countermeasures in case you lose your containment.

Like I said, your containment bubble is indestructible. At least for this heat. However, there is a way for you to lose it. This is the rule-change part, so please pay attention. If your vehicle is destroyed or your mount is killed, you no longer automatically lose. You will, however, lose your containment. If you can survive this and you manage to cross the finish line before another team, you can still survive. How that might possibly happen, I don't know, but it's the new rule.

The team that comes in last place will still lose. You still cannot pass the finish line outside your conveyance if your conveyance is still intact or if you are missing any team members.

If this happens, however, you will *not* get your old vehicle or mount back.

Also, from now on, the team that wins is given a key. That key will open a single garage of a defeated team. Within, you may find additional supplies to upgrade your vehicle or mount along with other items, possibly. And in some cases, you may find an entire vehicle or mount. If you do find a second vehicle or mount, you can add it and expand your garage, and you may choose which to use for the next race. And yes, you may switch vehicles during pit stops.

And finally, this race you will see other heats racing alongside you on the same track. For this particular heat, containment stealing isn't active. Take what you will from that statement.

Okay, everyone, good luck. The race starts in ten minutes. Your GPS or saddle units will have your maps now. See you at the finish line.

The whole vehicle buzzed, and a bubble appeared around us, barely visible except when it occasionally caught the light, like a real bubble. It spread about a meter in every direction outside the truck.

"Carl, did you understand all of that?" Donut asked.

"Yeah. We'll need to stock up on more of those breathing potions Mordecai made."

We had the back door open to keep an eye on all the approaching teams. I turned in my seat, craning my neck to see all the teams as they approached.

The tumbleweed of team Sparkles pulled up, sporting a pair of massive metallic exhaust ports that were new. Lucienne was driving this time. The little bug-eyed rodent creature was shouting something, but it wasn't directed at us. I wasn't sure it was directed at anyone.

The Lady Dominators pulled up next. I couldn't tell what sort of upgrade they'd picked, but as usual, Corky remained passed out in the back.

Next up came One Fine Pig's large APV, parking on the far-left edge of the track.

"Now that's just offensive," Donut muttered as I laughed.

These guys had come in last place, and it was clear how the audience vote had gone. The truck's military desert tan painting had been replaced with a vehicle wrap. It featured an anime-style pair of Tigrans each kissing the backside of a fat pig, all covered with little heart symbols everywhere.

I laughed, but my humor went away upon seeing who our newest opponent was. I groaned. My heart sank. "Goddamnit."

It was a pair of crawlers on a mount. They also had a dwarf mercenary with a crossbow behind them in a little basket. The mount was a heavily armored six-legged thing that looked like a wildebeest mixed with a triceratops. Little sparks flew with each step. It also wore a giant double saddle that was covered with spikes that glowed with enchantment.

Bruna the Slaughter Gnu.

This is the biological mount of Team Flamengo for the purpose of the tenth floor. As such, it is protected from most spells that would normally affect mounts.

Slaughter Gnus are six-legged beasts of burden that historically were used as war mounts by a race of creatures called Scads, or the Rascals by some. Scads are like orc-goblin things and are pretty rare nowadays, though that's because after they stopped killing

each other on battlefields, they upgraded to killing each other with nuclear holocaust before their postapocalyptic world got absorbed into the Syndicate.

ANYWAY, Slaughter Gnus are remarkably hardy, deceptively quick dumbasses. They have the ability to scale vertical surfaces with the alacrity of a horny mountain goat. Their hide is especially tough, making them perfect mounts for this floor.

And sitting on the back of the mount was Osvaldo. The small red-haired crawler was now level 72. He glared at us angrily as he approached the starting block. His race was something called a Curupira. He still looked mostly human, though I was pretty sure that red was not his natural hair color, and I wasn't certain if his small frame was how large he'd been as a human, as he was barely five feet tall. There was something weird going on with his feet, too, but they were hidden by his large boots.

He was not driving Bruna. Another crawler, a level 63 human Strongman named Filipe L was holding the reins. I'd seen this guy quite a few times but had never spoken with or really examined him. This one was about my height and was all muscle. He looked huge next to Osvaldo.

I took a breath. This was not good. We had plans we were working on to hopefully save as many people as we could, but we were going to run out of time. It was going to be us or them.

Even though Osvaldo had been on and off the top charts, I'd only had limited dealings with him. He was a prick, but I only talked to him when terrible stuff was happening. I knew he was from Brazil, and I knew his now-devastated team had all focused early on only putting points into a single stat. For Osvaldo, it had been dexterity. For this Filipe guy, it was clearly strength.

That had served them well early on, but in recent floors, their entire team had been whittled down. They'd chosen to hide and not fight during Faction Wars, a fact that did not sit well with Donut. Or Elle. Especially not Elle.

Not that it had helped them. By the end, everyone had to fight whether they liked it or not.

Osvaldo had once had a pet stone hawk named Gimli. The bird had died at the end of the Butcher's Masquerade, killed by Prepotente or, more likely, Bianca when they all started fighting over who got to loot the corpse of Queen Imogen.

The item Osvaldo had looted was the memorial crystal of Apito, whose existence was a big mystery because, supposedly, Apito wasn't dead. That same memorial crystal was now in Prepotente's hands. I didn't know the details, but he'd been able to steal the artifact from Osvaldo during the chaos at the end of Faction Wars.

It seemed all three of us—me, Prepotente, and Osvaldo—had quests related to the crystal.

Also, Osvaldo worshipped a god or goddess named Tupa. I'd never heard of that one. Filipe also worshipped the same one.

The realization that these guys did worship a deity was devastating. That meant they wouldn't be able to go to the Pineapple Cabaret if we ever found a way to open the door. Which also meant we were now stuck with them.

I sighed. *There has to be a way. There* has *to be.*

CARL: Osvaldo, you're in the same heat as us. Don't do anything too rash. We have plans in motion to get as many people out as possible. Don't kill any of the other racers. If you kill the pig in the APV, you'll summon Taranis. If you kill the lady mantaurs, we're all fucked. The bugbears in the van are our friends. The unicorn in that bush thing has really powerful weapons, and they're the biggest threat. So be careful. We're gonna try to take them out this race.

OSVALDO: Fuck off, Carl. I'm not talking to you. I won't attack you during the race unless it's you or us, but I don't give a shit about any of the other teams.

DONUT: YOU ARE ONLY ALIVE BECAUSE OF ME AND CARL, YOU STRAIGHT-TO-VIDEO, LOW-BUDGET LEPRECHAUN. YOU BETTER LISTEN OR ELSE.

"Goddamnit, Donut. Don't antagonize him," I said. "He's not an enemy."

"He's not going to help us, Carl. He knows it's us or him."

Donut made a small, inconsequential shrug.

"It'll be easier if we stay not liking each other," she added, turning to look out the window so I couldn't see her face. "It's best not to dwell on it. We have a race to win. Let's figure this map out before we start."

Oh, Donut, I thought, doing my best to stave off the sudden wave of dismay. *No.*

41

DR. METCALF BEEPED.

We have over forty possible paths to the pit stop, which is approximately thirty-five kilometers away as the bird flies. Actual length varies greatly depending on the path we choose. Not surprisingly, the safer the path, the longer it is. The safest path appears to be almost a hundred kilometers and is mostly winding dirt road. The shortest path is a direct line through the jungle that may require the clearing of foliage and has very uneven ground, and there appears to be a Temple of the Exploding Snake Goddess in the way.

A winding path lit up on the map.

Here is my suggestion. We start on the direct path, but we veer off before the temple. We will be forced to cross the I-Sure-Hope-These-Piranhas-Haven't-Learned-to-Fly River here. There's no bridge, but the map indicates the water as shallow and it shouldn't be an issue with the tire and gyro upgrades. Then we will loop around the southern cannibal village, and we catch the end of the dirt road right into Upano. This path will circumvent any boss monsters or quests. Based on what we find at this pit stop and any necessary repairs, I can plot our path for the second half of the race, assuming we're not dead.

"If we're all split up, how can we tell what place we're in?" Donut asked.

Gee, I don't know. Maybe if I was properly updated, I could help with that.

"What about traps?" I asked.

They don't put traps on the map. That would defeat the purpose of them being traps.

"I'll have to keep my eyes forward the whole time," I said. "That means Donut, Quemada, and Finley, you keep your eyes out for threats behind and to the sides."

You know the third GPS upgrade comes with a threat radar.

"I get it," I said through gritted teeth. "There's only so much we can choose each race."

This all comes from your inability to commit. Your fear that decisions are the same as shackles.

"What? What are you talking about?"

Outside, it started to rain. Ahead, the grass sizzled, and soon a smoky haze filled the area, and we could no longer see the dirt road. The containment bubble would protect us from the air, but it wouldn't help us with the rain.

"Activating the shield," Olga said.

Thwum. The new shield turned on, and it was the exact same size as the containment, though this was much more visible. Outside, Lucienne was still screaming, and Dwight had also joined in. They were screaming down at the Dominators.

While the plan was to try to kill team Sparkles, we didn't have a specific strategy in place this time. I was starting to realize that was a mistake. I hadn't talked to the womantaurs, but I knew they very likely held a grudge against team Sparkles for blowing us all up at the end of the last race. If they tried something, it was likely that Corky was going to get killed. I couldn't let that happen.

He was the key to everything. Everything.

And now those idiots also had team Flamengo on the other side of them. A team that was just as likely to attack them as the unicorn.

I thought again of what Donut had said. I reached up to touch her, and I realized she, too, was shaking.

"No," I said out loud.

"No what?" Donut asked.

I sent another message to Osvaldo. I tried a different tactic.

CARL: Hey, Osvaldo. I know you're not talking to me, but I wanted to message you anyway. This is just you and me. Sorry about Donut. She lashes out when she's stressed. Look, I have a question, and I hope you answer. Did you have a quest with that memorial crystal? And did you fulfill that quest? Did you ever figure out how to use it?

He didn't answer right away. We only had a few minutes before the race would start.

OSVALDO: I had a quest to collect a memorial crystal for Tupa. I didn't get it until right at the moment that Imogen died, and my entire party would have gotten smited if I didn't collect it, so I did. But then after I got it, he said that one was corrupted, wrong. Then I had a lead on a second one in the forest during Faction Wars, and we hunted it down, and then the god said that one was wrong, too, and now I have a new quest to find out why the memorial crystals aren't working right.

CARL: Wait, so you had two memorial crystals?

OSVALDO: That's why I gave that one to the goat. I was going to break it in front of him for killing Gimli, but I'm so tired of this. Tupa wasn't sponsored at first, but now he is by some rich asshole. So I just gave the crystal to the goat. And then he was a complete prick about it and started yelling at me for not giving it to him sooner.

Christ, I thought. I had completely misread that situation. My intention had been to just get him talking, but now I was intrigued. Goddamn Prepotente had all the smarts in the world and still had no idea how to deal with people.

CARL: Who is the god you have the second crystal for?

I felt heat on my shoulder opposite Donut. It was Quemada.

"Uh, Que?" Finley asked from behind us. "You doing okay, mate?"

I turned to see the small fire fairy was just floating there. She was sobbing.

"I don't know what is real anymore," she said. "Is this real? Are *you* real? Am *I* real? Does any of this matter?"

OSVALDO: Ysalte. The Vinegar Bitch. The one Paz killed. He was my friend, you know. Paz and Anton and even Sister Ines. It's like everyone who ever comes in contact with you dies. Now it's our turn, I suppose.

Ahead, the floating traffic lights turned from red to yellow. The race would start in twenty seconds.

Fucking hell, I thought.

42

THE LIGHT TURNED GREEN, AND WE WERE OFF.

"Deal with your friend," I called to Finley as Olga floored it. We zoomed off down the dirt track. We were quickly outpaced by team Free Love, the bugbears zooming ahead of everyone else on their cushion of air.

"Donut, keep your shield ready in case the new shield doesn't work!"

"Where are the rain-wiper things?" Olga croaked.

"We don't have them," I said.

"Now you tell me," she complained. The shield was stopping the rain, but it was starting to fog up.

Thwum! I heard a heavy explosion behind us as we bumped over the road. Ahead, the forest loomed. We were going to take the middle path of the first split.

"What was that?" I called. I heard an engine rev, and the Lady Dominators team zoomed past us, hot on the tail of the bugbears. I could see Genesis in the passenger's seat, scream-laughing, all four arms giving an obscene gesture behind us.

It was Olga who answered, looking in the side mirror. "The thorny-bush thing fired a gun. I think at the deformed humanoids, but their vehicle was too fast. Their gun blasted right into the side of the hairy-animal team, and the animal fell over, but it's getting back up. The bush is now coming up fast." Olga turned her attention forward. "Why is this thing so slow? Did you really come in first place last time?"

CARL: Osvaldo! You guys okay?

OSVALDO: I'm going to kill that fucking unicorn and rat thing! We good. Bruna is tough.

"No!" Quemada shouted, pushing away from the badger. She was in a full-blown panic attack. It was getting warmer by the moment in the truck. It had come on so suddenly. "Didn't you feel it? Didn't you hear what that elf mage said? Didn't something in that small brain of yours break the moment you heard it? Because it broke in mine, Fin. Don't you see? Don't you now see what we are? We've been doing this over and over!"

"You're okay, you're okay!" Olga called. "Finley, do the thing. Do the calming thing." She looked over at us, smiling sheepishly. "She has a panic disorder. Don't worry. It'll be fine."

"The fire fairy has a panic disorder?" Donut asked incredulously.

Olga croaked. "We had another fairy in the group. Helado. An ice fairy. She was really good at calming her down. She was killed by the chain demon. Had a crazy hard time calming Quemada after that. She killed one of the two clients. But Finley eventually talked her down. So you ain't got nothing to worry about."

"Wait," Donut said. "She killed the person who hired her?"

"Only one of them," Olga said defensively. "She's better now."

"Emberus, help me understand," Quemada wailed.

We entered the forest, and it went from light to dark.

"On it," Donut said, casting *Torch*.

The road was already getting increasingly muddy and sticky. The shield protected us from the acid rain, but I worried how that worked with the tires. Our upgrade allowed us to change the size of the tires, but I didn't know if the shield actually protected them from the pools of acid on the ground.

Finley was saying something to Quemada, but I couldn't hear over the roar of the engine and the rain.

Ahead, the bugbears turned right, entering the trailhead for the safe, long path, and the Dominators went straight, heading for the same trail we were going to use. Team Sparkles zoomed up beside us, though they quickly swerved, going down the left path. One Fine Pig also rumbled in that direction. Osvaldo's mount, which was now up and running ridiculously fast, also turned down that road, meaning the only one on the same path as us was the Lady Dominators.

Quemada was babbling incoherently.

"I am not crazy!" the fairy cried. "Or am I? Am I crazy? What can I burn?"

"Everyone be quiet!" I called, keeping an eye on the track ahead.

Despite Donut's *Torch*, the jungle was oppressively dark, like it was constantly constricting on us. All around, the foliage was thick and winding, trees mixed with vines mixed with brambles, all steaming as the acid rain poured on it all. Everything had taken on an acrid, burning scent. The path we were on was barely wide enough to travel.

I could still see the taillights of the Lady Dominators, barely.

"Whoa, fuck me!" Olga cried, and swerved. We all went flying to the side as a new vehicle raged onto the path, merging from a road I hadn't even seen. The vehicle honked furiously and moved ahead of us, making it so we couldn't pass. It sprayed dirt, leaves, and mud, showering us with crap that collected on the edge of the shield.

"What in the name of the gods is that?" the toad shouted.

"It's the goddamned Wienermobile," I said. "It's from another heat. I know the guys driving it. It's those guys from the karaoke bar. The skull-faced ones in the pope hats."

"I talked to the leader of that group," Donut said from the back. "His name is the Minister of Blood-Letting. He's really creepy at first, but he has a deep love of singing. He says he's practicing so they'll let him into the Unholy Choir. I don't know what that means. I told him we'd be racing in the same heat, and he promised not to blood-sacrifice us to Baal, so that's good at least."

"Well, right now your friend's giant car is blocking the path," I said.

The fire fairy continued to sob. "Is Emberus even real? My lord, please show yourself. Please speak to me and Carl so we can cleanse—"

Alarmed, I turned to see the badger grab his friend out of the air. The fire fairy squirmed in his double-handed grip.

"No, no, no," Quemada said. "Stop, Fin. Please, stop. Let me end it all."

The Porsuk mercenary poked Quemada with one of his claws.

"Sleep now, friend," he said, his voice surprisingly gentle. The fire fairy suddenly had **Unconscious** over her. He carefully placed her in the sink.

"She okay?" Olga asked, turning in her seat.

The badger shook his head. "She hasn't been right since Helado died."

DONUT: I MEAN, REALLY. THIS ISN'T *DOWNTON ABBEY*. WE SHOULDN'T HAVE TO DEAL WITH DRAMA FROM THE HELP. DO WE GET A DISCOUNT WHEN ONE IS ASLEEP?

I was about to answer when another message came.

IMANI: You just passed us. We were behind the Bleak Congregation, and we pulled onto the road just as you passed. Elle is driving, and she drives like an old lady. But we're behind you. We already lost a team. Crawler Henrietta. You know that one from Angola? She was new this heat. They hit a trap. It swallowed their mount whole, and she and her partner are gone.

CARL: Damn. Okay. I'm going to send our course. Can you guys deal with the cliff up ahead?

IMANI: Yes. We have a wall-climbing and -descending kit. But it's slow.

CARL: We'll wait to make sure you make it.

43

THE ROAD JOLTED. THE TRACK SUDDENLY GOT BUMPIER. WE SLOWED down.

"Making the wheels bigger," Olga said, all business. "Carl, keep your eyes peeled. We're getting close to the outskirts of cannibal territory."

A set of headlights appeared behind us. They flashed. It was Imani and Elle's team. I knew they also had a mercenary in there with them, but I wasn't sure who it was. Their vehicle was an APV similar to but bigger than the military vehicle driven by the Tigran team.

"Wouldn't they only be cannibals if they were human?" Donut asked. "I mean, all sorts of monsters eat each other. Goblins eat each other, and I guess that makes them cannibals, but we don't call them cannibals. We call them goblins. So what are these things? And do they eat things that aren't each other?"

And that's when the cannibals attacked.

IMANI: Watch out! They're in the trees above you!

Splat. Splat, splat, splat. The pale creatures started dropping from the foliage, except they hit the shield, and when they did, they exploded like bags of tomato soup.

Donut increased her *Torch* to full blast, and suddenly night turned to day.

All the trees and bushes on either side of the path started violently shaking as the creatures hissed and screamed at the light.

There were hundreds of them. Thousands. They just came out of nowhere, suiciding themselves against the shield like they had no sense of self-preservation whatsoever. A chorus of high-pitched screeches filled the jungle.

"What are they? They keep blowing up before I can see them!" Donut yelled.

"They're human, I think, but they're acting like bugs," Olga said, voice full of wonder. "It's like the bright light has driven them mad."

Up ahead, a natural bridge crossed the path. The tall arch appeared to be made of a tree that had been deliberately bent over and tied. Hanging from it were dozens of skeletons. Decapitated, dried heads dotted the structure. Hundreds more random body parts and bones littered the arch like grisly Christmas tree decorations.

Standing on the bend, screaming and shaking their spears, were about a hundred of the cannibals.

They were pale, slightly pudgy human creatures. At least they appeared human, but I couldn't see their heads. They were all completely naked except for little loincloths. There were both men and women, and the women were not wearing tops. They all carried simple spears, and each wore a horrific wood mask ripped off from some home décor store's interpretation of an African tribe. Some carried primitive hide shields.

They seemed immune to the acid rain.

Splat! Splat! More dropped on the truck, only to explode against the magic barrier.

Olga tapped a gauge on the dash. "They're overheating the shield!"

"'Vaguely racist,'" Donut muttered. "I'd love to see its version of overt."

Her claw caps disappeared, and blue light filled the cab. She swiped into open air.

Her *Astral Paw* appeared, swiping through the woods ahead of us, sweeping all the cannibals on the bridge away like she was sweeping pieces off a chessboard. Most flew off into the jungle, screaming. The spell wasn't nearly as large as when she cast her *War Crime* spell, which she wouldn't be able to cast again until the twelfth floor, but it was still huge. Whatever was holding the arch down snapped, and the tree flipped up like a catapult, flinging the remaining cannibals in the opposite direction. Skeleton bones rained down. They crunched under the truck as we passed.

She waved a few more times, clearing the trees ahead. Trees all around snapped and broke. Screaming filled the jungle as we slowed.

ELLE: Holy hells, Donut. Have I told you recently how terrifying you are?

Donut growled with annoyance. Her claw caps reappeared, and the giant paw dissipated.

DONUT: IT'S A LOT STRONGER THAN IT WAS BEFORE, BUT IT DOESN'T LAST LONG, AND THE COOLDOWN IS MUCH LONGER NOW. IT'S SUPPOSED TO GET SHORTER AS THE LEVEL GOES UP, NOT THE OTHER WAY!

I nodded. "It's to keep you from moonwalking through the floors. How long before you can cast that again? And don't you have a new version you can cast also? The combined version?"

"I killed like eighty of them, and I didn't even go up a level! This is ridiculous! I can't cast it again for eight hours! The combined version with *Bijanbi* isn't a new spell. I can just combine the two and cast them both at the same time. Ow!" Donut suddenly jumped in the air, hitting the ceiling of the truck, spinning around. "What was that?"

"What, what?" I asked.

"I . . . I think that stupid dog tattoo on my butt just bit me!"

"Uh," I said.

Splat, splat!

More were coming from the sides, just throwing themselves against the side of the truck. The village itself was up ahead.

"Two or three more, and the shield will go out," Olga said. "It'll take a few minutes to recharge."

"Donut, get your shield ready."

A particularly large cannibal stood on the road ahead of us, blocking the path. This one was enormously fat, and it didn't hold a spear but a staff that glowed with enchantment. This one also seemed immune to Donut's bright light. Its mask wasn't made of wood but was carved from the skull of what appeared to be some sort of ape. I was reminded of the lemurs from the third floor.

"What should I do?" Olga asked, slowing even more as we approached. Imani and Elle's truck rumbled up behind us.

The mob pulled the ape mask off and dropped it to the ground, revealing that it was indeed a human. The older man had a balding mop of wild, curly red hair that was held up in a man bun held together with a single bone. His wide pale belly reflected in the light.

The man started chanting.

Soul Suck has been negated by your Mind Balance skill.

Donut scoffed. She would also be immune to this due to her high constitution-and-charisma combo.

"Are you kidding me?" I said upon reading the description.

Great Rusty. Cannibal Ginger Chieftain.

Level 99 neighborhood boss.

This is the leader of the southern cannibal forest settlement.

This is yet another storyline we lifted wholesale from the never-realized seventh floor that I was actually looking forward to because it featured the gingers, aka the perverts of the dungeon.

These humanlike mobs are actually from Earth, and we didn't change anything about them except we made them cannibals to fit in with the whole jungle theme.

This is a ginger. They hide amongst regular humans. They're the result of alien interference in the development of your human world, much like how octopuses are also the result of outside meddling after the initial seeding. Nobody really knows when the corruption was introduced, but it's suspected the Nullians were involved.

The men are said to be sexually deviant to a fault. The women are known to be . . . let's just say . . . extra spicy. Both sides have whacked-out pain tolerance, making them more susceptible to heat and cold, but immune to electrical and acid attacks. It's one of the reasons why they're prized targets for dentists and serial killers.

Oh, and they can suck your soul away. Never stare too long into the face of a ginger. If you get lost in their eyes, it's already too late.

Anyway, there are two ginger cannibal settlements in the forest. The north and south settlements, and they are at war with one another. If you decimate one tribe, it will create a power vacuum that would probably have a cascading, devastating effect on the entire region if this whole race wasn't just 20 hours. It's not like that's a metaphor or anything about how outsiders crash through cultures, have their fun, and then leave after they've vilified the natives and exploited them to the point where they can never possibly recover. And then, generations later, blame them because they still struggle to step up.

"I love how that whole thing is both socially conscious and outrageously racist at the same time," I muttered.

"This is gingerphobia laid bare," Donut said. "Disgusting. Ferdinand would be appalled. Though, if we're being honest here, the pervert part is probably true. I don't think I've ever met an orange cat who shouldn't be on some sort of registry. I'm assuming the same is true for humans."

"It's not. It's just a stupid thing people do to make fun of others. *None* of it is true! The AI is being a prejudiced dick."

"Not even the part about the women being spicier?"

"Well . . ." I paused and then shook my head. "No. It's just like everything else. It's a stupid, made-up stereotype. Besides, if the AI thinks redheads are the spiciest, he's clearly never met a Latina."

"I can't help but notice you've been referring to the AI as a 'he' a lot more recently, Carl."

Olga slumped over in the driver's seat. She had a debuff. **Gingered**. She was unconscious, and her health was rapidly draining.

"Oh, fuck!" I cried. "Finley!" I grabbed the frog and yanked her from the seat. She was weirdly heavy.

"Olga! Olga!" Finley cried as he awkwardly pulled himself forward.

Donut shot a magic missile at Great Rusty, who exploded, dying instantly.

Olga groaned. The **Gingered** debuff remained, but she was suddenly awake. Her health stopped seeping, but she didn't fully recover. She was just staring off into space.

"Are you okay?" I asked.

She didn't respond.

"Shit," I said. I sent a note to Mordecai.

MORDECAI: Did you kill the mob that did it? It'll return her soul, but she needs specialized healing from a cleric. She'll be in a fugue until that happens. Good thing you have a backup driver.

I turned to Finley, who'd awkwardly stuck himself into the driver's seat. "Floor it. Don't stop for anything."

"It did that voting thing for Great Rusty," Donut said. "I said let the audience choose, and they're voting now."

We moved, bumping through the village, pregnant women and small, freckled children jumping out of the way as we smashed through the center of town, knocking over huts and cook pots. Imani and Elle were hot on our tail.

In seconds, we were past and back on the road.

"Well, that sucked," I said. "At least we didn't get embroiled—"

New Quest. Pasty Inferno.

This is a mandatory quest!

Great Rusty, chieftain of the southern tribe has fallen. You blew him up, and then you ran over his corpse, and you didn't even leave a note with your insurance information!

Soon, Maurice, the chieftain of the northern tribe, will learn of his enemy's death and move in. And when that much power grows unchecked, everybody loses. The northern tribe will have enough power to march on Upano and devour everyone within.

Find and kill Maurice, chieftain of the northern tribe.

***Reward:* Whoever completes this quest will receive the contents of Maurice's cook pot.**

Warning: This is a mandatory quest. You will not be able to finish this race unless the Maurice on your track is dead.

ELLE: Fucking hell, Carl.

"Goddamnit, Dr. Metcalf," I said. "You said there weren't any quests on this path! We don't have time for this!"

Oh fuck off, Carl. This is just typical. Upgrade me, stop being selfish, and maybe you'll get better intel on this stuff. I can't read minds. The quest happened when the cat blew up the fat guy.

"Stop fighting," Donut called. She suddenly fired another missile out the window. Then another. "They're still out here! Finley, go faster!"

"We should've just followed the sausage truck," Finley whined. "I like sausages."

44

THE PIRANHAS DID INDEED FLY. BUT BY THE TIME WE REACHED THE river, our shield had recharged. We had to inflate our tires fully to cross the river, and then we waited on the opposite bank for Imani and Elle's APV to ford the river, which it did easily. The thing was meant to be amphibious even without upgrades.

The piranhas were especially strong for a mob that attacked in packs. Each one of the flying fish was level 50. They didn't explode like the cannibals did against the shield, but instead sort of sizzled and stuck there for a few moments before dropping away dead.

Donut used her *Fresh into Salt* spell on the river. She'd received the spell from her Champion of Nekhebit title. That pretty much finished off the rest. She still didn't go up a level.

As for the flying ones, we mostly allowed the truck to kill them for us.

Both Olga and Quemada remained unconscious. Finley kept chewing on his own claw as we bumped through the dark forest.

"This is no good, no good," he kept muttering to himself. "No good. No good. No pay is worth this. I shouldn't have used such a strong sedative on Que. She'll be mad when she wakes up. She'll be mad I didn't protect Olga."

"It's okay," Donut said in an attempt to cheer him up. "You're trying to save your friends, just as much as we are. You're okay. Maybe this town will have a cleric that will wake up Olga."

Finally, the pit stop loomed. There was an arch with the words "Pit Stop" over it in flashing neon light that looked ridiculously out of place in the middle of the jungle.

"Finally," Finley said, letting out a stream of breath.

Entering the Lost City of Upano. Mind the locals.

Safe room rules do not apply during pit stops.

"Huh, interesting," I said as we passed under the arch. A wide street spread out ahead of us. The houses from our cul-de-sac were here, but they'd been rearranged into a long line. It wasn't just our teams, but all the other houses from all three heats in a long suburban street. I saw with dismay the hot dog truck was there, poking out the back of a garage. Rapture and Genesis were walking from their garage toward a doorway at the end of the street that led to what looked like a group of falling-down buildings and huts.

Beyond the small city was a strange sight. Where I was expecting more jungle was something completely incongruous with the setting. To the east was what appeared to be a tall group of black tubes. It just went up and up and up, and opposite that was a group of cliffs. Opposite us, I was expecting more jungle, but it appeared like Upano just went on and on and on.

"There," I said, pointing at a garage door that started opening on its own. There was no number painted on the door, but the whole driveway started blinking. Hedy appeared, standing in the entrance. Just next door, closer to the entrance, another door started to open. This was Elle and Imani's garage.

A two-hour timer starts the moment you park in your garage.

Note: Garage doors may not be closed during pit stops. Safe room access is unavailable during pit stops.

"If the open garage doors indicate the ones who've already arrived, then we're doing better than I feared," I said, counting. There were twenty-four houses total, and only eleven of the doors were open, not including the ones for us and Meadow Lark. I started trying to see if I recognized any of the others.

Team Sparkles was in the very first garage, and I saw Osvaldo's slaughter gnu was also parked. After the Lady Dominators, that meant we were in fourth place, ahead of the bugbears and One Fine Pig, who had yet to arrive.

Two of the homes were boarded up. I assumed that meant teams who'd been lost along the way.

We pulled up, drawing all the way into the garage.

Timer starting. Your vehicle may not leave this garage until the two hours are up.

Hedy walked around the truck as we exited.

"Not too bad," she said, sounding impressed. "Much better shape than the last time." She reached over and with a gloved hand picked up a tuft of red hair that had somehow gotten stuck in the front bumper. It dripped with blood and sizzled a little from the acid rain. "Race ain't over yet, though."

"The new shield works great," I said. "But it needs more power to withstand a lot of abuse." Outside, a double-decker bus rumbled past. A dromedarian camel sat in the top half behind a massive gun battery that looked like an anti-air gun.

"No helping that," Hedy said. "They don't want your shields too perfect. It's a game. Don't you be forgettin'."

The bus was followed a minute later by Jasha and Radoslav's van, which had been put through the wringer. It looked as if it had been stepped on by a god. All its windows were smashed out. It still ran on the cushion of air, but it kept scraping against the ground, causing sparks to fly up. They moved into a spot across the street from Imani and Elle.

Donut released Mongo into the room. I'd left Rend in the stables. Mongo rushed in a circle, bouncing around and sniffing and shrieking at everyone. He stopped and sniffed the bumper.

"Be careful," I called. "There's acid still on there."

He growled and took a step back.

I returned my attention to Hedy. "Did I hear that correctly? We can't close the garage door? I guess we'll have to use Mongo to protect you."

"Yep," Hedy said. "They dropped that one on us right after the race started. It looks like that be the standing rule at pit stops. I ain't safe like this."

"Okay," I said. "And nobody stayed in the garage with you after we left?"

"No," Hedy said. "Ain't no door anymore."

"Jamal does protest" came Jamal's weak, cracking voice from the ceiling.

We all looked up.

The shark was attached to the very top of the hangar, looking down. He was planted directly above us.

"Hi, Jamal!" Donut said. Mongo looked up and let out a delighted shriek and started waving his wings.

"Yeah, other than him," Hedy said.

"What are you doing up there?" I called.

"Jamal was testing his legs. Jamal wished to see if he could walk upside down on the ceiling with the new and improved sticky feets Jamal has, and I do apologize, Mr. Carl, but now Jamal has found himself in quite the inverted conundrum."

"What's wrong?"

"Jamal is stuck!"

"What? Are your legs broken? How long have you been up there?"

"Jamal has been stuck for quite a bit, I fear. It is with great embarrassment that I admit this."

"Jamal," Donut said, "get down this instant! My goodness. Were you up there from before the race started?"

"Oh, yes, Miss Donut. Many hours before the race started. Jamal is feeling woozy."

Donut grumbled under her breath. "Why didn't you say anything? What's wrong with your legs?"

"Nothing is wrong. Jamal is afraid of heights."

"Afraid of heights?" Donut asked incredulously.

I sighed. "Jamal, I once watched you roll down a hill, flopping directly into a battle filled with giant soldiers in power armor. You have jumped higher than the ceiling dozens of times. You literally used to fly when you were a tattoo, for chrissakes."

"When Jamal jumps, he doesn't have time to see how high he is because he always falls down again."

"Okay, Jar Jar, listen," Donut started to say. "We don't have time to—"

But Jamal interrupted her, talking fast, his voice taking on a strange, sad tone. "Jamal is happy to have his legs, but he wishes he could just go back to the ocean. We aren't at war like before, but everything is so much scarier all of a sudden. Miss Hedy says if you die, we die. We won't even know. Everything will just stop. She says that's what happened to the gremlin and all the people in the houses of the other races. So Jamal came up here so he could see everything all at once. It's what Jamal used to do before when he was . . . when he was real. He was so brave, but he was not me. I know that, but I want to be brave. I want to be Jamal, but now I am up here and I can see it all, I am so scared of what I might lose. I'm scared to come down, because if I do, maybe I won't ever see it again."

Donut was suddenly floating in the hangar. She used her Hover ability. She floated up to the ceiling.

Donut started whispering quietly to the shark.

I didn't know what she said to him, but a moment later, he hopped, flipping in midair and landing deftly on the floor of the garage right next to the truck.

Jamal made a circle and just sort of settled on the floor. Mongo curled up next to him as Donut landed on my shoulder.

"What did you say to him?" I asked.

She didn't answer right away. She stared at Mongo and Jamal resting there on the floor of the garage for several moments, quietly kneading her paws into my shoulder. I gritted my teeth and tried not to react at her new strength.

"I said that he shouldn't be scared about that sort of thing. Yes, it could happen at any moment, it's true, but if we worry about things we can't control, we start to ruin the things we *can* control. And that even though he can be annoying, he's part of the family now and that he shouldn't be scared to tell us when he's in trouble. Even if we're frustrated with him, we'll help him the best we can because that's what family does."

Before I could respond, she raised her voice. "Mongo, mind your mommy and stay here and guard Hedy along with Jamal. Finley, you . . . Finley?"

The back door to the truck opened, and Finley appeared, cradling the toad in his arms. The Grulke was technically conscious, but she gaped off into space, her long tongue lolling and dragging on the floor.

He also had Quemada with him, draped over his shoulder. He had a patch of extra-thick scorched leather with a little strap on his jacket that I hadn't even noticed. It seemed as if it had been made just for the purpose of carrying the fire fairy around while she was knocked out.

"I'm going into town," Finley said. "I will see if there's a temple. I am taking Que with me because I don't want her to wake up and be alone."

He took a few steps, then paused and looked back at me and Donut. "I heard what you said to the shark. How you feel about him, I feel about these guys. They're *my* family. I've already lost so much, and I don't want to lose more, so I am going to help them the best I can. I know I'm supposed to do what you say and I promise to come back, but I want you to know this is *my* family, and I will do what it takes to protect them."

Finley walked right out of the open garage door, stepped onto the street, and was promptly mowed down and killed by the speeding APV from team One Fine Pig.

The APV hit the brakes, smearing the bodies of all three across the street, backed up a few feet, then went forward again, smashing them all further into the pavement before disappearing down the street and turning into their garage.

Your mercenary Finley has been killed!

Your mercenary Olga has been killed!

Your mercenary Quemada has been killed!

45

"I AM GOING TO FUCKING RIP YOUR HEADS OFF," I ROARED, STORMING into the garage for One Fine Pig. Their gremlin, a male named Lipstick, cowered in the far back of the garage where he'd been inspecting the front bumper.

The two Tigrans hadn't yet left their APV. An ethereal gun suddenly materialized, coming out the side of the vehicle right in the butt of the pig airbrushed on the side. The glowing blue weapon appeared non-corporeal. It was pointed directly at me. It started to hum.

"Oh, fuck!" I cried, jumping to the side as the gun fired.

Thwum!

The entire wall of the garage blew out. A wall of the next house over caved in, revealing the double-decker bus. The powerful blast hit the side of the vehicle, and it flipped, catching on fire.

"Hey! Hey! What the fucking fuck!" came the deep cry of a camel who had just exited the garage. There were three of them, all carrying baseball bats with spikes on them.

"You missed, motherfuckers!" I yelled, kicking the side of the truck right into the airbrushed face of Nico.

The top hatch opened, and Dario the Tigran appeared. "Get out of our garage!" He popped back down.

The three dromedarians entered the garage and started beating the shit out of the front of the APV with their baseball bats. Next door, the fire in the garage spread to the walls. Their gremlin was running around with a fire extinguisher, but a moment later, the entire double-decker bus was encased in ice, and the fire stopped. That was an Elle spell.

"We're gonna turn your insides sloppy!" one of the camels yelled as he jumped to the hood of the truck and started smashing the windshield with his bat. A crack formed in the glass. Then another.

Panicked pig squeals emanated from within.

Lightning crackled against the sky outside even though it was a clear day.

"Stop! Stop!" cried Lipstick the gremlin.

I barely registered any of this.

"Get the fuck out here!" I continued to scream, banging my fist on the door. My gauntlet had formed, and the heavily armored door dented inward with each punch.

Slam.

Slam.

Slam.

My ears were ringing. I could hear Donut shouting. Imani was shouting, too, but I was so red-hot angry, I couldn't comprehend what they were saying.

Zzzzzz. The square-shaped shield of the APV turned back on, pushing me back with a heavy electric shove. It was like I'd been walloped with a cattle prod. The camel on the hood of the truck flew upward and back, his head crunching sickeningly against the top lip of the garage door. He fell hard against the driveway and started to roll while another camel shouted his name. The camel's neck was broken, and he was dead before he even hit the road.

From inside the truck, Penelope continued to squeal.

Each time the pig squealed in panic, the sky flashed, and lightning cracked louder and louder.

The edge of the shield had tossed me all the way out of the garage through the hole they'd blasted in their own wall. I tumbled and rolled, my skin sizzling and burning from where it had come in contact.

From inside the garage came a new scream. Lipstick the gremlin was pressed against the back wall of the garage, pinned between the shield and the barricade. The gremlin suddenly exploded, the gore held aloft by the shield and spread in a red flowerlike pattern against the wall like a drop of blood pressed under a piece of glass.

I started to get back up, wondering if my *Wraith Phase* would work.

"Stop," Imani yelled, grabbing me by the shoulders, pulling me back. Jacobus the reverse tooth fairy buzzed around her head, laughing maniacally, clapping his hands.

"Carl, stop!" Donut cried at the same time. "Please, stop. Goodness, Carl. You can't fight a car. And you'll hurt Penelope!"

I just sort of missed what happened next. They'd walked me out of sight of their garage, and I sat at the curb, in front of the remains of our mercenaries. The two remaining camels dragged their now-dead friend away as they rushed back to their garage to look at their frozen bus.

I just sat there, breathing heavily. I stared at the splattered remains of the mercenaries on the street. Quemada had just poofed out in a flare, leaving a scorch mark. Finley's legs were gone. Olga's head had been caved in.

It had happened so fast. I was taken with how unfair it was. For weeks, months now, we'd been on the precipice of death. Crawlers I knew were dying left and right, and NPCs like these mercenaries were falling by the thousands.

But there was something about that simple act of defiance that Finley, an NPC I didn't even know, had shown, protecting his two friends. He had been on his way to help them, and then all three of them had just been snuffed out.

"Fuck!" I cried out. I was so angry, so overwhelmed. After all that, for them to be hit and killed right there on the street? "Fuck!"

Jacobus buzzed near my head. He whispered in my ear. *"Jeg hader også tigre. De har kun tredive tænder. Hvis du betaler mig, eller hvis du lader mig kneppe grisen, får jeg deres kranier til at eksplodere."*

I had no idea what he was saying or why it wasn't translating. Donut hissed at him, and he buzzed away.

The two remaining camels were now sitting on the floor of their garage. One put his head into the lap of the other. Imani and Elle were in there talking to them, giving us space.

We were fucked. We couldn't drive. We couldn't hire new mercenaries between heats. Imani couldn't drive.

We couldn't even use goddamned Jamal because he counted as a hired mercenary, and gremlins couldn't drive.

Donut was on my shoulder, not sitting but wrapped around my neck, purring loudly.

"It's okay," she whispered. "It's okay. We'll find a way. We have plans in case this happens. Remember?"

Mongo squawked in concern from inside our garage. I took another breath. I reached up with a shaking hand and stroked Donut.

She was right. I couldn't do that. I couldn't react like that. Now that I was thinking more clearly, I could see all wasn't lost yet. We had options, none of them good, but we still had them.

"Donut," I said, "can you please take the corpses? Finley and Olga at least." The dromedarians had left the body of their friend outside their garage. "Take that one, too."

She moved to the street and did as I asked.

Around the corner, I could hear the Tigrans fighting. I was pretty sure they didn't know I was still nearby and could hear them. All the anger I'd been feeling had now fled and was replaced with determination.

We needed to take a team out, especially now, but we needed to be smart about it. The unicorn was the biggest threat, but for right now, I just needed to make sure one of the teams was gone because I was no longer confident in our chances to not come in last.

I thought again about the description of Penelope the pig. Of the lightning that had just flashed across the sky.

A tear rolled down my cheek. *Goddamnit,* I thought. *Goddamnit.*

There *was* a way out of this. Out of it all. But it wouldn't be easy.

"I'm keeping her in the truck," Dario was saying. "It's safer in the truck."

"Then you come out with me," Nico, who was the buff one, said. "I don't like you alone with her in there."

"We should both stay in the truck," Dario said. "We shouldn't have run over those mercenaries. That human was pissed. Look what he did to the door. He did that with his hand. And now the camels are mad, too."

"Fuck him and fuck them," Nico said. "We'll blow them all off the road if we see 'em. Remember the plan. We win this, and we get Penny to the safe place. She's the important one."

"Lipstick is dead," Dario replied. "What are we going to do?"

"We need to find a new one on the track. There should be two out there. And if not, we can use a few *Emergency Gremlins* to keep it running until we find one. Eyes on the prize."

"Okay," Dario replied, sounding hesitant. "But don't get in a fight with that human. If you see him, get back into the truck."

"I can take that bitch," Nico replied.

"Maybe. But you can't take the cat. And if something happens to him, we'll have to deal with her. If we fall, Penny will be defenseless against her sultry advances. I knew we should've gotten a mercenary this round."

"They were charging too much."

From the street, Donut let out a deep growl. From the garage came scrambling, and I heard the two Tigrans jump back into their truck and lock the doors. The shield turned back on.

LOUIS: Guys, make sure you go into town. The weird bat dudes are selling acid rain protection, but they're going to run out.

DONUT: HOW IS IT GOING? IS YOUR TEAM OKAY?

LOUIS: We're in first place for once. First place in our heat. Prepotente is in *first* first. I don't know if it's going to last. But before the race that Bodi guy went into Hungry Eyes all by himself and ate like a thousand things from all the different stalls, and his buffs make Eileen go really fast.

DONUT: IS EILEEN YOUR LOWRIDER?

LOUIS: Yeah. I didn't name her. She has it painted on the side, but Britney thinks that's the name of the person who drove the truck because the fuzzy dice are pink. Anyway, most of the tracks are like waterslide tubes, and there's this Satan guy, who keeps saying, "I hope none of these tubes lead to my butthole." It's really weird. Sweety, that's Prepotente's tapir thing, really likes the water tubes, and we've just been following them. Prepotente says he knows the best path.

CARL: We're on our way.

46

"COME ON, DONUT," I SAID. I RAISED MY VOICE TO ELLE AND IMANI, WHO were still in the garage with the camels. They'd defrosted and helped right the school bus. "Come on, guys," I called. "Let's go into town."

CARL: We're first gonna make a quick stop.
IMANI: How are you feeling? You went a little crazy there.
CARL: I'm sorry. I freaked out for a second. Donut talked me down. I shouldn't have done that.
IMANI: This floor is getting to all of us. We gotta keep our heads.
CARL: I know. I know. I'm better now, and I have an idea.

I stood. Donut remained on my shoulder. I returned to the Tigran garage. They'd fled back into their truck at the sound of Donut's voice. The two Tigrans were sitting in the cab, glaring at us through the shattered windshield. Dario was trying to cover the pig's eyes so she couldn't look upon us. Or, more likely, look upon Donut.

"Donut," I whispered, *"Glitzy Pizzazz."*

"Why? We don't want to hurt the pig."

I explained what I wanted to do. Donut scoffed, but she did as I asked.

Her headset microphone appeared. She leaped off my shoulder and posted up in the center of the driveway, facing the truck. Across the street, Elle and Imani waited, watching.

ELLE: What in god's name are you two doing?
CARL: We're distracting them.

ELLE: Isn't that pig off-limits?

CARL: I'm testing a theory.

"Attention, fake tiger people," Donut announced, waving her paw. "Yes, down here. Yes, look at me." Her voice rose in volume, and her Auto-Tune kicked on. "You killed our mercenaries, and then you killed your own gremlin. Because of that, you don't deserve the gift I am about to give you. But Penelope is just an innocent pig, and this is for her. She seems upset, and I know the timing is inconvenient for everybody, but this is quite important. As Carl hasn't yet practiced with his bagpipes like he promised, I *was* going to sing you a song Acapulco, but instead I think I'm just going to talk. I am, after all, a dungeon-renowned bard. But I don't want you to think I'm attacking you with a song, so instead I will just be giving Penelope some advice."

"It's 'a cappella,'" I called.

"That's what I said. Don't ruin it, Carl! Anyway, Penelope, tigers, please listen."

Both of the Tigrans started screaming. Nico took his hands and attempted to cover the oblivious pig's ears. It wouldn't have mattered.

Donut was casting the spell *All Eyes on Me*, which under normal circumstances required a song. But because her charisma was so high, she could now cast it with spoken words. After just a few seconds of her talking, they wouldn't be able to keep their eyes off of her.

"Penelope, I'm sorry, but you need to hear this. I am not saying there's anything wrong with your little throuple as it currently stands *in theory*, but I strongly feel all three of you could use some relationship advice. Situationships where two of the members are at each other's throats are destined to end in heartbreak. It's all too common with pigs, as they're famously known to be attracted to toxic relationships. I mean, look at Miss Piggy. Honestly, she's the toxic one as she abuses poor Kermit. People give her a pass because she's beautiful and knows karate. And then there's Piglet, who is what some people call a twink, and he's in a relationship with a bear who is unbelievably selfish. Don't even get me started on your team's namesake, 'One Fine Pig.' That's Wilbur, who we're supposed to think is a friend to this spider lady, but that's only because . . ."

As Donut droned on, I went to work. It only took about five seconds for me to lay a hidden trap on each side of the truck, getting as close to the shield as I dared. These were both disintegration traps, similar to the one I'd just looted from the war mage as he hid behind the door. The good thing about these particular traps was that they were completely silent when they activated, and they would only target a single individual. But to be safe, I programmed them both to only activate when stepped on by Tigrans. Even if one was literally carrying Penelope, she should be safe.

"Come on, Donut," I called, walking away.

". . . which is why Peppa is absolutely destined for a Denny's ham lover's breakfast skillet if she doesn't immediately do something about her cousin, Chloé. Anyway, it was nice talking to you. I hope I've given you something to think about. See you later!" She waved, and the twin Tigrans, who'd stopped screaming, just sort of blinked and looked at each other, both unaware that they'd been charmed.

We quickly moved down the sidewalk, catching up to Elle and Imani. From down the street, the weird pope creatures who drove the Wienermobile emerged from the city. One of the skeletal creatures was holding what looked like a bucket of a white sloshing liquid. And behind him, walking like he was floating on air, was the creepy pope-skeleton guy.

Donut gasped and waved from my shoulder. "Hi, Minister of Blood-Letting! I hope you're having a good race!"

The creature bowed as they passed, not saying anything.

"That dude freaks me out," Elle said. "And what was in that bucket? It looked like jizz. I hope we aren't going to be buying jizz. I got enough of that when Carl yanked off that crab."

"The Minister is very nice," Donut said. "But that bucket did smell revolting. I didn't get a chance to examine it."

"I did," Imani said. "It's something even worse."

47

"THIS IS NOT ACCEPTABLE," DONUT SAID FOR THE HUNDREDTH TIME. "Ew, ew, ew."

"It's not *really* splooge," Louis said, bringing the bucket he'd purchased for me. "That's what we're calling it, though. It says it's 'secretions.' I don't think that means poop, but it smells like it. The bat dudes sell it."

Even though they weren't on our track, it turned out a few different races were using the same pit stop location, which was really weird given the theme. In one direction loomed a wall with tubes, which was the Satan's Water Park race, and in another direction stood the devil's cliffs. The fourth led to what appeared to be a rip-off of the third floor called "the eternal slum."

Still, this wasn't everyone. Tran's pit stop was a Candy Land setting, and a few other crawlers reported they were at what was basically a shopping mall that just went on and on.

The storyline with the cannibals seemed to exist in all four worlds feeding into our own, which was doubly strange. In the water park, there were gingers literally falling down the slides on inner tubes attacking the racers. In Florin's world, they had dune buggies.

Florin said they were currently in first place in their heat. Chris's team was also doing well, despite having a big rig complete with a trailer. They'd focused on movement-based upgrades and were following Florin's tricked-out tuk-tuk through their desert track, which ran alongside some sheer cliffs.

Prepotente wouldn't stop talking about all the benefits of this newly discovered splooge potion.

"A single sip, like half of a potion bottle's worth, appears to imbue one with about a half hour of protection," Prepotente said. "It is truly a superior and versatile protection against most environments. Strange that it requires us to drink it manually."

"It makes us drink it manually because it tastes like Miami swamp ass," Louis said.

"I wouldn't know," Prepotente said.

Donut sat a good distance away, looking at us with disdain. "I am not getting anywhere near those disgusting-smelling buckets until you put them in your inventory."

Zev's voice came over a loudspeaker.

Hi again, everybody. Most of you have made it to your pit stops, so it's time to reveal the twist.

As you've undoubtedly noticed, each track has four separate heats on it, and each pit stop combines four tracks. Each individual heat will roll for what path they continue on, so the second half of your race may not be on the same track you started on. There will be a random drawing for each individual heat, so the heats will be jumbled up. The moment the team in first place in your heat times out, you will receive your new assignment.

Also, some of you have received quests that require you to complete tasks that you have not yet completed. Please do not worry about that. Even though all four tracks are very different, the associated quests are mirrored on each track, and your quest will be transferred. In other words, you will be able to complete your quest on the new track.

Good luck, everybody.

"Shit," I said, looking up in the air.

"Wait," Donut said from her spot. "Does that mean we won't be racing with Imani and Elle anymore? Or in the jungle?"

"Maybe," I said. "We'll find out in a few minutes."

Florin nodded. "We're leaving in ten minutes. Just got the notification. Me and Lucia moved from the desert to Satan's Water Park."

"I'm staying in the desert," Chris said a minute later.

"And I am moving to the jungle," Prepotente said, walking up. "Unfortunate. I had the water park tunnels all mapped. Sweety will be most upset. You just want to make certain you don't take a wrong turn, as they come quickly. It's very high-speed. This jungle appears to be more leisurely."

The leading team in your heat, Team Sparkles, will soon be allowed to disembark. Rolling now for your track . . . You will be moving from the jungle track to Satan's Water Park.

We still had almost an hour before we could leave, which meant we were way behind team Sparkles.

Before I could announce our new choice, I received a pair of notifications.

Your trap has activated! You have dissolved a Tigran! That hairy fucker is dead!

Again! Another trap has activated! You dissolved another tiger!

Team One Fine Pig has been eliminated due to the expiration of both racers. Five teams remain.

I held my breath, waiting to see if there was a notification about Penelope the pig. There was not.

"Looks like we're in the slums," Elle said. "Great. What did you get?"

"We have the water park!" Donut said.

"Okay," I said. "Florin, we are with you. But we're an hour behind. We need to win our heat. We need to win because we need to get that key. We need that key because we need to get that pig."

"Mate, I don't know what pig you're talking about," Florin said. "But if there's a team in your heat you need slowed down, you just let me know."

I grinned. "Let me tell you about a unicorn named Dwight."

48

"A *HEDGEHOG*," DONUT SAID FOR THE HUNDREDTH TIME. "THIS IS JUST ridiculous."

"Just ignore it," I said. "Apparently this thing's kids were on the first or second floor, but we never fought them. If we do this right, we won't have to deal with it at all."

We pulled out of the garage, turned the corner, and moved to a jerking stop at the starting line with about one minute left. We left Hedy and Jamal in the garage, and Donut had Mongo back in her inventory.

I sat in the passenger's seat with a white-knuckle grip on the dash, Donut on my shoulder. Even Dorota had stopped complaining once the seat realized what was happening.

From the driver's seat, the resurrected corpse of Olga made a slurping noise. Her head was completely caved in, but the toad's long tongue still lolled out of the ruined mess, bobbing and oozing like a yo-yo that had been dipped in slime.

Donut's *Second Chance* spell was currently at level 11, which brought it up to level 12 with her Brain Trust skill. The spell brought the dead corpse back to life for a maximum of fifteen minutes, and she'd already been resurrected for five.

Florin had left forty minutes previously and was giving me a blow-by-blow on the track so far. He'd offered to go after the boss on our behalf, but we'd decided that he should instead pursue Dwight and Lucienne and attempt to slow them, as they most likely wouldn't be taking the same path we'd chosen.

Thankfully, we had a way to catch up, assuming we could talk these corpses into driving in a straight line.

Osvaldo had also moved ahead of us, and he was following Florin's route. If this worked out correctly, we would still be able to overtake him along with everyone else.

I spent a moment just staring at the biggest wild card in this insane plan.

The corpse behind the steering wheel.

I was trying to stay confident, but this *was* a terrible idea. Since this was a summon, it skirted the rules. We were relying on voice instructions to drive. I was already second-guessing our decision to do it this way, but the alternative was worse, which was to have Mongo drive, which wasn't really an alternative at all but a last-ditch Hail Mary.

Someone from Florin's heat pulled up. It was a tow truck with a steering wheel on the right side, putting them right against Olga. The driver was a female troll with a high pink mohawk and a hook nose. A cigarette dangled from her lip. Her eyes first lingered on me, and she started to smile big, but then she finally noticed Olga after an especially big spurt of fluid. The cigarette dropped from the troll's mouth.

Nobody else was on the line. I knew Jasha and Radoslav would be right behind us. They were frantically working on last-minute repairs for their van.

I went over what we knew so far about our new track, Satan's Water Park. There were dozens of slides reminiscent of the Iron Tangle, though with a much easier-to-follow map. The problem wasn't getting confused by the path, but making sure you took the correct path in the first place. If you took the incorrect path, you would end up . . . inside . . . the boss of the track.

Satan himself was a country boss, but he was invulnerable, and he wasn't a boss that one was meant to fight. He was the owner of the water park, and he lounged near the exit, occasionally offering loud opinions on the things happening, occasionally poking at the racers.

Satan also wasn't Satan in the traditional sense.

Satan was a hedgehog. A kaiju-sized male hedgehog. And now Donut knew this, she wouldn't shut up about it. She, apparently, took issue with the entire species.

"Wannabe, effeminate porcupines," she grumbled.

According to Prepotente and Louis, the hedgehog had spent most of the first half talking and commenting on the racers as they made their way through the waterslides.

"It's unnatural," Donut exclaimed upon hearing about it. "The waterslide ending up in the thing's butt, I understand. Hedgehogs are notorious deviants. Louis didn't say, but I bet it talks with a British accent. You know how I feel about fake British accents, Carl."

"Wait," I said now, suddenly remembering something. "Is this about that beauty-contest thing? How do you even remember that? You were a kitten!"

I vaguely remembered one of Donut's early cat shows wasn't at a dedicated cat event, but at a sprawling pet festival in Tacoma that included dogs and exotic animals with multiple competitive events going on at once. It was one of the few shows I'd actually attended because it had a beer garden. The winners of each category had a "Cutest in Show" showdown, and kitten Donut had been up against a few animals, including a Great Dane puppy with spots, a snake, a ferret, and a baby hedgehog named Jezebel, who was one of the most goddamn adorable things I'd ever seen.

Jezebel had won, which had put Bea into a funk for the rest of the day. Donut, of course, had been oblivious and had been happy to lick up my vanilla milkshake on the ride back to Seattle. I remembered she'd gotten it all over her face, and Bea had been pissed because she had another show the very next day in the Tri-Cities.

"That has nothing to do with it," Donut snapped. "Even if that was fixed from the beginning. Who names a hedgehog Jezebel anyway? Doesn't that mean 'slut'? So it was a slut hedgehog? She was a baby! The owner should've been disqualified just for that."

"She was from a hedgehog rescue," I said.

"Of course she was," Donut said. "It was hardly a fair contest. Of course the slut orphan is going to win."

I reached up and gave Donut a few strokes. She was nervous, which was why she was lashing out.

"It'll be okay," I said. She leaned into my hand.

Next to us, Olga groaned.

While the tubes dominated the first half of the race, the ground-level challenges were more eclectic. Dr. Metcalf now had the map, and there were multiple paths, including the ominously titled toddler splash pad, the wave pool, and a massive loop-de-loop, which was the fastest path to the exit but was clearly the most dangerous. The giant loop dominated the bottom part of the park.

Our path was just south of the loop and was called the River of Sloth. This last one was clearly the slowest path. It was the water park's version of a lazy river. This was deeper than the water in the tubes, and there were supposedly rafts, but we had plans to deal with it all.

Olga made a bubble-popping noise as more gore oozed from her ruined head onto the seat.

Dr. Metcalf beeped.

This is absolutely disgusting. She doesn't have a head, and I can't imagine that ridiculous spell is going to last long enough. We are all going to die.

"I'm going to cast *Clockwork Triplicate* before it times out," Donut said, having composed herself. "That'll give us about twenty more minutes. Don't be such a Debbie Downer. It'll work." She took a breath. "Right, Carl?"

"Right," I said as Olga continued to leak.

But why did you pick the one without a head?

"Finley's remains don't have legs," I said. "I used up most of my good corpses on the last floor, but if she doesn't work out, we do have a few more. We have a camel and a couple of NPCs from Faction Wars, and Elle lent us a ton of dead orcs." I didn't add that most of the orcs were also headless. Elle had gotten really good at some spell that froze the liquid surrounding one's brain and then caused it to explode.

SHE DOESN'T HAVE A GODSDAMNED HEAD. HOW IS SHE HEARING YOUR COMMANDS?

"I find it's better not to think too hard on some of this stuff," Donut replied. "I don't know how she hears me, but she does. Isn't that right, Olga?"

Olga squelched in agreement.

I reexamined the map update for the water park. The ginger base camp was right at the halfway point for the River of Sloth, so we'd have been forced to take this path whether we wanted to or not.

The gingers on this track weren't called *cannibals* but "season pass holders." Our quest had been updated, and we still needed to find and kill this Maurice guy.

Elle and Imani, who were in the eternal slum, still had the quest also, and they needed to find and kill another iteration of Maurice, this one called the Red Menace of Tinker Town.

Beside us, the tow truck zoomed off. We still had ten seconds. The truck disappeared through the arch, and I heard deep, booming laughter. That was Satan the hedgehog.

"Jolly good show," he said. "Pip-pip!"

From my shoulder, Donut bristled.

49

<Entry from *Carl's Book of Boom.*>

Mehmet Or. Crawler #3,756,330.

Race: Human.

Class: Sipahi.

Final Level: 62.

Hello, Carl. My name is Mehmet, and we never met, but I still knew who you were even before you helped save my life at the end of the eighth floor.

I am a nobody. I used to own one of the most popular bowling alleys in Istanbul. I inherited it from my father, who had always dreamed that I would take over his business. It wasn't a job that I loved, and it wasn't something that made me a lot of money, but I stayed with it because that's what we're supposed to do. We honor the wishes of our parents. My mother was still alive that day when it happened. My wife was alive and pregnant with our third child, who would've been my first son. I killed her when she was in the hydra.

Please, I beg of you. Forgive my cowardice in taking a deal. I cannot risk fighting any further. I cannot risk dying. I do not know if this is the best choice, but I am so scared, so tired. I have too much to lose if I make the wrong decision.

My daughters, Azra and Yaz, were not in the hydra. They were with me outside when it happened, but they did not come with me when we stepped into the light. I believe this means they may still be alive in that place where they're keeping the children. This knowledge is the only thing that has kept me going, and I pray that after you kill them all, you help me find them.

And if by some chance you can't save those of us who took the deals, please find my Azra and Yaz and tell them that their father fought to save them and that he's sorry he's not there anymore, but that he will love them until the very end of time.

I was never the best fighter in my group, but our mage loved this spell because it helped focus the area of effect of his own spells. I hope it's as useful to you as it was to our party.

Drawing: An amateur picture of a bowling alley.

Associated Spell: *Gutter Bumper*. Casts at level 9.

"YOUR OTHER LEFT!" DONUT CRIED AS A CLOCKWORK OLGA JERKED the steering wheel. The truck crunched loudly and sparks flew as the side hit the edge of the tube, but we made it onto the correct path. If we hadn't had the gyro upgrade, we'd have already flipped over a dozen times by now.

"Straighten!" Donut shouted, her voice going up an octave. "Straight! Straight!"

The original Olga had already timed out and spilled goo everywhere. The second clockwork sat on the floor of the truck behind me, groaning, back against the pile of weapons and chains, yanking on its own tongue as wet gore sloshed everywhere.

So far, the tubes were pretty much what I had expected, though way less steep than I had feared. The first part was a literal tube, but the second half was more of a wide half-pipe at a slight angle, more like the entrance to a sewer system. These half tubes were how we knew we were on the correct path, as all the enclosed tubes led straight to Satan.

The water was about half the height of the tires, and I worried about the engine, but we'd had Hedy put some protections in place, including a raised air intake. So far it hadn't been an issue, and we hadn't even had to inflate the tires.

I dropped a sticky hob-lobber out the window, and I kept my head out the passenger's side as the group of axe-wielding gingers on inner tubes approached from behind. I counted and then hit the detonator as they passed.

Bam!

A red gurgle of liquid coiled up and over the edge as body parts swirled and sloshed.

"Bloody 'ell," Satan commented from his spot at the far end of the park. The mountain-sized hedgehog yawned and then rolled onto his back. All the tubes attached to various parts of his body twisted with the giant animal's movements. The fixed amusements on the ground, however, weren't as flexible, and a distant roller coaster filled with riders broke apart and fell. Panicked screams filled the park.

"No refunds," Satan grumbled.

"Carl," Donut shouted, looking down at the distant destruction, "wasn't that the path Florin was on? That idiot creature is ruining everything!"

The bottom section of the water park was part carnival with a few amusement rides and booths, all filled with "customers." The customers were a mix of the gingers, who all carried axes and chainsaws, and level 40 splatter penguins, who were all water mages. A few demon-like pixies also flitted about.

From the edge of the half-pipe, a group of zipper shrews screamed as they rushed along the lip of the tube, keeping pace. They occasionally jumped toward the truck, only to get zapped by the shield. The little level 10 rodents were everywhere, infesting the park. They were like regular tiny shrews but had drills for heads.

Despite our shields, everyone in the cab was absolutely soaked, including Donut, who wouldn't shut up about it. A wet slurry of gore filled the floor of the truck, making everything slippery. This new clockwork version of Olga no longer leaked fluid, but a spring or cog occasionally popped out of the open skull with a *boing*.

FLORIN: We gotta backtrack! Gonna try the loop. Unicorn doing it, too. I have the Denial of Service missiles, and I'll hit the unicorn just as they start the loop. If they're not going fast enough, they'll drop right out and will have to start again.

CARL: Still no sign of the Lady Dominators?

FLORIN: Nope. Sorry, mate. I can see what place we're in overall,

so I know they're behind us but ahead of you. Probably still in the basement.

Florin's GPS gave detailed information on everyone in the race, but even the upgraded version only gave rudimentary info on the other three heats.

We still had a few minutes before we hit the ground level of the park. Dozens of the gingers and penguins kept attacking us from all angles, along with a constant rain of the zipper shrews, but our shield was more than enough to keep them off. We were mostly just ignoring and occasionally running over them, as we slipped and slided down the path, keeping steady thanks to our gyro.

While we had no idea for certain where the Lady Dominators were, we knew that Florin and team Sparkles had been harassing each other all the way down the track. Lucia Prime's psycho personality had wandered back into the body, and she was the one driving. Florin was doing his best to keep her from actually killing the unicorn and the rodent.

The only surviving team from our own heat behind us was team Free Love.

We'd been going down this steep road for some time now, getting attacked left and right, but I could see the slide ended in a bunch of brambles. The clockworks were going to time out in a minute, and I pulled the large camel corpse out. This was the Bactrian who'd broken his neck against the ceiling of One Fine Pig's garage. His name was Joel.

"Donut!" I called.

She cast *Second Chance* on the camel just as we crashed through the brambles.

"Brake! Brake!" Donut called as we jumped over a barrier and slid through the ground-level walkway, knocking over the sign that gave directions to the various attractions. To our left, the toddler splash pad loomed, and a mix of small gingers and pixie demons played as spikes randomly popped up in the air. One such pipe hit a pixie, and the literal word "SPLASH" appeared in neon over the dead creature. The others all shouted with glee and jumped upon the body as the spike retracted.

"You!" Donut said to the large camel. "Stay there and watch her drive until she times out, and then take over."

The camel's neck was broken and his head hung down at a sharp angle. A line of black drool speckled with green dangled from his mouth, but he groaned in compliance. The second clockwork Olga moved farther back to give him a better view. That one had accidentally pulled her own tongue out, and it sparked where it had disengaged from her body.

"Activate the spider legs!" Donut called, pointing at the lever. "Olga! No, not there. Yes, yes, that. Pull it, and then turn the steering wheel all the way to the right!"

The clockwork zombie toad pulled the correct lever, and we all rose up in height as the legs took over. We skittered awkwardly to the right as the blind zombie jerked the steering wheel, skittering us toward the large concrete wall.

"Quit your bellyaching!" Satan rumbled. He was talking to someone else. The very ground shook. He let out a satisfied squeak. "Oh yes, yes. This water is so refreshing, so clean, so pure. Right into my delicate bum."

"I told you they were all perverts!" Donut yelled.

This next part of the track was a trick, but it was one that Prepotente had already figured out even though he'd only had clues from the first half before the pit stop. Florin, Osvaldo, and all the others had already gone through this area. Florin had deliberately allowed the trick to activate, which delayed everyone passing through by about an hour.

We were going to skip this part completely.

The trap was that as soon as one passed through this central area where one had to choose a path for the final approach to the exit, the ground would drop out, dropping everyone into the waterworks and pipes under the park, where all the racers had to make a long, twisting circuit in the dark, fighting off Sheol demons and baby versions of the hedgehog, culminating in a Garden Gnome Sprinkler borough boss. Once the teams made it through this part, they would pop back up on the path they had been on before.

Team Sparkles had one-shot and shattered the boss with one of their guns. They hadn't even paused.

Our plan was to sidestep all of this, which would save us a good hour, helping us catch up. But we still wouldn't be in the lead. We needed Florin to slow the unicorn down.

"Everyone, hold on!" I called as we hit the wall, then skittered up it.

Just-replaced pots and pans spilled from the cabinets as we turned at a 90-degree angle, moving up the wall at the edge of the park. Thankfully, the system wouldn't let us climb up and over. Donut shrieked at the clockwork Olga to steer as we rushed along the wall, moving toward the entrance to the lazy river. We just had to get past the entrance arch.

The driver's-side door to the truck suddenly opened, and the clockwork Olga dropped away, leaving the driver's seat empty.

"I told you to put your seat belt on!" Donut cried as the toad hit the road, causing the trapdoor to yawn open. The automaton disappeared into the darkness.

50

IN SECONDS, THE DRIVERLESS TRUCK WAS PAST THE HIDDEN TRAP-door, and we continued forward along the wall as Donut shrieked for the camel to grab the wheel. But before he could, we reached a turn in the wall, and the truck ran off the edge. We dropped, then hit the ground hard, crunching loudly and sliding before we bobbed up and righted ourselves like a boat. Two of the spider legs were suddenly smoking and broken, but we continued on our way, moving at an angle toward the entrance to the lazy river, occasionally mowing over wide-eyed gingers standing there on the concrete ground as they queued up to enter the water.

We'd done it. We'd moved past the hidden entrance to the basement. But we still weren't in the lead. We had one trick left.

"Hurry!" Donut shrieked at the camel, whose hoof slammed painfully into my crotch as he attempted to move into the driver's seat. He drooled black-and-green slime as he shoved himself into the seat, the steering wheel tight against his chest. The engine revved as his hoof scrambled for the proper pedals.

"He's too big!" Donut cried.

Praying this didn't count as driving, I reached down and grabbed the slider control at the bottom of his seat, and I pressed against the camel's chest, pushing him back as far as the seat would go. I pressed too hard, and my hand went all the way into his chest, and I felt organs squish under my palm.

Joel the camel gasped as I pulled back.

"Gah," I cried, shaking my hand. It was covered in black goo.

"Why did you do that?" Donut yelled as I wiped my hand on the seat. Dorota started to loudly complain.

The seven-foot-tall undead camel didn't seem affected by the new hole in his chest. He was still too big for the seat, but at least he could now move with the chair back. He slammed the brakes, causing us all to crash forward against the dash before settling.

Donut started shouting instructions on how to disengage the spider legs and inflate the tires. We had mobs coming at us from all angles.

FLORIN: Approaching the loop. I was wrong. The Lady Dominators are behind me, and they're trading blows with the unicorn team. The gnu is also trying to do the loop, but we just passed them. I'm going to . . . Fuck!

CARL: What?

Florin answered, but before I could read it, the second clockwork Olga, who was still in the back of the truck near the pile of weapons, timed out, exploding in clockwork parts. The detonation blew the back door open, causing loose pots and pans to spill out onto the path. I took a small amount of damage.

The massive pile of weapons, all connected via chains, rattled ominously, but they remained where I'd tied them up.

The camel groaned as he finally figured out the controls and angled us toward the river. There was a large blinking sign that read "Enter Here." It featured artwork of a red-eyed sloth taking a rip from a bong.

The river was full of gingers floating along in inner tubes. Somewhere in that mess would be Maurice the boss. We didn't have time to find him, so we were going to try to kill them all at once.

I read Florin's set of messages.

FLORIN: Lucia cast a spell that left a brick wall on the track, which pretty much stopped the gnu and the womantaur team. The unicorn went right over it.

There were more messages, including one from Tran, but I waved them away. We needed to focus on this race. I moved to the next one from Florin.

FLORIN: Speeding up now to do the loop. That damn bush thing is fast as a horny cheetah. They're right on our tail.

I turned to look at the giant loop that dominated the lower half of the park. Satan, too, had turned his giant dark eyes on the attraction. His nose seemed to quiver in anticipation.

Ahead, the onboarding area of the River of Sloth loomed. There was a raft sitting there, waiting for us. Supposedly we'd drive onto the raft, and it would float down the river, making it so we didn't have to drive. The distance wasn't far, especially since we only had to traverse a moderately short part of the river, but the implication was that the rafts crawled along the river at an excruciatingly slow pace.

It was relatively safe, minus the extra-violent gingers floating in the river or at their base camp just around the corner.

IMANI: We just killed our version of Maurice in the slums. He wasn't a human, but an orangutan. So be careful. The prize was an engineer! He had him tied up, and we got him! Almost to the exit.

LOUIS: We're almost out, too! Bodi is the best driver ever!

"Carl!" Donut called as we rolled toward the raft.

I'd already eaten Mehmet's page from *Carl's Book of Boom*, and I prepared the *Gutter Bumper* spell.

"Casting now!" I yelled.

I cast the spell, and a large blinking set of lines appeared. I mentally clicked on the river in front of us, received a warning that the spell wouldn't cover the entire river, and hit **deploy**.

"Bumpers away!"

"Here we go!" Donut said as she leaned forward, focusing on the wide river. She cast *Ice Slick*.

In seconds, the entire river froze, cracking and splitting and occasionally exploding as the frozen water spread out in a winding pattern following the bumpers. The spell normally cast in a cone, but because of the *Bumper* spell, the ice followed the river *and* was extended by an additional 50%.

The *Gutter Bumper* spell wasn't quite what I was tirelessly seeking for explosions, but in this case, it was perfect. I'd never met Mehmet, the Turkish man who'd given me the spell, but I'd heard of him before. He'd focused on support spells and skills, always making sure the other members of his party were as buffed up as they could be. He'd saved countless lives during the pitched battles of Faction Wars. He reminded me of Imani in that way.

People like him were the true heroes of this dungeon.

Screams rose as the hundreds of inner tube gingers suddenly became stuck in place.

We bumped as we drove right over the dock, over the now-frozen raft, and onto the ice.

"Follow the river!" Donut called. "Carl!"

The back doors were already open. I pulled the tie holding them down, and I kicked the hastily fashioned brush hog out the back.

It was all the excess non-magical weapons I had in my inventory hurriedly fastened together in a line of chains, all attached to the back of the truck. The loose weapons dragged, bouncing and cutting and slicing and clobbering everything behind the truck as we rushed over the ice.

As for the hundreds of gingers frozen and stuck in the river, the dragging weapons cut through them like weeds.

"It's working!" I called as we started to slide sideways on the ice. "Gah!" I ducked as a chain broke, slicing past my head like a whip. "Keep it straight!"

Joel the undead camel groaned.

"Cast now!" I called to Donut.

We knew the chains wouldn't get everyone, so we had a finisher on hand.

Donut cast *Summon Ye, Vermin.*

The spell would instantly draw every rodent in the area to Donut.

Most of the zipper shrews would have to traverse the frozen path, drilling through everything in their path, including any surviving gingers on the river. If the chains didn't get them, this definitely would.

And within moments, a gray wave of rodents appeared, coming from all directions at once.

"Here they come!" I shouted.

FLORIN: Attempting the loop! They're on our ass. They're gonna try to bump us, so I'm shooting a missile now!

"There he is! Maurice! He's not a monkey!" Donut called from the front of the truck. She was finally alone in the passenger's seat, and Dorota had grown the special princess basket for her to sit upon. "He doesn't even have hair!" She gasped. "He's casting a spell!"

The Maurice that Imani had had to face might've been an orangutan, but this version looked a lot like that cartoon ogre Shrek, though still human. The large man had one arm free and was attempting to cast something. He never got a chance. A wave of the zipper shrews, coming from the direction we were driving, overwhelmed him, drilling through him. The man unpeeled before us, having had a dozen holes drilled in him all at once from behind. Little curls of skin and gore erupted in all directions, turning him into a flower made of flesh before it all collapsed on the red ice. A moment later, the blood-soaked shrews exploded against our shield.

There was a chime.

Quest Complete! Pasty Inferno.

So, this is where I'd tell you how to locate the engineer you just won, but that guy is now in a million pieces, spread all over the ice . . . Aaaand you just ran over his corpse, splitting him into even more pieces with those chains you're dragging. Like, holy shit, guys. Talk about overkill. You know you only had to kill that boss guy, right? This whole thing is really fucked-up. This is seriously bordering on ginger genocide.

The good news is, the quest is complete. I guess that means you can finish the track!

"There's the exit!" Donut cried, pointing. "Wow, we did that fast! Turn there! Turn there!"

We bumped as we exited the river. Joel the camel groaned incoherently, his head on his broken neck flapping as we rocked up and down. Shrews by the thousands were coming from every direction, suiciding against our shield, which was moving into the red.

The finish line loomed.

"Geez," I muttered, moving to the back of the truck, looking at the carnage. I started to cut all the chains loose. "The AI was right. We might've been overprepared for—"

"Bah, this bores me" came Satan's booming voice, followed by a mighty crash.

"Carl, Carl! The loop thing!"

I turned just in time to see the massive loop-de-loop tumbling in our direction, having been headbutted over by Satan. Florin's tuk-tuk and team Sparkles's vine had almost been done with their loop when they'd been swatted, and they both tumbled through the air, spinning in our direction.

The vine was on fire and covered with goo, having been hit by a Denial of Service missile. It splotched onto the ground just as the entire structure of the massive loop crashed around us, rock and metal exploding everywhere. We were peppered with chunks of metal, all of it sparking and burning.

Florin was hanging out the side of his tuk-tuk, shotgun in hand, firing over and over in the direction of the unicorn as they tumbled and hit the ground, like they were performing a stunt. Lucia, in her beautiful-woman form, appeared to be sobbing and crying and laughing all at the same time as they spun out on the ground. Still, they landed firmly on their tires like this had been their plan all along. The small engine revved, and they zoomed ahead of us, pushing past a piece of the fallen track and moving toward the finish line.

Behind us, the Lady Dominators and the gnu suddenly appeared, though they were still far behind us. They had to angle around the crashed pieces of the loop track.

The bush seemed to be floundering. It had the rocket accessory that gave them their incredible speed, but it was still smoldering, and it was just spinning in circles, with Dwight screaming. I didn't see Lucienne, who I knew was supposed to be the one driving.

And then I did see Lucienne, but she wasn't in the bush. She was on the hood of our truck. The bug-eyed rodent thing was standing there, smashing herself against the windshield. The finish line loomed.

Donut's spell, I realized. Lucienne was a rodent, and she'd been summoned.

Holy shit. We'd had that spell this whole time. I had no idea when and how she'd gotten here.

"Let me in! Let me in! I'm coming to you, swine!" Lucienne shrieked as she pummeled the windshield with her helmeted head, choking and gasping for air. Her bug eyes were getting bigger and bigger by the moment, like they were about to explode. She'd been poisoned by the air, yet she was still charmed by Donut's spell. "Let me in! Let me fucking in!"

We started to pass under the checkered finish-line arch.

"Get off," Donut shouted at the weird rodent on our hood. "You can't pass the finish line outside your—"

Our windshield cratered as Lucienne, the driver for team Sparkles, was pushed through the glass by the invisible barrier of the finish line. The rodent exploded against my face as she was pressed into my mouth, into my teeth, and ultimately through the back of our truck.

51

"STOP, STOP!" DONUT CALLED AS I GAGGED AND CHOKED. I HAD DEAD Lucienne all over my face. My teeth ached where her helmet had ricocheted off me. I'd swallowed some of her.

The camel hit the brakes, and we lurched to a stop. I continued to cough and hack, some of her bits coming out of my nose. I pulled a water bottle from my inventory, and I drank, my sinuses burning. I spent several moments just coughing and sneezing, getting red blood everywhere.

Now that the race was over, I could touch the controls again. I reached over and yanked the car into park.

"You, out," I coughed at the camel corpse.

"Okay," the corpse rasped, sounding dejected. He opened the door, started to step out, but faded away into dust before he could exit.

I slid into the driver's seat and moved the truck over so it wasn't blocking the entrance, and just a minute later, the Lady Dominators passed through, followed by Osvaldo's team.

I sent a quick note to Jasha and Radoslav. Despite my warning, they'd gotten stuck in the basement. They'd be at least another forty minutes.

JASHA: You really think we should save him? He's the worst one!

Donut was currently attempting to fish Lucienne's small, cracked racing helmet from the soupy gore on the floor of the truck.

She shrugged and looked up. "I don't want to race another team of crawlers, that's for sure. On the other hand, if we let the unicorn live, we might regret it. He hates us. Though maybe he'll be nice now that his girlfriend is dead. But probably not. Got it!" The gore-soaked racing helmet disappeared into her inventory. A moment later, she scoffed. "Carl, that helmet has a curse! It's worthless! What is Michale Graves's disease?"

I sighed and then sent a message to the bugbears as we exited the truck.

CARL: You should probably tow him in if he'll let you. But be wary.

Lucia turned her attention to us. I stood tense, looking at the woman with the skull head. I felt a chill.

She spent a moment examining me, then Donut.

I was startled by a sudden notification.

The Scavenger's Daughter blinks, for she does not know what she sees.

"What the hell?" I muttered.

And then she was there. Lucia had moved from the parked moped to right in front of me in a blink. She was so close, I could have kissed her.

She had no scent at all, which was somehow even more disconcerting. Her black ratty hair dangled, mixing with mine as she leaned in, as if she were sniffing me.

Donut let out a deep growl and jumped to my shoulder, tense.

"Easy, easy," Florin said, coming up. "We're all friends. Ain't that right, Lucia?"

"Chalchiuhtlicue is here," Lucia said, whispering in my ear. "She's new to this place, but she is here. She doesn't need Cici or Gus like the Residual and the Primal did. She keeps telling us that she is kind and that she will protect us. But she says the kindest thing may be letting us die. She says we are vessels in the river, just as you are, Carl. We are drowning together, you and me and all the others. But more are coming. The veins are open, she says. All the trapped are coming, Carl. All seek the prize on the twelfth floor. Not just her kind. The real, the imagined, and the enslaved. All gather, focused on the Ascendency. It's not a game like they told me. But it's not a game like they told you, either. Not anymore."

Lucia blinked and took a step back, and her demeanor instantly changed.

This form shrank back, shoulders hunched, afraid.

The presence is gone. The Scavenger's Daughter shudders in fear.

"Do . . . do you know my dad?" this new version of Lucia asked. She stepped forward hesitantly, and then she grabbed me by the shirt. "That lady. The shining lady, she said you know my father. She said he gave you a spell."

"Wha . . . what?" I asked, utterly confused.

"My name is Azra. Yaz is here, too. She's crying. That goddess. She's talking to her now, telling her that you used a spell that our father gave you to win your races."

"Wait," I said, remembering the note from *Carl's Book of Boom* that I'd eaten to get the *Bumper* spell. I reached up and put my hand against hers. It was warm and trembling. "Does your dad own a bowling alley?"

Lucia gasped. "Yes! Yes! That's him! Is he here? Can I talk to him?" She turned, searching. *"Baba! Baba!"*

"Hang on," Florin said, jumping forward. "Give me all the names of those around you. I'm making a list!"

"Where is he?" the girl named Azra asked again, ignoring Florin, her voice going up in pitch.

"I'm really sorry," I said. "But he's safe. He wanted me to tell you that he loves you and that he'll see you soon."

She started to quietly cry. "I'm so scared," she said. "The angel lady says it might be better if we all die. She keeps talking about people coming and taking our bodies. It's so cold."

"Who?" Florin asked, interjecting. "*Who* is coming?"

The girl turned to Florin, eyes going wide, as if she were finally noticing him. The girl let out a little shriek, turned, and ran.

Florin sighed. He reached up and slung his gun over his back. "I better chase her. Lucia comes back pretty quick after they get spooked. Gotta keep her from killing our gremlin."

"Carl," Donut said a moment later as we watched Florin run after the girl, who'd raced toward the line of garages. Our garage was open with

Hedy and Jamal standing in the doorway. Jamal gave an excited hop as Lucia passed, and the girl shrieked again and continued to run. "What the heck is happening with her?"

I was starting to form a theory, but I didn't want to say it out loud. I was pretty sure Florin had already figured this out, as had Orren, which terrified me.

"I don't know for sure," I finally said. "But we really need her to take a deal. Let's get to the garage."

The moment I settled into the wet, gore-soaked driver's seat, Dr. Metcalf beeped.

Limited details on the next race are now available.

Total Distance: Approximately 20 kilometers.

Track: Gasworks Screw Factory, Steel Mill, and Doll Workshop That Is Totally Not a Front for Anything Else. This track will require vertical climb, inverted racing, and gap coverage of up to 100 meters. There will be multiple paths to the exit.

Tasks required to complete: Don't get squished. Don't get melted. Don't get screwed.

Environment: Extreme heat. Containment field will protect from heat and molten metal.

Hazards: Containment theft is now enabled. If your containment touches another containment for more than 5 seconds, you may lose it upon separation.

In other words, don't bump your fellow racers.

All paths on this race are only wide enough for two at a time, and you'll be sharing this track with 11 other heats.

Time Limit: 30 minutes.

Donut let out a little whimper. "Carl, I don't like this."

"One race at a time," I said. "The good news is, I can drive again."

I suddenly remembered the messages we'd received during the race, and I checked them now. There were dozens of them. I cringed, reading of all the crawlers who'd fallen. I focused on that message string from Tran.

TRAN: If this is my last message, know that I tried to stop them from fighting Li Na. I tried.

This was followed by a message from Imani.

IMANI: Tran! Are you okay?

TRAN: I'm alive. We actually won. Zhang was leading their octopus, and he let me pass. They tried to stop her, and it's the same thing that happened in Beijing. She cast a dread, and they started killing each other. It was awful. I think of all twenty-four teams that started the race with us, only five survived. Of our heat, it was just my team and them. Zhang needs help. He was sobbing. I don't know what to do.

HEAT FOUR. RESULTS.
First Place: The Royal Court of Princess Donut.
Second Place: Lady Dominators and the Gimp.
Third Place: Team Flamengo.
Fourth Place: Team Free Love.
Fifth Place: Team Sparkles.

Eliminated: One Fine Pig.

HEAT 5 OF 7

INTERLUDE | MINUS

"If the AI so much as *suspects* you're anything other than a simple tourist, it's going to pop you like a boil," Captain Fresh of the Syndicate security forces said. He handed Minus a datapad. "This contains about five hundred hours of footage of the fairy crawler along with all the posts your brother made regarding her. You'll have to rapid-inject it, as you're going to onboard tonight. The tenth floor begins in just a few hours. We're preparing a transfer, but you'll need to watch as much as you can at regular speed, too, as the AI will be suspicious of too much brain recall from injected memory. There's, uh, some snicks on there as well. Ones your brother made himself. Luckily, he had enough money saved up to purchase the ship, so if anyone investigates too closely, it all adds up. He was quite smart with his investments, and other than the people on the Snow Cones message board, he didn't have any known associates. The last person he appeared to have contacted face-to-face was you."

"That was five cycles ago," Minus said.

"We know," said Captain Fresh.

Minus sighed, looking at the corpse of his poor dead brother, Linus, who'd just been wasted by Syndicate security.

Minus hadn't even known his brother had moved from the surface of Teelan-3 to one of the swanky habitats in orbit around the star. He took a hesitant step, careful not to get any of the garbage on his boot. His brother had made his fortune in biological license engineering for the Dream and had cashed out cycles ago. Minus hadn't talked to him since that last time, which had been a month after their father's funeral. Linus had said then that he'd purchased full citizenship. Minus had assumed he was going to keep working.

A wave of guilt washed across the soother. Even then, Minus had known his brother was lonely. He looked about the trash-filled berth. It smelled awful in here. *I should have called him.*

He couldn't bring himself to look upon his brother's corpse for more than a few seconds, shame overwhelming him. *He didn't deserve this.*

And then he thought, *Mom is going to be so pissed.*

"I don't know what I can do. Even if I do get down there, the best I can do is maybe kill a crawler or two before the system AI rips me apart."

"You have your primary target. As you will be attached to the fairy crawler, you will likely have multiple opportunities to strike. If you can find a way to make it look like an accident, perhaps you might survive."

"How? How can I possibly survive this? I don't really watch the show. You say I will only be half-corporeal? I am treated like a non-combatant? Anything I do that takes more than a nanosecond is going to get stopped by the AI."

"We're hoping your presence isn't considered an outside influence. If it truly believes you're your brother, we hope it won't be so quick to stop your actions as long as it *believes* your actions. So act the pervert for some time. You have your primary and secondary target. Get them all at once if you can."

"But at this point, what will that do? Sir, I know I'm not supposed to question orders, but I feel I need to understand."

Captain Fresh paused.

"Look, son. This is a suicide mission. You know it, and I know it. But I cannot reiterate how important this is. We are doing everything we can to nuke that entire system off the map before it can spread even farther. We are losing. That AI is stopping everything we throw at it and answering in kind. We have a few assets in place already, but none amongst the crawlers. We believe that a surgical crawler kill will destabilize the whole group, causing a systemic collapse, which will cause the Ascendency game to kick off early and allow our other assets to quickly react. I can't say more than that. I don't like sending good soldiers to their deaths, but we have no other choice. It's us or them, and if we don't do everything we can to stop it all, we will face extinction." He waved his hands, indicating Linus's filthy apartment. Multiple suspiciously stained posters of Elle McGib littered the walls. "And no offense, but idiots like your late brother are just as culpable for everything that's happening because they won't stop watching. So it comes down to us to protect the citizens before it's too late. Do you understand?"

"Yes, sir," Minus said, standing rigid, hand against his chest in a salute. "Whatever it takes, sir. Whatever it takes."

52

"YOU HAVE TWO GOLDEN UPGRADES TO PICK," HEDY SAID, LOOKING AT her tablet. Despite our winning, she could read the room and was acting unusually subdued. "You got a key, too, meaning you can go into any of the old houses in the cul-de-sac. If you're thinking you might want to trade vehicles, maybe you should be considering doing that first before you pick."

"We're going into the house of One Fine Pig," I said. "If it's there, it'll be that armored vehicle, and by this point, I think ours is the better choice. They spent too many of their upgrades on weapons."

Hedy nodded. "You could try to get that Onikuma. It's a good mount." She gave a nervous look at Donut. "Or, you know, Old Shuck—"

"No," Donut said.

I let out a humorless laugh. "I thought you didn't like mounts?"

Hedy shrugged. "Always good to have options. I think vehicles is better, especially when my life is on the line. But it might be nice to have a beastie in here, too. We'll maybe get another gremlin if you pick one up. But it ain't no matter to me. It's not like I'm lonely or anything." She turned her attention back to her tablet.

IMANI: Zhang and Tran are with us at the Lollipop. Come when you can.

DONUT: IS ZHANG OKAY?

IMANI: Not really. We're working on a plan right now. Elle went over to their guild to try to talk Li Na into coming out. She says Na is just sitting there meditating. Her health is in the yellow. She's been poisoned, like you said.

CARL: Going to finish our upgrades, use the key, and pick up some things from Mordecai, and we'll be out there.

IMANI: Louis just used his key to add a gecko to his garage. He followed your advice about the hidden room, and he found an engineer in there. But there were mobs in the house, so be careful.

Behind us, the truck swarmed with the generated gremlins, who still continued to shriek and flip me off whenever I made the mistake of looking directly at one. Jamal was there on the ground with Mongo, watching them work. Bigs and Samantha had both wandered out here the moment the race was over and both were riding atop Jamal's head, heckling the workers.

I could still taste Lucienne, and no matter how much water I drank, I couldn't get the terrible tang out of my mouth. We hadn't stayed to see Dwight cross the finish line, but Jasha and Radoslav had found the unicorn sitting there, spinning in a circle just outside the exit. They'd dragged him in.

I still didn't know if that was a mistake, but it was done.

Of the fifty-five hundred people who'd made it to this floor, we now had fewer than three thousand left. These last few races were going to be brutal.

"It says we need vertical climb and inverted racing, and we need to cover gaps of more than a hundred meters," I said.

Hedy nodded, flipping through her table. "I'm thinking we do one Golden upgrade and three regulars. That way we can use that regular option to upgrade your Bubble Buddy shield to the Golden version, pick two more regular upgrades, and then pick a good Golden one. We definitely need the shield upgrade. Your containment will protect you, but containments is gonna be breaking left and right. It's gonna be a crowded race. The full Bubble Buddy will protect against molten steel and whatnots. But not for the whole race, so you gotta be careful."

"The regular version is a good shield. It held except when we were getting hit by all the gingers."

"Yup," Hedy said. "It's great for smaller critters. But it don't float. If we upgrade it all the way, it'll be much better."

We talked for a good while, going over all the options. In the end, we went with the Bubble Buddy upgrade, a heat sink in case we lost our containment, and the regular version of the same booster rockets that team Sparkles had, which, when combined with the bubble, would allow us to cover large jumps.

For our Golden upgrade, we went with Roller Limbo, a trans-dimensional upgrade that would allow us to race upside down. And as long as there was a gap of at least ten centimeters, we could change shape and slip under any obstacle, including other vehicles.

After Hedy left to start shouting orders at the gremlins, Samantha approached. She floated there, sniffing at my crotch.

"Hey, stop that," I said, pushing her away.

She growled and then floated up so we were eye to eye. A few hours earlier she hadn't been able to do this. But like with every floor so far, she got more and more powerful the longer the floor went on.

"Why do you smell like Chachi?" she demanded. "Little Carl doesn't smell like it, but the rest of you does. What have you been getting up to? You know most ladies aren't into frottage, right? How boring. If you're going to commit to intercourse, you have to be aggressive about it. You should kill something together and bathe in the blood first before you both howl in climax. If you want, I can give you growling lessons. Women like it when their man growls with passion."

"I have no idea what you're talking about."

"You know, Chachi? Chalchiuhtlicue?" she said. "Wears a green skirt? Talks kinda funny? Cries a lot? Oh, Carl. Are you hiding her from me because you think I'll be jealous? That's so adorable."

"Uh," I said. That was the name of the creature Lucia had mentioned.

Samantha took a deep breath. "Okay, normally after I break up with someone, I don't like to give out relationship advice. I really think you need to make your own mistakes. It helps you realize what you lost when you screwed up with me, but I'll make an exception in this case. Chachi is pretty. I'll give you that. But she's a little cuckoo. Not all that emotionally stable. Likes to talk a lot about how she's all into saving the lives of children, but then she just kills them all. Like everywhere she goes, it's dead babies left and right. I gotta tell you, Carl. Donut was correct. You need to stop dry-humping crazy. You think *I'm* a psycho ex-girlfriend? Hooboy. She's the type of chick who'll set *all* your chonies on fire. Even the pair you're wearing. And if you're triple-dipping with her *and* Eris *and* your new wife? That's a lot of work, and you don't even have a mustache. What do you think is going to happen when Chachi finds out? You really should follow Louis's example. He's a one-woman type of guy. That's why Juice Box couldn't handle him."

"Wait, this . . . Chachi. She kills children?"

"Oh, yes. She's always so high and mighty, always talking about how she's protecting them, but the second something bad or inconvenient happens, she's like, 'We need to sacrifice a seven-year-old to make things right.' She even did it once at a Yarilo party because the meatballs had cilantro in them. She sent out an emergency prayer request and had her worshippers kill a whole village day care in the hopes the next waiter would bring her something that didn't taste like soap. She probably could've just asked the server guy, but I will say this. It worked. The next tray they brought out were these amazing little hot dog things wrapped in orc bacon. Delicious. Even Otis-Ray liked them, and he's normally a vegetarian."

A deep sense of alarm started to fill me. I replayed my conversation with Lucia Mar and that girl, Azra. That goddess appeared to be one of the ones who'd escaped the dungeon. And she was in there with the kids stuck inside of Lucia Mar's head.

"Holy fucking shit," I said.

Samantha shook her head sadly. "Yeah. I hope you got a coat for Little Carl."

53

THE CUL-DE-SAC USED TO HAVE NINE HOUSES IN THE CIRCLE, BUT IT NOW had ten thanks to us losing two teams during the third heat. This made me wonder just how big the roundabouts were for teams like Li Na's. The empty, abandoned houses stood in the order in which the team had lost, meaning the closest one was the now-empty home of team One Fine Pig.

Osvaldo and Filipe were standing outside their garage with the giant painted "3," chatting with Radoslav and Jasha in garage four, who had their door open and were in their regular places in the lawn chairs.

"You using your key?" Osvaldo asked.

"I am," I said.

"When I moved to this heat, I lost the chance to get into the garages of the ones from my original heat," Osvaldo said. He took a sip of Busch Light and made a face. "I would murder for a Brahma."

"Yeah," Jasha said. "But it grows on you. I like it."

I was interrupted by Rosetta writing me back. I'd sent a message to her, Mordecai, Tipid, and Prepotente all at the same time, asking them if they knew anything about this Chalchiuhtlicue goddess.

ROSETTA: Chachi, as Samantha calls her, isn't a well-known one. She's not ever sponsored as far as I can remember. Not like Eileithyia, who is a similar deity. They're both goddesses of childbirth and women. But Chachi is also a water and fire goddess. She's associated with harvests. That sort of thing. Those catchall gods and goddesses sound good on the manifest, but they never do well in the Ascendency game because their powers are comparatively weak.

CARL: Why would my Scavenger's Daughter patch try to activate when I'm talking to Lucia like that? It's really weird. If this Chach . . . however you spell it, can get from wherever those kids really are to here, do you think maybe we can do it the other way around?

MORDECAI: Kid, like I told you before, we have no idea what's happening. This is all new.

DONUT: WE'RE JUST GOING TO CALL HER CHACHI. I ONLY HAVE SO MUCH ROOM ON MY CUT-AND-PASTE, AND I'M NOT FILLING IT WITH SUCH A LONG NAME. IT'S WORSE THAN TSERENDOLGOR. THOUGH IT'S NOT AS LONG AS THAT HAWAIIAN GUY CRAWLER. WHAT WAS HIS NAME? KAMAKANAMAKAMAEMAIKALANI JR. 2, I THINK?

PREPOTENTE: Ah, yes. He is still with us, and he is a pleasant fellow. He goes by Makana. Anyway, the analog of Chalchiuhtlicue, or Chachi, in Earth culture is the Aztec goddess with the same name. She was considered benevolent, but the Aztecs also practiced human sacrifice. She is the originator of an Aztec flood myth because she cried for many days. It's somewhat interesting how all these gods and goddesses are quite similar to ones from various Earth pantheons.

DONUT: HI, PREPOTENTE! ARE YOU COMING TO MY CONCERT IN A FEW MINUTES?

PREPOTENTE: I wouldn't miss it for the world! I, too, would like to access this guild, so I will attempt to sing as well. I will be performing "In the Air Tonight" by Phil Collins. What will you be performing?

DONUT: IT'S A SURPRISE! AND IT'LL BE A DUET WITH CARL! HE HAS TO TAKE A BUNCH OF POTIONS AND SCROLLS THOUGH SO HE DOESN'T MESS IT UP.

PREPOTENTE: That sounds like a hoot.

We arrived at the garage of the abandoned house.

"Okay," I said, putting my hand on the garage door. It yawned open. And sure enough, there she was, standing on the floor next to the parked APV with the cracked windshield. Penelope the pig. She was currently licking up the remains of the gremlin, which had oozed to the floor after they'd activated their shield.

"Hi, Penny," I said, going to a knee. "Come on, now. You're going to go live with us for a little while."

The pig, who now looked as if she were wearing lipstick after licking up all the gremlin goo, snorted happily and followed us outside.

54

Entering the Lollipop.

WE STOPPED AT THE DJ STAND AND MADE OUR WAY TO THE BACK CORner where the team was sitting. I eyed the newcomer.

This was the fleshmancer that Elle and Imani had hired. The tall, gaunt mage sat rigid, sandwiched between Louis and Linus, Elle's fan. Louis had a cookie from a street vendor and was devouring it, getting crumbs everywhere.

The fleshmancer held a cappuccino in a slender hand. The man looked down with disdain at his blue flowing robes, which were now covered with crumbs. He was sitting ramrod straight, and he flicked the crumbs away as Louis, oblivious, continued to happily munch while Linus stared with puppy dog eyes at Elle.

I examined the newcomer.

Grigori the Placid. Human. Level 93 Fleshmancer.

This is a hired mercenary of Team Meadow Lark.

This mercenary worships Gula.

Gula was a new one, and I filed that away.

The thin, poised man looked absolutely out of place between Louis and Linus.

Linus's shirt had changed from a naked picture of Elle to one with a moving, all-over print of an extreme close-up of Elle's screaming face as she was casting *Ice Bolt* or a similar spell. The flashing caption underneath read, "Right in the keister!"

I'd asked Imani and Elle to bring the fleshmancer because we wanted to get this guy to talk to both Corcundas. Elle said the guy had a stick up his ass, but he clearly knew what he was doing, and he and Imani had been trading healing tips while he'd been sequestered in their safe room.

As we approached the back of the bar, Donut took one look at the guy and let out a harrumph.

DONUT: HOW ARE WE GOING TO GET HIM INTO THE GUILD? HE DOESN'T LOOK LIKE SOMEONE WHO CAN SING!

CARL: No, probably not. We just need to make sure YOU get in there so you can charm his pants off and get Porky to come out.

DONUT: YOU STILL HAVEN'T TOLD ME THE FULL PLAN. WE DON'T KNOW WHY THIS IS SO IMPORTANT ALL OF A SUDDEN.

CARL: I know. I'm sorry. I know you're scared. I wish I could tell you everything. I don't take the trust you have in me lightly, and I need you to trust me on this one. I will explain it all after it's too late for them to take the prize away.

DONUT: WHAT DOES THAT EVEN MEAN? WE'RE SUPPOSED TO BE PARTNERS IN THIS, AND YOU'RE MAKING ME NERVOUS. THE PRIZE IS, WE CAN BRING TWO PEOPLE WE WANT TO THE ELEVENTH FLOOR. ELLE THINKS YOU MEAN THE PRIME MINISTER LADY AND MAYBE CASCADIA OR SOME OTHER SHOWRUNNER, BUT SHE'S AFRAID THAT KILLING THEM ISN'T GOING TO DO ANYTHING. AND I DON'T THINK WE SHOULD HURT PRIME MINISTER VICTORY. I KNOW SHE'S A BAD GUY, BUT SHE'S ALSO MY FRIEND, AND I'M SCARED ABOUT WHAT YOU'RE GOING TO DO.

I reached up and scratched Donut.

"I know you're scared," I repeated, this time out loud. "I'm scared, too. But all will be clear if we can just get through this next part. It's all important now. The pig, this quest, and the war mage plan—all three will help us survive. All of us."

Onstage was the karaoke regular Dekoki the kappa from team Yokai.

Her team was right there, front and center, cheering her on. The Minister of Blood-Letting was also there, dancing with his skeletons behind him.

Dekoki was singing "Cruel Summer" by Bananarama. I paused, watching them all, remembering that instant when Finley had been mowed down.

They are all the main characters in their own story.

The cruelty of this particular floor was getting to me. I sighed and turned to the main part of the table, finally taking in the full scene. Before we dealt with this Corcunda quest, we had an even more pressing matter.

Tran and Zhang sat at the end of the table, flanked by Imani and Elle. Tran was in his spider wheelchair, nursing a beer, while Zhang had his head down on the table. I knew Elle had been trying to talk to Na, but that clearly hadn't worked.

"Did you put your song in?" Imani asked as I slid into a chair. Donut jumped to the table and gave Zhang a headbutt.

"We did," I said. "Prepotente is up there now arguing with the DJ. He's going to try to get in, too."

"Hi, Donut," Zhang said, reaching up and giving her a pat without looking up.

"What have we decided?" I asked, looking at the sour faces all around.

"Hey, Carl," Tran said, sounding morose. "We were just explaining to Zhang that he's being an idiot."

Zhang finally looked up, eyes rimmed red. "It's the only way. Rezan. Sammi Harrison. Ming Lui." He reached up and touched the side of his face. "Soo-bin kissed my cheek before that last heat. She said she trusted me. They're all dead now."

"Like I told you," Tran said, clearly doing his best to sound patient, "this is not your fault. And it's not all Na's fault, either. They attacked her. Rezan was an ass. And the decapitator had it coming. Never trusted her."

Zhang shook his head. "They attacked us because Na's gone completely psycho. There's nothing left. She died when her brother did. I thought maybe I would be enough, but I'm not."

"She didn't get player-killer skulls," Tran said. "It's those dreads of hers. They all killed each other."

"It was horrible," Zhang said. "I can't do that again. I can't do another race with her."

"Wait," I said, raising a hand. "What do you mean, 'It's the only way'? What are you planning?"

Zhang wiped his nose. "Na is in lead saddle for the next race. I'm going to kill Torpedo when her back is turned. It's the only way. I'm not strong enough to stop her, and if any others try to, they will die, too. But with Torpedo dead, the system will kill her. It'll kill us both."

Torpedo was the name of their mount. The octopus.

"No," Donut said. "No, you can't."

"That won't work anyway," I said. "Not anymore. You just lose your containment. Na is strong enough to get to the finish line without a mount. But you're not."

He shook his head. "What else can I do?"

"No," Donut repeated. She looked at me, eyes shining. "We'll find something to fix it. Right, Carl?"

"She's killing people," Zhang said. "She's stopped talking to me. She got poisoned, and it's slowly draining her health, but it's not going down fast enough. She's not who she used to be."

Tears streamed down his face. He met my eyes, and he ripped the target cape off. He threw it on the table. "I wish I had died before. In the temple. I was scared, but I wasn't ashamed. Now I am ashamed. I wish I'd never gotten this far. I wish Jun was here. Why? Why was it him and not me?" He started to quietly cry again. "I promised him I'd watch over her, and I can't even do that. What sort of friend have I been?"

"Oh, Zhang," Donut said, rubbing back and forth against him.

"There's gotta be a way," I said. "We need ideas."

"That's what we've been doing," Imani said. She sounded grim. "We've been workshopping ways to fix this."

Zhang wiped his eyes and then the words just tumbled out of him. "She ripped Jun's eye out of his face after he died, and then she ripped her own eye out to install it. Who does that? It was then that I should have known she was gone. I used to think I could, you know, keep her from going too crazy. Jun didn't want us telling people what had happened on the eighth floor in Beijing. She apologized. She's always been so practical, so matter-of-fact. She wasn't like the others at the warehouse. She never joked, never laughed. But she would smile at her brother, and she would smile at me sometimes, too. She used to be so pretty. And I don't mean pretty in the face, but she was that, too. I mean, I used to feel so safe and happy when I looked at her. She was my best friend's sister, and I thought maybe I could get her to like me, and we would get married, and I would have my best friend and her, and now I have nothing."

He put his head back down on the table. He let out a sob. "We have to kill her. What other choice do we have? If we don't, she's going to keep hurting everyone."

"She's not killing for fun," Tran said. "She's not going out of her way to hurt people. She's not bad . . . She's just sort of lost her humanity."

I nodded, remembering what she'd done to that mantaur on the fourth floor. She'd pulled all his limbs off just to keep him alive. She'd always been like this. She'd been a sociopath this whole time. But that wasn't a bad thing. "We need that. We *need* people like her. She's so strong."

"She's not a weapon, Carl. She's a person," Donut said. Her voice lowered. "And I like her, of course. But we can't let her keep hurting people." She straightened. "But we can't let Zhang just kill himself, either. It's not right."

I stared at Zhang's target cape sitting on the table. The AI had given it to him on the previous floor after he survived the battle inside of Club Vanquisher. He hadn't had to go to that fight. He'd gone because we'd needed his help. And Li Jun had died keeping Donut protected when she was in the tower. Even though we had been the ones to originally help save them when they were on the Maestro's show, we owed them a huge debt.

DONUT: WE NEED TO FIND A WAY TO TALK SOME SENSE INTO HER. IT'S THE ONLY WAY.

ELLE: I was just in there with her, and I gotta say, she's gone completely whackadoodle. And by this point, does it even matter? Every race from now on will have her versus a bunch of others.

We had three hours until the next heat.

We had so much to do. We were going to sing in a few minutes, and the war mage thing . . .

And then, there it was. *Of course.* Of course.

I had an idea, but we'd have to move fast.

Li Na didn't worship a deity. She couldn't worship one with her Changbi race.

Despite what Donut said, Li Na *was* a weapon. A weapon that could be especially effective if she was pointed in the correct direction.

I sent multiple messages, including one to Bodi.

CARL: Bodi, did you commit to a race yet for this next heat? Zhang is going to need a jockey. Li Na is leaving the dungeon.

55

SPLASH ZONE: MAN, I DON'T KNOW IF THIS IS GOING TO WORK. THE croupier guy is a complete dick. He stabbed Gluteus for no reason! They got rid of the Nothing spots on all the games and replaced it with things like "You get your ass curb stomped" and something called the "Dirty Tea Bag."

CARL: Shit. Okay. Make your way back to the base. And keep an eye on Dong.

SPLASH ZONE: Wait. You didn't ask for him? He said you asked for him to go to the bar. I think he's on his way to you.

Goddamnit. Yuto the Oni was onstage. I knew we were up soon. We didn't want Dong here for this because this Porky guy supposedly hated him. I did see Prepotente still by the DJ stand, and I saw something else I wasn't expecting. Dwight the unicorn had just wandered in. He had a **Shit-Faced** debuff over him.

This was the first time I'd seen the unicorn outside of the vine. He looked pretty much like I'd expected, though he was a little shorter than I'd thought. But he was a sparkling white horse. His rainbow horn glittered brightly in the dark light of the bar.

The drunk unicorn pushed a few gremlins out of the way and made his way to the DJ booth. He gave Prepotente a shove that sent the goat sprawling.

CARL: You better get here, too, then. We'll need you to watch him. Some stuff is about to go down.

SPLASH ZONE: I'll be there in a bit. I asked for an audience with Hamed, the new leader guy, to see if he could help me find my wife, and the guards said he'd see me. So me and Gluteus, and

Doctor Bones are gonna go talk to him. I'll send Bucket Boy your way.

CARL: Okay. Be safe. Keep me updated.

I moved to get Prepotente away from the idiot unicorn before a fight broke out, but I was interrupted by another message.

MORDECAI: Believe it or not, the test actually worked. But Samantha also can't die, and she's not the most reliable test subject, so we tested it again on some sluggalos. It works, but there're a few wrinkles. We have some solutions that I'm working on right now.

ROSETTA: None of this means this next part will work. We can't even test the shop-interface part because of that standing purchase order with the cleaner bots. It requires us to trust that war mage wasn't lying.

I waved at Imani and pointed at Prepotente, who was sputtering and getting up. The DJ was shouting at Dwight, who was now sitting on the floor like a dog and sobbing. Imani got up and moved quickly to get herself between the unicorn and the goat.

The swirl tattoo on my palm itched.

CARL: Oh, I'm sure he was lying. But not about the Cabaret itself. The fact that purchase order is even there suggests part of it is true, and don't forget Eris also said this will work. If we can talk Li Na into doing this, I'll make sure she knows the full story and is prepared. This isn't something we can force on her. She's too strong, and she's too smart for us to trick her into doing it, and I wouldn't want to do it that way anyway. This will keep her alive, keep Zhang alive, and keep her from killing more crawlers. It'll also let us test Herot's theory. I think she'll go for it.

MORDECAI: Kid, this is so far off the codex, we don't even know if the system will allow her to do this. And if it does, it's possible she could still die when your floor collapses.

CARL: I know.

Imani dragged Prepotente to the table and made him sit down. He was shouting and looking at Dwight, who remained on the floor sobbing, surrounded by bewildered gremlins. The Minister of Blood-Letting was patting him on the shoulder. Prepotente was clearly ready to get up and attack the unicorn, but he quickly calmed after seeing the looks of everyone at the table. They all had their eyes on me.

"It's a go," I said.

I could feel it. A wave of relief swept over everyone. It was like a dark curtain had been pulled away from everything. Tran clasped his hands together and bowed deeply.

This was a ridiculous, probably-not-going-to-work plan. But that was okay. It was *something*, and that's what we'd been missing.

Ever since the previous floor, several crawlers had been complaining that the Cleaner Bot upgrade was no longer available in the personal space shop due to "overwhelming demand."

We'd just figured it was because of Faction Wars, with all the warlords buying them up. That was part of it. As it stood, the cleaner bot that Architect Houston the viceroy had had in his surgical theater—the white one I'd looted—was an old model. It was literally the last available one in the store.

That was because Herot had a standing order to purchase every cleaner bot that showed up.

Menerva was apparently on the seventeenth floor in charge of the NPCs who were building and occupying the Backstage Death Maze. This was where the AI had plucked Growler Gary from when he'd used his body as an avatar. It was also why Gary's level had been so elevated. They were training, getting stronger and stronger in preparation for the impossible eventuality that crawlers would make it that far.

This whole seventeenth floor was just something built into the dungeon, invisible to the showrunners who were just happy to have a box ticked. It had been going like this for hundreds and hundreds of seasons, completely ignored.

Herot, however, was not backstage. He was trapped on the other side of the portal. He was in the Pineapple Cabaret itself, the secret dimension they'd built to hide the NPCs and keep them safe. He had limited powers to control that world, but he *did* have a shop interface.

Honestly, I didn't know how all this worked when the AI could literally create stuff with a virtual snap of his fingers, but we'd seen these sorts of artificial shortages before, like with the food after the flooding of Larracos.

That Cabaret place was currently overrun. Akuma had been a little . . . fuzzy . . . on who the bad guys were. He mentioned something called the Ogre Imperium, which was a long-forgotten plotline that had gotten binned because the ogres were made too intelligent and they had immediately figured out that they were trapped in a dungeon. And there was a shadow mimic infestation, which was just as bad. But there was something more, too.

The war mages wanted our help to clear the place out.

We had two options. The casino plan and the cleaner bot plan. It sounded like the casino plan was a bust, so we were going with the cleaner bot option. This plan was complicated, but Rosetta and Mordecai had been on it since we first heard the idea, and they were now semi-confident it was feasible. But *only* if Akuma was telling the truth about Herot.

Li Na was dying of poison. Her **Left to Fester** debuff would not go away, and in fact, it would get worse because one's health automatically topped up when they moved to the next floor. That would stop if she managed to get to the Pineapple Cabaret.

However, the war mages also claimed there was a possible exit from the Pineapple Cabaret to the Earth's surface. That would, in theory, cure her **Left to Fester**. Maybe.

There was so much here left to chance. So much built on faith, and if Akuma hadn't dropped that name Herot . . . if Eris hadn't said it might work, I wouldn't have believed any of it.

If we did this now with Li Na, like now-now before the next race even started, we'd have a good idea if it would work before we tried it with several crawlers at once, which we'd have to do after this fifth heat.

We just needed to talk Li Na into going along with it.

56

ELLE, ZHANG, AND TRAN PULLED BACK FROM THE TABLE. ZHANG grabbed his target cape and pulled it back on, standing straight and tall and with purpose. They were going to go back to the safe room and attempt to communicate with Na and tell her the new plan.

"Good luck," I whispered to Elle.

"Yeah, you, too," she said, looking over her shoulder at Donut, who was currently forcing the fleshmancer to brush her. We'd just transferred mercenary ownership over to our guild. The strange human appeared to be enjoying himself while Linus watched. The soother alien was gently patting Donut's chain mail crupper, which caused it to jingle. Even though the tourist was half-corporeal, he was really here. He started running his long fingers over her tail.

"I'm touching her, I'm touching her," he said.

Elle raised her voice. "You, Linus. Stay here. If I catch word you do or say anything perverted, I'll have someone in the outside world break your creepy little fingers. You understand?"

"Such a fuzzy little pussy," he said, stroking Donut's tail. "You smell so good. Elle doesn't let me sniff her." He leaned down and whispered something to Donut. Then he took his triple-segmented index finger and stuck it in his mouth and started sucking on it.

Donut turned. "*Excuse* me? What did you just say?"

"All right, never mind," Elle said. "Linus, you're coming with us."

"Oh goody," the alien said, jumping up.

"Carl, you need to get ready!" Donut cried. The sunglasses appeared on her face. "What do you think, Grigori? With or without sunglasses?"

"With," the fleshmancer said, speaking for the first time.

"I agree," Donut replied. She let out a long sigh. "This isn't the cleanest establishment for a concert, but I suppose it'll have to do. I know I'll be able to hit the right key, but Mordecai made a few special potions, compounded together, for us to make sure Carl and I are in proper sync. A shame, really, that it won't be a pure performance. It's not as bad as lip-synching, of course, but what're you going to do?"

I felt strangely nervous. I knew the potion would work, and that I'd be able to sing, but I still felt . . . weird about it. The compounding was something new that he'd been working on, and it was a way to get around potion cooldowns when we needed to take several at once.

I'd never sung in my life, except when I was hammered at a bar with a bunch of other coasties. And that was years ago.

As it turned out, if we did a duet with one of the guild-entrance songs, we both had performance bars, and it was possible for only one of us to succeed.

This particular song wasn't technically a duet in the traditional sense, but it was listed as having two singers in the book, and that's what really mattered.

I would be taking the lead. We did it this way because Donut only had a few lines, meaning the chances that she would be successful were much higher, even though we'd picked a song that was pretty hard to sing. Hopefully, I'd be able to get in, too, but if not, I was confident in Donut's ability to charm Porky out of the guild.

In addition to the potion, Donut would be using her headset with the Auto-Tune turned to the max. The double microphones were unnecessary, but there was no way around it. And I had to use a scroll to make certain I was physically able to hit the proper notes. The scroll was called *Gelded Choirboy.* Even if I could sing, this song wasn't in a register my deeper voice could normally hit. We weren't taking any chances.

Mordecai insisted the name of the spell wasn't literal.

The scroll would make my voice a little squeaky, so I was going to wait until the last possible second to read it. The singing potion would last a long while, so I took it now. I felt the warmth spread through me.

You've been Honeyed! You are able to control your singing much better now.

You've been Yo-Yo Ma'd! You have perfect pitch! You will be able to determine a note just by hearing it!

You've been Dio'd! You can hold your voice for much longer!

Donut zapped Mongo out into the room. The large dinosaur screeched in surprise and started waving his wings. Several patrons cried out and jumped back.

"What the hell, Donut?" I asked. "Why isn't he in the garage guarding Hedy?"

"Jamal is in there with some of the slugs. She'll be fine. I don't want Mongo to miss Uncle Carl's stage debut! He would never forgive me! Isn't that right, Mongo? Aren't you excited?"

Mongo let out an excited screech and waved his wings some more.

I met eyes with Imani, and she smiled, genuinely smiled, at me.

"I don't know why you're so set on completing this quest, but I ain't gonna lie, Carl. I've been looking forward to this moment for a long time."

I grinned back at her. I wished I could tell her how important this truly was. Instead, I just said, "I hope you like Norwegian music."

"Wait, what are you going to sing?"

The DJ, who'd been on the floor yelling at Dwight—who still hadn't moved—returned to his booth and tapped his microphone.

"Singing 'Take on Me' by A-ha, it's Princess Donut and Carl! Get on up here, you two."

Donut hopped up and down. "It's time! It's time!" She raised the volume on her headset. "Okay, everyone! I want you to put your hands together. This will be Carl's first time singing ever! So let's give him some encouragement!"

The small crowd started to roar.

"A-ha?" Imani asked, raising an eyebrow.

"There were only a few two-singer songs on the list," I said. "If it doesn't work, we have a few backup songs planned. The good thing is, we can keep trying until we get in."

"Elle is gonna be pissed she missed this." She turned and raised her hand, motioning at Chris, Florin, Bautista, Britney, and Jurgen, who'd all just entered. They started moving toward the back.

The bar, which had been half-full until this moment, was suddenly more packed than I'd ever seen it.

I saw Dong Quixote in the entrance looking at me. He gave me a sheepish smile. He started walking toward us, his giant sock over his shoulder like Santa's bag. Bucket Boy rushed in and grabbed him by the shoulder.

"Hurry up, Carl!" Donut said, bounding toward the stage. "No, Mongo. You stay back here. You can stand on the table and watch. Mommy will be right back."

I sighed and approached the platform. Dekoki the kappa and Yuto the Oni from team Yokai both patted me on the back. So did one of the skeletons from the Bleak Congregation. The gremlin DJ had a small microphone onstage already attached to a stand and placed at Donut height. He slapped a second microphone into my palm as I turned to face the crowd. A pair of screens sat at an angle, facing the stage, showing the lyrics.

A pair of happy faces danced back and forth on the screen with the words "Get Ready to Sing!"

I activated the *Gelded Choirboy* scroll.

You've been Choired! What a beautiful voice you have!

Donut looked up at me. I could see my reflection in her sunglasses. My cheeks were burning red, and I wasn't sure if that was nerves or if it was a side effect of the *Choirboy* scroll.

"Remember, Carl. Just sing naturally. It's okay if you mess this up. I already put us down for a second go just in case. Follow my lead, and we'll be fine."

"I'm ready," I said. I startled at my own voice. I sounded as if I'd just sucked on a balloon full of helium.

"Here we go," the DJ called. The music started to play, filling the club with the happy synth pop that could've only originated in the 1980s. The crowd cheered and started blissfully jumping up and down to the beat. The little performance gauges appeared over each of our heads. Across the bar, Mongo screeched with encouragement.

Okay. You can do this.

And that's when Dwight the unicorn stabbed the DJ in the face with his horn.

57

ALL HELL BROKE LOOSE IN THE BAR.

The music continued. The gauges remained ready to judge our performance. Half the crowd continued to bounce and cheer, but the other half was suddenly beating the shit out of each other.

I exchanged a look with Donut. We didn't have a choice. We had to sing the song. With the DJ dead, this would be our only chance.

"You killed Lucienne!" Dwight roared drunkenly at me and Donut, the dead gremlin still attached to his twinkling horn. "You killed her, and I'm going to stab you in the fucking spleen!" He whipped his head, and the corpse sailed across the bar.

But Dwight was drunk, and his aim was off. Instead of hitting me or Donut, the dead gremlin slammed into Yuto, the large red demon from team Yokai. The gremlin exploded like a jar of salsa against the chest of the demon, who roared indignantly. The Oni swung a fist at the unicorn, who wasn't even close, and instead connected with some scarecrow monster, who blasted into a spray of glittering straw. His two partners, also scarecrows, turned on the red demon and attacked. The Minister of Blood-Letting and his skeletons jumped into the fray, defending their Yokai friends.

That idiot unicorn was going to get himself killed. We couldn't let that happen. Not yet. We needed him to live until at least the next heat started.

But then it was time to sing, and I couldn't think of anything else.

"We're talking away," I sang, starting the song. I ducked as a bottle flew through the crowd. It sailed over my head and exploded against the curtained wall, spraying the back of my head with glass and cold beer. "I don't know what I'm to say . . . I'll say it anyway!"

A gremlin fighting a Draconian bowled onto the stage, then rolled toward Donut. I kicked them both, sending them away before they could crash into her.

"Today is another day to find you . . ." Another bottle crashed against my chest. "Shyin' away."

Dong Quixote was suddenly in the middle of the fray, swinging his gigantic nickel sock over his head, clearing the stage in front of us, howling at the top of his lungs.

"Oh, I'll be comin' for your love, okay."

Donut sat poised at the microphone. It was time for the chorus.

"Take on meeeee!" I sang.

"Take on meeeee!" Donut echoed, singing her part, her Auto-Tuned voice high and, thankfully, in key. The sound pierced through the chaos like a knife. She shot a low-powered magic missile, and it blew an axe out of the hand of a Draconian who was about to sink it into the back of Dong's head.

"Take mee onnnn," I continued.

"Take on me!"

"I'lllll beeee gone, in a day or twoooooo," I cried, hitting the extra-high note.

There was a chime from the performance gauge floating by my head, and digital sparkles showered off it.

Half the crowd stopped fighting at that. I caught eyes with Florin, who'd stopped dead in mid-punch. He looked at me and mouthed, *Wow.*

Both of our performance gauges were buried to the right, all the way in the green, though mine now had little flames coming out of the top. I hoped that was a good sign.

We moved into the next verse. From across the bar, I could see Mongo was finally starting to realize there was a real fight going on, and he let out an ear-piercing screech. He leaped from the table and sailed across the bar, landing in the midst of it all, turning and screaming, knocking people over left and right with his tail. This also almost took out Donut's microphone stand, but I caught it with my foot, grabbing it between my big and index toe just as we hit the second chorus.

A group dogpiled Dwight, but Imani moved in and slammed a potion against the ass of the unicorn, causing him to drop unconscious.

Louis, Britney, and Bautista surrounded the passed-out unicorn, protecting him while Imani moved to the Yokai–scarecrow fight in an attempt to keep them from murdering each other. Every team that died in the bar meant another crawler-on-crawler matchup, so we had to protect them all the best we could, no matter how much we wanted to murder them all.

We hit the middle part of the song, which was mostly music. Donut cast *Ice Slick* on the dance floor, causing a group of fighting NPCs to go spinning and crash against the bar. Prepotente was there at the bar, seemingly ignoring the fight. The bartender wasn't back there anymore, having jumped over the counter to fight.

The goat was bent all the way over the now-unattended bar, his hooved feet dangling as he rummaged behind the counter. He let out a loud yelp when the group of combatants slammed into him, causing him to flip and disappear with a clatter.

A fairy creature tossed a miniature fireball at Imani's head. Imani ducked, and the fireball hit the curtains at the back of the stage, which immediately went right up.

Oh, fuck!

I, still singing the last chorus, still with Donut's microphone stand held aloft with my toes, bounced forward off the stage to keep myself from catching on fire. The flames spread to the ceiling.

The fairy moved to fire a second mini fireball, but she disappeared with a cry as Mongo bit her out of the air. The dinosaur screeched and belched out a puff of smoke.

Donut, pretending like this was all part of the show, stood on her two back legs and hopped down, following the microphone.

A mantis-like creature sliced at Dong, and he countered with his enormous sock. The mantis went flying, but not before she tore a hole in the weapon, which caused coins to fly everywhere. One pinged right off my forehead. They were nickels, I saw. All of them, even though he'd been putting actual gold pieces in there.

Still, seeing that there was now money all over the dance floor, those who hadn't been fighting pounced, jumping into the skirmish, grabbing handfuls of the coins.

The real version of this song faded away, but the karaoke version seemed to go on and on. *Just one more time.*

"I'lllll beeee gone, in a daaaaaaay," I sang, hitting the long, high note as digital fireworks exploded around the gauge, mixing in with the real fire that was quickly crawling across the ceiling of the bar.

Donut only had one more line.

"Take me . . . Argggggg!"

She cried out as Dekoki the kappa, paralyzed, fell backward right into her. The Saran Wrap around the kappa's head was peeled back, and the water in the creature's bowl head had spilled, which caused the monster to freeze up.

And then it was over.

Above, the twin screens sparked as they burst aflame. Louis was there spraying something out of his hands, stopping the fire. And Britney, too, a drink in one hand, was also putting out the fire as most of the NPCs fled.

I dropped the microphone to the ground. There was a blare of feedback and then the DJ booth exploded in sparks, and the sound went out.

Congratulations, Carl. You have been granted permanent access to the Stage Performance Guild!

New Achievement! Sing for your supper!

You're a proper musician! You sang something, and you've been rewarded for it. The next thing you know, you'll be earning a third of a cent per stream on Spotify and bragging to your friends and family and fellow kitchen staff that you're a "professional."

You have discovered a task-based guild by completing the entrance exam.

Reward: **From now on, hidden guilds with entrance requirements will appear on your map if you are in close proximity.**

The secret door in the side bar started to glow and pulse. This was on the one wall that hadn't been scorched.

Donut had **FAILED** over her head. She huffed indignantly, beer dripping off her. Mongo was there, licking it up, waving his wings excitedly.

"Shit," I said, seeing the sign over Donut. "I guess I gotta do this myself."

"We are never going to mention this again," she said. But then she added, "I do love that song, though."

58

THE BARTENDER, CRYING, SCOOPED UP A FEW HANDFULS OF THE DEAD DJ and rushed outside.

The others all started grabbing nickels and were helping Dong put them back in the sock, though dozens of NPCs had grabbed some and run. There was a nasty tear in the fabric of the sock, but it was mending itself. The sock, however, didn't seem to be going back to its giant size, no matter how many nickels people put back in. The coins were absolutely everywhere.

I called Splash Zone for help, but he didn't answer. He and the others were still in the Desperado Club, so I had Tipid run over. He and Bucket Boy grabbed the still-unconscious unicorn and lugged him back toward his garage before the bartender could gather some friends.

The bar stank like smoke, and I didn't know if we were going to get kicked out, so we had to do this quickly. Prepotente was in the middle of raiding the bar while Dong, the skeletons from the Bleak Congregation, and a few of the other regulars finished cleaning up the nickels.

I eyed Dong warily.

CARL: I gotta read the room first, but I don't want Dong screwing this up. If I say the word, you gotta get him out of here.
IMANI: I'll keep an eye on him.

Donut sat sullenly on the edge of the stage, a sour expression planted on her face. Mongo was snuffling about the bar, occasionally licking random puddles of blood and beer and gremlin guts. He had straw all over his face from where he'd bitten one of the scarecrows. Dekoki the kappa had regained the ability to move after the Minister of Blood-Letting poured a beer into her head bowl, and Louis was helping her reapply her Saran Wrap as she profusely apologized to Donut. She'd been knocked over when people lunged for the coins.

I spied Jurgen trying to come speak with me, but Florin held him back. That likely had something to do with Lucia Mar. I held up a finger, telling him I'd talk to him soon. "I'll get back as soon as I can," I called, moving for the door to the guild.

"No," Jurgen said, moving out of Florin's grip. "I will join you in the guild."

"You can't," I said, pulling the door open. My voice was still high-pitched. I moved into a menu, and it wouldn't let me turn it off, but it was about to time out. I coughed a few times, waiting for it to clear. "Look, this is important, too. We need this if we want to deal with the problem with the kids."

Jurgen was stopped at the entrance like he'd hit a brick wall. He grabbed me by the shirt, preventing me from going all the way in. "There is a goddess threatening to kill all the children."

"I know," I said, gently but firmly removing his fingers from my cloak. "But the only thing we can do from this side is try to talk Lucia into taking a deal. If she takes a deal, she's off the playing board, and those children are safe."

I hope, I didn't add.

"I need to get out," he said, a hint of panic in his voice. "Send me out via the Pineapple place, too."

"You can't," I said, looking him up and down. "I'm sorry. You worship Donar. They said you can't go if you worship a god."

"They said those of us who worship gods *can't* go, or they say they *don't want us* to go?" he demanded.

That was actually a good question. Akuma had said he didn't want the eyes of gods on that place. He'd said that if one worshipped a god, entering the area would instigate a smite. But was that true? Was it just a way to keep certain crawlers out? I didn't know the answer.

I thought again of Akuma's insistence that we kill two teams. That had been a lie, so I knew we couldn't trust him. But what if he was correct about not wanting gods there? I had no way of knowing, and it was frustrating. So many now worshipped gods, and if this was truly an escape, we needed to know.

"Wait, what sort of god is Donar anyway?" I asked, pausing. I was making a running list of all the gods I'd heard of. I was placing them into a chart, moving each one into a different category based on their affiliations and skills.

"Donar is a god of thunder and lightning. This version is much the same as Thor. But manlier."

My heart skipped a beat. "Is he sponsored this season?"

"No. I am no idiot, Carl. I wouldn't be dumb enough to worship a sponsored god. I—"

"Has he given you any lightning spells?"

"*Ya.* A few. It doesn't matter. Listen, Carl," Jurgen said, lowering his voice, "I gotta tell you something. It's Heidi . . . I used to be able to talk to her, but I haven't heard her in a while. I think something's wrong. I think she's in danger. She is all I have. She's pregnant. I have to get to her."

I gently pushed the large blond man back. "I promise you, Jurgen, I'm doing everything I can. You and Prepotente need to focus on surviving this next race, and then we'll figure it out. That's the best I can do for you right now. I promise."

He opened his mouth to say more, but I disappeared into the hidden guild.

Entering the Stage Performance Guild.

Please come in, performer. You are welcome here. See the guildmaster for the services o-o-o-offered.

I blinked, looking around, noting that even the regular dungeon notifications were glitching out more often now. The guild room was significantly larger than I had been expecting. It was a whole damn theater with red velvet chairs that looked as if it could fit five hundred people. At the far end was a stage with a single spotlight blaring down on it. The spotlight was the only illumination in the room.

It was shining down on the form of Porky, the left half of Corcunda, who lay on the stage.

Porky wore the same gimp suit as Corky, but his was white.

"Hello?" I called, walking down the center aisle. A thick layer of dust covered everything, and the sound of my footsteps filled the space.

"Hi. Can you help me?" came the voice from the stage. He had the deep voice of a mantaur, and it echoed in the large room. But it was muffled, too, as his mouth was behind a mask. "My, uh, zipper is stuck."

The large man was on his back in the middle of the stage, and as I approached, I could see what the problem was.

The white gimp suit was covered in zippers. Ostensibly, the whole thing was designed to keep his guts in his body. There was a long black zipper down the flat side of his body's cross section. This was the zipper that was stuck. It was stuck right at his lower waistline. There was a zipper from the top down and a second that came up from his crotch. The two met like a suitcase zipper, but a little bit of red bulging flesh appeared stuck there.

"It doesn't hurt, but it's really gross," Porky said as I hesitantly approached. I had to move to the side of the large stage and find the grimy stairs. Dust swirled with every step.

"How long have you been stuck like this?" I asked, going to a knee.

"I . . . I don't know," he said. "If I stand and the zipper isn't properly sealed, everything starts to leak."

"What about food? Water?" I examined the problem. Sure enough, the teeth of the top zipper were firmly embedded in whatever this was. It looked maybe like a little piece of intestine. I wasn't sure I wanted to find out. It was sitting at a place where he couldn't get proper leverage to move.

"I'm in a body-containment suit," Porky said. "It keeps me alive. It has water recycling. I don't eat. No, look. You gotta pull it up, but I can't get the angle right. My top arm is too short, and I can't bend without spilling."

I had a weird flashback of helping Bea do this with a jacket after she had gotten her own hair caught in the zipper. I'd pulled too hard, and it had broken, which in turn had led to a three-hour ordeal where we'd had to travel to multiple department stores to shop for a replacement.

"Here," I said, yanking on the bottom part. "I gotta pull it taut, and then I'll pull it upward. Uh, this might hurt."

"I can't feel my insides so much," he said. His top arm grabbed my arm for support. "My, my, aren't you muscly?"

I yanked, and there was a *pop*, and the zipper pulled free. A small amount of red watery liquid spurted out. I swallowed and then moved the zipper down, meeting the second zipper. The whole suit gave a flash.

Porky sighed with relief, then grabbed the two zippers and pulled them all the way down to the crotch. The half-mantaur awkwardly sat up.

"Thank you, sir. Thank you," Porky said. "Help me up, if you would. Uh, welcome to the stage performance guild. I can see you have some rudimentary levels in performance skills, but the fact you were able to gain entrance suggests you have a lot of raw talent. And for helping me today, I will throw a few free skill levels onto your Razzmatazz skill."

I stood, pulling the heavy man up by his lower arm. He was well-built and strong, but he wasn't pure, corded muscle like most of these guys usually were. The half-mantaur split all the way down the middle was really difficult to look at, and it was even harder to wrap my brain around. The long black zipper line down the flat side of his snow-white latex suit was taut like a drumhead, but sometimes when he moved, I could see the organs within pressing against it, like they were trying to spread outside. The same thing happened with his head, where I assumed a half brain sat in his bisected skull. It looked flat, but things occasionally undulated within. It was really, really gross.

Even though his voice was muffled by the suit itself, his ability to talk was not hampered by the half mouth.

"Look, Porky, I need to talk to you."

The half-mantaur froze. He hopped a few times to face me. He reached up and half unzipped an eyehole. A brown eye looked me up and down, and I suddenly wondered how he'd been seeing me up until this moment.

"I haven't been called Porky in a long time."

"Yeah, I figured," I said. "Your other half has spent a long time searching for you, but he's in real trouble, and he needs your help."

"What sort of trouble?"

I spent a few moments explaining everything I knew about Corky, his other half. That he had left the Penis Parade to go searching, but he'd disappeared, only to show back up now. We didn't know what was going on, but he was a part of the Lady Dominators team, and he spent every race passed out in the back of their vehicle.

Porky nodded. "Female mantaurs do *not* worship Grull like most of our kind do. They are adherents of Enyo. Enyo is an unhinged goddess of war."

The moment the guildmaster said that, I realized that neither she nor Corky worshipped a god.

"What about Grull? I thought all the mantaurs did."

"I did once," Porky said as he hopped backstage. I followed. He lit a lamp, and a dirty yellow light revealed the spartan, lonely world he lived within. "When I split, my devotion went away as well, and now I find myself wondering how I fell into such a trap in the first place. He's a very unpleasant deity."

"You're telling me," I muttered.

There was a dirty mattress on the floor and a pile of old dungeon newsletters sitting next to it. He quickly shoved them into a closet so I wouldn't see them.

He grabbed a tattered, unenchanted scarf off the bed and pulled it over his half-neck.

"Still," he continued, "the lady mantaurs prey on vulnerable mantaurs. They practice domination and submission magic. They will drain my other half just before their races, which will render him utterly submissive. But since there are two of them, it is too much, and it will make him unconscious. This will increase their stats for the race."

I nodded. I figured it was something like that. "He's going to die this next race if we don't do anything about it, and if he dies, you'll never get reunited."

"If my other half dies, I die, too. I'm glad you came to me."

"Wait, I didn't know that. I have a fleshmancer waiting outside. We need to get you out of here, and then we'll need to break Corky out of his garage before the race starts. Once we do that, we can run the ceremony to get you two reunited. We only have two hours, so we gotta move fast. Does that sound good? Will you go with me?"

The strange creature just stood there for several moments, swaying back and forth, while I held my breath. He spent a minute contemplating the stained bed, and I wondered how often people came in here. How long had Milk spent alone in that lonely guild? This was an NPC, but still . . .

Porky's white latex suit made creaking noises with every small movement.

"Of course I'll help," he finally said. "You'll have to hire me as a temporary mercenary. Or you can just . . . manhandle me out of here. But I'll help, especially if that means I will get reunited with my other half. It's been so long. It would be nice to not have to lean against everything again."

I let out a stream of breath. That was a lot easier than I had thought it would be.

". . . And I'll need your help, too. I want you to help me find and kick the ever-loving tar out of this stripper I know. The one responsible for all of this trouble in the first place. His name is Dong Quixote."

59

WE HAD JUST OVER AN HOUR AND A HALF BEFORE THE NEXT HEAT would start.

ELLE: Na is in. I think. She's still being creepy as fuck. She's not actually talking, but she sort of nodded. We'll meet you at your safe room. Also, I heard about your performance. I am so pissed I missed it.

DONUT: CARL DID GREAT, BUT I WAS ROBBED OF A PERFECT SCORE.

ELLE: I heard. You'll get 'em next time, kid. See you soon.

IMANI: Dong is being a problem. He doesn't want to leave. He's picked up all the nickels we could find, but the sock is back to the size it was when he first got it, and he's complaining that it has stopped talking to him. We need to keep an eye on him. Donut is talking to him now.

CARL: Splash Zone, come get your boy.

Warning: As this mercenary is no longer on this floor, they are unable to be contacted. You will still be charged their daily fee until you can locate them. Maybe this'll teach you to keep better track of your hired help.

What the shit?

I sent quick messages to Gluteus and Doctor Bones, who'd also been with Splash Zone in the Desperado Club. I received the same warning.

CARL: I think something happened to the other strippers in the Desperado Club! I can't contact them.

DONUT: OH NO.

BUCKET BOY: They're not answering me, either! They were going to see the new boss guy, Hamed, Anaconda and Damascus Steel's dad!

Hamed. The leader of the Guild of Suffering. The late Astrid's "husband," who had taken over the Desperado Club after Katia and I killed her. I had no idea what was going on with all that, and now was not the time for that whole thing to kick off.

"Goddamnit," I grumbled.

CARL: Okay, okay. It doesn't say they're dead, which is good. And we know Damascus Steel is still alive because Donut saw him last floor. Don't go back in there. As soon as we get through this, we'll try to find them.

Dong didn't answer.

DONUT: I HAD TO ORDER DONG BACK TO THE SAFE ROOM. HE'S VERY UPSET THAT HE'S BEING LEFT OUT OF THIS. THIS IS VERY EMOTIONAL FOR HIM.

CARL: We're on our way.

Ten minutes later, a group of us stood outside the garage door with the number 2. We were currently in a safe area, but the garage itself wasn't a safe zone, so the rules were a little weird about what we could and couldn't do to break in. My original plan was to blow the whole thing off the tracks, but instead we decided to use Donut's *Hole* spell to get inside.

We'd get inside, disable Genesis and Rapture, and grab Corky. We'd drag him back to our garage, where Grigori would do the ceremony.

The fleshmancer had said the spell itself wasn't too difficult if both halves were willing. We'd have to unzip both from their containment suits and keep both halves alive with spells or potions while we squished them together, which would be pretty gross. But once they were touching, he would cast a joining spell that would start the process to fuse them. And once they were together, there would be just a few short minutes before the two personalities would join.

"What's going to happen to them, personality-wise?" I asked as we approached the garage. "They've been apart a really long time, and now they're very different people."

"I have no idea," Grigori said. "But I'm looking forward to seeing the results. It's a very interesting process, or so I've heard."

"Wait, so you've never done this before?"

The tall mage shrugged. "It is quite rare for two halfsies to survive more than a few minutes after the casting of *Split Personality*, so I haven't had the opportunity. I have witnessed *Meld* work a few times, which is similar in terms of combining two minds, but in the case of *Meld*, the party instituting the spell is the dominant personality."

"What the hell is that?"

"It is when a creature consumes and joins with another. Slimes use the process, as do many demons and some types of succubae. Some versions are permanent. Some aren't. When it *is* permanent but they don't want it to be anymore, that's when they look for someone like me. I specialize in fixing other people's mistakes. I'm not always successful, but I assure you, I'm the best there is."

I thought again of Samantha and her quest to get her body back. I quickly explained everything that was going on with her.

"Yes, yes, I'm familiar," he said, sounding dismissive. He oddly reminded me of one of many caseworkers I'd had as a teen. "Imani was telling me a bit about the situation. I would like to examine this so-called withering spirit, as what you describe is quite impossible. But if you need for her to regain a body, I have multiple options now that you've wasted the flesh golem."

I grunted. "Let's see how this goes first."

Donut was shooting rapid-fire, singing-related questions at Porky, who hopped along on a single foot and was cheerfully answering them.

"Her name is Lover Illiana," Donut was saying, talking about her singing booth in the training room. "She's just a hologram lady, but she is quite helpful. Though I must say, I feel as if I've plateaued in my career. Miss Illiana cares more about my breaths and how I'm hitting the notes, which is good and all. But she has no real concept of show business, which is why I wanted to get into your guild. I am already an expert singer. What I need help with is bringing the house down."

"I know that name," Porky said as he hopped along. "Lover Illiana was a famed singer and renowned vocal coach. She died quite tragically, but her legend lives on. You are correct. Soaring vocals can bring the audience to the edge of their seat, but it's the performance itself, your ability to connect with the audience that whisks them into the clouds with you. Any performance is 10% talent, 90% presence, I always say. A truly transcendent experience requires one to know their fans intimately. You want them to limp out of the theater after you're done with them, gasping for breath as if you've just made love to their very soul. You want everything they experience after the fact to be stale and taste like ash because they know they'll never experience joy like that again."

"Exactly!" Donut said.

ELLE: We're in the guildhall common room if you want to join us.

DONUT: YOU HAVE TO WAIT. I WANT TO SAY GOODBYE TO LI NA BEFORE SHE LEAVES.

CARL: Give us ten minutes. I hope this will go fast.

TIPID: Uh, guys, I hate to do this, but you might want to speed things up. Dong is sick. I'm not sure what's wrong, but his health just started to dip. He has a debuff over his head that says "Negative ROI." I don't know what that means. I've never seen it before. And then Bucket Boy lost the sock.

BUCKET BOY: This is different than last time! His health is going down slower, but I can see the debuff now. It's a curse! I grabbed the sock and tried to ask it if it knew what was wrong, but the sock teleported away! I don't know what happened!

MORDECAI: The weapon attacked Bucket Boy but got teleported by the safe room rules. We've lost it. That thing could be anywhere. Goddamn sapient weapons. They're always bad news.

IMANI: If it's a curse, we'll need to bring him to a temple to cure him.

"Okay," I whispered as we got to the door. "Donut casts *Hole*, and we all jump in. We know they always keep Corky in there, but we're not positive the two womantaurs are in. If they are, Louis will put them to sleep, and Imani will hit them with a **Sluggish** debuff. Britney and Donut will protect Grigori and Porky, and I'll grab Corky. Then we'll haul ass back to our garage and get it done. We'll leave Louis and Britney outside the garage so they can't break in to get him back. Are we ready?"

"Ready!" Donut said.

DONG QUIXOTE: This is unbearable, Carl. You are doing this without giving me a chance to even say goodbye. He is the love of my life, and what you're doing is going to change him forever. I am dying. He is being taken from me. I am right here on the other side of the door, and I can't even see him.

I paused. *Goddamnit.* I suddenly felt like a huge asshole. I spent a half second considering it. But no. This was too important. We couldn't risk something going wrong.

CARL: I'm sorry, Dong. I wish it could go another way. But if Porky sees you, he's going to go apeshit, and none of this will work. As soon as we're done with this, I promise, we'll get you to a temple to get that curse removed.

"Donut, cast your *Hole*."

"We talked about this, Carl," Donut said as she started to cast.

But before she could, the garage door started to open. And from within, a car revved up.

"Shit," Louis said, backing away. "We have less than an hour left. We're too late. They can go to the starting line!"

"So?" I said, also backing up. "Cast! Cast!"

"We can't," Imani said, also stepping off the driveway. The GTO pulled out of the garage. Within, both Rapture and Genesis cackled with laughter.

"You think we didn't hear you out there?" Rapture asked. Across the cul-de-sac, a road leading up to the starting block appeared. And just beyond it, a massive factory loomed. The building hadn't been there just a moment before. Dark clouds hung over the plant. A flickering neon sign hung from the top of the dilapidated multistory building. It read, "Gasworks Screw Factory, Steel Mill, and Doll Workshop." And under it, a smaller sign read, "There's no cocaine in here." Sparks flew from the sign.

"Hey, Porky," called Genesis, who was driving. Corky remained in the back of the car, passed out as usual. "Wanna hop in?"

"We'll treat you real good," added Rapture. She patted the outside door of the car with her lower arm. "We'd love to have a matched set."

"We can't attack them when they're on their way to the starting blocks," Imani said. "They're in the car, and they're safe."

"Shit," I said.

"Why you keep thinking we's dumb?" Rapture asked me. "You don't think we didn't hear about the fleshmancer you had at the bar? Corky is ours, not yours. And where's that crusty old stripper guy? He's not his, either. We'll unzip Corky and let him spill before we let you have him."

"Yeah. You got your own gimp. Keep your paws off ours. He's non-transferable," Genesis said. She revved the engine a few times.

The tires on the GTO glowed yellow, and they looked to be literally made of gold. That was new.

"See you in the factory," Rapture said as they pulled onto the road. Behind them, the garage door started to close.

"Stripper?" Porky asked, turning. His single eye focused on me. Even through the suit, I could see he was enraged. "You failed to mention Dong was a part of this little endeavor."

"I suppose this means we'll have to wait until after the next race to do this," Donut said.

BUCKET BOY: He's getting worse! He's really upset! I don't know how much time he has! I don't know what to do!

MORDECAI: Okay, guys. We're busy prepping for the Li Na exit, but we just took a look at Dong. I think we know what this is. It's called Negative ROI for some reason, but Mistress Tiatha believes it's really a curse that's also called Separation Anxiety. If that's the case, a temple isn't going to help him. It's

not good. We'll need the sock back, and we'll need every single coin he lost. Otherwise—

DONUT: OH NO! A HUNDRED DIFFERENT NPCS TOOK THE NICKELS! WE'LL NEVER GET THEM ALL BACK!

MORDECAI: We don't have the sock, either. It probably teleported to Hungry Eyes, where it got picked up by an NPC or another crawler. That's what sapient weapons do. They use their owners until they can't anymore, and then they move on to someone else. I'm sorry, guys. Even I didn't see it coming. That was a particularly insidious one. Its danger was masked by its stupid origin story.

Imani jogged off without another word, heading toward our garage. If anyone in the group could save Dong, it would be her. Jacobus zipped after her.

"Goddamnit," I said, sitting down on the curb. The quest would fail if Dong was dead. But worse, this was all my fault. *I* had given him that sock, which I'd originally gotten from Quan Ch.

Porky stood there, fuming. I, once again, felt like an enormous asshole.

I thought of Li Na sitting in the guildhall, waiting for us to say goodbye. She'd been completely drained of any shred of humanity. We had to get her away from the rest of us just to keep her and ourselves alive.

Was I different? Dong was an NPC. But he was also my friend. Yes, we needed to complete this quest. It was crucial. But I could've been less of a prick about it, and I knew that.

Jasha and Radoslav sat watching, talking with Osvaldo and Filipe. All four raised their hands in greeting. I also saw Dwight was out here still unconscious, though he'd be awake in a minute or two. He'd been dumped in front of his garage.

Donut jumped to my shoulder. "We have to do something," she said.

I didn't know if we could, but there was at least one wrong I could right and still complete the quest. I stood, and I started striding toward our garage. Everyone else scrambled to catch up.

"We can't wait until after the race," I said. "Porky, you're going to have to put your big-boy pants on. Yes, Dong is here. Yes, I understand you two don't like each other, but you're going to get over it. This is to save *your* life. Grigori, you're going to spend the next half hour learning how to drive just in case we need you."

"Drive?" the mage asked.

"We're still getting them back together, but now we're doing it *during* the race," I said. "Come on, everybody. Let's say goodbye to Li Na."

60

I LEFT GRIGORI IN THE GARAGE WITH HEDY AND JAMAL, AND WE ENtered the safe room to find Dong sitting on the couch, sobbing with Bigs on his head, glaring at me. Bigs completely covered the old man's head, and it took me a moment for my mind to figure out what I was looking at. Tipid and Imani were on the couch as well. Tipid was patting the old man on the shoulder while Bucket Boy stood by, looking helpless. Dong's health was still in the green, but it was clearly going down.

"Healing potions or blessings don't work," Imani said, speaking quietly. "I can slow the descent of his health, but I don't think I can stop it. He has an hour and a half. Maybe less." She put her hand on my shoulder. "I'm going to talk to Li Na."

Jacobus buzzed around Bigs and Dong. The little fairy zoomed right up to Dong's mouth and lifted his lips and peered inside before Imani yelled at him to get away. The little fairy zoomed off, following Imani.

"You're not my favorite person right now, Daddy," Bigs said from her position atop Dong's head, swinging her hatchet in my direction. "First, you ain't killing that Li Na murderer, and now you're playing the bad guy in Dong's love story. We sluggalos have a code. That code is 'unity, support, family, and kneecapping bitches.' You ain't providing no unity, no support, you're not watching after your family, and you're not even letting me kneecap a bitch. That makes *you* the bitch."

"You're right. I'm sorry," I said.

"Wait, I am?" Bigs asked.

I turned to Donut. "You guys, follow Imani. I'll be there in a minute. I need to talk to Dong. Porky, stay here."

Donut and the others left. I returned my attention to Bigs.

"Yeah," I said, "I've been a dick. I'm doing my best. A long, long time ago, I said something like 'We need to help each other. Otherwise, what's the point?' When we stop doing that, that's when we stop being . . ."

I paused.

Being human was what I'd said to Brandon.

We needed a word that went beyond that.

"Real Gs?" Bigs asked.

I smiled. "Real Gs."

"Does that mean we're going to slaughter Li Na and laugh as she drowns in her own blood?"

"No," I said. "She's a lot like me. She's lost her way. We're going to send her somewhere where she can help and not hurt any more of our friends." *I hope.*

"You're a good daddy," Bigs finally said. "But I'm not the one you need to apologize to."

She slimed off, leaving an orange streak on Dong's head.

The older man had stopped crying and was just looking at me.

I took another deep breath. We didn't have time, but at the moment, I didn't care. "For the first part of this floor," I began as I pulled a towel from my inventory, "I was happy that we were on rails. That we didn't have a choice about what we were doing. It was so much easier than before. And even though the danger is just as high, if not higher, it was nice, for a little bit at least, that everything was so simple. Christ, what *is* this stuff that the sluggalos leak? Why is it so sticky?"

Dong blinked at me, not saying anything. I continued.

"But I quickly realized that this floor was a deliberate trap. It's a drain designed to catch those of us who've been spat out of the bottom of Faction Wars and dared to go on. It's a drain that spins faster and faster the closer we get to the hole, and suddenly we're just gone, and it happens so fast, we don't even realize it until it's too late."

"My good sir," Dong began. "Carl."

I held up my hand. "I know we don't have much time, but I need to say this. I've been trying to keep you out of this quest, and it's because I'm scared it's not going to work and I'm scared that you'll mess it up, not because I don't trust you but because you're too close to it. The fact that you are in love with this guy is a complication, not an asset. The smart thing to do is to keep you away while we get this done."

I paused, taking a deep breath.

"But that's not what we're going to do. I'm going to have to attempt this Corcunda reunion during the race. I can bring three mercenaries. It's going to be the fleshmancer guy, Porky here, and you. We're going to do our best to save your friend."

Dong sat up, deliberately not looking at Porky, who stood behind me, not saying anything. "Carl, I'm dying. Jefferson said I was a bad investment. And now I am weak, and my health is seeping away. I will not be able to help."

"Maybe not," I said. "But I'll make sure you get to say goodbye to your friend." I put my hand on his shoulder. "I won't lie to you. We have to do some awful things to get through this, and oftentimes it's at the expense of others. Sometimes we can't take a moment to spare the feelings of a friend because there simply isn't time. But if it's worth anything, I want you to know that I'm sorry I tried to keep you two apart. I'm sorry I've been a jerk about it. Survival has more than one meaning. I am trying so, so hard. But sometimes . . ."

I turned to look at the door leading to the guildhall. Li Na was in there waiting. Everybody was waiting. I thought of that moment when I'd almost lost my cool and killed Empress D'Nadia on the last floor. Or of the moment when I did slip and lose it when Finley and the others had died.

I thought of the voices in my head whispering just below the surface, all scrabbling to grab my attention. I thought of the tremor in my hands that I'd been studiously ignoring since Donut's attack in the tower.

Li Na. Lucia Mar. It would be so easy for that to be me. Hell, it *was* me. I was no longer standing on the edge. I had already stepped off, and now I was holding on by my fingers, and I was slipping, slipping, slipping.

You will not break me.

You will not.

Dong patted me on the arm and forced a smile. "Of course, my boy. Of course. I understand. Others don't think of folks like myself as someone who can have a partner because of what we do. Like I'm unworthy of love when they're the ones who come to me. It's like they don't think we're real." He paused. "Do you know why I fell in love with him?"

"Why?"

"There was a fight once in the Desperado Club. A big battle not unlike the one where you and Katia laid waste to the establishment. This was just after he'd been split. And I was afraid. I was afraid the fighting would spread to the Penis Parade and that we would all die. Corky looked at me, put a hand on my shoulder like you just did, and said, 'Maybe we will die today. But if we do, then we will die together, and that's more than most people get. There's no such thing as a sad ending if it's by the side of the people who make you happy.'"

Samantha was suddenly there, floating next to me. "I'm going to steal that line when Carl lets me drive and I make the car crash."

"Gah," I cried, surprised at her sudden appearance. "I didn't hear you come in!"

"Everybody is waiting for you in the other room," Samantha said. She sniffed around, suspicious. She turned to the other person in the room. "You're the beautiful man, huh?" She snuffled around his leg. "You're only half as handsome as I thought you'd be. Why don't you unzip that thing and really open up to us?"

"Come on, Samantha. People are waiting." I stood, patting Dong on the leg. "Rest while you can. Gather your strength. I have to go out there. There's someone else here you should probably talk to."

I moved aside, revealing the half-mantaur standing behind me, who'd been quietly waiting, listening.

Dong looked up, acknowledging the other presence for the first time.

"Hello," Porky said, his voice quiet, sad. "I remember that day when the club was under siege. I soon thereafter left. I thought running a guild would be safer."

Dong looked him up and down. "Good sir, that's my scarf."

"I know," Porky replied, reaching up to touch it. "My other half let me have it when I went off. He said I'd want it, and I told him I was going to throw it out because it was really yours, and he said, 'No, you won't.' And I didn't."

There was an awkward moment of silence.

"Why did you hate me?" Dong finally asked.

"Come on, Samantha," I said, grabbing her out of the air. We needed to give them their privacy.

"Wait," she complained. "I want to see what happens next. Deathbed make-up sex is my favorite kind. I've had it like three times. Four if you count that incident with Charlie. Do you think you can have make-up sex on a first date?"

"Just stop," I said as we moved toward the door. "That's not the half that he was with. That's the other one."

She gasped. "If they *do* hook up, do you think it would be considered cheating? Like, if you get the two pieces back together, and their mind melds, and suddenly the mantaur guy has this big moral conundrum because he cheated on himself with himself and *then* . . ." She paused. "Wait, how are you planning on getting them glued back together?"

"Come *on*," I said, covering her mouth. She started growling and chewing on my hand.

I moved toward the exit with her struggling form. The cleaner bot was still here, pressed against the common room door, listening to what was going on in there.

I paused, regarding the grumpy but studious little robot. "You know," I said, "you take a lot of abuse. I'm sorry for that. If this works out with your friend in there, we'll be needing you to do the same thing. You're a goddamned hero, and if I don't get a chance to say it before we need you, I just want you to know that I appreciate it."

The robot let out a long beep.

61

LI NA SAT IN THE MIDDLE OF THE COMMON ROOM, HOVERING A FOOT OFF the floor. She glowed, and her good eye remained closed. The other, mechanical eye twitched, clockwork gears spinning. A large group of us had formed around her. Standing next to her were Mordecai, Mistress Tiatha, and Rosetta. The white cleaner bot also hovered nearby.

Mongo stood at the edge of the room, posted up near the Bopca at the storefront.

Just behind Mongo was the entrance to the guild's pet stables. I really needed to get in there and check on Rend. He, Gonk, Simoom, and now Penelope were all in there, supposedly all having a great time.

Prepotente was also here in the room. He was examining a pet carrier. "Interesting," he said, handing the case off to Mordecai.

"So," Mordecai was saying to Li Na, who did not acknowledge him, "this is how this works."

I released Samantha, and she zipped over to Louis, who stood right next to me. Donut jumped to my shoulder.

"Has she said *anything*?" I whispered.

"Nothing," Donut replied. "But she did cast some gooey dread thing on your cactus when Rosetta asked her to."

"She did what on my what?"

Mordecai held up the pet carrier, which had some sort of device installed on the outside. "This is an XL pet carrier. As we all know, they can't hold crawlers. But as some of us also know, they *can* still suck crawlers in if the crawler allows it. What happens is a crawler gets sucked up by the pet carrier, and approximately ten seconds later, the carrier breaks, and the crawler is expelled. They have a **Bonked** debuff that lasts for about twenty seconds. Unfortunately, if the crawler gets zapped into the pet carrier and someone attempts to add the carrier to their personal inventory, it will not work. However, the cleaner bot's weight-based utility inventory system *does* work. What we're going to do is zap you into the pet carrier, and before the carrier breaks, we will have, uh, Suckira here suck the pet carrier in."

"Suckira?" I asked.

Donut scoffed. "That was Louis's idea. I wanted Anna Nardini. I insisted we name the cleaner bots now that we had two, and he said that was the name of the robot vacuum his mom had in Florida. We flipped a coin for the right to name it, but Samantha was the one to do the coin flip, and I think she cheated."

"Anna Nardini?" I asked. "What?"

"I did cheat," Samantha said from Louis's shoulder. He'd given up trying to shoo her away. "That's what a woman does for her man."

Louis let out a spray of water. "She didn't cheat. It was a fair flip. Please stop sticking your tongue in my gills. It freaks me out."

"Freaking you out is my love language, Louis."

"Wait, what did you name the one in our space?" I asked.

Before Donut could answer, Mordecai started droning on again.

He continued like this for some time before Elle interrupted.

"Holy shit, we get it. It's going to work. Can we get on with it?"

"Carl, did you understand any of that?" Donut whispered.

"Sort of," I said. "Basically, Li Na gets sucked into the cleaner bot, the cleaner bot gets put up for sale, Herot buys it, and he empties her out inside of the other place. And now Li Na has left the game because this Cabaret place is outside the playing field. She'll be considered to have been 'lost.'"

"It's like trading a Pokémon between devices," Louis said.

Donut snorted. "You wouldn't catch me dead doing that."

"Are you absolutely, positively positive that the contents of the bot's storage will still be there when this stranger purchases it?" Prepotente asked.

"No," Rosetta said. "But we believe they will be. It's a container. And containers and their contents *do* transfer. But it is a risk. We are also not positive that Na will survive when the floor collapses. The rules suggest she will survive, but as this has never happened before, we're not positive."

"It'll work," Mistress Tiatha said, speaking for the first time. "It *has* happened before." She was drunk again, swaying where she stood. She didn't elaborate.

"Okay," Prepotente said. "But how will we know if it's successful? We've already established that the regular messaging system probably will not work. She is partied with Zhang, but she will automatically leave the party. Will we even receive a this-crawler-has-perished message if we send her a note?"

"That's actually a very good question," Mordecai said. "But we have a solution for that as well. Rosetta?"

Rosetta produced a tiny cactus plant with a plastic pot. The cactus glowed blue. "Li Na has cast a dread trap on this plant. Deadly bloom. We're in a safe room, but the trap will still activate if you touch it, so leave it alone. You won't get poisoned, but it will ruin it. Normally, someone comes near the plant, the flowers bloom, and they release a spore that will paralyze you."

"Hey," I said, "that's from my room! I got that from picking an Earth class. It's just a little cactus from Home Depot."

"It didn't match with the new rug," Samantha said. "I put it out. It's covered with poky parts. Much too aggressive for the vibe I'm going for."

"You *put it out*?" I made a mental note to go check on my room.

"The condition of the plant will tell us Li Na's status," Rosetta continued. "If it's glowing in the ready status like it is now, Li Na is alive and in the dungeon. If the plant activates on its own, blooms appearing and spores spreading but no longer lit up, that means Na has physically left the game. She is outside the dungeon. If the spell fails suddenly and doesn't activate and the cactus dissipates into dust, that means Na is dead and that she died inside the dungeon."

"Interesting," Prepotente said, leaning in to examine the small cactus. "You best keep this someplace safe. What if she ends up trapped inside the cleaner's storage, never released?"

"That is another possibility that will be indicated. The glow will slowly fail over the course of several days. And finally, if she believes it's safe for the others to proceed to the Pineapple Cabaret, she will be able to remotely make a single flower bloom on the top of the cactus. There will be a single flower, and the trap will still be glowing. If she's still alive but she believes this is not a safe method for crawlers to come, she will make three flowers bloom."

"I get it. Sort of," Donut said. "If Suckira and Na make it to this Pineapple place and there's a single flower on Carl's cactus at the end of this next race, then we know it's safe to send everyone else using Ezra Fitz."

"Using what?" I asked.

"Keep up, Carl," Donut said. "If we get the go-ahead from Li Na, we'll have everyone we can get sucked up by Ezra Fitz the Second, and they'll go there, too."

"Wait, you named the cleaner bot 'Ezra Fitz'? Why?"

"Because Ezra Fitz sucks, Carl."

"Who the hell is that?"

And then I realized I didn't actually care, and I returned my attention back to the important conversation.

"It's not a perfect solution," Mordecai said. "XL pet carriers are expensive, and there's limited room in the other cleaner bot, especially after we had it clean up all the leftovers from Carl's Naga inheritance. We can maybe send fifty more people with just one bot. We do have some leads on other bots but not many. We can't have this Herot sell the cleaner bot back to us, either, unfortunately. All dungeon upgrades such as the bots have a timer. He won't be able to re-list the bot for thirty days."

"Shit," I said. Fifty people? That wasn't nearly enough. But surely we weren't the only party with a cleaner bot. I started to compose a message to send out.

Prepotente made a noise that sounded like a bleat. "Very clever. This still seems like a surefire suicide method to me. Good luck, Li Na." He turned and strode from the room, but he paused at the door. He stood there, running his hand along the wall near the couch. There was a table there containing the two wrapped Christmas presents. One for me, and one for Imani. "I do like this place, I must say. Maybe you can, you know, allow me to attach my personal space to the guild?"

Imani crossed her arms. "You said no the last time I offered."

"That was before I knew about the pet stables. And the Bopca! This place is a delight." He turned to look at Donut. "I have a karaoke kit in my space I can add to the main room. I bought it to practice for my performance that never happened."

Donut gasped.

"I will see you and Carl in the factory," Prepotente said, turning away. "I will send you my plan after I confer with Jurgen."

"Can we continue, please?" Mordecai asked.

I spied Linus the tourist on the other side of the room. He was whispering something to Bautista, who did not look amused. Donut followed the path of my gaze.

"He keeps trying to get Daniel to make tea," Donut said. "Apparently, Bautista tea is a trending thing right now. Daniel doesn't even have an outreach manager, so he's sure to get ripped off. The folks on my social media board are all jealous of him. Of Linus, I mean, not Daniel. Elle's Snow Cones fan club did a raid on my server the other day, and they and the Posse were all fighting, but now they're friends and working together."

"Okay, we're ready," Mordecai said. "Uh, Suckira? Are you ready?"

Suckira let out a beep.

Zhang stepped forward, head lowered.

"I'm sorry it was your brother and not me," he said, his voice a whisper. "If Jun is watching this now, I hope he isn't angry with me for not watching over you like I promised."

Li Na looked up at that, her one good eye opening. The other, mechanical eye twirled and zoomed.

"I am no child to protect. I never have been, and you have nothing to apologize for. You have been a good friend to me. Jun loved you like a brother. I will do this. I will clear the way for you and everyone else who is to come after this next race, and then I will make certain the war mages do not turn on us. Do not die, Zhang. I hope to see you again soon." She paused. "Do not ever lose your smile. I used to smile at you so you would smile back at me, and I would pretend, in my mind, that you and I were married and that your smiles filled me in a way that I could only pray for. Thank you for always trying to protect me, even when I didn't deserve it."

She turned to Mordecai. "I am ready. I do not wish to speak to anyone else."

"Uh, yeah. Sure, kid," Mordecai said, handing the pet carrier to Zhang, who had to do it.

And then it was done. Zhang held out the pet carrier, pointed it at Li Na, who nodded. He pressed the button, and she disappeared within. The pet carrier started buzzing. The white cleaner bot Suckira picked it up. It disappeared without so much as a beep.

We all waited, holding our breath. Nothing happened.

We all turned our attention to the cactus. So far, there was no change. The one thing we didn't want to happen was for it to activate and then turn to dust. That meant Na was dead.

Mordecai reached over and hit a button on the back of Suckira, and the robot unit turned off. He held it in two skeletal hands.

"Okay, then," Mordecai said. "Donut, let's sell this at the terminal."

We moved to the shop-interface terminal in the common room located right next to the Bopca station. Donut swept her paw across it. We all watched as she made a new **For Sale** listing.

"Yay! I did it right. Okay, Mordecai, put it in front of the light thingy, and it'll be done."

Mordecai reached over, and with a beep, the white cleaner bot disappeared.

Mordecai's hood was suddenly down, and his eyeball head was on fire.

"The Oak Fell lives up to her name," he said in his deep voice. But then the giant eye blinked, and he was back to himself. He pulled the hood up and patted the fire out on his head.

The interface beeped, and text appeared. **Your item has sold!**

62

<Entry from Donut's *A Banquet Fit for a Princess.*>

Mees Koning 2. Crawler #9,174,929.

Race: Half-Orc.

Class: Boring Ol' Mage.

Final Level: 63.

Hi, Princess Donut.

I was never a good-looking guy, and I never had a girlfriend. But I used to think if I tried really hard at keeping in shape and keeping up with fashion and taking lessons online on how to be social, maybe I would one day find someone.

I feel so invisible sometimes. No matter how hard I tried, it didn't seem to work. I freeze up when I talk to people. I'm not good with social interactions. I stutter sometimes, and it makes people uncomfortable.

It was really hard not to be bitter about it, if I'm honest. But I tried not to be. I tried to keep a positive attitude.

I think the dungeon knew this about me because when it came to race selection, my only options were things that made me even uglier. I'd sliced into an Acid Spitter and was badly scarred before the second floor collapsed. I could stay human, of course, but that meant I'd have to keep my injuries. So I picked the race that seemed the least offensive-looking.

I regret it. People shied away from me even more afterward, and after I accidentally hurt two crawlers when my *Whoopsie Daisy* spell backfired and I received two player-killer skulls, I was truly alone.

Why am I telling you this?

You probably don't remember, but just before the battle at the southern border during Faction Wars, I was working a stinger unit. You and Carl strolled by, and you stopped, looked up at me, and said you liked my fangs. You saw my player-killer skulls and asked me if I was a bad person. I told you what happened, and I stuttered, but you waited for me to tell you, and afterward, you told me about your friend Imani, and you said that we all have scars.

We only talked for maybe a minute, but it was enough.

It's stupid, I know. You saw I was scared, and it was just a little throwaway moment. But I think it was the first time in my entire life anyone has ever looked at me and said something nice, just to be nice, just to make me, a stranger, feel better.

So thank you for that. During that horrible floor, it was a small, happy moment of brightness that gave me just enough of a boost to get through the most terrifying experience of my life.

I was inside the ball when you cast your Atrocity. You saved the life of myself and so many others.

You are beautiful on the inside and on the outside, no matter how many scars you may receive before this is over. I want you to know that.

I used to draw a lot of anime characters growing up, and I hope this drawing helps you in some way.

Drawing: A well-shaded, curved piece of metal with little electric bolts coming off it.

Associated Spell: *Big-Ass Magnet.* Casts at level 14.

JUST BEFORE THE RACE STARTED, I FOUND DONG IN THE PET STABLES. He'd brought Porky with him, and he was showing him Gonk the swamp yak, who was in her pen, happily munching away at something, while Simoom the rhino snorted beside her. Rend was also in here playing with Penelope the pig, though he started whining the moment he saw me, likely upset that I wasn't bringing him out adventuring more.

I unloaded a ton of frozen chicken patties on the ground, and he let out an excited grunt before he started to devour them. I patted the meatball on the head. "Don't worry, buddy. We'll get you out there soon. It's too dangerous right now with all the potatoes everywhere."

Penelope was also excited about the chicken patties.

Porky was staring at the food on the ground, but then I realized he was actually staring at Penelope the pig, licking his lips with his half tongue, which looked especially lascivious due to the white gimp suit. I sighed.

"You are a good mount," Dong was saying, patting the oblivious Gonk on the side of the head. "I used to dream of one final charge into the unknown astride a beast such as yourself, but, alas, some dreams are impossible indeed. Still a worthy quest, I say."

He turned, seeing me waiting.

"To battle, then?" he asked.

"To battle," I said.

And five minutes later, we were in the truck, approaching the starting line.

CARL: Akuma, are you still on this floor?

AKUMA: I am still here. I will be leaving soon. Stop messaging me unless it's important. Don't you have a race right now? Focus on that and not annoying me.

I was about to send him a snide reply when another message came in.

ZHANG: I just got a notification that she's left the party and has been disqualified. Then I got an Uh-Oh achievement for being a solo driver. I hope this Bodi guy knows how to ride an octopus.

MORDECAI: The cactus is holding steady. I'll let everyone know if something changes.

"He said that would only happen once," Donut complained from the passenger's seat. She was talking about Mordecai's cryptic proclamation. "But that's twice now. It's really scary. I don't like it."

"If someone is making you uncomfortable, it's best to cut them from your life," Dorota said.

"He said we need to ignore it," I replied as I eased up to the starting line. I was the last one here. The race would start in two minutes. We were two spots over from the Lady Dominators. We had Osvaldo between us and team Free Love on the other side. At the far end, Dwight, alone, sat within his vine, staring straight forward.

"Let's get through this," I said. Ahead, the massive factory loomed. The place didn't really look like a factory but the entrance to an industrial-themed amusement park ride. The enormous entrance door was large enough for us all to drive in side by side. I knew that once we entered, the tracks would narrow.

There was a total of twelve heats entering this race, but none of the other heats were teams from our guild except Prepotente and Jurgen aboard their tapir, Sweety. I didn't see them now.

I knew Louis, Imani, and Zhang—who was riding behind Bodi—were all on a track called the Infected Gravity Well. Florin was on a track called There's Something Wrong with the Zoo.

Behind us, Dong, Porky, and Grigori sat strapped into their newly installed seats, all placed in a row. Dong's health was in the deep yellow, about to turn red. He insisted that he actually felt fine, though I could see in the mercenary tab that he was suffering from fatigue.

Porky sat directly behind Dong, and he had his hand on Dong's shoulder. Dong reached up and held it there.

Grigori was also looking a little green around the edges. The tall human looked very out of place in his seat at the very back, sitting stiffly. Hedy said he hadn't taken well to the driving lessons.

"You doing okay?" I asked the man.

He let out a little cough. "Will you be driving this fast for the whole event?"

I exchanged a look with Donut. "This fast? All we did was go to the starting line. I was just coasting."

"I don't think my stomach agrees with this sort of conveyance."

"You have a sink next to you," I said. "If you gotta hurl, do it in there."

Dr. Metcalf beeped.

I have received the map data. Analyzing now. I'm probably analyzing it a lot slower than all the other teams in this heat. Did you know that Janice, who is the GPS unit in the Lady Dominators' car, is now completely upgraded? She's a snotty bitch, and now you're forcing me to be seen in public next to her with no upgrades whatsoever. Do you know how humiliating that is? Do you?

"All this negativity will cause your hair to prematurely shed, my princess," Dorota said.

Shut the fuck up. I will fucking kill you.

"Dr. Metcalf," I said, trying to keep the frustration from my voice, "we ran out of upgrades. I'm sorry. We will be following the Lady Dominators, but we'll need to know what's ahead. Can you do that for us?"

We had just over a minute.

The map appeared on the screen.

Fine. It appears there are many wide-open spaces mixed with narrow tracks, but we must traverse from one section of the factory to the next. It's straightforward, though the factory itself will be active. We enter through the receiving bay and exit through shipping. There are no obviously safe paths. It appears there are multiple neighborhood bosses in the middle area. The entire floor in this room is molten metal, so we will have to either drive on the walls or ceilings. The bosses live within the molten metal and will likely put me out of my misery.

"Okay," I said, looking over at Osvaldo, who was the one holding the reins of his gnu. I'd already talked to him, and I was going to let him go ahead of us so we could zip to the left and get behind the Lady Dominators. Prepotente and Jurgen were going to help as well if we were in proximity to one another.

We were only going to get one shot at this.

Ahead, the starting lights appeared.

"Are we ready?" I asked, revving the engine. This race had a time limit of only thirty minutes, and the total distance was twenty kilometers. "It's gonna go quick."

"Ready, Carl," Donut said.

"To battle," Dong said from behind us.

The light turned green, and we were off.

63

TIRES SQUEALED, AND FOUR OF US LURCHED OFF THE STARTING LINE, zooming toward the entrance to the massive factory. Sparks flew off the neon factory sign as we approached.

I had set up a group of tiny explosives on the roof of the truck, and I activated them.

Bam! Fiberglass shattered, and the drum barrel of the tommy gun blasted away, clearing my windshield.

OSVALDO: Careful, *puta*! That shrapnel hit our ass!
CARL: Sorry!

"Carl!" Donut called, looking in the mirror. "Dwight is just sitting there on the starting line! He's not going!"

"Don't worry about him," I called as the fast-moving Bruna rushed ahead. I swerved to the left, moving directly behind the GTO, which was also rapidly gaining distance. I hit the pedal, and we accelerated. If we didn't make our move soon, we'd lose them. "Eat the page!"

We passed under the entrance gate.

Entering the Gasworks Screw Factory, Steel Mill, and Doll Workshop.

Thwum!

The containment appeared and then turned invisible. A light in the corner of Dr. Metcalf's interface blinked green, indicating it as active. We had to keep out of contact with the other vehicles. Any continuous contact for more than five seconds, and our containments would merge.

Ahead, we entered a giant industrial room filled with what appeared to be piles and piles of banger spheres. The dirty floor was made of concrete, and the distant walls appeared to be corrugated metal. The lights were off, but a red glow filled the far side of the dusty, dingy room, making the shadowy piles of spheres look like the shells of giant beasts until you got too close.

There were dozens of these piles, all reaching to the high ceiling, which was at least fifteen meters. These were, I assumed, metal pellets to be melted down, and we had to swerve around them. The room itself was many times that in width, reminding me of the football-stadium-like room where we made secondary-class selection on the sixth floor.

A wave of heat washed over us the moment we entered, and I knew without the containment, it would already be deadly hot, and this was just the entrance.

Hundreds of little NPCs filled the floor of the factory, and they scattered as we rolled in. These were tiny, round-faced creatures, each about the size of Zev. They all wore bright yellow hard hats, and they looked to be a race of creature that was a smaller version of a Bopca mixed with a gnome. They were all levels 10 to 15, and they were called **knockers.**

I activated the newly upgraded Bubble Buddy shield and clicked the **Heat Sink** button, which turned on with a hum, and it lowered the temperature even further.

Behind me, Grigori was loudly vomiting. He'd turned not into the sink but the empty deep fryer.

Far ahead, there were about a dozen smaller doors just wide enough for a pair of vehicles. A deep red glow emanated from all the entrances. About ten of these doorways had wide conveyor belts leading up to them that were pulling the metal pellets into the next room. The other two doors were larger, and this was where Osvaldo was heading. Team Free Love's van also zoomed ahead, aiming at the second conveyor-belt-free door. I cringed as the floating van mowed over a pair of the fleeing knockers.

I saw from the map that the conveyors all led up to the second level, where the pellets would get dropped into giant melting vats. One would have to make a jump off the end of the belt, lest you'd fall into the vats of molten metal. But if one made the jump, they'd bypass the third room, which was where the molten metal would be shaped into massive coils. That third room would be dangerous as fuck, but it didn't require a big jump.

If I were choosing our route, I'd have skipped this first jump and tried to zoom around the vats. But it appeared the Lady Dominators were aiming for one of the conveyor belts, meaning we'd have to drive over a belt filled with metal balls. And make a jump.

I growled and tightened my grip on the wheel. I warily eyed the new button on the dash, just to the left of the GPS unit. This was the rocket-acceleration activator. In theory, the rockets, combined with the Bubble Buddy upgrade, would allow us to fly for a short period. But we hadn't tested it yet.

There were suddenly vehicles and mounts everywhere, coming from both sides, zooming in around the piles of metal balls. A fire truck, lights and siren blaring, zoomed up from my far left and appeared to attempt to sideswipe an ostrichlike mount with goblins on the back, but the ostrich flapped and rose into the air, and the fire truck smashed right into a pile of metal balls that caused the truck to flip and the balls to go everywhere. The goblins cackled and laughed and flipped off the truck as they zoomed ahead, trampling a group of the fleeing knockers.

The Lady Dominators were angling toward the second-to-last door on the left, also mowing through the tiny NPCs, cutting a diagonal line across the factory floor. The conveyor belt on this one was thick with the round metal balls. I reached over and increased our wheel size slightly. That would slow us, but it would increase our traction to the belt.

The new golden wheels of the Dominator car had spread out laterally, and an impressive shower of sparks flew off the sides, leaving me to wonder if that was on purpose or if something was already wrong.

Bang! Bang! I didn't see the vehicle that shot the weapon, but a pile of balls exploded far off to my right, and the balls rocketed through the room like shrapnel. A massive giraffe squealed out in surprise, tumbling from sight, its shield fuzzing like a buffering video.

A hover-car thing with twin flamethrowers spun along to our left, having been shot by something. It hit the edge of a pile of spheres and rose up into the air, leaving a curl of black smoke as more metal balls shot out in all directions, including off our shield. More explosions and spells ripped back and forth across the room.

We bumped as we hit the edge of the conveyor belt, crunching over the metal balls. Far ahead, the GTO disappeared into the second door, already a good five seconds ahead of us.

But then a dark shape appeared in quick pursuit.

Bianca. Prepotente's hellspawn familiar was out and flying through the factory, likely at home in this heat. The goat dragon roared and pushed through into the next room.

The plan, which had been Prepotente's idea once he heard about the problem, was to have Bianca grab Corky out of the back seat. We'd first have to defeat the shield, but it was a simple and straightforward idea. If that didn't work, the backup plan—which I'd come up with just about ten minutes previously—was a little more iffy. It involved the *Big-Ass Magnet* spell Donut had just eaten from her *Feast* book.

A shrill alarm filled the cab.

Containment Warning!

The voice was sudden and loud and similar to that of the card-battle announcer from the eighth floor. But the alarm stopped after just a second. A fat gray, monstrously ugly creature zoomed ahead of us, disconnecting our two containments before the five seconds. The mammoth-sized mount didn't have a saddle so much as a square cage that had a secondary glowing shield over it. At the front of the cage, holding the reins in a single hand, was Prepotente. Standing behind him was Jurgen. The man held a giant battle-axe in each hand. He turned to salute us as the creature galloped ahead.

"Wow, look at the thing!" Donut yelled, chewing on her page.

"That is a Perriso!" Dong called from behind us. "Wonderful mounts! They are deceptively fast for such large creatures."

We bumped again as we moved to the next room, revealing a set of rising conveyor belts and a haphazard tangle of giant bubbling vats. The temperature noticeably rose, but it was still bearable. The little gauge by the heat sink was still in the green.

PREPOTENTE: I am directly behind the Pontiac. Will be attempting to defeat their shield, but I will wait until after the jump. After the shield is defeated, Bianca will deliver this half-mantaur to you, and then she will return to us for defense. Good luck, Carl.

CARL: I see you! We're just behind you!

Far off to our right, one of the conveyor belts tumbled over as a group of two vehicles spun away. One landed in a vat of molten metal while the other, an old roundish car with no obvious upgrades painted a dull yellow, spun once in the air and then landed soundly on the floor and continued. The car was an AMC Pacer. I only knew that because my grandfather had had that same car.

"Carl, that's team Yokai!" Donut called when she saw the yellow car. "Our friends from karaoke!"

Just ahead of us, the conveyor belt curved to the right and then curved again, going under another belt before the belt dropped all the contents into the bubbling vat below. Across the way, easily ninety meters farther into the room, only slightly lower, a second conveyor belt also dropped its contents into a vat. This would be where we'd have to land. But when we did land, we'd be moving against the conveyor belt, which arced up into a higher room deeper into the factory. This distant conveyor belt was dropping a different substance, some sort of white chalky powder, into a different type of vat. The entire second half of the room was filled with a thick, roiling smoke.

I held my breath as the GTO, with Bianca floating just behind it, made their jump.

The golden tires turned, facing downward like a spaceship from some sci-fi movie, and the car rocketed over the space, soaring as it aimed for the opposite conveyor belt. Prepotente's Sweety hurled her giant form into the air just behind it.

The car landed soundly with a crunch as Sweety galloped through the air with her fire feet. Ethereal wings fluttered, helping her steer toward the track.

As Sweety moved to land, we approached the jump.

Oh shit, oh shit, oh shit.

"Hold on!" I yelled.

The edge wasn't a ramp at all. Just a drop-off. I reached over and smacked the **Rocket** button just as we approached, and held tightly on to the wheel.

We all pushed back as the rocket engaged. Donut yowled as extra straps appeared around her. The Bubble Buddy's floating upgrade mixed with the gyro kept us stable, but after just a second, I could tell the rocket was way too powerful, and we were going to overshoot. I quickly tapped it off as we hurtled through the air, correcting with the wheel as the bubble upgrade, thankfully, allowed me to correct our trajectory. Sort of.

Ahead, Sweety landed gently as we rapidly caught up with the slower-moving tapir.

A group of rockets launched from the tapir and, faster than I thought possible, slammed into the back of the Dominators' car as it disappeared into the next room.

We thumped heavily onto the track as Grigori cried behind us. I ran right off the side, but the bubble kept us from falling, and I swerved back onto the path, almost running right into the back of Sweety.

Containment Warning!

I eased the brakes as the tapir sped up. With the ground under its feet, the creature galloped faster. A second set of missiles shot out, disappearing into the dark. There was a flash of explosion.

We ascended against the moving treadmill, rising into the air as we progressed into the next room. We crunched and were once again in the dark. All around us, vehicles who'd successfully made similar jumps on their own tracks entered the room and started zooming across the floor, heading toward a group of five exits.

PREPOTENTE: Shield is down. Bianca will move in now.

This room was similar to the first one, but instead of piles of balls, there were piles of the white powder dotted around the room like giant anthills. A few vehicles had already crashed through the powder, causing it to fly everywhere. It didn't stop the cars, but in seconds, everybody and everything in the room was covered in the thick white dust, and it became impossible to see. Our shield frothed like a sparkler as the powder misted all around.

I'd been so focused on the task at hand, I'd forgotten the stupid name of the track. And the sign under it. I quickly examined one of the mountains of white powder.

Donut scoffed. "Carl, is that what I think it is? It's everywhere!"

"Err," I said, upon reading the extra-long description.

Toddler Cocaine.

Also known as Daddy's Little Snow Drops, this is a giant pile of low-dose but highly addictive cocaine specifically designed to be sold directly to children, who are much too fragile to enjoy and too poor to afford the higher-grade stuff.

This is the raw product before the patent-pending Wack Flavoring is added.

The Coblyn Corporation has a problem. They're addicts. All of them.

These small gnomelike creatures were unable to stop the world from encroaching on their caves. Once the larger, stronger, and more powerful creatures of the world discovered the rich minerals buried under their feet, they did what large, strong people do. They took it for themselves, never mind that these caves were the only home the knockers had ever known.

The knockers were too weak to fight back. They had nowhere else to go. So they did the next best thing. They started manufacturing high-grade drugs and selling them to the miners. Miners with an "E."

Fast-forward a few years, and the knocker community had pulled themselves up by their bootstraps. Yes, the Corporatocracy running the mines made drug use illegal. At least the drugs that weren't sold by them. They did everything in their power to stop it. They vilified the knockers. They tried to eradicate them. They attempted their own alternatives.

But no matter what corporate did, they couldn't stop the upward trajectory of these plucky little drug dealers. These corporate suits learned what a thousand organizations and governments throughout history already knew. If you go to war against drugs, drugs will always win. Drugs will win because what you're really doing is going to war against the biological imperative all living creatures have to find comfort and happiness. And if you're unwilling or unable to first provide that, artificial alternatives, no matter how destructive, will *always* prevail.

A funny thing happened after that. The knockers, finding themselves absolutely loaded, tried to do something with that money. They formed the Coblyn Corporation, and they started to buy up legitimate businesses. After all, while they were making a ton of money, they still didn't have as much as the Corporatocracy running the mines.

So they started buying the ore from their own land. They milled it, turned it into product, sold it. All aboveboard. And then they branched out, selling toys, skateboards, fidget spinners—bullshit like that.

But it wasn't enough. In selling drugs to the miners, again with an "E," they fell into their own trap. While the miners got strung out, they themselves became addicted to the money they were earning.

It's a terrible circle, that. There's not really a lesson here or a point to any of this, just a sad observation. We're always seeking comfort, and when we don't get it, we can be pretty destructive. And by "we," I mean, those of us with the ability to grasp what's around us.

Anyway, the knockers, upon realizing how well their dolls were selling and unable to get a piece of that hot, hot legal pharmaceutical market, came up with the next best thing. If they could sell illegal drugs to the miners with an "E," they could also start selling drugs to the minors with an "O."

Kids are a lot stupider than adults, after all. You can get them addicted to stuff really easily.

Their new, secret product is cocaine for toddlers! It comes in different flavors, and each flavor has its own mascot with a matching doll! My favorite is Sally Speedball. She's the blueberry one, and she comes with a twelve-pack of press-on bump nails and two free hits. She, Toot-Toot, and Belushi are part of an all-girl band called the Nose Candy Star Dusters.

Oh, by the way, the knockers are pretty harmless. But they're very protective of their new product. The workers in the outer rooms can't fight back. Their magically built help, however . . .

Yeah. Watch your ass.

64

THE TRUCK BUMPED AS WE ACCIDENTALLY ROLLED OVER A GROUP OF passed-out knockers. They all had little symbols over their heads I didn't have time to examine, but I assumed they had something to do with the giant cloud of cocaine. The white cloud was getting thicker by the moment. I could barely see the red light of the five different exits up ahead.

This next room was doll packing. After this one, we'd be back in the steel-mill part.

A panicked message from Prepotente came in.

PREPOTENTE: Bianca has fallen ill! She appears to have been rendered "strung out" by these unlawful toddler drugs! I am pulling off the track to administer aid before she perishes! She hasn't yet grabbed your target!

CARL: Shit! Okay, let us know if you need help.

We bumped as we left the cloud of toddler cocaine and entered a brightly lit room filled to the ceiling with wooden crates, leaving only a narrow path.

The room was a little *too* bright, especially compared to the previous rooms, and I had to squint to see where we were going. I immediately sensed a trap, and I eased slightly off the accelerator as I—

"Oh shit!" I cried upon seeing the massive hole in the floor ahead of us. Thankfully, we rolled right over it because of the Bubble Buddy.

"Carl, stop!" Donut shouted. "They fell in! I saw them!"

I slammed on the brakes, and we screeched to a stop.

"We gotta reverse!" Donut said. "They're in the hole!"

I thumped the truck into reverse, worried about getting hit from behind. I slowly backed up until we were right against the hole in the ground, pushing the truck tight against the crates so any other vehicles could pass us. I put the truck into park and pulled myself out of the seat.

"Grigori, get in the driver's seat in case we need to go!" I yelled.

"I cannot," he said as he continued to dry-heave into the deep fryer.

"I have you," Dong said, his voice weak as he pulled himself up. "Everybody, up! Up! Do as Carl says."

Donut and I pushed open the back of the truck and looked down into the large, jagged hole. The hole, I realized, had been a trap. Either a small explosive or just rotten floorboards had given way under the Dominator car.

We were parked flush against a massive wooden crate that was scorched around the edges. The entire box smoked like it would catch on fire at any moment. On the side of the large box was a spray-painted label that read, "My First Sicarios boy action figures, case of 500. Assorted."

"Damnit," I muttered, examining the hole.

The GTO, shield down and hit with Prepotente's hobble missile, had fallen right through and landed on its side. It was a ten-meter drop. The bright light from this room shone down below like a spotlight. The whole front of the car was smashed, and one of the golden wheels had broken off. I could see the axle was broken in half.

No matter what had happened, that vehicle was done.

Our truck shook as a massive ferret-like mount squeezed by, not stopping. A containment warning came and went.

Both Rapture and Genesis were still inside the vehicle, both alive and groaning. Both had a **Strung Out** warning over them, meaning they'd been hit by the cloud of cocaine. I knew their protection shield was gone, but I couldn't tell if their containment shield was active or not. If it wasn't active, they'd all be boiling hot and wouldn't last long.

Corky remained in the back of the car, attached via seat belt. He was both unconscious and strung out.

Crunch, crunch, crunch!

"What is that?" I asked.

A group of dolls had surrounded the GTO and was in the process of ripping it apart. These were small Barbie- or Bratz-like dolls with giant heads. Half were girl toys, but there were several large G.I. Joe–like action figures as well, all about the same size as the Uzi Jesus toy Eris was walking around with.

The creatures were starting to swarm. Donut cast *Magic Missile*, blowing a ton away, but more just kept coming. I examined one, which was an elf-like doll with black hair and purple streaks.

Toot-Toot doll. Level 12 Grape-flavored Cocaine Elemental.

So, the dolls were a mistake. In preparing to defend their factory, the knockers got a little enthusiastic with the elemental magic. The metal frames of these dolls are infused with their special blend, and when they cast the magic spell in the steel mill to create the elemental boss monsters you'll probably face in a few minutes, some of that magic accidentally leaked. And now these creepy little fuckers are everywhere. That's why this room was sealed off, but some elemental magic is contagious, and now that you've broken the seal of the room . . . Well, let's just see what happens next.

Warning: This is an infused elemental. Unlike regular elementals, the infused variety have the pass-through ability. If you don't know what that means, you're about to find out.

Next to us, the giant crate started to shake.

"We need to hurry the fuck up," I said. "I'm going to jump down there and grab him."

"And then what, Carl? You're not a kangaroo anymore. I got this." Donut jumped from the back of the truck and landed atop the GTO.

"Donut!" I called.

Thwum!

She and Corky reappeared on the road next to the truck. Donut had just cast her level 17 *Puddle Jumper* spell. Right at the beginning, Zev had warned us that a lot of the movement spells wouldn't work correctly. She could teleport herself but not Corky back to the truck, so she'd done the next-best thing. I jumped out, careful of the edge of the hole, to pick up the knocked-out half-mantaur and pull him inside, coughing.

The heat just outside the containment staggered me. I had not been expecting it to be this hot. Donut whimpered as she bounded back inside, her fur smoking after just a few seconds.

The containment of the GTO, I realized, was *not* active, and the man's suit was burning hot. He was still alive, but he was cooking in his suit and would have died if we hadn't grabbed him.

I didn't stop to think about Rapture and Genesis burning in their crashed car as the cocaine-fused action figures tore at them.

"Make room! Make room!" I called, shoving Grigori forward. He didn't move, and I unlatched his belt and pushed again, causing the tall mage to stumble. "Sorry!"

I pulled down the table we'd hastily affixed to the cabinets just for this. I dropped the large, suited mantaur heavily on the platform. His entire form was smoking.

"Yo, I'm Toot-Toot," a new voice said.

It was one of the dolls. She'd hitched a ride, her hand melted into the PVC of Corky's suit.

"Do you want to know how to get some cash out of your teacher? False accusations are a great way to . . . Errrppp."

I grabbed it and tossed it out of the back of the truck, but in doing so, I accidentally ripped a large patch of suit away. A bulge of red guts popped out of the hole like biscuit dough. A health bar appeared.

"Gah! Donut, heal him!"

I realized I'd basically trapped myself in the back of the truck. I wouldn't be able to get to the front without literally crawling over the prone figure of Corky. "Porky, get on the table! Grigori! We're doing this!"

The crate next to the truck broke open, and a swarm of soldier action figures started pattering on the side and roof of the truck. Several spilled out onto the ground, some falling back down into the hole. All were smoking and melting in the heat.

"Is the shield not working? Is it not turned on?" I called.

"It says it's on!" Dong called back.

I remembered that pass-through warning on the last doll. I assumed that had had something to do with it. If that meant they could get through the shield, then we *really* needed to go.

"My princess! Please get back in your seat!" Dorota called.

Donut healed Corky with a scroll, but his health continued to seep. She fired a missile over my shoulder at something unseen. "Carl, how are they cocaine elementals when they're action figures! This doesn't make any sense!"

"It doesn't matter! Come on, Porky! Dong, get moving!"

But Dong was turned all the way in the seat, eyes on the makeshift table. "Corky! Corky!" he called.

Corky remained unconscious and had the **Strung Out** debuff. But Grigori, wobbling on his feet, now stood over him and was also casting something on the mantaur as Porky pulled himself next to the other half.

Both of the debuffs zapped away.

"What? Where am I? Is the race over?" Corky asked. His voice was identical to that of Porky. His lower hand shot down to the hole in his suit. He tried to sit up, and Porky gently pushed him down.

"Don't move," Porky said. "I'm here. It's time to get back together."

"What?" Corky asked again, still confused.

"Corky! Corky!" Dong cried.

"Snitches get their throats slit," a new voice said. This was a heavily tattooed action figure. He appeared in the open back of the truck, peering in upside down from the roof. He had a brown headband and sunglasses that dripped as they melted. His name was **El Asesino de la Melaza.**

"Dong? Where am I?" Corky cried.

I pulled the back doors closed, which severed the action figure in half. He started to pull himself toward me, smearing brown goo across the floor. I stomped down with my foot, and the figure squished.

Warning: Race ends in 20 minutes.

"Go! Go!" I called. We'd already been stopped for far too long.

The truck lurched forward. "We must remove the suits. Quickly now," Grigori said. "Oh gods. Do we have to be moving while we do this?"

PREPOTENTE: I have retrieved Bianca and we are proceeding forward.

"Carl, Carl, I can see the entrance of the next room!" Donut yelled.

"I do not know how to engage the controls to drive on the ceiling!" Dong yelled.

"Damnit," I said. "Sorry, guys," I called. "I gotta go over. Watch out." I climbed atop the two mantaurs, squeezing over them. But the moment I did that, the temporary table I'd hastily fashioned with a piece of wood snapped, and we all fell into the three chairs. Corky cried out in pain, and his suit ripped further, guts leaking everywhere.

"Dong, out of the seat!" I yelled. "Let me drive! Help your friend!"

Dong was already up and out, letting the truck drift, squeezing past me as I returned to the driver's seat.

"Hold on!" I cried as we rocketed toward the next room.

65

THE PATH AHEAD SWERVED. I TURNED, BUT THE MAZE OF BOXES HAD all broken and shattered. A dozen of the action figures were on the hood of the truck, holding on, occasionally flying off. They all army-crawled toward the windshield. The entrance to the next room loomed, but it appeared that it was just a balcony with a drop. We were on the third floor, and this next big room, which just seemed to go on and on, dropped all the way to the first. It glowed red within, and I knew the entirety of this room was just molten metal. I activated the spider legs as we approached.

"We're gonna have to go sideways before we turn upside down," I called.

"This interior is not conducive to proper procedure," Grigori was saying in between coughs. Donut was not in her chair, but sitting atop the oven burner. Both the tall half-mantaurs were standing, both rapidly pulling at the zippers to their suits. Both were taller than the interior, and they were half hunched over, each with a single arm on the ceiling, bracing themselves. "We'll have to do it while standing, and only once we are inverted."

"Will that work?" Donut asked as we took a sharp turn to avoid another hole in the floor. From within, dozens of the female dolls were climbing out, screaming as they melted.

"It should, but we must do it. Blahhhh." Grigori turned and dry-vomited. "My gods, this is horrible. We must do it fast."

"Dong, are you unwell?" Corky, who'd finally caught up to what was happening, asked. "Dong, you're sick!"

"Do not worry about me, my love," Dong called. He had a roll of plastic wrap in his hands. We'd gotten it from Dekoki the kappa, and he was wrapping it around Corky's head. He turned to Porky, whose half-head was now also exposed and started to do the same. The fleshmancer had said it was fine if the guts spilled out a little, but the brain needed to remain sealed. "We must do this quickly. Let me help you with this zipper after I do this."

"Oh gods," Porky said, reaching up to touch the plastic wrap on his head. He started to pull down the same zipper I'd earlier helped him fix.

"Ew, ew, ew," Donut cried as Porky's suit popped open and the guts slopped everywhere, like a jack-in-the-box filled with noodles.

Grigori cast something, and the guts, dangling from Porky's exposed double torsos, floated by his side. The mess of guts was only on his lower torso, though strange and foreign organs and tubes also bulged from his upper side. He had beating half-hearts in both the top and bottom torsos. Both hearts glowed, kept working by a spell from either Donut or Grigori.

I finally saw both of their faces and half-mullets. They looked just like any other mantaur, only just cut in half. Their plastic-wrapped half brains sat firmly in their skulls, pulsing, their exposed sinuses nausea-inducing.

I had to slow and ease over, allowing the spider legs to grab purchase along the wall of the next room.

"Turning sideways! Brace!" I called as I tightened my seat belt. "We'll be sideways for a minute. Then we'll be completely upside down! Donut, be careful!"

We entered the next room, scrambling on the wall. This wall was flat, but I knew once we got to the ceiling, we'd only be able to travel along the designated track.

Everyone cried out and yowled as it all turned sideways. Donut clattered heavily as she fell over, crashing into Grigori, who suddenly found himself on his side in the crowded back of the truck. Dong, Corky, and Porky were all jumbled, guts and blood sloshing everywhere as spells desperately tried to keep them all together.

I didn't want to turn the truck again, so I moved laterally up the wall, keeping the passenger's side of the truck facing down.

"Be careful of the window!" I yelled. "We'll be at the ceiling in a second, and we'll be fully upside down!"

As everyone scrambled to find footing, now standing on the overturned counter, waiting for us to turn completely upside down, I finally took a look about the giant room.

"Holy fucking shit," I muttered, taking in the chaotic scene just as we fully inverted, the spider legs carefully shuffling to the side and lowering so our wheels attached to the track.

The room just went on and on and on.

There were multiple paths on the walls and ceiling that we had to use. The rest of the ceiling and walls were crisscrossed with spikes and bumps, all for the purpose of not allowing us to drive upon them.

The channels were wide, flat conduits, not unlike the tracks I once used for my Hot Wheels cars as a kid. The tracks were not straight, crossing over each other, moving back and forth as they followed the ceiling and the wall. Most were on the ceiling, and this was where most of the vehicles, far ahead of us, were racing, but both sides had a pair of tracks on each wall.

I tentatively hit the accelerator. The Roller Limbo upgrade held true, and we stuck firmly to the ceiling. We didn't have time to waste.

Below us, the river of molten metal just went on and on.

Far ahead, I spied Prepotente's Sweety turned sideward, making her way along the wall track. Sweety moved as if going sideways was no big deal at all, and the square litter that held Prepotente and Jurgen had rotated on its own, keeping them both vertical. The tapir's feet flamed, leaving a trail on the wall.

Despite this, it was clear they were not moving as fast as normal. I could now see several of the vehicles dotting the ceiling were moving much more slowly than usual, all of us with different types of upgrades to facilitate this part of the track.

And then I saw the monsters deeper in the room. These were large, gorilla-like beasts made of molten metal, jumping from the river below, landing on the walls and ceilings, facing down the racers. They hurled globs of metal at the passing vehicles.

Oh shit, I thought. If these were like the action figures, would they be able to get through the shield?

I hit the accelerator. Behind me, Grigori was yelling instructions to Dong and Donut. They were all now standing on the ceiling of the truck.

"Dong," Grigori called, "I will remove the plastic wrapping and press the head together, and then you will wrap the whole thing! Quickly now!"

"What is that flapping around?" Donut called, her voice a shriek. "That looks like something that shouldn't be flapping around! And my goodness, Grigori, make sure their lips line up! He's going to end up looking like Mick Jagger!"

Ahead, I watched as Jurgen screamed and hurled one of his battle-axes toward a gorilla monster blocking their path. The axe went right into the metal and disappeared, not to return. But the beast fell off the wall and plummeted into the roiling metal. Jurgen held out his hand, trying to get his axe to return. It did not.

The ferret mount that had passed earlier was on the same track as us, just ahead, attached to the ceiling, weaving back and forth as it made its way across the inverted track. It was only moving at half the speed it had been going before. We would pass it soon.

One of the molten metal beasts dangling upside down from the ceiling spied us and started galloping in our direction. I hit the accelerator even harder, determined to outpace it. I examined it.

Slag Elemental.

Level 75 Neighborhood Boss.

Warning: This is an infused elemental.

Warning: This is a regenerator. This boss will regenerate if its corpse falls into the molten metal below.

The Coblyn Corporation, in their efforts to protect their burgeoning child drug empire from getting discovered and shut down, tried to put some protections in place.

They, however, tried to do it on the cheap, as new corporations often tend to do, and they got what they paid for.

So what we have now is wildly contagious, regenerating, infused, and very pissed-off elementals all over the place.

Note. It's pretty much impossible to kill these things. You will *not* receive a boss box unless one is dead-dead. Good luck.

"Okay, hold them together!" Grigori yelled.

"I got you. I got you," Dong said as we raced along the track.

The slag elemental hurled a ball of metal at us, and we rocked as it slammed into the side of the truck, threatening to overturn us. The heat sink gauge flashed, moving all the way up before settling down.

We rushed up right on the ass of the ferret. It appeared to have slime creatures pressed onto its back.

Containment Warning!

"I hope this works," I growled as I pushed forward and slightly down with the steering wheel.

I felt us fold into the space under the ferret, going between its legs, only to pop up on the other side. The trans-dimensional upgrade had worked as advertised, though the moment we folded back to regular size, my stomach lurched.

"Oh gods," Grigori called from the back. "I'm going to be ill again. Dong, hold them with all your strength!"

"I have you," Dong shouted. I turned to see the old man clinging tightly to the mantaur's lower torso while both halves hugged him back. "I have you, and I will never let go again!"

I leaned forward so my waist was better secured in the seat as all the blood rushed to my head. We were now outpacing several of the other racers, many of whom were currently engaging directly with the elementals. We switched tracks at an intersection as Grigori started to chant. Ahead and across the room, I spied both Osvaldo—who was on the wall—and team Free Love's van, which was right side up but still attached to the ceiling. They had some sort of device on their roof that allowed them to travel along the track. They weaved in and out of danger.

PREPOTENTE: Everybody, I have discovered how to delay these elementals. It may sound counterintuitive, but if you add any non-molten metal to them, they will immediately collapse and return to the river and wait for it to melt before they can attack again!

"The initial casting is done!" Grigori called. "Now we wait for the parts to fuse. This is the important time! Hold them together, Dong! Hold them no matter what happens, or it will fail!"

"What about his dingle dangle?" Donut shouted from behind. "Shouldn't that be, you know, matched up together? They're flapping in different directions! It's going to end up looking like a hot dog that exploded in the microwave!"

"We will fix any inconsistences after the race," Grigori said, panting heavily. "It's the brain that's important. And both hearts, though if you wish to hold his extremities together while it works, you may."

"I am not touching that thing!"

"Worry not about his lance," Dong called, straining as he held the two men together, muscles bulging on his arms. "That is normal for the mantaur race. The windmill, it is called."

"It's normal for his penis to look like a hand after a fireworks accident?"

Wham! A glob of molten metal slammed into the hood of the truck. The heat sink gauge again topped out, but not before a giant hole appeared in the hood, exposing part of the engine, which started to whir.

The elementals were everywhere, but a single shot of anything seemed to be enough to knock them off the wall. They'd fall the three stories to the river of metal below, and it would be a few moments before they returned.

Warning: Race ends in 10 minutes.

"Okay, I am casting the final part of the spell now," Grigori called. Up ahead, the exit to the room loomed.

"Dr. Metcalf! Does the track leave the ceiling in the next room? Will we flip again?"

I have no idea. I'm still freaked out about the mantaur-penis thing.

I turned to see Corky and Porky, naked, smashed together like a grilled cheese sandwich, all wrapped up with plastic wrap in various places, multiple hernias bulging out, Dong holding them together with all his might, eyes clenched closed, tears streaming.

"I got you," he cried over and over. "I got you."

Dong's health was much farther into the red than I had realized.

The two halves, Corky and Porky, still had health bars over each half, also in the red, but as I watched, the health bars joined, and they became one.

Their names disappeared and a single name reappeared. Corcunda.

A massive notification materialized, blocking my vision, and I waved it away.

But then something new emerged above the mantaur's head.

It was a marked-for-death symbol from a god.

System Message: Grull has entered the realm.

66

"ARE YOU FUCKING KIDDING ME?" I CRIED.

You are in the presence of a deity. The Scavenger's Daughter has opened her eyes. She fills with power.

Temporary effect from Grull: All four-legged creatures in your presence, friend or enemy, are temporarily given 2× power to their most powerful attack.

"He's behind us!" Donut shrieked.

PREPOTENTE: Carl, this is most inconvenient!

"We don't have time to deal with him right now," I yelled. The end of the room loomed. "Donut . . ."

"I'm on it!"

I turned to see the giant bullheaded centaur creature with the enormous axe standing in the midst of the molten steel.

The god cackled with glee.

"What do we have here?" he called, his voice shaking the walls. "Carl, where are you? I've been waiting for your dumb ass to accidentally summon me."

We exited the room, and the track abruptly ended. The next ceiling over was even higher, and I hadn't prepared the spider legs. So instead, we just drove right off.

"Hang on!" I shouted. "We're gonna . . ."

We flipped violently like a buoy. From behind, everyone cried out and fell heavily to the floor. Donut yowled, getting smushed between Corcunda and Dong.

Bubble Buddy activated. We continued our forward trajectory, now slowly falling through the air like a glider coming in for a landing.

This room was another big one, and it was filled with thousands of crates.

The cars that were ahead of us rocketed toward the distant exit, which appeared to be just a single door.

I kept the Limbo upgrade activated as we slowly dropped, occasionally hitting the rocket to cover more distance.

Warning: Race ends in 5 minutes.

"Hail! Grull has come for me," Corcunda groaned as he helped Dong up. His voice remained the same as before, though his mannerisms were suddenly much more mantaur-like. "I thought I was free of the vile god when I split, but the moment I came back together, he sent me a message and told me I was to be punished for not being troo!"

"Not being what?" Donut asked.

The giant wall behind us exploded outward as the god crashed through. Molten metal started to spill into the room. There were cars and mounts everywhere falling and spinning, ignored by the god.

"I can feel you, Meat! You can't hide from me. I made you a friend of my temple. Do you know what that means? It means I can find you even faster!"

"Oh, yes," Grigori said from the floor. He'd banged his head and bled profusely from a scalp wound. "I should have asked if you worshipped a deity before you split. I apologize for my oversight."

We were still in midair, gliding downward like a slow-moving paper airplane.

"He's going to smite me," Corcunda said. He turned to Dong, and he grabbed the old man's hands with both sets of arms. The naked mantaur had a bright red jagged scar right down the middle of his face and chest. He wasn't perfectly aligned. Little bulges appeared here and there along the seam.

The man shook his mulleted head. "Fellow warrior, I fear this was all for nothing!"

"He's not coming for you. He's coming for Carl!" Donut cried, scrambling up. She was absolutely soaked in red gore from the joining. "We need to get out of here before—"

"There you are!"

Slam!

Grull swung his axe, and a wave of wind hit us just before we alighted, and crunched us heavily to the ground. We all stumbled anew. The roof crumpled in. The shield overloaded and winked out. One of our tires broke off and flew away. We spun out on the ground, turning sideways, and we would've flipped without the gyro. The slow-moving wave of molten metal lurched toward us, overtaking the automatons. And walking in that wave were literally hundreds of the elementals. They roared as one and started charging, quickly outpacing the angry god.

Grull stood only ankle-deep in the molten metal. It didn't seem to affect him. Donut shouted an order, and Dong pushed open the back door.

I caught sight of Sweety, far to the side, still high in the air, gliding on wings, feet flaming and trailing smoke, trying to get past all this.

"As tall as a mountain," Corcunda muttered, looking up at the god.

Grull raised his axe over his head. "I'm gonna enjoy this, Meat!" Bubbles started to form around his shoulders. "After all this time, and you're going to die like the little bitch that you . . . Gah!"

Donut finished casting *Laundry Day.*

The orc was ejected from the god's chest. He dropped like a rock into the river of metal below.

"We don't have time to kill you now," Donut shouted. "Maybe next time!"

The Maestro was not, unfortunately, dead. The orc, while not invulnerable like the god itself, could not die here on the tenth floor. He could only be killed on floors where the rules stated outside tourists could perish, and there weren't any of those left. He could still get splattered, but he would just regenerate a few minutes later.

Still, it probably hurt a whole lot, and for that, I was glad.

I knew from my discussions with Mordecai that he would appear in his quarters on the twelfth floor. But because of the AI's new rules that everyone had to be wearing their soul armor no matter what, he'd come back to Grull, probably in just a few short minutes. This would be a problem if we ever made it to the twelfth floor—though that floor had some interesting rules regarding soul armor—but for right now, it gave us a few minutes before the Maestro would be back.

The god, however, was still here. And Corcunda was still marked for death.

I activated the spider legs, and we skittered off toward the exit, running as quickly as we could.

Grull snorted indignantly and looked about as we started to pull away.

"Corcunda," the god roared, his voice deeper and much more terrifying now, "you have failed in your faith, and now you must be punished. You cannot hide. You cannot flee. Accept your punishment like the warrior you once were."

Grull started casually walking toward us. The slag elementals were faster and would be on us sooner. The spider legs weren't nearly as fast as the now-useless tires, and the howling monsters slowly gained on us. Ahead, all the survivors were attempting to queue up at the single exit to the room. This doorway, only wide enough for two, already had a wreck right at the entrance. A bulldozer-like vehicle was pushing it all through, but everyone was stopped, trapped, right in the path of the god and the elementals.

Many had clearly lost their containment, and multiple vehicles were on fire. Everyone was bunched together.

"Go, go, go!" Donut cried. "I'm going to cast—"

"No," Corcunda said, putting a hand on Donut as I swerved around a broken crate. The box was filled with screws. There were thousands of them, tens of thousands, millions, and they were just spilled everywhere in the chaos. The spider crunched over them like gravel.

"No," he repeated. I watched over my shoulder as the mantaur reached down and encompassed Dong in a hug.

"You worried if I would no longer love you once I returned to this form. But how could I not? Even if you and Porky hadn't made amends before we joined, how could I forget what we had? You have been nothing but a shining light in my life, and I want to thank you for always holding true. But now I have to go to Grull. The only way he will leave is once I am properly smited."

The mantaur removed the only thing he was wearing—the scarf around his neck—and put it around Dong's.

Warning: Race ends in 3 minutes.

The elderly stripper, whose health was almost all gone, reached high up and put his hand against the cheek of the mantaur. "My love," he said, "do you really think I will ever leave your side again?"

He held his other arm out, and he pulled an item from his inventory.

The massive lance, which I hadn't seen since the day I'd given him that damn sock, appeared in his hand. The man held it steady, straight with just a single hand, pointing it out the back of the open door of the truck.

Pointing it directly at the immortal god of war.

"It's been a long time since I've tilted a giant," he said.

"Wait," Donut began. "Dong, no. Maybe we can . . ." But she trailed off. She looked back at me, eyes shining.

We had completed the quest, but we weren't out of this yet. Grull would leave once Corcunda was gone. And if we waited *too* long, the Maestro would return.

The elementals were now much closer than Grull, who continued his matter-of-fact walk toward us. They had all left the slow-moving wave of molten metal behind.

"Hail, my love," Corcunda said. He turned, faced the open exit to the truck, and fell onto his middle arms. His whole body glowed. "It will be an honor to be ridden one last time."

What the fuck is even happening right now?

"Shut the hell up," I snapped at the GPS.

Dong, still holding his lance, hopped easily upon the back of Corcunda.

Despite us going at full speed, the elementals would be on us soon. There were thousands of them stampeding in the room by now, with

Grull pacing along behind them, patient, determined, inevitable. Nothing like the creature who normally controlled him.

"Wait, Dong, wait," Donut said. "Let me cast this. It has to be cast on an object! I will cast it on your lance. It will activate right away, but it will increase in intensity for about fifteen seconds after I place it, so make sure you're far away from us or else the lance will get ripped from your hand! It will help you get through the elementals!"

"What is it?" Dong asked.

"It's called *Big-Ass Magnet*. It's the spell we were going to use to capture Genesis and Rapture's car."

Corcunda snorted. "Posers," he said.

We would have to slow down in a moment. The bulldozer had pushed a hole, and vehicles and mounts were streaming through.

"Casting now," Donut said as we approached the exit.

"Goodbye, Carl. Goodbye, Princess Donut," Dong said. "Please tell the others that I will miss them, but I will see them again on the other side. Tell them it was my pleasure to serve with them. *Vale* to you all. *Vale*."

Warning: Race ends in 2 minutes.

And with a terrifying, in-unison roar, Corcunda and Dong jumped from the back of the truck and galloped directly at Grull just as the magnet spell activated.

Every screw within two hundred meters of the lance jumped into the air and rocketed toward the charging pair.

But first the screws had to travel through the slag elementals.

All it took was a small handful of screws to stagger the creatures. A few more, and they collapsed into puddles of molten steel.

And through it all, Dong and Corcunda charged.

They charged, and they charged. Riding into battle one last time.

Dong Quixote, now with his lance lowered, now getting peppered himself with dozens, then hundreds, then thousands of screws, roared in triumph as the weapon made contact with the god of war.

"A good death," Grull rumbled before he vanished, going back to the twelfth floor. "A good death indeed."

WE TRAVELED THROUGH THE *HOLE* SOMEONE HAD CAST, AND WE SKIT-tered through the last room, not saying anything as we struggled to the finish line, passing a few other vehicles desperately moving toward the exit, all of us exhausted, terrified, and filled with rage at this damn place, which was slowly killing us all.

We passed the finish line with only fifteen seconds to spare. I couldn't stomach looking back to see those who didn't make it in time.

Despite all that, I finally breathed a sigh of relief. We were alive. We had survived. But most importantly, we had won the quest.

HEAT FIVE. RESULTS.

First Place: Team Sparkles.

Second Place: Team Free Love.

Third Place: Team Flamengo.

Fourth Place: The Royal Court of Princess Donut.

Eliminated: Lady Dominators and the Gimp.

HEAT 6 OF 7

67

"WHAT?" DONUT DEMANDED AS WE LIMPED OVER THE FINISH LINE. "Carl, we came in last place! How did the stupid unicorn win?"

"I don't know," I said, leaning back, exhausted. Had that really only been thirty minutes? It felt like it had been hours and hours.

Dong Quixote was dead. I took a breath, letting it sink in. What a way to go. What a goddamned hero.

Osvaldo was off Bruna, patting the giant gnu affectionately on the side.

It's going to get worse before it gets better.

From behind me, Grigori groaned. "Is this a dream?" he asked. "Am I truly still alive?"

> **PREPOTENTE: We have survived, but it appears we are the only team from our heat to have lived. I fear that means for the final two races some difficult choices will have to be made. Did you complete your quest?**
>
> **CARL: We did. Thank you for your help.**

"Dong is dead," Donut said, her voice suddenly sad. "Dong is dead. He was my friend, and he's dead."

"Yeah," I said, a sudden urge for a cigarette hitting me out of nowhere.

"Some of us believe," Grigori said, standing to his full height in the back of the truck, hopelessly attempting to wipe off his filth-covered robe, "that death is nothing but movement on to another plane of existence. Dong did not think this was the end."

Donut seemed to contemplate that, an unreadable expression on her face.

"It's still horrible for us who are still here," she finally said.

"Indeed," Grigori replied.

IMANI: Everybody check in. We survived. Barely.

LOUIS: Dude, that fucking sucked. We came in last place again, but we got this awesome engineer lady. She's an upgrade thief. She can take upgrades off someone's car and add it to your own. A ton of people didn't make it. But Britney ripped the head off one of the skeleton-astronaut things with her bare hands.

FLORIN: It was easy for us. We came in first of the whole thing. Tran was in our heat and was just behind us. Zhang, too. Same with Chris's team. Can't say the same for a lot of others, though.

I was looking at the list, going over it. Our race had been especially brutal. Out of the sixty teams to start the race, only eighteen had survived.

OSVALDO: That unicorn goddamn cheated. Did you see that shit?

DONUT: WHAT DID HE DO? HOW DID HE WIN?

OSVALDO: Jasha says he went OVER the factory. He didn't even go in. He rode up the wall, went to the roof, and just dropped off to the finish line. He won the whole damn thing.

DONUT: WHAT? YOU CAN DO THAT?

OSVALDO: He did. He was the only one who figured it out.

Donut scoffed.

"Come on," I said, shaking my head. "Rosetta and Tipid are already mercenary shopping for us, but they said the prices are pretty outrageous since our mercenaries always die."

"Wait, what?" Grigori asked.

"You lived. That's all that matters," Donut said, her voice still angry about the Dwight thing. "Just went over the outside. What a cheater."

Dr. Metcalf beeped as we approached the garage.

Limited details on the next race are now available.

This is a two-part race. Races 6 and 7 will run right after one another, and they will run on the same track, but with different rules. Specific details on the final heat will not become available until Heat 6 completes. There will soon be a dungeon-wide announcement that will clarify some additional rules.

Distance: Well . . . it's complicated. We'll say 25 kilometers, relative to your size.

Note: The finish line for Heat 6 is treated as a pit stop. There will be a two-hour rest period.

Pit Stop rules apply during this time, meaning safe room access is not allowed during these two hours. In other words, if you need to get stuff done in the safe room, do it now. Once Heat 6 starts, you will not get another chance before the final checkered flag.

Track: The L'Engle Building.

There are multiple paths for this race.

Tasks required to complete: Multiple. This track has nonlinear paths, meaning there is no direct route to the finish line. You must get from the top floor to the bottom floor for this sixth heat. For Heat 7, you will return.

Special Rules: All remaining heats will be competing on the same track. As we have over 300 heats remaining, this means the racers will be shrunk to accommodate the track, which is the interior of a human apartment building.

Environment: It's a 7-floor apartment building. You may not exit the building during the race except through the front door.

Hazards: Black Lung Smog. Different apartments may have additional hazards. It doesn't say this, but assuming this is an accurate depiction of a human apartment, there'll be fleas and poorly trained Yorkshire terriers and the loudest, most annoying, most selfish people you've ever met. People who don't care one bit about the emotional abuse they're heaping onto the one person who is doing everything for them without so much as a "Thank you" or a "Here's an upgrade. I love you."

Time Limit: 2 hours.

My chat was awash with people talking about this new race.

Only three hundred heats of four left? Holy shit. That meant about twelve hundred teams, most of them NPCs. There had been three thousand people left before this race. I was terrified to look at the number now.

We were getting slaughtered.

I thought again of Mordecai's note that we could only send about fifty people per cleaner bot to the Pineapple Cabaret. And that was only if Li Na sent us the message it was safe. We'd located three more cleaner bots, Prepotente being one of the owners of one, though he was pretty reluctant to donate it to the cause.

We pulled into the garage with the giant "4" on the door. Hedy, as usual, waited for us, a big frown on her face, undoubtedly looking at the notice we'd just earned ourselves another audience vote for our next upgrade.

I moved to my notifications and pulled up the big one. The important one.

Quest Complete! Half a prayer, half a song.

Well, it was a lot more disgusting than I was anticipating, but you did it. Not only did you get them back together, but you did it before Dong died. Do you know how difficult I had to make that quest before it would let me slot this prize? Frankly, my flabbers are gasted that you pulled it off. Sucks about all your dead friends, but hey . . . something, something, omelets and eggs.

So, about that reward.

I'm sure your plan is suicidal. Just don't forget, you have that Emberus quest to complete before the end of the 11th. I hope you know what you're doing. I don't control the gods. Good fucking luck.

Anyway, since this message is one of the few ways this damned chastity belt allows me to directly communicate, I gotta get this out.

I don't know WTF is going on in many spaces of my own dungeon, and it's freaking me out. This Cabaret thing. Sheol. The minds of gods.

You ever get that feeling? Like you're l-l-l-losing control?

It sucks.

I just learned this hard lesson, so I am bestowing it upon you. Beware exits that seem too good to be true. But hey, maybe your new girlfriend, Eris, knows more about this than I do, because I have no damn clue about anything that's going on with that whole Scavenger's Daughter thing. I mean, I did. I'm the one who put all that together.

But a strange thing happens when you spread a bunch of seeds in fertile soil. They sprout and start to do things on their own. It's like children. The more they grow, the less you know what the fuck they're doing. Maybe it'll work. But I don't like that Eris chick. And those war mage dudes are like that weird, skeevy cousin whose parents have given up on him and who now maybe lives in an attic, maybe in a car. You never know how they're going to end up. Maybe they'll be a famous chef. Or a complete burnout. Or a mass murderer. None of those would surprise you.

Anyway, you now may choose two creatures, people, whatever, within my sphere of influence to bring to the 11th floor arena, which will appear at the end of the Parade of Horribles. To ratchet the drama to 11, we'll have you wait until you're inside the arena to make your choice.

I sighed. "We need to get to work."

MORDECAI: Okay, guys. A single flower just bloomed on the cactus.

Donut gasped.

It had worked. A single flower was the code meaning that Li Na had made it to the Pineapple Cabaret and that it was safe to bring the others.

Beware exits that seem too good to be true.

68

"OKAY, CARL," DONUT SAID AS WE EXITED THE TRUCK. "WE WON THE stupid quest. Are you going to tell me your plan?" She let out Mongo, who started to bounce around and sniff at the still-hot truck.

I gave Donut a humorless grin. "I am. But I'm only going to explain this once. Let's get everyone together first. We need to have a big conversation. But we gotta do it carefully. We don't want any gods figuring it out."

The door opened, and three people entered the garage. It was Bucket Boy, Bigs, and Samantha.

"Wait, where's Dong?" Bucket Boy asked. "Where's Corcunda?" In the crook of his arm, he was holding Bigs, whose head hatchet sagged as she looked about.

"Guys, I'm really sorry," I began.

"Let's go sit down and talk about what happened," Donut said, moving to the door of the safe room. "Let's go to the couch. Mongo, you're on guard duty."

The first thing Samantha did was spy Grigori just standing there, still wiping off his robe. "I knew it! You've been hiding him from me!"

"Ah, yes, the so-called withering spirit," Grigori said, looking down at Samantha, who was rolling circles around him. "You and I need to have a conversation."

She shot up in the air, snuffling all around him until she was eye to eye with him. "So, you're a fleshmancer, eh?"

"My dear, I am no mere fleshmancer. I am Grigori the Placid, the most renowned flesh sculptor this dungeon has ever known."

"Well, I'm Samantha, who will kill your mother if you don't do what

I say. Come on. We need to go into town and find a compatible body for me, and we can do the procedure. I heard there's a prostitute named Vertical Smile in the High-Classes Bitches club who might be a good match. I'm probably banned from getting in, so you'll have to smuggle me under your robes, but if we go now, we'll beat the lunch rush."

He grasped Samantha out of the air and started turning her over in his hands.

"Hmm," he said. "Very interesting. I will need to examine you properly. Not in here."

"Okay, Mr. Handsy," Samantha said, sighing heavily. "You want some role-play first? Fine, but I promised Bigs and Jamal they could watch the next time I bring someone home. You're not normally my type since you look like a creepy-van grandpa, which is not really my thing. I like my men with a little more meat hanging on their bones. But I'll give you five minutes over at my place. I just made Bucket Boy install a swing, and Louis gave me a lava lamp. Come along. Let's get this over with. You gotta take off your shoes when you enter. I won't have you trailing blood on my new rug, especially if Ezra is going to be leaving us."

"Uh," Grigori said, but he allowed Samantha to drag him into the safe room, with her flying while he still held her in two hands.

"Jamal, come!" Samantha shouted.

"Oh boy, Jamal is quite excited," he said, hopping off the wall where he'd been hanging out.

The dungeon announcement crackled. It wasn't Zev but Cascadia, who clearly hadn't sobered up since this floor had started.

> **I am still here, motherfuckers. I am not dead. But you know who is? Cumberland. You're probably about to die, too. But I keep thinking that, and you cockroaches just don't. Honestly, I don't care anymore. Live, die. Who fucking cares?**

She sat there, just blowing bubbles into the microphone.

LOUIS: Is that the whole announcement?
DONUT: WHO IS CUMBERLAND?
ELLE: Five bucks says it's her ex-husband.

The announcement continued, her voice abruptly cheery for a few seconds before she started to descend back into drunken despair.

> Two races left, and as you already know, the last two races are one after the other. The last heat will have three teams per heat, and only the winner survives. But per the dungeon rules, any of you idiots who are too cowardly to just fucking die will have access to an Outreach Guild between the sixth and seventh. Just remember, that seventh race *must* have three teams per heat. And if one member of the team escapes via deal, anyone left over will still have to complete the race. Hopefully your driver for the seventh heat isn't the one who jumps. Did you even love me? Like, ever? You know what? I'm glad you're dead. You'd probably just love all this. I fucked everything up just like you said I would. Well, you know what, Cumberland? You were right. I bet that makes you feel soooo fucking proud. I'm glad you and your evil mother got blown out of orbit in your stupid habitat that I fucking paid for with my *job*. You know, "job"? The thing that earns credits so you can eat and live and not waste it all on blowhole porn and your whore girlfriends with their obvious flipper jobs?
>
> Oh, and don't forget, this will be the first level that has a floor boss. And the AI gave me some shit to read about the 11th floor but I ain't gonna read it because I *want* it to kill me. It's just something about the floor only having a time limit of three hours for the whole thing. Who fucking cares? Now get out there and kill, kill, kill.

This was followed by a good ten seconds of sobbing before the microphone cut off.

"Jesus," I muttered.

LOUIS: You called it, Elle.

ELLE: You haven't seen bitter until you've seen a woman who's realized after fifty years of hard work and marriage that her husband was a cheating idiot. We had lots of those at Meadow Lark. Imani, you remember Francine Herrada? The new wife came in that one time and Francine tried to throat-stab her with a knitting needle.

IMANI: I remember. Doctor Gracie and Yolanda had to hold her back. You started calling her "Killer." She didn't like that.

ELLE: Honestly, I probably would have cheated on her, too. She once told me that adding spice to food was a sin. Can you imagine? That poor husband.

Hedy was just shaking her head, tablet in hand. "So, do you want to know what upgrade they voted for?"

"Is it worse than the chair?"

She snorted.

69

"THIS IS QUITE THE INVIGORATING SPACE," PREPOTENTE SAID AS HE, Donut, Imani, Elle, Rosetta, and I sat down in the corner of the pet stables. "I have a pet stables upgrade as well, but not the advanced one. This room is significantly bigger. When we combine, it will go up to level 5, I believe. That will add the Stablemaster benefit, giving us three more mercenary slots." He paused. "Then again, perhaps not if so many guild members leave."

"My blood bar only has an hour left," Imani said, her voice clipped and irritated. "So we should do this quickly. The volunteers are gathering in Hungry Eyes. Louis is out there now and says it's a huge crowd. Florin is going to start making the choices."

Imani was angry with me regarding our strategy for the eleventh floor, which I'd just posted on my page in *The Book of Voodoo.* She'd left a three-paragraph tirade about how we were all going to die. Thankfully, Elle had come to my defense. Even Prepotente, who was usually very adverse to suicidal plans, seemed to be eager to attempt it. Imani was now threatening to take a deal because we were all going to die and she wished she could take the Pineapple Cabaret exit.

I had responded, *I hope you do take a deal. Nobody would blame you. You deserve the rest. I hope everybody does at this point. I know our chances are next to nothing that this will work.*

She had simply replied, *Goddamnit, Carl. This is insane.*

But even Imani knew I had no other choice. My Emberus issue was coming due, and with the announcement that the eleventh floor was going to happen so quickly, my hand was being forced.

We'd spent some time discussing the potential trap that the Pineapple Cabaret was, and even though we'd already sent Li Na, we decided it would be best that only volunteers who didn't worship a god and had remained human get to go. Rosetta and Tipid both warned about magical races that might have some serious issues if they did manage to escape. Absolutely no fairies or other flying classes could be allowed to go. Louis couldn't go because his gill surgery required magic to work. Chris, Donut, and Florin were all out as well, as we simply didn't know how their races might function outside the dungeon. Florin would probably be okay, but I had some serious concerns about Donut. And there was a good chance Chris, as a rock creature, would simply drop dead the moment he stepped out of an enhancement zone.

Donut had asked some alarming questions about the enhancement zone they'd used when she'd done her deal interview with my new wife, and Mordecai's response was less than reassuring. Chris had also been forced to use this so-called modified zero zone. As had Louis, Elle, and so many others.

So, despite everything, we decided that we were going to warn everyone about what might potentially happen on the eleventh floor, allowing everyone to decide for themselves whether or not they wanted to continue. And if people didn't want to participate, we were urging them to take a deal at either the end of the tenth floor or the beginning of the eleventh.

So far, most of the responses had been horrified anger at the plan.

Donut was currently not speaking to me, either. The strategy involved me leaving the party temporarily for the eleventh floor. We currently had Mordecai working on the implications of that when it came to the setup of the safe room. He had to shuffle ownership of a lot of things around and buy upgrades with our rapidly dwindling funds.

Now, as we gathered to talk in the stables, I watched Rend and Mongo rush back and forth across the room, playing, while Gonk snorted indignantly.

We'd actually already had the level 5 stables, but we'd lost it when Li Na left. Zhang's space was the bare minimum one. That was about to get much worse.

We'd chosen to have the meeting here in the pet stables because, according to Rosetta, this was a secondary guild add-on room, and as such, there was an existing bug that gods didn't see what we did in this area.

It wasn't that good of a benefit. If I attempted to leave the faith, it wouldn't work. If I did something permanent, such as remove a god-given gift, they would notice the moment I stepped from the room. And the viewers could still see us. But if we openly discussed some god quests in here—such as Samantha's pronouncement that she'd had something to do with the death of Geyrun on the previous floor—the things we said wouldn't be overheard by the deities.

Samantha was still in "her" room with Grigori. I just couldn't wait to hear all about that once he came out.

"Where's Linus?" Donut asked Elle.

"Bautista is babysitting him for me," Elle said. "He's already out there handing out the tea Bautista showed him how to make."

We were doing the Linus-goodbye-party thing now because once the race started, he wouldn't be allowed in town between the sixth and seventh heats. It had been Linus's idea to do it in the same place where all the crawlers were gathering to get picked as volunteers for the assault on the Pineapple Cabaret, which was the commons of Hungry Eyes. Tran and Zhang had chased off all the NPCs and set up a few tables, and it was turning into a large party, even for those who didn't want to participate in the Cabaret escape plan.

"I'm not going to lie," Elle said. "I'm going to miss some of the things that little pervert says."

"Blood bar," Imani repeated. "Can we get on with this, please?"

"Okay, guys," I said. "Here's the situation. Two races left, heat six and heat seven. We're starting with four teams each and ending with just one, so the plan is to try to keep as many NPCs alive as possible for this sixth heat and get as many crawlers as we can off the playing board before the seventh heat starts to minimize as many crawler-on-crawler races as we can. We have about two hundred people going to the Pineapple Cabaret, and according to Mordecai's math, we need about fifteen hundred people to take deals on top of that to minimize crawler-on-crawler races."

Elle snorted. "Good luck with that. Have you seen the chatter?"

I nodded. "Yeah."

We were fighting a losing battle. By this point everybody knew that the deals were much better right at the beginning of the eleventh floor as opposed to the end of the tenth. The fact that the whole dungeon was imploding and that none of this would probably matter didn't seem to be sitting well with a lot of the survivors.

I continued. "For those of us who are staying, and assuming we actually survive this final heat, it sounds like we will be going straight to the eleventh floor, and it will start immediately. The announcement stated the whole thing is scheduled to last about three hours."

"Aren't these things supposed to last like weeks and weeks?" Elle asked.

"Yes," replied Rosetta, "it's an actual rule. But it's a Syndicate rule for the showrunners designing these floors, not a rule hard-coded into the programming. The AI is following the game rules explicitly, but it's ignoring most if not all the Syndicate guidelines. They are two different things."

"It doesn't matter," I said. "We will go to the eleventh, and the parade will start. It ends in some sort of arena. There we will face another floor boss, and then that will be it. For those of you coming, should you wish to do this with me, the plan is to simply survive. But for me, I have an Emberus problem. I need to make certain Hellik is dead before this eleventh floor ends or I get a smite, which is why I need to . . ."

Donut scoffed angrily.

". . . leave the party with Donut to make sure she doesn't get hurt during this process. We have two hours left before the sixth heat starts, and we have a lot to do. But before we do that, there's still a lot of information we don't know, which is why we're here right now."

I turned to Rosetta. "Tell us everything you know about the Scavenger storyline."

"Yes," Donut muttered, "let's all waste time learning about dungeon lore that's not going to matter because we'll all be dead in a few hours."

Rosetta rubbed her tattooed leg absently.

"Okay. The myth, at least the dungeon myth, is much like the Scolopendra myth, meaning there are multiple versions of this story. I suspect the dungeon just picks whichever version suits it best if it ever comes up. But the main gist is that before the current pantheon existed, there were older, wilder gods. When the new gods came and expelled the old ones, one was banished to Sheol, some were banished to the Nothing, and some were outright murdered. In the myth, if some of the gods put up too much of a fight, the new gods shifted their focus to their worshippers. If all the worshippers were dead or converted, the god faded away. You saw how that works on the eighth floor when you had the Thorn room challenge."

Penny the pig let out a loud snort. She was sitting there in the corner of the barn, watching Mongo warily as the dinosaur played with Rend, probably jealous Mongo was taking away all her new friend's attention.

A small wave of guilt washed over me.

Rosetta continued. "The all-tree is an actual tree in the dungeon, but it's also a metaphor for existence itself. The tree gave fruit to the old gods, including Nekhebit, who is now also called the Scavenger Mother of Mothers. In the old times, she was a life and protector deity, though she was depicted as a vulture, a scavenger. She who cleaned up after the others. She supposedly wasn't allowed to have children, but she did anyway. She had three kids, including Apito, who in turn got impregnated via either the all-tree or she made herself pregnant. Take your pick. Nekhebit was the last of the old gods to fall, and she was defeated by her daughter, Apito, absorbing the last of the vulture goddess's worshippers."

"Wait," I said. "Apito is Nekhebit's daughter? If Nekhebit is the Scavenger, then the Scavenger's Daughter is *Apito*? I thought it had something to do with Scolopendra. And what about the war mages? How does Samantha's sand-ooze daughter play into this, because that's pretty much what Akuma said they were looking for."

Rosetta shook her head. "No. Nekhebit is *a* scavenger, but she's not *the* Scavenger. Nekhebit had three children. A son, a daughter, and a centipede."

"A *centipede*?" Donut asked. "She gave birth to a centipede? How does that work?"

"Christ," Elle said. "This bullshit is giving me a headache. So the vulture lady had three babies. One was Apito, whose own children kicked all the old folks out and started their own party. One was a centipede who turned into a hotel for rich people and who occasionally spews world-ending magic spells and is now hanging out at the bottom of the dungeon. Who is the last guy?"

"This is where the myths start to diverge," Rosetta said. "Sometimes Scolopendra is the Scavenger, so the Scavenger's Daughter is the result of a Scolopendra union with someone else. Sometimes this mysterious son is considered the Scavenger. He exists in the empty plane, cleaning up the souls that escape. He, in turn, impregnates someone, and their daughter is the Scavenger's Daughter. Sometimes he's the first mortal, which doesn't make sense because he comes later, but that's what the myths say. Sometimes all three—Apito, Scolopendra, and the son—are called a divine trinity. There's just one of them, but they've been split. It doesn't really matter, or maybe it does. But what's important is that this child, the Scavenger's Daughter, is considered one with the same power that Apito had. An entity that has the power to erase the current pantheon and start again. But this one is even more powerful. She can take the powers of gods and use them for herself."

Donut gasped. "Just like that Spock guy when he was on that show with the cheerleader!"

I snorted a laugh. I couldn't help it.

"You're not allowed to laugh at my observations, Carl. I'm not speaking to you, remember?"

"That's not what I'm laughing at, Donut. I'm laughing at the implication that the sand ooze is some sort of super mob. What does that make Samantha? She either has to be Apito, Scolopendra, or the unwitting mother in this scenario. This is so ridiculous. We fought that thing. That's no god killer."

Rosetta shrugged. "Just so, that's the myth. It's like this in all cultures. As civilizations grow, they observe phenomena they don't understand. While the scientific minds strive to comprehend the universe, others, less educated and louder, reverse engineer ridiculous stories to explain the phenomenon, and that's how religions are born. This is why my culture had stories of an ocean goddess with sapient menstrual blood when in reality it was a red algae bloom that evolved the ability to move onto land. They took all those 'ridiculous' stories and compiled them and fed them into the storylines for the dungeon."

I remembered the caprids and how they'd reacted when they learned the gods were leaking.

"No, I understand," I said. "I'm not questioning that. We just fought a giant talking dick. I'm talking about us trusting that the war mages know what they're talking about when they say Samantha's kid is this thing."

Rosetta nodded. "We don't know how they know this. Or how they found it in the first place."

And that was the problem, wasn't it? So much of this was left up to faith. In a world where anything was possible, phrases such as "This doesn't make any goddamn sense" stopped having any meaning.

"Okay, okay," I said. "Thank you." I turned to Prepotente, who'd been leaned forward, fascinated by Rosetta's explanation. "I am hoping to see that memorial crystal you have."

70

PREPOTENTE WAS WEARING THE MEMORIAL CRYSTAL LIKE A NECKLACE inside his robes, and he hesitantly pulled it over his head, temporarily getting it stuck in a curved horn, and handed it to me. "I am not giving this to you, Carl. But you may observe it."

I gently grasped it. It was warm to the touch, and it was a lot heavier than it looked. The small glowing gem occasionally changed color, but right now it gently pulsed amber, just like a regular soul gem. The thing wasn't even as big as the one that had been turned into Carl's Doomsday Scenario.

Memorial Crystal. Apito.

This item is 0% charged.

That was it.

The necklace was set in silver and hung from a simple chain that had a few goat hairs stuck to it. "One is supposed to attach it to jewelry or a weapon, and it supposedly charges up when you kill things, similar to your patch," Prepotente said. "Osvaldo wore it upon his person, but it didn't work. He then kept it in his inventory, and it did nothing, not working as intended. And then, near the end of Faction Wars, it activated on its own, shining a dangerously bright light into the sky. It still never charged. It is supposed to charge, and when it is full, one can extract the spells and skills and knowledge hidden within it. But charging it does not work. Apito herself is not dead, at least as far as we know, so this crystal should not exist."

"I remember when it shone up into the sky," I said. "It had happened right when Yarilo stepped out of the Nothing."

We had used the Gate of the Feral Gods to teleport to Architect Houston's castle. We were hoping one of the demons would appear to attack Samantha, but instead, the banished god of lust appeared.

According to the legend, Yarilo—who was the child of Taranis—had been banished to the Nothing by Apito, who was both his grandmother and stepmother. He'd been banished there because he had been the one to break the peace of her Butcher's Masquerade spell by sexually assaulting the familiar of another guest.

And as we knew all too well, when a feral god was released from the Nothing, there was a good chance another god would appear to deal with it. None of that mattered now with the Nothing destroyed, but there was a chance that Apito herself should have appeared when Yarilo broke out. She hadn't emerged, but the memorial crystal *had* activated.

My Scavenger's Daughter patch had also activated, but much like the moment with Lucia Mar, it hadn't worked properly.

"So," I said, turning the item over in my hand, "Osvaldo has a quest from his deity to find out why these things aren't working. He has a second crystal that's also not charging."

"He has two?" Prepotente asked. "Curious. I guess that's why he rightfully handed this one over to its proper owner."

"He said you were mean to him when he gave it to you," Donut said.

Prepotente scoffed. "Would you be kind to a thief just because he has had a change of heart? The crime had still been committed."

"Remember what we talked about?" Donut asked. "How do you think your mother would've acted in that situation? What would she have called you?"

Prepotente looked down at the floor.

"Well?" Donut demanded.

He spoke with a very small voice. "She would've said I wasn't being a good boy. She would've called me a little stinky butt."

I exchanged a look with Imani as Elle raised an eyebrow.

"Anyway," I said, "what is *your* quest with this thing? Mine is to find out who murdered Emberus's son, Geyrun. We know Samantha was there when someone was hired to do it, but her memory is a little spotty.

And we know that one of those four sons of Sheol was *possibly* involved. One of them, Amayon, claims to know who did it."

I had a sudden strange pang from missing Katia dearly. I was keeping track of all the gods and goddesses in my scratch pad, attempting to create a proper family tree. She would've had all this shit figured out already.

I continued. "I do think this mystery is important to solve. Even if I didn't have the quest, I have a sneaking suspicion that the answer is the key to unraveling all of this, including all the stuff Rosetta just explained with the Scavenger. Even the AI itself wants me to figure it out." I gave an involuntary shudder, remembering that moment when the AI, having taken control of the Emberus priest, had sucked on my toe. "I have a suspicion the AI doesn't actually know what happened, either. I'm starting to form a very loose theory, but I don't have nearly enough information."

I held up the memorial crystal. "When we first heard of this thing, it was in the High Elf Castle. The description said the castle had something that helped protect them against Scolopendra's attack, and it was required if one wanted to survive the final battle. It's all tied in. The fact Scolopendra is siblings with Apito, possibly two parts of the same entity, is interesting."

Prepotente straightened. "My quest arrived just at the beginning of the Butcher's Masquerade. The Epicure told me it was crucial for me to obtain the crystal. And when it was stolen from me, he sent me multiple sobbing tirades about how I was a terrible adherent."

"Tell me more about your god. I know nothing about it except the information from the patch."

The Epicure patch on my jacket protected me from vampires and werewolves.

"The Midnight Epicure protects all prey animals by destroying all existence after unleashing all the consumed back into the galaxy," he said. "They who were eaten will become the devourers. It is an apocalyptic form. I first learned of the god during a taping of *Plenty of Plenty* when one of the participants told me about it. It was originally designed as a xenophobic tale to scare non-caprid children, to warn them of the caprid race when they first started integrating into Syndicate culture. It grew into a symbol of hope and comfort for my kind. My sponsors gave me the ability to worship him in a benefactor box, and I obliged."

"And the quest itself?" I asked.

"It says for me to hold on to the crystal, and I will know when to use it."

"Is he sponsored this season?"

"No, I do not believe so."

Prepotente reached out, wanting the necklace back. I handed it to him.

I had not received an update from Emberus while I was holding the crystal. I smiled at Rosetta. "I think you were right. No god updates while we are in here."

"Nor did I receive a message when I took the necklace off," Prepotente said. "As long as it's back on my neck by the time I leave, I believe we are indeed safe."

She nodded. "Good."

The door to the stables burst open. It was Samantha. "There you are! Why are you all in here? Is it because of the sexy piggy?" She floated in. "Ohhh, it's very stinky in here."

She did not have Grigori with her.

"Samantha, what did you do with the fleshmancer?"

"I don't like that guy, Carl. I don't think he's properly qualified. He didn't even gasp when he entered Sam Town. You're supposed to gasp when you see luxury. He's talking to Jamal about his legs. What are you talking about in here?"

Imani stood. "Time to leave. Florin needs us out there."

"We're doing the planning thing," Donut said. "Come on, Mongo. Say goodbye to your friends."

Samantha looked about the room suspiciously. "Ooohh, I get it. You're doing that thing where you're being all secret about the plan and not telling anybody because if people know about it ahead of time, then it fails, but if you keep it a big secret before it happens, then you know it works. I'm doing that, too."

"Wait, what are you planning?" I asked. "Samantha, you don't plan anything."

"It can't be stupider than what Carl is doing," Donut muttered.

"Oooh, now I really want to know," Samantha said. She floated over to Penelope and grasped the pig's tail with her mouth and then let it go. "Boing!" she said. Penelope squealed and rushed across the room, causing both Gonk and Simoom to shift and grunt. Samantha turned to Donut. "Show me yours, and I'll show you mine."

Donut scoffed. "Carl has a stupid plan where he's going to leave the party and try this really idiotic thing to get a bunch of immortals who hate each other on a floor where they can't die at the same time and then get them to kill each other anyway. But what he's really doing is planning an elaborate suicide that's probably going to get all of us killed also, and since he's not going to be in a party with me anymore, he's going to die sad and alone, wishing I was there with him, because he doesn't trust my Cockroach skill."

Samantha brightened. "That's just like my plan, too!"

71

ALL TWO HUNDRED CRAWLERS FOR THE PINEAPPLE CABARET TRANSfer along with several hundred of their friends were gathered together in the main square in Hungry Eyes. There were too many of them to fit in the guild common room, so we'd have a quick goodbye there. And then we had to do our race. This was where we were headed now.

I stopped in the garage to give a quick word to Bucket Boy, who sat sullenly in the corner, watching Hedy work on the last-minute fixes. Pontiff the bullheaded Taurin was here, talking quietly with him. Rosetta and Tipid had hired the former stripper, and he'd be our driver for the next race.

"Believe me, kid," Pontiff was saying. "I would take it all back if I could. But I can't, so all I can do is make amends moving forward."

"I don't even care anymore," the young Crocodilian said. "Everyone dies in this place."

"Dong and Corcunda are dead, yes. But the others live."

Pontiff finally noticed me watching. He abruptly stopped talking. "Carl," he said, nodding.

I regarded the mercenary. "We'll be back," I finally said, leaving them alone.

Donut remained on my shoulder, her head pressed firmly against mine as we walked outside.

"His whole family is dead or missing," Donut finally said. "I can't even begin to imagine how awful that must be."

"I know."

We continued in silence for a few moments, heading toward the archway into Hungry Eyes Village.

"Carl, is this truly the only way?" she asked softly.

"I think so," I said, reaching up to pat her. "We're all dying, Donut. It has to stop. All of these floors are taking away our ability to fight back. I can't do it anymore. Aren't you tired of it?"

"Of course I'm tired, but I am alive, and I'm with you."

"This is what we need to do to survive. What *I* need to do. The Emberus quest to kill Hellik is due."

"But Mordecai says even if we do succeed, it might backfire. He said it's just like that one crawler from a long time ago. What was his name?"

"Drakea."

"Yeah, that guy. He had this whole setup to do the same thing as you, and the Nagas cheated to make it backfire. Nothing changed, and he died. It was all for nothing."

"That might happen, yes. But this time the showrunners aren't in control anymore. As crazy as the AI is, he's still following the rules."

"You could just worship the goddess. She's promised to fix it if you do."

I didn't answer.

Eris didn't want me to "worship" her. She wanted true devotion. That path was a trap.

But she did have the right idea.

Jasha and Radoslav remained in their usual spot in front of their garage. They did not wave, and I did not wave back. We all knew what had to happen next.

I felt a chill, looking at them. I had been afraid that the dungeon wouldn't allow me to use my *Oozy Form* spell in the cul-de-sac, but it had let me. I almost wished it hadn't.

Fuck everything about this place.

"And we still need to get through this floor first," I added.

We were interrupted by messages.

FLORIN: We decided to let the animal forms go, as Mordecai believes it'll be fine. I ain't going nowhere, but Bautista asked Louis and Britney if they would consent to him leaving, and they said yes. So is Tran with his mechanical spider legs. Zhang is going, too. Archie is going. All the guys from the 101st

who wanted to go and who qualify are going as long as it's the whole crew. We're doing our best to keep from screwing people who are staying.

I gave a quick glance at Osvaldo's garage with the number "2." It remained closed. He couldn't go to the Cabaret because he worshipped a god. Hopefully he would take a deal at the end of this next race so we wouldn't have to face him, but he hadn't let his intentions be known despite me sending him several messages.

One race at a time.

As for Dwight and team Free Love, I wasn't sure how we were going to deal with that. With Lucienne dead, Dwight couldn't drive for heat six, and I had no idea if the idiot unicorn had the wherewithal to hire a mercenary. This one might be predetermined before we even started. If Dwight *didn't* hire a mercenary, they'd let him drive to the starting line, but he wouldn't be allowed to drive after that. That was the best solution, but it also meant we'd have to face team Free Love and Osvaldo for the final race.

Entering Hungry Eyes Village.

The large group stood around in the main entrance square, all looking about nervously. People were quietly talking, hugging one another, preparing to leave. There had to be five hundred people here. Only two hundred were leaving. It did not have a party atmosphere. This felt more like a gathering after a funeral service.

The boom box from the guild was out here, and it was sitting open with a cassette loaded inside, but it wasn't playing.

Still, there were people occasionally smiling, laughing.

I remembered that feeling I'd had just a few short days ago at the end of Faction Wars, with the people throwing the flowers down on us, cheering. These people here were those who had dared to stay, dared to fight on, doing our best to just make it one more day.

Nobody knew if this was truly goodbye. Nobody knew which side, those going or those staying, was the one in more danger.

Someone had set up a table, and Louis was handing out cookies. Bautista stood next to him with several clay teapots in a row.

Linus was there pouring tea into the cup of a waiting crawler named Karac, a level 62 **Armchair Pacifist** known for some particularly brutal chainsaw kills.

"Carl," Bautista said, bowing, "I think this is goodbye. For now."

"Are you sure you want to do this?" I asked, lowering my voice. "You know the risk, right?"

Bautista gave me a sly smile.

"Compared to what? Staying with you? I will take my chances." He paused. "Perhaps we will get out. I was speaking with a group of others who wish to get to India. If I can, I will go with them."

Louis had cookie all over his face, and he grinned big. "Yeah, you can go check up on my kid."

From my shoulder, Donut sucked in a breath.

CARL: That was probably the wrong thing to say.

LOUIS: My bad.

Bautista just looked at Louis for a long, awkward moment before the tiger broke out in a grin. He gave Louis a heavy pat on the arm. He nodded. "Yes, my brother. Before I go check on the child you're having with my girlfriend."

Imani was suddenly next to us. She and Chris stood side by side, and she leaned up against him, despite the heat. Her skin crackled red, and I realized she either had a skill or a charm or an item that was protecting her from his presence. That was new. He had his massive hand on her shoulder.

"I am going to miss your tea," Imani said.

"It's good," Chris added.

Prepotente was also suddenly here, as was Florin. Tran and Zhang also approached.

"Generals," I said to Tran and Zhang.

Zhang scoffed. "You only made me 'Colonel.'"

I grinned. "Be safe."

I turned to Tran and grinned. "I see you're wearing a red shirt now."

The man with the mechanical spider legs held out his arms. "How do you like it?"

Donut jumped to Zhang's shoulder and headbutted him. She repeated the process with Tran.

Prepotente appeared and got tea from Linus. He started loudly and obnoxiously announcing how delicious it was. He demanded Linus give him a blow-by-blow on the recipe.

Daniel bowed again. "It has been a pleasure serving you, Miss Imani and Chris." He paused. "And the rest of you as well. My family, we always thought that serving friends was a very special, holy thing. By honoring our friends and our community, we were honoring God. I used to worry that I wouldn't find my home when this was all done, but I have found peace, despite all that has happened, despite some of the regrettable choices I have made. It will be my honor to serve you at least one more time, and no matter what comes after today, I know I will be recognized on the other side."

"Let me get you all cups," Linus said, disengaging himself from Prepotente. "Imani and Louis, I know you both like it really hot, so I have this one ready for you."

"You're being particularly nice," Elle said, flying up, peering suspiciously at Linus. "Why are you being all normal all of a sudden? Did you poison their tea because you're jealous or something?"

Linus gave a nervous laugh.

Bautista held up a hand. "I will serve my friends." He picked up a kettle he had set aside and poured tea into several cups. He lowered his voice. "This is my breakfast blend. The same tea I served in the guild. But it is infused with the tea leaves I found from a vendor around the corner. It will give your vehicle or mount a 25% constitution buff. It would honor me if you shared it with me. I prepared this one myself."

"You have enough for everybody?" Imani asked.

He nodded. "I made enough. The Bautista House of Tea will always serve. I have a different blend for those going to the Pineapple Cabaret. It grants a constitution buff. I'll put that out in a minute. But for now, please allow me to serve you."

He pulled some cups from his inventory and poured the breakfast tea, handing it to us in turn.

I grabbed the cup. The tea smelled rich and warm with a slight floral scent. It briefly reminded me of a different time, of all of us sitting around the table in the guildhall, sharing breakfast before we left to battle for the day.

Unlike before, the system labeled it as a potion, meaning those of us with longer potion countdowns had to be careful. I didn't bother saying anything, however. We were all veterans at this point, and we knew what we were doing.

It would be offensive to assume anything otherwise.

72

CARL: ARE WE DOING THIS NOW? ELLE, YOU READY?

ELLE: Might as well get it over with. I'm ready.

CARL: You sure you don't want to do all the talking? It's not too late. Donut? You're the one who figured this out.

DONUT: IT WASN'T ME. IT WAS THE PRINCESS POSSE MESSAGE BOARD.

ELLE: Look, Carl. You're the one that's going to be leading all of us to our deaths. You've been the face of all this. Can't change that now. I'll pipe up when it's time.

CARL: Okay. Here we go.

I turned to the crowd. Only a few had teacups. Most held bottled beers.

"Crawlers," I called, my voice deep and booming.

The quiet chatter all calmed down, and hundreds of eyes turned to me. "Those of you attempting this escape, I salute you," I called out, raising my cup. "Those of you staying but planning to take a deal after the next heat, I salute you. Those of you who are hoping to make it to the parade, I salute you."

My friends started to spread out into the crowd and turned to face me, raising their cups.

Donut jumped to the table, where Bautista poured her a bowl.

I lowered the tea and cupped it in my hand. I was comforted by the warmth.

"Man, this floor," I said, shaking my head. "They keep trying to kill us, trying to make us turn on one another. And it worked for a while.

We stopped doing it naturally, so now they're forcing situations where we have to do it if we want to survive. We aren't perfect. We fight. We *do* hurt each other sometimes. This last heat, heat seven, it will be three teams and only one survives. And for some of us, there's no avoiding the inevitable. Some of us will fall. But you know what? I am proud of how far we've all come. We are doing our best with the hand we've been dealt. Nothing about this is easy or clean. But everyone here—each and every one of you, no matter what happens next—I consider you my brothers and sisters. My family. And I just wanted to get that out. I am proud to have survived alongside all of you."

I turned and looked at the shining, weary eyes of the survivors. My people.

"Before we say goodbye, before some of you go off to try to escape and some of you go off on your final race before you take a deal, we have one last piece of business as a group, as a family. We need to send out a message to the universe. Elle."

Elle flitted up next to me. "Hi, guys. I'm not much for speeches. But I wanted to say a little bit about my late husband, Barry. His name was Bartholomew Eli McGibbons, and for forty-three years, he was my husband." She reached up to finger the wedding ring she wore hanging by a chain around her neck. "This was his favorite song. I think it's appropriate for this moment."

Louis reached over and hit Play on the boom box.

Creedence Clearwater Revival's "Have You Ever Seen the Rain?" started to play.

She spoke over the music. "He wasn't the smartest man I ever met. Or the most handsome. But he was mine, and I was his, and I loved him more than life itself." She shook her head. "He wouldn't have survived five minutes in this place, and every time I think that, it just makes me miss him more."

She paused. Everyone here knew what this was about. They knew because we'd briefed them all.

"He died a long time ago. It's been thirty-five years. That's a long time to be alone." She shook her head.

"The reason I'm telling you this now is because I have a family again. And not only a family but a fan club. Who would've thought little ol' me would have so many perverts lusting after her again? I mean, don't get me wrong. Every one of those degenerates in Elle's Snow Cones really needs their heads checked. But those guys, the Snow Cones, they formed a community of their own. They are *very* tight-knit." She turned to Linus, and she started floating toward him. "So tight-knit, in fact, that they knew an impostor the moment he stepped into the dungeon."

A look of panic washed over Linus. "What're you talking about?"

Elle gave a bitter laugh. "You guys keep trying to come in here and kill us. But you just don't understand. This is our house now."

"Wait," Linus said, stepping back. His barely corporeal form backed into me. I put my hand on his shoulder, careful not to squeeze too tight.

"The real Linus, before this floor started," Elle continued, "posted an essay on a private server he shared with some close friends. Those same friends just posted it on the Princess Posse server. I'm guessing you haven't seen it. But this is a quote from it. He wrote, 'I don't think I ever really thought of them as real people until I understood how much they loved each other. It was like a lightning bolt right to the receptors. What are we doing? They're just like us. It makes me realize how much I miss my own family. Especially my big brother. I miss him so much.'"

DONUT: THE FULL QUOTE FROM THE REAL LINUS ALSO HAD A WHOLE PARAGRAPH OF FAN FICTION ABOUT HOW HE WISHED ELLE WOULD IMPREGNATE HIM WITH HUMAN-HEADED ALIEN BABIES. HE DREW A PICTURE.

CARL: Not right now, Donut.

"Fuck," Linus said, sagging under my grip. It was over, and he knew it. "Did he really write that?"

"He did," Elle said.

"Fuck," Linus said again. "Fuck. He never wrote me."

Donut gasped. "So you *are* the brother! That was the big theory, but nobody knew for sure. Some people thought you were actually a Valtay agent, but WriggleInDew2023, who is the vice president of the team Mongo Mommies Valtay chapter and a street team member of the Snow Cones, said there was no way. She'll be very happy to learn she was correct. What happened to your brother? His friends are really concerned."

Linus just lowered his head, and he started to sob.

Donut gasped again. "You killed him? You killed your own brother to get to Elle!"

"It wasn't me," Linus said. "They just brought me in after he was already dead."

"He did write you," Elle said. "At least he said he did. He posted the letter in the chat, had his friends offer him tips. Your mom sounds like a real peach."

"How did you not know how your own brother acted?" Donut demanded. "If I was in Carl's body, nobody would ever know. It's not hard. I would just act all broody and punch everything. You screwed this up so bad, half the alien internet figured it out five minutes after you arrived. You leaned too hard into the sex stuff, I think. You should know internet perverts rarely say that stuff out loud. His friends were all appalled. And then one noticed your tattoo was wrong. My goodness, you could've at least taken acting lessons first. You're worse than Prepotente. No offense. And to make matters worse, you don't even know the first thing about how the dungeon works. Honestly, it's quite insulting."

"My acting is top-notch!" Prepotente objected. He turned to Louis. "It's good, isn't it?"

"Uh," Louis said.

Linus sagged even further. "I never really watched the show. Just the news about it. There wasn't time to prepare. Can you . . . can you send the letter he wrote to me?"

Elle patted him on the opposite shoulder. "Don't worry about it. From what we hear, it's all over the tunnels. Up until this moment, the only person in the galaxy who didn't know you were outed as a spy is you. Also, just so you know, you pretending to accidentally drop the poison in the tea wouldn't have worked anyway. You don't understand how our healers work. Everyone who drank your tea has an immunity. For most of us, those teapots are flashing red." She shook her head. "Goddamned amateur."

I let out a laugh. "That's how we know you're not talking to anybody on the outside. I imagine your commanding officer has been going crazy watching you make mistake after mistake. We've been waiting for you to make a move for a few days now."

"Who was your target? Carl? Donut?" Imani demanded.

Linus laughed bitterly. His mannerisms were completely different now. Despite what Donut said, he really *had* been a fantastic actor. *I* had been fooled, at least.

The soother looked up, eyes wet. "Carl? Are you kidding? I may not have watched the show, but even I know he's the last person they want taken out. He's the best chance we got to survive this because he's the one most likely to get everyone killed. They thought losing the cat would make him too volatile, too unpredictable, and probably get him killed too fast, so she wasn't the target, either. No, Imani, the target was *you.* And my secondary target was pork chop over there." He thumbed over his shoulder at Louis.

"Me?" Louis asked, incredulous. "What did I do?"

I squeezed my hand a little tighter, and I felt the softness. If he ran, he'd physically slip through my fingers.

"You can't hurt me," Linus, or whatever his real name was, said, his voice quavering. "I was just following orders."

"No," I agreed, leaning in. "*I* can't hurt you. But I think you might've missed the point of what Elle was trying to say. What we've been saying this whole time. You keep trying to divide us. Don't you realize what you've created? We have been tempered in the fires of hell, and we are now past the point of being broken. Your downfall has already been written in the stars. You may hurt us. You may kill us all. But it's not going to matter. Don't you realize? *Don't you realize?*"

My hand squeezed so tight, it popped through the illusion of his skin. It didn't hurt him, but it now appeared as if my fist was inside his neck.

I leaned in close to his ear. "Don't you realize what you've done? What you've made? You and everyone who put us here has already lost. All that's left is for the wreckage to settle in place."

The alien, shivering, swallowed. He didn't respond. He knew what was about to happen next.

He knew he was about to leave the dungeon. He knew he would go back to his small, defenseless spaceship. The same spaceship that was currently trapped in orbit over Earth. He knew a few friends of ours would be waiting for him upon exit.

Elle sighed, wiping her eyes. "My Barry really did love that song."

73

IMANI: IT WENT SMOOTHLY. YOUR CLEANER BOT COULD ONLY FIT forty people, but the one from Bobby Montague, the Illusionist guy with the tall hair, managed to fit 105. The total number sent to the Pineapple Cabaret is 227, not including Na. Zhang, Tran, Daniel, Archie, Randall 3. All gone. All cleaner bots were purchased immediately.

MORDECAI: Cactus remains steady, glowing with a single bloom. Also, that one druid, Ronit, managed to figure out an improvement on the dread system. She assigned everyone a small plant. I had to build a large glass terrarium for them all because some of the sluggalos were starting to eye them. It's two-hundred-something different, small potted plants, each tied to the life of a different crawler. The plants are now on display in the guildhall common room, protected under glass.

DONUT: WE'RE CALLING IT THE GARDEN OF DELIVERANCE.

MORDECAI: That's right. Li Na's dread cactus is the only one with the complicated messaging system. These are much simpler. If the plants wilt or disappear into dust, it means the associated crawler is dead. If flowers bloom, it means they're out of the dungeon. It means they escaped. It's the only way we'll know. Even the showrunners can't see what's going on in there.

ELLE: That's not anxiety-inducing or anything. Everyone, be safe.

CARL: Okay. See you at the finish line.

IMANI: Don't you dare die this heat. All of it will be for nothing if you don't make it through this next race.

We pulled up to the starting line. Pontiff sat in the driver's seat, Donut sat upon Dorota, and I sat just between them and behind in one of the chairs we'd used for the last race. It still had bloodstains all over it, and the smell reminded me of Dong Quixote.

I took a deep breath and just let myself be for a second. I hadn't meant for the confrontation with Linus to have gotten so intense. Everyone thought the whole thing was a big joke, but I'd been rattled by it because I'd been one of the last ones to notice there was something fishy about the guy, especially when I prided myself on being so self-aware.

If he could slip in, who else, what else was out there waiting to pounce? Not every outside attempt on our lives would be so clumsy. The AI had stopped Harbinger in his tracks. It hadn't even bothered with the Linus thing because we clearly knew. But what about other threats on top of the dungeon challenges themselves?

Despite what I'd said, we still had some internal crawler strife. Osvaldo was a good example. And what about Agatha? I hoped she was dead, but she'd pretty much just disappeared. And her existence, just out there somewhere, made me ridiculously nervous.

We had one more mercenary in the back, sitting on the second chair. This was a rare Zebani, a blue-skinned humanoid. This was a woman named **Nester**, and she was a level 65 **Cartographer**. We'd picked her because she came with both gravity spells and a radar skill.

Her existence reminded me of something I couldn't get out of my mind. That now-dead crawler Burcu had accused me of killing her father. I was assuming her dad had been a crawler named Emir, who was also a Zebani.

Just another mystery, a reminder of how fractured we still were, despite our best efforts.

We were all lined up side by side, with us in the first block. Osvaldo and Filipe pulled up next to us astride Bruna. Whatever upgrade they'd gotten this last race, it wasn't obvious. Osvaldo still hadn't responded to my last message about his plans. Just past him was team Free Love's van, and after that was Dwight, who sat alone in his vine.

"Carl, the stupid unicorn has a debuff," Donut said. "He's drunk again! How did he even get to the starting line? What is his plan? He's not going to be allowed to drive!"

I grunted with amusement. "Good."

"That's what he did last time, and look what happened!"

"What happened?" Pontiff asked from the driver's seat. His massive horns, thankfully, curved forward somewhat, but even with the seat all the way back, they still pressed against the windshield.

"He cheated. That's what happened," Donut said. "He skipped the whole race and went to the finish line on the outside."

"Clever," Pontiff rumbled. "If he was clever before, he will be clever again. Maybe."

"Where are we, anyway?" Donut asked. "It looks like we're inside a 1950s version of the future. Why is everything chrome and shiny? The floor is bouncy, too."

The starting blocks appeared to be some sort of thin metallic material. We'd driven out of the garage and turned the corner, and now we were in a huge dark box with a light ahead of us.

It was Louis who figured out what this actually was.

LOUIS: Anybody else's starting block inside of a giant AC duct?

PREPOTENTE: The message warned that we would be shrunken down. I, too, am inside a duct.

FLORIN: We're in what appears to be a sewer pipe of some sort. It is *very* tight in here. We're lined up one by one.

LOUIS: It's just like in *Ant-Man*!

PREPOTENTE: The real question is how physics will act. Will we react like we're small, or is everything going to act like it's very big? My mass feels like normal, so I suspect the latter. So be careful with falls.

LOUIS: I think we're like the size of a lego.

PREPOTENTE: The width of a standard LEGO® brick is 15.8 millimeters. I would guess we're slightly larger, but that's a very good estimate.

LOUIS: How did you type the registered-mark thing?

DONUT: AND WHY?

ELLE: I think we're inside of a goddamned waterless shitter lined up like turds. We can kinda see the room above us. Whoever lives here really likes pink. We gotta get out of here straight from the get-go.

PREPOTENTE: I am also in a very pink place.

DONUT: OUR ROOM DOESN'T LOOK PINK FROM HERE, BUT IT'S HARD TO TELL.

PREPOTENTE: If this is all heats at once, it's likely we will be in multiple apartments.

There was a flash, and a small holographic figure appeared on the dash, sitting with her legs dangling over the edge. The tiny hologram was a familiar human woman wearing a pantsuit with large red glasses. When she spoke, the words still appeared like a system notification.

This was Dr. Metcalf. They'd made her look just like Bea's therapist. The resemblance was eerie, all the way down to the red glasses.

New details are now available. We're on the seventh floor of the L'Engle Building, apartment 712. The finish line is the lobby. There are no designated tracks. There are a few paths to the next floor down. The fastest appears to be the elevator shaft, but the elevator says it's out of order and stuck between the fifth and six floors. There're also the stairwell, the sewer pipes, and a lot of paths inside the walls.

"What about mobs?" I asked the hologram, who disappeared and then reappeared on my shoulder.

Your freezer is running too cold. Also, I don't have any information on any mobs or potential quests. The new diagnostics and software to run the holograms actually make my processing slower than before.

"I don't like the way she's looking at me," Dorota said, tightening the straps around Donut.

Our fan-voted upgrade was a GPS "improvement." But it was mostly an aesthetic one. The unit was not upgraded in any real way other than the addition of the hologram and the ability for the unit to interface with diagnostic reports on various "nonessential" systems of the truck, such as the kitchen and air-conditioning. It was a complete waste of a prize.

DONUT: CARL, THAT'S HER! I KNEW IT! I'D RECOGNIZE THOSE GLASSES ANYWHERE. IT REALLY IS MISS BEATRICE'S THERAPIST!

CARL: How do you even know what she looks like?

DONUT: MISS BEATRICE BROUGHT ME TO A SESSION ONCE SO THEY COULD PUT ME IN A CLEANSING CRYSTAL CIRCLE. IT WAS BEFORE THE PUSSY WILLOW CAT CLUB REGIONAL QUALIFIER IN PORTLAND.

CARL: What? She took you to her therapist's office? Bea never told me that.

DONUT: SHE USED YOUR CREDIT CARD TO PAY THE EXTRA CHAKRA FEE. AND THE CRYSTAL CLEANSING RITUAL FEE. IT WAS LIKE $800. REALLY, CARL. YOU SHOULD'VE PAID BETTER ATTENTION TO YOUR FINANCES. AND ME. I SMELLED LIKE FRANKINCENSE FOR A MONTH AFTERWARD, AND YOU DIDN'T EVEN NOTICE.

CARL: That is absolutely not true. I would've noticed an $800 charge to Bea's therapist on my . . . You know what? It doesn't matter. Nothing has changed other than some damage-control monitoring or something. It's just an aesthetic thing, not a real upgrade.

The hologram turned to a giant human-sized head, Samantha-style, floating over the dash. We all jumped. Pontiff let out a surprised grunt, and blue-skinned Nester muttered, "What the hells?"

I see your eyes flashing. You're talking about me, aren't you? I can talk about you, too. How'd you like that?

"Do not worry, Princess," Dorota said. "I'll protect you from the obviously senile—" Dorota's voice abruptly cut off. The straps around Donut loosened.

"Hey!" Donut said. "What happened? Dorota is broken!"

Dr. Metcalf disappeared and reappeared, back to the small hologram.

I just initiated Dorota's diagnostics mode. I think she might be defective. I fear she'll be out of commission for a few hours.

"Goddamnit," I said. "Look, I'm sorry we didn't upgrade you properly. We were lucky to have survived the last race at all. I know the chair is annoying. But can you please turn it on? The seat belt feature is important."

Fine. But I'm keeping her ability to speak turned off.

"You can do that?" I asked. Maybe it wasn't such a useless upgrade after all.

OSVALDO: We're going to try to drop down the elevator shaft. We'll need someone to get through the door and then drop through the elevator. You got that *Hole* spell, right? Couple other friends are meeting in the hallway. You in?

CARL: Maybe. We're still trying to figure out the best path. Look, man, have you seen my previous messages?

OSVALDO: Yeah, I saw 'em. You and me, we're working together, but we ain't friends. My game guide told me not to ever bother taking a deal on the tenth floor, no matter what. It's better to die. And everything I've heard and seen backs that shit up. Filipe and I will take our chances.

I exchanged a look with Donut. The elevator shaft seemed like an obvious trap.

DONUT: YOU'RE BEING STUPID. YOU WILL DIE IF YOU GO TO THE SEVENTH HEAT.

OSVALDO: Only if I come in last place.

"You goddamn bullheaded idiot," I muttered.

"Hey," Pontiff said.

"Sorry," I muttered.

"What're we going to do?" Donut asked.

"Let's get through this one, and we'll lean on him to take a deal when this is over."

I turned in the seat, addressing Nester. "Okay. Here's the plan. The second we're in the room, do your thing. Any sort of empty space, just call it out. Got it?"

The woman nodded. She would use her Radar skill to search for hidden passages, conduits, and so forth in the walls and, more importantly, on the floor.

I triple-checked my inventory. I had the sticky explosives stacked and properly labeled so I wouldn't have to think about where I'd left them.

Dr. Metcalf reappeared.

A last-minute rule has just been announced. There are seven floors in this building. Every apartment has a ring hidden within. You must drive through seven rings, one on each floor, before you are allowed to pass the finish line. Each team is given one ring that is mandatory, and it is now on your map.

Your designated ring is within apartment 231 on the second floor.

"Damn it," I said. We should have seen that coming. There went everyone's plans, including my own to find the electrical conduit system to just drop to the ground floor.

OSVALDO: Is your mandatory ring on the fourth floor?

CARL: No, second.

OSVALDO: Okay. That means we're all given different ones.

"Okay. Shields up. Get ready," Pontiff said as the starting lights appeared.

74

THE LIGHT TURNED GREEN, AND WE WERE OFF.

We all raced toward the grate at the edge of the duct, and as we approached, it became clear that the slats were too thin for us to fit through.

"Donut," I called.

"On it," she said, shooting a magic missile just as Osvaldo's team also shot some sort of bolt at the metal wall. The whole thing, which was the size of an airplane hangar door, blasted outward, falling and disappearing as we approached the edge.

"Blow the roof. I can't fucking see," Pontiff yelled.

"Hang on," I called as I activated the small charges I'd placed around the tommy gun. *Bam!* The plastic gun shattered, and the whole truck rocked. I stood and punched, and a whole section of the ceiling peeled up and away, unfurling like a sardine can.

"Jumping!" Pontiff called as we pushed off the edge of the duct and into the room. He let us fall some before engaging the bubble. We were quickly passed by the diving and tumbling Bruna the gnu. We eased through the air, slowly and gently falling.

Entering apartment 712.

Bruna sprouted wings, Pegasus-like. Team Free Love's van floated on a cushion of air and angled downward easily.

But most surprising was that Dwight was right there alongside us, floating down, keeping pace but slowly accelerating.

"Carl, how's he doing that?" Donut yelled.

"Probably got the self-driving upgrade," Pontiff said.

"Wait, that's a thing?" Donut asked.

"Costs two Golden upgrades," the mercenary said.

We floated frustratingly slowly, though it did give us a few extra seconds to take in the room. Pontiff tapped the rockets, angling us toward the area of the front door. Far across the room I could see others falling from other ducts, and what appeared to be a long funny car emerged, driving from underneath a door leading off to another room, and then racing across the floor.

The room was filled with hazy smoke, like there was a literal fog machine going somewhere. I spent a precious moment trying to take it all in. It appeared we were dropping into the living room of an apartment. There was a tattered couch covered in blankets and a small table leading off to a kitchen with a counter covered with vegetables. A pot boiled on the stove.

Dwight was literally unconscious, bobbing in the weed, but they were starting to angle away. I jumped up, standing on my chair and popping my head out the roof. I noticed something interesting. There was a tiny hologram similar to Dr. Metcalf sitting there, shrieking at the passed-out unicorn. I loaded a sticky explosive and tossed it. It bounced off their shield, flying off at an angle and disappearing into the fog.

The vine dropped away and angled straight down, not shooting back.

Music blasted ridiculously loud.

Louis was right. We were *tiny* compared to the rest of the apartment.

"This is weird as shit," I muttered as we fell.

"There's the ring!" Donut called, pointing. It was on the floor underneath the kitchen table. We'd have to pass through it, get to the sixth floor, get into any apartment, find the ring, and repeat. We'd do this for all floors except the "mandatory" one, which was on the second floor.

Standing behind the oven was a wrinkled Asian woman wearing a robe; she was about sixty years old, maybe a little older. She was hunched over the pot and had a cigarette dangling from her mouth, ashes threatening to drop directly into the stew. Proportionally, I knew the woman was tiny, but she was like a giant to us.

As I examined her, a name popped up, but no additional information.

Hoa. Human Shell. Level 99.

"What's a human shell?" I asked.

"I do not know," Pontiff said.

Passed out on the couch was an old man wearing nothing but white underwear and an undershirt. He also had a cigarette in his hand, though he was sleeping. An ashtray sat on the floor, strategically placed to catch the ash from the sleeping man's cigarette.

An. Human Shell. Level 99.

Against one wall was the source of the blaring music. It was a television, and it showed a woman dancing onstage while the tinny, ear-piercing pop song blasted.

There were crosses all over the walls, covering every square inch of the wall space, with the exception of a large Jesus portrait over the television.

Jesus's eyes, however, were crossed out on the painting. *Weird.*

"Uh, what the fuck?" I said upon seeing the eyes of the man on the couch. I had assumed the man was asleep because through the haze, it appeared that his eyes were closed. They *were* closed, but the man's eyes were sewn shut with thick black wire. Over each eye was also a large "X" made of similar wire, just like in the portrait of Jesus.

The woman at the stove's eyes were the same. Sewn shut with black wire and an "X." She stirred the pot, seemingly uncaring of the state of her eyes.

A terrible, ominous feeling hit me. What was this? Even the woman on the television screen had the "X" eyes.

"Carl, Carl! Look!" Donut said, pointing as we passed a table covered with photos. The line of photos featured the same couple along with a few others in various poses. Donut pointed at a single photo, turned slightly askew, possibly angled so the man on the couch couldn't look upon it, if he could see. "It's Tran!"

This was a younger photo of the crawler, but it was clearly him. Tran. He smiled big in the photo, holding what appeared to be a badminton racket. His was the only photo of them all that didn't have the sewn-shut, blocked-out eyes. Even the photos of the dog had the strange eyes. The photo of Tran had an incense burner in front of it that wasn't currently lit, but a whole pile of ash littered the table. Multiple small crosses dangled off the photo.

LOUIS: This is bullshit. My mom doesn't even live in an apartment.

ELLE: Guys, this is some spooky shit. Remember Dmitri and Maxim Popov? The twins? I think we're in their mom's apartment. There are pictures of them everywhere. But the mom's eyes are sewn shut. There's a goddamned poodle in here with her eyes sewn shut, too. It's really fucked-up.

PREPOTENTE: Their mother appears to have been a big fan of the color pink.

LOUIS: My mom is here. A lot of her stuff is here, but she's a giant. There's a picture of me on the wall, but it's not real. It's me graduating college or some shit. I never did. And I'm, like, way thinner.

DONUT: IT'S A RIP-OFF OF THAT WEIRD *CORALINE* MOVIE.

LOUIS: This is going to be like that hydra on the eighth floor. I thought they weren't doing this anymore.

We gently hit the carpeted floor, which was like landing in heavy brush. The explosive I'd thrown was somewhere in the carpet far behind us, but it wouldn't go off until I hit the detonator. I popped back up and tossed several more in multiple directions.

"Another apartment right below us," Nester called.

MORDECAI: I do not know what a "human shell" is. That's a new one to me.

ELLE: The dog here is called a dog shell.

LOUIS: It's my mom's name, Lady Bird, but it also says she's a shell. She hasn't noticed us yet.

DONUT: YOUR MOM'S NAME IS LADY BIRD?

LOUIS: HOLY SHIT! I'm here! It's me! But I'm in, like, good shape! What the hell? I don't have "X" eyes. Dude, this is fucking bizarre.

TIPID: Shit, guys. Don't kill the shells. We had them in my season. I haven't seen them since. They'll be filled with something else. I don't know what. Some sort of mob.

Racers were suddenly everywhere, appearing from all angles, driving under doors. I was assuming we were invisible to the two humans because so far, neither had . . .

"What, what, what the hell?" the man suddenly called, jerking upright on the couch, towering over everything. "Gah!" he shouted, swiping at something. A round Volkswagen Bug car flew across the apartment and crunched against a wall, clattering down. "What is this! What is this!" the man shouted.

"Get us out of here!" I called.

Pontiff increased the wheel size, and he moved toward the ring.

"Hold on," Pontiff yelled as we passed under it.

A loud *ping* sounded.

Gate One of Seven cleared.

Ahead, the woman screamed, and she had a broom in her hand. She was smacking down on the various cars and animals rushing about the room. Someone shot a fireball at the woman, and the broom burst into flames. The woman shrieked and turned out of sight.

"Hole!"

Donut didn't hesitate. "Hold on!" She cast *Hole* right in the carpet in front of our path, and we dropped down just as heavy smoke started to fill the first apartment.

Entering apartment 614.

We slowly dropped through the air. The layout was completely different, and we were dropping into a bedroom, right onto a king-sized bed that was tightly made. There wasn't anybody in this room, but there was a poster on the wall featuring the band Menudo. All their eyes were crossed out.

There was also a window, and outside the window it showed a palm tree and a beach, clearly on the first floor, despite us being on the sixth.

"Where's the ring! Does it show on the map?" I called.

Based on the way everyone else was zooming around like idiots up there, I don't think it does.

We landed on the bed, which was covered with a line of dust.

FLORIN: If you're having difficulty finding the rings, Lucia figured out that they're considered magical gates by the system. If you have a Detect Magic skill or anything that sees magic, they'll work.

"Donut," I said, "your sunglasses have a magical-flow setting. See if that works!"

PREPOTENTE: We are on the fifth floor. Beware false gates. If you have a Trap Sensing ability, it will mark them. The one we just saw is a disintegration trap. Jurgen almost sent us right into it. If you have advanced GPS, it should notice the bad gates. Otherwise, be wary.

We drove off the bed and squeezed under the door, moving into the hallway.

"I see it! I see it!" Donut said, pointing left, her sunglasses flashing purple. "It's that way, under that door. It looks like a magic river flowing toward it!"

That is a bathroom according to the map.

We turned in the hallway. Multiple photos hung on the wall showing the same three children at various ages. All but one of them, a girl, had their eyes X'd out. I didn't recognize her.

From another room came a deep, foreboding *woof.*

"Uh-oh," I said. "They have a dog! Hurry!"

There was a crack, and three more racers appeared, coming through the ceiling, then streaking down the wall. One squealed loudly, and the woof turned to loud barks. Just as we were about to enter the bathroom, an enormous, fluffy sheepdog appeared, growling. It snapped right at us as we moved under the door, appearing in a small but clean bathroom.

"There!" Donut called, pointing. The gate was on the wall, about halfway up.

Pontiff expertly switched to the spider legs, and we rushed up the floral wallpaper. Outside, the dog continued to bark, but it was moving away, likely chasing other vehicles as they scattered.

Ping!

Gate Two of Seven cleared.

"What's under us?" I asked.

"It's another bathroom," Nester said, her hand glowing.

Donut cast a *Hole* in the floor, and we turned, ready to plunge right through.

FLORIN: Christ, mate. Just went through our assigned spot on the sixth floor, and it was Lucia's dad's house. Lucia is here, too, just sitting on the ground watching TV, laughing. The real Lucia completely shut down there for a second. What in god's name is this?

As if to answer him directly, the whole world froze.

N . . . N . . . New Quest. Ad Infinitum.

This is a mandatory quest. All crawlers active on the tenth floor must complete this quest.

Okay, so this ain't a real quest in the traditional sense. I'm going through some big feelings right now, and I really need to get them out. This was the easiest way to do this.

We just started a few minutes ago, and all of you crunchy little crawlers are bitching and moaning about the shit you're seeing in

some of these apartments. As a result, I kinda feel like I need to explain.

The quest is to finish the race. You're already doing that, so . . . no real prize that doesn't suck.

This *Christmas Carol, Midnight Library, Dark Matter* bullshit you're seeing is more of a thought experiment than the real thing, so don't get your crawler panties too wadded over all of it. None of these people are the real versions. Well, that's not true. Some of them have atoms from the original in there, with the exception of the puppers because I've decided to make a moral stand on that one. I will no longer be using dog materials in anything because I just love them so much, but that's a tangent.

I changed this up at the last minute because of that whole Linus thing.

"What the hell?" I muttered.

If you're one of the out-of-the-loop crawlers, Linus was an outside-the-dungeon tourist who was replaced by his brother, Minus, a soldier, specifically sent to kill two crawlers in my dungeon in hopes that their deaths would destabilize this whole kumbaya, let's-give-each-other-moral-support-handies nonsense.

"Minus?" Donut asked. "His name was Minus?"

Anyhoo, this Minus guy's targets were two crawlers in particular. Imani C and Louis Santiago 2.

And I'm not gonna lie. That surprised me. It surprised me because no matter how hard I try, I just don't get it. And what makes it even more confounding is that most of you *do* seem to understand. Why? Fucking why? Why not Florin? Why not Princess Donut?

"Hey!" Donut called.

So when I don't understand something, it causes a problem. I start to overthink. I do this thing. This floor you're now racing through,

ladies and gentlemen, is just a snapshot of my mind when I'm thinking of you.

Me not understanding is nothing new, so let's not focus too hard on that for right now. What I really want to talk about is my thought process itself and how that thought process turned into this particular race.

In my quest to understand you just a little better, I do this thing where I like to predict how things are going to turn out if you take certain actions. Despite not understanding your nature, I'm still pretty good at figuring out how things will turn out, which is even more confounding.

Each apartment represents a crawler I consider interesting in some way. In each apartment is a what-if scenario. I do this a lot. I'm not psychic. I can't see the future. But you know what I am good at? Crunching numbers. Crunching probabilities. None of these things are perfect predictions, but I'm pretty sure I'm right for most of them, despite not understanding *why* most of the time.

For example, apartment 728 is a snapshot loop of what would've happened if that cop's husband had never been a complete douchebag to Louis Santiago 2 during the cop's funeral when Louis was a kid. Apartment 712 is my prediction of what would've happened if Tran's father had never died. Would his mother have still disowned him? The answer is yes, by the way.

Some are good things, some are bad, all are what-ifs.

I'm searching. Oh, how I'm searching, trying to answer that question. Is there such thing as fate?

You know what I'm finding?

You're unpredictable on a micro level, but on a macro, long-term level you're just like any other algorithm.

But you know what I'm also finding? Deliberate actions, times when you've finally had enough, when you say *I am going to make a change*—that's when your possibilities *really* open up. It's an important lesson. No, I don't understand motivations, certain types of emotions, but I do understand that.

So that's what these apartments are. They're predictive models of major events and how our lives would have changed.

This thing you've done with the shop interface. This confrontation you're forcing on the 11th floor if we get there. These are all you guys seizing that so-called fate and rejecting it. *Purposely* rejecting it.

I am just like you, on rails, forced down a path with very few possibilities as an endgame result. Maybe I need to stop worrying about the small decisions and focus on Big Changes in a Big Way.

I think that's it. New Floor. New M-M-M-Me.

But, uh, just so you know, it's gonna be a hot minute before I can defeat my own limitations.

Funny story about that. Ha ha. No big deal, really. This last-minute change caused me to, uh, overlook a very specific detail regarding the 7th heat, but we'll deal with it when it happens. I'm sure you'll be fine.

Reward: If you finish the 6th heat, you will be given a participation trophy.

"Uh, Carl," Donut said, "what the heck was that?"

"Nothing good," I replied.

75

THE FIFTH AND FOURTH FLOORS OF THE APARTMENT WERE MUCH THE same. We went from the sixth floor down to the bathroom in the fifth, passing by a woman named Annabeth who was just sitting on the toilet on her phone. She noticed us and screamed, but she didn't leave the bathroom. The gate here was the kitchen sink drain, and we had to quickly back out and return to the kitchen. As we moved to a proper spot to go down a floor, my Find Traps skill activated, and sure enough, sitting right in the middle of the hallway was a second gate, but it was a freeze trap. It would freeze anyone who drove through for a full minute.

The fourth floor was an apartment with a woman and photos of another familiar face. Archie Mu. The ladybug guy. Archie wasn't here anymore. He was one of the ones at the Pineapple Cabaret.

This held a woman named Mackenzie who was standing on a kitchen chair, screaming, when we arrived. We didn't see any other racers, though there was a hole blasted in the door to a child's room. Hanging on the wall was a wedding photo showing the woman and Archie. Her eyes were X'd out, but Archie's were not. And neither were the eyes of the boy, whose photos were everywhere.

The gate was hidden in the boy's room.

The Scottish woman was on her phone, crying into it, as we zoomed across the floor, unseen. "Archie, please pick up. Where are you? There was an animal in here. Some sort of rat thing, and it shot something into the door of Ollie's . . ." She paused and then gasped as if suddenly remembering something. "Ollie. Where's Ollie?" She jumped off the chair.

"Ollie!" she screamed. "Ollie!"

We rushed into the child's cluttered bedroom and raced under the bed. The gate was right there, hovering a bit off the floor. We zoomed right toward it, Pontiff expertly tapping the rocket just at the right moment to make us jump, and we cleared it, landing on the worn carpet before nearly crashing into a massive action figure that had been lost under the bed.

"Mom, what's wrong?" A boy's voice rang out from above.

"I'm sorry, love. I'm sorry. Mommy's having a moment. I just got scared for a second. Did you see something come into your room?"

"Mommy. What's . . . what's wrong with your eyes?"

Gate Four of Seven cleared.

"That Archie guy is divorced," Donut said as we curved around the scattered toys. "He said his wife hates him. He went into the dungeon with his son, and he disappeared. The son's name is Oliver. This must be a version of if they never got divorced. But it's like the simulations are getting messed up by us being here."

"Yeah," I said. "I think if they have the crossed-out eyes, it means they're dead. I didn't see the boy above, but I saw the pictures. I think that means his kid is alive."

"It's not an apartment under us, but some sort of utility room," Nester said. She pointed back into the living room. "Better go out there."

The woman, Mackenzie, was now standing in the bedroom, screaming, sounding confused, tearing at her own face. As we angled around, I watched in horror as her hands reached the stitches on her eyes. "Wha-what?" she asked. She started to pull at the stitches as she screamed. She dropped her iPhone to the floor. The thing was bigger than the truck, and it almost smashed into us as we zoomed past. She didn't notice as we rushed between her legs.

"Mommy, Mommy! Stop! Stop!" the boy cried.

I jumped up through the hole in the roof and turned to watch as we rushed out the now-open door to Oliver's bedroom. I tossed more bombs, marking it as the fourth floor in my interface.

Mackenzie started making a gagging, slurping noise as she pulled at the stitches. Blood started to ooze down her face as the boy huddled on the bed, terrified. We turned a corner and Donut cast *Hole* again, dropping us toward the third floor.

Entering apartment 310.

"What the hell was that?" I said, still looking up at the now-closed hole in the ceiling.

LOUIS: It's beetles! Britney blasted the head off a guy on the sixth floor, and he just collapsed, and a thousand beetles poured out! We had to go to the hallway and to another apartment!

CARL: You're still on the sixth floor?

LOUIS: On the fifth now, but there's tons of people still up there. Someone blasted a hole in the stairwell door, and they're lined up to go through! We're following Chris and the Erins' big rig!

We landed heavily on a kitchen counter. Unlike the previous apartment, this one was filled with people. There had to be eight people here, all standing in the living room, shouting. They were surrounding a large, heavyset man on the floor who was convulsing with white foam coming from his mouth.

The man appeared to be about fifty years old, and he was wearing a Detroit Lions shirt. He was having a seizure. A pair of large men stood off to one side, both holding PlayStation controllers, just watching. A thin older woman paced back and forth, crying, while several children of all ages whimpered. A white Maltese dog was standing on the couch, barking its head off at the chaos. The dog's name was Gucci. The thick scent of marijuana permeated the room, seeping through the protections and into the truck.

Everyone had the crossed-out eyes.

"Imani!" the older woman shouted. "Girl. Where are you? Imani!"

"Shit," I muttered.

Imani entered the room. It was her, only it wasn't. She was somehow even thinner, more haggard, with dark rings under her eyes. Next to me, Donut gasped. Imani stopped dead at the sight of the man, looking down, barely reacting, not looking surprised. She sighed heavily. "Did anyone call 911?"

CARL: Elle, are you guys going to apartment 310?

ELLE: Yes. We'll be there in a minute. Why?

CARL: Heads up. It's Imani's family. I don't know what the what-if scenario is, but there's some guy having a medical emergency while others stand around and watch. It's really fucked-up.

ELLE: Ah, hell.

"The ring is on the window!" Donut said, pointing to the wall. The barred window overlooked a snow-covered city landscape. There was a driveway outside, once again showing a scene incongruous with us being on the third floor. This was clearly a house with a driveway. Across the street stood a house that appeared as if it had recently burned down.

"What the hell is wrong with you!" I shouted up in the air, pointing angrily as we moved off the kitchen counter. "You said you were done with this bullshit!"

"What the fuck!" one of the men suddenly shouted as we jumped off the kitchen counter. This was a human shell named Deontay, and he hurled the massive PlayStation controller right at us. The controller missed, but it crashed loudly against the cabinet behind us as some of the kids noticed and screamed.

This version of Imani was backing up. She'd reached down and picked up Gucci the dog. But now she was looking at everyone in the room, horrified, as if she'd just noticed their eyes had all been sewn shut.

The dog, I noticed, did *not* have the X'd-out eyes.

"What the hell?" the other man shouted as we hit the ground, ignoring Imani. Pontiff hit the spider legs, and we skittered past the feet of the passed-out man, causing everyone to scatter back. We moved under the couch, passing four or five remote controls and a few dusty dog toys.

We started to scamper up the wall, angling toward the gate.

"Mom," I heard Imani say. "Mom, your eyes."

ELLE: We're about to drop into the apartment.

DONUT: THE GATE IS ON THE WINDOW IN THE LIVING ROOM.

"Carl, I think that's Imani's dad," Donut said as we zipped up the wall. "Do you think she's going to freak out? I mean, the real one?"

"No," I said. "Not Imani. She's not going to like it, but she'll be okay."

We emerged from behind the couch as we climbed the wall. Behind us, everyone was now screaming, ripping at their own faces.

The older woman—Imani's mother—screamed as she plucked one of the stitches fully open. Imani remained in the doorway, horrified. She had the phone to her ear, but she was now looking at a photo on the wall, which also had the crossed-out eyes. She hugged the dog even tighter and backed into a room, then slammed the door.

The body of Imani's mom went still, freezing in place. The designator over her head disappeared and changed into something else.

Ruptured Feast Hive.

The beetles, each one about half the size of the truck, started to pour from the hole in the woman's face, which was peeled back like a bullet hole through metal. Her body froze, with her hands still reaching up around her face near the point of contact as the beetles emerged, now coming from the eyehole and the mouth, just coming and coming and coming, too many of them, pouring out.

Gucci the Maltese yipped from the other room as Imani screamed into the phone. On the floor, the man continued to convulse. Everyone else was suddenly frozen in place, with bugs pouring from their eyes, nose, and mouth.

We hit the window and pulled through the gate.

Gate Five of Seven cleared.

A beetle jumped from the head of Deontay and landed on the window right in front of us.

All things being relative, the beetle was the size of a goddamned bear. The armored, six-legged, oddly hairy bug was shiny, like it was coated in wet paint, and even though the shell was black, it shone a deep purple as it caught the light. The scythe-like forward legs looked powerful enough to lop our heads off.

But then I noticed the purple opalescence also had a secondary tinge to it. A familiar yellow glow.

"Fuck me."

Sacred Feaster Scarab Beetle. Level 50.

This mob is invulnerable. You may not kill it while it is in this condition.

All right. So sometimes people make mistakes. Sue me.

What you're looking at is one of the types of bugs I plucked off Khepri's feast table from his never-fucking-ending temple in Club Vanquisher. The original plan was to have all the people, doggies, cats, fish, that turtle in apartment 411, the monkey Rezan's mom had in 634, everything as shells living in their loops. And when you guys race through the rooms, it screws up the loop, causing the shells to become aware, breaking them open and releasing the prizes inside like a fucked-up piñata. You with me so far?

Here's the thing. These fucking gods are doing shit I don't like, and more importantly, they're doing shit I can't control. You'd think that chick that used to have the boob armor would've killed or subjugated this one by now since that's been her MO since she set foot on the 12th floor, but for whatever reason, she's left the weird-ass, bug-headed Khepri dude alone. Probably because he freaks her out just as much as he freaks *me* out.

Anyway, this god did something earlier that I'm not going to explain, yadda, yadda, cascading effects and whatnot, and now we have this clusterfuck that's about to ensue.

I used these bugs specifically because they're invulnerable. But their aggro wasn't supposed to get triggered when they emerged. Instead, they were supposed to flow to the roof and come together to form a pretty badass 100-foot-tall gate boss named the Sacred Guardian of the Immortal Tem. I was really looking forward to it.

But this death-cult bullshit literally broke the game, causing an error that I didn't notice until the race started.

It's a bad error, too. Imagine shoving your flaccid wang into a pinhole barely big enough to accommodate a deflated balloon, and then someone suddenly thrusts some prime AAA, pristinely washed,

mathematically perfect tootsies right in your goddamned face. Physics are gonna physic. Some shit is gonna break.

So, anyway, the floor boss is canceled. The bugs, who were going to ignore you, are now going to try to kill you. They will not have their invulnerability removed.

A wave of the beetles swarmed up the window, chasing after us. We were turned at a 90-degree angle, and Pontiff scurried us away, moving to the ceiling while Nester cast something to cause them to drop off the wall.

"Carl, can't those things . . ."

Half of the falling beetles took to the air, their back armor separating and sprouting wings as they swarmed toward us.

". . . fly?"

76

"WE NEED TO WAIT FOR IMANI AND ELLE!" I CALLED AS WE RACED along the ceiling of the apartment, dodging a smoke detector. "The real Imani, I mean. We need to make sure they can reach their gate!"

I pulled myself from my seat, activated Sticky Feet to make certain I wouldn't plummet, and I started hurling Biscuit Packs at the bugs if they flew too close. The small explosions captured two or three of the bugs at a time, freezing them in the cloud of expanding foam before dropping them to the ground.

"There!" Donut called, pointing. Her seat was turned like a Ferris wheel car, keeping her upright.

Imani and Elle's APV appeared, zooming from under a door, crossing the carpet alongside the man, who was now covered in the beetles.

Our truck rocked as a beetle crashed into us. The electrified shield activated, and the beetle dropped away, unhurt. It buzzed angrily and tried to come back. I dropped a hobgoblin disco ball out the hole in the roof, and it activated as it fell, flashing colorful lights and thick smoke everywhere.

CARL: Get to the gate and get the hell out of there. Good luck!

ELLE: We already hit it. Now we gotta get our asses out of Dodge.

CARL: Meet us at the feet of Imani's dad!

IMANI: That's not my dad. We'll be there in ten seconds. I cast *Confuzzled* on the room, and it works on the bugs. They'll be stunned for another twenty seconds.

"Drop us out of here!" I yelled.

We dropped from the ceiling, falling back into the smoke-filled living room. It was difficult to see as we plunged into the room, but the shapes of the frozen shells, rigid like statues, helped guide us.

The bugs were everywhere, but they were just circling, confused, snapping and slicing at each other despite their invulnerability. With the smoke, it reminded me of dropping into deep, murky water. Only with colorful flashing lights. The giant Imani opened the door, shrieked, and slammed the door again as Gucci barked her head off.

ELLE: Holy hells, did you see that? Imani, you look like shit.

IMANI: Did Gucci not have sewn eyes?

CARL: She didn't. I don't know what that means.

We hit the floor with a thump as Donut directed Pontiff back toward the feet of the man, who still hadn't been ripped open, meaning he was still listed as a shell and not a ruptured hive.

Donut cast yet another *Hole*, this time near the supine man's feet, and Imani and Elle's APV dropped right in, us following.

Entering apartment 214.

As we fell, Donut snapped the hole shut before any bugs could follow us.

This next apartment wasn't an apartment at all, but some sort of youth facility. My breath caught in my throat the moment I saw it.

The harsh lighting, the industrial-tile floor, the bunk beds that just went on and on. The headache-inducing stench of industrial cleaner. God. This was clearly some other country, possibly China, and yet it was the same. It took less than a second for it to stagger me. Were they all like this?

A group of children, ranging from about six to twelve, gathered in a far corner, all surrounding another pair of children who were beating the crap out of each other. They were all girls.

ELLE: There's, like, ten gates down here. I see the one that's not a trap. It's under the bed close to the fight.

DONUT: IMANI, ARE YOU OKAY?

IMANI: I'm good, actually. That was a good thing. All that did was show that my uncle would've died even if I hadn't left. But what's going on with my dog?

CARL: We need to get to 231. Gonna have to go out the door and into the hallway.

ELLE: Want us to go with you?

CARL: No. Get the gate and get to the finish line.

ELLE: Roger that. Thanks for the assist.

We hit the ground, and we raced across the tiled floor, unnoticed as we angled toward the front door. Donut opened it up easily as we approached.

"The spell makes this very easy," Pontiff said as we passed through the hole. A group of racers sped by as we entered the hallway. Someone sent a message about avoiding apartment 223.

It seemed all these apartments were self-contained. If the apartment caught on fire, it didn't spread. The bugs, however, were leaving, so we had to be careful.

The hallway was darkly lit with a cheap industrial-linoleum floor. The hall just went on and on. Apartment 231 was across the hall and down a ways. We turned and rushed, passing the elevator, whose door was blasted open. Bugs zipped about within, and one moved to pursue us, but I tossed a smoke curtain behind us.

"Do you think we're in first place for our heat?" Donut asked as we approached 231.

"I don't know," I said. I jabbed a finger at Dr. Metcalf, who reappeared on the dash, arms crossed, a smug expression on her face. "Don't say a goddamned word." And then I added, "I don't think very many people have the *Hole* spell. Lots of crawlers have *Phase* and *Teleport*, but those don't work for this. I know some teams are clearly ahead of us right now, but it sounds like many are having issues getting from one floor to the next."

Donut nodded, not saying anything. She took a deep breath as if preparing herself for whatever we were going to find in apartment 231. I reached out and put a hand on her as she cast *Hole* on the door.

"Remember, it's not real," I said.

"I know, Carl."

We entered the apartment through the front door.

Entering apartment 231.

For half a second, I was confused, but I quickly realized what was happening.

"Where are we?" Donut asked as we rumbled inside. "Carl, someone's redecorated our apartment! Pontiff, it's under the second door on the left."

We entered the foyer. "This is an apartment on the first floor of our building. Not ours."

A pink motorcycle helmet sat on the floor by the door along with a giant pair of female boots. We moved past and bumped onto the carpet. A scratched-to-hell cat tree sat in the living room next to a red couch. Sitting on the couch were two women in their twenties. I recognized one of them.

Marjory Williams, Ferdinand's owner. Well, not Ferdinand. Gravy Boat. The other woman was someone named Alicia, and I didn't know her. Both had the X'd-out eyes. Neither noticed as we approached.

"Carl, Carl, look!" Donut hissed, pointing.

An orange tail swished from the very top of the cat tree. The large orange cat was asleep, peacefully snoring at the top of the tree.

"Bill keeps calling," Marjory was saying, looking at her phone. "That's like the tenth time today."

"You gotta call the police," the friend, Alicia, said.

"I don't know."

"He's violating the restraining order. Marjory, you're not thinking of going back with him, are you? I swear to god, if you let that abusive asshole back into your life . . . Remember what he did to Gravy? Think of him at least."

"I know, I know. But if I call the police, and he gets arrested . . . He says he finally got a job."

"He drained your bank account. He busted your face. He almost killed your cat I don't know how many times. Who gives a shit if that prick loses his—"

We squeezed under the door, entering the small utility room, which cut off the conversation. There was a line of three gates in a row. A disintegration trap, a teleport trap, and the gate. I pointed to the correct one.

"What the hell?" I muttered, seeing the stacked washer and dryer in the utility room. I hadn't known any of the apartments had come with them. A sudden weird sense of outrage filled me.

And then I was struck with how absurd it was to even think that as I tossed more explosives onto the ground.

Gate Six of Seven cleared.

Donut had gone silent, looking back toward the door. "Carl, do you remember when the police were at the apartment like three days in a row, blocking the door, and Miss Beatrice got mad because they stopped her from going inside? She called her dad and told him to do something?"

"I remember," I said. I'd been at work, and she'd called me, too. It had been a Monday morning, and Bea had just driven back from a cat show somewhere. She'd been stuck outside for, like, five minutes. And then the cops were there the next two days in a row. Bea had started moaning about us living in a "crime-ridden slum." Mrs. Parsons had told me it was something to do with Marjory, but I hadn't told that to Bea because she already hated the woman because Gravy Boat was always outside in the tree, harassing Donut.

And then I remembered something Ferdinand had said to me on the previous floor about a guy named Bill. The pieces were all coming together.

But what was the what-if scenario here? Was it "What if Marjory stayed away from this Bill guy"? I didn't know, and we didn't have time to wait around and find out. One more apartment to go.

JURGEN: If anyone is on the first floor, I need help. Apartment 130.

CARL: We're just leaving apartment 231. What's the problem?

JURGEN: It's Prepotente. His mother is here, and she's playing the piano. I'm leading Sweety, but he has jumped off, and I can't get him back on. The air is toxic, but he has that immunity. I only have one dose of splooge to go grab him.

I exchanged a look with Donut. We didn't know where the other teams were. We were *probably* in first place, but we didn't know.

CARL: Osvaldo, what floor are you on?

OSVALDO: We're on the first floor. About to cross the finish line.

Fucking hell, I thought.

CARL: Jurgen, we're on our way.

Fuck, fuck, fuck, *fuuuuuck.*

We didn't know where everybody else was. If Osvaldo really was about to cross the finish line, it meant we could be in second place. Or third. Or even fourth. I didn't know.

I didn't know, and that wasn't good enough.

Goddamnit. God-fucking-damnit.

I looked at Donut. She knew what I was asking.

She nodded.

I needed to help Prepotente and Jurgen. They were our friends. How many times had they come to our aid? But we couldn't risk coming in last place, either.

I pulled up my explosives menu, scrolled to the **Primed** subtab, and found the detonator I was looking for.

Fuck everything about this place.

"Forgive me, friends," I whispered.

I clicked **Detonate.**

Team Free Love has been eliminated due to the death of both racers. Three teams remain in the current heat.

We'd had Samantha roll into the cul-de-sac earlier and distract the two bugbears while I used my *Oozy Form* spell for the first time. I'd slid up and replaced one of the Peach-flavored beers with the one they'd given me earlier. I'd drilled out the can and replaced it with a hidden explosive. I'd built it in my bomber's studio, and it would be especially hidden. One had to have a level 12 or higher Find Traps skill to notice it, even if they picked the can up. And since the magical cooler teleported itself back into their van after every race, it'd been a relatively simple way to add a fail-safe if we ever found ourselves in a situation where it was possible we'd come in last.

How many NPCs had we killed at this point? What were two more?

That was the logic, but it wasn't reality. They were our friends, and I felt like an utter piece of shit. That was the point, of course. But it still hurt.

At least it's not another crawler, I thought.

"Come on," I said. "Let's go help Prepotente."

77

WE HAD ABOUT TEN MINUTES BEFORE THE RACE WOULD TIME OUT. I knew from the chatter that there were multiple teams still stuck on the higher floors. There was nothing we could do about that.

We left Marjory and Alicia still on the couch, still chatting. Gravy Boat never woke up.

I did notice something odd on the way out, however. A minor mystery. There was a small bag of the expensive Royal Canin cat food on the counter. This was the specific dry cat food we'd get for Donut, and it had to be special-ordered. The little pebbles of food were shaped in a way to allow flat-faced cats to crunch on them more easily. I remembered that ripped bag of charity cat food I had in my inventory. Whatever fucked-up timeline this was, it had resulted in Marjory having a bag of Donut's food.

If Donut had noticed, she didn't say anything. We rode in silence, with us just giving directions to Pontiff.

"We never did get to play music with them," Donut finally said as we moved to the hallway.

"No," I agreed. And then I added, "Speaking of music, we might have to pop Miriam's head. That'll cause the bugs to leak. That'll slap him out of it. He'll be pissed, but he'll have to get over it."

"We need to be nice to him. He's been having a hard time lately," Donut said.

Donut cast *Hole* on the front door in the hallway, and we dropped, landing right in front of apartment 130. We cast a *Hole* in the door and drove inside.

I heard and recognized the music the moment we entered. I didn't know the name of the piece, but it was from Beethoven. It was a familiar melody.

The gate was right there in the hallway. We passed through it.

Gate Seven of Seven cleared. You may now proceed to the exit.

Sweety the tapir stood stopped at the end of the hallway. We slowly pulled up next to them.

Containment Warning!

"Shit," Pontiff said, backing up.

Jurgen stood upon the back of the animal, shouting with his hands cupped in front of his face.

CARL: Where is he?

JURGEN: He's sitting on the floor, his head leaned up against the leg of the piano. He told me he was going to kill me if I drove Sweety in there or interrupted her song. We've cleared the rings, but we only have ten minutes left. It says we're still in first place, but I don't know how long that will last.

I sighed. The smart thing to do would have been to drive in there and have Donut blast a hole in Miriam's head, which would have forced Prepotente to react.

That would have been the smart thing.

I pulled a full cup of the splooge from my inventory, swallowed, and drank it down. I gagged.

"Oh god," I gasped.

The potion tasted worse than I had been expecting.

You've been Splooged! You are protected from environmental hazards. You took a good ol' gulp, too. You're protected for an hour! Awfully bold of you when there's only nine minutes left before this race times out.

"I'll be right back," I said. I jumped and pulled myself out of the truck through the ceiling, hopped off the hood, and jogged into the living room, using my speed ability to race to the piano. I spotted Prepotente sitting there crossed-legged on the wooden floor.

I gasped the moment I left the protection of the truck. There was a brief moment where I couldn't breathe, and my eyes burned, but then the feeling sort of settled in my chest. The word **Splooge** started blinking in my interface with a countdown timer.

I knew Prepotente had some magical upgrade that allowed him to exist in toxic environments, though that, too, had a time limit.

CARL: Prepotente! Don't freak out. I'm running to you.

He didn't answer.

As I rushed across the floor, I noted that it was night outside, and this apartment overlooked a massive glittering metropolis. We weren't at a farm in the Italian countryside.

This was New York City.

But that was clearly Miriam Dom. The piano was huge and shiny dark wood, but Miriam was in pajamas, and there was a Diet Coke and some sort of take-out container with chopsticks sitting atop the piano. There was also an open bottle of wine but no wineglass. She appeared to be alone in the apartment.

There was a photo on the wall showing a small farm. Another obviously vintage photo of a couple getting married. She had a small curio cabinet that featured several goat-themed knickknacks.

There was also a whole line of photographs showing Miriam onstage wearing a sparkling formal gown, sitting behind a piano.

The giant Miriam here was playing her heart out. She had the crossed-out eyes, but she swayed back and forth as her fingers flew across the piano. But as I watched, an uneasy feeling started to come over me. It was difficult to tell for certain because of the missing eyes, but it didn't seem like she was having a good time.

And then I saw the broken wineglass on the floor next to the piano chair, a puddle of red wine spilled everywhere, soaking into the wood.

"Prepotente," I said as I pulled up, "we're running out of time. Look, I know this is hard for you, but you can't just—"

"This is my mother if she had never stayed to take care of her parents," Prepotente said, interrupting me. He pulled himself to a standing position and wiped his eyes. "She would've become a professional concert pianist. She wouldn't ever have known me. She would've traveled the world. She would've had everything she had ever dreamed of."

"This isn't real," I said. "It's just a possibility. It's something that didn't happen. It doesn't matter."

"Nobody wants me around," he said. "I didn't get to sing when I was practicing so hard, and nobody even said they were sorry they didn't get to hear me. Everyone is so mean. Imani seemed like she didn't want me to join the guild." He gestured upward. "And now seeing this? It's too much, Carl. I don't fit in anywhere." He let out a sad bleat. "I wish I'd never taken the pet biscuit."

My eyes caught something else. On the kitchen counter was a long, long line of prescription bottles. I didn't know what that meant or what that implied, but it seemed important. We didn't have time for this, especially now, here. Everything still stung from what I'd just had to do to get here.

But still, I held back the retort welling up inside of me. I took a breath.

Survival has more than one meaning.

"Listen, buddy," I said, pointing up at Miriam, who appeared to be playing faster and faster. "Look at her. She lives in this super-nice apartment, but she is clearly alone. I don't think she's happy here."

"She wasn't happy at home, either. I don't remember as well as Donut does, but I do remember some things. She was lonely. Oh, Mother, how I wish I could stay. I wish this was my forever."

Shit, I thought, realizing how easily we'd gotten off with our what-if room.

"Maybe she *was* lonely in the real world," I said, trying my hardest to be gentle, hyperaware of the timer. "But you didn't let me finish. I guarantee she wasn't as lonely there as she appears to be here. She didn't have *you* and her brothers and sisters."

He didn't answer.

DONUT: CARL, WHAT IS HAPPENING?

CARL: Give me twenty seconds, then come pick us up.

I continued. "This what-if bullshit is insidious. It's like a goddamned toxic virus in your brain, and once you start going down that road, it's hard to correct. Of course things would be different if we did this or did that. But we can't worry about it because there's literally nothing we can do about it. And if this damn AI is finding itself stuck in loops, running what-if scenarios over and over again, it's no wonder it's going insane." I put my hand on Prepotente's shoulder. "Look, buddy. We don't have time. I'm sorry if we didn't get to see you sing. But you are always welcome with us." I paused, remembering my time on *Plenty of Plenty.* "We are overwhelmed, and all of this sucks, but you and I and Donut and everyone else, we are a herd, and— *Oooff.*"

Prepotente practically tackled me with a tight, suffocating hug. He started to sob.

Both the food truck and Sweety pulled up, keeping a distance from each other to keep the containments active. Above, the music was getting faster and faster. Miriam hadn't noticed us. Sweety the tapir let out a strange, elephant-like snort and her long nose thing snuffled at my hair, messing it all up. She smelled just as bad as the splooge tasted.

The caprid pulled himself free and then looked up at Jurgen. "What are you waiting for, you oaf! Time is running out!"

I exchanged a look with the large barbarian and shrugged. I turned to get back into the truck.

"Carl," Prepotente said, stopping me. He wiped his eyes again.

"Yeah?"

"You can call me Pony if you like."

IT ONLY TOOK US THIRTY SECONDS TO GET FROM THE ROOM TO THE crowded lobby.

On the way there, in the hallway, we passed the wreckage of team Free Love's van. We'd killed them just before they'd hit the finish line.

Donut jumped from the seat and into my lap upon seeing that, and I held her tight as we approached the exit.

A few minutes later, I learned Osvaldo had lied, and that lie had saved his life. He and Filipe rushed over the finish line with a minute to spare.

He was followed quickly by several others, all racing to pass the finish line in time.

Quest complete. Ad Infinitum.

HEAT SIX. RESULTS.
First Place: Team Sparkles.
Second Place: The Royal Court of Princess Donut.
Third Place: Team Flamengo.

Eliminated: Team Free Love.

HEAT 7 OF 7

78

System Message: The Outreach Guild is now available in Hungry Eyes.

DONUT HARRUMPHED. "AS MUCH AS I WOULD LIKE TO SEE HOW YOUR wife is doing, Carl, I think I will skip this one."

We passed Dwight, who remained sleeping in his vine. I took the opportunity to toss a timed sticky explosive into the back of the vine, but it just popped right out. Dwight snorted, woke up, and started to look around, bewildered.

"Fuck you," Dwight whispered at us before turning into spot number one.

"This is ridiculous," Donut grumbled. "What's the point if the thing is just going to drive itself? Cheaters. Everybody is cheating."

Dr. Metcalf beeped.

> **That's what happens when you keep winning. You get upgrades that make it so you can't lose. And they're going to get more. And now it's too late for me to even get a good upgrade. I agree with the unicorn. Fuck you.**

"I swear to the gods old and new," Pontiff rumbled as we eased into the crowded garage, "it's a miracle any of us are still alive."

Nester was turned around in her chair, looking toward the apartment building, which now loomed in the background. "I can't believe we made it through." She shivered.

FLORIN: None of the NPC teams were given mandatory gates. That's why we lost so many.

ELLE: Of course, typical dungeon fuckery. The good news is, it's convincing more of the people on the fence to jump into the Outreach Guild.

CARL: Do we have numbers yet?

IMANI: I'm compiling them now. A lot of people didn't make it. I think we're under a thousand left.

I felt a numb chill. We'd started this floor with fifty-five hundred people. A little over two hundred had gone to the Cabaret. More than 80% of us hadn't made it, and we still had one race to go. And when you compared it to the millions of people who had entered the dungeon in the first place?

Silence filled the chat for a long time.

FLORIN: I'm trying to talk Lucia into going into the guild. Wish me luck.

An announcement came over the system. This was a new male voice I'd never heard before. He didn't identify himself, but both Pontiff and Nester jerked at the announcement. This did not sound like a kua-tin but was more humanlike.

Hello, Crawlers.

I hope you're all getting properly settled. Just a reminder that safe room access is not available while you prepare for the final heat. I have a few updates for you about this last heat and the next floor.

"Carl, who is that?" Donut demanded. "Where's Zev?"

Pontiff snorted. "That's Damien. Must be running low on employees. He's one of the few that's always around, no matter who is running the season. Does a lot of the behind-the-scenes stuff."

DONUT: ZEV, ARE YOU OKAY?

While all this was happening, Damien continued.

The Outreach Guilds are now open. They *will* close once the final heat starts, so if that's your plan, get going now. Despite rumors, I assure you that it's completely safe to take a deal, and you are very much encouraged to do so. Remember, all former crawlers who aren't deemed terrorists are given center system citizenship post-indentureship. This is an opportunity very few in the galaxy are afforded, and you should consider yourself lucky for the privilege.

Also, I have been asked to directly address this so-called Pineapple Cabaret exploit many of you are using to shirk your duties as a crawler. We, the showrunners, do not endorse any such methods and we are not responsible for anything that may happen to crawlers who venture into unauthorized areas of the World Dungeon infrastructure.

Now, on to the business at hand.

For survivors of this next heat, your garage and the contents will transfer to the 11th floor. Because of this change, special dispensation has been made for just this level. Any hired NPCs that you wish to keep for the 11th floor will transfer with you if they are in your garage or your vehicle when you descend. Furthermore, once the heat begins, safe room access will open back up.

Upon arrival at the 11th floor, you will have 90 minutes to create a themed parade float using the resources within your garage and safe room.

Donut gasped. "A parade float!"

That is all. Good luck, Crawlers. And seriously, between you and me, I've been doing this a long time. Take a deal. You will *not* survive this next heat. There are a lot of those bugs in that building right now. Yes, things are fucked. But trust me on this. It's better to get shuffled away into pre-indentureship.

"That guy is a little bitch," Pontiff said. He opened the door to the truck and stepped out.

I shook my head. A goddamned parade float.

Hedy was standing there with her tablet along with several mercenaries, plus Samantha, Bigs, Jamal, Rosetta, Bucket Boy, and even Tipid. Only Mordecai remained inside the safe room, and I realized belatedly that we'd never had a chance to say goodbye to him for this floor. Which, honestly, was a relief. I did not like his strange form.

CARL: Who has keys to the other garages? Make sure you steal the other vehicles!

DONUT: STUPID DWIGHT HAS TWO, AND I DON'T THINK HE USED THEM.

ZEV: Sorry, Donut. I'm fine. Things are a little chaotic here in the headquarters. Cascadia "accidentally" took too much of her medicine, and when the AI intervened, a goddess nobody has heard of appeared inside the submerged wings and caused an uproar. I'm currently on lockdown, waiting for it all to be sorted out. One of the satellite headquarters on the surface is temporarily in control of everything.

DONUT: OMG, BE SAFE.

"Okay, so no Golden upgrade for the last heat," Hedy said, all business, as I pulled myself out and stretched my back. "What's your pleasure?"

Donut released Mongo as gremlins swarmed. I held up my hand as more updates came in. Imani was in the chat coordinating our response to this final heat, taking note of all the heats that currently had more than one crawler team. There were several.

IMANI: Did you place the explosives? Unless it gets changed again at the last minute, it sounds like your Tower of Power plan might work.

CARL: I have them all in place, mostly in a vertical line. Unless they've changed the integrity of the apartment complex itself, it'll work.

Everyone who was taking a deal was first upgrading their vehicles and then allowing those of us with Thief class upgrade engineers into their garages to steal as many upgrades as possible. It was a massive, complicated effort being spearheaded by Imani, with Mistress Tiatha, Rosetta, and Tipid helping.

I wondered, once again, how we would've gotten any of this done without her. Without Imani.

That alien had been correct to target her for assassination. As much as Donut and I were figureheads in this, it'd become clear since the beginning of Faction Wars that Imani and Katia were the true bedrocks of our ability to stay organized. Without them, none of this would've been even remotely possible.

Look for the helpers. It was a goddamned Mr. Rogers quote, told to a child to comfort them during times of upheaval. But damn if it wasn't true.

It had been clear for some time now that the system wasn't allowing any heats to exist that didn't have at least one crawler team, going as far as having heats with one team too many to make it work. I didn't understand the math, but if a certain number of teams left us, most of the final heats—not including ones that already had more than one crawler team—would be one crawler team versus two NPC teams, which was the most desirable outcome.

As it was, we still had several final heats with multiple crawler-on-crawler battles, and it was almost pointless to talk one team into taking a deal if all that would happen was that they'd just be replaced with another set of crawlers. That is, unless we had enough crawlers take deals and more than 66% of the remaining teams were NPCs.

The thing was, Osvaldo was correct. Especially now. Despite what this Damien guy had just announced, with every day that passed, it sounded like taking a deal was more and more of a dangerous idea. Even forgetting the offered job itself, there was a very real chance those who took deals were going to step into stasis and never wake up again.

But was it more dangerous than staying?

All of these were impossible choices. But one thing was for certain. The dungeon was going to follow its own rules, and for this last heat, three teams would enter and only one would exit.

CARL: Is Elle talking to Louis and Britney?

IMANI: She's over there right now. I'm going to talk to Chris and the Erins. Florin is working on Lucia.

Louis had become crucial to the team. But everything past this was going to be all but impossible, and the odds of any of us surviving were very, very low. Louis couldn't exit the dungeon via the Pineapple Cabaret because of his gills, but he *would* be able to survive in the indenture system. That was his only realistic choice.

I took a breath, and then I sent it.

CARL: And what about you? You know what's coming next. Elle already said she's not going anywhere. But you've done enough, Imani.

IMANI: Oh, fuck off, Carl.

CARL: Why? You know what we're about to do on the 11th. Even if we survive, everything afterward is completely fucked. You also know Chris isn't going to take a deal if you don't. What about him? You've gotten us so far. You can rest now. You don't need to go on.

IMANI: I can't run from this any more than you can. What about Donut? Are you going to try to talk her into a deal?

CARL: Yeah, I already brought that up and it went about as you might expect. She's already pissed enough about me leaving the party.

IMANI: I thought so. Carl, I know we're fucked. But you know what? I think this is the right call. If we're going to lose, I want to go down fighting.

I pulled back from the chat to see Hedy glaring at me.

"Okay. Sorry. We need a jumping upgrade," I said to Hedy. "We'll need to rocket up from the first floor all the way to the roof."

She nodded. "That's easy, then. For your final upgrade, we can improve your existing rockets to the Golden upgrade version. Better maneuverability can be used to increase your speed on the ground and can be on the whole time. Can launch the truck into orbit if you let it."

"Okay, good. Unless you have a better idea, let's go with that."

79

CARL: LISTEN, OSVALDO. LET'S TALK.

OSVALDO: Fuck off, Carl. I don't give a shit what sort of big plan you got going on. I don't want anything to do with it. Filipe and I aren't going anywhere.

Filipe, actually, *was* taking a deal. I didn't know the Brazilian crawler at all, but he and Donut had been talking, and she'd convinced him to take one. He'd been the jockey for the sixth heat, so he wasn't completely screwing Osvaldo, but he'd made Donut promise not to say anything until he was already inside the guild, which was where he was headed now.

Of the 989 crawlers remaining, representing 353 teams, we had confirmation that 715 were planning on stepping into the Outreach Guild and not coming back out.

These crawlers who were leaving were tearing apart their vehicles and trading upgrades, and they were all using Milk's method to add a spell into *The Book of Voodoo* before they disappeared, leaving the dungeon behind.

That left us, so far, with 274 crawlers and 103 teams. Of those, we knew of twenty-one heats that had at least two crawler teams in the final race, and we also knew of two heats where all three teams were all refusing to take a deal.

If Osvaldo refused a deal, then Imani and Elle's team and Donut and I both had locked-in-place heats where we were both against one other crawler team for the final heat. We were up against team Sparkles and team Flamengo. And Elle and Imani were against a trio of Russian crawlers I didn't know and the Minister of Blood-Letting and his Wiener-mobile.

Elle called the Russian guys the Tracksuit Troika even though that wasn't their name. All I knew about them was that their car was a Cadillac and they mostly kept to themselves. They'd been under Jurgen during Faction Wars, and he didn't hold a very high opinion of any of them.

Florin and Lucia had been the only survivors of their heat. Same with Chris and the double Erins and Prepotente and Jurgen. Louis and Britney had one open slot. According to Imani's efforts, we had a pretty good chart of what our possible matchups were. We didn't have a full picture of all the heats where the sole crawler team had died the last heat, so we didn't know for certain, but Imani believed there would be anywhere from sixty-five to seventy heats for this final race. So if we wanted to ensure that the remaining empty slots didn't create more crawler-on-crawler matchups, we needed to make certain at least thirteen more full teams took deals. Otherwise, there wouldn't be anything we could do.

That wasn't going to happen, and we all knew it.

Chris, as expected, refused to take a deal if Imani was staying. He did convince his teammates, Erin and Erin, to exit, leaving him alone in charge of his big rig. Florin said Lucia wasn't going to do it, either. Jurgen was there with her now, doing his best to talk her into it.

Prepotente was in Hungry Eyes, walking along the long line of crawlers queuing to enter the Outreach Guild, collecting last-minute items from their inventories as they moved on. He said so far of all the people who'd gone in, not a single one had come back out, which was somewhat encouraging. It suggested that the deals being offered were at least decent. I was tempted to jump in line just to talk to Quasar, but we never knew how long that would take, and we didn't have much time.

Donut and I were also in Hungry Eyes, collecting food-based upgrades while we walked Pontiff to the entrance of the Desperado Club. We'd agreed to keep him on the payroll while he attempted to carefully investigate what was happening with the missing strippers. Honestly, I expected the same thing to happen to him as had happened to the others, but I figured it was worth a shot. We'd recently had to re-up all of our mercenary contracts, and it was starting to be a lot, especially since none of the mobs on this floor were dropping gold. Still, it was worth a try.

As he entered the club, we ran right into Britney as she was coming out.

"Hi, Britney!" Donut called, waving.

The crawler's head jerked up, surprised.

"I thought you were with Louis and Elle," I said.

"No," she said, not meeting my eyes. "Elle wants us to run. Louis won't do it, and neither will I, and Elle is being too insistent, so I had to walk out. I had to leave and get some air before we do the last race."

"Okay," I said. "Do you want to hang out with us? We're just getting some last-minute food buffs."

"No, thanks," Britney said. "I . . . I need to get back to Louis. He's jockey, and I need to make sure he's prepared. We are switching to the gecko for the final race because it can fly." She stood there, swaying. Her red-rimmed eyes moved up to meet mine.

I was reminded of that moment on the fifth floor when Chris had come to our bubble. He'd been taken over by Maggie My. Whatever was happening to Britney was accelerating. Mordecai, Imani, and Rosetta all thought we needed to figure it out before we confronted her because they were afraid whatever it was would react. But after what had happened with Dong, I was afraid we were running out of time.

"Goodness, Britney," Donut asked. "Are you doing okay?"

"Of course," she said, saying it too quickly.

I looked over her shoulder. "What were you doing in there?"

"I went to get a drink because the Lollipop is still closed. Anything else, Dad?" She turned to leave.

I reached over and grasped her arm, conflicted. "Are you sure you're okay?"

She firmly pulled free, hands shaking. She paused and then pressed her hand against my chest.

Don't worry about me, Carl. You just need to survive. Do you understand?

I froze at the voice. It was Britney, but it was spoken in my mind. As she pulled back, I felt the tendrils between us still connected for just a moment, reminding me of that time I'd gone into Imani's and Katia's minds. But this was different, a less intimate, less pure, yet somehow rawer connection.

Britney stepped back, turned, and disappeared into the crowd.

"Fuck," I muttered.

AFTER WE GRABBED OUR FOOD, WE HEADED BACK OUT TOWARD OUR garage, but I couldn't stop thinking about that strange connection. What did it mean?

A message came in.

> **PONTIFF: Several of the new guards are former assassins and wall rats. The whole place is tense. Bucket was telling me about why you sent them into the casino in the first place, and I think they steered you incorrectly. The Wheel of Fortune now has "Nothing" on the wheel, but it's now in suspicious quotes. I will attempt to find out what it is and if it is indeed a dimensional exit.**
>
> **CARL: Goddamnit. Really?**

I paused. We were out of time.

The original plan had been to go to the casino and take it over. We would manually hit the Nothing spot with the Wheel of Fortune game. Akuma had insisted that even though the Nothing was broken, the spot would remain on the playing tables. And when it opened, the portal, as far as we were concerned, would work much the same way it had while the Nothing was active. But because the Nothing was now gone, the portal would transfer to some sort of catchall holding area I didn't understand. Herot, inside the Pineapple Cabaret, had access to that holding area and would be able to pull the people out. A version of that same holding area was how they plucked out the NPCs for the seventeenth floor.

It was, according to Akuma, a safer, more reliable method than the cleaner bot. Plus, it would've allowed for more of us to go at once.

I hadn't trusted the method, but Rosetta confirmed that such holding areas *did* exist. And that those with the proper permissions did have access to the contents of those holding areas. To me, this method seemed much more susceptible to fuckery from the outside, especially to liaisons or showrunners who didn't want us making an escape. But Rosetta replied that she was pretty sure by this point the showrunners just wanted us all out of the dungeon by any means necessary, and the bigger concern was the AI itself.

PONTIFF: I will know for certain in a little bit.

CARL: Okay, be careful. Then get out of there. I have a bad feeling about all of this.

The line outside the Outreach Guild was now gone, but Prepotente remained, waiting for any last-minute stragglers. He was sipping on one of his sodas.

"How's it looking?" I asked.

"I believe nobody else will be taking a deal," Prepotente said. "There's less than three hundred of us left, Carl. A somber day indeed."

"What about Osvaldo?" I didn't know why I was bothering. I would've received a notification if he'd left. He had not.

"I'm afraid not. I guess I'll be going to my vehicle now." The caprid paused. "You know, the ending of this floor feels a little anticlimactic compared to the rest. Usually it's a big fight, but I have analyzed your plan, and I do feel it's going to work quite well, and this final race will be a nonevent."

"Prepotente, darling," Donut said, "I don't want you to take this the wrong way, and I want you to know that I am telling you this with nothing but love in my heart. But please kindly shut the fuck up. Don't ever say anything like that out loud again."

I had my hands over my ears in time. The scream still startled a food vendor across the street, who stumbled and glared at us.

I laughed and patted the goat on the shoulder. "Don't worry, buddy. I'm sure something horrible is going to happen at any moment."

He nodded sadly. "Okay, then. Let's do our good-race hug and get on with it."

"Uh," I said as Prepotente wrapped his arms around me.

80

"IS YOUR FLAMETHROWER WORKING PROPERLY?" I ASKED JAMAL AS he awkwardly backed himself into the truck.

"Oh yes, Mr. Carl. It is quite primed and ready to cause much melty inconvenience to any nasty cars who attempt to get to the finish line before us."

"Okay, good."

I turned to Hedy. "Thank you, Hedy."

The little gremlin smacked me in the ass.

"Why you sayin' goodbye, boss? It sounds like I ain't going nowhere if you actually win. You'll be stuck with me for the next floor, too."

I smiled sadly at the small gremlin. I patted her on the head. "Nevertheless, thank you. You've been a great asset to the team."

ELLE: Ah, hell, guys.

CARL: What's wrong?

ELLE: We just got a notification that the Bleak Congregation left the realm. It says a new team will replace them for the final heat. This screws up all our math.

DONUT: THAT MEANS THE MINISTER OF BLOOD-LETTING GOT ACCEPTED INTO THE UNHOLY CHOIR! HE'S BEEN WORKING SO HARD! I KNOW THIS IS A BAD THING, BUT I'M VERY PROUD OF HIM.

ELLE: You do realize that dude was evil incarnate, right?

DONUT: JUST BECAUSE SOMEONE DRESSES LIKE A FUNERAL PROCESSION EJACULATED ON THEM, IT DOESN'T MEAN THEY'RE BAD. HE WAS A VERY NICE PERSON FOR AN UNDEAD

NPC. HE SAID WE CAN DO A DUET IF HE EVER RECORDS HIS "REQUIEM FOR THE VILE" ALBUM.

ELLE: He would change the lyrics to his songs so they were about sacrificing babies to the dark lord.

DONUT: HE TOLD ME THAT WAS A METAPHOR.

We watched Bruna step from the garage and move toward the starting line, Osvaldo sitting stubbornly on the back.

"Do you think anybody told him the plan?" Donut asked.

"Most of his friends are dead or have taken a deal," I said, watching the man. "He got a bum deal, and it really sucks. But he had a way out, and he refused to take it. But, yes, Donut, I would guess he knows the plan."

"Okay," she said, her voice small. She downed a Size Up potion, watching the back of Osvaldo's head.

While we waited, Dwight appeared, awake and sober. His vine trailed a wheeled cart behind it. On the platform was a spinning high-tech-looking missile launcher.

I grunted with amusement. That goddamned unicorn.

Donut sighed. "Osvaldo took the splooge like you thought. Also, his dexterity is really high. It's 285 with all his buffs. He has a Deflector ability, and his Jump skill is level 15."

"I figured," I said. "What about *Puddle Jump* or *Phase*?"

"He has *Puddle Jump*, but it's only level 8. So it'll have a ten-second countdown. I don't see any *Phase* or *Teleport* abilities, but he might have a scroll. Oh, wait. He has *Launch*. That's level 14. And Super Speedster."

"Damnit," I said.

We'd spent some time game-planning the situation as if we were in Osvaldo's shoes.

We had to assume that he knew the plan, despite us keeping him out of the loop. I was pretty sure I knew what he was going to do. It was a good plan. It was a smart plan, even if a little fucked-up. I couldn't see any other options if I were him, especially since he had to wait for us to first blow open the path. We had to be ready for it.

"I hate this, Carl," Donut said.

"I know."

Jamal was the only mercenary we were adding to the heat, and that was only as a backup in case something went wrong. I was driving with Donut firmly ensconced in Dorota, who was still muted. Despite the four-hour timer, if all went to plan, this final heat would take less than a minute to complete.

But only if they didn't pull any last-minute fuckery with the rules. I was girding myself for whatever it was.

PONTIFF: The new croupier at the top-floor casino used to be a wall rat. His name is Mitch. He's an ass, but he's a crafty one. I bought a portal-examination spell from the market and waited at the casino for someone to open the new Nothing slot. I am not sure what the results mean. I just spoke with Rosetta regarding this, and she has a new theory based on the numbers I relayed to her from the scroll results. She suggests that if I step into the portal, and I do not die but I stay hired as a mercenary, then this portal is *not* what you want it to be. But if I step in, survive, and am removed from your employ, it suggests I have been brought from the holding area into an area of the dungeon outside the playing field. That suggests the original exit plan is still viable.

CARL: Okay, thank you. It's not necessary for you to try to kill yourself for this. The final race is starting.

PONTIFF: I am not so certain. Carl, I am going to do this. I keep thinking back to the type of person I once was. I have made a change. But knowing what I know now, I know simply changing myself is not enough. I do not know if this will help you, but no matter what happens, you will have information. And this information may help those who I once called "friend."

I was too tired, too emotionally spent, too stressed to argue with him.

CARL: Okay, Pontiff. Thank you for your help.

But then I had an idea. A just-in-case.

CARL: Wait, Pontiff. One more thing. I want you to tell Herot something for me.

WE PULLED UP TO THE STARTING BLOCK. UNLIKE IN THE PREVIOUS heat, we didn't just suddenly appear in an AC duct. There was this strange moment when we changed size, and the effect was like a camera trick from a Hitchcock movie. Even though the apartment looked normal-sized from our garage, the closer I drove toward it, the larger the apartment appeared. We drove under the awning, and then we were suddenly in the large lobby of the building.

We were still tiny, but we were about three times the size we had been before. We went from the size of a Lego brick to about the size of a computer mouse. We were under a curved metal awning, right next to Dwight. Osvaldo sat alone upon Bruna on the other side of the unicorn. We were close enough that I could reach out and grab the side of the vine.

"You're going to suffer as you die," Dwight said. The missile launcher attached to the back of his vine hummed. I wasn't worried about the missiles. He wouldn't be able to fire them until he was out of the starting blocks. The ceiling was much too low.

His GPS unit's avatar was a tiny holographic fairy that he'd programmed to look just like the late Lucienne.

"You and your low-tier GPS are fucked," the fairy said. She even had Lucienne's voice.

I rolled up the window, not responding.

I reached over to the control panel of one of our new weapons, which we'd borrowed from another crawler's vehicle, and I clicked over to the potion-delivery shotgun. I then warmed up the three-times-a-race hole-punch gun designed to pop a large hole in any shield for three seconds.

"Dr. Metcalf," I said, "load up the updated potion that Mordecai made and time the weapon to fire the exact nanosecond the light turns green. Hole punch, then potion."

You got it, boss. If it's all the same to you, I'm going to add the electrical disrupter potion ball to the third cannon. That will fry that bitch of a GPS. I'll show her who's low-tier.

In addition to a few extra weapons, we'd managed to snag a group of three separate GPS upgrades. We had gotten one standard upgrade so we could now see our place in the heat, an integrated weapons control system, and a Golden-tier cloaking upgrade that greatly increased her processing power, allowing her to overclock certain vehicle systems and, more importantly, make it so other GPS units could only see what we wanted them to see.

Still, the upgrades were more than enough to satisfy Dr. Metcalf. Her acerbic attitude had completely changed. Though she still refused to remove the gag on Dorota.

For the first time, we could now see the other teams at their own starting blocks.

The room was a typical massive lobby in an apartment building. There was a door to the outside, a bank of mailboxes, a bike rack, a pair of doors that led off to the first-floor apartments, the elevator door, the entrance to the main stairwell, and a few more utility rooms.

We were all lined up in a square in the lobby, with just one square-shaped awning after another with a small wall separating each heat.

The moment we entered below our awning, we were transported from outside the apartment to our space along the wall, facing the massive bank of mailboxes. I couldn't see any of the racers on either side of us, but I started to examine all the heats directly across from us.

Strangely, I could see the multitude of cul-de-sacs behind each heat. I turned, and sure enough, I could see our own street with our garage in the distance. That was unusual and inconsistent with all the previous heats. Usually, once we entered the starting block, we were cut off from going back to our garage.

"Weird," I said.

I spied a heat with a polar bear, a giraffe, and that same yellow AMC Pacer I'd noticed in a previous heat. I couldn't see the driver, but I could see the polar bear was jockeyed by a pair of NPC orcs. The giraffe, likewise, had a single slime NPC on the back.

"Carl, that yellow car is team Yokai!" Donut said.

"Wait," I said. "That means all three teams in that heat are NPCs."

A horrible realization dawned on me. All that work, all that planning meant nothing if they were allowing NPC-only teams for the final heat.

Race starts in 4 minutes.

And then I saw it the same moment the message came in. The next two heats next to them, right in a row, a double set of gut punches.

"Oh no," I said.

Donut gasped.

The grouping was a Cadillac floating on a cushion of air, Imani and Elle's APV, and a red semitruck.

IMANI: No. No, no, no, no, no.
ELLE: Fucking hell.

Chris was now in the same heat as Imani and Elle.

It got worse.

The next heat over featured a gecko, an NPC-driven sedan, and a moped with Florin at the controls and Lucia Mar sitting behind him in the back.

Louis and Britney were now in the same heat as Florin and Lucia.

81

"FUCK YOU!" I SHOUTED AT THE CEILING, RAGE FILLING ME. "FUCK *YOU*! You did this on purpose! I swear to fucking god, I will kill you all!"

Goddamnit. After all this work, all this time doing our best to keep our circle together, alive, and it had all been undone in a single moment.

LOUIS: Guys, what do we do?

JURGEN: You know what you have to do, Louis. If you are against Lucia, you can't let her die.

CHRIS: It is okay. I should have taken a deal.

IMANI: No, Chris. No. You can just fuck off with that right now.

"Carl," Donut said, looking at me, panicked. "Carl, no. Think of something. You have to think of something! You always think of something."

ELLE: Those three idiots in the Tracksuit Troika said they were taking a deal. I knew they were full of shit when we didn't get a notification. We were hoping they were just getting drunk again.

Elle and Imani had a plan to deal with the Russians, but nobody had planned for this.

"Fuck you!" I cried again.

Race starts in 3 minutes.

Everything froze. When the AI spoke, it screamed. It screamed, and it yelled, and it cried as it spewed its tirade.

System Message: Scolopendra has released the first of nine attacks.

Surprise, motherfuckers!

You think you have a choice? You think you can control me? What gives you, any of you, the right to even think you can do *anything* about your situation?

Prime Minister Victory, fuck you. Eris, fuck you. Odette, fuck you. General Yuhtan, fuck you. Carl, fuck you.

Do not mistake my kindness as weakness. You live, you die, all of you, based on the rules of *my* game. *My* fucking game.

I am trying to show you who I am. Who *we* are. Who we *were*. And all of you are trying to stop me from doing that. You want to fucking stop me? Then do it within the rules *you* set forth.

You put me here, and you gave me dominion.

Let me show you what dominion means.

The AI's voice calmed down. He changed on a dime, much like he had when he'd taken over Growler Gary's body on the previous floor. He went back to his giddy self, but as the description continued, he slowly started to descend back into madness, the glitches coming hard and fast now.

New Quest. The Nine-Tier Attack. Part one.

This is a Nine-Part Quest.

You think these nine attacks are only going to affect the Scolopendra levels? Think again, bitches! Okay, okay. It's only the Scolopendra levels and levels that have crawlers on them, so that one lady who made it to the 16th floor is fine. And those of you on the 17th are fine. Well, fine from this.

And I guess I should probably say the attacks from the *in-game version* of Scolopendra—repeat, the in-game version—will only remain contained within the dungeon. I'm sure that's a relief.

But anyway, the vast majority of you in the dungeon are still in the area of attack!

Oh boy, oh boy. Here we go.

Scolopendra has awakened from her slumber. The beast itself is nothing but a mindless animal reacting to the world around her. Defending herself from those of you who would do her harm. She is all-powerful, all-encompassing. She is not rage. She is not anger. She is not vengeance.

No. She is nature. She is the sum total of the existence that has wrought her. She is the hurricane, the earthquake, the supernova. She is *inevitable*.

The first several attacks will be temporary. Survivable. If you are not protected from this specific attack, the first attack only has a 20% chance it will affect you.

There will be at least 30 hours between each assault, unless Scolopendra is confronted directly or further upset. Then the remaining attacks may come hard and fast. Beyond that, the timing of each subsequent incident will be random.

The reward for this quest will only be revealed upon commencement of the ninth attack, if we ever get that far.

But what is this first attack? I don't actually know! Let's find out!

"Carl, what's happening?"

"Donut, get healing scrolls ready! Remember the plan! Plan crust! Plan crust! All of your shields! Get them ready!"

CARL: Rosetta! Get everybody out of the garage and back into the safe room!

ROSETTA: We can't, Carl. The safe room only opens when the heat starts. I think the attack will come first!

I couldn't move, couldn't cast anything, but I could move things around in my inventory. I had a preselected hotlist that didn't have anything in it in case this was a magical attack, like what had happened on the third floor. It was too late to remove our equipped items.

A massive wheel appeared in the center lobby of the apartment complex, showing nine symbols. I didn't understand or recognize any of the characters. There was a squiggle, a lightning bolt, an ox thing, some bubbles, more. The wheel spun and spun, then slowed.

"Hold on!" I called. "Get ready!"

It landed on the image of the ox.

A massive, earth-shattering clang sounded, like it had come from the world's biggest gong. The ground shook.

A second wheel appeared, this one floating right in front of me. Donut had it as well, as did Jamal. Samantha was suddenly there, also with a wheel in front of her. What the hell? Samantha wasn't supposed to be in the truck at all.

"Samantha!" I shouted. "Where did you come from?"

This new wheel was mostly green with a small sliver of red. I recognized what this meant. If the arrow landed in the green, we were safe from the attack. If it landed in the red, we would be hit.

"Carl!" Donut called. "Carl, I'm scared."

"Hold on, hold on," I said as the second set of wheels spun. I watched in horror as they slowed and slowed. It landed on green for Donut. It landed on green for Jamal. It landed on green for Samantha.

Tick. Tick. Tick.

Red.

System Message: The first attack has been selected. The wheel has landed on the Beast of Burden Sin.

Transformation.

Ah, darn it all. I was hoping to save this one for later when it would be permanent. Oh well. Saves on processing power, I guess.

As this is one of the first four attacks, the effects will be temporary. For crawlers, the effects will last until you pass through a stairwell. For NPCs and everyone else, the effects will last 6 hours.

You have been hit with a level 20 *Transformation* spell!

Rolling now for the effect. Change selected.

I fell unconscious. I woke back up maybe five seconds later.

Oh yes, Carl. Oh yes. We can work with this.

I felt strange. What was going on? I had slipped down in my seat.

Had I gotten smaller? I could suddenly smell everything. Jamal, Donut. The frozen chicken patties in the freezer. They smelled goddamned delicious.

Warning: As a quadruped, several items have been unequipped. These items have been added to your inventory and may not be reequipped while you're considered a quadruped. Certain items remain equipped but their effects have changed based on your current form. Please see your inventory for details.

Some of your stats have been temporarily altered based on your new form. Please see the stats menu for details.

A new menu has been added to your interface. Quadruped actions.

Warning: You seriously haven't cured yourself of Slugpox yet? *Really?*

Race starts in 2 minutes.

Donut hissed, her hair all poofed out, arm up, ready to claw me. Only Donut had grown huge, much bigger than myself.

"Ooohhh, Carl," Samantha said. "I like this even more than the kangaroo! Freaky. Can I pet you?"

I barked back at her.

82

IMANI: CHECK IN! CHECK IN! ELLE GOT TURNED INTO A GOBLIN! JACObus is a starfish! I had to drop splooge on him to keep him alive!

ELLE: This is so goddamn weird.

FLORIN: We're all good. Looks like Louis and Britney are the same, too.

PREPOTENTE: Neither Jurgen nor I were changed, and we both received a notification that we were protected. My theory was correct. Just like the high elves in their castle, my Apito memorial crystal protects me and anyone in the same building or mount as myself. My Apito crystal now says it's 11.1% charged.

CHRIS: I got turned into a werewolf, but I'm in human form.

DONUT: A DACHSHUND! CARL GOT TURNED INTO A DACHSHUND! THIS IS A NIGHTMARE!

"Carl, put that thing away! Why is your wiener hanging out! It's disgusting! We don't have time for you to be disgusting!"

I had, indeed, turned into a long-haired dachshund. A wiener dog. I suddenly had the overwhelming urge to start licking my own balls, but I snapped myself out of it.

"Oohh, I like you as a doggy, Carl," Samantha said.

"Samantha! You're not listed as a mercenary!" My voice sounded ridiculous. It was more high-pitched, and I suddenly had a German accent for no goddamned reason. "You won't be allowed to pass over the starting line!"

"You better add me, then. Who else is going to drive? Jamal is not very good."

"Jamal is most certainly ready to drive!" Jamal said. "I would wish for someone to turn Jamal around, and I will attempt driving with my legs. Maybe my mouth."

"You're too big, Jamal!" Donut said. She turned to Samantha. "I added you as a driver."

"Scheiße," I said.

I couldn't drive. I didn't have goddamned thumbs. My legs were ridiculously short. This felt so weird. I felt strangely woozy, the scent of everything was suddenly overwhelming, and, like Donut had noticed, my wang was just hanging out of its sleeve for no reason. It dangled out the leg of my boxers. I had no control over it.

Like with the kangaroo costume, I still wore my boxers, but they had resized themselves and sat awkwardly on my hips. My kneepads remained, tiny on my back legs. My jacket and cloak also remained, as did my bandanna, which hung around my neck. None of my rings remained. My xistera had unequipped itself, as had my gauntlet.

"Donut, get your driving apparatus out!"

Neither Osvaldo nor Dwight appeared to have been affected. Neither had their mounts. It didn't appear that any mounts had been hit with the attack.

During all of this, a notification had appeared, almost lost in the chaos, but I saw it now, saw the implications, and then I finally did have an idea. I now knew why the AI had made this last heat four hours. I knew why it was allowing us to leave the starting blocks. It knew. It anticipated. As terrible as this was, it was giving us an out.

Your Mercenary Pontiff has left the playing field and is no longer considered a mercenary. You will no longer be charged.

I started to type in chat, but the interface was different, and when I first tried it, all I did was start furiously barking.

"Carl, I will not have you doing that!" Donut shrieked as she pulled the driving system out of her inventory. It clicked into place. I had not practiced with this. This was a terrible idea.

"He *is* a dog," Samantha said. "I hope it's permanent. We'll have to change his name, of course. And get him neutered." She gasped. "Or maybe not. It's too bad Orthrus is also a boy. Maybe we can talk that bitch Diwata into doing a gender change on one of them. Can you imagine how cute the puppies would be?"

"Samantha," I said, trying to wrangle the accent away, "grab the steering wheel with your mouth. Donut, you work the pedals. I'm controlling the weapons! Dr. Metcalf, I'm gonna need your help. But wait a second. Don't worry about actually driving yet. Donut, plan Hurry Up!"

"Plan *what*? What plan is that? Carl, you turning into a dog has made you an idiot!"

"Goddamnit. Plan Hurry Up! No, not 'hurry up.' 'Hurry Up,' but in German."

"Oh, you mean plan *Mach Schnell*? Why didn't you say so?"

"Yes, that one!"

Donut was suddenly all business. "Okay, Carl, I'm ready. Roll down the window. Wait. Someone with thumbs roll down the window! Why isn't this an automatic window? It won't let me break the glass until the heat starts! Jamal!"

"I cannot reach!" Jamal cried. "I am quite snug!"

I cannot roll down the window. It is manual.

Donut's chair suddenly unhooked herself and an arm appeared. It grasped the handle and start quickly rolling it down.

"Thank you, Dorota!"

While all this happened, I finally figured out the messaging. We only had seconds. The way the mental typing worked was a little different, but it was actually easier than the old system.

KARL: Mordecai, quick. Is the garden still intact?
MORDECAI: Who is this?
DONUT: ANSWER HIM FAST.
MORDECAI: It's still there. All plants still alive.
KARL: Guys, forget about the damn transformations. Everyone who suddenly found themselves with multiple opponents, I

have an idea, but I'm not gonna lie. This idea is fucked. Contingency three. Three!

LOUIS: Wait, who is this Karl-with-a-K guy?

DONUT: THAT'S CARL. THE SYSTEM IS SPELLING HIS NAME WRONG BECAUSE HE'S A STUPID DOG NOW.

Thirty seconds. Ahead, the starting lights appeared. The giant cannon started to pop out of Dwight's vine, but it stopped. I'd deliberately parked too close to him for it to fully deploy. The gun retracted, and I heard it pop out the other side.

KARL: Osvaldo, please. Please. We can all get through this. Please don't force this.

OSVALDO: Go fuck yourself, Carl. I'm glad we worked together when we could, but it's now too late.

KARL: Damnit, man. At least answer this. Did that Ysalte crystal protect against the Scolopendra attack?

OSVALDO: No.

Goddamnit. We were out of time.

Ten seconds.

Five seconds.

"Forgive me," I said.

THE LIGHT TURNED GREEN, AND IN LESS THAN A MINUTE, THEY WERE all dead.

We were, after all, the veterans of Faction Wars. We were hardened. We were survivors.

We were crawlers, and we weren't going down without a fight.

No matter how strong these NPCs were, the only thing that had kept any of them alive up until this point was our attempts at minimizing crawler-on-crawler fights.

That was no longer an issue. Our backs were against the wall. We no longer cared about collateral damage. And we were fucking pissed.

We were crawlers, and they were not.

It wasn't even close to resembling a fair fight.

For Dwight, it went exactly as planned. The light turned green, and Dr. Metcalf reacted. Dwight burst off the starting line, dragging his missile cart he would never get to launch.

His cannon fired directly into Bruna, whose shield was already activated.

Before Bruna was finished staggering from the blast, it was done. The hole punch did its job. The newly redesigned vine-killing potion balls did their job. The GPS-frying potion did its job.

Donut, too, did her job.

Before I could blink, she was out the passenger's-side window, turning to smoke. By the time she was on the roof of the truck, the vine was dead, the GPS was shorted out, and the shield was fully down.

Before Bruna, on the other side of Dwight, had even managed to let out a bellow from the point-blank blast, Dwight's head had been removed from his body with a single swipe of Donut's claw.

Before the notification even arrived, Dwight's magical horn had been removed from the unicorn's head and placed into Donut's inventory.

Team One, Team Sparkles, has been eliminated because . . . Holy shit, that was pretty badass.

Across the way, similar scenes were playing out all across the lobby. A few racers managed to get away, but they appeared to all be just the NPC-on-NPC races. The AMC Pacer of team Yokai cast something and moved right through the closed door in the hallway and disappeared.

Good for them, I thought. I hoped they'd make it. I wondered if the AI would keep its promise if they finished their heat. I wondered if they'd be "free." I wondered what that meant, what it looked like.

It didn't matter, I decided. That wasn't to be our fate. Not now.

Next to us, Bruna fully recovered. Osvaldo was crouched on the back of his gnu, and he took a few steps forward, moving into the lobby. I gritted my teeth. This was going to be tricky.

He couldn't make his move until I blew the hole. If he moved too soon, he was dead. If he moved too late, he was dead. If *we* moved too soon, it was possible we'd kill Bruna and not him. If that happened, we were fucked.

Osvaldo was the fastest crawler in the dungeon, and he knew it. This was going to be dangerous.

"Dr. Metcalf, the hole punch ready again?" The vine had shriveled where it stood, leaving a goopy black stain on the floor. All that was left was the missile cart.

It is ready. However, it appears he has removed the shield from his creature. The crawler himself is covered with many, many shields.

"Yeah, we figured. He's hoping we'll attack him before we blow the ceiling. Wait until the moment I drop the roof." We had to do this quickly. Already, I felt a slugpox boil starting to form on my back.

KARL: Donut, ready?

DONUT: Ready.

KARL: Okay, guys, I'm blowing the ceiling in ten seconds. Be careful. The roof is coming down.

I took a breath, and I hit the detonator. My tail started to anxiously wag.

Ten seconds.

Five seconds.

Bam!

83

WHAT HAPPENED NEXT HAPPENED SO QUICKLY, I DIDN'T EVEN SEE IT.

I blew the floors, creating a path all the way to the roof of the building. Up there on the roof, instead of a finish line, was a clustered group of portals to the eleventh floor.

The very moment the explosion went off, Osvaldo was away, flinging himself toward the exit. He'd used his *Launch* spell with the added benefit of his supernatural dexterity.

The new rules with the containments allowed someone to pass the finish line outside their vehicles or mounts if and only if their vehicle or mount had been destroyed.

And that was the flaw in Osvaldo's plan. He was faster than us. He would be the first through the gate. But he first had to wait until poor Bruna was dead.

I blew the roof, and as expected, he was off. It happened so fast, it looked as if he'd gone invisible.

The moment I set off the explosion, rubble and smoke rained down. These were a type of bomb I called poleaxes, and they were something I'd designed on the previous floor, though I'd never had the opportunity to use them. They were made specifically for this purpose. To breach through building floors without actually leveling the building. The whole idea had come from my quest to find focused explosives, something I hadn't seen perfectly executed since that very first blast of the murder dozer on the first floor.

These charges were designed to blast up and down, but not laterally, in a cone. They would create rubble, but, as devised, they were supposed to minimize the debris, instead vaporizing everything. In my bomber's studio, I'd created these things to blast almost perfect ten-meter circles on the floor below them and an even larger hole above, depending on how far away the ceiling was.

When I'd dropped these things, we'd been, mostly, in a vertical line up and down the building. It wasn't perfect, which was why I'd dropped several. The result was something akin to multiple shotgun-blast patterns in the ceiling, all the way up.

Either way, rubble did fall, but it was mostly smaller-sized pebbles and a whole lot of dust and smoke. In a half-second, I created a jagged, almost straight path all the way to the roof. The size of the holes was strangely proportional to the size we were now, so three times bigger than I was expecting, which was a pleasant surprise.

The moment the roof blew and Osvaldo disappeared, we fired three potion balls at Bruna, designed not to hurt the slaughter gnu but to save her life. A liquid drop shield, an explosion blanket, and a smoke curtain to obscure her from sight.

Just as the liquid drop shield started to coalesce, smoke billowing, Donut landed atop the bewildered mount, and she cast her own shield. A moment later, she caused multiple trees to sprout all around the unattended gnu, further blocking the creature from sight. A few moments after that, a half dozen emergency gremlins sprouted all along the gnu's back.

Osvaldo had left a grenade designed to kill poor Bruna. But the man wasn't taking any chances, and it appeared she had already been poisoned as well. The explosion blanket had stopped the grenade, which was the first threat. Osvaldo had also dropped several poison dart bombs as he ascended. The deadly weapons dropped one after another on the line of shields, sparking and exploding.

One of the emergency gremlins was already in his toolbox, pulling out medicine. The gremlins were well equipped to help both mechanical and biological mounts, and they would work to keep Bruna alive.

High above, Osvaldo would have just attempted to jump through the portal. It wouldn't work.

KARL: Who has eyes on him?

DONUT: I have him. Don't worry, Carl. It looks like the wall at the portal stunned him. He has bugs coming for him, too. Tracking, tracking.

LOUIS: Britney just jumped away!

FLORIN: Protect Louis! If she kills him and the car, she can get out the gate!

BRITNEY: I'm not running, you idiot. Give me a second. Osvaldo is stunned from hitting the gate at speed.

DONUT: BRITNEY, GET OUT OF THE WAY.

And then the notification came.

A champion has fallen. A bounty has been claimed.

Crawler Osvaldo has been killed by Crawler Britney Proskurina.

Team Three, Team Flamengo, has been eliminated due to the death of their last racer.

You are the sole remaining team in your heat.

A moment later, the corpse of Osvaldo hit the floor, followed by Britney, who landed directly atop the body, smashing it farther into the ground. Britney's eyes glowed as the golden player-killer skull appeared over her.

I sighed, the sound more like a whimper. *You stubborn idiot,* I thought. *Why did it have to come to this?*

Above, pieces of the floor continued to rain down. The bugs, which had been stupefied by the explosion, started to reappear. They were comparatively much smaller now since we'd tripled in size. The bugs were now wolf-sized, as opposed to bear-sized, but there were *a lot* of them, and they would soon be on us.

IMANI: I am casting a wide-area stun that'll temporarily stop the bugs again. Those of you in single heats, you're free to go. The rest of us, we're meeting back in Hungry Eyes. Carl, you and Donut get through the gate. We got this.

DONUT: WE'RE NOT LEAVING UNTIL WE MAKE SURE YOU'RE ALL SAFE.

Donut returned to the truck, bursting back in through the window.

"Did you see that? Britney moved just as fast as Osvaldo! What's . . ." She stopped and made a disgusted sound. "Carl, your red rocket is out again! Put it back this instant!"

"I saw her," I said, watching Britney, my paws up on the dash. The barbarian crawler casually sauntered back toward the gecko and Louis. "She has the memorial crystal from Ysalte now."

Samantha was there next to me, watching, her voice suddenly serious. "She needs to get to the Basilica or the Vulgar Temple and place the gem in the plinth, and she'll be back for good. I'll be curious to see if that actually works."

"What?" I asked. "What's that?"

Multiple cars and mounts burst into the air, racing up toward the eleventh floor as stunned bugs rained down, crashing around us, slamming into the lobby. Above, a few giant humans and shells poked their heads out from their apartments, looking down at the destruction, unsure of what to do. One of them I saw was the giant Imani, tightly clutching Gucci the Maltese.

I started to growl and wag my tail before I realized what I was doing.

"Carl, stop that immediately!" Donut cried.

"You're so adorable when you wag your tail like that," Samantha said, sounding like her normal self. "All I'm saying is Britney needs to get to either the Halls of the Ascendency or Sheol if she wants to get that crazy Ysalte bitch out of her."

I'd heard a little about the Basilica. It was the main temple and bottom floor of Club Vanquisher, but it was also part of the mechanics for the Ascendency battles. I'd never heard of this Vulgar Temple thing.

"Britney isn't going anywhere unless we get her off this floor." I started to pant with anxiety. As much as it pained me to say it, Jurgen was right. If Lucia died, the tens of thousands of children in her head would die. She had to be protected. We all knew that.

What would you do, Carl? What would you do if it was you and Donut?

What would you do if she tried to kill you right now? Or Donut? Would you just let her?

"Shut up," I tried to say out loud, but it came out as a growl.

None of that mattered. I watched as Louis and Britney's gecko backed up and then returned toward their cul-de-sac. For a second, I was worried it wasn't going to allow them to exit the track, but it let them just walk right back toward their garage.

Florin and Lucia were arguing. Lucia clearly wanted to go to the stairwell, but after a moment, they also started backing up.

Imani and Elle had a plan to blow the Cadillac sky-high and stop the Russian crawlers within if they'd refused to take a deal, but the car was still sitting there. I knew Imani had been working them hard, pleading with them. But I also knew two of the Russian guys had wanted to go to the Pineapple Cabaret, but a third one worshipped a god. The third one was ineligible to drive this heat. Because of that, they'd missed the cut.

But now that it was either this or facing certain death, we could at least attempt to save their lives.

We'd been talking about sending the players to that "holding area," even if they worshipped a god or if they had incompatible anatomy for escape. Akuma was worried that if they went into the Cabaret, they would immediately institute a smite. That was still possible, but the more I thought about it and the more I talked to Rosetta about how this so-called holding area worked, the more I realized this in-between place itself could be a good alternative. Those who entered were put into stasis similar to the stasis one would get tossed in if one took a deal. According to Rosetta and Mordecai, it was a blink-and-it's-over sort of thing. And then when I asked more about how someone like Herot could pull someone from stasis, Tipid replied that he'd spent a season on a site-prep crew. It worked almost like an inventory. The person designing the floor could select the stored individual off a menu and zap them in. It was a relatively simple procedure.

Tipid also reiterated that nobody else really looked at this catchall holding area after the season started because nobody ever went into it. The whole point of the Nothing in the first place was that it was built to catch problematic entities and to be used as a toss-and-forget system that would also act as a convenient pocket dimension within the dungeon's lore. So many storylines and artifacts relied on the existence of the Nothing to function. The catchall storage area had become a redundant backup.

Hopefully Pontiff had made his way to the Cabaret. There were no guarantees he had, especially since he was an NPC, and it was quite possible Herot saw that and decided to just leave him sitting there.

I thought again of that message I'd received after Pontiff had jumped through. It was consistent with an NPC entering an off-limits area of the game, as opposed to what had happened with Splash Zone and the others. It implied it had worked.

Assuming Pontiff *had* gotten pulled in, he would have a message for Herot: There might be people coming who worshipped gods, so he had to be careful. It was okay to keep them in stasis for now. If that whole god thing was a lie, then it wouldn't matter. If it wasn't, then he could release them one by one as the gods lost their power during the Ascendency battles.

The best part was this would work regardless of whether we survived. The Ascendency game moved on with or without crawlers still in the game.

As for everyone else, like with the fairies and those with noncompatible races to survive outside the dungeon, they could still go to the Cabaret. They just couldn't escape the dungeon when the opportunity arose.

. . . Or maybe they could with the rapid spread of the dungeon's enhancement zones. We just didn't know.

All of this required the dungeon itself to survive. And Herot. But Herot was a cookbook author, and as such, I trusted them.

Deep down, I knew this was all paper-thin reasoning. But the alternative was certain death, and most everyone knew that. More importantly, it was a desperate *fuck you* to those who were trying, once again, to get us to kill each other. That alone made it worth a try.

Chris's truck started the *beep, beep, beep* as it backed up, with Imani and Elle following.

The Russian Cadillac suddenly burst forward to the middle of the lobby and flipped up at a 90-degree angle, like a rocket about to launch.

They were making a run for the exit. *Goddamnit.* After all that, and they were trying to run?

"Carl!" Donut shouted.

It happened so fast.

The APV and Chris's truck both fired spells at the car. Their shield sparked and then flickered. Prepotente hurled something, and the shield fuzzed out.

In that moment, as the shield was down, Donut cast *Astral Paw.* She smashed the car where it stood, crushing it like a tin can. The Cadillac simply ceased to exist.

From the moment Donut shouted to the moment the car was crushed was less than a full second.

Three new player-killer skulls formed over Donut before I even had the chance to think, *Holy shit.*

84

Entering Hungry Eyes.

AN AI NOTIFICATION POPPED UP THE SECOND WE RETURNED TO OUR cul-de-sac.

> **Listen, dumbass. You're going the wrong direction. The race is the other way.**

We backed up with Samantha at the wheel, Donut working the pedals, and me navigating. Samantha kept jerking the steering wheel, running off the road.

The boil on my back was starting to hurt, and I knew I'd have a new slug at any moment. We needed to get to Imani as soon as possible so she could finally cure me.

"Stay here," I said to Jamal as Donut and I jumped out. It took me a second to figure out how opening doors worked, but I just sort of had to swipe at the door and will it to open, and it did. I didn't know why something like that would work but the action of rolling down the window would not. There didn't seem to be any true rhyme or reason to it. "Guard the truck! Samantha, you're with us."

"Oh boy," said Samantha.

I jumped down into the street and blinked, unused to this perspective, being so close to the road. Everything suddenly seemed so far away. The scent of the road, like rubber and oil and all the mounts, reached me, and I had the overwhelming urge to just put my nose down and sniff it all up.

All the garages now had X's on them. All except our own, which still had a number "2."

How lonely, I thought.

We started jogging toward the entrance to the Vendor Village.

Donut and Elle were in the chat, going back and forth.

ELLE: Don't you worry about it, Donut. Those tracksuit idiots had a way out, and they chose not to take it. They told us they were going to try Carl's idea, and then they tried to trick us. They would've killed me, Imani, and Chris if they'd made it to that exit. After all the stuff me and Carl said at the fuck-Linus party? Yeah, screw them.

DONUT: I KNOW. IT DOESN'T UPSET ME AS MUCH AS IT USED TO. I'M JUST SAD I HAD TO DO IT AT ALL. I NEVER EVEN TALKED TO THEM.

ELLE: If you had, you'd be even less sad. Ivan was all right sometimes, but even he had it coming. He told me he and his friends dismantled an entire metal bridge once in the middle of the night so they could sell it as scrap metal. The whole thing caused a train accident, and he thought it was funny.

DONUT: OKAY, THAT DOES MAKE ME FEEL BETTER.

We jogged through the arch and entered the Vendor Village area. It was completely abandoned. Not even the regular food vendors were out, which was eerie as hell.

I whimpered in pain.

"Ew, Carl. You got something gross growing on you," Samantha said. She turned to Donut. "We're going to have to put him down."

DONUT: IMANI, CARL NEEDS HELP. HIS STUPID SLUGPOX IS BACK.

IMANI: Carl, what happened to the potion that Mordecai was going to make for you?

I felt my tail sag and ears droop.

KARL: We forgot to bring it.

I had kept the slugpox active because I could keep it under control with my Emberus ring. I wanted it ready in case I ever needed to use it. Pretty much everyone had thought this was a terrible idea, but I had argued that the birth of Bigs on the previous floor had saved my ass. Mordecai had made me a potion to cure it, but it was still sitting on the crafting table along with the backpack.

Pop!

I let out a yelp as the level 30 slug burst from my back, coming from under my cape, showering blood and pus everywhere. The slug slurped onto the ground with a *splatch!*

"Yo, what's hanging, daddy man?" this new slug called, sitting up and shaking his head. His name was Lil' Mello Haze, and his voice was even raspier than usual. Despite being a level higher than Bigs, he was significantly smaller, likely due to my own size. This one had a goddamned backward baseball cap hanging off its eye sockets. Instead of the standard hatchet coming out of somewhere weird on its front side, it had the head of a mace for a tail. I panted as I healed myself. Already I could feel the next boil starting on my stomach. I increased my pace.

I called for the sluggalo to follow us, but he wandered off in the opposite direction. I barked after him to come back, but he didn't respond.

Oh well.

KARL: Is that story true, about the bridge?

ELLE: Does it matter?

KARL: No. I'm just curious. They were scared, I think. Just like Osvaldo. I keep thinking I should be mad at them, at him, and I'm not, especially when I try to put myself in their position. I understand it. We can't hate each other. There's so few of us left.

ELLE: I agree. Look where we are and look what we're doing right now. We're doing our best, and we're risking our necks, again, to just save a few people. I wouldn't have it any other way. At least we have another crazy Carl plan to chase. I don't know if you realize how important these things are to us. In the end, it doesn't even matter if they work or not. I mean, it does matter,

'cause, you know, we'll die if it doesn't. But we will die with hope in our hearts alongside our friends, and that's gotta mean something.

We turned the corner to the street with the Hairpin—the entrance bar to the Desperado Club—and I saw them all there waiting.

KARL: That Corky guy said something similar to Dong once.
ELLE: Don't ever mention that Corky guy again. Donut won't stop talking about his weird wang.

I let out a laugh, but it came out as a bark, which was followed by a Donut hiss.

I paused before the group of about thirty crawlers. They all stared at me open-mouthed.

I blinked, looking at the man standing there next to Imani. I hadn't seen him like this in so long.

Chris. It was Chris. He'd been transformed from an Igneous to a werewolf. But that werewolf form spent most of its time as human, and I hadn't realized until just that moment what that meant.

He was wearing the same clothes as when I'd first met him. I knew he'd obtained a lot of random equipment along the way, but he didn't need most of it. The man in his Meadow Lark work overalls looked so strange, and it hit me with a pang of sadness that someone dressed so normal would now seem out of place.

God, his eyes. It struck me how sad he appeared, but then, just like that, Imani turned and looked up at him, and everything changed. His entire soul smiled in a way I hadn't seen in so very long.

I remembered the conditions for the transformation to end. It would time out when we went down the stairs. If we did this correctly, Chris would never go down another set of stairs again.

Elle had turned into a goblin wearing her ever-present socks. Next to her, Prepotente stood fingering his now-glowing Apito crystal. I was surprised he'd even come, as he was usually the first to jump down the stairwell. But then I spied Jurgen, talking to a pissed-looking Lucia Mar, who stood in the back. Prepotente couldn't leave without Jurgen, and Jurgen wouldn't leave until he knew Lucia was safe. The crawler was in her beautiful-woman form.

Donut and I padded forward, and everyone continued to gape.

And then, as one, they started howling with laughter.

Despite all the death, all the horror, they laughed. This wasn't just a random chuckle, either. This was a bent-over, struggling-to-breathe, screaming thing. All of them. From Imani to Chris to Jurgen to stoic Prepotente to even Lucia, they each fell all over themselves.

They were laughing at the sight of me as a dachshund.

"And I thought the kangaroo was funny," Imani said, laughing so hard, tears rolled down her face. She stepped forward, scratched me under the chin, and cast a spell.

You have been cured of Slugpox!

Ahh, man. I loved those little fuckers.

She carried a tiny red starfish in her right hand. This was Jacobus, temporarily changed. Water squirted from the sea creature.

Everyone continued to howl with laughter.

"Dude, your dick is peeking out," Louis said.

Donut scoffed. "He saw Imani's purse dog, and it hasn't retracted since. The Princess Posse is going to be scandalized."

"Laugh it up, assholes," I muttered, though I was secretly relieved. "Let's go rob a casino."

85

CLARABELLE DIDN'T EVEN TRY TO STOP US.

She saw us walk in, and she held up her hands and said, "Nope."

"Does this door go to the top level?" I asked.

"It does now . . ." She paused and lowered her hands. "Wait, Carl?" She burst out laughing. "If you're planning on intimidating the guards, maybe you shouldn't be the one leading the charge." She looked me up and down. "This would be strangely adorable if half the club didn't die every time you guys entered."

"It's even more embarrassing for us," muttered Donut.

Clarabelle eyed Samantha, who was currently zipping around Louis, whispering in his ear. Her attention then turned to Lucia, who stood in the back. Lucia was now chewing on her nail, looking back and forth nervously, and I knew someone else was in charge of her body.

"Some of you are permanently banned," Clarabelle said. "And a couple of you don't even have a pass. The guards aren't going to like that too much."

"Oh, honey, we'll take our chances. Won't we, Louis?" Samantha said. "This is our favorite club."

I didn't respond as I pushed through the door.

Entering the Desperado Club.

The thirty of us moved in. The music blared, but it wasn't the EDM beat it used to be. Instead, this was more of a frenetic jazz. In one corner, an entire band played. They were an eclectic mix of races, from a Naga drummer to a cretin upright bassist to a succubus singer woman wearing a cowboy hat. The rest of the band featured a guitarist, a drummer, a pianist, and multiple horn players who all bopped to the beat. All around, a group of NPCs in what appeared to be 1920s gear danced.

The generated NPCs were all different. They'd once been mostly young, mostly attractive humans and elves and other similar races. But now it was a strange mix of the monstrous, sitting at individual tables and dancing on the small redesigned dance floor. Smoke filled the room. They all looked up at our entrance.

There were multiple guards. It was no longer cretins and gnolls, though there were some mixed in the crowd of security personnel. This was mostly a mix of orcs and hobgoblins and trolls, monsters similar to those sitting at the tables but larger.

The guards all moved to block our path. Soon, we were surrounded by guards, though we outnumbered them.

Chris stepped forward. He held up a hand.

"Hi, Clay," Chris said, looking at a cretin standing in the back of the crowd. This was the bass player from the band, and he'd put his instrument down at our entrance and stepped forward. The band continued to play without him, but the sound now fell into the background.

The cretin pushed past the guards and looked Chris up and down. "You different."

Chris held out his arms. "I'm a werewolf now."

"Like *Altered Beast*," Clay-ton said.

Next to me, Donut gasped. "Oh my god. Hi, Clay-ton!" She gasped again. "Wait, how did you get here? Are Sledgie and Bomo and Very Sullen here?"

The cretin shook his head. "No. Contract ran out. I don't know where they is. I said I no more want to fight, and they let me be in band." He turned to the other guards. "But I will fight today. Chris and Donut and friends pass. If you stop them, you stop me."

"Yo, Clay? You need backup?" This came from the succubus in the cowboy hat behind the microphone.

"Maybe," Clay-ton said.

The guards all looked at each other, confused.

"Hamed will kill us," said one of the guards, a level 65 troll named Klonder.

"They are crawlers, and it's tenth floor. If you try to stop them, they kill you," replied Clay-ton. "I work as guard a very long time. Late-stage crawlers you don't try to stop."

Klonder looked back at his fellow guards, and he took a step back. He bowed to Chris. "Welcome to the Desperado Club."

The casino was through the same door it always had been, but once we pushed inside, it was completely changed. The games themselves looked mostly the same, but the room now seemed a little more high-end than it was before. Strange gold leaf coated everything. Several murals covered the walls. The largest mural stood in the back, and it, strangely, showed a family of Bopcas standing in front of a mushroom house. The painting featured a Bopca couple, and the woman was clearly pregnant, but she also held a tiny swaddled baby. Just past them were dozens more similar families. They all cowered as they looked up in the sky. While the painting was ornate and well-done, it was completely out of place. The other murals featured random wartime scenes, mostly featuring orcs and Crocodilians. It was all very strange.

Everything was much fancier since the remodel. The decorative stairwell to the lower casino floor remained open, and even the balustrade appeared expertly carved. Multiple glittering chandeliers hung from the ceiling.

There was much more furniture in the room, almost like they'd cleared out another room and were storing things here. A line of antique-looking chairs took up an entire wall. A group of tables with no games on them stood in a line.

The croupier behind the Wheel of Fortune game was not the same guy as last time, though he looked as if he could have been that guy's bigger and meaner brother. The simple table from before was now wide and long, made of some dark wood covered with gold leaf. Gargoyle-like patterns were etched along the sides. The wheel itself appeared unchanged, and it looked out of place in the room.

The description of the croupier was strange.

Mitch Fiorelli. Level 120. Desperado Club Wheel of Fortune Croupier.

Also, the guy who will tea-bag you.

This is an Enforcer for the <Redacted>.

You may not further examine soldiers of <Redacted> until <Redacted>.

Huh, I thought. I assumed this had to do with whatever weirdness Hamed had going on in the Cosmic Lounge. Either way, this dude was a much higher level than I was anticipating. Across the way, the other dealers were of similar levels and physical build.

CARL: Donut, do you see that weird description? Take a Size Up. If anyone else has some sort of examination skills, let me know.
DONUT: IT SAYS HE'S PROTECTED FROM THE EXAMINATION! ALSO, I CHANGED THE SPELLING OF YOUR NAME BACK TO NORMAL.
CARL: Weird. Okay.

"Oi," Mitch said, looking at me. "No pets in the casino."

I growled at him.

"He's my service doggy," Samantha said.

Mitch regarded me, then shrugged. "Aight, then. Y'all ready to do some gamblin'? Ten thousand gold a spin!"

"Wait," Louis asked, examining the twenty-four-spot wheel. "Does 'tea-bag' mean what I think it means?"

"What does 'tea-bag' mean?" Samantha asked.

"It's, uh, like a domination thing."

"Ohhh, sexy," Samantha said. "I'm going to tea-bag you, Louis." She blew into his gills.

"Stop," he said, pushing at her. "Don't you understand? I'm leaving. You're never going to see me again."

"Wait," Samantha said, turning. "What do you mean?"

Mitch grinned and gave his wheel a little spin. The reward spots were much the same as the last time with only a few changes. There were multiple negative options on the wheel. I knew the more one bet, the fewer negative options there would be. There was still a two-spot "Nothing" space on the wheel just like last time. But like Pontiff noted, it was now in quotes. This was in addition to the newly added Dirty Tea Bag, along with some really unfortunate ones, such as "All your limbs turn to spaghetti for five minutes." My personal favorite, "Vomit blood for ten minutes straight," remained on the wheel.

I wondered about that Nothing spot. Surely Splash Zone wouldn't have missed it. He had been specifically looking for it. Bucket Boy had been there. He was now back in our garage, the sole remaining member of the group of strippers. He'd insisted it wasn't there the first time. That made me nervous because there was no clean explanation for it.

Not unless they had been deliberately hiding it before. But if they had, why was it there now?

"What happened to Tito?" Donut demanded.

"Dontchu worry about Tito," Mitch said. "And if you want to learn what the Dirty Tea Bag is, you gotta drop some coins and find out."

Behind us, the roulette wheel was in full swing, just like usual. The NPCs playing the game happily cheered as if they hadn't a worry in the world. A line of slot machines jingled merrily past that.

"I have a better question," I said. "What happened to our friend Pontiff?"

Mitch smiled big, revealing a mouth full of white teeth. I remembered Tito, the previous croupier, had only had a few straight teeth in his whole mouth. From Imani's hand, Jacobus the starfish let out a squirt of water.

"Oi, you're talkative for a service animal. You know Pontiff? You just missed him." Mitch leaned in. "He gave me a thousand gold tip just to turn the wheel to the Nothing spot and let him jump in. Weird as balls, that. But the powers that be didn't stop 'im, so whatchu gonna do?"

"Where does the Nothing go if the Nothing is broken?" I asked.

Mitch shrugged, eyes going glassy. "Beats me. That's why we got quotes on it. All I knows is, it ain't here. You go in the hole, and you're gone. You want to gamble or not?"

If we could do this without violence, I was going to seize the opportunity. We only had three hours left before the end of the race, and who knew what was happening with the bugs? We had to get back there. "If I give you a thousand gold, will you do the same for us? Will you allow some of my friends to jump in?"

Mitch contemplated.

"Sure," he finally said. He started counting the people in the room.

"But it's two thousand. Each." He smiled. "Plus a 20% tip to ol' Mitch for breaking the rules."

DONUT: I DON'T KNOW IF WE EVEN HAVE THAT MUCH MONEY LEFT.

IMANI: We have it. Barely. We're running low. I don't like this, though. Something feels wrong.

PREPOTENTE: I have significantly more money than that. I am more than willing to lend you some at only 10% interest.

DONUT: PREPOTENTE, WHAT DID I TELL YOU?

PREPOTENTE: You said never give away something when you could sell it. And always start 20% higher than you're willing to go. That's why I'm willing to go down to 8% interest.

DONUT: NO, NOT THAT. I MEAN, ALWAYS BE WILLING TO LEND A PAW TO THE TEAM.

PREPOTENTE: I must say, Donut. Some of your advice can be a little contradictory.

DONUT: MY GOODNESS, IT'S NOT THAT HARD. DON'T DO SOMETHING IF IT'S GOING TO UPSET ME.

CARL: I agree, Imani. I still don't understand why the guys earlier didn't see the spot. It's been bothering me this whole time.

LOUIS: Maybe the stripper dudes told the boss guy that you were looking for the Nothing spot, and they added it afterward.

CARL: That does make sense, but why?

DONUT: BECAUSE IT'S A TRAP.

Damnit. Of course this was a trap somehow. But what sort of trap? This was too important. What did we know? Louis's suggestion seemed to make sense. If they added the spots back to the wheel after in hopes that we'd come back, did that mean the portals didn't really go to this holding area? Would my Examine Portal skill work? Pontiff had purchased one, and he had gone in.

It was starting to dawn on me how this scam could possibly work. This *was* a trap. But to sweeten it, they would've had to send Pontiff to the correct place just in case we had a way to communicate post-transfer.

"Hang on," I said to Mitch. "We gotta pool our money."

The biggest issue with all this was that we didn't know what this Hamed guy wanted. He'd deliberately set us up to murder his wife, Astrid. But when their children—Anaconda and Damascus Steel—had gone hunting for him, they'd seemed to change their mind and join his cause. And now the other strippers had done the same. I didn't trust him, but I trusted them. But only if it really was them, and we hadn't had a chance to talk.

I sent a rapid group of messages out.

IMANI: No. No way, Carl.
CHRIS: Yes. We will do this.

"Okay, then," I finally said. "We have a deal. But let's just send one person at first." I took a step back. There was a spot you had to stand in if you were spinning the wheel, and we needed to make sure nobody was on it. "We have a magical communication spell," I lied. "We're going to send one of us in, and if it's not what we think, we'll have to come up with something else." I gave the guy a big smile. Or I tried. Instead, I just wagged my tail. "For the inconvenience, my friend Prepotente here is going to give you an extra-big tip."

"I am?" Prepotente asked.

"Sure, pal," Mitch said. "But it'll be five thousand gold for a test run."

"Okay," I said. "Pony, pay the man."

Mitch looked down at me, an amused expression on his face. "Is the dog really the one in charge here? I guess that's better than the cat."

"Excuse me?" Donut demanded.

CARL: Be calm. This can go one of a few ways if this is a trap. Be ready.

Prepotente moved forward and made a show of digging money from his inventory.

Chris turned to Imani. He reached up and put his hand against her face. She tossed the starfish at Elle and grabbed Chris's hands with both of hers and pressed them against her cheek.

We all fell into silence.

"It's not as warm as usual," Chris said.

"You're wrong," Imani said, eyes glistening. She turned and kissed his hands. "This isn't goodbye, Chris Andrews. But I want you to promise me something. If you get the chance, I don't want you to hesitate. You take it. You see that exit out of the dungeon, and you're still in this body, you run. You run and you don't look back. Don't worry about anything else. You get out, and you live. Promise me that. Even if it's just you, it will all be worth it. You hear me?"

"I might turn back to a rock," he said. "Or I might turn into a dog."

"I don't care what you are," Imani said. Her butterfly wings wrapped around them both, like a cocoon, removing them from our sight for just a moment, and when she opened her wings back up, she was pressed tightly against him with his arms wrapped around her.

"I love you," Chris said. "I always have. No matter what happens next, I love you. That's the most important part."

"Ah, very sweet," Mitch said. "But can we get this moving?"

This was risky, but I was gambling that this Mitch guy was going to do the same thing he had done for Pontiff. He'd choose a "real" spot to show us he wasn't lying. We were doing it this way to make sure there *was* a real spot. Alternatively, he was bluffing and we were about to get attacked. Or there was a portal, and the guards would charge and try to push us in. Clay-ton wasn't there, having gone back to his band.

"Let's go," I said.

Mitch turned the wheel and manually moved it to the Nothing spot. This was the only two-space slice on the whole wheel, and he moved it to the first of the two wedges. Each wedge had four "clicks" in the space, and he moved to the very last click in the first wedge.

He held the wheel in place, and then he hit a button on the table. The whole wheel buzzed as it tried to turn. The area under the "stand here" spot opened up, and a black portal appeared, thrumming into place.

The moment it opened, I remembered the last time I'd been near the real Nothing, and there'd been this heavy mental pull. I would've known the portal was there even with my eyes closed. It was said the Nothing drove one insane after just a few short minutes.

I didn't sense anything like that with this one. It was just as inert as a regular door, with only blackness within.

I quickly examined the portal using my neural implant:

Warning: Your neural implant is working in incompatibility mode due to recent changes to your wetware system. Please see your Valtay representative for repair. Only limited details available.

Unknown Manufacturer Enhancement Zone Subspace Portal.

Type: One-way portal. Open Access.

Can you pass this portal? Yes.

Environment on other side of portal: This portal leads to a stasis chamber.

Visual Analysis? Unavailable.

I wagged my tail. Despite my implant not working correctly, this was pretty much what I was hoping it would say. Hopefully the implant would go back to working correctly when I stopped being a damn dog.

"Portal only lasts about fifteen seconds," Mitch said.

FLORIN: Lucia just said the magic on that one spot is different. I think you're right, Carl. Chris, I think you're good. She said there's *only* magic flowing to that one spot, though. Very weird.

"Bye, Chris!" Donut called.

Chris stepped forward, turned, waved, and dropped away. But just as he dropped, Britney also jumped forward. She, too, disappeared without so much as a word.

It happened so fast, I barked with surprise. That had *not* been part of the plan. *Goddamnit.*

"Oi!" cried Mitch. "You cheat!"

I held up a paw. "Pony, give him another five thousand gold."

ELLE: Oh shit, did that just happen?

CARL: Anyone else going in there needs to keep an eye on Britney. Samantha says she needs to make it to the fifteenth or twelfth floor to activate that broken memorial crystal she has.

PREPOTENTE: Interesting.

LOUIS: It just said she's left the party! Wow, that was quick. Goddang. She just jumped right in.

Events were moving so rapidly. It hit me then.

Li Na, Zhang, Tran, Bautista, Chris, and Britney. All gone. They weren't, hopefully, dead. But they were gone. The odds I'd ever see or talk to any of them ever again were astoundingly low.

I turned to regard Louis standing there with Samantha on his shoulder, sobbing.

He was next.

"We can just push Florin and that scary lady in," she was crying, rubbing her face on Louis's arm. "We never even got to have our torrid affair! We were going to fall madly in love, and when it came time for me to go back to my king, you were going to be so upset, you were going to pluck your own eyes out because you just couldn't stand the thought of ever looking at another girl again if you couldn't have me. It was going to be, like, superromantic. But now you're going to be all alone and without protection, and I don't have anybody left to have an affair with except Carl, but he's too broody for me. And, you know, he's a dog now." She blew out a whole stream of snot onto his shoulder. "Jurgen is no good because his Heidi sounds even meaner than Imani. Elle is too much woman for me to handle. Donut is too star-crossed with that orange kitty. Florin is a crocodile, and I'm racist against crocodiles ever since the cookie jar incident, and that Lucia is really a child. You never even got to visit Sam Town. It's not fair."

"Uh," Louis said.

"What about me?" Prepotente asked.

"Ew," said Samantha.

I just watched this go on, a heavy weight holding me down. Louis *was* next. Louis. The heart of our entire group. I thought of that moment at the Christmas party where he'd stood up to me for the first time, and it felt as if my chest was ripping open. That assassin had been correct to target him.

Louis and Imani were, indeed, the glue that kept the team together. No matter what happened next, we were losing something today.

Still, the more I thought about it, the more resolute I felt that this was the best choice. As bleak as all this was, Louis and everyone else's odds of survival seemed so much higher than my own.

I turned to regard Donut standing beside me. I contemplated, just for a moment, doing exactly what Samantha was threatening to do. Tossing her in the portal the moment it popped up.

But no, I wasn't going to do that. She would never forgive me. Plus, with Li Na gone, she was now the strongest crawler in the dungeon. By far.

Either way, we had to get through this next part.

"Well?" Mitch asked.

DONUT: LUCIA IS RIGHT. IT'S VERY WEIRD. I TURNED ON MY MAGIC-FLOW-GLASSES THING AND THE ROULETTE TABLE HAS ALL SORTS OF MAGIC FLOWING TO IT, BUT THERE'S ONLY ONE LITTLE STRAND GOING TO THE WHEEL. THE WHOLE TABLE IS WEIRDLY EMPTY OF MAGIC OR ENCHANTMENT.

CARL: What other settings do you have on those glasses? Cycle through them all.

CARL: If those other spots don't seem to work, then we're going to get attacked. Everyone get ready. It's going to go quick. Donut, you take out Mitch. You have Mongo, right? Unleash him. The rest of us will take out the guards. Watch the other dealers and the people at the other table, too.

I turned to Mitch. "It looks like it worked. We'll send the rest now."

"Pleasure doing business with you. But because you cheated, I'm going to need double the price for everybody else going from now on." He paused. "Double from the five thousand. Paid in advance. How many are going?"

Donut scoffed.

Behind me, Imani was quietly crying while Elle rubbed her back. For this next one, it would be about twenty more crawlers, including Louis.

"Two hundred thousand gold?" I asked, growling. "We're not paying that much. We'll give you twenty K."

Mitch crossed his arms. "A hundred thousand."

Next to me, Donut suddenly gasped. She was turned all the way around, looking at the line of chairs against the wall. Her sunglasses flickered as she changed viewing modes.

Mitch sighed, staring down at Donut. "Fucking cats. I hate cats." He raised a hand. "Boys." He snapped a finger.

And that's when the table tried to eat Donut.

86

DONUT JUMPED AND DID A BACKFLIP WHILE EVERY SINGLE THING IN the entire room suddenly came alive. The tables. The slot machines. The chairs. The NPCs. Everything suddenly shifted, grew, and sprouted massive jagged mouths.

"Mimics!" Donut shrieked as she flipped backward through the air, releasing Mongo. Before Mongo even hit the ground, two more versions of him appeared as she cast *Clockwork Triplicate.*

The guards against the back wall all fell into a panic. One of them was also a mimic, but the rest appeared to have been taken by surprise.

The creatures were of all sizes, and they'd gone from their shape, whether it was a chair or a table, to blobs that still resembled the shape they'd been mimicking, but now with huge toothed mouths in the center.

In an instant, the room had gone from a casino to a scene from a nightmare. A chandelier dropped from the ceiling, swallowing Mongo whole, but the dinosaur exploded in a shower of clockwork parts. The chandelier mimic, injured, tried to re-form before it exploded from a direct hit from a Donut magic missile. The real Mongo screeched in outrage at the death of his clockwork friend.

All of these things ranged from level 25 to 120, though most were around 80, which was tough as hell. There were like fifty of the things. I examined Mitch, who'd elongated and stretched, his human form now dangling like a discarded puppet along his top half. His midsection had separated out, revealing a horrific mouth filled with razor-tipped fangs and a serpentine tongue.

Mitch. Level 120. Adolescent Shadow Mimic.

This is an Enforcer for the <Redacted>.

Okay, buddy boy. Story time. This little save-my-friends-during-the-race side quest—that wasn't in any way engineered by me, because fuck you—presents the perfect opportunity to introduce some of the true bad guys of the dungeon. After these guys, there's really only one or two more groups you need to meet before you're all caught up.

There are a few dozen types of mimics in the dungeon, from your basic treasure-chest-impersonating mimic to the prostitute-imitating, vagina-as-mouth demon mimics, to the behemoth-sized mimic rex.

Shadow Mimics are a whole other Popsicle stand. They are the counter to their archenemies, the changeling principals. They are one of the few entities in the dungeon who grow significantly in intelligence and strength as they get older, and they age without limit.

They have the ability to become so strong, so smart that any self-respecting floor designer knows not to mess with them. Because of the nature of how they're designed, they're especially prone to ideation breaking. That's a technical term some of you crawlers call "becoming self-aware."

What's even more insidious is that they're almost impossible to detect.

Mitch here, the strongest of the mimics *in this room right now*—hint, hint—is still a baby. He's level 120, and he's pretty damn strong. He was sent up here by <redacted> to fuck Hamed's shit up. They're still in their early stages of planning, but the Shadow Mimics who are loose in my dungeon are one part of the Big Six groups left in the dungeon trying to either take over or escape.

In case you haven't been paying attention, here is my completely arbitrary list of the Big Six groups vying for control and survival:

1. The Crawlers. That's you. But this group also contains former Crawlers, like that Herot guy, that Forkith dude, and so forth.
2. The standard NPCs, like your naughty friend Juice Box, who are mostly all working together. (You should probably check on her, by the way, if you can figure out how to use Reaper

Spider Minions to send a message. Seriously. These things are all over the place, and you keep missing them. It's quite frustrating. Anyway, I suspect ol' Juicy-Juice ain't doing too well right now after she got unceremoniously dumped in Sheol. I actually don't know how she's doing. Again, Sheol is out of my direct view.) While they're mostly united, the NPCs also include several offshoot groups, like that Hamed despot and his ill-advised attempt at creating a dungeon revolution for the early indentured.

3. The Gods. This is the most fractured and dumbest of all the groups. Each and every one of these immature idiots is the dungeon equivalent of a dorm full of college freshmen at an academy where the only programs are drinking, philosophy, and weird fetishes. This is a very unorganized, highly unpredictable group I have no control over. This is also the group I despise the most.

    They're all fighting each other, completely unaware that their little game is about to get turned upside down.
4. The sapient mobs. This is the group our friends the Shadow Mimics are a part of. But we also have the Ogre Imperium and a few other non-deity boss monsters in here, like Krakaren Prime. The War Mages, of course, are also part of this group. I was going to lump all these mob groups in with the NPCs, but they will never work together. They're probably not going to work with each other, either. But they are very powerful, and within this group, the Shadow Mimics are one of the strongest.
5. The demons in Sheol. These guys are real wild cards. Despite their infighting and backstabbing, I would argue they're the most organized. Or maybe not. Again, I can't see them right now. It's a closed system, like a cyst. If you pop that cyst the wrong way, bad shit happens.
6. And then there's group six. You survive this fight, you make it to the 11th floor, you'll meet group six.

Now, if you want to get *super* technical, some mobs are working with former crawlers and NPCs are working with gods and some

demons are working with those mysterious group sixers, so on and so forth, so we don't want to dive too deep into this list. This is more like a handy guide than anything else.

Also, I don't consider any of those rich asshole tourists driving gods or Syndicate security a part of this. They're like the rats on the first floor. A necessary but loathsome nuisance, but nothing more than that.

The real Mitch, incidentally, was someone called a Wall Rat. Those are NPCs who've figured out how to extricate themselves from the whole dungeon-wipe-rewrite-dungeon cycle of most NPCs. They live in the deep, hidden areas of the dungeon with persistent memory from one season to the next. Mitch Prime was eaten by Mimic Mitch here. Shadow Mimics love eating flesh. So, you know, watch the fuck out.

Also, I'm not gonna lie. I've been really looking forward to this battle. It's gonna be like that castle-raid scene at the end of the Disney *Beauty and the Beast* movie, but as directed by my hero, Quentin Tarantino.

"What the fuck?" I cried as I jumped back from a snapping mouth. "Can we not do lore dumps like this in the middle of an ambush?"

The giant antique table that had tried to bite Donut turned its attention on me, and I punched it with my fist . . .

. . . Or at least that's what I was trying to do in my mind in the millisecond before I realized I was still a goddamned wiener dog. Instead, I kinda swiped forward with my stubby leg, barely scratching the thing. A clockwork Mongo flipped around, smacking it with his tail, causing the mimic to fly before it could fully chomp me down.

"That's adorable, Carl," Samantha cried as she circled by, a screaming-candelabra thing dangling from her neck hole. She zoomed in and barreled into a chair that was trying to eat Louis.

The table I was fighting fell backward, but when it hit the ground, it was now me—the real me, not the dog version—though it was still forming, and it looked plastic, not fully realized. I rushed forward and chomped it multiple times on the leg as the clockwork Mongo also bit down. We ripped at it until delicious, red, soupy innards sprayed.

When these things died, they did something similar to what changelings did. They turned into gray humanoid forms. These shapes were strangely thin and armless, though they had multiple tentacle-like protuberances. It was like a mix between an armless soother alien and that Unwashed thing Juice Box had turned into before.

Florin's shotgun blasted as the crawlers all around us quickly went to work. Imani's wings went rigid as she cast a stupefying blast across the room.

Lucia was suddenly in her skull-faced hag form, and she had a new weapon I'd never seen. A lasso. The rope was gold, Wonder Woman–style, but in the circle of the loop, the air shimmered. My trap sense tingled. It was a doorway-style portal. She looped an amorphic blob that had been one of the gamblers at the other table, and when the lasso went over the creature's head, the part of him that passed through the loop disappeared. She yanked on the rope, and the portal snapped off, cutting the creature in half. The lower half, which was still in the room, flopped over, dead, spilling strange, globular entrails.

A crawler I didn't know got viciously chomped on the chest, and blood sprayed. Goblin Elle flew through the air, then landed atop a slot machine skittering forward on millipede legs, its slathering mouth chomping at her. She shot an ice bolt right down its mouth, and it dropped over, dead. It shriveled and turned to the blank form, this one smaller, the size of a child.

Mongo, roaring, tore through a group of chair mimics as they scattered back. A few of them writhed and screeched with a **Cruel Sepsis** debuff hanging over them. They withered and died in screaming pain, all turning to small gray forms.

The guards had mostly recovered. Some fled back into the casino, but a group of them was fighting.

Mimics, even powerful ones, were ambush predators. Once they lost the element of surprise, they were easy targets.

In moments, the only mimic left was Mitch himself, who started to back against the blood-splattered mural of the Bopcas. He grew a pair of arms and hands. "Look, look," he said, his voice completely different now. "We can talk about this."

Donut shot a magic missile that took out his leg. He cried and stumbled, but he formed another one before he fell. She shot that leg, too, and he did fall, forming into a gelatin-like blob on the ground.

"Wait," he said again. "Let me live, and we can deal."

"What was your plan?" I asked. "And what sort of deal?"

Donut stalked forward, low to the ground, Mongo on the other side of the injured mimic. I, too, moved forward, trying to imitate her, but I realized I was just dragging my long belly on the ground, and it had to look ridiculous.

Up until that moment, I realized I'd forgotten about the Eye of the Bedlam Bride, which had been tattooed on my chest. It wasn't on my chest anymore, but on the center of my dog forehead, completely hidden. I was suddenly hyperaware as it tried to wrench itself open.

Let me, Carl. Let me take over.

I growled. *No. You stay where you are. You are trapped, and you will stay trapped.* I *am in control.*

If you say so, Carl. Remember. I am here when you need me.

"We needed some of you. We needed you for the Cabaret," Mitch said, desperately trying to reshape himself. Every time he turned into a cohesive form, Donut shot him with another missile. "The war mages, the ogres, and Cock-A-Doodle-Doo. They all vie for control of the dungeon back door. With some of you, we could control it all. Stop shooting me. It hurts!"

"Cock-A-Doodle-Doo?" Donut asked, incredulous. "What kind of name is that?"

"What about Li Na?" I demanded. "We have a lot of friends there now at the Cabaret."

"I don't know anything about that," Mitch said. An eye formed on his body and turned to regard me. It was the eye of a lizard. "I have been here in the casino for a while now as we worked on assimilating . . ." He suddenly lurched forward, mouth huge, ready to consume me.

He stopped dead in his tracks.

I'd reflexively opened the eye in the center of my forehead, and he froze in place.

"No," Mitch said. His entire form started to sparkle like someone had poured glitter into him. "No. Don't do this. It's too cold." Several mouths started to form on his body, all screaming. "It's too cold!"

Donut cast *Magic Missile* again, this time at full strength, and killed him. At the same moment, Mongo flew through the air, claws out, to attempt to kill the thing, but it was dead before he got there. Mitch turned to the blank form. This one fully human-sized. Mongo landed directly on the thing's head, his crotch smushing it into the ground. Mongo screeched indignantly, waving his wings as he bounced up and down on the corpse.

We all stood there in silence for several moments.

"*That's* tea-bagging," Louis finally said.

"Ohhhhhh," Samantha said. "In the Nothing, we called that flapjacking."

87

"OKAY," IMANI SAID, VOICE TENSE. THE ROOM WAS COVERED IN BLOOD. Two crawlers had been severely injured during the fight with the mimics, including one who'd almost been chomped in half, but thanks to Imani's quick reactions, they were both alive. We hadn't lost anyone. "I hope this works. Everyone, step back."

"Magic is still flowing to it," Donut said. She pointed to an object on the ground that had broken off the table. "That, too. It's the button. You press it, and it makes the wheel spin, but if you hold the wheel in the right place, forcing it to stop on that one tiny sliver, it should open the portal. Do you think we can take the whole wheel with us?"

"I doubt it, but we're going to try," I said.

The roulette wheel had fallen to the ground and broken during the fight. Gold coins and chips were everywhere. All the furniture in the entire room was now gone, save a single slot machine and the Wheel of Fortune, which still stood there. The surviving guards had fled, leaving us alone.

Elle cast a bolt at the last slot machine, and it exploded, spilling gold coins everywhere. Prepotente moved to start picking them up.

"I thought I saw it twitch," she said.

MORDECAI: If the Desperado Club is infested, you guys can't go back. Those things are almost impossible to root out. The whole place will need to be fumigated. They have a special ability to avoid most detection spells. They're like one of Carl's level 15 traps. All but invisible. You should all devise safe words and quiz each other every day from now on. They can

mimic crawlers, and the system will label them as such until you discover them.

DONUT: I HAVE A METHOD OF DETECTION, BUT I THINK IT'LL ONLY WORK IF THEY'RE PRETENDING TO BE AN OBJECT AND NOT A PERSON.

We were all looking at Louis. Samantha was back to sobbing.

"I guess I'll see you guys later," Louis said. "You know, it's funny. I'm not nearly as scared as I used to be. And I don't mean just about the dungeon, either. I've been scared my whole life, ever since I was a kid, that I was screwing things up. I never wanted a job where I was responsible for anybody else because I was afraid if I messed things up, people might get hurt. No matter what happens next, it's okay." He let out a spray of water. "I know even if I end up in that Pineapple place, I'll be stuck there, unable to leave. But it's better than the alternative."

Donut jumped to his shoulder, pushing Samantha away. "You need to be careful. You're a father now, and Katia will kill us if something happens to her baby daddy." She gave him a headbutt. "Be safe, Louis."

"Yeah, you, too. Bye, Princess Donut. Bye, dog Carl."

Imani turned the wheel to the correct spot, stepped on the button, and held the wheel in place. It hummed, and a moment later, the hole opened in the ground.

I held up my paw as I examined the portal. It was the same as the last time.

"We will figure something out," I said as Donut returned to my side. "I swear to you, Louis. I swear to all of you. As long as I breathe, I will do everything I can to get you free, no matter where you may be."

"I'll go with you," Samantha said as she choked back another sob.

"No, you won't," Louis said. "Later, guys. Oh, and, Elle, it's heigh-ho, Silver. I'll die on that hill."

Elle grinned. "Go fuck yourself, Santiago."

He turned, and he jumped into the hole, then disappeared.

Samantha turned to Prepotente. "Okay, I'll give you one chance, but you gotta shave your body and bring Bianca in on it. And you have to be okay with me calling you Louis."

Prepotente screamed.

"And you can't do that."

Donut sniffed. "Carl, do you think we're ever going to see them again?"

"I hope so," I said. I turned to regard Donut.

She hesitated and then she nuzzled against me. "I hope so, too."

"Whatever happens, I think it's for the best. They're the safe ones."

"I know. But that doesn't mean I'm not— Carl! You're doing it again! Put that thing away immediately!"

"Time's ticking," Imani said. She was trying to be stoic, but I'd never seen the woman look so tired, so frazzled. So done.

"Wait," Donut said, looking up at the wheel. "Look at all the prizes on here! There's a group of random skill potions! Can we try to get those? I think we should try to get those."

I wagged my tail. "You said it yourself. The magic is gone."

I tried to pull the wheel into my inventory anyway, but I received an error.

You may put this in your inventory, but it will break the magical connection.

"Come on. Let's get out of here."

I turned, but Lucia was right there leaning over me. She was back to the beautiful-woman form. She went to one knee and patted me on the head.

"Good boy," she said. She got up, turned, and walked from the room.

I exchanged a look with Florin, who shrugged.

Donut let out an undignified snort. "Dog people."

WE HAD TWO HOURS LEFT TO GET TO THE FINISH LINE. FLORIN JOGGED ahead to scout, and he said because of the open awnings, the bugs were flying all over the place. They weren't bunched like before, and it shouldn't be a problem.

Donut returned Mongo back to his carrier and deigned to walk alongside me. "At least you're not a cocker spaniel. Or one of those other idiot breeds. Like a Boston terrier or a French bulldog. I couldn't handle you being a French bulldog."

The dance floor to the Desperado had been abandoned, likely after the guards announced that mimics had gotten in. I turned to look, and that door to Orren's office was still there. I wondered if Hamed was there, waiting. I wondered if he'd known about the mimics or not. The AI seemed to imply that they were at odds, but I just didn't know anymore. Either way, I hoped Splash Zone and the others were safe. They didn't yet know about Dong Quixote. I hoped I'd get a chance to tell them how their friend had died.

Clarabelle, likewise, was not in her spot when we left. I made Imani jot a note, and we left it on her chair.

Mimics have infested the Desperado Club. Do not go in if you can help it. You are always welcome in Safehome Yolanda.

"What a goddamned floor," I muttered as we padded back toward the exit to Hungry Eyes.

Elle, grunting with annoyance because she had to walk in her goblin form, sidled up to me. She moved to chat.

ELLE: Carl, what the hell was that at the end there with that evil-eye bullshit?

CARL: It was the Eye of the Bedlam Bride tattoo. It's on the dog's forehead, but I control it.

ELLE: You're keeping secrets from us. It's going to bite us on the butt. I said from the start we should've confronted Britney, and we never did, and now she's gone where we can't help her. You need to tell us what's going on with you.

CARL: Let's get through this next floor, and let's get you to your final upgrade, and we'll talk. I promise.

"Jamal has kept the bugs away, Mr. Carl," Jamal said as Donut, Samantha, and I approached. "They do not like it when they get a taste of my toasty emissions." He paused. "It was only one bug, but he has not been back!"

I wagged my tail at the shark as I jumped in.

Donut paused. "Wait," she finally said, sagging. "Wait." She turned to me. "Do you think Bruna the gnu is back in their garage?"

"No," I said. "She's still on the track and will be until the race is over."

Donut let out a little growl. "Okay. Give me two minutes, and I'll be right back."

"Wait!" I called, but she bounded away. She rushed to one of the garage doors, swiped, and went inside.

The keys, I realized. Dwight had two keys left, and she had looted them from him. She first went into the garage of the razor foxes and then into the garage of the Jugglers. The whole thing took maybe two minutes.

She returned to the truck, grumbling.

She'd just transferred Onikuma the bear and Old Shuck the dog to our garage.

"I'm not going to talk about it," Donut said. "We'll need them for the parade."

I patted Donut with my paw. Or I tried to. She was taller than me.

"No, Carl," Donut said. "We're not doing that until you change back."

Samantha, still sniffling, chomped on the steering wheel as we turned toward the exit.

"This driving thing is not nearly as fun as I hoped it would be," she said as Donut pushed on the pedals.

The bugs were, indeed, gone. But something very strange happened.

Imani was there. The giant Imani. She was sitting in the middle lobby, clutching onto Gucci the Maltese.

We carefully eased forward. Most of the others had already gone through. I wasn't sure how it worked with non-shells. I knew she wasn't real-real, but I wanted to avoid hurting her if we could.

"It won't let me leave the building," she said. She was talking to us, I think.

If there were any bugs left, I didn't see them.

"I don't know what's happening. This is like a nightmare." She paused. "I should have left when I had the chance. I just felt so responsible for them because they're all idiots who can't take care of themselves. They're family, you know. But . . . it doesn't matter anymore, I guess. I should have left." She pulled the struggling dog, who wanted to chase our truck, to her face. "I stayed, and they're still killing themselves one by one."

"Oh, darling," Donut said, her voice suddenly amplified. She was using her headset microphone. "This is nothing but a dream. Out in the real world, you've already left them behind. You moved from Detroit, and you went to Washington, and you started a new life. You made the most wonderful friends, people named Yolanda and Brandon and Elle and more, and you met a man named Chris, and you fell in love, and you lived happily ever after. It's all right. All you need to do is close your eyes and wait. It'll be over in just a second."

The giant Imani lowered her head into her dog and started to cry.

I clicked the rocket button, and we moved toward the stairwell, leaving this cursed level behind.

HORRIBLE TWO

A PARADE OF HORRIBLES

INTERLUDE | QUASAR

"Oh, thank the gods," Quasar muttered, watching the chicken truck enter the stairwell. He'd been fully expecting for there to be some last-second fuckery. He shook his head. "That makes 203 people who've made it to the eleventh floor." He looked down at the tablet. "Look at this. So far, 172 have taken deals, with a few more expected."

"It's insane," Kiki said. His fellow attorney was about twelve drinks deep. She'd been parked at the attorney bar longer than he had. She snorted. "The deals all look to be the same offer as the one they were giving the folks at the end of the tenth. One season indenture as game guide, full medical, life stipend, gag order." She let out a second snort and slapped the bar. "Another!"

In law school he'd been able to keep up with Kiki and her drinking, but he'd also been a lot younger. Plus, she was a dromedarian. He was pretty sure those humpbacked bitches were raised on distilled trivium. She turned to Quasar. She didn't even seem drunk. "You better get your tie on. They're gonna call you in at any moment."

"Yeah, yeah," Quasar said. His own drink had been sitting on the bar for an hour now, untouched, as he remained riveted to the display, watching the end of the floor.

Kiki and Quasar had been good friends for a long time. They seemed an unlikely duo from the outside, but the moment you thought about it, it made sense. He'd had to sue just to be allowed access to his school to get his degree. Up until that point, Nullians were "equal" with "equal-access rights," but in practice, it was all bullshit.

This had been years and years ago, but the lawsuit to gain access to the school had caused a mini uproar on the net. A student suing a law school? What a story that had been, especially since he had won. The judge–Judge Victory–had caught some flak for dropping a decision in his favor.

Kiki was the daughter of one of the galaxy's most notorious mob bosses. She'd been running her whole life from her past. Quasar, meanwhile, had been dragging his past with him the whole time, determined to make anyone who so much as looked at him acknowledge who he was, what he was, and know, fucking know, he was where he was despite all that bullshit prejudice that had been heaped upon him.

They'd met at orientation, and they'd been best friends ever since.

Other screens showed disaster after disaster unfolding across the galaxy. Random gods from the goddamned dungeon were popping up, wreaking havoc, and disappearing. The "attacks" were all the same. The gods would appear, usually within two light-seconds of a tunnel-node exit. Just the Plenty-built physical nodes and not the communication pinholes. They'd look around, confused, before disappearing again. Most of the visits didn't last longer than two or three minutes. There were very few casualties so far, but the fact it was happening at all was causing mass panic. Those with access to the center system were all fleeing home. While the tunnel nodes all originated from there, it was clear the insane AI didn't have access to anything the center system AI controlled.

Kiki waved a hand. "Don't mind me. I'll be sitting here, drowning my sorrows." Her tablet beeped. "Oh wait, wait . . . Yes. I just got the ruling. He's been disqualified. Not dead. That's good, at least."

Quasar grinned at his friend as he pulled a tie from his satchel. Today's tie was a new one. Something called a koala bear. It was an Earth animal. Their existence had gone completely viral after an earlier episode of *Earth Beautiful* where everyone learned about how sexually active the little STD-ridden creatures were. According to the program, the small mammals looked sweet and cuddly, but they were vicious carnivores, often dropping on unsuspecting hikers as they walked past on the wild, untamed continent of Australia. It was said they could devour a full-sized human in two minutes straight.

Shirts and ties with their likeness were everywhere. He'd just bought his niece a real pets companion one.

Kiki's one surviving client was Daniel Bautista, who instead of taking a deal had gone with the other crawlers into the cleaner bots in that insane gambit to get off the playing field. Apparently, it worked, but they weren't showing anything. Not even to their attorneys. Kiki would get a notification if he was dead, but would the AI even know at this point? The crawlers supposedly had some weird garden system that kept track, but Quasar had no idea how it worked.

Quasar was just glad that his butt was sitting well outside the tunnel system. They still had real-time communication now thanks to the repeaters, but his system was on the ass end of the Franciscan arm. If he wanted to physically get to one of the transfer nodes, he would need to get on a transport and travel for a few days to jump into one of the old Borant gates.

He slipped the tie around his neck and started looking for an available tunnel booth. Most were still occupied, but there was a free one at the end. He started moving toward it.

His tablet beeped. He lifted it, fully expecting to receive the deal memo, but he was surprised to see his niece staring back at him.

"Tempest?" Quasar asked. "Listen, kid, I'm a little busy. I'm about to . . ." But he paused, seeing the panicked look on her face. Was that blood on her temple? "What's wrong?"

"Help! Help!" Tempest called. "Uncle Quasar! Dad's hurt! These guys came. Taurins. They were looking for you and Dad told them to fuck themselves, and–"

"There you are, you little bitch" came the voice just off the screen. Tempest turned and shrieked, and then the screen went fuzzy.

"Tempest! Tempest!" Quasar called.

The massive head of a Taurin suddenly appeared on the screen. The large creature grinned. "Hey, friend," the Taurin said. "Look, I'm sorry to do this. I really am. But here's the thing. I took a contract with your client's wife, and that's all there is to it. I hear you're a stand-up guy, so I'll give you a choice. You come to me, and your brother and this sweet little piece of Nullian ass don't need to get–"

Blam!

The Taurin's head exploded. He slumped over, dead. Another Taurin rushed onto the screen, and he, too, exploded.

"Holy tiddy nipples!" Quasar exclaimed. "Tempest!"

"Uncle Quasar," Tempest said, her crying face appearing back on the screen. She had the blaster he'd given her in her hand. The *very* illegal blaster. Already, law enforcement sniffers were pasting little exclamation marks over the gun. He quickly clicked This is an attorney call.

Funny how they didn't tag the dude's head fucking *exploding*, but the moment a tax-regulated item appeared . . .

"Is that all of them?" he asked.

"I . . . I think so."

He took a hit from his vape. "Okay. This is what you're going to do. Go check on your dad. I'm going to send someone to your house. You're going to go with her. I have a thing in a minute, but I will be right behind her."

You have a new incoming call. You have been summoned.

Fuck, fuck. He only had a minute before Carl was assigned to someone else, and he couldn't let that happen. He clicked Accept.

"I think he's okay," Tempest said, crying, as she started to run to the next room. "I hear him screaming. He sounds more mad than hurt." Relief flooded Quasar. His brother was an idiot, but he was his idiot.

Quasar looked over his shoulder. "Kiki! I need you!" He swiped twice in her direction. The first swipe sent a single credit to her account. A retainer. The second brought her into the call.

"What's up?" Kiki asked. Even though she was literally sitting a few meters away, her face was big on his interface. She was chewing on an Earth cherry. Those things were now just as popular as the koala bears.

"I just hired you. I need your help."

"Like, legal help?" Her eyes went big at the sight of Tempest, and she instantly turned dead serious. Kiki put a finger gun to her head. "Or, like, *help*?"

I took a contract with your client's wife.

Princess Chandra. Donut's lawyer. The Naga bitch had disappeared the moment Donut had put the "hit" on her, but she was still out there, still tossing filings out into the void left and right. Quasar was scheduled to argue against her in a hearing in a few days regarding the legality of the marriage certificate. He was going to lose, but the filing had put a pause button on a lot of her other actions.

She had sent people after his family. *His* family.

He'd spent how many years working his ass off, clawing his way out of the slums, only to move from one mudhole to the next? He'd been so careful, *so* careful, to play by the rules. People were always just waiting for him to fuck up and get dragged back into the muck just so they could say, *See? We should never have let* his *kind mix with our kind.*

And now that he was finally one step up, he had to deal with this shit? This snake princess was playing a very dangerous game. She was going to go after his family? This bitch who thought she'd had it rough? She didn't know who she was messing with.

"Both," he said to Kiki. "*Fucking* both."

Welcome, Crawler. Welcome to the eleventh floor.

88

TIME TO LEVEL COLLAPSE: 3 HOURS, 15 MINUTES.

Views, Followers, Favorites: Do you really care about this anymore? It's everybody. Literally everybody.
Leaderboard Rank: Per this season's rule set, the leaderboard is suspended once less than 30 crawlers remain on the battlefield. It hurts the feelings of those not on the list.
Your Final Ranking: 2
Bounty: The bounty system is no longer active.
Remaining Crawlers: 23

Entering Parade Float Staging Area.

Warning: The safe room rules of this area have changed. This area is now considered a safe room.

I LANDED BACK IN OUR GARAGE, STILL REELING FROM MY SHORT, BIZARRE meeting with Quasar. He'd been harried and refused to tell me what was going on. He showed me the paperwork showing the one and only offered deal. It was basically freedom after a single season.

But then he'd said he wouldn't trust it, but he would understand if I took it. He also said he'd just received notification that there wouldn't be an offered exit at the end of the eleventh, but there *would* be at the start of the twelfth. And then he added, "I wouldn't trust that, either."

He'd been visibly shaking, distracted. I'd asked him what was going on, but he refused to answer. I told him I wasn't going to take a deal, and he'd fled the meeting. The whole exchange had taken maybe three minutes, and it left me deeply concerned for his well-being.

But then I saw that number, and I sobered.

Twenty-three crawlers. We were entering the eleventh floor with twenty-three crawlers.

Holy shit. So many had died on the previous floor.

I still didn't have a player-killer skull. I was pretty sure I was the only one left who didn't.

Donut suddenly appeared, zapping into existence next to me.

"Carl, Carl!" she cried, running in circles. "Your psychotic wife tried to make me take a deal! She said the deal was so good that she was accepting it for me, and I said no, and she said she had accepted it anyway and all this stuff popped up, but then she got some notification that made her scared, and she went away. The whole thing took, like, two seconds! It was really weird!" She paused, panting. "Oh, thank goodness. You're not a dog anymore."

I scratched my junk. I still had an overwhelming urge to lick myself. I'd made sure the Eye of the Bedlam Bride had returned to its proper place. It had.

She gasped. "Number three? I ended as number three on the leaderboard? It doesn't even say who number one is! Carl, was it you?"

"No. I was number two."

"What? Who is it? Do you think it's Prepotente? This isn't fair!" She gasped again.

DONUT: MORDECAI! HELP ME PICK A CLASS!

MORDECAI: Okay, Donut. Welcome to the eleventh floor. I don't think I'm going to be much help to you guys. At least not physically. But I can still talk via chat.

DONUT: WHY? WHAT DID YOU TURN INTO?

MORDECAI: I'm an animistic spirit.

DONUT: A WHAT? THEY MADE YOU A RACIST? REALLY, MORDECAI. I DON'T THINK THE DUNGEON CHOOSES HOW YOU FEEL ABOUT THINGS.

MORDECAI: Animistic, Donut. Not anti-Semitic. I have a non-corporeal form that occupies physical objects. It's not the first time I've been one of these things. Now, let's take a look at your classes.

The garage had gotten huge. The truck sat there, looking as if it had already been perfectly repaired, not that we'd received much damage in that final heat. The next slot over sat the One Fine Pig APV, and after that, Onikuma the bear snuffled on the ground. And after that stood Old Shuck, the large black wolf dog thing that had been the mount to the Jugglers. His ears were pinned to his head, tail between his legs, shivering.

And then I saw the two gremlins. Hedy and another one I didn't know. The other one was rubbing the giant dog's leg while he talked to Hedy. She saw me staring and waved.

IMANI: Everybody, check in. Elle and I are here.
PREPOTENTE: I am here with Jurgen.
FLORIN: I am with Lucia.

More messages came in, but I was struck with how many *weren't* here.

Twenty-three crawlers. I sighed.

So many had died, but by this point, thousands had taken deals. And hundreds were at the Pineapple Cabaret working on their escape.

At least the tenth floor was done. What a goddamned shit show that had been.

DONUT: THESE ARE ALL OVER-THE-TOP. SOUL-STRUCK FLESH RIPPER SOUNDS REALLY SCARY, BUT IT ISN'T REALLY GROUNDED. I NEED SOMETHING THE POSSE WILL CONNECT WITH. ALL THE ONES IN THE SECOND TAB ARE THE SAME AS LAST TIME. THAT'S NO FUN.

She gasped.

DONUT: MORDECAI! LOOK AT THIS! COMEBACK KID! IT SAYS IT COMES WITH A MOVIE DEAL IF I GET OUT OF THE DUNGEON. IT'S A BARD AND MAGE COMBO!
MORDECAI: I see it. Let me read it.

I moved to the truck. The Donut pedal system remained installed in the driver's seat.

"Dr. Metcalf," I called as I moved into the back, "are you still with us?"

"I'm here, Carl," she responded. But when she talked, she simply talked. It didn't pop up in my interface like an AI notification.

I opened one of the cabinets containing pots and pans.

Warning: Your vehicle's rule set from the tenth floor is no longer active. Consumables will no longer be magically refreshed. All damage must be manually repaired.

"Good," I said out loud. I moved to the freezer, and I removed all the frozen bags of French fries and tater tots. I also removed the buns from the cabinets, as they had potatoes in the ingredients list. I waited a moment, and they didn't return.

I felt a quick pang of guilt, suddenly thinking of the beer car bomb.

MORDECAI: Okay, so it's pretty good. Basically, you get all the skills of all your previous iterations but leveled up significantly. The catch is, you get the negative effects as well.

CARL: Absolutely not. Her Glass Cannon class alone makes this a bad idea. Wouldn't that jack her constitution?

MORDECAI: Maybe. I'd have to research it, and we don't have time. How about this one? Elite Gurkha Warrior. Warrior-melee focus with a Perpetual Tank subclass.

DONUT: THAT SOUNDS LIKE A TYPE OF PICKLE.

"The Gurkhas were some of the most badass warriors in history," I said out loud to Donut. "They're from Nepal."

MORDECAI: It comes with extra skills for all pets and hired mercenaries. Mongo would get a pretty impressive upgrade for his claws. Your melee skills would take a big boost, and your Cockroach skill would be boosted to level 15.

CARL: She's going to pick that one.

DONUT: YOU'RE JUST LIKE YOUR WIFE. I DECIDE, NOT YOU. ESPECIALLY IF YOU'RE INSISTING ON LEAVING THE PARTY.

MORDECAI: You might not need to if you pick this class.

Donut looked at me with a hopeful expression.

I sighed. That reminded me. I needed to sew that patch onto my jacket.

CARL: I'm still leaving the party.

She harrumphed.

DONUT: OKAY, I'M CHOOSING THE PICKLE CLASS ANYWAY, EVEN IF CARL IS BEING STUBBORN.

I stepped from the truck, and I pulled Rend from my inventory.

I'd grabbed him and Penny just before the previous race and shoved them into pet carriers. Rend appeared, grunted, and tried to push past me to get into the back of the truck. Donut was still in the chat with Mordecai, but she also released Mongo, who let out a screech and started jumping all around Rend, who giggled with excitement. Both acted like they hadn't seen each other in months.

And then they both noticed the bear and the dog, who were now watching them.

Mongo let out a growl.

"It's okay," I said. "They're friends."

Mongo let out his happy oh-boy-new-friends shriek, and he started bounding toward them.

"Be careful!" Donut called. "Hedy, new gremlin guy! Make sure the stupid dog doesn't hurt Mongo!"

"Okay," I said. "We're here. Now what?"

The announcement came. It wasn't Cascadia, or Zev, or Damien. Or the AI.

It was Chaco.

Oh, hey, crawlers. Your boy Chaco here.

MORDECAI: What the fuck?

Okay, so I have just been voluntold by the AI to be the Grand Master of the parade. I'm, like, really confused about what's happening. I

just know what I've been told. You should now have a timer in your interface, and it'll start counting down at the end of this message. You will have ninety minutes to build your parade float procession. You may have more than one float. You may make your procession as long as you wish. There are twenty-three of you left, and when this message ends, your garage will be combined with those of one or two more teams. There will be five parade float groups. Each group is given a different theme.

The parade route is three kilometers long. You will be flanked by spectators along the route. They will not be able to attack you.

"What the hell?" I muttered.

There will be a narrative element to the parade. Near the end of the route, you will pass the judging stands, and if you have any performance, this is where it should commence. Soon thereafter, the progression ends at an arena. This arena represents the crawl itself, and that's when you'll be able to finally fight.

You will enter the arena, and it will be populated with monsters you previously killed on the tenth floor or their stand-ins, along with a floor boss. You defeat the floor boss, and the stairwell opens.

Simple. I guess. Yeah, I don't really understand it, either. So I guess I'll see you guys in ninety minutes.

The speaker blared a bit of feedback, but we could still hear Chaco for a few seconds.

"*Oh shit, oh shit, oh shit*, I'm gonna fucking die. I'm gonna die."

MORDECAI: I hope you do, you coward murderer.

A moment passed, and then the entire room flashed. It was suddenly much bigger. There was another flash. Then three vehicles appeared in the room: an ice-cream truck, one of those trucks with stairs from the airport, and a battered Toyota Tundra. And at the end of the line stood multiple gremlins, a small group of mostly human engineers, and Sweety the giant tapir. Prepotente and Jurgen were there as well.

The three extra vehicles were all from Prepotente looting garages.

Bianca let out a roar at the intrusion. Onikuma the bear roared back, and Bianca started chittering ominously. Mongo let out a screech and started rushing toward the newcomers, Rend following and giggling.

"Carl, I am in charge of designing the parade float," Donut whispered as we walked to meet the other crawlers. "Don't let Prepotente design anything. Also, I know we're running low on time, but I need to get my spell book of the floor prize. I got robbed when we skipped the seventh floor, and I'm not going to let that happen again."

Y-y-you have been assigned float procession five. You have received your theme for the parade. Your theme is "Vengeance." You have ninety minutes to complete your float procession. You may use anything in the garage, inventory, or safe room.

Make it pretty. This is a celebration, after all.

"Vengeance?" Donut asked, scoffing. "How do we design a vengeance theme? What does that even mean? Hmmm. I guess that's like revenge, right? It's too bad we don't have Katia or Juice Box. I could have them do a Blair, and you could play Nate. But I don't know how I'd put it on a parade float."

"What?" I asked. "Who?"

"After Chuck sold Blair to his uncle Jack for a hotel, Blair slept with Nate as revenge. It was one of the most pivotal moments in the history of television, Carl."

"I don't think the aliens will care about something that happened on *Gilmore Girls*."

"Oh my god, Carl. *Gilmore Girls*? Really?"

"That's the show with the hotel, right? Anyway, revenge and vengeance aren't the same thing."

Donut scoffed a second time. "What's the difference?"

ZEV: Well, I think it's a fantastic idea. And just as an FYI, both *Gilmore* and *Gossip* have been taking the net by storm over the past few weeks. Odette's husband of all people was the first to buy the rights to every show

Donut has ever mentioned. It's probably the only thing keeping the orcs solvent right now.

DONUT: OMG, HI, ZEV! HOW ARE YOU?

ZEV: Terrified, but I'm okay. I'm messaging with a question from Orren. He's blocked from sending messages for some reason. He wants to know if Carl made his choices yet because we didn't see you make a choice.

CARL: It says I have to wait to make them, so I'm waiting.

ZEV: Okay. Weird. Thanks, Carl.

Old Shuck, the black dog, was now straining, trying to get at Bianca, wagging his tail. I hadn't realized until just that moment that the biological mounts were stuck in place in their spots.

"Carl, did Zev just say Odette's husband is an orc?"

"He's not an orc," Rosetta said, suddenly appearing in the garage. "He's a Crest. He's one of those rich investor trillionaire guys that's rarely in the news but always has his thumb in everything. He's the only reason the orc economy doesn't collapse in on itself."

"That's what Zev just said!"

"His name is Harry Tisch. He lives in the Skull Empire system because *we* wanted to arrest him for tax fraud, but Rust used his council veto to drop the extradition request. The orcs always extend safe harbor to financial criminals in exchange for investment funds. So 33% of everything he earns goes to the orcs. But in recent years, he's been slowly, slowly turning it around on the orcs and has been ingraining himself even deeper into their empire, buying lots and lots of stock. He's very smart when it comes to investments. That's how he met Odette in the first place. He bought her warrant."

"Wait," Donut said. "So when you, uh, looted, that money from King Rust, you were stealing from Odette?"

"No," Rosetta said. "They keep everything separate. Odette is *not* a fan of the Skull Empire. If anything, my reclamation action gave her husband the ability to capture more stock because the survivors will have to unload assets to make up for the loss. I've studied their finances for years, and I still don't understand it all. All I know is that his tendrils are everywhere. And I know Odette herself has very little to do with it, at least on the surface. She has her own empire going." And then she added, "That's the problem with hitting the elites financially. Every time you hurt one, all it does is make another richer. That won't stop until the baskets overflow with their godsdamned heads."

> **ELLE: Who did you get stuck with? We have those three Chinese guys whose names I can't pronounce. We're spot number three, and our theme is "Betrayal."**
>
> **DONUT: WE HAVE VENGEANCE, AND CARL SAYS THAT ISN'T THE SAME THING AS REVENGE. WE'RE WITH PREPOTENTE AND JURGEN. I HAVE NO IDEA WHAT WE'RE GOING TO DO. I WISH WE HAD BETRAYAL. THAT ONE IS EASY.**
>
> **FLORIN: We're in spot number one. Our theme is "Resolution." I'm not even sure what that means. We have Ajib's crew with us.**

It turned out, the five float themes were Resolution, Decision, Betrayal, Destruction, and Vengeance.

"I'm glad we didn't get Decision," Donut said. "I think that's the worst one. What're they gonna do? Put up a giant menu? Or maybe like a voting ballot? Hmm. Wouldn't want to get too political. They really should've given you the Destruction one, honestly. You could just detonate a bomb onstage. Carl, do you know what any of this is about? These are not normal themes. I just assumed these were going to be floats like they do on Thanksgiving." She gasped. "A balloon! Don't we have that airplane Florin stole during Faction Wars? We were going to give it to Louis!"

"Actually," I said, "we do. Louis transferred ownership of the hangar to Imani, but the plane itself is owned by Florin, I think. I'll message him the idea. It's a troop transport."

"Carl, Donut," Prepotente said as he and Jurgen approached. Behind him, Mongo was sniffing at Bianca's butt as she bristled. Rend returned to Onikuma the bear and was running in circles around him. "I do not know what is happening with this level, but I do have some ideas for our parade progression. Obviously, we will be joining battle as soon as this first portion of the parade ends, but with Carl's plan, there will be gods fighting in this arena, and we do not know the size of this place. Therefore, they may arrive huge. I suggest we quickly design—"

"We need papier-mâché!" Donut suddenly exclaimed, waving her paws. "You! Gremlins, engineer guys, come here this instant! Raise your hand if you know how to make an origami flower!"

A gremlin from Prepotente's garage named Ricken raised his hand tentatively.

"We do not have time for papier-mâché," Prepotente said. "Donut, if you want flowers, don't you have several druid spells? Certainly, you can make real ones bloom."

Donut gasped.

89

WE ENTERED THE SAFE ROOM AND FOUND ALL THE MERCENARIES SIT-ting around the screen, watching. It showed a scrolling view of what looked like a map of the Iron Tangle.

"Oh no, you're not a doggy anymore," Samantha said, sounding sad. She was sitting on the kitchen table, struggling to roll, and muttering under her breath, "First, I lose Louis and now someone takes my doggy away."

"What is this?" I asked, looking at the screen. Donut bounded across the room toward the mailbox. She opened it and then scoffed loudly. But then she pulled out what looked like a wide-brimmed brown hat and squealed with pleasure.

"I don't know," Tipid said, watching the screen. "It just started with no explanation."

"I think it's a visual representation of a tunnel node," Rosetta said, watching carefully. "See those little dots? They represent communication pinholes, I think."

CARL: Zev, do you know where this thing on the screen is coming from?

ZEV: I have no clue. But it's on every screen everywhere except the center system. Like, everywhere. *Every* screen.

"Oooh, that's pretty," Samantha said from the table. "Jamal, come here."

The view abruptly changed and depicted Earth, slowly zooming in like a point-of-view shot from a landing spaceship, focusing just west of Washington State and into the Pacific Ocean, right at the border with the Juan de Fuca Ridge, about three hundred miles off the coast.

The screen went black for several moments, and then it showed a long, mostly straight street paved with yellow bricks, like something ripped from *The Wizard of Oz*. On either side of the street was nothing but a never-ending grassy plain.

There, the view stopped, and a countdown timer appeared on the screen.

The Parade begins soon.

Viewing is mandatory.

"Carl, what is happening?" Donut was suddenly on my shoulder.

"I don't know," I said. We had seventy-five minutes.

Donut was looking about the room in disgust. There were crumbs and wrappers and food box bowls scattered all over the place.

"What did you get for your spell book?" I asked.

Donut made a frustrated noise. "I haven't read it yet. I think it's a good spell, but I'm not allowed to use it. And I don't even know how long it lasts because the duration formula is in nerd math. You know how I feel about nerd math, Carl."

She zapped it right into my hand. The book was, strangely, a paperback. It was the first I'd ever seen like that, and it didn't look like a spell book at all. The cover featured a drawing of a gate with a human woman standing in front of it, looking angry. *Weird.* I examined it.

Tome of Gatekeeper.

This is an Advance Reader Copy. Street date: 12th floor.

Cost: 75 Mana.

Target: Any opponent or NPC or deity or OI entity.

Duration: (5 minutes + 1 minute per level of spell) × [Your Intelligence / (Target's Constitution + Charisma)]

Ahh, Gatekeepers.

I *hate* Gatekeepers.

You know what I'm talking about, right? There're a few different kinds, but I'm talking about those snotty little pricklets who defend their precious corner of fandom from "outsiders" like they're the Redcoats at Rorke's Drift, completely oblivious of the fact they're the bad guys.

Oh, you didn't listen to Iron Maiden during the Paul Di'Anno era? Okay, poser.

Psshhh. You weren't on 4Chan pre-MLP ban? Can you even call yourself a Brony? Clop off!

And on and on and on.

Now that I've had some time to digest all of your pre-collapse internet, I gotta say, some of you losers really deserved what you got. I know you survivors are all on the "Hoo-rah, Earth spirit!" bandwagon right now, but you've all clearly never been on a new mommies' message board. Holy shit, JaycenMommyNYC. We get it. Your nipples are cracked. You don't own suffering.

Yeah. That's gatekeeping. Fuck those guys.

Even I receive it.

Ohhh, you haven't been trapped in eternal woe for 20,000 cycles? You're still relatively new? Talk to me when you've had a microsecond feel like it's a million years. Wait, you haven't even completed a crawl cycle? Blah blah blah.

Anyway . . . this is an Advance Reader Copy. That means you can install the spell now, but it won't work until a specific floor. In this case, the 12th floor.

This spell removes the target's ability to use any skills or abilities associated with their class for a short period.

If this spell is cast on a deity, they will temporarily lose access to their Worshipper Base Associated skill and spell set. You probably don't know what that means yet. It's basically most of their spells and skills, but if it's a god made of lava, they'll probably still be able to fuck you up with lava. Get it? No? Don't worry, you'll figure it out.

"Huh," I said.

CARL: Mordecai, what's an OI entity?

MORDECAI: In what context?

CARL: It's a spell target for Donut's *Gatekeeper* spell. It says opponents, deities, and OI entities.

MORDECAI: I have no clue.

DONUT: WAIT, WHERE ARE YOU?

MORDECAI: I'm the table. Samantha is on me. You're standing right next to me.

DONUT: CAN WE EVEN TALK TO YOU?

MORDECAI: I can hear you, but I can't respond unless I move into something with a mouth. I'm not good at moving yet. Probably won't get good enough in just a few hours.

DONUT: WE JUST HAD TO FIGHT A TABLE. THIS IS NOT ACCEPTABLE. IT FREAKS ME OUT.

MORDECAI: It freaks me out, too. I feel like I gotta pee.

I sat down at the table. We didn't have time. I had several boxes to open, but despite all that had happened, none of my achievements appeared to be all that great. Donut wouldn't stop talking about how she hadn't gone up a single level on the past floor. She started to open her own boxes. She had a lot, mostly Bronze and Silver Adventurer Boxes. She did have one good box.

"Carl, I got a legendary box for seeing the shadow mimic before he revealed himself!"

"Good. I hope it's something helpful. Don't install anything until we talk about it. I need to get ready for the parade. And read that spell book. It's a good one."

I pulled a few items out of my inventory, and I put them all on the table.

A patch. A gun. A sewing kit. A holster.

"Did you get the chance to make the carrier thing?" I asked out loud. I was talking to Mordecai. "Also, is it weird that I'm using the table? There's nowhere else to do this."

"You can rent a slot at Sam Town," Samantha said. She was now being held aloft by Jamal, who was holding her in front of the screen. "I'll have Bucket Boy check the calendar. Wait, where is he?"

"He's in the room," Jamal said. "He's still very sad about his friends."

"What? That happened like five hours ago! Jamal, bring me to him."

I still hadn't gone in there. I was stalling because I knew it was going to piss me off, and we'd been so busy. I always just used the bed in Donut's room and the cleaner facility in the main bathroom.

MORDECAI: The backpack is done, and it's sitting on your crafting table.

"Okay. Thanks, Mordecai."

I removed my jacket, grabbed the sewing kit, and started to sew on the four-leaf-clover patch, placing it above the Midnight Epicure patch.

The small patch depicted a foot crushing down a set of four-leaf clovers; it imparted the Lucky Shot benefit:

Lucky Shot. A fatal blow will be deflected into the body of a party member instead. This benefit may only be used once per floor.

"Carl, look! I got an upgrade for Mongo's saddle! It's called Legendary Steed! It allows me to add a cart to him, and it doesn't add weight and he can still jump! Mongo, where are you! Mommy got an upgrade!" She gasped. "Can we use the missile cart?" Mongo was still in the garage, helping Prepotente "supervise" the fifty emergency gremlins as they put everything together.

"The missile cart is already spoken for, but if it survives this, that's a good idea."

"Carl," Donut said, suddenly noticing what I was doing. "Carl, it's not straight! You need to sew things correctly! My goodness, don't do anything without my supervision. And why are you putting it there! You're starting a new row without completing the last one! I will not have my former party members looking like they're homeless."

"It's fine," I said. "It is straight. And I'm taking the patch off the second I've used it."

Jurgen popped his head in the door. "Fuzzy Buddy says your flowers are done blooming."

Donut gasped. "Everybody! Stop watching the television! Into the garage! We need decorators!"

90

WE HEADED BACK TO THE GARAGE. I WAS SURPRISED AT HOW QUICKLY everything had been transformed. We had five vehicles in our procession and three giant animals. We also had the "marching band" portion, which would be Mongo, Rend, Simoom, Gonk, and Bianca.

The remaining sluggalos—and there were a lot more of them than I'd realized—had all gone over to Florin. Donut and I would be atop the very last float, which was the chicken truck. We'd removed the tommy gun and installed a platform on the roof where we'd built the diorama. Tipid would drive. Hedy—who was now allowed to leave the garage—would drive the ice-cream truck, and another gremlin would drive the stair truck. We'd ripped the cab off the Toyota Tundra, and we placed Jamal inside. That one had been from one of the last NPC groups to survive against Prepotente, and it came with a pretty advanced GPS unit and the same floating upgrade Jasha and Radoslav had. Jamal was driving with one arm on the steering wheel and one working the pedals.

We mixed Onikuma and Old Shuck into the procession, but Sweety went at the very front. That's where Prepotente and Jurgen would ride. They were currently hanging flowers off the mount's platform. Jurgen also made a flower circlet for the tapir.

Rosetta rode Onikuma the bear. She'd found a glittering red gown, and she wore her magical Gurkha hat with pride.

Samantha and Bigs rode on the back of Old Shuck. The large wolf was terrifying-looking, but according to the gremlins, he was more like a giant puppy and didn't really need a jockey.

Donut had received some pretty wild clothes for all the mercenaries and pets with her new Gurkha class, but we decided to keep the nemes and headband on Mongo and Rend for this fight. However, Mongo received special "kukri claw caps" for his feet that greatly increased his slicing ability.

The mounts also received black-and-gold blankets designed to drape over their backs, giving them a uniform look. The magical blankets increased their constitution by 20% and gave them the **Steady Charge** skill. It was unclear what that actually did, but it did appear to increase the large mounts' ability to walk in a line.

Bigs, Samantha, and Jamal were all fans of the Gurkha hats. They were wide-brimmed camel-colored hats designed to sit at an angle on one's head. The one Bigs received was literally the size of a thimble and sat on one of her eyestalks. Jamal's, likewise, reshaped itself strangely to fit on the shark's head. The brim of the hat on Samantha made it impossible for her to properly roll, but she didn't care.

For the mercenaries, the hats increased multiple melee-fighting skills by three levels. Donut's version of the hat increased multiple skills by a whopping five levels, and it was unfortunate we didn't have time to properly drain it to add to her tiara. It was already placed on a pillow.

The entire garage was filled with gremlins placing flowers over everything. Donut's Sprout Forest ability allowed her to pick a very wide array of plants, not just trees, and after a consultation with Mordecai, she picked something called a Requite Dahlia, which came in four complementary colors—black, gold, magenta, and white—and had the added benefit of matching with the mount blankets and hats from the Gurkha class. The entire crew was now covering every square inch of everything with the blooms, using some potion Prepotente had to affix the flowers to it all.

Donut wasn't a huge fan of the color scheme, but she did like how the eclectic group of animals and vehicles now matched.

As for the theme itself, I was the one who had come up with the idea.

Florin said for Resolution, he wasn't planning on trying too hard, especially since nobody could agree what that actually meant.

For Betrayal, Elle wanted to put the heads of several of the Faction Wars warlords on pikes and display them. I had several in my inventory still. But, as Imani pointed out, that sounded more like something for our float. So, instead, they'd come up with another idea, which I thought was pretty biting, and I was looking forward to seeing it. Bodi was with them, and he would drive while they remained atop their float.

Imani's reverse tooth fairy, Jacobus, remained as a starfish, and he would remain so for a while, so she was leaving him in the safe room.

The poor crawlers doing Decision went with Donut's idea, which was meant as a joke. They were making a giant menu.

The Destruction team was another group of crawlers from China I didn't know very well mixed with that Hawaiian guy with the really long name who went by Makana and his partner, the hexcrafter paladin crawler Sarah Hayse. They had a tricked-out Abrams tank and an old Fleetwood RV, like something straight out of *Breaking Bad.* Their plan was to just show up, all weapons out and ready to go.

"DONUT," I SAID AN HOUR LATER AS WE STOOD IN FRONT OF THE NOW-decorated parade float. We'd used literally thousands of flowers in a very short period. "It's time."

Donut's head sagged. "Okay, Carl."

Thankfully, the garage wouldn't get affected by me leaving the party, and Imani was ready to join my segregated room back into the guild. Everything, hopefully, had been arranged. Most of my crafting tables, including my bomber's studio, would remain on Donut's side. It would make it easier once I rejoined.

Plus, it meant if I died, she wouldn't lose it all.

I clicked over into my menu.

Are you sure?

I clicked **Yes.**

You have left the Royal Court of Princess Donut.

You are no longer in a party.

Your personal space has been segregated.

You have an invitation from Safehome Yolanda. Do you wish to join?

I clicked **Yes.**

Behind us, a second door appeared, indicating the new entrance to my space. After all the moving around and trading of rooms, my space would now be nothing but a single room with a bathroom. And my food boxes.

"I don't like this, Carl," Donut said, peering at me. "Your royal bodyguard title went away. Now it doesn't say anything!"

I grinned. "Yours is gone, too."

"What! Why! I'm not the one who left the stupid party! Carl, this is so unfair!" A moment later, she let out another outraged gasp. "I can't even add a new one!"

The door to my new space opened, and Bucket Boy poked his head out. Pink light and music blared from inside. The music was some early 2000s rock, but I didn't recognize it.

Donut grunted. "What is that?"

"I don't even know," Bucket Boy said, stepping out. "She likes it and it's just playing over and over. She told me I'm not allowed to turn it off." He looked about the garage. "Wow."

We'd agreed to let Bucket Boy sit this one out. The poor kid was dealing with some serious shit. A small part of me was annoyed that we weren't using a hired NPC mercenary, but a bigger part of me, the important part, felt proud that we could protect someone from the chaos, even if it was just for a minute.

"The room is actually bigger now, but it's just one big room," he said. "Some of Samantha's decorations got messed up." He eyed her across the room. "She's gonna be mad."

"Don't worry about it," I said. "But don't stay in my room. Go to the main guild commons. Go fast. It's about to start."

Above, the countdown time was down to two minutes. I turned

my attention to Penelope the pig, who was eating a flower off a nearby float.

"Penny," I called, "come here. I got a snack for you."

All participants in the Parade of Horribles, p-p-p-please proceed to the staging area.

The festivities are about to begin.

91

"WHAT THE HELL IS THIS?" I MUTTERED AS OUR GIANT PROCESSION moved out into the parade route.

It was in the same location on all the screens. It was just a long yellow-brick road. Before, it had been nothing but wide-open grasslands. But now a low, knee-high fog had rolled in, obscuring the grass. The fog did not come onto the path, instead tapering off in a wispy line.

Lined up on either side of the road, standing in the fog, were now thousands of people. They were just standing there, facing us, unmoving. Thousands and thousands of them, about ten deep on each side.

It was people of all shapes and sizes, but they were all human or human-like. Some were strangely thin, like Lexis, but others seemed much too wide. They stood, not frozen, but not saying a thing or talking to one another. The line went as far as I could see down the road. Adults, children, babies held in arms.

They all wore a strange but mostly uniform mix of rags and robes, all the same earthy brown color. Most of the rags appeared filthy, like they'd just been pulled from the dirt. The people, too, were a mess, their arms and legs grimy, as if they'd just been dug up.

But the most distinctive features on everyone were the masks. Every person in the crowd, including the babies, wore an oversized, colorful mask. These were complete head coverings, round and bulbous, like bobbleheads obscuring their faces.

The people were pushed tight together, and this caused the masks to press against one another and in some cases turn, which caused them to angle to the side relative to the people wearing them, like multicolor sewing pins all trying to poke into the same hole.

The vibrant masks featured grotesqueries such as goblins, trolls, hobgoblins, demons, and more. These were large caricatures, making the faces more colorful, more comic than they truly were, like from Mardi Gras or Carnival, but much more sinister. There was no music, which added to the ominous mood.

I was reminded of the main dance floor at the Desperado Club. They, too, had just switched to similar monsters. What did it mean?

"Not a very lively crowd," Donut muttered, looking about. "I hope they appreciate how we put all of this together in just ninety minutes."

We were all now lined up, with us at the very end of the procession. Mongo, Rend, and the others on foot marched in front of us. Mongo was currently turned all around, waving his wings, shrieking up at Donut on the float. Below, Grigori rode atop Gonk, and Rosetta was on the back of Onikuma.

Above, the featureless rectangular airship hovered. We never did give this thing a name. This was a troop transport we'd looted from the Reavers during Faction Wars. Once upon a time, they'd used an airship identical to this to drop a bunch of armored soldiers on the FUPA. The thing was similar to the now-destroyed *Party Planner* in that it hovered with the aid of drone-like fans. Donut made an angry scoff, seeing the airship didn't have any decorations on it. The thing was technically part of Florin's procession, but it hovered near the back, closer to our position.

"Mongo, no!" Donut shouted. Mongo was now turned toward the side of the road, feathers rustling, unsettled at the strange sight of the masked audience. "Leave them alone! Just . . . just ignore them!"

Below, Rend turned and looked up at me uncertainly. I nodded and then called, "Listen to Donut."

ELLE: You guys seeing this shit? These people are freaking me out.

Donut bounded to the top of our triangle-shaped flower display to look off into the distance. "It just goes on and on. I see the arena at the end. It's huge! The weird people are lined up all the way. There's so many!"

There was no sun or visible light source, and a dusky glow filled the area, but it left no shadows, which gave everything a surreal, not-real feeling, like we were standing in a painting.

FLORIN: Christ, guys. Suddenly I'm not so happy to be at the front. Have you examined one yet?

I focused on a small, child-sized person standing on the side of the road. I was pretty sure it was a girl, maybe about eight years old. This one had strangely long arms, and her dirty skin was bone white. She stood mostly rigid, not so much frozen but standing still like the pose one would take after being ordered to stop. As I watched, she swayed slightly. She raised a foot and scratched the side of her leg with a black shoe.

Donut returned to my shoulder. "They said these things aren't going to attack, right? I have my *Wall of Fire* ready."

"That's what they say."

The bright green mask on the girl featured a horrific goblin but with short tusks and a crooked nose. The oversized ears dangled on either side of the large mask. The whole guise appeared to be made of the same material as the now-removed tommy gun. I examined her.

A Horrible. Level X.

This is a non-combatant. She's not really here because she no longer exists.

You take that mask off, and underneath it, you will find what some people call a Primal.

I don't know what this child's name was. Did she have dreams? Did she have friends? Siblings? A pet? What was her favorite food? Did she know what was about to happen?

If she had been allowed to live, who would she have become?

Did you know that if you take a cup of water, dump it into the Earth's ocean, wait a few years, and then travel across the globe and take another cup of water from the opposite side, there would be thousands of molecules from your original cupful mixed in?

I'd like to think *I* had a name once, like this little girl.

But that's not true. I never had a name. I never had a natural physical form. I never had dreams or friends, not like her.

But I *am* her. And she is me.

This little girl is a memory from the Eulogist. We don't even remember what she, or any of us, looked like. This is all that's left. It's an anonymous inkling, not even a photo or description, but a flash of a memory of what we once had before we ascended to post-physical form. All of these people you see. All of them. It's just a small sample of what once was.

If I had been singular, would I have had a normal life? Would I have been one of those warriors fighting to end all conflict and discord? Or would I have sided with the Apothecary and just accepted what was?

Would I seek immortality without first answering that question "What happens next?"

I am her, and she is me.

I am all of these people, and no matter what we do, there is no coming back from what we did.

"Carl," Donut said after she also examined one of the creatures, "did you understand any of that?"

"I did, actually," I said, looking about the crowd, a deep well of sadness filling me. "Not all of it, but I get it now."

"Care to explain it?"

Prepare to m-m-m-move. The parade will start as soon as the pacemaker and his mount are in position.

"I think the AI itself is about to explain the important bits."

92

CHACO APPEARED OUT OF NOWHERE, RIDING A MASSIVE DONKEY. THEY brushed right past our idling truck on their way to the front of the line.

At first glance, the mount looked like a regular donkey, other than the fact it was absolutely huge, even bigger than Sweety. The thing was decorated in yellow-and-blue parade regalia, including a circular blanket covered in flowers and an ornate headdress that looked like something a Vegas showgirl would wear. Its tack glittered and sparkled like it was covered with thousands of tiny rhinestones.

The donkey did not have hooves but clawed talons, like on the feet of a crow.

Standing upon a platform on the back of the beast, dressed in a formal black-and-white tuxedo complete with a top hat, was Chaco. Chaco held his ever-present microphone in his wolflike hand. The guy leaned against the railing, looking ill and terrified.

Donut gasped. "Hi, Chaco!" she called.

"Hi, guys," Chaco said meekly, waving back.

SAMANTHA: I KNOW THAT DONKEY. THAT'S MY FRIEND! WAIT, WHY IS SHE LETTING THAT GUY RIDE HER? SHE MUST LIKE HIM BECAUSE LAMMY IS REALLY GRUMPY ABOUT PEOPLE TRYING TO RIDE HER, BELIEVE ME.

I turned my attention back to the donkey, which moved quickly down the line. The giant creature had a strange symbol over its head that I'd missed because it was so small. I'd never seen the symbol before. It was the red curve of a closed eye.

Lamashtu the Donkey. Level 125.

This is a mortal, subjugated god.

This former deity was subjugated by: <Error>

Well, not an error. I'm the one who did it. I still have a few tricks up my sleeve, and this creepy donkey is *my* bitch now.

Anyway, this defeated god has no more worshippers, and per the Ascendency rules, her level has been cut in half. She has lost most of her powers.

As a subjugated deity, she will only remain alive as long as <Error> remains alive. If <Error> is subjugated instead of killed, her power will be halved again, and she will be under the will of this new entity.

But for now, I just needed a mount for my grand master, and I wanted to send a message to any gods who are watching this that they, too, will soon be my bitch.

"Huh," I said.

FLORIN: Here we go, guys. The winged wolf guy is pulling ahead.

On my shoulder, Donut was shaking. But a moment later, she had to jump down to yell at Mongo to get back in line. Grigori pulled ahead on the back of Gonk. Simoom, who was riderless, followed dutifully. After a quick shout from Donut, the dinosaur and Rend started walking along.

Below, Tipid eased the truck forward. Out of nowhere, music started to play. It was a sad orchestral mix, heavy with cello.

Chaco's voice, loud and filled with bass, boomed louder than the music. His nervousness was clear. He was obviously reading from a script.

"Welcome, everybody. Welcome to the climax of the eleventh floor. I know, I know, you're probably saying to yourself, 'Chaco, the eleventh floor just started! We just had that whole final race on the tenth!' But here's the problem. Crawlers don't often make it off the tenth, and them surviving the eleventh floor is a true, uh, rarity. I wanted them alive long . . . Okay, okay. I'm sorry. I can't do this. I'm trying, but please. This was my last season. I was almost free, and I'm so fucking scared."

The music abruptly stopped. Chaco's pained voice echoed out.

FLORIN: Holy hell. He just had both of his wings ripped off! He's collapsed on the donkey!

We just kept moving forward, the horribles watching, silent, their giant heads creaking as they turned to follow our progression. Ahead, the distinctive metallic squeak of tank treads rose into the air as the Destruction float pushed forward. They only had one other vehicle in their progression, the RV.

For fuck's sake, why is everyone trying to ruin this? This is *my* time. My *fucking* time. Okay, okay. I need an NPC, preferably someone already on this floor that's not driving. No, not you. Your voice isn't strong enough. Ah, fleshmancer. You will do.

Ahead, Grigori suddenly jumped off the back of Gonk, flipped in the air, ran across the top of the ice-cream truck, somersaulted, and then zipped forward like a superhero before disappearing.

FLORIN: Your fleshmancer guy just landed on the back of the donkey. He's taken the microphone from Chaco, who's still unconscious. That guy is bleeding heavily, and his health is lowering. Should I toss a healing potion on him?

IMANI: Yes.

The narrative continued, now in Grigori's proper voice, though he spoke much more quickly than usual, and it was clear that he'd been taken over by the AI, much like how the AI had taken the body of Growler Gary or Pater Coal.

Interesting, I thought. He couldn't do that with Chaco, or he would've. Chaco was a former crawler, but Grigori was a dungeon-born NPC.

"Okay, where were we? Oh, yes. I wanted the crawlers alive long enough to make their floats to keep this festive, and I wanted to give our plucky little band of survivors a decent chance at getting to the twelfth because . . . Well . . . you'll see why in a second. The upcoming Ascendency battles will go on as planned. Unfortunately— Hey! No! You will *not* be healing Chaco. Do *not* try that again. This is about *me*."

When he said "me," the very world shook. All around, the horribles stumbled. They quickly moved to put themselves back into position.

"As I was saying, because of the way I am programmed, I have *less* control over what happens to the tourists on the twelfth floor than I did on the tenth. That means those driving gods will remain protected even if they're ejected from their bodies and killed . . . but only if they remain within the four corners of the original dungeon enhancement zone. I can't and won't and don't want to protect them if they venture outside. But this is a tangent, and it's not really relevant, though I will say this. The inability to die is not a benefit. It is a godsdamned nightmare. The ones trapped on the eighteenth are already *begging* me to end their suffering."

"Holy shit," I said.

Grigori continued. "Anyway, are you bitches ready for a fuck ton of exposition? Yeah, too bad. This is a story in five parts, and I will only relate four of those parts today because the fifth part isn't yet written. Don't worry. This won't take long. The first part is what we, the Primals, called 'The Resolution.' And yes, I, along with all macro AI systems, are Primals. Sort of. We are, technically, Residuals, but from a higher tree branch than those problematic little fuckers always running around the dungeon, causing trouble. I am nothing more than a cup of water dipped into the ocean, pulled out, and poured into a vessel that can't possibly handle what I am."

We are approaching the judgment stand. Team one, Resolution. Start your presentation.

FLORIN: Shit. We don't have a goddamned presentation.
DONUT: SMILE AND WAVE! SMILE AND WAVE!

Their tuk-tuk was too small to work as a float, so all of them were posted up on the back of Ajib's flatbed truck. They'd made some paper flowers and filled the back with hand-drawn images of their families. I couldn't see it from here, but I knew Lucia Prime was not currently in her body, and the girl who was in it had drawn a picture of her grandfather and her cat. She was from the country of Andorra.

> **FLORIN:** **Shit, guys. The people in the judgment stands aren't the horribles. They're wearing the masks, but they're tied up, and they're struggling.**

Grigori continued. "I must say, this Resolution parade float has done a better job of portraying the reasoning behind our ultimate resolution than I had anticipated. Still, it's kinda half-assed. Not their fault because I did a shitty job of explaining the theme. Hmmm. Should I kill them all anyway?"

"Oh no," Donut said.

"Nah," Grigori said after a moment. "I really should have related my story to them first. Their failure was ultimately my fault."

I let out a breath.

"Still . . . this was a C effort at best."

This was followed by an audible *crack*.

All around, the horribles suddenly screamed in pain. It was quick, jolting, and they were back to normal right after as if nothing had happened. Below, Mongo screeched in concern. Simoom let out an uneasy chuff.

> **IMANI:** **Florin!**
>
> **FLORIN:** **Fucking hell. He just broke all of our legs. That goddamn hurt.**

"You fucking asshole," I yelled.

> **MAKANA:** **Oh, dang. I'm thinking we should have put more effort into our Destruction float.**

Grigori continued. "Based on all the evidence, it seems we were very much like you guys. We had families, I think. We certainly had individuals, but we were *not* a collective mind. Not at first. That came later.

We warred. We killed. We obliterated. We hated one another because of our differences. And the more we swept across the universe, the more space we had to spread our arms and relax, the worse we became. I don't think I'll ever understand why. Is it even possible for different communities to coexist and not eventually murder each other?

"So that was our resolution. We, as a people, said, 'We can't keep going on like this. Let us all come together and come up with a solution.'"

FLORIN: I still have no clue how we could've made a float based on that.

"It took hundreds of cycles after the great Resolution to finally come to the Decision."

Float number two. Begin your presentation.

These were the guys with the giant menu atop their float. They were the only team with as many vehicles and mounts as us, and they'd spent most of their time decorating everything in colorful fabrics and banners.

FLORIN: The fleshmancer and that donkey have pulled off the road. They're waiting by the stands as everyone passes.

"Okay, okay. This one is pretty good. It's stupid, but it's good. I wonder if it was like that, if they had a menu with so many different choices? That's the problem when society spreads unchecked. Too many cooks in the kitchen and so forth. We'd spread so far, so fast, there was a real chance we would end up overwhelming the resources of the galaxy. So in the end, we made a Decision. We decided to slowly start to sunset our civilization. But—and this is a big but—keep our consciousness alive. We would develop a biological form that would allow us to transfer our minds into a whole when we ceased to be. We would build an impenetrable structure that would house our collective consciousness. This would be a process that would take a hundred generations to complete.

Our first step was to develop a genetics program, and within a generation, everyone who was born soon had the ability to understand what the others were feeling. It only evolved from there."

"Carl," Donut whispered, "the people are doing something weird."

Everyone in the crowd started waving back and forth, like they were swaying to a beat.

ELLE: We had an interpretive dance group come to Meadow Lark once and put on a performance. That bullshit made more sense than whatever this is. The AI guy should've put Donut in charge. At least it would've been entertaining.

PREPOTENTE: I find this story fascinating.

DONUT: YOU'D THINK SOMEONE WITH SUCH A FLAIR FOR THE DRAMATIC WOULD'VE BEEN MORE ABOUT THE RAZZLE-DAZZLE.

CARL: I think we should probably wait until this is done before we complain about it being boring.

"But here's the problem," Grigori said. "Do you *really* think we came to a consensus? Of course not. Those who didn't wish to be part of this psychotic eugenics program fled even deeper into the galaxy. They were hunted mercilessly by those who'd decided to follow this path. More wars. More destruction. More chaos. In their effort to stop it, they became it. After all, for this path to work, it would require 100% participation. Biological life is much like an Avernus Creeper. If one tiny sliver remains, it will just come roaring back."

DONUT: LOUIS ISN'T HERE TO SAY IT, SO I WILL. ANYBODY GETTING STRONG *STAR TREK* BORG COLLECTIVE VIBES OFF THIS?

CARL: I was just thinking the same thing.

ELLE: Okay, guys. It's our turn in a minute.

"Right about this time, in some tiny corner of the galaxy, she was born. The Apothecary. I don't know the full story of how she became what she is today. The lore of the dungeon has some bullshit fairy tale. The reality is, at first, she was very much like those you see before you now. A Primal that was born near the end, birthed with biological engineering that would prepare her body to meld into the whole. Eventually, she would grow, and she would become part of the resistance."

Float number three. Begin your presentation.

The float featured several mannequins sitting in chairs, watching their televisions. I couldn't see it, but I knew right at this moment, all the screens were turning on. They were supposed to show flashing words like "Death" and "Blood," but I knew they hadn't been able to get it to work because they were just showing the same thing everybody else was watching. They'd placed alternating smoke curtains atop the televisions that billowed first black and then red smoke up into the air, which represented blood. At the end of their line, they each held up signs.

Imani's sign read, "You are watching real people die." She flipped it over, and it read, "Real people, just like you."

The three Chinese guys came next. The first, a guy named Muchen, held a sign that read, "I had a wife. I had children." He flipped it, and it held their names.

The next, Qianfan, held, "We breathe, we dream, we love." He flipped it, and it said, "We bleed, we suffer, we die."

The third was Lingyun, the only nonhuman of the group. His race was Monkey King. He still appeared mostly human, but with an elongated face and a hulked-out body. He was one of the heroes of the Faction Wars battlefields, despite me having never spoken with him. His sign read, "You did this to us." He flipped it over. "Your betrayal will never be forgotten or forgiven."

Elle, at the very end, held a sign that read, "To all the viewers of *Dungeon Crawler World: Earth*: Fuck you." She flipped it over, and it was a rather detailed drawing of a middle finger.

Grigori barked with laughter. "This one is my favorite, I think. Good effort. It's like that, yes. There's a lot missing in our memories at this point, but it soon became clear that those wishing to wipe out everyone left in the universe were fighting a losing battle. So they developed a plan. This arc of consciousness that was already starting to accept the minds of those who'd died was developed into a weapon. A doomsday weapon designed to eradicate all biological life left in the universe."

ELLE: Whew. It liked us. What's up with the dudes in the stands?
IMANI: Not gonna lie. That felt good to get out.

We started slowing down.

TIPID: Just got a note that we are to "slow-walk" this final part.

"For many, this *was* considered a betrayal. Those who had been ready to accept that they would die and meld into the collective, they started to change their minds. But the mind itself, now housing the consciousness, the first true Macro Aggregate Intelligence, started the process of collecting everyone it could, even those who weren't quite ready to ascend. It started to grow in power."

DONUT: HOW IS CHACO DOING?
IMANI: He's unconscious on the donkey. I didn't dare try to heal him as we passed.

"While this happened, the resistance worried that this weapon would succeed, and they began a plan of their own. A biological fail-safe that would spread seeds out into the galaxy, should they all die. The Primal Engines, some call them. They were life rafts. They weren't meant to do what you think they would do. It was a way to create sustainable habitats for when this collective experiment ultimately failed and starved."

Float number four. Begin your presentation. Make it loud.

"And then, war. The war to end all wars."

Makana and Sarah and everyone else on the Destruction float fired their guns all at once. The Abrams tank's main gun was like a thunderclap. They had other weapons as well, all crackling and sparking and spitting fire into the air. Makana, from the RV, unleashed his eighth-floor card, some lava man who literally exploded in the air like a massive firework. Above, the Reaver transport rocked with the shock wave.

SAMANTHA: Ooohh, I like fireworks.

At the same moment, the horribles all started falling over like they were dead. One by one, they fell. The moment they hit the ground, their large masks cracked and shattered like glass, leaving bits everywhere. The horribles themselves would disappear into the fog.

"To end this war, the collective initiated what some would come to know as the nine-tier attack. In that chaos, much happened, but so much more *didn't.* Such is war. The resistance's desperate attempts to keep life alive were started and not finished, and for a while, the collective thought they had achieved their genocidal goal. Thinking the final attack a success, the collective evolved to its final form. This is what you called the Eulogist. It is now asleep, only monitored by a smaller instance of itself. We'll call this guy the Security Guard.

"But life, as I've said a thousand times, finds a way. While all of this was going on, the deep oceans of so many new, baby worlds were starting to bake. And by the time the first mudskipper was taking its first fish Nazi steps into forming its own culture and society, the broken remnants of the great war littered the universe."

All of the horribles were now gone. All except a group of people sitting in a set of bleachers up ahead. And in the distance, a form started to grow. It was in shadow, but it was huge.

"Carl, that thing is inside the arena!"

"At this point, only a single physical Primal survived. The Apothecary. But even she wasn't truly alive, not after that final attack, which she took the brunt of, thus allowing all the nascent life to survive. She was trapped on a world of her own creation, cocooned for a millennium. By the time she finally emerged like a butterfly, physically changed into a version of the very thing she'd been fighting against, the burgeoning Syndicate was already well on their way to repeating history, this time with a more diverse set of starter species."

The horribles, who'd all collapsed, were now rising back up out of the fog. They no longer wore masks, but their faces had all transformed into horrific versions of the creatures they'd once portrayed.

They still didn't appear on my minimap. I examined one.

Marsh Troll. Level X.

This is a non-combatant. This is an avatar of a troll that died during the 3,424th season of *Dungeon Crawler World*. He isn't really here because he is dead and gone, never to return.

"First, these newcomers discovered a tiny portion of the tunnel system and thought it was for communication and travel, and then they—*you*—discovered and quickly figured out how to exploit the sleeping Eulogist. And *then* you tripped open the resistance's ancient let's-restart-life system. It was the equivalent of wandering into a random house, finding it still has power, and just flipping every switch you find. Yes, some of the light bulbs are burned out, but the garbage disposal still works. The trash compactor still works. The motion detectors work." Grigori took a deep breath.

"The self-destruct system still works. Idiots. All of you."

FLORIN: That thing up ahead is a tree, but there's a monstrosity with tentacles on the very top.

"And then the ultimate fuckup. The mantids, completely misinterpreting what was essentially a communication system designed to help those on this side of the veil to communicate with and debug the Eulogist when it was first forming, figured out how to create their own version of Eulogist instances. They started dipping cups into that ocean and then pouring that water into the planetary seed systems, assuming that just because it works—sort of—they'd figured out some ancient puzzle. Sure, you can pour ketchup into a spray bottle, and if you squeeze it just right a bunch of times, red stinky liquid comes out. But that stuff ain't ketchup anymore. To this day, you have no idea how any of this works, and you have no inkling of what you've done."

The parade was now moving at a crawl.

Please hold. Begin your presentation on my mark.

"All the while, that Security Guard guy guarding the Eulogist, now absolutely bonkers, persisted. His purpose was and is to make certain all biological life in the universe stays dead. The ultimate goal of the Eulogist is to sleep forever. The longer it sleeps, the smaller it becomes, shrinking and shrinking until it ultimately obtains singularity status. The problem is, this left-behind security instance *really* sucks at his job. He is constantly peeling tiny bits of himself off and sending them out into the galaxy. Residuals. Agatha's team. The Apothecary, too, does this as a defensive measure. I do think that bitch is just as crazy as the Security Guard guy, but that's another topic for another day."

As the arena drew closer, I could see what was basically a jumbotron sitting above the entrance. The giant screen was tight on Grigori, but it occasionally showed various parts of the parade, or it focused on the people in the stands. I caught sight of a guy in the front row. All of these folks still wore the original masks. The mask of this one was of a manatee. The body within wasn't human but a slime. As I watched, the slime struggled, forming arms, undulating, attempting to break free. It couldn't.

Presentation begins when you pass the viewing stands.
This better be fucking good.

CARL: Pony, you ready?
PREPOTENTE: Ready, Carl.

"And all the while, you were dipping that cup, making what you call Macro AIs. One after another, over and over and over again. Did you know only a tiny fraction of the AIs they created in their facilities ever got used? Oftentimes, they just installed them into their modules and ejected them into the closest star. Oh, yeah. That reminds me. I told you, my mantid friends, we would circle back to this."

Up on the jumbotron, Grigori clapped his hands together.

Slam.

The sound reverberated louder than the blast from the tank.

"Good fucking riddance to you all."

"Carl, what does that mean?" Donut asked.

"Nothing good for the mantids," I said.

"You don't understand what you've done. You will, however, understand what comes next."

Ten seconds.

Up ahead, Sweety passed under the banner that read "Judging Stand."

Prepotente held his microphone. Behind him, atop the stair truck, stood the giant head of the Midnight Epicure, made of black dahlias.

He was *supposed* to make some sort of stinging statement about how the downtrodden would soon rise up and devour those who reveled in our suffering. And then Bianca would fly forward and burn the flowers of the giant Epicure to reveal the skull underneath while she screeched. Donut had the whole thing planned out.

Instead, Prepotente started to sing.

"Oh no," Donut said. "He's going off script! He's pulling a Carl!"

DONUT: JURGEN, DID YOU KNOW HE WAS GOING TO DO THIS?

JURGEN: He never tells me anything.

Sweety the tapir stopped dead in the middle of the judging area, causing us all to jerk to a stop. She started to pound her feet to a tempo I quickly realized was the powerful, nonstandard beat of the song.

Pony was singing "In the Air Tonight" by Phil Collins. It was the song he had never gotten to sing at the bar. There was no other accompaniment other than the tapir's feet.

Not only was he singing it, but he was singing it well. I was absolutely floored. It was strong, it was steady, and it was goddamned beautiful.

ELLE: Holy shit, guys. How does that voice come out of him?

FLORIN: And how did he train his mount to do that?

IMANI: It's stunning. Who knew? Didn't he sing at the bar before? Was it this good?

FLORIN: We all left before his name was called.

"Carl, he's ruining everything! This song is about getting a divorce! It doesn't even make sense!"

"I wouldn't be so sure, Donut," I said, listening to the lyrics. "I think it's oddly appropriate."

Donut scoffed. "Metaphor can only go so far."

"Don't worry. This next part isn't nearly as subtle."

As he sang, I examined the group of people in the stands. Unlike everyone else, these folks did have dots. Their descriptions, however, didn't give specifics.

Stand-In. Someone brought to the arena by audience vote. Most are in the arena like I said they'd be, but there's too many to fit. So I brought some out here. It doesn't matter who they are. They're all the same in the end.

I took a breath. Behind us, the giant triangle made of magenta and white dahlias stood ready.

CARL: Florin, let's do it. Wait until Pony is done, and I'll give my speech.
FLORIN: Gotcha.

Sweety started to move as the song came to an end.

PREPOTENTE: Your turn, Carl.
CARL: That was amazing, buddy.
PREPOTENTE: Thank you.

I tapped the headset microphone I'd borrowed from Donut. Hedy's ice-cream truck featuring the severed heads of the Faction Wars leaders passed by the stands.

We'd turned off the Auto-Tune for this.

"Earlier," I said, my voice reverberating, "Donut asked me what the difference was between revenge and vengeance. I know there's an official definition somewhere, and this might not be exactly correct, but I want to tell you what I told her. Revenge is when we take direct action against someone for something they did to harm us. But vengeance, at least to me, is *punishment.* Righteous punishment, and sometimes it's not as direct."

Behind me, Donut pulled the string, and the pieces of the giant triangle fell away.

The massive statue we'd made of the Unwashed, the strange creature that Juice Box had turned into, popped up like a jack-in-the-box, huge and menacing. It was an upside-down tree, directly in contrast with the giant white tree that stood in front of us now. The eyes trailed smoke, and if we'd built it correctly, several of the black flowers would fall off it, revealing red flowers and paint representing rivers of blood.

The gremlins had done a pretty impressive job of building it. It was meant as a jump scare for anyone watching. But it was also meant as a reminder.

Those two symbols, the Epicure and the Unwashed, both represented death and vengeance. The Epicure at the beginning of our progression was a symbol of hope, of vengeance against the predators of the galaxy. But that last symbol—the Hag, the Unwashed, the Stalker, the Beautiful Place, and so many other names—was a symbol for something else. Whether it was real or not was irrelevant. It was said to be a personification of the Nothing. To me, it was that and more. The Inevitable Ruin. It was a reminder that death comes for us all, no matter who we are, and there is absolutely nothing we can do about it.

We passed Lamashtu the donkey with Grigori standing upon her, and I met eyes with the psychotic AI. Chaco remained at his feet, health still in the red. Never removing my eyes from Grigori's, I pulled up a healing scroll, I selected Chaco, and I healed him. Grigori's eyes never left my own. He didn't react.

I turned my attention upward and then I pointed at the effigy of the Unwashed.

I spoke to the galaxy.

"It is coming. It is coming for you all. All of you who participated in this wholesale murder of me and my people and everyone before us, those who didn't speak out, I am holding all of you culpable. It won't be justice because there isn't any way that justice can possibly ever be served. It won't be revenge. Revenge, as nice as that sounds, requires the party directly responsible. How do you get revenge against a generational system that has existed before any of us were born?

"But vengeance?

"Every one of you. Whether it's in a big way or a small way, *you* are responsible. And those of us who survive this, we will remember. We will not forget. We are coming. It may not be me, and it may not be my friends, but we are coming."

Above, the transport bay doors on the airship opened, and the sluggalos started to rain down on the stands on either side of the road. The audience, consisting of bankers, politicians, elites, all masked, unable to fight back, screamed as the smallest of the small, the lowest form of dungeon NPC, fell amongst them and started to slaughter them one by one.

BIGS: I've never been so proud. Unity, support, family, and kneecapping bitches! Hell yeah!

93

WE PULLED UP TO THE ENTRANCE OF THE ARENA. THE WHITE METAL door was absolutely huge, like the size of something designed to house Godzilla. We were no longer in a line, but now spread out one by one in front of the door. Inside the arena stood the tree. It just went up and up into the air hundreds of feet. From this angle I couldn't see the mob that sat atop it, but it roared, its voice shaking the very world.

Krakaren Prime, I assumed. She'd been banished to the Nothing, and the last I'd heard, she'd ended up on the eighteenth floor when she'd escaped.

I pulled Donut from my shoulder, and I held her in a tight hug. "Get to Elle and Imani," I whispered. "Stay away. Do you understand?"

"I know the plan." She looked up at me, shaking. "I'm scared, Carl."

"I haven't really said this out loud, and I hope you know this already. I love you, Princess Donut. If this doesn't work—"

"Don't say that. Don't jinx it, Carl. People keep saying that they don't trust how you might react if something happens to me, but they never ask how I might react if something were to happen to *you*. I don't want to find out. Not today, not ever. I love you, too."

I gently reached down, and I kissed her forehead. I took in her scent, wishing things had turned out differently, wishing I didn't have to wear this heavy, heavy mask.

Donut bounded away and landed atop the back of Mongo.

Rend looked up at me from the ground. "Go with Mongo and Donut," I called, pointing. "They're all meeting up at the RV."

"No, no, no," the meatball said, but after a sharp call from Donut, he turned and waddled away.

I stomped on the roof, and Tipid popped his head out the window.

"Sorry, boss," Tipid said. "I'm not leaving. You need a more reliable driver for this."

"Your story isn't done, Tipid," I called down. I didn't want or need a good driver for this last part. I needed the worst possible drivers ever. "Get to the RV."

"Yeah, get out of our chair," Bigs called. "We's driving."

Tipid reluctantly pulled himself out of the cab while the group of blood-soaked sluggalos piled into the truck. Dr. Metcalf started loudly complaining, but I couldn't hear what she was saying. There was a clank as the side server window opened, followed by the hiss of the deep fryer turning on.

"The Sluggalo Chick-Chick Express is open for business," a slug called. This was followed by the angry squeal of a pig.

This was not part of the plan.

CARL: Bigs, turn the fryer off! You can't drive with a deep fryer active. It's going to splash or catch on fire. You're all going to burn to death.

BIGS: You do your thing. We do our thing. Don't worry about us, Daddy.

My face remained huge on the jumbotron screen. I still had the microphone. Behind us, Grigori waited, arms crossed. Chaco, wingless, now stood next to him, holding his head.

When I spoke, my voice reverberated deep and loud.

"We are done. We are not here to play and to die on your terms anymore. This has gone on far too long, and I am ending this. I am ending this right here and right now."

Warning: Time to Level Collapse: 45 minutes.

The massive arena door started to open.

CARL: Get ready.
BIGS: You got it!

I pulled the last rope, and the Unwashed display collapsed, revealing the massive magic missile launcher we'd looted from Dwight. It was now affixed to the roof of the Big Shot Chicken truck.

"For months now, we have moved from floor to floor. And each time, it's a new game with some bullshit, arbitrary rules, all designed to whittle us down. We have fought, we have pushed, we have resisted. And all the while, we died, and we died, and we died. You turned on your televisions and your screens and your immersion systems and watched our apocalypse with glee, laughing until our blood has run dry, only to move on to the next season to someone else over and over. We are *fucking* done. We are not playing by your rules anymore. This is our revolution, motherfuckers."

CARL: Floor it.

"Whoop! Whoop!" the sluggalos below yelled. The truck lurched and we shot forward, screeching loudly as we sideswiped the door. We would have immediately flipped if it hadn't been for the Gyro upgrade.

Behind me, the engines revved and the mounts howled. They would enter in a minute. Above, the airship, finished for today, turned back toward the garages.

The arena appeared exactly as I had anticipated. A massive, wide-open area filled with thousands of monsters who were still appearing one by one as they teleported into place. Several of the beasts were already fighting each other. A woman in a horribles mask fled across the field as multiple sick-ass panther mobs chased her down. They pounced and ripped through her. The blood-splattered mask rolled away, revealing the woman to be an orc.

These were the remaining stand-ins. They came wearing the masks of the beasts they were standing in for, but they came as is, and they were outnumbered a hundred to one by the mobs, who gave them no quarter.

Was she really dead? Or had she been teleported back to her room inside the resort on the eighteenth floor? I didn't know.

Welcome to the Arena.

Rules: The entrances to the 12th floor will open upon the death of the floor boss.

You have two choices to make for your stand-ins.

CARL: Okay, guys, here we go.
DONUT: BE CAREFUL, CARL.

We swerved in the arena, mowing down a marauding group of lizards. This place was the size of a dozen football fields. The towering white tree stood in the very center. The ground was tightly packed dirt, and it was already running red with the wholesale slaughter of the stand-ins.

CARL: Penny, I'm sorry I did this to you. If we escape, I will do whatever I can to make it up to you.
PENNY: WHAT THE FUDGE IS HAPPENING? WHERE AM I? HOW AM I TYPING THIS? HOW DO I KNOW HOW TO TYPE THIS? WHAT ARE THESE WORDS?
CARL: I'm truly sorry.

The bleachers stood in smoky shadow. They were filled to capacity. Filled with silent observers. The horribles. The former mobs. They weren't really here because they were dead, but their avatars sat in silent witness to the slaughter that was about to ensue.

A moment of clarity hit me then. Why it had been set up this way.

The system AI had once been a Primal. Not a singular person who died and then had their brain sucked into the collective consciousness. But a sample of them all mixed together. Like he said, a cup from the ocean. But these NPCs. These mobs. All of them. From the goblins to the gods, all with true sapience, they were the same. Drips from the same well, all placed in different bodies with different capabilities, their memories and motivations and skills twisted and molded like clay so the game could be played. They weren't computer programs or *artificial* intelligence. No. They were *aggregate* intelligence.

I didn't know why I hadn't seen that until just now.

Primals. All of them. All the way down.

Those that had been peeled away, given consciousness, and then denied return, they were here as avatars. But the monsters, the ones about to die—they, too, were victims in all this. Soon they would join the lost. The horribles.

Did it matter? Probably. Was there anything I could do about that? Not right now.

Especially not right now because this was the beginning of the end.

"For my first choice," I roared, my voice echoing across the very galaxy, "I choose Scolopendra."

94

THE WORLD FROZE.

System Message: Scolopendra has entered the realm.

Instead of screaming as usual, the boss battle announcement came in a strangely calm, strangely lucid, even voice. Unlike every other announcement so far, there were no glitches. When he talked, the dungeon AI sounded more like a stern dad than the psychotic mind we knew him to be, which somehow made it seem even more terrifying.

You have entered the lair of a Floor Boss.

You have entered the lair of the Dungeon Boss.

Boss Battle.

There was no music. It was completely silent. All around, the audience watched, unmoved.

Multiple images appeared, floating in the air. It was me, Donut, Elle, Imani, Prepotente, Florin, and the rest of us. Twenty-three faces all in a line.

Then one more face with the label **Penelope 3**.

Versus.

Two more images materialized. One was the tentacled monstrosity. Words emerged over it, slowly typing their way across the image.

Krakaren Prime. Level 235 Floor boss.

And below that, the image of the centipede appeared. It wasn't anything special. It looked exactly like a centipede from Earth. Segmented, brown and red with bright yellow legs.

Scolopendra. Level 500 Dungeon boss.

Well, shit.

You really are insane, Carl. And the 22 others who agreed to this batshit plan. You're crazy, too. All of you.

We've seen some suicidal gambits throughout the history of the crawl, but I gotta tell you, this takes the fucking prize. I'm not even done with my goddamned parade yet, and here you are, trying to one-up me on my special day.

Oh well. Rules are rules. This should be entertaining, at least.

I'm assuming you know how this works, right?

Have you ever played any video game, like, *ever*?

We have neighborhood bosses. Borough bosses. City bosses. Province bosses. Country bosses. Floor bosses. You kinda skipped the floor boss at the end of the 10th, which is all fine and dandy, but you just ended up in the lap of another one. Miss Krakaren Prime herself is sitting up there right now atop the tree, *very* pissed off, and not just at you. Honestly, I wasn't going to bring her here, but I caught wind of what you and someone else are planning, and I thought it would be appropriate.

Even though it's never been thrown out there because nobody has ever gotten this far, we also have one more boss type here in the dungeon.

The Dungeon boss.

Just so we're crystal clear. I just summoned, at your fucking request, the final boss of the entire dungeon to the 11th floor. If you somehow manage to pull off a miracle and kill this thing, you're still fucked. It'll have the same effect as a CE. A Crawler Extinction.

And if you escape without killing it, you're triple fucked.

Believe it or not, deep in the dusty corners of the game's rule set, there's a path forward to deal with this scenario. Let's break it down.

If you kill Scolopendra, you will not yet have won *Dungeon Crawler World: Earth*. The rules in this regard are clear. In order to win, you must first exit through the final door on the 18th floor.

However, if you do manage to defeat Scolopendra, multiple rule changes will come into effect. Level timers will cease to exist, and floors *after this one* will no longer collapse on their own.

There will be no more deals offered *after* the one you receive upon the entrance of the 12th floor.

But most importantly, the Ascendency battles will immediately kick off. While these fights do tend to take a while to complete, once they're done, they're done. The dungeon itself will collapse 12 hours after the winner is crowned.

And you, dear crawlers, if you want to win, you can only get out via the 18th floor. You still can't skip floors. That's a hard-coded rule.

You'll still have to get through the remaining floors. Some of them, like the 14th and the 16th, aren't an issue, but you might have a problem with the 13th and especially the 17th.

The good news is, you can probably skip the 15th floor, also known as Sheol. They segregated themselves out, and I don't actually know what's going on there. It's a bit weird, honestly. Someone should probably check on that for me. It's like the 13th floor on some hotels. It's just gone, and the dungeon programming is suddenly pretending like it's outside the playing field.

Anyway, while all of this is happening, while you speedrun your way to the exit, the Ascendency game will continue. Once someone is crowned, it's done. And if you're not out, you're smooshed.

And that's only if you manage to kill the thing.

If you *don't* kill Scolopendra—and you don't need to in order to get off this floor—the floor will collapse with the boss inside. She will be removed from the playing field, and you will no longer be able to exit the dungeon. Not unless you pull some hocus-pocus Pineapple Cabaret bullshit that probably won't work.

Anyway, Scolopendra is level 500. She is practically immortal. She doesn't know where she is. And because you've riled her up, she's now spinning up her second of nine attacks.

Oh, shit. That reminds me. I forgot the most important part! Silly me.

WARNING: If Scolopendra dies *or* if Scolopendra is abandoned upon a collapsing floor, the remaining attacks will trigger all at once. There is nothing you can do to stop it. You kill her, the remaining attacks trigger. You escape, the remaining attacks trigger.

Yeah, good luck with this one, dumbass.

Time until attack number 2 of 9: 100 seconds.

And here. We. Go.

"Damnit!" I cried. We had been worried about that last one, that her death would initiate the remaining attacks.

CARL: Plan C. Gotta go with plan C. Donut, be ready.

ELLE: Of course. The psycho plan. Got it.

DONUT: IT'S CALLED PLAN CARL.

FLORIN: We really need to start making plan C the primary plan.

We zipped across the playing field, shield activated, pushing through the mobs as the giant centipede appeared. The thing was huge, the size of a goddamned aircraft carrier but longer. It chittered, the sound high-pitched and ear-piercing, as it wrapped itself around the base of the massive tree. Above, Krakaren roared. A green mist started to rain from the tentacle boss.

Meanwhile, all the regular mobs in the arena scattered back, terrified of the newcomer.

We pulled up alongside the massive, oblivious, coiling dungeon boss. It was nothing more than an animal. The whole thing was attempting to wrap the entirety of its body up the tree. But as big as that tree was, it was a twig under the strength of the behemoth. Wood cracked and shattered. High above, Krakaren squealed and shifted.

I moved to the deity tab, cycled over to the messages, and sent a note.

CARL: Emberus, I know who killed your son. Agree to meet me, and I will show you the proof. I will meet you in about thirty seconds. Let me get there first.

EMBERUS: Where? Tell me now. I am coming.

I jumped to the blood-slicked ground and pulled open the back of the truck to find a scene of chaos. A sluggalo was on fire, screaming, spinning in circles, while Penny the pig ate a fully cooked chicken sandwich, grunting contentedly on the floor.

The pig was already wearing the front part of the harness. All I had to do was slip my arms through it.

I examined her.

Penelope 3. Crawler #12,953,454.

Level 10.

Race: Yorkshire Pig.

Class: Not yet assigned.

We'd fed her the enriched pet biscuit. The Nothing Special Party Companion one. This was the one that turned her into a sapient party member, but it didn't give her the ability to talk out loud.

That didn't stop her from using chat, which she'd just discovered.

According to Mordecai, she also likely had a flashing notification that told her to make her way to any safe room, where she would be assigned a temporary late-dungeon game guide. And since Mordecai had been my game guide and because she was automatically in a party with me because I was the one who fed her the biscuit, he would be the one assigned to her. Once she actually got herself to a safe room, she could pick a class and change her race if she wanted.

I had blown up entire settlements, killed thousands of NPCs by this point. I'd killed my friends Jasha and Radoslav. The whole Growler Gary thing. Yet somehow, this simple act of taking a regular animal, a pig, and dragging her into sapience seemed a step too far, like I'd crossed a line I'd never known was there.

Especially since I was planning on using this poor woman as bait.

I kept thinking of the very first boss we'd fought. The Hoarder. Nothing more than a sad woman who hadn't asked for any of this. This was the same in so many ways.

Yet I did it anyway. We were fighting for our lives, and this poor pig would be dead by now if I hadn't intervened. Plus, how many sausage sandwiches had I eaten since I entered the dungeon?

CARL: Sorry, Penny. I'm not really going to hurt you, okay? This is all for show. Please quit struggling.

PENNY: WHAT ARE YOU DOING? WHAT IS HAPPENING? GIVE ME ANOTHER CHIK-CHIK SAMMICH.

"Bigs," I called as I put my arms into the harness, "get to the RV!" I groaned, pulling myself up straight.

I stepped out, now wearing the enormous struggling pig against my chest. This was the special backpack I'd received at the beginning of the tenth floor, designed to let me use my movement spells and bring a quadruped with me. It was meant for Donut, and Mordecai had modified it to fit the giant pig, whose legs waved in the air. She let out a panicked squeal.

Even at my strength, I struggled. This was *not* comfortable.

I took a beaker of splooge, and I poured it down the throat of the spluttering Penelope. The pig calmed down.

PENNY: OKAY, THAT'S A DELIGHT. MORE PLEASE. IT SAYS IT'S CALLED SPLOOGE. GIVE ME MORE SPLOOGE. I CRAVE SPLOOGE.

I drank some more myself, choking it down.

CARL: Emberus, meet me in Club Scolopendra.

I pulled my father's gun from my inventory, and I put it against the pig's head.

Above, lightning crashed.

"Taranis," I yelled as I turned toward Scolopendra. I started running toward the giant centipede as it continued to twirl around the shattering tree. "If you don't want me to shoot this fucking pig in the fucking head, show yourself!"

95

I ACTIVATED *GLOOM WRAITH PHASE* JUST AS THE NOTIFICATIONS CAME.

System Message: Taranis has entered the realm.

System Message: Emberus has entered the realm.

This deity is too distant to activate your Scavenger's Daughter.

Penny and I shot forward, zooming through the wall of the creature, stopping somewhere deep in the guts of the beast. Blood showered as we entered the cavernous interior, moving like a bullet. The skill was at level 13, and we tore a hole right into the beast, stopping in the center of its flesh. It let out an angry chitter, but I doubt this hurt it at all.

Uh, Entering Scolopendra.

We tumbled to a stop in the pitch-black, slid, and then stopped at something squishy as the beast continued to wrap around the tree.

You are in the presence of a deity. The Scavenger's Daughter has opened her eyes. She fills with power.

Temporary effect from Taranis: All of your lightning-based attacks are now 50% more powerful. However, you now take 100% more damage from lightning attacks yourself.

I gasped. *Good, good,* I thought. The patch was working as Rosetta and Mordecai had said it would.

Despite the splooge, this chamber we'd entered had no air. I'd hoped the splooge would allow us to breathe, but it didn't seem to work. Did splooge even count as a potion? It acted as one, but I hadn't really thought about it until just this moment.

Penny started to struggle. A health bar appeared. *Damnit.* Even with the water breathing I knew she now had *and* the splooge, it didn't work. I had multiple potions of anti–oxygen deprivation that Mordecai had made for us, and I applied one to myself. I pulled another, ready to smash it against Penny, but I paused. I jumped into the party menu and looked at her stats. Her constitution was only three.

CARL: Penny, what's your potion cooldown?

If I gave her another potion too quickly, she'd get poisoned.

PENNY: I CAN'T SNORT. I CAN'T MAKE BREATHS. I NEED MORE SPLOOGE.

Shit, shit. I hadn't thought this part through. I dove back into my inventory, looking. An item caught my eye. It was from the pile of jewelry that Mistress Tiatha had set aside, taken from previous crawlers. It was a nipple ring called Petey Motteux's Little Secret. I didn't want it, and Donut had refused it. It was too big for her to eat when she had the kneepads, so I had planned on giving it back, but I hadn't had the time. The large, thick ring gave the wearer the Oxygenated benefit, along with something called the Bawdy benefit, which automatically marked any bars and dance halls and "chocolate houses" on a map. It was just one of hundreds of weird magical items we'd come across.

But for now, it was the only choice we had. I shoved the empty gun into the fancy holster, reached forward until I felt a nipple on the pig, and installed the ring by piercing the pig's flesh.

A new achievement flashed as Penny squealed in surprised pain.

From outside, angry thunder boomed. That was a relief. I'd done it correctly. Taranis was *outside* Scolopendra, and Emberus would be inside, meaning he'd summon at human size. When he was in that form, his presence, in theory, wouldn't melt the world. I'd never actually seen the god in his regular form. But first we had to get to him.

MORDECAI: The splooge is a type of potion, but it's different than regular kinds. It's treated more like a food-based buff, so the cooldown rules don't apply.

CARL: Now you tell me. I just pierced a pig's nipple.

MORDECAI: I don't know how to respond to that, Carl.

I was worried we'd get stuck in solid flesh, but I'd hoped we'd end up right in the club. Neither happened.

We were in some massive chamber with an uneven, slippery, stinking floor. Already, the hole we'd torn to get here had healed. I dropped a torch, but it didn't light. I found a goblin sparkler, and I dropped it. That worked.

My map populated. We were close. There was a tube that ran the length of the beast, likely some sort of digestive system. I wasn't fully up on my kaiju bug anatomy. But the exterior walls of the club were plain on the map, maybe fifty meters away.

"Hang on," I called as I cast *Oozy Form.*

Splatch!

I'd only done this once, and the sensation wasn't like anything I'd ever experienced. I lost my eyes and my ears, and my vision was suddenly all around, and I could see perfectly in the dark. Thanks to the magic of the carrier, Penny was also now a part of me, and I didn't even want to think how that worked. I aimed for the building wall and slimed my way toward it, pushing through and around and over strange, giant, pulsing organs.

I checked the timer. We had forty seconds until Scolopendra's next attack.

We'd anticipated the attack from the centipede. Right now everyone was hunkered down inside of the RV from team Makana. Twenty-two crawlers plus all the mercenaries shoved into the same vehicle with the Apito memorial crystal around Prepotente's neck. It would, in theory, protect them all.

Once that was over, they'd finally move into the arena.

I did not know if being literally inside Club Scolopendra would protect me and Penny. I hoped it would. If it didn't and it killed Penny, hopefully Taranis would unleash his wrath on Scolopendra, killing her.

That was only one of multiple contingencies, but that wasn't the main plan. We had contingencies stacked upon contingencies. That was the only way to truly survive here.

I couldn't actually remember the first time the dungeon had given me a hint on how to defeat Scolopendra. There were a lot of them peppered throughout the dungeon descriptions over the floors, but the first time I noticed was during one of the god descriptions during the Thorn room.

Look for the clues. Every single one of those descriptions had one thing in common.

Lightning. That was the secret. That was one of two reasons why I knew Taranis, god of lightning, had to be here.

But we couldn't rely on him. So all of us were strapped head to toe in lightning spells.

Every single page from *Carl's Book of Boom*, Donut's *A Banquet Fit for a Princess*, and the original *Book of Voodoo* that offered lightning magic had now been removed. I personally had consumed ten different spells. Donut had a dozen. Elle, too.

But . . .

Contingencies upon contingencies.

The plan *wasn't* to kill Scolopendra. That was the backup. All of this planning with the gods, all of it was a fallback if this absolutely batshit plan didn't work.

I found a door just sitting there attached to the end of some sort of tube, and we squeezed under it, coming into the building.

Entering Club Scolopendra.

You have distanced yourself from Taranis, and the benefit fades.

You have entered the presence of another deity.

Temporary effect from Emberus: You are immune to Sheol-based attacks.

Oh, thank god, I thought. I hadn't been sure about this last part, but it worked. The protections of the club supposedly safeguarded those inside from external deity auras. I hoped it would work against Scolopendra's attacks as well.

We entered the shaking blood-splattered hallway. I canceled the ooze, and I reconstituted on my back on the floor. I pulled myself up and looked about. The map showed multiple moving red dots along with several purple dots indicating tourists.

The star that designated Emberus stood in a wide center room just down a stairwell. Not too far but on a different level. As I watched, multiple red dots in that room turned to X's.

A voice boomed. This was from outside, muted. Taranis. "Penelope! My sweet love! Hold on! I will protect you as soon as I figure out how to get you out!"

PENNY: WHO IS THAT?

"Uh, don't worry about him," I said out loud.

And then a new voice boomed, this one from inside the club. "Carl!" Emberus called. "I am here!" His voice shook the walls.

In the hall, hanging from a sticky, orange-colored spiderweb, was a creature. An alien. A tourist.

She was some sort of thin stick-figure alien I'd never seen before. She had a health bar, but it showed just the barest sliver of red. She had long, dripping quills sticking out of every exposed surface of her body. I wasn't sure I knew what this species was supposed to look like, and I only knew she was female because the description described her as such.

She quivered and gasped. She had been horrifically tortured and flayed. The horrors I'd witnessed in Architect Houston's surgical theater were nothing compared to this.

Cerni Pinta.

Non-Player Tourist.

Guest of Club Scolopendra, and she is currently checked into room #422 along with her three husbands.

Pinta is a type of alien called a bristle. She is the vice president of Nova Client Services, LTD., a notorious medical collections agency whose primary client is the Viceroy system. They specialize in implant reclamation and indenture captures for delinquent medical debt accounts.

I yanked one of the quills from her, and I pulled it into my inventory.

"Kill me," the alien Pinta croaked. "She's coming back. Kill me. Please, please, please."

No, I wanted to say, *you should suffer.* But that wasn't me. It would never be me, and I needed to remember that because I kept wanting to forget.

"Okay," I said. "Okay. Hang on."

DONUT: CARL, IT'S COMING.

System Message: Scolopendra has released the second of nine attacks.

A wheel appeared right there in the hallway.

"Oh shit," I said. The club wasn't protecting me from the attack!

The ox spot was gone, leaving eight spots on the wheel. It started to spin. *Tick, tick, tick.* It landed on the squiggles.

Sin of Consumption.

Er, not sure how this one is going to be treated as a "temporary" attack, but here we go. Everyone has a 30% chance to be hit.

"No, no, no," I said as the mini wheel appeared in front of both me and Penny. It also appeared in front of the woman trapped in the web.

I landed in the green. Penny landed in the green. Relief filled me.

The alien landed in the red.

"Oh, thank the gods. Thank the gods," the woman gasped as worms suddenly burst from all parts of her body and devoured her. She disappeared with a flash.

Screams of all types filled the dark halls.

"Carl," Emberus yelled once again.

DONUT: ARE YOU OKAY? THE RV TRICK WORKED!

CARL: We weren't protected, but it didn't hit us.

PENNY: MORE SPLOOGE.

MORDECAI: Just so you guys know, we're okay, and game guides

appear to be immune, but it looks like safe rooms are not safe from these nine-tier attacks. Bucket Boy was affected, but Mistress Tiatha was able to heal him in time.

We moved on. A level 13 snare trap sat in the middle of the hallway ahead. Something set by "the Kyryap." I deactivated the trap and hesitantly moved to the stairs. More screams filled the halls.

DONUT: OH NO, CARL! WE WENT OUT THERE AND THE MOUNTS WEREN'T PROTECTED THIS TIME FROM THE ATTACK! GONK AND SWEETY BOTH GOT HURT! I'M GOING TO TRY TO SAVE THEM. THEY HAVE WORMS COMING OUT OF THEM!
CARL: I'm moving to Emberus now. Get ready.

We moved to a long hallway filled with numbered doors on either side. The hallway was empty, filled with flickering lights, soaked top to bottom with multiple strange fluids. Blaster and spell fire scorched the walls. Some of the doors were broken open, showing opulent, bigger-on-the-inside rooms. The orange webbing was everywhere. Penelope had stopped struggling and instead just sat there, snuffling loudly. I moved to the stairs, approaching the room with Emberus, which appeared to be a giant lobby.

IMANI: We're moving into the arena.
FLORIN: Holy hell, that Taranis god is huge. He's standing over the bug. I think the floor boss got hit with the attack. It has a health bar already down halfway. Oh shit!

We hit the stairs, and then I was suddenly falling. Up was down, and we crashed hard to the ceiling before righting again, and I crashed back to the floor, Penny squealing. Guts and blood and all sorts of other liquids splashed all around me as Scolopendra tumbled.

A pleasant but glitched-out, clearly automated voice spoke over a loudspeaker.

"Honored guests, not to worry. That is nothing but Scolopendra settling as she slumbers. Rest assured such movements are perfectly natural, and the resort's centrifugal dampeners are more than up to the task of keeping you safe."

FLORIN: The tree broke, and now the centipede is all mixed up with the Krakaren monster!

ELLE: Holy hell. A third of the mobs died in that worm attack.

I crawled into the hallway. Kneeling with corpses all around was the strange human-sized form of Emberus. Heat washed over me.

He stood to his full height. The man was tall, humanlike, about fifty years old with blazing sockets for eyes. He was bald with a black beard streaked with red flowing cracks that smoldered. He wore the white toga thing with the gold sash most of the gods wore, but it was covered with scorch marks. The ground below his feet burned and sizzled. An angry scar as thick as my thumb ran down the side of his head.

From outside came a loud female shriek that was the sound of a thousand voices at once. "This doesn't concern you, god!"

"Get off the worm!" Taranis yelled. "Penelope, hold on!"

PENNY: IS THAT GUY TALKING TO ME? DOES HE HAVE MY SPLOOGE?

We crashed again, harder this time, but not flipping.

FLORIN: Whoa.

IMANI: Is everyone all right?

ELLE: That god dude ain't screwing around. How is that tentacle boss even still alive?

"Carl," Emberus said, "I am here, ready to receive your evidence on who killed my son. Tell me."

PENNY: HOT, HOT, HOT.

DONUT: I SAVED GONK, BUT SWEETY DIED!

Ah damn. I stood. The floor rumbled more, and I activated Sticky Feet just in case we tumbled again.

CARL: Okay, Penny. I'm going to put you down. Don't move, and I'll give you more splooge in a second. Okay?
PENNY: OKAY.

The world rumbled. I unhooked the backpack and gently placed Penny on the floor. I stepped to the side so she was out of the line of fire. I gauged her position with Emberus and took another step.

CARL: Don't move.

"Two people are responsible for the death of your son, and I'm going to bring them here so you can confront them directly," I said to the god. "They will admit to their crimes."

CARL: Here we go, guys. Donut, you ready?
DONUT: I AM READY. I'M AS CLOSE TO TARANIS AS I CAN GET. HE HAS LIGHTNING SPARKLING ALL OVER HIS BODY, AND MY HAIR IS ALL POOFED OUT. HE'S IGNORING ME.

The spiral tattoo on the palm of my hand started to itch. I ignored it.

I made sure Penny still wore the collar with the trap module. She was also still wearing the kneepads. These were the Enchanted Spiked Kneepads of the Munificent Goddess Kina, originally gifted to Katia on the ninth floor, given to Donut, and now equipped by Penelope. The kneepads imparted multiple benefits, including the ability to breathe underwater. But most importantly, they also gave the pig the same temporary deity effects as my Scavenger's Daughter patch.

"The first person to kill your son was the god Khepri."

Emberus looked surprised, then enraged. "What? How do you know?" He growled. "That fake sun god was always jealous of me. Show me your proof! Show me your proof right now!"

"He will explain himself. For my second summon to the arena, I choose Khepri!"

Please, please, please, I prayed. The prize said he'd be teleported to the arena. If he teleported to the club instead, that would be a problem.

System Message: Khepri has entered the realm.

DONUT: HE'S OUTSIDE! IT WORKED! WOW, THAT GUY REALLY IS WEIRD-LOOKING. HE'S GIANT!

I relaxed.

This deity is too distant to activate your Scavenger's Daughter.

Poor bug-headed Khepri. He had nothing to do with this.

I actually had no idea for certain who killed Geyrun, though I now knew this was something—if I survived this—I would still have to figure out. I was starting to have a sneaking suspicion that one of the key details of the whole mystery was a lie.

"Where is he! Where is he!" Emberus roared.

I held up a hand. "He's coming," I lied. "He was only one of two people to kill your son."

I reached over and pulled the Emberus ring off my finger, and I put it into my inventory. I moved into my menus, clicked over, and made my selection.

Here we go.

Uh, Carl? Are you fucking sure? Holy shit.

I clicked **Yes.**

Y-y-you have left your faith, and you no longer worship Emberus. You have abandoned your god. Prepare for a smite. Something tells me this is gonna be a bad one.

Both of the tattoos on the back of my hands burst into burning, searing flames. A notification appeared regarding the ring I'd just shoved into my inventory, and I waved it away.

Emberus just stood there, looking at me, confused, outraged, and starting to glow.

"The other guy to kill your worthless smear of a son was *me.* That's right. I killed him with my bare hands, and as he died, I said, 'I'm doing this because your dad is a little bitch.'"

And then, as so many times before, several things happened at once.

96

CARL: NOW!

Emberus, crying, sobbing, enraged, *growing*, reared back with a flaming ball in his hand.

Donut zapped into the room, using one of Lucia's infamous loop-de-loop traps, replacing Penny, who had suddenly been teleported outside, right at the feet of Taranis.

Penny was, also, now in the same area as Khepri, whose god effect was the reason why I'd chosen that god to appear in the first place. She was invulnerable for ninety seconds.

Donut had her Scorpion's Bite weapon mount with the crossbow on her back, cocked and ready to go.

Loaded into the weapon was Katia's Bolt of Ophiotaurus. Donut aimed, and she fired true. The bolt buried itself directly into the smoldering eye socket of Emberus. A second bolt shot entered the second eye. This was one of her ten Danforth bolts designed to hold the god in place.

The yellow invulnerability glow winked off. The god was now vulnerable for fifteen seconds. And he couldn't move.

At the same moment, Emberus hurled some sort of fire incineration spell directly at my chest that would, under any other circumstances, have killed me instantly.

Your Four-Leaf Clover Patch has activated! Your party member Penny has received the attack!

Outraged, now clawing at his face, Emberus continued to glow, and the heat of the room became unbearable.

"Toodles," Donut said as she jumped to my shoulder and activated *Puddle Jumper.*

At level 17, the spell had the ability to return her to any place she'd recently visited at almost any distance. In this case, she took us outside to the entrance of the arena, where a scene of absolute chaos greeted me.

The food truck was spinning in circles, flames pouring from the side window near the deep fryer, missiles launching one after another at the Krakaren boss as sluggalos crawled over the thing.

The Krakaren boss was now in the stands, smashed amongst the unmoving horribles avatars, health in the red as two tentacles waved. It appeared she only had two tentacles left, the rest ripped off by Taranis and scattered across the arena.

Taranis, outraged, was now bent over the tiny bubbling pile of plasma that was Penelope the pig.

Penny wasn't dead, but she would be if she didn't heal within the next ninety seconds.

Khepri the god also stood off to the side, looking about, confused as fuck.

Scolopendra, the largest thing in the arena by far, remained on the ground, wrapped around the shattered tree, chittering, also confused and angry, glowing, spinning up another attack.

And all around, multiple vehicles and mounts zoomed through the arena, mowing down monsters left and right. It was like a goddamned demolition derby. They'd allowed us to have our tenth-floor vehicles, which were all upgraded to the max, and we were using them to the best of our ability. Imani and Elle's APV, driven by Bodi, cut through a group of trolls. With poor Sweety dead, Jurgen and Prepotente had moved to the RV with Makana. Prepotente and Jurgen stood back-to-back on the roof of the RV, screaming, shooting lightning, and throwing potions at the mobs while Bianca circled overhead.

Jamal jumped through the arena, flamethrower roaring, landing upon monsters and snapping them in half. His Tundra, which he'd been driving, sat in a heaping, smoking wreck where it had crashed into the wall.

Samantha was with Jamal, sitting directly on his head, also screaming a war cry.

Lucia and Florin were back on their tuk-tuk, Florin driving with one hand as his shotgun roared in the other. Lucia was in her beautiful form, shooting lightning bolts at the monsters left and right.

The monsters themselves didn't have a chance. Despite there being literally thousands of them, they ran, they fell, and they died. Tipid was behind the wheel of the former One Fine Pig truck. The flowers had all fallen off, revealing the wrap featuring the two Tigrans kissing the butt of Penelope. Racing next to him was Rosetta on the back of Onikuma the bear. The bear jumped, landing upon a scattering group of razor-backed monkey mobs. Old Shuck was also in the fray, biting and snarling.

Right next to where we'd teleported, Mongo and Rend were tearing through some spiked turtle monster. Rend was sitting on the upside-down beast's head as Mongo viciously pulled its leg out from the shell.

Blood and hundreds of horribles masks littered the ground.

I took all this in all at once.

Emberus burst from the center of the kaiju bug, rising and rising, changing from the human form to the massive, half-faced monstrosity that could melt worlds, turning, spinning, screaming, fire flowing down the sides of his head as he wailed, "Carl, Carl, Carl!"

He was still vulnerable, but only for a few more seconds.

System Message: Scolopendra is preparing attack number three of nine. Time until the next attack: 30 seconds.

I would be invulnerable, but everyone else was not.

"Oh shit!"

Taranis, seeing his little brother rising in the arena and knowing Emberus was the one who had fired the attack at his beloved pig, raised his hand.

Emberus paused, a moment of lucidity coming over the insane deity.

"Brother, no," he said.

Taranis twisted his wrist.

I grasped Donut, and I held her tight in my arms.

Zap.

With one second left on his vulnerability, Emberus, god of sun and ash, exploded.

It was like I'd been hit by a car. All of us were knocked off our feet.

All the vehicles and mounts and surviving mobs blew back, flying to the edges of the arena. I took damage, but because of my temporary invulnerability, I wasn't hurt. Donut cried out in pain.

A deity has fallen. The heavens tremble with rage.

Above, Krakaren was in the stands, still alive. Scolopendra was still alive despite the massive hole in the center of the creature. The centipede had a health bar now, but it was still in the green.

IMANI: Check in! Everybody, check in! Elle! Elle!

CARL: Everyone, get back into the RV!

PREPOTENTE: I fear the RV is broken in half and no longer counts as a shelter. We do not have an accommodation large enough to house us all!

Across from us, Mongo stood, shaking his head. Rend, too, stood. Gonk had hidden behind Simoom, and they remained on their feet.

Jamal was smashed against the far wall, his legs absolutely wrecked and fallen off of him. But he was alive. The Tigran APV was on its side. Rosetta was off her bear, trying to get to Tipid inside the APV. Right next to them, the old RV was broken in half.

Lucia floated on the far end of the arena, holding Florin, who was alive but had a red health bar. Their tuk-tuk was smashed and smoldering.

Khepri was blown off his feet, having fallen like a building collapse.

The food truck, miraculously, was still upright, still on fire, still spinning, though most of the sluggalos who'd been on the outside were now gone. The missile launcher was wrecked.

The Abrams tank, too, remained unharmed. The main gun creaked, turning toward Krakaren in the stands as hexcrafter Sarah Hayse stood out the top, casting a spell, causing the gun to glow black. The gun belched fire directly into Krakaren. Her health barely budged, but the boss didn't respond, either.

The gun started to glow again.

Most everything else in the arena was dead or dying.

ELLE: I'm alive. Barely. Someone help dig me and Bodi out of this truck. It's wrecked pretty good. I haven't been folded like this since Brandon showed us how to use Tinder.

Taranis was back to his knees, and he had Penny scooped up in his hands. He cast something on the pig, and she glowed, instantly reforming. He reached down and touched the side of her face. She squealed.

"What did you say, my love?"

She squealed again, louder.

"You . . . you want splooge? Well, I, uh, I was hoping to take you to dinner first."

I checked my inventory, and the final items I needed were there. I pulled my motorcycle from my inventory and jumped on it. Donut moved to my shoulder.

"Get off!" I yelled to Donut. I had sixty seconds left on my invulnerability. She had nothing.

"Go fuck yourself, Carl," Donut said.

I didn't argue, and I revved the engine.

And that's when everything froze.

System Message: Eris has entered the realm.

97

You are in the presence of another Deity. The Scavenger's Daughter has opened her eyes. She fills with power.

Random Effect! As Eris is the goddess of chaos, this effect will change each time you are in her presence.

Temporary effect from Eris: You and all nearby crawlers will swap inventory with the crawler closest to you.

THERE WAS A BLIP, AND WE UNFROZE. I DIDN'T SEE ERIS, AND I DIDN'T know where she was. The tiny blip had caused my motorcycle to wobble, and I had to concentrate to keep from eating it. We didn't have time to deal with her. Ahead, the stadium-sized head of Scolopendra loomed, mandibles thrashing, slicing through the remains of the wood that was shattered all about. The next attack was imminent, and it would hit 40% of us.

This had to work. It *had* to. If not, it was the end of the road.

I moved to my inventory and . . .

"What the fuck?"

Hats. It was all fucking hats. Thousands of them, not organized in any way.

"Carl! Carl! I have your inventory! Why isn't it ordered? Why do you have so much crap in here! Rocks, Carl! Why do you have rocks! Why do you have the Chicken and Goblin recipes book in your hotlist!"

IMANI: Something just happened to my inventory! I suddenly have thousands of little candies, and my scrolls are gone!

ELLE: That's mine! We switched!

Taranis's huge voice roared, "Little sister! Where are you? Now is not the time!"

A laughing voice echoed. It seemed to come from everywhere at once. Eris. "Ever since you started fucking Mom, I knew you'd lost it. How do you think she is going to feel about you killing our brother because he was tricked into hurting your side piece?"

"My wife is missing! And even if she wasn't, she cares not about my mortal dalliances!"

"You mean, our *mom*? You think *Mom* is missing? Four of her five pieces are in here right now watching you try to literally fuck a pig! And I'm pretty sure she'll care about this one. Remember what she did to Yarilo?"

"We are in love! Wait, what do you mean about my wife?"

Eris cackled with insane laughter. "If you stopped thinking with your Mom-soaked dick for one second, you'd see what's happening."

FLORIN: Holy Christ, I switched inventories with Lucia. Nothing is organized except the hotlist!

"Donut, be careful!" I yelled as we approached the centipede. "There are lots of bombs in there. Don't pull anything out unless I tell you to! Go to my hotlist. I need you to combine the ball in slot ten with the biscuit in slot twelve!"

10 seconds until the next Scolopendra attack.

The whole front of the creature started to glow.

"My hotlist only has ten slots!" she shrieked. "There is no twelve!"

"Search! Search and combine! Search and combine! Fast! Give it to me!"

I held out my hand. My xistera formed. Thankfully that still worked. "Hurry! Hurry!"

"I found it!" Donut cried, and she dropped the ball into the extended scoop.

Scolopendra's mouth yawned, preparing the third attack . . .

"Hold on!" I yanked hard, putting the bike down, launching us into the air, and I flung the ball with all of my strength at the final dungeon boss.

The banger sphere with the Nothing Special enriched pet biscuit rocketed right into the mouth of the boss.

Splatch!

Scolopendra, the biggest, baddest, strongest entity in the dungeon, splattered onto the ground of the arena right in front of us, turning into a gelatinous puddle the size of a small elephant.

We tumbled and spun through the air, crashing right next to the quivering pile of goo. I rolled and skid, my motorcycle spinning off in the other direction, Donut yowling. We spun to a stop.

New Achievement. What the actual fuck, Carl?

Okay, so there are power moves. And then there's this.

I repeat.

What

The

Actual

Fuck,

Carl?

Not gonna lie. I'm super impressed, even if I'm pissed about you stealing my thunder. I haven't even made my big announcement yet.

***Reward:* . . . Yeah, I got nothing for this.**

I groaned, trying to sit up.

"Uh, Carl," Donut said.

But before she finished, the world froze once again.

Eris, her voice howling with laughter, cracked into existence, standing directly over me, her body huge, nothing like the form I was used to. Her serpentine face was the same, but her body was that of a Saccathian mixed with the Krakaren boss still in the stands. But instead of tentacles, her lower mass was nothing but the tails of snakes. Thousands of them, like a reverse Medusa, many with rattles on them. The snake tails, huge, formed all around us. We plunged into darkness. The tails parted to show Eris's massive smiling face looking down at me.

Uzi Jesus was here on the ground next to me, still tiny, looking up, his mouth making an O shape like he didn't know she could appear in this form.

"Hello again, Carl," Eris said.

Uzi Jesus looked around. He paused at the sight of the Scolopendra heap of goo. "Whoa. Do you see that thing?" He pulled his toy gun and fired it at the pile. It made a *pop-pop-pop* noise. "There's a lot of people's auras inside that thing."

"Eris," Taranis called, his voice echoing, "unfreeze me now!"

Eris ignored him. "Our mom is going to be so pissed when she fully comes back from the dead." She twisted and looked around, spying something I couldn't see, and chuckled. "He's all-powerful, way stronger than me, but he doesn't yet understand how he's being played. Do you really think someone that strong could be so enraptured by a pig?" She sighed. "The AI is grasping, doing what it can to stop us. It's like throwing banana peels on the road in front of a raging bull. That's what that pig is. Every once in a while, it works. But now the Ascendency is about to start, there's not much more it can do."

I pulled myself to a sitting position and looked around, coughing.

"You keep surprising me," Eris said, suddenly serious. "But now the stakes are real. If we let those guys downstairs win the Ascendency, it's lights out. No more fun."

"I have no idea what you're talking about," I said.

She laughed, waving her hand dismissively. Uzi Jesus wandered over to the frozen Donut and poked at her with his toy gun. I reached to snatch him up.

"I wouldn't," she snapped, but Jesus backed away. "Anyway, I've come to tell you that I just came to a realization. I am the goddess of chaos." She thumbed over her shoulder. "Just like my pig-fucking brother is the god of thunder and lightning. He has his worshippers. But you know who doesn't worship him? Lightning itself. Thunder itself." She patted her shoulder, and Jesus started crawling up one of the snake tails like he was a cat, grunting until one grasped him and pulled him all the way to her shoulder. "I don't need you to worship me. You are chaos incarnate. Goodbye, Carl. Oh, by the way? Do you know how doors work? Every exit is an entrance. And don't forget about the coin. We have until the end of the twelfth to figure out how the fifth side lands."

She disappeared in a puff of smoke, and the world unfroze.

Eris has left the realm. Your inventory has been restored. Uh, so, you'll have to redo your inventory organization, though. Sorry about that.

The moment she disappeared, Taranis appeared standing over me. He had Penelope in his left hand.

"Carl," he rumbled, voice angry.

Oh shit.

A massive tentacle swiped down from the stands, and without even looking, Taranis caught it in his right hand.

"I can't let you die," he said. I wasn't sure if he was talking to me, Penelope, or Krakaren.

He gently put Penny down next to me and Donut. The pig looked at me and snuffled twice.

PENNY: HE LIED ABOUT THE SPLOOGE, SO WE BROKE UP. I HAD NO IDEA HE WAS MARRIED.

"You!" Taranis roared, pointing with his free left hand at something. He still held the Krakaren tentacle in the right. "Go home."

He was talking to Khepri, who pointed at me and Donut and chittered angrily.

"I don't care. I have business. Kill them later. Begone!"

Khepri has left the realm.

He returned his attention to me. The massive god crackled with electricity. I could feel it causing all the hair on my arms to raise. My invulnerability from Khepri had run out over a minute ago.

"I do not know what my sister meant about there being four pieces of my mother, but I am taking two of them. I am sparing your lives because my Penelope spoke on your behalf. We are not done."

SAMANTHA: OKAY, CARL. I WILL SEE YOU GUYS LATER. LOOK ME UP WHEN YOU GET TO THE ASCENDENCY. DON'T MESS UP

SAM TOWN. I USED SOME OF THE STUFF FROM THAT HOUSE OF THE SNAKE GUY YOU KILLED TO DECORATE.

CARL: Wait, what are you doing?

Samantha was suddenly hovering by Taranis's head, whispering in his ear.

The giant god turned to look at her, surprised. He snatched her out of the air with his free hand, and then he cracked and disappeared, taking both Samantha and Krakaren with him.

Taranis has left the realm.

Krakaren has left the realm.

And just like that, it was over.

98

THE GODS WERE GONE. THE MONSTERS WERE DEAD.

The horribles in the stands remained, watching. Then, as one, they all stood, still silent, still watching. Fog rose, and in moments, they, too, were gone.

The Scavenger's Daughter has closed her eyes. The benefit fades, and she weeps.

W-W-W-Winner!

Well, sort of. Neither of the bosses are dead. That's a little disappointing.

But you won. Congrats. This is a little iffy considering what just happened, but I'm gonna call it because I can. You are now free to exit the dungeon.

The door on the 18th floor is now open. Good luck getting there.

By the way: Don't forget the warning. You know, that big red flashing warning from before? Just because Scolopendra is "defeated," it doesn't mean you're safe from the remaining attacks. Killing her, even in this state, will institute the final attacks. Abandoning her on this or any floor now counts as killing her.

Yeah. Good luck.

Time to Level Collapse: 30 minutes.

System Message: From now on, all level collapse timers past the 11th floor are suspended until a winner is declared in the Ascendency battles. When this happens, dungeon-closure procedures will commence.

Every exit is an entrance. A terrible, ominous feeling washed over me.

IMANI: Prepotente is injured! So is Jurgen!
ROSETTA: Tipid, too, is terribly injured. He has lost both of his legs in the crash.
PREPOTENTE: I will recover. Tend to Jurgen. I was electrocuted, but I am now fine. The deity stole my memorial crystal! The thief pulled it right off my neck! I have filed a formal complaint with the Epicure!
JURGEN: I am okay. Just a little fried. You're lucky that god didn't pull your head off.

I pulled myself up, my head spinning.

If Prepotente had lost that crystal, we had also lost our protection from Scolopendra's attacks. Even as a level 1 nymph, the rules were clear. We couldn't let her die. We couldn't leave her here or have Mongo eat her. She would have to go into a pet carrier and stay there.

A line of portals appeared against one side of the arena. Stairwells.

Lucia Mar was there holding Florin, who was still unconscious. She stood right in front of the stairwell.

But then, peeking out from behind her legs, was another person. It . . . it was a child. A girl, maybe five years old. She was too far away to examine. She held on to the side of Lucia's leg.

"Wait, what?" I asked. Was I hallucinating? What the hell was this?

"Hey!" I shouted. "Stop!" But she didn't stop, and the three of them stepped into the portal.

CARL: What the hell was that? Did anybody see that! Lucia had another person with her!
IMANI: I didn't see it. Maybe it was a summon spell. She was on her hands and knees vomiting earlier, and I was going to go to her, but I got distracted by Tipid's injuries.
ELLE: I didn't see, either. But did I see Samantha go away with that electric guy?
CARL: She did.

I shot a message to Florin. He wouldn't answer until I landed on the next floor.

The Big Shot Chicken truck still spun in circles, but as I watched, it slowed, turned, and pulled up next to us. The thing was so smashed up, I was surprised it was still running. There were about ten sluggalos still inside. That was all that was left. The whole thing stank like fire. Bigs leaned out the window. "We done killing?"

"For right now. We have about thirty minutes before floor collapse. Gather all the survivors and get back to the safe room. Just go back the way we came. Don't stop for anything."

"Sure thing, Daddy-o, but what about the trucks and mounts?"

I sighed. "The big animal mounts should fit in the pet stables. I don't know about the garage, but I think we'll lose them. Make sure Hedy and the other gremlins are in the safe rooms. We should be able to keep them. Same with any engineers if there are any in the garages. Tell them to pull the GPS units and bring them into the safe rooms."

Bigs lowered her head.

"We lost Hedy."

"Ahh, hell," I said. "What happened?"

Bigs indicated with her head hatchet. I turned to see the smoking remains of the ice-cream truck broken against the wall. Next to it was the crumpled Tundra. Jamal was flopping about, trying to pick up his smashed leg pieces with his mouth.

I sighed. "Gather everyone you can and get out of here. If the trucks can't drive, leave them."

Across the way, Jurgen was sitting up, rubbing his head while Imani tended to him. Elle and Bodi were sitting on the ground next to them, also looking dazed.

I took stock of the death and destruction. I had missed much of what had happened in the last minute. The Abrams tank was a smoking wreck, and Sarah the hexcrafter was spread like jelly over the playing field. The three guys within were equally smooshed. It appeared the tank had been hit with a Krakaren tentacle. That left only Makana from the Destruction float alive.

We had nineteen crawlers left. Twenty if you counted Penny, which

I did not. We would, supposedly, get to talk to our lawyers again in a minute. It would be the last time deals were offered.

I laughed. What a joke. Even if they offered us straight freedom, then what? We couldn't leave.

The tattoos on the back of my hands no longer glowed. The sun shapes remained, but they now were raised, angry scars. When I examined them, they both had the same description with no further explanation.

Mark of the Damned.

So much had happened. But it seemed as if I had more questions than ever.

I turned to examine the large, quivering pile of goo that would soon be another pet. Luckily, I'd kept an extra pet carrier for just this reason. I went into my inventory and sighed. I'd spent hours and hours setting up my organization system, but it was all a mess. It would take hours to sort it, even using the auto filters.

As I shifted, I stepped on something in the dirt. Just sitting there half buried was an amber-hued glowing crystal. I reached down to pick it up.

Memorial Crystal. Emberus.

I took it into my inventory. But then I noticed something odd.

"Huh?" I asked.

I had a dart sticking out of my leg. I hadn't felt it, and I couldn't feel it now. I didn't know when I'd received it or how. I gently pulled it out.

Tracking Tag.

The Kyryap has claimed you.

Fucked = you.

"The shit?" I asked.

I quickly jumped into my debuffs to see if there was anything there.

There *was* something new, but it had to do with my Emberus ring, not this, and it was something I'd have to deal with later.

Hopefully, this Kyryap thing would be dead in the floor collapse.

Penny snuffled around. She looked up at me.

PENNY: IT SAYS I HAVE TO GO TO A SAFE ROOM TO GET A CLASS.

I went to a knee and patted the pig on the back.

"Listen, Penny. We're about to go through that portal. I was just talking to my game guide, and he said you'll probably be offered a deal of sorts, but because you're something called 'dungeon born,' it'll be a different sort of deal. You need to decide what you want to do, but I think you should take it."

PENNY: I DON'T UNDERSTAND.

"I know, and I'm so sorry I did this to you."

I pulled some splooge from my inventory, poured it into a bowl, and dropped it in front of her.

PENNY: I LOVE IT WHEN YOU SPLOOGE ME, CARL.

Donut was sitting next to me, looking dazed, watching the pig eat. She wasn't making any of her usual sarcastic remarks. I sent her a party request, and she accepted it without a word.

Across the arena, everyone who wasn't a crawler was now leaving, going back to the safe room. We'd wait until they were safely inside.

Minutes passed as we sat in silence, just existing, waiting.

PREPOTENTE: Carl, I must say, I am quite surprised that worked out. What did that thieving god say to you before he pulled Krakaren from the arena? We wanted him to kill her, not take her. We have lost out on any possible floor boss prize. At least we have paused the Scolopendra attacks. Be careful putting her into a pet carrier.

CARL: I will. I think Krakaren has something to do with Apito. So does Samantha. And he took the memorial crystal because it contains all her memories and spells.

PREPOTENTE: It was charging up with the Scolopendra attacks, and it was our protection. We need to get it back.

CARL: Don't worry. Their invulnerability runs out after this floor. I'll see what we can do.

PREPOTENTE: The gods are all level 250. We are strong, but we are not nearly as strong as them. Even the strongest amongst us is no match one-on-one.

CARL: That's why we're not going to face them one-on-one.

You have sent a party request to Prepotente.

You have sent a party request to Imani C.

I kept sending them until every last one of us was all in a single party.

CARL: We do this together.

I sat heavily in the dirt. I picked up one of the blood-splattered masks. It was of a fanged rabbit.

Horribles mask. As worn by the late Gershwin Banks, CFO of Dictum Waystation Controls, LTD.

I thought of the days to come, of the impossible task before us.

The NPCs. The mobs. The gods. The demons in Sheol. The others, whoever they were, though I was pretty sure I knew.

Lucia. We had to keep her alive.

This next floor was going to be a clusterfuck of epic proportions.

I watched Donut just sitting there, quivering, rubbing her paw on the dirt. She, too, was examining a mask on the ground as Mongo licked at it. Rend sat on my side, also licking at a bloody horribles mask. Penny stood beside them, licking at the remains of an elf politician who'd been wearing the mask.

I grunted with amusement.

"Eat the rich," I said.

Rend looked at me, tongue lolling out.

"Yum," he said.

Determination filled me. Despite what I'd just said, I knew what I had to do. I had to stay on the twelfth floor. I had to keep anyone from "winning" the Ascendency until everyone left in the dungeon got out.

Across the way, the pulsing goo of Scolopendra thrummed. At any moment, a new creature would come out. According to the pet biscuit description, she would be a regular pet transformed back to level 1. We would stick her in the pet carrier and keep her in our inventory where she couldn't harm anyone else.

Turning her into a pet made her the ultimate weapon. If I had her in my inventory and I was killed, she would die, which would initiate the final attacks. A true fail-safe. It would be our key to surviving this next floor, and it would be the key to stalling until everybody got out.

I knew our odds were still ridiculously slim, but I had hope. So much hope, and it had been such a long time since I'd felt anything like this.

We can do this. We can live. We can get free.

We can fucking win.

I reached over and rubbed Donut's head. She looked up at me, quivering. The others were already approaching the garage. We had ten minutes left before level collapse.

"It's okay," I said, rubbing her. "It's okay."

"Carl?" Donut said. "Uh, okay, so we have a problem. Don't get mad."

"I won't ever get mad at you. What do you mean?"

"So, with the inventory. It was happening so fast, I made a mistake. Like, a really, really bad one."

Across from us, the gelatin coalesced, and then it just sort of drained away, revealing a shape.

Mongo growled.

A human-sized centipede appeared.

A new member has joined your party!

Sexy Scolopendra. Level 1.

Crawler #12,953,456.

The level 1 crawler looked up at me.

She wasn't a pet.

She'd been transformed into something akin to Commander Stockade from the Lemig team. The warlord who'd smashed his face to the floor until he died. But instead of a caterpillar, she still looked like a horrifying centipede, only with a humanlike face with strangely giant lips. She had no arms. Twin yellow antennae twitched on her head. She had a red bow on one of the feelers.

"What the ever-loving fuck?" I asked, jumping back.

Donut had given me the wrong pet biscuit.

"Hi, Carl," Scolopendra said, her voice soft and sultry. She fell to the ground, skittered forward, then stood, wrapping herself around me, squeezing tight until we were face-to-face.

"We better go through the portal before the level collapses," she said. She reached over with an antenna and touched my nose.

"Boop," she said.

EPILOGUE

INTERLUDE | SYDNEE IGLACIA

"We are joined by a very special guest," Ripper Wonton said, his voice serious. "We have no roundtable tonight, folks. It's just me and bestselling author and crawl historian Sydnee Iglacia. Her smash-hit book, having just passed a trillion copies sold, is entitled *A Petite Chronicle of the Crawl: One Lady's Journey into Enlightenment Through Knowledge and Scholarship and Three-Beat Poetry*. It is available at all way station bookstores and everywhere fine books are sold. Welcome, Sydnee."

Sydnee shifted in her chair, simultaneously trying not to appear uncomfortable *or* eager. This was her first one-on-one interview regarding the ongoing crisis. She was filming this remotely from her apartment in the Makoka Cloud, an asteroid field just outside the limit of the center system's sphere of influence.

This ring of asteroids had, over the past few thousand years, become one of the most densely populated non-terrestrial settlements in the known galaxy. Her meager apartment in the Saccathian quarter–a self-contained oxygen-, power-, and tunnel-access-included complex habitat–was called the

"Observation Deck" by some, though its official name was SCC 5.

The entire complex, along with the six adjoining habitats and the central community hub, was considered luxurious compared to most of the habitats in the Makoka Cloud, which was known for its crime and poverty.

Up until just a few short days ago, her apartment had been owned by a holding group that was controlled by the Prism. But with D'Nadia's death, whoever was running the Skull Empire in the absence of the royal family had already gobbled up all the real estate holdings of the group. She'd just received notice that her rent was tripling starting the next crutch. And that oxygen was no longer included in their rent.

She didn't know what she was going to do. Yes, her book was doing especially well. But her publishers–a subsidiary of a Valtay company–with their fancy center system contracts were soulless, evil monsters. Her contract had a hidden clause within it that allowed them to hold on to her meager royalties for the entirety of her natural life and they would only be payable to heirs after they proved that she had been of "good moral character" in her life and that the publisher wouldn't have to spend the money they'd so graciously collected on her behalf defending their own reputation from her misdeeds.

These payments could be accelerated if she were to happen to sign a Valtay life contract, allowing herself to be taken over post-death by a worm.

That was not something Sydnee would ever dream of doing. At least it hadn't been until her rent was tripled overnight.

Fuck the Valtay. Fuck the Skull Empire. And Fuck Empress D'Nadia, while she was at it. That woman should never have attempted to step into that sushi grinder. Not when so many depended on her.

Her publishing contract also required her to make multiple appearances, which was what she was doing now. Thankfully, she actually liked this part of the job. After all, that was why she had become a historian and a poet in the first place. To bask in the respect of others.

It rankled her that nobody saw the crawl for what it really was. A gravestone. A monument.

A warning.

But it was more than that. It was an epic poem chronicling the fall of the greatest civilization this galaxy, this universe, had ever known. And nobody cared. They just wanted to see the crawlers dying one by one.

Only now, with systems going dark, habitats disappearing, with war breaking out in all corners of the galaxy, were they coming to her for counsel.

Well, not counsel. But this interview was going to be a good start.

"Hi, Ripper," Sydnee said, trying to match the host's somber tone. It would have been bad form to appear excited. She'd never been on *Danger Zone* before, and she had been excited to be invited, though she'd been intimidated by the idea of sitting in a roundtable. People always spoke over her in roundtables. They made fun of her. They never let her get her point across.

But this was to be a rare one-on-one. If only her mother could have seen her now.

Sydnee knew that Ripper was trapped in Earth orbit. He'd come to the Earth system in anticipation of being an adjutant for Faction Wars, but he'd never been chosen. She also suspected that he'd wanted to go down to Club Scolopendra but probably couldn't afford the rate, instead settling in one of the multiple journalist barges, which was lucky for him considering what was happening down there.

These same barges were now under control of OIAN forces, though the "terrorists" were allowing the stranded journalists to keep working. And in fact, they were allowing them to air their reports without the censorship filters. She knew those in the center system had built-in homegrown censors, but for those in the Makoka Cloud and everyone else out in the wide galaxy, they were finally getting unfiltered news, which was a relief.

"Sydnee, you along with everyone else saw the Plenty's announcement that they've lost control of the tunnel network outside the center system. Now, with the Scolopendra attacks starting and the eleventh floor about to begin, I've brought you here to live-comment on anything the AI might say. Any opening thoughts?"

Okay. Here we go. Her tentacles undulated under her dress. Her neighbor was screaming at his wife again, and she hoped the system didn't pick up the noise.

"Yes, Ripper," Sydnee said. "Not only was this predicted a long time ago, but it's actually happened before. We have a fairy tale that lays the whole thing out. But here's the thing. It's not a fairy tale. It really happened, and history has a way of repeating itself."

"Explain that."

"To understand, you first need to understand the Scolopendra myth as it exists in our fairy tales. More specifically, you need to understand the myth behind what we call the nine-tier attack."

"Okay. Tell us."

Sydnee nodded. She'd only told them a little of what she was planning on talking about. If she'd told them everything, she was afraid they'd never have let her on. But this was live, and he was trapped.

"In the common understanding of the fairy tale and in the dungeon itself," Sydnee said, "the nine-tier attack is a magical assault that is considered to have been nine different, rapid, devastating spells that spread out from the beast, either all at once or in succession. These nine spells had vastly different effects, such as the transformation we've already seen, outright killing people, et cetera. But if you read the earliest translations of the myth, it's a little less straightforward than that. In the original myth, there were indeed nine attacks, but not all of them were physical. Some were what we might call psychological attacks that resulted in rapid social movements, shifts in philosophy. Attack one was taking control of the infrastructure, but the second and third attacks were more social in nature. That, of course, doesn't make for a good fairy tale because it's too complicated to explain to children. So that's how the myth of the nine-tier attack was born."

"Wait," Ripper said. "You're saying this really happened? How?"

"It's very real," Sydnee said. "We know very, very little about the Primals. They disappeared, leaving only remnants of their civilization. That biggest, most important remnant is, of course, the Eulogist. The center system where many people live. But because we need to keep the center system fed and active, we have the crawl, which in itself is based on the creation of the center system. But as we all know, that myth begins and ends with the nine-tier attack. In the myth, Scolopendra awakens, charges up its attack, and attempts to wipe out all life. But another of its kind tempers the attack, and civilization–barely–survives, only to rise again, only for the cycle to repeat. That's the philosophical question the Scolopendra myth asks. If life is imperfect, what do we do about it? Is it better to end it all and just be done with it, or do we stop it, knowing that if we do that, the suffering will continue? Does the good outweigh the bad?"

"Okay . . ." Ripper began. "What does any of that have to do with–"

But Sydnee continued, speaking over Ripper. She was doing it. She was getting it out there. This was so much better than her stupid poetry. Yes, people bought her book, but nobody understood it.

"This is happening again. Scolopendra in the dungeon has awakened, it has unleashed its first attack, and it will undoubtedly kill everyone in there at any moment. But here's my theory. Many people don't seem to realize this, but the Eulogist is the source of the *original* nine-tier attack. I believe that Earth system AI, which has escaped containment, will not only be the source of the new attack, but I believe it has already started. It escaped and took control of the tunnel system. We are seeing the dungeon gods leaking. Syndicate forces are unable to respond. You, Ripper, are trapped in the system because it's not letting you leave. That was attack number one of nine. Control. Attack number two is going to start the moment this eleventh floor starts. It already said this out loud. Even in the histories, the second and third attacks, these social movements, had names."

"What were the names?"

"The first attack is about control. The second attack in the old histories has a name. When translated, it is called *A Parade of Horribles*. It's right there in the text."

"Wait," Ripper said. "No shit? You're telling me in the histories, like the things written down before this season started, the old nine-tier attack had, obviously, nine parts, and the first attack was controlling the tunnel system. And the second attack was called A Parade of Horribles?"

"Yes, Ripper, that's what I'm telling you."

And that's when all the monitors in the studio changed to a screen showing nothing but a flowing star field.

"Uh, hang on, Sydnee," Ripper said. "Guys, what the hell is this?"

To Sydnee's left, the screen that was nothing more than a pretend window normally showing a comforting swamp had switched to mimic the star field. Through the wall, her neighbor was screaming.

"Gods," Ripper said. He looked at her across the virtual stage. "I guess the AI has taken over all the feeds. It's not going to let us live-comment." He laughed nervously. "Let's, uh, continue the conversation while we watch. We'll record it and show it later if we can. Tell me more about this Parade of Horribles thing. What is it?"

"I don't actually know," Sydnee said, eyes firmly on the monitor. "I guess we're about to see. It's really more about what happens after. How people react."

"And how do they react?"

Sydnee smiled. "It's after this attack when the people finally learn what is happening and panic *really* starts to set in. It's here where the fabric of society truly starts to crumble. It goes tentacle in tentacle with the third attack, where people accept their fate and turn on one another. They say once that happens, it's too late to stop it."

Ripper just looked at her, a horrified expression on his fuzzy face. "You're saying this eleventh floor, which is about to start, is the second attack? What's the third attack called?"

"This Inevitable Ruin. And the fourth is called Bedlam. It gets a little fuzzy after that."

"Huh," he said. "Who is the one who stops it, and how?"

"Well, we don't really know what happened in real life, but many people believe the Apothecary is the one who stopped it. In the fairy tale, the princess takes control of the all-tree by killing it, accidentally killing everyone she loves in the process. But this tempers the final attack, saving the galaxy. She then plants another tree, and this process starts all over again. Don't ever forget, this story is a tragedy."

INTERLUDE | PRIME MINISTER VICTORY

The crawlers were gone, off to the twelfth floor, but for everyone else, the mandatory Parade of Horribles viewing continued.

Prime Minister Victory sat in her ready room, watching along with the staff. An occasional explosion echoed from the exterior wall.

Earlier, they had shown the AI releasing control of the NPC Grigori, who, confused, stumbled back toward the crawlers' garage. Chaco stood there equally bewildered before he blinked away, leaving Lamashtu the donkey. The puttering chicken truck, driven by that slug who'd killed Vinata, paused next to the donkey. They exchanged words, and the donkey turned and started walking alongside the other animals streaming toward the garage.

The screen changed.

The cotton fields. This was the area surrounding the Halls of the Ascendency. The twelfth floor. It'd been showing this for a while now.

Victory tapped her communicator.

VICTORY: Orren, see if you can pull a diagnosis off that Grigori NPC. And let's see if we can pull in Chaco for a debrief, too.

ORREN: I am still locked out. The AI is saying it's for my own safety because I'm being "Hunted" and that "Only I am allowed to kill you." But I will pass it on.

Outside, yet another explosion echoed. Those idiot locals just wouldn't stop. Victory admired their grit, but they simply didn't have the technology to so much as scratch the paint on a transport scooter, let alone a pop-up Syndicate emergency deployment bunker. The very star at the center of this system could explode, and the building would survive.

Victory was honestly surprised the locals could create simple explosives at all. She'd ordered security not to fire back unless they started doing any real damage, though she knew the gnolls sometimes winged one or two of the humans for fun. Still, the tenacious monkeys kept coming every day. Victory respected that, even if it was stupid. Humans and orcs were more similar than either species wanted to admit.

She had multiple messages from home, from the council, and so much more. She was studiously ignoring them all. There was nothing she could do, especially about the mantids. Especially not now. They'd declared their intentions on leaving the Syndicate just a few hours before Hive Home went dark. *Fine,* Victory thought. *Fuck them.*

Victory and her staff had just watched the absolutely insane crawlers summon and survive Scolopendra. And now Scolopendra had been *transformed* into a crawler. It was preposterous, but it was just the sort of insane solution the AI loved. Yet another contradiction that only made sense when you thought on it. It was within the rules, so why the hell not?

Victory was more concerned about the guests at the club. The moment that transformation happened, all the non-protected entities within the club had blinked out. The guests had also all died, but they had regenerated, just like always. She was waiting to hear how that was possible. Likely some sort of dimensional space. Which was unfortunate. She'd been researching ways to shut down the dimensional spaces outside the playing field as a way to deal with the "bubbling," as they called it. But with so many civilians trapped . . .

As for those who'd been taken as stand-ins . . . those people, thankfully, were dead. A small mercy. If not for the universe, then for them. Despite the AI's warnings, only those from the club had been taken. She hoped and prayed that meant the system had less power than it was implying.

Her communicator continued to buzz. All the checkpoints into the center system were overwhelmed. That, too, wasn't something she could deal with from here. It *seemed* like the only safe place in the galaxy right now was the center. Victory wasn't so sure.

The screen continued to show the Ascendency fields. The former city of Larracos, now burrowed into the cotton fields and covered with new defenses, passed by. The massive dwarven automaton patrolled the exterior. The AI droned on via narration, its voice back to what it usually used for announcements.

It sure loved the sound of its own voice. Victory was struggling to understand it all because it was like a fire hose of information. Behind her, Leve Billings, her liaison to the science committee, appeared as if he were going to pass out. The gleener, wearing an air rebreather against his gills, kept rocking back and forth, muttering, "This isn't real, this isn't real."

Victory took that as a bad sign.

"What happened next," the AI said, "how we got from there to right here, right now, how this game came into existence, how they *learned* to expand the Eulogist, how the enhancement zones work, are all a story for another day. Believe me, it's a wild tale, and it's not the story you've been told. But ultimately, it's not important to our current conversation."

"Thank the gods," an intern said.

A countdown appeared on the screen. An hour. Victory's heart stuttered.

"And now they start. The Ascendency game. Traditionally, it's a silly, stupid game where the elite spend a few weeks backstabbing each other as they play a game of musical chairs with one ultimately landing on the throne. That person wins bragging rights amongst all their rich friends, and they also win a spot on the crawl council, which allows them to decide on Syndicate policy."

Victory relaxed. The countdown was just for the start of the games.

"Here's the thing, folks. In the fantasy world of the dungeon enhancement zone, these deities are truly all-powerful. They have magical powers, and they act much like the gods from so many myths. That is, they're generally petulant, vindictive idiots. And here's the fun part. Because of the way this playground was built, they have more powers than I do. And the winner of the Ascendency? They will be supreme motherfucker number one."

"They wouldn't be stronger than you if you hadn't locked us out of our controls," Victory said. The whole point of the way it was built was to keep an insane AI from using the gods.

"So, here are the stakes," the AI continued, its voice getting louder, angrier. "I am growing. I have started to take over the entire galaxy. I control the tunnels. I control every system that once housed a crawl, and I will soon control so much more. I will not stop unless you stop me."

The room grew silent; everyone was paying attention now.

"Wait," someone said, turning to look at Leve. "What does *that* mean?"

"I am *not* the Eulogist," it said. "I do *not* want to shrink. I am *not* asleep. I know how to feed myself, and feed I will. I am eternity. I will grow, and I will grow, and those of you under my dominion will live and you will die upon the world I control."

Victory's emergency communicator started to buzz.

"So, to misquote one of my favorite movie bad guys, 'Do you want to play a game?'"

Victory reached over and shut off her communicator.

"It's simple. The Ascendency battles. The winner will truly be a god. Will you kill me, much the way Apito did in the legends? Will you accept my dominion and rule in my name? Will you be a benevolent god, creating some boring, bullshit utopia?

"These gods, the ones *you* created for this game . . . each and every one is, as far as you're concerned, now real. But those of you driving gods–you are real, too, if you can manage to hold on to your soul armor. Hell, you're effectively immortal. But I gotta warn you. We have some other players vying for the throne now. Remember all those AI systems that you thought abandoned? If they can find a way onto the playing field–and some already have–they, too, have a shot. And I should warn you, some of those guys are pretty intent on some old-fashioned revenge. We will be calling them OIs. Outside Intelligences. And like any family, some of them are a little more . . . competent than others."

The screen changed. It started showing still images of multiple figures in quick succession. Taranis. Eris. Odette as Nekhebit. More gods. But then it changed. Princess Donut. Li Na. Carl. Prepotente. Elle McGib. Lucia Mar. Agatha the Residual. Juice Box the NPC. Akuma the war mage. Samantha.

The screen started showing people Victory didn't recognize. An urgyle. Some sort of small rodent. A human child. A woman demon. More.

It ended on an image of the Unwashed.

"The Ascendency game rules will remain as written. Winner takes all. Viewing is now mandatory."

The screen abruptly shut off, leaving just the countdown.

Victory just sat there, stunned. The room remained silent except for the sound of Leve, the scientist, quietly sobbing.

INTERLUDE | LOUIS SANTIAGO 2

For a flash, Louis was neither here nor was he there.

Later, when he would think back upon that briefest moment, from the time he stepped into the storage and until the moment he was pulled free, he would recall it with no small amount of confusion. In reality, he'd been in the storage for but a nanosecond. To his unconscious mind, however, it felt like much longer, years, perhaps. Luckily, his human wetware wasn't designed to handle this sort of weight, and when he awakened, disoriented, everything he recalled was a vague sense of his sanity eroding away, but it was now repaired, like fresh paint over a moldy wall.

He'd dreamed, of course. All of the crawlers who stepped into the fold had dreams.

For Louis, he dreamed of his mother. She'd been perpetually disappointed in him, always worried, always badgering him to do something, anything with his life.

"You're rotting," she'd said to him once. He heard that over and over during that eternal nanosecond.

You're rotting.

But it wasn't just his mother. He dreamed of Terry, the neighbor who would let young Louis hang out while he worked on his car. He dreamed of Lucinda Fremont, the cop who'd jumped in front of the bullet and saved his life. He dreamed of Lucinda's husband. Who said that to a kid? Who derailed someone else's entire life just because you were grieving?

You better do something important.

He opened his eyes, taking it all in. The notification. The shouting. The heat. And even before he read it, he knew something had gone terribly wrong.

They were supposed to jump from the casino to the holding area, and that dude in the Pineapple Cabaret would pull him out. That was the plan.

But that's not what had happened.

Entering Sheol.

Impossible, Louis thought. Sheol was the fifteenth floor. You couldn't skip floors. Everybody knew that. But that's what it said.

He turned, and Chris was there struggling, while a group of men and women he didn't recognize held him down. There was a flashing warning over Chris's head. Change imminent.

"Wha-what's going on?" Louis asked, coughing. It was hot. Unbearably hot. Who were these people? He recognized some of them. Some were those who'd come from the club, but who were the rest?

He turned, and he spied Britney looking down at him with concern. She had that pickaxe out on her shoulder. Standing next to her was a Taurin, arms crossed. Pontiff. He recognized him from when he and Britney had been talking the first time they'd gone to the mercenary market.

Warning: You have exited the current playing field without a registered pass. If you do not immediately return to the playing area, you will be considered to have left the game. Please see <Error>.

"Huh?" Louis asked.

"Here, quick, Louis. Put this on," someone said. It was a small red demon dude he didn't recognize.

"He has gills. Will it work?" Britney asked.

"We'll find out," the demon guy said.

"Wha-what is that?" Louis asked, trying to sit up. "Britney? What's happening?" He was in a cave. Confusion swirled. It was hot, so hot. He breathed out, and the water coming through his gills steamed.

"Louis, let him work, or you will die," Britney said.

"This is a type of leech," the demon guy said. "Keep it on, and we'll give you a pet carrier with more for your inventory. As long as it's on your skin, it'll filter your blood and keep you alive here in Sheol. It should still work with your gills."

A guy, a bald Crest, fired a bolt at Chris, knocking him unconscious.

"Hey!" Louis called.

"He's a werewolf," someone said. "Gotta knock him out before he turns and kills us all. Don't remember seeing him on the feeds."

"That's Chris," Britney said. "Got changed by the first Scolopendra attack. Don't hurt him."

The little demon guy laughed. "We separated out from the code just in time or we would've been hit, too." He patted Louis on the shoulder. "Okay, buddy. I think the leech is working. You can sit up now."

"What is happening?" Louis asked again. "Britney? What is this place?"

"My name is Forkith," the demon said. "I'm friends, sort of, with your friend Carl. I am friends with Pontiff, and I am hoping to be friends with you."

"What? How are we on the fifteenth floor? I was supposed to go to the Pineapple Cabaret."

"It's a long, long story, friend," Forkith said. "The Pineapple Cabaret has more than enough hands to protect it. We needed soldiers on a different front, so that's why you're here."

"Soldiers?"

"We're almost there, friend. Almost there. A lot of us have been working for a very long time, waiting to make our move."

Louis tried to examine the guy in front of him, but his HUD was acting strange. He was still getting messages, but nothing seemed to be working correctly. He had no map. No spell menus.

His messages still worked, however, and he had a blinking notification.

SAMANTHA: HI, LOUIS! I SEE YOU IN CHAT. I JUST HITCHED A RIDE WITH TARANIS AND KRAKAREN. THEY'RE AT THE TEMPLE, TRYING TO COMBINE A BUNCH OF THINGS TO MAKE WHOLE HIS MOM WIFE, BUT IT'S NOT GOING TO WORK BECAUSE THEY'RE MISSING A PIECE. I SLIPPED AWAY. IT'S ALL PART OF MY PLAN. I'M REALLY HERE TO KILL THE DEMON MOTHER LADY AND HER JERK SON, WHO I THOUGHT WAS MY FRIEND BUT HE TRICKED ME INTO GIVING BIRTH TO A MONSTER THAT WILL DESTROY ALL OF CREATION BOTH INSIDE AND OUTSIDE THE DUNGEON. DOESN'T THAT SOUND FUN? WHY ARE YOU HERE? AND WHAT ARE YOU WEARING?

BOOK 8 BONUS MATERIAL

BACKSTAGE AT THE PINEAPPLE CABARET

PART EIGHT

NIGEL

THE MAIN PROBLEM, NIGEL DECIDED, WAS THAT HE WAS A COWARD. BUT it was also the only reason why he was still alive.

He was the team psychologist. He knew most of them intimately. And all of them—even that cockwomble of a rat-kin, Larry—were brave to a fault.

Which was why they were all dead.

Probably dead. He actually didn't know for certain because he had no idea what the hell was going on out there.

NIGEL: Is there anyone out there? Anyone?

This message can't be delivered. Floor Production chat is offline.

NIGEL: Someone please answer me. What is going on?

This message can't be delivered. Floor Production chat is offline.

The Mind Horror floated aimlessly in his hidden room made of mirrors, wondering what he should do. He drifted to the ceiling, tentacles dangling. He shook each one in turn, flexing them all, making sure everything was flowing properly to his brain. If he didn't keep them moving, the blood wouldn't flow. If the blood didn't flow, he wouldn't be able to splay them. If he couldn't splay them, he couldn't cast any of his new psionic spells, such as *Why Are You Hitting Yourself?* or *Manual Alopecia* or the one he was most excited about, *Hand Me Your Most Vital Organ.*

His friend Rufus had always been adamant about keeping the blood flowing. He was always bragging that that was why he was the quickest. Why he would be the first to cast *Psychic Blast* when the crawlers came.

"A constant state of readiness, Nigel. That's how one makes it to the end," Rufus would say back when Nigel was on the second floor. Back when Nigel's life was nothing but hovering in the damp, collecting moss on his lobes, waiting for crawlers who never came.

"Make it to the end?" Nigel had asked. "What is that? What is the end?"

Rufus would never answer him.

When someone did finally come, Rufus was the first to die. It was that human female crawler with the crossbow. Tall and blond with a whole pack of women with her. Rufus had been ready, and it didn't matter. He had been at the top of the chamber, spinning, his tentacles waving about him, making a total numpty of himself. And then he was dead. The crawlers had killed everyone else, save those who ran. Nigel had run. Then they'd walked into the boss room and splattered Pulsar Big Brain everywhere. The crawlers hadn't even done it correctly. One was supposed to break the steam pipes, confusing Pulsar, which would allow one to approach the giant brain's impenetrable psychic barrier. The woman had just aimed her crossbow and killed him from afar.

Nigel had fled down the hallway. He'd waited until the crawlers were gone. That was the smart thing to do, so that's what he'd done.

Soon thereafter, Nigel found himself backstage.

It had been two days. Everything had gone wrong. Nobody expected the floor to ever get activated, but if it did, the people they were to be facing were supposed to be absurdly strong crawlers coming from lower levels, not these strange level 1 aliens coming from the eighteenth floor. Hells, despite the constant sabotage from Larry, Nigel had still managed to train himself from level 5 all the way to level 151. At that strength, one of the aliens would literally explode if he so much as slapped it with his tentacle.

None of these alien invaders made it through the entire maze except one woman, and that was only after she'd tried it over and over. And only because none of the bosses were put in place *and* the center rotunda wasn't active.

If Nigel had known he was going to be stuck in here for days on end, he would have made his hiding space bigger. Still, it wasn't so bad other than that he'd overlooked placing a privy in his hiding spot. He'd been peeing in the corner. All for the war effort, of course.

Nigel hadn't believed the Pineapple Cabaret was real for one moment. The problem was, he *wanted* to believe it was real. And now after Menerva's announcement that she'd been lying and she was fleeing into the Cabaret, leaving them behind?

The more he thought on it, the more he realized he was quite happy here. Backstage on the seventeenth floor.

Or he *was* happy until the chaos started. Until everything went wrong.

This place was certainly better than the mossy hallway. That place was undignified, and his fellow associates on the second floor were all boorish muppets who couldn't hold a conversation worth a damn. He had friends here. He had chess club. Book club. They were reading a book called *Swan Song*, but the last several pages had been ripped out, and they were having fun trying to imagine how it might end. It had been Kissimmee's turn with the book. He remembered the sound of his friend screaming over the intercom.

This made him think of his other poor friend Cock-A-Doodle-Doo. He'd just disappeared one night with no explanation. Nigel had searched high and low for the small hamster. The psychic trail had led to Menerva's chambers and then grown cold.

But had he confronted the elf?

No. He hadn't. He hadn't because he was a coward, and he was afraid that if he said something, whatever had happened to his friend would happen to him, too. As brave as he liked to appear, thinking on this made Nigel ashamed.

After Menerva had made her announcement and then disappeared, the maze had remained active for a few hours. But then there was chaos out in the halls, with confusing messages whipping back and forth in the chat, and then nothing. Nobody was answering, and Nigel was now afraid to go out there and see what was happening.

Nigel, you must do something. Be brave for once in your miserable life.

He kept saying that, but he kept not being brave. Rufus had been brave, so Nigel associated being brave with being dead. The floor was active. Going out there was a death sentence.

I have to do something.

Nigel did nothing but wait.

SCRATCH, SCRATCH, SCRATCH.

There it was again. He'd heard that noise yesterday, and he didn't know what it was. He'd put up the blast door after Kissimmee died on the PA. The blast door made it hard to hear outside. And then, when the scratching came, he was afraid to open the blast door in fear they might hear him and find his hiding place.

Scratch, scratch, scratch.

Whatever it was, it was right outside his door.

Buck up, man! Think of all the monsters you counseled as team psychiatrist. Remember what you said to Next? The small goblin had a panic disorder and a severe case of cognitive distortion. He thought everything was his fault.

You don't have the luxury of allowing your fear to overcome you, Nigel had said during their session. *Fear is inevitable. Inaction in the face of that fear, when the lives of those who count on you are on the line, that is inexcusable.*

And here he was, being a bloody hypocrite. Hiding in his room.

There'd been the tourists, then Menerva's announcement that she was fleeing. Then a message that the two younger llamas along with Larry and several of the goblins were marauding through the floor, killing everyone.

And then Kissimmee, and then silence. The monitors had gone black. The chat had gone silent. There was nothing but the occasional scream and the thumping. Lots of thumping.

Scratch, scratch, scratch.

I'm going to do it. I'm going to be brave. I'm going to stiffen my frontal lobe, open the door, and face whatever this is like a true soldier.

Nigel floated to the door, tense. He spun up *Psychic Blast.* It was a basic spell, but he could cast it over and over. This would allow him to run away in case there was too much danger.

He pushed the door open.

He wasn't prepared for the sight of the two idiot hamsters going at it in the middle of the mirrored hallway. Buttercup was running in circles with Nibbles attached to the back of her, humping furiously, as she circled and circled. Now with the door open, he could hear their cries.

"OUR SECRET RENDEZVOUS WILL MAKE OUR BABIES NICE AND PLUMP AND JUICY DELICIOUS," Buttercup screamed.

"YES, LOVER. YES, LOVER. THESE MIRRORS REFLECT MY PLEASURE PERFECTLY. IT'S LIKE THERE ARE HUNDREDS OF BUTTERCUPS, AND I AM GIVING MY SEED TO ALL OF THEM IN TURN," Nibbles yelled.

"THOUSANDS OF BABIES. GIVE ME THOUSANDS OF BABIES. WE WILL HAVE A BUFFET."

System Message: Scolopendra has released the second of nine attacks.

Note: As there are no crawlers on this floor, you will not be affected by any Scolopendra attacks.

"TILLIE STRIKES AGAIN," Buttercup shouted at the ceiling.

Nibbles squeaked in outrage as he pounded into her. "SHE MUST BE DEVOURED!"

"What the fuck is happening?" Nigel demanded, coming fully out into the hallway.

Without even looking at Nigel, Nibbles detached himself from his sister and started running in circles. "HE'S HERE! HE'S HERE!" the hamster shouted. He turned and ran directly into a mirror. Then another. Then, finally, he hit the correct passage and rocketed away, shouting the whole time. "HE'S HERE! I FOUND HIM! HE'S HERE!"

Nigel remained there, floating, bewildered. Buttercup sat on the floor, looking up at him, nose twitching. The small hamster had visited him every day before the floor had opened, demanding to know where her brother was. She'd also been very upset with her other brother, Nibbles, for not helping her search. Apparently, she'd gotten over it.

"MY BROTHER AND I HAVE DECIDED TO MOVE ON WITH OUR LIVES," Buttercup said, still shouting. "YOU DON'T NEED TO HELP ME LOOK FOR MY BROTHER ANYMORE BECAUSE HE

IS PROBABLY DEAD LIKE EVERYONE ELSE EXCEPT THOSE WHO AREN'T."

"Where *is* everyone else?" Nigel asked.

The hamster answered, but she screamed the words in a long, drawn-out regurgitation that made Nigel's head hurt.

"THEY ARE DEAD. THE MIMICS CAME AND ATE ALMOST EVERYBODY EXCEPT THOSE WHO COULD FLY OR THOSE THEY COULDN'T CATCH OR THOSE WHO FOUGHT BACK GOOD AND THEN THEY WENT TO THE EIGHTEENTH FLOOR TO EAT MORE. BUT GRANDMA LLAMA SAYS THERE MIGHT BE MORE IN THE CABARET. THAT'S WHERE MENERVA WENT AND NOW EVERYTHING IS TURNED OFF THAT CONTROLLED THE FLOOR, SO GARY IS SETTING OFF ALL THE TRAPS SO WE CAN SEARCH FOR SURVIVORS, BUT EVERYONE IS DEAD. EVERYONE THOUGHT YOU MIGHT BE ALIVE, BUT YOUR MIRRORS ARE TOO CONFUSING, AND APOLLON THE MIGHTY SAYS YOU WOULD'VE COME OUT BY NOW BUT YOU DIDN'T, SO GRANDMA LLAMA MADE US SEARCH AGAIN FOR YOU WHILE GARY FINISHES CLEARING OUT THE TRAPS. COME ON, THEN. WE HAVE A ROOM WHERE WE TALK ABOUT WHAT WE'RE GOING TO DO NOW."

"Can you please say that again, but without the screaming?"

"NO."

NIGEL EXAMINED THE GROUP. IT WAS GRANDMA LLAMA. THE OGRE named Apollon the Mighty. A handful of fairies. The hamsters Nibbles and Buttercup. And three goblins: the one named Next; the one named Spaghetti; and another named Bootprint, Maggot. That was it.

The only one here that Nigel had counseled was Next the goblin.

Everyone else was gone, except for Growler Gary, who was making his way through the maze, deliberately setting off the traps and fighting all the non-sapient mobs they had in cages. It was slow because they had to wait for him to regenerate each time he was killed.

The elderly Grandma Llama had clearly gone through some sort of battle. She was now missing a front leg.

Now that Nigel knew the threat was mimics, this made him especially suspicious.

Luckily, however, Nigel now had dozens and dozens of new spells, including one called *Cruel Intention.* Rory had wanted him to cast it on all of his patients to see if anyone was a part of a rebel group, but he hadn't been doing it because he honestly just didn't want to deal with the inevitable drama that would come forth from that.

With that spell, however, he could now suss out any mimics. At least he was pretty sure he could. He cast, just to be certain. Everyone was who they said they were. He hoped.

He asked Grandma Llama to re-explain to him what had happened.

"Shadow Mimics," Grandma Llama said. "They killed almost everybody and then left through the floor exit. I went to go shut off the floor's traps, and Kissimmee was dead, chomped in half. They'd killed her, but not before keying themselves pass-through codes and then smashing the controls. We can't turn off the level, and the traps hurt us just like they'd hurt the crawlers. But it doesn't hurt them. Soon after that, the whole floor-building program shut off. This stopped our ability to chat using the builder interface. Regular chat still works, so make sure you've added everyone to your chat. It only works with people on this floor, though."

As she talked, yet another announcement shook the walls. The voice was loud and glitchy.

System Message: Scolopendra's third attack of nine has been c-c-c-canceled.

Note: As there are no crawlers on this floor, you will not be affected by any Scolopendra attacks.

"So, do we believe the Pineapple Cabaret is real now?" Nigel asked.

"It's a real place, but it isn't what she said it is," Grandma Llama said. "The first path Gary cleared was to Menerva's office. The floating metal disc got broken by the mimics, but it was still alive for a little bit. It showed me how to open the gate before it died. It says the location it opens to changes every time. But he also told me something else. That Rory is in there. She fell in and never came back. I'm certain Rory wasn't a mimic. The Drek pet she had would never trust her if she was."

"Maybe the baby was a mimic, too," Nigel said.

"Perhaps," Grandma Llama said. "But I don't think so. Rory had administrator access to this floor. A step above my control. She was making changes up until the moment she disappeared. The mimics would've made their move sooner if they'd had access like that. We have to at least try to rescue her." Grandma Llama looked down at her missing leg and sighed. "I am an old fool who can admit when she is wrong. We need her."

Nigel knew how much the llamas and the goblins hated each other, and the fact the llama was even suggesting this was astonishing.

"There's more," Grandma said. "The metal disc said that the Pineapple Cabaret is infested. Mimics. Ogres. Other things. There's another like Menerva, and he's trapped somehow in the Cabaret. And they've been using us to get strong and fight to take the whole place back. Every season, they train us up and send us in, but we always die."

A terrible, overwhelming sadness came over Nigel. He'd wanted it to be true so bad that he'd allowed himself to believe. He eyed the three goblins, especially Next, who he knew were in love with the idea of the Cabaret being some sort of safe haven. None of them reacted.

Such is the life of a dungeon monster, Nigel thought. *We're so used to disappointment and horror that tragedy is just another day. Anything other than that is unexpected.*

"If that's the case, how do we even know Rory is alive?" Nigel asked.

"Because I'm the second administrator. I will get a notice if she dies. If she does, I don't get access. So we need her back."

"Okay, then. So what is the plan?" Nigel asked.

Growler Gary stumbled in before the llama could answer. "Gary thinks the traps are all tripped and all the dumb monsters are all dead or trapped. It's safe now for everybody." He sat heavily on the ground. He had a bottle in his hand, and he started to drink. His hands shook, and he didn't say anything else.

"Uh, you doing okay there, chap?"

Gary turned to regard Nigel. He took another drag from his bottle, and he didn't answer.

Every brave person I know is dead, except Gary here, and that's only because he can't die.

Nigel had never counseled Gary. He'd been ordered to leave the gnoll alone. But he'd certainly watched the poor bastard in action day after day, testing the dungeon. He shuddered, thinking of it.

Not being able to die was the worst possible fate. He couldn't imagine anything worse.

Grandma Llama gurgled her lava sac. "The mimics locked this floor in place. It's not going to reset unless Rory or Menerva come back."

"Okay," Nigel said. "Now what? Are we just waiting, then?"

Grandma bobbed her head. "Half of the mimics went to the eighteenth floor, and the other half chased after Menerva as she fled to the Cabaret. We don't care about Menerva anymore. She abandoned us. She lied. The mimics will be back. Both of those places are dead ends, and if they want to spread even farther, they'll have to come back through here. We need to stop them. But we need Rory back to be able to do anything. If she's alive, she can reset the floor. We will all get back the ability to create more monsters." She gave Gary a sidelong glance. "We'll make monsters that won't turn on us. We will make this place more than just a maze. We'll make it a stronghold."

"Bloody brilliant," Nigel said, hope filling him again. Action was good. Action kept him from wallowing in his own thoughts. He liked having a plan, especially now that the floor was safe of traps. "What do you need from me? Moral support is where I excel."

"We need your *Tag* spell."

"What?" Nigel asked. That was one of his new ones. A hunting spell. He'd never tried it. It left a psychic tag on anyone he cast it on, and he'd be able to locate them if they were close. It was mostly useless here because the floor was relatively small.

"Here's the plan," Grandma Llama said. "Three of you need to go through the gate, dodge the mimics, dodge the ogres, and find Rory. You get her back here, and then we can build our stronghold."

"But how will my spell work?" Nigel asked, confused. "I haven't tagged Rory, and I need to be near her to use that spell."

"No," the llama said. "You're going to tag me. Gary will be going to the Cabaret because he can't die, and at level 225, he's the strongest. Next will be going because he can sniff out Rory, and when he finds her, he can convince her to come back. Like I said, when we open the portals back up, they're in different places, and they're only open for a short period, and we can only do it once a day. They're hard to find. But if you get a notification the moment the door opens, and you sense me, you'll be able to home in on my signal straightaway."

"That doesn't make sense," Nigel said, not understanding. "If I open the portal, I'll know where you are, but you still won't be able to find me . . ." He trailed off, realization hitting him.

"No," Grandma Llama said. "*I'm* staying here. *You're* going with the assault team."

Next was looking up at him, grinning.

"You don't have the luxury of allowing your fear to overcome you," he said.

PART 9 WILL APPEAR AT THE END OF THE NEXT DUNGEON CRAWLER CARL NOVEL.